Night Warriors

Warriors, Book 3

Brenna Lyons

Bearing Armen

Fireborn Publishing Copyright Statement

Bearing Armen
Includes:
Bearing Armen © 2004/2005/2009/2015 by Brenna Lyons
The Warrior's Man © 2014/2015 by Brenna Lyons
Damsel in Distress © 2014/2015 by Brenna Lyons
Mother's Son © 2014/2015 by Brenna Lyons
Print ISBN: 978-1-943528-14-1
First Fireborn Publication: October 2015

Cover Artist: Brenna Lyons
Photo Credit: Dollar Photo Club
Bearing Armen & The Warrior's Man Editor: Kathryn Lively
Damsel in Distress Editor: Anne Logston
Logo copyright © 2014 by Fireborn Publishing and Allison Cassatta
Licensed material is being used for illustrative purposes only. Any person depicted in the licensed material is a model.

This book is written in US English.

PUBLISHER

PO Box 5216
Haverhill, MA 01835

Dedicated to...

To the little loves of our lives.

To Beth, who's always wanted a Warrior of her own. I promised you James, and I always keep my word.

To all the ladies and gents of Ebh's list and the Weyr Live. You're my first 'writing home.'

To open communication and a happy family.

My husband, a most worthy man, who has proven himself over and over again.

Glossary of Warrior Terms

Beast- Beasts are what humans erroneously refer to as vampires. The stories humans tell are obviously not correct, but you can't expect a human to get everything right.

Blutjagd- The "blood hunt." Warriors crave battle with the beasts, as the beasts crave blood. Warriors are tied to beasts in that they sense many of the beasts' special powers. A Warrior can feel the use of coercion, feeding, and other controls of humans. They also feel other Warriors engaged in *Blutjagd*, the death of beasts and Warriors in their range, and the presence of nearby beasts that are not fully ghosted. Rigorous battle training will quell the *Blutjagd* for short periods of time.

Elder- One of the original beasts, the Stone stealers who were damned for their crimes against the Stone and the Warriors. The elders are gifted with powers turned beasts are not, including the ability to reproduce with a *Blutjagdfrau*, the ability to turn other beasts, and the inability to be killed by anyone but a Warrior.

Endspiel- The point in printing when a Warrior must either seal printing or go insane. A Warrior who feels printing may not progress should break printing long before this point. Note that they are rarely smart enough to do so.

Fluch- The Warrior's curse, passed from father to son or daughter. The *Fluch* may be removed from a daughter but never a son. If the *Fluch* is not removed in the *Zeremonie der Freiheit* by the time the menses begin or the *Zeremonie des Schutzes* is performed before freeing, the daughter is cursed to become *Blutjagdfrau*, a female Warrior. Because elders target

Blutjagdfrau as mates, Warrior fathers will go to any lengths to free a daughter not marked by the Stone.

Ghosting- A talent that both beasts and Cursed Warriors learn to harness. Ghosting can hide the physical form of Cursed Warriors or beasts and all they hold or carry from each other and humans. In a lesser strength, it can "blur" the image of the user so that humans do not note the passage in particular but still see a person there, which avoids accidental collisions. Even a ghosted beast cannot hide uses of power that a Warrior can track. Warriors sometimes ghost in tandem to remain visible to each other but not other Warriors or beasts.

Krankheit- The "sealing sickness." In the final stage of the transformation between human and Cursed Warrior, at or about the sixteenth birthday in males and a year after the start of menses in females, the sickness strikes. The young Warrior will suffer nausea, vomiting, a high fever, disorientation, dizziness, and may become incoherent. It is usually the only time in a Warrior's life that he or she becomes ill, save morning sickness in a *Blutjagdfrau.*

Printing- Like imprinting, a Warrior becomes tied to his mate for life. He cannot choose another if she's lost, cannot be unfaithful while she lives, and cannot ever divorce or otherwise dissolve the union. A printed Warrior is the most stable of men, unless his mate or children are endangered or lost. Then he will suffer the printing madness and may have to be killed by his house. Likewise, a Warrior who breaks printing, even early printing, will suffer for it. A Warrior who breaks printing too close to *Endspiel* will face the madness.

Veriel- The Mad Elder. The Destroyer of Lives. The Mad Deceiver, who led the traitors and freed the elders from the Stone. The most hated and hunted of all the beasts. Fixated on one woman, he would destroy the world to own her. At least, that's what the stories say of him.

Warriors- Also called Cursed Warriors, *Krieger der Nacht*, *Soldat der Nacht*, or Sons of the Stone. The Warriors were an ancient race of protectors who spawned the beasts and now are driven to hunt their former brothers to extinction.

James:

Armen and Dangerous

Tarot: Nine of Pentacles

Tarot Card: Nine of Pentacles

The Nine of Pentacles is the perfect card for Beth Havens. She is a woman accustomed to relying on herself and depending on the meager resources she has to support her two daughters alone. A widow left with twin infants to raise, Beth doesn't have much, not even family to depend on. She resists depending on others, which makes dealing with the free-spending James Armen just a little hard to swallow.

It's also a card of discipline and self-control, of sacrifice to reach a goal and pursuing something better for yourself. Beth lives for the day when their lives will be better. She has a timeline in mind to make this happen, and she has a plan in mind to get there. She will sacrifice everything from every pleasure of her own and even her health to reach that goal in the long run.

Beth is a woman of high moral fiber. She takes only what she must to survive. She's gracious, even when she is turning you down. She resists the appearance of impropriety as much as the actual acts. Every move she makes is weighed: what it will gain her and her girls against the moral implications, and she willingly, though painfully, turns down any avenue that she deems a morally empty venture.

Little does she know that her usual methods will have to bend just a bit to reach what she really wants in life.

Chapter One

Thursday, November 30, 1978

"Damn it," James Armen grumbled, staring at the hamburger in his hand in longing. "Is it too damned much to ask to get a meal in?"

The sense of a beast nearby was eclipsed by the sense of its coercion of a victim.

"Apparently so." He took one bite, tossing the rest over his shoulder, knowing the rodents of the city, scurrying and flying alike, would finish it off.

The beast wasn't far. James made the distance in a few short minutes. He swallowed a sigh at the sight of the woman, enthralled, unbuttoning her coat slowly while the beast watched. It was a disgusting thing to order her to do, especially if it intended to let her keep the memories of this degradation.

However, the fact that the beast was sloppy, completely engrossed in his play to the exclusion of all else, would aid in James's job. He unsheathed his sacred weapon and took the beast's heart in annoyance, cleaning his blade on its foul clothing before letting it fall, his eyes watering at the stench of beast blood.

"I gave up my dinner for a waste of skin like you," he growled, unghosting. Now he'd have to return home and properly clean his blade, or he'd smell faintly like a beast all night long. The damned thing hadn't even had the decency to give him a fight to take the edge off his need to hunt. A kill without battle was almost worse than no kill at all.

"Oh, God."

He turned to the victim, sheathing his weapon before she could see it clearly. As he'd expected, she was pulling her coat shut, shaking, confused.

"Are you all right?" he asked, leading her away gently.

"What...what happened?" she managed thickly, looking back at the body they'd left behind.

"He was robbing you," James lied. "He had a knife and—"

"No. He had fangs and...and glowing eyes."

He winced. "If you tell someone that, you know they won't believe you."

She stopped cold, but her eyes didn't challenge him as he expected. She fumbled her watch up, her pale face draining of all remaining color. She turned, swearing softly.

"What is it?" he asked. "Can I help?" James didn't question his reason for offering that. It was a weakness most Armens shared, the knight-like inability to leave a woman in need to fend for herself.

"No." She sobbed, pushing his hands away. She ran full out, crying.

"Damn this." James fought his natural inclinations, then gave into them, gritting his teeth and loping after her.

The woman darted from alley to street to backstreet. James could have caught her easily, but he didn't want to stop her; he wanted to find out what made her cry...and solve it. That's what Armens did.

Finally, she stopped at a row house and knocked, stifling her tears.

The door opened, and an old woman scowled at her. "You're late, Beth."

"Yes, I know. I... Oh, Alice."

"Come in. They're waiting to go."

James furrowed his brow, sliding silently toward them, ghosting. The women disappeared inside. What was Beth late for? Who was waiting for her? And why would these people make her frantic?

* * * *

Beth Havens wiped at her cheeks roughly, managing a tight smile as Melissa waved her hands from her seat in the playpen. She reached down and picked her up, hugging her younger daughter by an hour to her chest, avoiding Alice's eyes. Beth knew what she'd see there.

"You can't keep doing this," Alice stated.

"It will never—"

"Happen again. I know. How many times have you told me that, Beth?"

Her heart sank. *Please... I need this sitter. No one else reliable will watch the girls for a price I can afford.* Beth lifted Melissa's coat from the corner of the playpen and slipped it on.

Beside her, Alice did the same for Michelle. "I had plans tonight."

"Oh, God. I am so—"

"Sorry. I know."

"You know I—"

"Don't usually have the misfortune of coinciding with my schedule. You did tonight." She set Michelle in the double stroller, placing her hands on her ample hips.

"You know—" Beth began.

"I know you need this arrangement. I know it's been difficult for you to keep house and home together since Ethan died. I know you don't *mean* to inconvenience me, but you have more than once."

Beth held her breath, praying that Alice wouldn't send her packing.

"It can't continue this way."

"I guarantee—"

"You'll guarantee me this. Every time you're late, there will be a five dollar late fee."

Breathing became difficult. Beth pulled the bonnets from her pocket, trying to fathom how she could possibly arrange never to owe that fee.

"Starting now."

Beth turned to her, sick at the thought of paying it this week. Rent was due, and the cabinets were nearly bare.

"I mean it, Beth. If you don't have the late fee by Monday morning, don't bring the girls back."

"Alice—"

"End of subject."

Beth bit back tears at that. There was no way she could come up with another five dollars in her weekly budget. There was nothing else she could give up and still have food and an apartment. But without childcare, she would lose her job. There had to be some way to convince Alice.

What? Are you planning on telling her that you're late, because a vampire attacked you? The man who'd saved her had been right; no one would believe that.

A knock at the door interrupted her inner argument. Alice marched to it and opened it.

Beth's heart seemed to stop beating, and she barely noted Melissa patting at her shoulder. Her mystery man was standing in the doorway—a wad of money in his hand.

Alice looked from him to Beth and back again. "May I help you..." she asked, hinting for an introduction Beth wasn't capable of giving.

"James, ma'am," he offered.

She shot a hard look at Beth, but what answer could Beth possibly give? She didn't know this man, and the only thing she did know about him, that he'd killed a vampire, would hardly sound sane.

He didn't hesitate. "It's my fault Beth is late," he lied. "I...caused her extra work. Please, take this." He pushed the money at Alice again, his expression pained.

Alice stared at the money in shock. "It's too much," she breathed.

It *was* too much. The bill on top was a ten, and even if the rest were ones, it wasn't small change he was handing over.

"I've inconvenienced you, and I've inconvenienced Beth. Please. Look on it as a bonus for your fine work." James tucked the bills into her hand, staring at Beth and Melissa.

Michelle made a grumbling sound of complaint and bounced in the stroller, no doubt a warning that it should be moving and she'd be happier if it were doing so. He locked on the movement, rounding Alice and striding toward her, his eyes wide in wonder.

Michelle turned to him, waving her fist his way. James crouched to her level, and she touched his face. Beth held her breath, biting back hysterical laughter as he kissed her daughter's wrist.

* * * *

James reached out and took the bonnet from Beth's hand, settling it on the little girl's head, covering her blonde curls, chuckling as she fought the process. *Twins!* He could barely comprehend how lucky she was to have two precious baby girls. They were beautiful babies.

A few moments' delay, and I would have orphaned them. I considered ignoring their need for a damned hamburger! He swallowed a cry of dismay at that thought. It was the truth. Ani help him, he'd honestly considered taking the time to eat at the risk of this woman and her children.

Never again. He touched the baby's chubby cheek, managing an honest smile as she honored him with one of her own. "I'll see you home," he assured her.

"That's really not—"

He snapped his gaze to Beth and the other baby, rising to his feet slowly. She took a deep breath, meeting his eyes steadily. James lifted the child from her arms, untangling the baby's fist from her mother's shoulder-length, slightly-darker than honey hair. He strapped her into the stroller behind her sister, topping off the job with the second bonnet.

Then he smiled at the sitter. "Good night, Alice."

The silver-haired woman straightened her dress with a blush. "And to you."

James rolled the stroller onto the front porch.

Behind him, Alice whispered to Beth, "That man is one you grab onto and hold tight, dear."

He smiled at that, lifting the stroller down the single step to the sidewalk. Why couldn't he pursue this? *Not that I have much of a choice with my family history. Armens are fond of saving the ladies in distress and bringing them home as mates.*

If Beth were willing, he could have more than he'd ever dreamed of. Few Warriors were lucky enough to have a daughter, and two were unheard of, even when they adopted daughters in.

His smile faded at the sight of Beth, her amber eyes assessing him. She wouldn't be easy to court. She was a sensible woman. On the surface, his life wouldn't seem a sensible choice.

"You didn't have to do that," she began cautiously.

"It was nothing." It was. Most Warriors carried much more than that for emergencies. In truth, James had been lax by carrying so little pocket money. "Which way? Or should I drive you?"

She blushed. "No. It's close, but you don't have to—"

"I do." Step one. "There are dangerous beings about."

Beth scooped her shoulder-length hair behind her ear, motioning him east and falling into step beside him. "I'll pay you back," she stated proudly. "In two weeks—"

"There's no need to. It was my fault you were late."

"It was the vampire's fault...and my own. I was already late." She grimaced, as if admitting that was painful for her.

"You don't owe me anything." James rolled the stroller around a heave in the concrete.

"I don't need your charity," she snapped.

"It's not charity. It's a gift."

She shot him a wary look. "You don't even know me. Why would you give me a gift?"

"I didn't. I gave your daughters a gift."

Beth looked away, seemingly rattled by the concept.

James ached to take her hand and comfort her, but he had no doubts that she wouldn't allow that. It simply wasn't fair. The type of woman he wanted most was least likely to accept him in her life. Why couldn't he just be happy with the typical blade chasers?

He turned to a door as she did, subconsciously matching her movements. Beth unlocked it, and James removed the baby from the front seat, anticipating her dismissal at the door.

She turned back, looking at the stroller and then James, her expression pained. "I can get them—"

"I need to talk to you." He tried to state it calmly, but it came out as a plea.

She hesitated, glancing at the door nervously.

"Please. Have I done anything to prove myself untrustworthy?"

Beth looked as if she might say that he had. She sighed, shaking her head.

"It will only take a few minutes. You have my vow."

She lifted the other child and pushed the door wide. "Park the stroller beneath the mail slots," she instructed, heading for the stairs without a backward glance.

The baby in his arms yawned widely and snuggled into his shoulder, and James bit back a laugh. Even if Beth refused his bid for a relationship, this moment was priceless to him.

He followed her up the stairs and into a cramped apartment. Beth breezed through the front room and into the kitchen, removing the baby's coat and bonnet and setting her in a playpen. She turned on a pot of water already set on the stove. She peeled off her own coat, revealing a trim body, maybe a touch on the thin side but still nicely rounded.

James took her hint, removing the coat and bonnet from his little charge. He glanced into the refrigerator as Beth opened it, then away to the baby in his arms, his heart aching as she stuffed her thumb in her mouth. There was little in the fridge, and what there was inside seemed to be primarily for the babies. He smoothed his hand in circles over her back and promised his protection silently.

"What did you need to talk to me about?" Beth asked, setting two glass bottles in the pot to heat.

His head spun. James had to make his continued presence a sensible move. "I want to offer you protection." He didn't stop to consider how he'd justify that to Carrick.

She went still, staring at the stovetop. "What does that mean?"

"You know what's out there, Beth. You know about the beasts."

Beth turned, looking at her girls in horror. "They'll come back?"

James cursed his inability to lie to her. As much as he'd like to lie to gain the advantage, it would be dishonorable, and he wouldn't do it. "Probably not, but anything is possible." After all, Veriel had fixated on Corwyn's mate. The thought of a beast doing the same with Beth made his stomach clench. "What I want to do is a simple thing—just an amulet and a blessing that keeps them from harming you."

She fingered the silver cross at her throat.

"As you saw tonight, it doesn't work. What I offer does." He paused, gauging the effects of his words on her. "For your girls. I offer them protection as well. If something happened to you—"

"Yes." Her voice was a strained whisper.

He sighed, relieved that she'd accepted his offer.

Beth stepped toward him, watching James pull the amulet from his jacket pocket. He settled it over her shoulders and cupped his hand behind her head, whispering the words of protection. He didn't hesitate, pressing his lips to her forehead, then releasing her immediately.

She stared at him, touching the spot he'd kissed, moving her mouth as if she couldn't decide what to ask first.

"It's required," he assured her.

Beth cleared her throat. "And this will work?"

"Guaranteed, as long as you keep the amulet next to your body."

"But the girls—"

"We typically pin them to the inside of a child's clothing until the age of four. Do you have spare diaper pins?"

"Yes. Of course." She retrieved two from a Life Savers stacked bowl set on the counter, offering them to him.

James accepted them, then stared at the sleepy baby in his arms. "I need to know your name, princess," he hinted.

Beth darkened. "You're holding Michelle. Melissa is in the playpen."

"Michelle. What a beautiful name for a princess."

Chapter Two

Friday, December 1, 1978

"What's troubling you, James?"

He ground his teeth at the sound of Carrick's voice, acknowledging that his moment of truth had come—literally.

"Oh, no. When one of you won't answer me, I know it's bad news." His grandfather settled on the couch across from James. "What is it? Did you lose a sacred weapon? Or break one? If you did, you're forging the new one. You know that's the house rule. Did you lose an amulet?"

"I—offered protection to...someone last night."

The old lord's bushy white brow rose in a way he hadn't seen since Kord Maher had delivered himself for judgment after spending the night with the Lord Farmer's daughter. "There was no feeding," he noted.

He shook his head, feeling his cheeks heat. "No. There was no feeding, Grandfather."

"Would you care to explain why you offered protection to someone who hadn't been fed upon?" The bitter edge in Carrick's voice spoke of punishment—or worse.

James prayed to Ani that his grandfather wouldn't revoke protection. He started to ask the same of Syth, then decided his house god being Stone god made Him a bad choice to ask for something so outrageous and added a second prayer to Ani. With a woman and children involved, surely She was a better choice to ask for aid. On a whim, he added a prayer to Tes. She was female and known for granting unusual wishes.

Carrick cleared his throat, demanding an answer.

"It was actually three amulets," James admitted. *Maybe if I'm honest, Carrick will let them keep the amulets. Please, Ani—*

"Three? You committed three amulets to persons who are not marked without *my* permission to do so?"

He nodded miserably.

"This tale had best amuse me, James."

He sighed. "It's a widow with two babies. She was attacked, and I couldn't... I can't bear to think of them unprotected."

Carrick stared at him, a look of calculation on his face. "Do you intend to take this woman as your mate? Do you have interest in it?"

"If she'll have me. I—I don't understand this feeling, Grandfather," he admitted. "I just met her, and I already ache to touch her, to soothe her, to—"

He laughed long and hard, wiping moisture from his eyes. "The right one is often like that. Just ask Kord about what the right one will do to a man." Carrick sobered. "Have you considered the difficulties of bringing human boys into a Warrior household? It might not be wise."

James chuckled in spite of the seriousness of the situation. If Carrick refused him... No. He wouldn't think about that. "They're girls. Twin girls, ten months old, the most beautiful I have ever seen, much like their mother."

The old man looked at him in shocked silence, no doubt remembering his sister and niece.

"Michelle and Melissa," James sighed, touching the shoulder Michelle had cuddled to, a smile curving his lips.

"A true treasure," Carrick croaked. "Never forget what a treasure they are."

* * * *

"Oh, Beth!" Mrs. McKee called out.

She turned, pulling the check from her pocket and offering it to her landlord.

"I can always count on you."

Beth managed a smile, though she was still slightly heartsick. If it wasn't for James Armen, she'd have either lost her child care or her apartment. She turned back to the stroller.

"I let the delivery boy in," Mrs. McKee continued.

She went still, her mind working fast. "Delivery boy?" Who would send her a package?

"With the groceries. I imagine he made it here before you. They're quick on weekdays."

"Is he still here?" If he was, Beth would have Mrs. McKee call the police. Beth hadn't ordered groceries. She'd planned to go to the store after the girls' nap, but she never bought more than she could carry in the stroller. The two-dollar fee for delivery was more than she could afford.

"No. He left just a few minutes later."

"You're sure?"

"Of course." She sounded offended by the question.

"I'm sorry. I don't like to take chances, being alone with the girls..."

"Of course, dear."

Beth scooped up the diaper bag and hung it over her shoulder, then hoisted a baby onto each hip. She looked up the flight of stairs, already weary though she hadn't climbed a single one. The walk seemed to get longer every time she did it.

By the time she'd reached the top, her legs and lungs ached and her arms shook in exhaustion. She wouldn't be able to carry them both at once for much longer. Then what would she do?

Just the thought of leaving one at the bottom made her ill. If the lock on the door was more reliable, she might not feel so nervous about it, but it wasn't. More than once, she'd come to the door and found that it hadn't latched correctly and could be pushed open.

Shifting them both onto one hip and using the wall to support their combined weight got harder every day as well. Beth got the upper lock open and launched inside, lowering the girls to the living room rug. She shut the door, sagging against it. Lord, but she was tired.

Melissa and Michelle didn't share that concern. In a heartbeat, they were on hands and knees, crawling across the floor in search of trouble.

Let them, she decided. The apartment was largely safe. What could it hurt to let them roam?

"The groceries," she reminded herself. Beth had to find out if she'd been burglarized.

She laughed harshly. What was there to steal? The only thing of real value she owned was her necklace, pitiful as that was. She'd even sold her wedding band to survive a particularly hard month.

It was better to check, she supposed. The television was on its stand and the radio was on the counter next to the fridge. The 'valuables' were safe.

But, there was still shopping to do after naptime. Beth prepared herself for the bad news inside and opened the fridge, choking on her sigh.

"My God." Her mouth watered at the sight of the stocked shelves.

The top shelf held three gallon jugs of milk, a half gallon of orange juice, one of apple, and one of grapefruit. The bottles of mixed milk and formula had been moved to the door to make room for the rest. There were salad greens and baby carrots in one drawer, assorted fresh fruits in another, and lunchmeat and cheeses in the last. The shelves were packed with margarine and butter...

Beth touched it, afraid she was dreaming. "Butter." She laughed nervously, then forced herself on, cataloguing the rest.

There was cottage cheese, two types of jelly, condiments, eggs—two dozen, and a huge package of steaks.

Certain that it hadn't ended there, she closed the fridge and pulled open the lower freezer drawer. There were meats of every kind, frozen sides, and...

"Ice cream." She hadn't had ice cream since just before the girls were born.

Beth shut the freezer, mindful of the electricity she was wasting with it standing open. She stared at her pantry cabinet, barely breathing. Her hand shook, but she eased it open, catching a bag of chocolate chips as they slid out.

"Baking supplies, canned fruit and vegetables, cereal and oatmeal, cookies and crackers, rice, spaghetti, sauce, macaroni and cheese, chips, wine..." Her head spun, and she could only see the front row. She set the chocolate chips inside and closed it, staring at the handle for a long moment.

Who would do this? Who could afford it? A wild guess that Ethan's parents wanted to mend bridges lit in her mind, then disappeared amid a flurry of images of the tense months after Ethan died...and earlier, when they'd been engaged and newly married. No. They'd never have done this.

But, who did that leave her with? She had no one who would spend this kind of money on her, even if they had it to spend, and no one Beth associated with on a daily basis had this kind of money to spend.

A high-pitched squeal sent Beth in search of the girls. She found them beside the coffee table.

Melissa patted a stuffed bear that was nearly her seated height, a white bear with a pink bonnet that she'd already pulled to the back of the bear's neck. Michelle had hers hugged to her body, peeking around the beige furred face topped by a pink peaked hat with a matching veil, the type typically seen on damsels in distress...or fairy tale princesses.

"Princess?" A memory pulled at Beth.

Michelle. What a beautiful name for a princess.

"He wouldn't dare!" But, she knew James would dare it. The man obviously had no concept of frugal spending. The money he'd handed Alice as a 'bonus' would pay Beth's bill for a month or more, if—as she suspected—most of the bills were the size of the ten on top.

"At least you two chose the right bears," she muttered.

This was insane. Why would he...

Beth pushed away the thought that James expected a sexual repayment. That didn't sound right. He'd kept his distance the night before. Aside from the kiss on her forehead, which he claimed was necessary to 'seal the amulet,' he hadn't laid a hand on Beth, hadn't hinted that he wanted a reward for saving her, hadn't come on to her in any way.

And...she trusted him. Beth couldn't say why she did, but there was something about him that made her trust him with her daughters, herself, her home...

Then he's doing this, because he feels sorry for us.

Her initial gut response of anger faltered at the memory of all the food at stake. Without conscious plan, the mental math of how long this food would last played out in her mind; speculations about the uses the extra money in her budget could be put to for the duration followed.

Beth bit her lip, torn.

James had money to burn and wanted to burn it for her benefit...hers and her children's. What did it matter if he did? He could spare it, and he would tire of them and move on soon enough.

No. She didn't need to examine the reasons it was wrong. It was.

As it was, the state provided her with food stamps and medical coverage for the girls, but that wasn't charity; it wasn't a free ride. Beth paid taxes into the system that helped support them. She looked forward to the day when they wouldn't need the subsidies. *When the girls are old enough to spend the after school hours alone,* she reminded herself.

Still, Beth cringed at the idea of them alone...ever. There was no question that the day would come, but she couldn't deny that she wished it wouldn't.

She stared at them, managing a tight smile. Michelle was laying on her bear, seemingly intent on an early nap on her new pillow. Melissa chewed on the bear's bonnet, teething avidly now that she had something other than her fist to do it on.

"I can't accept it," Beth decided, her voice betraying her misery at the idea, though she knew it was right. The bears were one thing, but the food was too much.

There were two listings for Armen in the phone book, neither one for James Armen. Beth sighed, took a deep breath and called the first number.

A groggy-sounding man answered on the second ring. "Connor here," he half-yawned.

"Sorry," Beth managed. "I was looking for James." She wound the phone cord around her fingers, hoping he knew James.

Connor snapped awake. "Is it an emergency?"

"No. I—I'm sorry I bothered you." She started to hang up the phone.

"Wait!"

Beth gasped at the bark of an order, but she found herself obeying, bringing the phone back to her ear.

"That's better. I'll have James contact you, but I need your name to do that."

"It's Beth...Beth Havens."

"Protected or..." He trailed off, hinting at a more intimate relationship.

"Protected," she assured him, her face burning.

"If you're a protected, I can—"

"This was a mistake," she breathed. "I'm sorry I bothered you." Beth hung up, ignoring Connor's demand for her not to.

She stared at the phone, considering her options. He'd said James would call. Beth decided to wait until nightfall, then try the other number.

* * * *

James grumbled a curse, reaching for the phone at his bedside and fumbling it to his ear. "Yeah?"

"Oh, good. I'm waking you," Connor growled.

He squinted at the bright light sifting around the heavy drapes. "Damn right you are. Who pissed in your Cheerios?"

"One of your protected by the name of Beth Havens."

From the first thud of his hammering heart, James was wide awake. "And?"

"Well I *would* give you the 'and,' if she'd given me the 'and.' Since she refused to talk to me—You really need to educate your protected better than—"

"I'll give her my direct number," James promised.

"That isn't the point, big brother. A protected needs to know—"

"I know what a protected needs to know, and so will she."

"But?" Connor was just too damned perceptive for his own good some days.

"I'll be giving her my direct number," he repeated.

Connor snorted in laughter.

"It's not what you think," James warned, praying his youngest brother wasn't about to let the others in on this.

"You haven't taken a special interest in this protected?"

"Obviously, I have."

Connor howled in laughter.

"She needs help, and—"

"And you're a Warrior of Armen. You'll be mated within a week. She'll be your own little haven."

The urge to punch Connor for the pun warred with the completely mad need to have her as his haven, and he as hers. But, that wasn't going to happen in a week, if it happened at all. "Don't count on it."

Connor sobered. "You're serious. Aren't you?"

"Yes. I am." And it damned well hurt to admit it already. James cursed his Armen roots, then winced as he realized he'd spoken the explicative aloud.

"Then I'm sorry." He sounded it, which didn't help James's mood.

"When it happens, it happens. Right?"

"Right. Well, give her a call. She's rattled about something."

His heart stuttered at the thought of Beth upset. "Thanks, Connor." He hung up, resting his hand on the phone. It took only a moment for him to decide to shower and dress. If Beth was upset, a phone call wasn't going to cut it.

Chapter Three

Beth winced at the knock at her door. She'd heard the lower door, of course, but she'd left it for Mrs. McKee to answer. Since Beth never had company, why would a knock be of any interest to her?

Except this one. The girls were both napping on their bears, Melissa with the bonnet strap wrapped around the thumb tucked into her mouth, and the last thing she needed was two cranky babies interrupted from naps.

Beth sprinted to the door and pulled it open, stepping back in shock at the sight of James Armen.

He put both hands up in a sign of calming. "You called?"

"Uh...yes. I suppose I did." *Don't be an idiot! He'd have to come pick up the food, anyway.*

"May I?"

"Wh..." Beth looked around, coming to the realization of what he was asking abruptly. "Oh, yes. Come in."

James strolled inside, stopping in the middle of the living room, chuckling. "They like them," he whispered.

She shut the door and headed into the kitchen, knowing he'd follow.

His voice came from just behind her. "Is there a problem, Beth?"

"The bears were very sweet," she began, then faltered, searching for a way to say the rest.

"But?"

Beth turned to him, noting his relaxed stance, his hands shoved in his jeans pockets, his feet parted. Was the man ever uncomfortable?

"But?" he repeated.

"The food is too much. I'm sorry, but I can't accept it."

"The fresh supplies would go bad before I could use them," he reasoned.

"I'll pay you for them," she offered. "But the rest—"

"Keep it. I'm hopeless in the kitchen. I live on pizza, gyros, and burgers out more often than not. The Colonel and I are on speaking terms, and cereal and hotdogs are about the extent of my prowess."

"Really?" Even Ethan had been able to manage the occasional burger or steak, and she'd thought he was the world's most lost man in a kitchen.

"Really. I can catch fire to a stove just boiling water." He grimaced. "And have."

Beth stared at him, nearly stunned to silence. "I'll pay for them all then...a little at a time. I'll be honest. I don't usually buy this much at once."

James seemed to consider that. "Would you entertain another possibility?"

Her heart pounded at what he might suggest. "No promises, but I'll hear you out."

"I'd just about kill for a home-cooked meal a few times a week without driving all the way to my parents' house to get it." He paused.

So far, this didn't sound so bad. "Go on."

"I know how much I pay for a decent meal out...a steak or roast chicken with sides and dessert. Maybe an eighth of what I spent on those groceries?"

"Probably." It had been a while since she'd experienced it, but that sounded reasonable.

"How many nights do you have off every week? Two?"

"Three. I work long shifts the other days."

He nodded. "Cook for me two of them...four weeks. Just dinner. If the arrangement is agreeable to you, maybe we could make it a permanent one. I supply groceries, and you cook me a few meals for it."

He waited patiently...to outward appearances, though Beth had the strangest feeling that her answer was vitally important to him.

"Let's get through the first eight meals," she managed.

This isn't charity. It's a second job, and even if it only lasts the month, it will be four weeks of food money that can buy the girls the next size up in clothes and shoes. That will put me ahead for the first time since they were born.

James smiled widely, nodding in what looked like gratitude.

"Aren't you the least bit afraid that I'll be a horrible cook?" she asked.

"Not in the least."

Beth couldn't force speech. He was putting an incredible amount of trust in her.

"I've seen you boil water without starting a fire. That alone means you're a better cook than I am."

She laughed at the absurdity of his logic. "Until tonight then?" she asked.

"If it won't be an imposition to have me over so soon."

She shook her head, surprised that it wasn't. For some reason, she was looking forward to spending time with James. "Six o'clock."

* * * *

James sat back, sighing in contentment. "Delicious," he complimented her.

Beth paused, her back to him. "I hope you're not full. Dessert was part of the agreement."

"I'm sure I can manage it." And, he'd smelled chocolate before he'd made it upstairs. Whatever she'd chosen to make, it was sure to be more good food.

She came back with a platter heaped with chocolate chip cookies and set it in front of him.

He rubbed his hands together, wondering how many he could eat without shocking Beth with his appetite. "Oh, yeah."

"It was short notice," she offered in what sounded like an apology. "How does apple pie sound for tomorrow?"

"If you make it, wonderful. In the meantime, I love cookies."

Beth sat, handing cookies to the babies, her face darkening and the edges of her mouth twitching up.

"Yes?" he prompted, plucking a cookie from the platter.

"I don't want to offend you."

"That's hard to do."

She smiled, a single laugh escaping. "I'd say you love food."

James laughed heartily, and Michelle echoed him with a squeal of delight. "My mother has accused me of that more than once."

Beth took a cookie, leaning forward on her elbows. "You really have four brothers?" she asked. She took a bite of the cookie, closing her eyes in pleasure.

He forced himself to think, the image bringing up portions of his anatomy that needed to shut up for now. "Sure do. You don't have any?" He popped the cookie he'd grabbed into his mouth, groaning as it started to melt away.

"Not a single one. No brothers. No sisters."

"Parents?"

She hurried to swallow another mouthful of cookie. "Dead. My mother when I was thirteen and my father when I was twenty-two."

He nodded, at a loss to offer sympathy for so monumental a personal tragedy. "Your husband?"

Beth smiled weakly, playing another cookie between her fingers. "Ethan and I didn't have much time together. Only sixteen months after we married, two years total."

"I am sorry. I know that's inadequate."

"It's not. It's sweet of you to say it. It...was just one of those things. He was killed by a mugger."

James fisted his hand on his lap. This was why he hunted, to keep this sort of senseless loss from happening, but while he was killing off beasts, humans were busy killing off each other.

Beth bit into the cookie, eyeing her daughters, probably trying to avoid looking at James. He'd made her uncomfortable, but he couldn't seem to stop himself from following the conversation out to the end.

"You have no family at all. Do you?"

"None."

"Not even Ethan's?"

She darkened. "None," she whispered.

James wondered at that, but he'd already pushed her too far. "So, are you going to banish me to White Castle and McDonalds for being a poor guest?"

Beth snapped a look at him, her eyes wide. She tried to talk through a mouthful of cookie, then stopped and swallowed. "You think you're a poor guest?"

"I ask too many questions. I'm sorry I made you uncomfortable."

She smiled, and his heart skipped. James would do just about anything to see her smile.

"So, is it Sal's Pizza for me tomorrow night?"

"Not tomorrow night or any night I'm off."

"But our deal—"

"If you don't want to—" she began, her smile fading.

"I do. Thank you, Beth. This means a lot to me." *More than you can possibly imagine.*

She picked up another cookie, offering it as a toast.

Chapter Four

Monday, December 4, 1978

James stared at the file in his hand, trying to internalize what he was seeing. Whatever went wrong between Beth and her in-laws had been explosive.

She'd taken her husband's name of Rice when they'd married, but that had lasted only until shortly after his death. The girls even shared her maiden name of Havens.

Ethan's parents lived only a few miles from Beth and the girls, a neat little home on the edges of an affluent area. Considering the girls' date of birth and when Ethan died, there was no question that his parents would have known about them.

That was where logic failed him. Gods, Michelle and Melissa were a joy! Warrior affinity for family disregarded, how could any grandparent turn his back on his flesh and blood, the only living links to a dead son?

He considered the possibility that they hadn't and dismissed it just as quickly. Beth wasn't happy with the situation; her reactions stated that clearly.

James sighed. Part of him wanted to question them, to learn what drove them to ignore their own family this way.

Another part rationalized that he had no right to do it. In fact, stirring the pot on a bad situation could force them to the boiling point.

Whatever was wrong between them, it was likely irreconcilable. That was all James really needed to know. He wasn't in this to secure aid for her; he was in this to become the person she could count on.

Chapter Five

Saturday, December 9, 1978

"Good God, James," Beth half-laughed. "I'll be cooking for you forever, if you keep bringing food with you."

He winked at her, smiling a sly smile. "You saw through my cunning plan." He set the sacks down on the countertop. "Does this mean you're sending me back to University Cafeteria food?"

She laughed. "I can't decide if you're afraid of that or you want it. I mean... You say it every time you do something you know might land you there."

James pulled bottles of root beer out of the sack, lining them up on the counter. He didn't answer her accusation, though the tension in his shoulders fairly screamed that he didn't want banished to crap restaurants again.

"Mmmm," she purred. "What do you have in mind for those?"

"I was wondering if you liked root beer floats."

"Love them."

He deposited the root beer between the girls' bottles, then pulled out a gallon of milk, rotating it to the rear.

Beth watched that move with a pang of guilt. Since he barely touched the stuff, James was obviously supplying it for the girls.

He turned, two bananas torn from a bunch in hand, his eyes narrowing. "Something wrong?"

"It just seems..."

"Yes?"

"I understand you buying things you eat and drink, but I really should—"

"It's no trouble. If I'm stopping at the store anyway, picking up milk and bananas is no inconvenience. Besides, maybe we'll make some banana splits later in the month."

"Carrying them up the stairs is—"

"Less of a burden for me than it is for you. You already carry two babies and their supplies up." He turned to the highchairs and started breaking pieces of banana onto the trays in preparation for dinner.

Beth took a calming breath, trying not to snap at him. "I have the money to—"

"Use it to buy other things you need. I know how fast babies grow."

"I can't use food stamps for that, but I can use them for food."

He went stone still, barely breathing. Beth swallowed hard, unnerved by his reaction. She prayed that he wasn't one of *those* people who looked down on anyone who was forced by circumstance to depend on the system for a while.

James went back to the bananas. "I guess you're right about that. Okay... I'll make you a deal."

"What kind of deal?"

"I'll bring the milk and juice."

"But—"

"It's heavy. I'll bring it."

She paused, noting the tension in his shoulders. "It means that much to you?"

"Yes. I hope you'll humor me."

"If I'm not buying the milk or juice, what's the tradeoff?"

"Surprise me. So far, we've been eating what I've provided. Introduce me to what you like to eat once in a while. A dessert...or a main dish."

"What if you don't like it?"

He chuckled, heading to the trash to dump the banana peels. "As you so aptly noted, I like food. I've eaten rattlesnake and moose."

Beth bit back a sound of disgust, curling her nose at the thought. "Snake?"

"My grandfather taught me never to offend my hosts. That means eating what's served. Snake's not so bad, actually...cooked correctly. I've tasted a lot worse. With your cooking, I taste much better, and someone who likes food would know."

She smiled, the first test of his tastes already in mind. If James survived cure tongue, he could survive anything she threw at him. "You may come to regret this."

"Never." His eyes were hot in an undertone of meaning she'd never noted from him before.

Beth forced her breathing to steady, abruptly aware of James as a man in her space: strong, handsome, protective, and very desirable.

Chapter Six

Friday, December 15, 1978

"I told you that you couldn't serve anything that would disgust me," he stated, taking another sip of the wine they'd opened after dinner. "You used just the right amount of salt to bring out the flavor of the tongue."

"Shhh," Beth managed through her stifled laughter. She leaned toward him, her nose nearly brushing his.

James felt his heart begin to pound. The urge to kiss her was nearly maddening. It had been almost two weeks since he'd taken release with a woman, ten days since he'd felt the urge to take it with anyone but Beth.

But, it was too early to expect a move like that, even now. She'd only allowed him to stay past the girls' bedtime twice so far, and this was the first time she'd allowed him to stay this late into the night...let alone had drinks with him. Being comfortable with him was not enough. Beth had to want him as a man, and he'd only seen the faintest glimpses of that in the last week.

She met his eyes, her giggles tapering off into a few hitching breaths. Her breath was sweet with wine and hot against his lips. He burned, the need to close that finger-width of distance driving him further toward madness.

Dear Tes, I haven't even kissed her yet and—

Beth eased forward, tilting her head to his, her eyes closing. He nuzzled her lips, his cock coming to life with just that encouragement. She moved closer, and he pressed his lips more firmly against hers.

She eased back, her eyes opening, looking at his lips in something akin to fascination. James bit back a groan as she licked her upper lip.

Then her body was pressed to his again, her lips parting to his, the kiss moving from a sensuous, slow exploration to an intense encounter in a few precious heartbeats. Her hand trailed up his thigh to his cock. James did groan at that, praying fervently that this experimentation wouldn't end.

It didn't. Beth traced him, learning his dimensions while their mouths mated fully. James took a wild chance, feathering his fingertips over her breast.

She went still, her mouth parting from his and her breathing coming in ragged gasps. He searched her eyes for some sign of either acceptance or refusal. Neither came; she seemed stunned. He started to move his hand away, certain that he'd overstepped her comfort.

"No," she whispered. "Please, James. It's been so long."

He nodded. "If you want me to stop—"

Her lips returned, silencing him. It was a deeper, less fevered kiss, full of aching promise. James tested her decision, fondling her breasts, acutely aware of every gasp and moan, every shift of her body.

Her hand pushed at his, and James backed away, nearly groaning that it was over. It took him only a moment to digest that it wasn't.

Beth unbuttoned her blouse and hiked it off her shoulders, her expression uncertain. He unbuttoned the first button on his shirt, searching her face for any sign that she didn't want him to proceed. He paused, then undid the next two and dragged both the buttoned shirt and t-shirt over his head.

She touched his chest, seemingly committing him to memory...or comparing him to what she already knew. He hoped the comparison would be a favorable one.

She just wants love play, he reasoned. Though he ached for more, it was unlikely that she was willing to let him take release fully with her...or more.

Beth reached for the hooks on the back of her bra. He circled his arms around her, kissing her as he accomplished the task.

He trailed his lips down her chin and throat, groaning aloud as she lay back over the arm of the couch, offering her breasts. James sucked at one, then the other, tasting her, reveling in her grip on his shoulders and the way she arched up for more.

"Please," she begged. Her hands nudged at his shoulders, not away from her but down.

James explored her ribs and abdomen, tasting the salt of new sweat on her skin. He paused at her jeans. She tipped her hips up, an inarticulate sound of longing giving him leave to proceed. If this was what she wanted, he would gladly comply, even if this was all she wanted and though he felt certain that not completing what they'd started would be torture for him.

Her musk was pungent, drugging his senses. The next few minutes passed in a haze of tasting her skin as he stripped the last of her clothing away. James licked at the rich honey coating her inner thighs, smiling as she draped one leg over his lap and the other over his shoulder, opening herself for more.

He teased her, stroking his tongue and lips up her thighs while she pulled at him, seeking to draw him in. She choked out a cry when he obliged her, her breathing announcing her rocketing ascent toward climax. He slowed, savoring every reaction, guiding her toward her pinnacle.

She shattered, her hands dragging up at him while moans escaped her lips. James captured her lips, and she responded in a fever. Beth pulled his jeans open and started pushing them away, her hands quaking lightly.

He went still. "Are you sure?" He wouldn't do this unless she was. He wouldn't convince her to it.

"Yes, James. Believe me, I know what I want."

That reminder seared him, but her husband was a former life, not a competitor for her affections. Beth had called him by name; she knew who she was with and wanted him. James intended to make the experience unforgettable for her.

Duty intruded, and he sensed her, reaching automatically for one of the condoms in his jacket. She watched it roll down his length, seemingly shocked.

James stroked his fingertips over her cheek. "I would never risk you," he assured her.

He smiled at her amazement. This went deeper than the rules of sanction. The babies were too young to risk her to another pregnancy. Carrying twins and single motherhood had taxed her system to its limits, and the few weeks of decent food and reduced physical load were not enough to replenish what she'd lost. If she became his mate, Beth would be in pristine health before he'd give her the choice of carrying his sons.

She nodded, her gaze settling on his cock, pleading silently for him to continue. Her hands traced his body, touching, testing, driving him near mad. She guided him in by his buttocks.

He resisted her pull, sliding in slowly, watching her eyes widen in rising concern. She was tight, amazingly so considering the fact that she'd delivered children. Perhaps it was the time without a man that had accomplished it.

"Dear Syth," he breathed. He forced his eyes to stay open, relaxing only when she pulled him deeper and showed no signs of distress or pain. "If I hurt you—"

"No. Please," she gasped.

James glided in to the hilt, capturing her squeal of delight in his mouth, praising the fact that her five feet eight allowed him to do so with little difficulty. He went still, listening for the girls, certain that she'd shy from him if they woke. He thanked Syth, Ani, and Tes alike that they slept on.

He slid back, then in again, their kiss less restrained. As if the storm broke, the rest was a blur of touching and tasting, moving bodies and whispers. When the end came, James muted his cry and hers with it. Slow, deep kisses followed and then the soothing brush of fingertips.

Finally, Beth's breathing was deep and measured. Her hands settled at his hips, no longer roaming.

James eased out of her, hiking his jeans to low on his hips. He smiled at her peaceful expression, sated, her lips thoroughly kissed. He lifted Beth into his arms and carried her to bed. James hesitated, then pulled the blankets over her and went to the bathroom to clean up a bit and dispose of the condom.

He stood over her and considered his next move carefully. There was no way he could conscience leaving her. Though Beth hadn't invited him to stay the night, he wouldn't allow her to wake alone and wondering if this was all that mattered to him.

A questioning gurgle solidified his plan. James turned to the cribs and scooped the two wide-awake girls to his chest, biting back a laugh. Joining Beth in bed would be presumptuous. Caring for her daughters, bedding them down in the main room, and allowing Beth to sleep would make his meaning clear.

Chapter Seven

Saturday, December 16, 1978

Beth sighed, snuggling under the blankets. She smiled, phantom memories of James's touch dancing over her nerves. Some prudent portion of her mind argued that she should be ashamed of herself. If her mother were alive to see this, Beth would be disowned in a heartbeat.

I deserve some enjoyment! There was never money for dinners out and movies. There were no grandparents to allow her a quiet picnic in the park.

But a fling?

Plenty of women did it, of course. They'd been responsible. A chance like this would likely never come again. Few men were looking for an entanglement with a woman with two small children.

She sobered. It was unlikely that James wanted a long-term relationship either, and their affair would have to end before the girls were old enough to understand...or to form a bond with him. In many ways, she'd been lucky that Ethan had died before they knew him.

Beth yawned and opened her eyes, staring at the clock, trying to force the blur from her vision. She blinked in disbelief. It couldn't be nearly noon! The girls— She scrambled from the bed and to the cribs, gasping, her heart pounding at the sight of the crumpled blankets and no babies beneath them. He wouldn't!

A happy squeal followed by a masculine chuckle reassured her that he hadn't taken her daughters far.

She relaxed her death grip on the crib side, forcing her heart to slow to a natural rhythm.

I'm being ridiculous. Hadn't she just complained that she had no time to herself? James had given her a wonderful gift, a chance to sleep as she hadn't since the girls had been born. Though they usually slept through the night these days, there was always housework to be done or some other chore that meant she couldn't really sleep when they did.

A smile curved her lips. She should thank him properly for what he'd done for her.

Beth pulled her hope chest open and dug out the silk robe Ethan had bought her for their first—their *only* anniversary. He'd given her the robe; she'd given him a silver watch and the news that she carried the children he'd never seen. He'd been killed three months later by a desperate young man—for ten dollars and the watch.

She pushed away the gloom and pulled on the pine-scented silk. Ethan was dead. Whether he'd approve of James or not was immaterial. He certainly wouldn't want her constantly worn and working either, no matter what small pleasure she carved out for herself.

She padded out to the kitchen, stopping in the doorway and watching James in amazement.

He sat there in nothing but his jeans, chuckling and feeding spoonfuls of oatmeal to the girls. It was so warm and cozy that she found herself smiling.

No. It wouldn't last. It was like a Norman Rockwell print, a slice captured in time that never comes again. Still, who would have thought a vampire hunter would be caught dead feeding a baby? And, he looked so comfortable doing it.

"Now," James crooned. "We've let your Mommy sleep in. We've had food and baths and gotten dressed. What would you two say to a nap in the car and shopping for Christmas dresses?"

Beth felt her face heat. "You know I'm here. Don't you?"

"Of course."

"I don't have—"

"Car seats for the girls?"

"You do?" she asked weakly.

"Don't worry. I didn't buy them. I borrowed seats from one of my brothers. He and his wife have no little ones at the moment...and no plans for more that I know of, so they won't be needing them back anytime soon."

"Good." She examined her relief in confusion. What did it matter if he'd bought seats? With his money, it wasn't a sign of anything significant. Maybe that scared her in itself.

"Then you'll come to lunch and for some Christmas shopping?" he asked cautiously, as if he'd scented her attack of nerves. "After all, you said you'd planned to do it today."

She weighed the idea of him leaving against the certainty that he'd end up having sex with her again if she invited him to stay. Either option carried a certain amount of discomfort for her, but the up side of each...

Be reasonable! I came out here, intent on seducing him again. Why would I want him to leave?

Because he was asking for things she hadn't expected him to ask for? Because he was doing things she hadn't? It was a weak reason to send the man packing, when everything he was doing was so overwhelmingly positive.

"Yes. I'll need a shower first, though."

James raked his gaze over her, and her body responded to the promise in his expression.

"The girls can nap just as well here," he suggested.

Beth nodded. "Yes. They can. Probably better, but they've never been in a car, so I don't really know."

As if agreeing, Michelle yawned deeply.

"Nap time," James announced, lifting Michelle and then Melissa onto his hips and marching toward the bedroom.

She hesitated, searching her memory and imagination for the best way to drive James as crazy as she felt. It had been almost a year and a half for her, and James was so different than Ethan, that she felt as hopeless as a virgin.

A protest from the direction of the cribs, most likely Michelle, reminded her that she was anything but a virgin.

Beth untied the robe and let it slide aside, leaning against the counter. James sauntered back in, stopping with a jolt. His cock hardened while his gaze made a slow inventory. That was all it took to make her ache to have him back inside her.

"Stay there," he rasped. James disappeared into the living room, returning moments later, nude.

He wrapped his hands around her waist, a sealed condom between them, lifting Beth to the counter. She parted her legs, allowing him to step between them. His mouth covered hers, his tongue delving inside as she opened for him. He was thorough, intense.

James pulled back, his eyes closed. "Do you want this?" he asked.

"Oh, yes." More than she wanted anything in life at this moment.

He smiled. "I know you want..." His fingertips stroked at her clit. He captured her whimper in his mouth, then eased away. "Do you want me to take you here? On the counter?"

Beth pressed to him, needing exactly that, something wild, something hot.

The rip of foil announced his preparations. Then he was inside her in one smooth, deep thrust. His hands supported her, positioning Beth for his possession. Their moans and pleas wove a tapestry of pleasure.

And then he tensed, swallowing a cry as his heat rocked the teasing ripples of her body's reaction into a wake of pounding waves.

For a moment, they held to each other, gasping for breath. Then a smile curved his lips.

"What are you planning?" she asked.

"Are you intent on shopping today?"

"Well... No. I suppose not. I prefer to get an early start when I do, especially this close to Christmas. Why?"

His lips caressed hers. "I'll take you tomorrow, bright and early."

"And today?"

His hungry look left no doubts as to his plans. Beth nodded, feeling abruptly lightheaded.

Chapter Eight

Sunday, December 17, 1978

"Where are we going, James?"

His smile widened. So, she finally realized that he was taking her away from home. "I thought we'd stop by the manor house and let Michelle and Melissa play with the other children."

"You're taking us to meet your family?" she squeaked. Beth looked down at herself in seeming horror, smoothing her blouse.

James took her hand, kissing her knuckles. "Relax. You look beautiful."

"What if they don't approve—"

"It isn't their place to approve or disapprove, and I've never seen them snub anyone that one of us cares for."

She looked over her shoulder at Michelle, biting her lip lightly.

"They'll love you...all of you. Trust me."

She nodded, pulling her hand away and looking out the windshield. Beth didn't demand that he turn around; that was a good sign, he supposed.

The house rose before them. Her mouth opened in an Oh of surprise, and her eyes widened. "My God... It's...it's enormous."

"It's full of family."

"Full? That..." she sputtered.

"Well, there is room, but when most of them come in for the holidays, the size becomes necessary."

He pulled the car up to the head of the drive and got out, flipping the seat forward. He scooped the diaper bag over his shoulder and lifted the sleeping princess onto his arm. Beth fell into step beside him as he rounded the car, Melissa peeking over the back of her shoulder.

The door opened before they reached it, and his mother rushed out, rising on tiptoe to kiss his cheek. Georgia's eyes lit at the sight of Beth and the babies. "Oh, James," she gushed, reaching for Michelle. She pulled her hands back sadly when she realized that the little girl was sleeping.

Beth shifted from foot to foot, then smiled widely, offering Melissa. "Would you like to hold her, Mrs. Armen?"

His mother blinked back what looked like tears, nodded, and accepted the baby. "What a baby doll." She smiled at Beth. "It's Georgia, dear. Please...make our home your own."

She swallowed hard, nodding.

James ground his teeth in frustration. He'd hoped coming here would put Beth at ease, but it seemed to be having the opposite effect.

The house was milling with women and children, but none of the men were in evidence. That was unusual. Even men who'd hunted the night before would be awake and interacting with family by now. It was only a few hours until dinner, after all.

Georgia guided them to the library. James raised an eyebrow at that. Michelle had proven she could sleep through a ruckus when the younger boys saw new playmates. If she wanted a quiet place, she would have suggested a crib in one of the nurseries. It was almost as if she was conspiring to keep their guests out of sight. None of this made sense.

"Where's Dad?" James asked, adding a look that requested an explanation to it.

Georgia placed Melissa on the rug, handing her a cookie from the tray Rachel brought in. She nodded to the doors, silently instructing them shut. Her voice was light, her smile tense. "Meeting with Carrick, the Warriors who were in residence today...and Corwyn Lord Hunter."

James looked to the ceiling in dismay. *Oh, dear Ani! I never would have brought them here if I'd known.*

"James?" Beth asked in concern. "What's wrong?"

"Nothing," he lied, his mind spinning. Perhaps Georgia was right. If they stayed in the library, Corwyn might leave without seeing them. Surely, one of the women was already passing the news to the Warriors to steer him clear.

"James," she said sharply, demanding an answer.

"It's all right, dear," Georgia soothed her. "One of our other guests... He lost a wife and child recently and... Well, his daughter would be not much older than your girls are."

Beth winced. "We should go."

"No," James and Georgia said together.

"No," James repeated. "It will be all right. Corwyn will be leaving soon. He never stays longer than an hour or two." He prayed it would be all right.

* * * *

Beth smiled, stifling a giggle at the 'lesson' in progress.

"Like this," Tim piped up, handing the wooden dagger to Melissa. James's nephew was a cute four-year-old who was the size of a typical seven year old.

Melissa wrapped her tiny hands around the hilt, and Tim released his prized possession to her.

"That's right," he urged her on.

The baby considered it carefully, then started to teethe on the edge. Tim sighed, but he let her continue.

Beth tried her best not to laugh, hoping not to offend the child-Warrior. James was less restrained. He howled in laughter, slapping his thigh with one big hand.

Melissa released her bite, smiling widely at his response. She squealed in delight, dropping the toy to clap her hands together.

The doors burst in, and a Warrior stepped into the room, standing over them, his hard eyes locking on Melissa. He took two steps toward her, coming to a halt as Beth scrambled to the floor and scooped her daughter up.

He met her eyes, and her heart hammered in fear. This man was crazy, and he wouldn't hesitate to harm her, though she didn't understand why. Was this the one who'd lost his daughter? Surely, he wasn't unbalanced enough to think Melissa was his?

James appeared at her side, drawing Beth to her feet and stepping halfway in front of her. She started to transfer Melissa to the hip hidden by his body, but James grasped her arm, shaking his head. Her protest died out as James untied the bonnet and pulled it off Melissa's head.

"Mother," James hinted.

Beth looked around at Georgia, watching her remove Michelle's bonnet. James's mother fluffed the baby's golden curls, and Michelle rubbed a fist to her eye, yawning and then looking around in curiosity at the new place she found herself in.

"Stand down, Hunter," James whispered.

Melissa patted Beth's chest, bringing her attention back to Corwyn Hunter...and the Warriors crowding behind him.

The man's expression had changed to one of pain and longing. He offered a tip of his head, unfisting his hands.

Melissa grasped James's shirt, twisting to lay her cheek on his arm, then stuffing her free thumb in her mouth.

James stroked the fingertips of his opposite hand over her cheek, his eyes still on the Warrior facing them. "It's okay, Baby Doll," he breathed.

Hunter cleared his throat. "My apologies for frightening you," he grumbled. "They're...beautiful." He nodded to James. "Protect them." That sounded like an order.

"You know I will."

"They are beautiful," he repeated.

Beth shifted further into James's back. "Thank you," she replied woodenly. She wanted to offer her condolences for his loss, but something told her that his pain was too raw for that.

He turned and left, slipping between the Warriors who parted for him. The oldest, an ancient man with snow-white hair, motioned to two of the others, turning toward the library while they followed Corwyn. The remaining two trailed the older man into the room.

"My apologies," the leader intoned. "You must be Elizabeth."

She nodded.

James turned to her, placing his hand on Melissa's back. "It's Beth, Grandfather. Are you all right?" His eyes offered comfort.

Beth managed a strained smile. "We're fine," she assured him. "Just shaken."

"I'm sure Corwyn wouldn't have hurt you."

The leader nodded emphatically. "Even if he'd wished to, he wouldn't have made it more than another step toward you. You have my vow on that, Beth."

"Thank you."

He offered his hand. "This wasn't how I'd envisioned meeting you, but welcome to Armen manor. I'm Carrick."

James lifted Melissa to his shoulder, freeing Beth to shake hands. But Carrick didn't shake her hand; he raised it to his lips and kissed it. She blushed at that.

The next Warrior did the same. "Aaron, ma'am. I'm James's uncle."

And the final one. "I'm Ben. James is my son. I'm pleased to meet you and..." He looked from one of her daughters to the other, fingering Melissa's hair. "Melissa." He nodded to Michelle. "And Princess Michelle?"

Beth realized her mouth was hanging open and snapped it shut. "Yes, but how could you know which is which?"

He smiled. "The three of you are all my son has talked about for more than a week. How could I get it wrong?"

Her heart leapt at that.

James cleared his throat, going red-faced, turning his attention to his mother. "Will dinner be ready soon? I'm sure we're all famished."

Beth dimly noted Georgia's response, too busy considering what Ben's comment signified to pay attention to anything else.

* * * *

Beth tucked the blankets around Melissa, noting James doing the same for Michelle. The girls were exhausted from hours of play with both children and adults. By the time they left the manor, not a single person there confused 'Princess' for 'Baby Doll.'

As James had foretold, his family adored Michelle and Melissa. Aside from the disturbing encounter with Corwyn Hunter, all three of them had been treated like honored guests. Georgia and Ben had even pressed them to return for Christmas Eve dinner. It had taken Beth less than a minute of self-argument to agree.

The reason for her disquiet was hard to quantify. Their presence was welcomed, even encouraged by his family, and yet... There was a tension unrelated to Corwyn Hunter; his family seemed to watch Beth and the girls, assess every move they made. When she'd taken time to deliberate, the entire room seemed to hold its breath until she answered. Even now, she wasn't certain whether they were happy that she'd agreed or bearing her presence for James's sake.

She wasn't exactly the typical girl next door that most parents hoped their sons would bring home. It would be understandable if they weren't happy about him taking on the responsibility for another man's children, especially since family was obviously so important to them. Michelle and Melissa were 'playmates' to the Armen children, but could they ever be accepted as 'cousins?'

James touched her cheek, bringing her back to reality. Beth turned to him, wrapping her arms around his neck, drawing his mouth down to hers. They came together, ravenous, needing the passion that they shared so well.

He lifted her, sweeping Beth out of the bedroom and into the living room. Hands pulled at clothing and shoes were toed off, a frantic race to disrobe. Beth bit back a moan, wiggling her hips as James pushed her jeans down her body.

God, had she ever been this crazy for Ethan? She pushed that question out of her mind, kicking the last of her clothing away as James did the same. Ethan was dead. She wasn't being unfaithful to him, and there was no use comparing James to him. There was no either/or; there was only James.

He rolled a condom down his length, his expression intense. She shivered, her nipples coming to points unrelated to the slight chill of the room.

There was no denying that James wasn't Ethan. The men were polar opposites. Ethan had been little more than Beth's five feet eight, a slight man with the body of a runner. He'd been blond and blue-eyed. Most of all, he'd been...a relaxed lover.

James pulled her to his chest: six feet three, broad, and dark. "You make me crazy," he breathed.

Beth nodded her agreement, at a loss for words. That was the other difference between them. Whether their lovemaking was slow or fast, with James, it was all-consuming, as essential as the beat of her heart.

He tipped her chin up on the shelf of his curled hand, stroking his thumb over her lips, sensitizing them, preparing them for his kiss. She kissed the pad as it reached the center of her lips again, hinting that she wanted more. His thumb retreated and his mouth took its place, questing for her response. There was no question that he'd find it a favorable one.

James straightened, lifting her by his handhold beneath her buttocks so that their kiss was uninterrupted. His cock slid between her thighs, and she gasped, trying to find a way to hook her legs around him comfortably. Until now, they'd always made love somewhere where she had support, even when he'd taken her from behind in the shower. This wasn't as easy as people made it sound when you had no support.

His mouth left hers. "No," he grumbled. "Leave it to me."

She settled into his hands. "Yes." *Show me.*

He lowered her around him, stretching her open at a maddeningly slow pace. Beth held to his shoulders, breathing in sharp little blasts of air. It felt so good that it made her head spin, and yet it wasn't enough.

"You do so much," he whispered. "Just let me—"

"Yes. I'll let you do whatever you want right now." *Just don't stop.*

James levered her up and down his length, pausing each time he filled her. She never knew what would spur him to motion again. Sometimes, he would wait for a sound from her, sometimes a movement, and sometimes meeting her gaze.

At last, she couldn't hold off any longer. James moaned lightly as she started contracting around him, his heat pooling inside the condom.

He stood there, naked, holding Beth in his arms, his cock buried inside her. Her body pulsed in aftershocks at the image they presented.

"I never would have let him hurt you," he whispered. "Any of you. You have my vow."

Beth kissed his chest, enjoying the mixture of musk and salt on his skin. "Corwyn Hunter?" He wasn't still upset about that, was he?

"I would have died rather than let you come to harm."

Her heart skipped a beat. He took his vow to protect her so literally.

"Let me share your bed," he requested.

She paused with her lips pressed to the hollow of his throat. "Now?"

"Tonight. Now, if you wish. I...won't make love to you there, if it disturbs you, but I'd like to hold you, to sleep with you in my arms."

The image was almost too much for her. How long had it been? Well, that was a stupid question. She hadn't shared a bed with anyone more than two and a half feet tall since Ethan, and she missed it...badly.

"Beth?"

"Yes. You can share my bed."

Chapter Nine

Monday, December 18, 1978

James smiled at the feeling of Beth pressed to his side in sleep. By Ani, this felt right. How could any Warrior question this? How could any of them settle for simple release for their entire lives and never print?

He grimaced. Yes, he was printing, and it was downright uncomfortable already. Every time he touched Beth, he ached to ask her to be his. Every time he made love to her, the urge to seal her to him made him crazy.

But, it was undeniably too early for that. She'd just met his family and was still ill at ease with them. She'd had to consider whether she'd have dinner with them again...and whether she'd let him share her bed.

"What are you thinking?" she whispered.

"This is nice."

"Then why are you scowling?"

He turned to her, grasping for a plausible explanation. One look at her breasts brushing his chest was his inspiration. "Just plotting how to arrange making love to you in a bed." He pinched her nipple lightly, watching her eyes dilate in renewed hunger. "The couch is nice..."

"And the shower."

"And the shower and the countertop, but I want to love you properly."

"James, I—"

He brushed a kiss over her lips, and she stiffened in response, her eyes widening instead of sliding shut.

"Not here and now," he promised. "Christmas weekend."

"But, how are we going to arrange it?"

"We'll get Alice to watch the girls for a few hours." He offered her a sly smile. "I'll offer her another bonus. She told you to hold on tight. She wouldn't begrudge you listening to her, would she?"

"She goes to San Diego to stay with her son for the holidays. Since I have the week between Christmas and New Years off, it's never been a problem for me."

"My mother then. Tim and Alex would love to have the girls there."

Beth hesitated. "She won't mind? I don't want to impose, James. Maybe I should—"

"She won't mind." He wound his hand in her hair, kissing her passionately. "Say yes," he pleaded. Who would have believed that the entire meaning of his existence could come down to the acceptance of one woman?

"All right...if it's all right with Georgia."

"It will be. She loves you and the babies. She's almost as happy that you're coming for Christmas Eve as I am."

Beth seemed about to question that when the first shouted complaint from the cribs sounded. James turned to his back, chuckling at Michelle, standing up, her hands fisted on the top bar.

"Good morning, Princess," he greeted her.

She clapped her hands, overbalanced, and landed on her diapered backside.

Chapter Ten

Sunday, December 24, 1978

James fidgeted, trying to calm his jangling nerves. Damned if his father wasn't right. Printing was more frightening than beasts on first night, more gut wrenching than a feeding, and a greater rush than *Blutjagd*.

He hadn't planned to do this so soon, but his printing had forced him to it. If he didn't change the status quo, the results would be disastrous. He just hoped he wasn't rushing Beth too much.

Of course, I'm rushing her. She's a sensible woman, and this is crazy.

"Fingers crossed?" he asked Melissa.

She smiled, bouncing up and down in her patent leather Mary Janes.

"I'll take that as a 'yes.'"

"Da-da-da-da-da," she babbled at him.

"I'm trying, Baby Doll. I'm trying my best."

Beth breezed into the kitchen, tucking spare sleepers and outfits into the dangerously-overstuffed diaper bag. "Have I forgotten anything?" she muttered, placing the bag next to the sack of milk bottles.

"No. I don't believe so."

She had already packed half of the girls' cold-weather clothing, a few lightweight alternatives in case the cold snap suddenly broke, blankets, toiletries, and food. He'd argued that there was milk at the manor...and bottles, but Beth had packed them, all the same.

He recognized Beth's nervousness, though he didn't understand it. She wanted to prove something to his family, though he couldn't name what she wanted to prove yet. Trying to convince her that she had nothing *to* prove was an exercise in futility, and so he let her continue this mad packing expedition.

"I'm sure I have," she fretted.

"Beth—"

"Balmex?"

"In the front pocket of the bag. Beth, I—"

"Spare diaper pins?"

"Underneath the Balmex. I want to—"

She touched the pile of items over the back of the chair closest to her. "Heavy coats, blankets... The winter bonnets!"

He grasped her by the shoulders as she started to turn away. "Beth, I need to ask you something before we leave."

"All right." Her expression was wary, leaving him wondering yet again what he was doing that made her so unbalanced with him.

James lowered himself to one knee, taking her hands in his. Her mouth opened in shock, and she looked ready to bolt.

"I know this is fast," he apologized. "You probably think I'm insane, but I want to spend the rest of my life with you."

Beth didn't answer. Her pallor convinced him that he wasn't imagining her failure to breathe.

He winced at his choice of words. How stupid was he? Beth was a widow; Ethan had literally spent the rest of his life with her and died all too soon for her comfort.

At a loss for something better to do, he pulled the ring box from his pocket and opened it, offering it to her.

She touched it with trembling fingers, seemingly torn. "It's too much," she gasped.

"I know it's too soon for you...and I don't mean to rush you." *If she refuses me, how will I survive the wait?*

Somehow. I have to give her time. She deserves that.

"I know Ethan hasn't been gone long." Maybe it was better to address the issue head-on.

Beth shook her head. "No. It's not Ethan. It's..." She motioned to the ring. "It's too much, James. I can't accept something so..."

He stared at the ring in confusion. It wasn't that large, only half a karat and no nested stones. Knowing Beth's tastes in simple things, he'd chosen a classic ring, smaller than he'd originally considered by far. It was a curse of printing that Warriors wanted to show off how precious their mates were in any way they could. Getting a diamond as small as he had had rankled, and she thought it was too big?

"You can have any ring you want," he managed, though he suspected size didn't matter to her as much as she protested it did. Beth had other reservations.

"I need time to think," she pleaded. "Would you—"

"As much as you need," he vowed. *As long as I can survive the wait, but how long is that?*

She shifted, obviously discomfited.

"Just promise that you'll consider it," he requested.

"Yes. Of course, I will." Beth fled to the bedroom.

James pushed to his feet, stuffing the ring back into his jacket pocket.

The sound of a raspberry brought his head around. Michelle stood next to Melissa. She met his eyes, then started chewing on the top bar of the playpen.

"Maybe I should have asked you to cross yours, too," he muttered.

Two pairs of solemn blue eyes were his only answers.

* * * *

"James!"

He grumbled a curse, pulling the car back under control. "The girls?" he asked, not daring to take his attention from the road. Where in the hell had this storm come from? He'd never seen one hit with this much ferocity, speed, and stealth. It was the meteorological equivalent of a beast attack.

Beth turned onto her knees on the seat, clutching the back, pale. "Good. I think they're amused."

He smiled, allowing the vehicle to coast to slow them down. With the suddenly-icy condition of the road, he didn't dare hit the brakes to accomplish the job. "They would be."

The car slid again, and Beth pitched toward him. James took his right hand off the wheel long enough to scoop her to his side, then set her on the passenger seat.

"Seatbelt," he barked, pulling the car back into the lane again. The wind sheers and ice fought him.

Beth fastened her belt, grasping at her door. "We should turn back," she managed, panicked.

"No. We're almost off the bridge. The rest of the way to the manor is less hazardous than taking the bridge again in this mess."

She nodded her agreement.

James managed to keep the car facing forward and in the lane, despite the elements, and before long, they were off the bridge. Beth relaxed slightly as the trees closed around them, affording a wind break from the worst of it. She groaned aloud as the moderate rain became a downpour so bad that he could barely see the road.

"It's okay," he assured her. "The manor is just over the next rise."

"Good." Her voice was worn nearly to exhaustion.

He pulled off the driveway and over the lawn, bringing her door as close to the front door as he could. James turned off the car, taking a calming breath. The battle wasn't won yet. They still had to get two babies and supplies safely to the house.

"Okay," he began, his mind working fast. "We'll wrap the girls in blankets and take them inside as fast as we can. I'll come back for—"

The front door opened, and three of his brothers marched out, supporting a tarp between them. When they'd created an overhang from the car to the house, Alec knocked on the passenger window. "Get them inside," he shouted over the howling wind.

Beth nodded, unbuckling her seatbelt and turning with James. They each took a baby, wrapping them in blankets. James soothed Michelle when she fought the process, and she settled down for the trip.

"Ready?" he asked.

Beth nodded, then launched out under the tarp, recoiling from the force of the storm as the wind whipped the rain sideways under it. Alec and Brad tilted the tarp down to act as a windbreak for her upper body, leaving Connor with the shit duty of the top edge.

Alec reached for her waist, hesitated, then urged her forward with a hand between her shoulder blades. "Straight ahead," he instructed.

She lurched toward the door, and James followed.

"Nice save," he complimented Alec as he breezed by. It would have been a shame to have to sock him in the jaw for laying hands on the wrong woman.

"Where are their things?"

"Back seat floor."

"Go. We'll get them."

James nodded and rushed inside, thanking Ani for his brothers' overactive sense of duty to the women and children of the household.

"Isn't she the sweetest thing?" Ben crooned to Melissa, cuddling her to his chest.

Nearby, Georgia helped Beth out of her sopping jacket, offering a towel for her hair. "Thank goodness you made it," his mother exclaimed. "James, get that soaking blanket off of Michelle."

He nodded, tossing it into the corner with Melissa's blanket and Beth's jacket. Michelle blinked her eyes at the sudden brightness. Rachel reached for her, and James resisted.

"You're wet, James," his sister-in-law reminded him.

He handed Michelle over with a grumbled 'thanks,' peeling off his jacket and hanging it to dry on the hook board.

"James," Alec shouted out.

"What is it?"

"We have the babies' gear. Where is Beth's?"

"She didn't bring any."

Beth darkened at that, berating herself for it, he was sure.

The door closed, and silence fell around them save his brothers removing their jackets and boots.

Georgia glanced around. "Are the babies dry and warm?"

Ben nodded. "Melissa is fine."

"Michelle, too," Rachel concurred.

"Good. Boys, go change."

His brothers scattered, proof positive of decades of heeding their mother's orders. James remained. His place was with Beth and the girls.

"Rachel," Georgia continued. "Helen is about Beth's size. Have her choose a dress for our guest, please."

James winced. Saying any of the women was about Beth's size was a stretch. A dress was necessary; no one could lend her jeans.

"Right away," Rachel called back, heading up the stairs behind Alec and the other men.

Georgia steered Beth toward the stairs. "You're shivering. We'll set you up with a hot bath, tea, and dry clothes."

Beth shook her head, seemingly mortified for some reason. "The clothes are fine. I really shouldn't—"

"Nonsense," Ben interrupted her. "The girls will be fine with us for a few minutes. You need to take care of yourself, Beth."

She looked as if she'd like to argue the point, but she didn't.

* * * *

Beth straightened the dress nervously. It was loose but not outrageously oversized. The problem was, it wasn't a style she would normally choose. The dress was cut low in front, panels of silky fabric creating a vee over her chest. Layers of skirt overlapped to create a ragged knee-length. She was wearing an evening gown...and in bare feet.

She took a calming breath and left the bathroom, heading down the stairs. The sounds of talking and laughing led her to the single largest room in the manor, the dining room. Conversations quieted.

Beth searched out her girls first. Melissa sat on Tim's lap on the floor, chewing on his wooden weapon again. Michelle stood between Ben's knees, marching her feet in place in preparation for walking, her hands fisted on the inner seams of his jeans. Without conscious plan, she looked for James next.

He hardly seemed to breathe. Beth was equally breathless as he rose and strode to her.

James cupped his hands around her shoulders, planting a soft kiss at the corner of her lips. "You're beautiful," he whispered.

Her face heated. "It's the dress—" she began.

"Not the dress. *You* are beautiful."

Beth smiled. It had been far too long since someone had said things like that to her.

"Do you feel better, Beth?" Georgia asked.

"Yes. Thank you." Beth's smile faltered at the sight of the crowd of people, easily three times as many as she'd met the last time they visited, and every eye was on her. She smoothed the dress self-consciously.

James turned her to his relatives, drawing her forward. "As you can see, most of the family is home for the holidays."

"Most?" she asked in dismay. Good God, there were more?

"We don't usually have this many, but—"

The one who'd helped her inside laughed heartily. "Big brother *finally* brings a woman home for dinner," he drawled. "Only beasts running wild could have kept us away. Oh, that's why Doug and Tina aren't here."

"On trail?" James asked.

"Unfortunately. He sends his regrets at missing you, Beth." His smile widened. "I'm Alec, by the way. Son number two." He nodded to the slight brunette beside him, nursing an infant. "My wife, Helen."

Beth nodded. "Thank you for the loan."

"Anytime," she replied cheerfully.

"Connor," another intoned.

Beth managed not to wince at the memory of hanging up on him.

He shot a look of amusement at James. "It's nice to finally *meet* you after talking to you that morning."

James cleared his throat, his expression one of warning for his relative.

Connor's smile widened. "Son number five." He hugged the redhead on his lap. "Aimee."

"Pleased to meet you," Beth grumbled. Since he hadn't mentioned her hanging up on him, she wasn't going to either. She'd find a time to apologize for it later. "I've met Brad and Rachel. Does that make Doug number four?"

"Sure does," James replied. He started pointing out his other relatives, firing off one name and relationship after another.

Beth nodded numbly, feeling as if she was on display, as if she was on trial. How would she fare? Would they think she was good enough for James? Or would they see the ragged, wet woman who had to borrow a dress?

Finally, Georgia called everyone to the tables for dinner.

To Beth's surprise, the women situated themselves and the children, sending the older ones to the secondary table—a monstrous table that would fill most formal dining rooms, a full three-quarters the length and width of the main table. The younger ones were settled at the main table with their mothers, strapped into highchairs when necessary, and babies in arms placed into one of the two playpens at the head of the table.

The older men took their places at the main table, and the young men and teen boys marched into the kitchen.

James got Beth seated, then strapped Melissa into a highchair at her right while Ben strapped Michelle into a second, on the other side of her sister instead of Beth. Taking the time to kiss Beth on the cheek, James disappeared into the kitchen with the other men.

Then they started streaming back in, carrying huge platters of food. Beth gaped at the turkey that had to weigh thirty pounds, the massive ham; bowls of potatoes, stuffing, gravy, and vegetables; trays of olives, cranberries, and pickles; boards of bread, cheese, and assorted butters. She stared in disbelief as people started filling plates, men passing them off to children as often as women did.

Alec settled a plate in front of Helen, grasping it and forcing it back to the table when she tried to pass it along to a young boy. He whispered something to her, his expression pleading. Helen blushed, then nodded, releasing the plate. Alec immediately started filling another, handing it to the boy in question while she ate the first. The third plate he filled, Beth assumed, was for himself.

"Beth?" James asked.

She glanced at him, noting the plate of minced food in front of him, blushing in the realization that she'd been so intent on her surroundings that she'd forgotten her children.

"Is this all right?" he asked.

Beth reached for the stuffing and added a spoonful to the plate. "A bit of this. They can eat the diced turkey and stuffing while I feed them the mashed potatoes and carrots."

James turned to the girls, nodding as he scraped the turkey and stuffing into piles on their trays. He raised a spoonful of potatoes to Michelle's mouth.

"You should eat," Beth protested, reaching for the plate.

He shot her the same pleading look Alec had used with Helen. "You need to care for yourself, Beth."

"But, my girls—"

"Let me do this," he whispered. "I want to do it, and my family expects that I will. Let me care for all of you...tonight."

Beth sucked in her breath at the double meaning of his words. She nodded, turning back to her plate, filling it slowly. She glanced at James often, noting his solicitous care in confusion.

* * * *

James laughed around a mouthful of turkey, feeling his cheeks burning. "Come on, Alec. You know I didn't want to marry her," he protested.

Connor laughed heartily. "Well, certainly not after she spent all night—"

"Connor," Aimee and Georgia warned together.

He glanced at the children listening in from their table. "Um...getting to know Kord Maher," he finished tactfully.

"Not before," James insisted. "Julia Farmer was too unsettled and wild for my tastes. And...she didn't do much for me, in all honesty. The right one should make you crazy."

Beth coughed on a mouthful of milk, her eyes wide.

He rubbed her back, watching her color return to normal. "Better?" he asked.

She nodded, though a fine tremor passed through her. Her gaze darted about, then settled on the playpen where the girls played. "They're getting tired," she noted, clearly hinting at more.

"The smaller nursery isn't in use," Georgia offered. "The girls can sleep there."

Beth gasped lightly. "You mean... Surely, you don't have room for us. We should head home...when James is done, of course."

Carrick leaned toward her, putting on his most endearing 'I'm being nice, but I am Lord' expression. "I'm afraid the roads are far too slick to travel tonight, and the storm surge is washing the bridge."

"Do you have room for us?" she repeated. "Any couch or bed will do. Even a playpen for the girls. I don't want to put anyone out."

James felt as if ice had settled in his stomach. He pushed the food around his plate, no longer hungry. It was obvious that Beth had no intention of sharing his bed...or even of admitting that they'd shared one in the past.

The room went silent. His brothers avoided meeting his eyes, and Connor winced. His parents stared at him, questioning James silently.

He didn't answer that question. He couldn't pressure Beth. He wouldn't convince her to willingness. If she chose to distance herself, James had to let her do it.

"If that's what you want, dear," his mother assured her. "The small bedroom next to the nursery is available."

Beth nodded, visibly relieved.

James forced his hand to unfist, allowing his fork to slide to the tabletop.

Chapter Eleven

Beth looked out the window at the pouring rain, her mind spinning. Marriage? She hadn't considered what she'd do if James offered to marry her.

Melissa sighed in her sleep, and Beth echoed it. Why wouldn't she marry him?

It wasn't the money. If anything, she was afraid his family would think she was marrying him for the financial stability he offered. Still, that wasn't her reason for shying away.

She'd proven her solvency to them already. There was little question of that. Though she hadn't packed clothing for herself, what she'd carted along for the girls would prove she wasn't completely destitute. But, they might still think she wanted the extras, the frivolous things like that lovely engagement ring.

Beth didn't doubt that she loved James. She loved spending time with him, laughing with him, making love with him. She enjoyed just talking to him over dinner and watching him play with the girls.

Neither did she doubt that he loved her, that he doted on both her and the girls. James would do anything for them, place his life on the line at the first sign of threat. Giving her heart to such a man would be all too easy for her.

Maybe that was what scared her so much. Beth had given her heart once and lost everything. True, he'd died and not left her. Had he lived, Beth couldn't believe that Ethan would have ever left her.

But, James had a dangerous job. What would happen if he died? What would happen if he tired of her? Somehow, she doubted that enforcing a divorce settlement on a vampire hunter would be all that easy.

Then there was family. Ethan's family couldn't even be bothered with his children. They'd never wanted him to marry Beth. She'd never been good enough for their only son. Worse, they'd blamed Beth for his death and refused to acknowledge their grandchildren.

Beth pushed away from the window and ambled down the hall to the stairs. Maybe a cup of tea would make her feel better and clear her head. It might even take her mind off Ethan's parents.

Think logically! James's family confused her. She couldn't seem to decide how they felt about her. Most of the time, she'd swear they were happy to see her with James. Then there were those odd tense moments. When she'd asked if they had room for her, for example. Their reactions had indicated that she'd done something wrong, but for the life of her, Beth couldn't figure out what that wrong thing might have been.

She walked into the kitchen, lost in thought.

"Good evening, Beth," Georgia called out brightly. "Is there anything wrong?"

She managed a strained smile. "Full mind," she admitted. "I thought I might get some tea to calm myself."

"Sit down. I'll—"

"No. Really... I mean, I don't want to be any trouble."

The older woman shook her head and took Beth's hand, tugging her toward the table. "James has been remiss. I can tell."

"Remiss?" she asked, sinking into a chair.

Georgia collected another cup from the cabinet, pouring tea from the pot already set on the table. For a moment, Beth wondered if James's mother had known she was coming down.

How could she? "Remiss?" she asked again. "How has James been remiss?"

"Has he asked you to be his bride yet?" she countered.

Beth felt her cheeks darken. She took a sip of the tea, trying to organize her thoughts.

Georgia smiled and patted her hand. "I will assume he has."

She nodded.

"Good. Now, what is it that has you so afraid to marry him?"

"I shouldn't—"

"Pish! It's my job to put new brides at ease when their boneheaded males forget to explain the state of affairs to them. I've heard them all. With four daughters married into this family, there isn't much I haven't heard. I'll assume your sexual relationship is healthy. It always is."

Beth choked on a mouthful of tea, clapping a hand over her mouth to stifle her gasp of surprise.

Georgia rolled her eyes. "Good gods! James has been intent on you for almost a month. If he hadn't bedded you by now, he'd be stark raving mad."

"He'd what?" She lowered her hand, realizing how garbled that must have sounded, and tried again.

She sighed. "When I find that son of mine... And I thought Connor left Aimee in the dark. James has to be the worst—"

"Georgia?" The woman seemed positively livid about something, so much so that Beth was strangely relieved that it wasn't her that Georgia was angry with.

"Warriors require sexual release often. I was stunned that you requested a separate room."

"Oh."

"You weren't afraid of my reaction, were you?" She seemed amused by the prospect.

"I suppose I was. In light of the facts, that almost seems laughable. You all knew we were..." She motioned her hand, even now uncomfortable with stating it.

"Of course. It's the usual way. Warriors have fierce drives."

Beth drank down another mouthful of the tea, considering this new information about him.

"They also mate for life."

Beth gaped at her. "They...never—"

"Divorce?" She shook her head. "When a Warrior takes a wife, he is biologically tied to her. Even if she dies, he never marries again. He's incapable of it. If you left him tonight..." She grimaced. "It wouldn't be pretty. It could drive him mad to lose you. You see... The ties have already started to form."

"How do you know?"

"I'm a Warrior wife and I'm watching my fifth son print. James is far gone." She smiled. "The fact that he's asked you tells me all I need to know. Considering your past, he would have put that step off as long as he could, giving you time to come to terms with a new man in your life."

Beth nodded, dumbstruck at the concept. "James...mentioned that he thought that would be a problem for me, when he asked me to marry him."

"Is it a problem?" It wasn't a demand for information. She seemed honestly concerned, but for Beth or for James, she didn't know.

"No. It's not. Ethan has been gone for quite some time. I've never had a real problem in that respect."

Georgia's smile returned, brilliant and warm. "At ease?" she asked.

Beth blushed, reluctant to admit that she wasn't.

Her smile disappeared. "Does the concept of printing frighten you? The concept of James taking you as a mate for life?"

"No." It didn't. At least she knew he wouldn't simply get tired of her.

"If you're worried about your girls—"

"I'm not. James dotes on them. Everyone does, actually. I don't really understand it, considering... Well, that really isn't important, I suppose."

"What isn't?"

Beth couldn't seem to form an answer to that. Ethan's parents were her problem, not Georgia's. Actually, they weren't even Beth's problem; they were more of a non-problem.

Georgia took her hand. "Has James discussed having a family with you?"

"No. Nothing like that," she assured her.

"Has he explained the Warriors' views on the subject to you."

"No. As I said, the subject of children has never come up."

"No wonder you don't understand." Georgia took what appeared to be a calming breath. "You've met the children. Have you noticed anything odd about them?"

"Aside from how quickly they grow..." Beth started to shake her head, then stopped in amazement.

"They're all boys. All of them are..." She looked to Georgia for confirmation.

"In our family, this generation—yes. Actually, in every family, this generation."

"But, they can't all be boys. Mr. Hunter lost a daughter." She stopped, gasping. "You don't lose your daughters, do you?"

Georgia grimaced. "No. Nothing of the sort. Warrior babies are the most hearty and healthy babies in existence. There are a rare few girls. There have always been only a rare few. They are simply not conceived.

"Females... *All* females are revered by the Warriors, by the household as a whole. Those they take release with are. Those they marry are, and their daughters are.

"A woman who mates with a Warrior is part of the family for life. If James dies, you would still be a member of this family, held in the highest regard. All women, wives and daughters, are protected fiercely by every Warrior of the house."

"Even if..." Beth ventured, wondering at this system. But, she'd seen it, hadn't she? She'd seen the Warriors waiting to eat, caring for their wives and children first. She'd seen them carrying the food to the table, taking a momentous but menial task from the hands of the women they revered.

"Even if they are daughters adopted into the family. You have no concept how precious and joyous we find having the girls here with us. Like you, they would be members of our family for life, no matter what happened to James. With your permission, we'd raise them as our own flesh and blood.

"The Warriors live and die by duty, drives and family alone. Our men would die for you and the girls tonight, if for no other reason than that you wear an amulet and have a blessing. It's their duty to do it."

Beth fingered the amulet. She hadn't realized how seriously they took the giving of one.

"The fact that James wants you as his mate drives them to protect you more fiercely. Walking out into the storm to protect you isn't their duty, but the boys did it, because you already have a place here and in their hearts.

"If you agree to marry James, you're family, and the Warriors are never more dedicated than they are to family. It's not the marriage certificate or adoption papers that seal the pact but your agreement to be bound as James's mate."

"Bound?" she asked.

Georgia chuckled. "If you tell James you wish to be his wife, he will allow the printing cycle to complete. He will...cement the chemical bond between you in lovemaking."

"It's that simple? He makes love to me, and it's done? But we've... I mean..." Beth bit her lip. She was discussing having sex with James's mother? When had her life gotten so strange?

"It's difficult to put into perspective, but James can fight the need to seal printing up to a certain point. *Endspiel* means the point of no return, the point where he must seal or go insane. Though Warriors are taught to turn away from a hopeless relationship long before *Endspiel*, I've never met one who could walk away while the slightest chance of success existed."

A niggling of unease ate at her. "You said James is far gone. How far gone is he?"

She shrugged. "He's a strong man and an honorable one. Warriors rarely admit their need...unless they are asked directly."

A sudden pang assaulted her, and Beth pushed to her feet, turning toward the door.

"Beth?" Georgia asked in seeming concern. "Is something wrong?"

"I need to talk to James." She started toward the doorway.

"If you need to talk more, I'll be here," she promised.

Beth turned back to her. "Thank you, Georgia."

"Warrior wives are always there for each other. We're mothers and sisters to each other. Someday, you may be the oldest Armen woman or the Lord's wife, doing the same for your son's chosen mate...or your grandson's chosen mate."

"If I am, I hope I live up to your example."

* * * *

James set the file Carrick had left for him on the nightstand and headed for the door. Someone was running up the stairs. It was too heavy to be one of the children, too light to be one of the men. If it was Cal, his cousin in training, James would offer correction. If it was one of the women, something was wrong.

He wrenched the door open, catching Beth as she nearly tumbled into the room. "What is it?" he asked. "Are you all right? Are the girls?"

She nodded.

He forced his muscles to relax. They were in no danger, and his *Blutjagd* was unnecessary.

"Can I come in?" she asked.

James hesitated for a moment, the reality of her in his arms, fifteen feet from his bed, scattering his senses. "Yes," he managed in a rough voice. *Stay here*, he begged silently. He led her a few feet into the room, then closed the door behind her.

Beth wandered to the window, staring out at the pouring rain. "Are you in *Endspiel*?" she asked bluntly.

He ground his teeth in frustration. If that was her reason, he wouldn't seal. She had to want to be with him, not just agree to be. "Not...yet." He hadn't lied but nearly. How close was he? Probably too close.

She turned to him, seemingly considering something carefully.

Lightening flashed, outlining her body.

James realized he was in motion when he was halfway across the floor to her. Beth didn't retreat. She closed the last stride to him, winding her hands around his neck, parting her lips as his mouth meshed with hers.

His entire body burned. It was a hunger, a craving only Beth could sate. James guided her back to the bed, stripping off his button-down shirt and opening his jeans in just those few steps.

He reined himself in. If he didn't clear his mind, he'd rip her robe off and ravish her. She was more important than that.

Beth sank to the bed, panning her eyes down his body. She untied the robe and eased the t-shirt he'd lent her up to uncover her curls. James shivered in need, yanking his t-shirt over his head and dropping it to the floor.

"You're crazy for me, aren't you?" she whispered.

"Yes. Everything about you makes me crazy to have you."

Beth pulled off the t-shirt, uncovering her beaded nipples. "Everything about you drives me crazy, too. I want you inside me...now."

James groaned at that; he would be insane before New Years. He followed her down onto the bed, granting her wish with a long, slow slide into her silken body.

Some traitorous corner of his mind protested making love to Beth half-dressed. Then she nipped at his chest, and James told the fool to shut up.

She clutched at the meat of his buttocks, pulling him deeper with each thrust. "You want to seal printing. Don't you?"

He closed his eyes, trying desperately to stave off the need. His thrusts became more frantic. "Yes. By the gods, I—"

"How bad do you want to?"

"With every cell in my body," he admitted. "All I can see is you, smell is you, taste—"

"Later," she gasped.

James opened his eyes in confusion. "Later, what?"

"Taste me later."

His mouth watered at that. Maybe she'd taste him again, as well. Gods, but he lost all control when she did.

"Give me your vow," she moaned.

"To taste you?" Nothing she was saying made sense.

"Give me your vow that this is forever."

He nearly climaxed from that alone. *It isn't the promise I need. I can't pretend it is.* "If you'll have me," he gasped, fending off his release.

"I want you."

James roared out a protest, losing his battle with self-control. He lay, trembling, his body emptying into hers, the calm that came with the seal at odds with his guilty conscience.

"What is it?" Beth asked, her eyes wide in concern.

"I didn't... I shouldn't have... It's not supposed to happen this way."

"I did something wrong, didn't I? Oh, James." She seemed on the verge of tears.

He shook his head, laying a gentle kiss over her lips, the enormity of his offense nearly crushing him. "No. It was me. It was my error." She hadn't asked him to seal, and he had. If she meant that she wanted him to make love to her and not marriage, he would have to face his grandfather's blade for it. The only consolation would be that Beth and the babies would be taken care of as if they were family members.

Tears welled in her eyes. "Oh, no. I wanted it to be perfect," she choked.

"It?" he asked, praying he wasn't reading more into her comment than she intended.

"Accepting your proposal. Telling you to finish...seal your printing. I'm—"

"Thank Ani! Thank Syth! Thank any gods who are listening and more."

"James?"

He brushed away the tear winding down her cheek. "I sealed to you. When you said you wanted me... In the heat of the moment... Thankfully, you really did mean printing."

"Then you'll marry me?" she asked, uncertain.

"I wouldn't survive losing you. I'd give everything I own just to have you with me."

"Just promise that I'll have *you*," she requested. "That's all I really want."

"I wouldn't dream of less, but there is one thing I have to ask."

She was abruptly serious. "What is it?"

"Can I put the ring on you now?"

Beth's laughter filled the room. "Since you won't return it for something smaller...yes."

"Do you want something smaller?" he asked, fully prepared to exchange the ring if she said 'yes.'

She shifted against him, gripping his cock with her inner muscles. "Mmmm. No. I don't." Beth gasped as he hardened within her again.

"Good," he growled. "Because it's only going to get bigger."

Michelle: Devon's Price

Tarot: Ten of Cups

Tarot Card: Ten of Cups

The Ten of Cups is a card of peace and family. Devon Kaufmann wants nothing more than a wife and family, and Michelle Armen is the woman he wants to fill that void in his life. A Warrior never knows peace the likes of which he does when he seals printing, and that is a state Devon avidly pursues. For a Warrior, the key to happiness is family.

Unfortunately, Michelle has been raised in a close-knit Warrior family as well. Torn, between the same need to find family with Devon and her individual need to retain her family ties in Armen, it seems they will never find the peace they seek. After all, how can she have both?

The book starts off with a tense game of cat and mouse between the mate-seeking Devon and the pleasure-seeking Michelle, but hostilities cannot last long between them. However, Devon's true test of restoring harmony comes when he has to earn James Armen's forgiveness and restore peace in the household after going too far in his printing madness.

Chapter Twelve

September 5, 2003

"Then I have your permission?" Devon Kaufmann asked.

James Lord Armen nodded. "Since your lord gave you leave to remain, you may do so in my range. The usual rules apply."

Devon smiled. "I've never had a holiday, Lord Armen. It would take an emergency to get me into battle...feeding, something I couldn't ignore as a Warrior. I doubt I'll be interfering in one of your tracks."

"I hardly—"

"Dad, have you seen—" a female voice began.

The lord raised his hand and jingled a set of keys hung on his fingertip, one eyebrow raised in a look of supreme amusement. "Next to the computer," he informed her. "You have really got to learn to keep a handle on your keys, Princess."

"Thanks, Dad. I don't know what I'd do without you."

Devon looked up as she passed his chair, biting back his laughter studiously so as not to appear rude to his hosts. His smile faded, and his gaze followed her.

She was enchanting, nothing like any Warrior-born daughter he'd ever seen. The woman had long blonde hair. He might have assumed she'd dyed it as some daughters did were it not for her stunning blue eyes. Even contacts couldn't turn brown eyes that perfect shade of blue.

She took the keys from her father's hand and leaned to place a kiss on his cheek, her breasts pressed tight into her halter and her jeans molded to a luscious backside. Her eyes met his, and she stood, offering Devon a shaky smile.

The Lord Armen cleared his throat. Devon snapped his gaze to him, feeling his face heat at the lord's inquiring expression, certain that he'd just blown his holiday in Armen to the Christian Hell.

The woman backed away and then turned for the door. "I'll finish that computer track this afternoon," she promised.

"When you have time," her father replied.

Devon didn't watch her leave, though he ached to. He didn't have leave to pursue her, didn't even have an indication that she'd welcome the move. And, he'd already pushed Lord Armen further than he should have.

"My daughter," the lord offered simply. His voice was calm and seemingly without censure.

"My apologies. Her appearance is—striking. She surprised me."

He chuckled. "You expected her to look like the typical Warrior-born. Most Warriors do unless they know *of* her."

"If you don't mind my asking... I mean, Warriors don't usually adopt children because of the risk of exposure, and—"

"My mate was a widow when I saved her. She had twin daughters, infants. I am the only father they have ever known, and I love them *as* my own."

Devon nodded, barely stopping himself from asking if there were two women like that running around in shock that any house had been gifted two girls, no matter how they came to be there, let alone ones that looked that enticing. The threat had been stated clearly enough. They were Warrior-raised, and the Warrior in question wouldn't hesitate to enforce the rules of sanction where his daughters were concerned. "I understand. I wouldn't dream of touching her without your leave to do so."

For a long moment, the lord stared at him. He looked toward the foyer and back to Devon. "Very well. Enjoy your holiday, Devon."

He nodded again, nearly shaking in relief that he hadn't offended his gracious host. That was one thing his father and grandfather would punish severely. "My thanks."

* * * *

Michelle stood by the stairs, watching the Warrior who'd been meeting with her father. Tim had told her it was Devon Kaufmann, when she'd asked. Even now, she wasn't sure why she was waiting for him. There was just something about him, something in his eyes that she wanted to see again.

The door to her father's office opened, and Devon headed across the foyer to the front door, seemingly deep in thought.

She hesitated, uncertain how to begin. "Well, well, well... What's on your mind, Warrior?" she drawled.

Devon stopped, looking at her in confusion. "Miss Armen," he greeted her with a courtly bow.

"Let me guess. My father didn't tell you my name." She ambled toward him, adding an exaggerated sashay that caught his attention immediately. Michelle smiled. It had never failed on human men, so she'd known it couldn't with an oversexed Warrior who wasn't related to her or mated already. "It's Michelle, by the way." She offered her hand for him to shake...or kiss.

"No. He didn't." Devon didn't take her hand. "Tell me your name, I mean."

Michelle sighed. "I'm certain my father won't kill you for a handshake," she ventured, trying to keep him talking.

In truth, her father wouldn't kill him at all...probably. She had autonomy. It was one of the things her mother had insisted on. Of course, the rules of sanction might still apply to Devon, since he was a Warrior and she the daughter of another house, autonomy or no. It was dangerous business for a Warrior to poach on the family of another.

Devon looked at her hand, his expression pained. "It wouldn't be appropriate," he replied.

She stepped to him, grasping his wrist, drawing his hand up to hers, noting his indecision in amusement. He didn't dare wrench his hand away, but he wasn't comfortable touching her either. He winced as she grasped it in her own but didn't pull away, resigning himself instead to shaking her hand properly.

"See? Not so bad, is it?" she asked.

"No," he admitted in a rough voice. "It isn't."

Michelle chuckled at his unease. "In America, it's considered rude to turn down the offer of a handshake, especially when you are a guest in someone's home. If you mean to stay for a bit, you should remember that."

"And how do you know I mean to stay?" he asked suspiciously.

Thank you, Tim. I owe you a beer for this one. "I'm not my father's best electronic tracker for my pretty face. I'm not that shabby at foot tracking, either." *Though, the pretty face does occasionally help with that.*

Devon withdrew his hand, and Michelle pasted on a smile to hide the sense of loss coursing through her.

"Are you?" he asked.

"I am. I trained specifically for it in college. I've always wanted to go into the family business, and this was my way in. I'm afraid I've made myself rather indispensable, though."

He ranged his gaze over her, and she gasped in surprise at the hunger in his expression. Yes. That was the look she wanted to see again.

"A woman of many talents," he noted.

Michelle shivered at the possible hidden meaning in that. "Some say so," she countered smoothly.

His smile disappeared. "I should—"

She grasped his arm as he started to turn. A fine tremor raced under her fingertips.

"I really should leave," he managed, though he made no move to do so.

"And if I offered to let you stay?"

He turned back, a fierce determination burning in his eyes that stole her breath. "If you do that, I will be forced to ask your father to give me leave to pursue you in any way you prove agreeable."

She forced a breath, wetting her upper lip. "I think I'd like that," she managed. She'd certainly be willing to help Devon enjoy his vacation properly, though she didn't want a permanent relationship.

He stared at her, perhaps shocked by her blunt acceptance. Or was he calculating how best to approach her father to take her up on it?

"Is that so?" James asked, breaking the moment.

Devon winced, turning to him, probably planning to offer an apology for speaking out of turn.

"Of course it is," she answered before he could speak. "I'm sure you're going to ignore my autonomy, since Devon is a Warrior, so why don't we just settle this now?"

Devon shot her a look of disbelief, then looked back to James, seemingly waiting for an explosion.

Her father's smile widened. "You want to pursue her?" he asked.

"By your leave alone," Devon replied hastily. "My intentions are honorable."

"Mine aren't," she warned. There was no sense letting either of them think she was in the market to be some Warrior's mate.

Devon half-turned to her, his expression assessing.

James chuckled. "Do you *still* want to pursue her?"

"Oh, yes." The hint of challenge was in his eyes.

Michelle raised an eyebrow in acceptance of that challenge. She'd never lost before, and she wasn't about to lose now.

"And if she refuses to mate, Devon?"

He seemed to consider that, clearing his throat, darkening. "If she refuses me, I must accept it."

"Very well. Since you seek a permanent arrangement, you have my leave to act as young lovers will." He paused. "Syth help you. You're going to need it."

Devon bowed his head in thanks, casting her another hungry look. Her father went back into his office and closed the door.

Time to put this game in motion. "Well, I do have to go into town," she informed him. "We could meet—"

"I'll come with you. I imagine we have a lot to talk about."

"Yes. Perhaps we do." A lot to talk about if he thinks he can order me around.

* * * *

Devon knew it was coming, whatever ultimatum was brewing in Michelle's pretty brain. They would understand each other perfectly before he was done.

"So, you accepted my suit," he prodded her.

Michelle pulled off the side of the mountain road and into a small grove of fruit trees, putting the truck in park. She turned to him, her expression starkly serious. "Let's get one thing straight, Devon. I'm not the mating kind."

"Mmmm hmmm," he murmured, smiling as her nipples came to points for him.

"I don't want to be sealed. I don't want to be the mother of your sons. I want a hot time in bed, and you keep giving me looks that..."

He unclasped her seatbelt and lifted her, turning Michelle astride his lap.

"Promise that," she gasped.

His half-erect length came to full attention, and he pressed her to it, rocking his hips to grind it against her. Her eyes closed in ecstasy and she rode him, groaning softly.

Devon pulled her head toward him, tangling his fingers in her golden tresses and taking full advantage of her parted lips. Her mouth was frantic against his, her tongue sliding along his while their bodies ground in mimic of what he'd soon have. Her nipple was already hard and ready when he tweaked it. Michelle jumped in response, then pressed harder against him. Gods, but the woman was hot!

Her hands pulled at his shirt, and Devon switched the engine off. The urge to take her on the grass outside the door was insistent, but that would be giving Michelle what she wanted. Devon had no intention of that.

He eased her hands away, dimly noting that she'd unbuttoned half of his shirt. Good. If she wanted him badly enough, he might just leave Armen range with a mate.

Michelle tried to pull back, but he clasped her head to his, swallowing her groan of protest. She sighed, moving against his thrusts.

The game was sweet torture, all the more so when her climax neared. She pulled at his clothes, alternately fought her climax and pursued it, and even escaped his kiss to plead with him. Devon nearly laughed at that, but it was more important that he make his point first.

Then the moment crashed over them. She stiffened, then eased into his chest with a ragged cry. Her scent was sweet and pungent, an assault on his aching body.

"Devon, I—"

"You want more?" he interrupted her.

"You know I do."

He brushed his lips over her forehead. "It's not fun, is it?"

Her brow furrowed. "What isn't?"

"Being unfulfilled. That's what release is like for me."

"Release is—" she started to argue.

"Experiencing a climax and wanting more. At least it is for Warriors who are ready to settle down. Let's get *this* straight, Michelle. It seems your father gave his leave, because I want more than release. Neither he nor I are comfortable with the idea of you sampling a little Warrior cock with no return."

She pushed away, settling on her knees beside him, seemingly livid. "How dare you! How do you know what my father—"

"Warriors understand each other well enough."

"So, you're saying you won't fuck me unless I agree to marry you?" she challenged.

"I'm saying I won't *fuck* you at all. Your father gave me permission to pursue you as my mate."

"He gave us permission to act as young lovers will," she shot back.

"A woman I pick up for release isn't a lover, Michelle. A lover is someone you want more with. Unless I have a reasonable expectation that you'll consider being my mate, you'll remain as unfulfilled as I am. Oh, I'll give you orgasms, mind-blowing orgasms, but to get what we both want... Both of us have a shot at it or neither does."

Michelle crossed her arms over her chest, her face crimson and her jaw tight in fury.

"I've given you enough to consider. I'll see myself back to the manor and my car while you finish your errands. Have a nice day, Michelle."

He didn't give her time to argue. Devon slid out of the truck and strolled away, savoring the taste of Michelle in his mouth and the sun touching his chest in the vee of his half-opened shirt.

* * * *

"That son of a bitch," she growled for the tenth time in the last hour. Four of them had been uttered before she'd regained enough composure to start driving again.

He'd rattled her horribly. There was no denying it. So far, Michelle had left her keys behind at two stores and left her credit card behind at a third.

"He is going to pay for this," she vowed. All of the Warriors learned that quickly enough. After the examples she'd made of Tim and Tyler, few had been stupid enough to try her again.

But that had been the typical male bullshit, their belief that they had the right to order her around, despite her autonomy. This was different. Her retaliation would have to fit the challenge.

For a moment, Michelle considered simply refusing him. It would serve him right if she called a halt now, coming out on top, one orgasm up on him. One...tremendous orgasm...

A smile curved her lips. Michelle pulled a three-point turn and headed back to town, a new plan in mind. Devon would pay. He wanted to leave her in agony? Two could play that game.

Chapter Thirteen

Devon opened the door to his hotel room, raising an eyebrow at the sight of Michelle. The little vixen was stretched out on his bed in the most alluring sky blue lace teddy he'd ever seen. He strode inside, locking the door behind him, trying to ignore the insistent ache of his now-erect cock.

"Cyber tracker?" he asked.

She smiled. "You did use a credit card to pay the bill. I told you I was the best."

"I won't deny that I'm surprised to see you here."

"You doubted my abilities?"

"No. I doubt your willingness."

"Well, my intentions still aren't pure, if that's what you mean."

He nodded. "Thought so."

"I guess you'll just have to convince me." Her smile widened.

"It's against the rules of sanction to convince you to willingness. You know that."

Michelle stretched her back, and Devon shifted toward her, noting that he could see the darkened tips of her breasts through the lace...the faint outline of her pubic curls, even the darker patch where her juices had wet the fabric between her thighs. The temperature in the room seemed to kick up ten degrees.

Her voice was dripping in invitation. "Oh, I'm more than willing, Devon. You just have to convince me to be your mate. You intend to do that anyway."

He nodded, his mouth watering.

"You made promises this afternoon," she hinted, stroking her fingers in little circles over her mound.

"I most certainly did." Devon stripped off his jacket, weapons belt, boots, socks, and shirts, then headed to the bed.

"Hmmm. Is your control that uncertain?" she mused.

He faltered, one knee raised over the bed. "What?" She was questioning his control, while she was dressed this way and in his bed, inviting him to take release with her?

Michelle stared at his jeans. "Afraid you'll give in and fuck me?" she teased.

Devon ground his teeth at her base description of what he wanted. "I fuck blade chasers," he corrected her.

Her eyes flashed in anger, and she turned away.

His anger faded into confusion. What the hell had he said to cause this response? "Michelle?"

She slid from the bed, reaching for a trench coat. "I'm hardly going to waste my time with you, if that's what you're—"

He made it to her in a single stride, taking her shoulders in his hands. Michelle tried to shake him off, but he pulled her closer.

"Let go of me," she ordered.

"Cool your jets."

She glared at him.

"Tyler taught me that one. Did I use it wrong?"

"Let go of me." Her voice was low in warning.

He ignored her. "You think I'm planning to take release with blade chasers while I pursue you, don't you?"

She stopped struggling and stared at him.

"I'm not."

"Then what are..." She faltered.

"You aren't a blade chaser, Michelle. If I give in, I'll still be making love to you. Remember that."

* * * *

Michelle stared at him, struggling for clarity. The wild urge to walk away assaulted her, then was silenced by her need...and her need for revenge for that afternoon. He hadn't paid for that. And yet, she couldn't shake this confusion.

Nothing seemed clear anymore. Her anger, for instance. What did it matter to her if he screwed a blade chaser?

Michelle tried to convince herself that she'd never get him to give in and have sex with her if he was releasing it with another woman. She reasoned that he wouldn't be suffering as she was if he did. She argued that it balked the idea of a level playing field.

None of those reasons stood up to scrutiny for long. She was jealous.

And I shouldn't be. Devon is a Warrior, a natural-born male slut.

Until they print.

But, she didn't want to consider that possibility.

Devon released her shoulders, holding her gaze. The unmistakable sound of a zipper made her gasp. He went still, his eyes questioning her. She nodded, and he stripped away his jeans and boxers.

Michelle panned her eyes over him, hungry in a way that the other men she'd slept with had never caused.

It was a solemn truth of Warrior-born or Warrior-raised daughters that they went to extremes. They craved Warriors or men who resembled Warriors in every way...or they craved men who couldn't be mistaken for Warriors in a pitch-black room. There was no middle ground, no slight dark men and no Vikings.

Her twin, Melissa, had gone the way of marrying a very human man. At five feet ten, with strawberry-blond hair and green eyes, Mack couldn't be further from a Warrior if he tried. Despite the scars he bore from the beast he'd stood up to in defense of Melissa, he was no Warrior and had no desire to play at being one.

Michelle had always favored tall, dark men. She'd masturbated to visions of visiting Warriors for years.

And now I get to indulge myself. She tossed her coat on top of the dresser.

Devon took the hint. He sealed his mouth to hers, taking the lead as he had in the truck. She wanted to complain about that, to turn the tables on him, but what he was doing felt too good to stop. His hands were everywhere, cupping her to his body, arousing her with practiced ease. He lowered Michelle to the bed, covering her with his body.

She pressed to his cock, gasping as he broke off the kiss, his eyes closed in pleasure. Devon fingered the lace straps over her shoulders.

"Yes," she urged him on. "Remove it."

He smiled wickedly. "Not this time."

Devon moved abruptly, rolling to one side and sliding down. In the time it took her to raise her head to question him, he'd started his seduction.

His mouth was hot and insistent against her breasts, the softness of his tongue at odds with the rough knit of lace. She groaned, fisting her hands in his hair. His fingers stroked at her clit, using the damp cloth to rocket her toward climax.

It took him only minutes to send her over. Michelle screamed in pleasure, gasping out a plea for him to stop when he continued pushing her on.

His head came up, a wicked smile curving his lips. "I promised to make you climax again and again, but—"

Her face heated. "I can take anything you can dish out," she attested, knowing it was a lie even as she uttered the words.

"I'm not done with you yet, Michelle." His hand retreated, leaving her drawing in ragged breaths.

She watched in disbelief as Devon sucked in his fingers, then released them and licked his lips, his gaze traveling down her body, making his meaning clear. The man was going to kill her this way.

But, what a way to go! She reached for the shoulder strap, intent on aiding him in his quest to taste her.

Devon pulled her hand away, smiling. "I like the teddy. Leave it on."

Her temper flared. "I like a man's tongue *inside* me."

He rose to his knees, spreading her legs around him. "I like a woman who knows what she wants and isn't afraid to demand it."

"But?" Her eyes settled on his rigid cock, and her frustration spiked. Of course, he didn't want to take the teddy off. It was a physical barrier between them.

He chuckled. "There's a nice feature to this type of lace, Michelle."

"What?" What the hell was he talking about?

Devon slid two fingers between the lace crotch and her aching flesh, stroking his knuckles up and down her seam.

"Don't you dare," she warned him. The outfit had cost her forty dollars, and while she knew that her father wouldn't bat an eye at the waste of that much money, her mother had imparted enough frugal lessons to her daughters to make her avoid such destruction.

He yanked the material to one side; Michelle winced, mentally preparing herself for the sound of ripping fabric that never came.

She arched up as his tongue dipped inside her, screaming harshly. This went beyond good; it outstripped every fantasy of a Warrior she'd ever had.

Devon eased back, his breathing buffeting her sensitive tissues. "Lace stretches, Michelle. At least, it does if it has a Lycra base."

The other outfits she'd purchased coursed through her mind. Most of them included lace panels. Michelle prayed they were the same type of lace.

Her musing was cut short when he went back to his play, his mouth doing glorious things that made thinking impossible. Everything came down to pure sensation, touches and sound, snips of color and smells so powerful they triggered the illusion of taste.

Michelle shattered, her hands tightening on his shoulders as his groan set off aftershocks. Her head spun, and her muscles were heavy in exhaustion.

Devon smoothed the lace over her, shushing her softly when she jerked away from the added sensation. He lay down next to her, stroking his fingertips over her stomach.

She shivered, gasping out a plea for him to stop. Her body was little more than live nerves, raw, powerful, painful even in pleasure.

"Enough for tonight?" he asked.

"Yes." Michelle felt her face darken in response to his mocking smile.

Devon started to draw the sheets and blankets over them.

That brought the world into focus for her. Sharing his bed wasn't in the cards.

* * * *

Michelle moved so quickly that Devon didn't register her intent until she was off the bed. By the time he was beside her, she had her 'come fuck me' heels on.

"What do you think you're doing?" he demanded.

"Going home."

"Why?"

She didn't answer. Her hand closed on the trench coat.

Realization that she'd come to him in nothing but the lingerie and coat caused him to harden more forcefully. He reasoned back his response. *I am not going to fuck her. I am not going to fuck her on the dresser.*

Common sense rocked him back to course. He snatched the coat away, shaking his head, trying to force words.

Michelle turned on him, her eyes wide in shock. "My coat," she demanded.

"You are not returning home this way."

"I came here—"

"No," he growled.

"Excuse me?"

Reason deserted him. "You cannot..." He motioned to her state of undress, vaguely aware of the pulse in his cock.

"If you'd hand me my coat, I'd be properly covered," she snapped.

He shook the coat, noting the faint jingle of keys from the pocket. "*This* is not properly covered. Not for a woman traveling alone at night."

"It wasn't dark when I arrived here."

"It is now," he managed through clenched teeth.

Michelle glared at him, then turned and strode to his discarded shirts. The lace molded to the curves of her ass as she leaned and snatched his button-down shirt up.

Gleaning her intention, Devon started dressing as well. He glanced at her, fastening his jeans, calculating how best to defuse her. *The keys.* He swept them from her coat pocket and into his jeans silently.

She turned, snatching the coat from his hand, pulling it on over the dress-like shirt as he retrieved his t-shirt and weapons belt. By the time she'd tied it, forsaking the buttons, he'd gotten dressed, save his socks and boots, sloppily though it was.

Michelle headed for the door, her posture stiff in anger. He bit back a smile as her hand dipped into the coat pocket and she stopped abruptly. She checked the other pocket, muttered a curse, then turned back, searching the floor around the dresser, giving him the time he needed to finish dressing and straighten his clothing.

Devon fastened the last buckle on his boots, stood and pulled on his jacket. "Ready to go?" he asked.

Her jaw tightened and her eyes narrowed. She raised her hand, palm-up. "My keys," she ordered.

"When you're safe at home."

"When you've walked me to my car," she countered.

He shook his head. Devon raised an eyebrow in challenge at her growl of frustration.

Her face went crimson in barely-leashed fury. "It's five miles home, Devon."

"Five miles you're not traveling alone."

"You have no right—"

"A protected obeys Warriors in matters of safety."

"You're not of my house."

"I'm a Warrior, and I know for a fact that you don't listen to the Warriors of your house, either. You're right. I'm not one of them; *I* won't put up with it."

Michelle sputtered for a moment. "I'll ask for a judgment," she warned.

"Then I'm guilty of seeing to his daughter's safety. Are you ready to go?"

She seemed to work that through, no doubt coming to the realization that the Lord Armen would side with Devon if it was presented that way. "Give me my keys and follow me."

He smiled. "Your brother says you are quite the driver. Attended a certain race-driving school and came out with flying colors? I don't think we'll be testing that tonight."

A smile curved her lips. "And how will you get back here? You're not using my truck."

"I'll manage."

"Fine. Suit yourself." Michelle preceded him to the truck, tapping her foot while she waited for him to unlock her door.

The trip back to the manor was tense. Michelle fairly seethed bloodlust, and her plotting was obvious.

At the house, she was out of the truck and striding up the walk before he caught up to her. To her credit, Michelle waited until they were halfway across the foyer before turning to him with her hand out in silent demand.

Devon raised the keys, letting them hover over her palm for a moment, then dropping them in.

"Thank you," she stated in a crisp voice that nearly crackled with ice.

James's voice broke the tension between them. "Nice night?" he asked.

"I think so," Devon answered brightly.

Michelle turned, unknotted the coat, and strode to her father, kissing him on the cheek. She whipped off the coat and placed it in his hands without a word, then sauntered up the stairs, clad to appearances only in her heels and Devon's shirt.

Devon choked at the display, envisioning an end to his days even as his errant body responded to the sight.

James chuckled. "Sleep well, Princess."

"I will," she sang back.

Devon snapped a look at the Lord Armen, certain his cheer had been for his daughter and his expression would hold a warning for Devon...or worse.

It didn't. The lord was still chuckling, folding the coat over his arm. He nodded toward Michelle. "If there was ever a human woman with the spirit of a Warrior, Michelle is it."

"I noticed."

"I warn you, she's not going to make your pursuit an easy one."

I could have used that warning earlier.

Oh, who am I kidding? I knew this wouldn't be easy. He nodded stiffly.

"You're prepared for the possibility of failure?"

His heart ached. "I have to be. Every Warrior does."

James nodded grimly. "You drove her home?"

"I couldn't risk less."

"Thank you for that. I'll drive you back."

"No. I think I need the walk to clear my head." *And work off my arousal.* He smiled. "I promise not to kill a beast unless it's stupid enough to attack me." He turned away.

"One more thing, Devon."

"Yes?"

"To put an old man's mind at ease... She was wearing something under your shirt?"

"Oh, it was something," he drawled. That settled it. He needed the walk to cool his blood.

Chapter Fourteen

September 22, 2003

Devon took a calming breath, nearly groaning as she repeated herself.

"I need more, Devon."

"So do I," he replied. He had to keep that in mind when the urge to sate them both properly called to him.

"I'll consider it," she pleaded.

He went still, forcing his mind to function. "What?"

"I'll consider your suit seriously," she vowed.

He ground his teeth, reining in his body.

"I said—"

Devon pressed his forehead to hers. "I heard you," he gasped. "I understand."

"I don't," she admitted. "I said—"

"Say it when you're calm, when your drives aren't talking for you."

"I will."

"When you do... If you do, I'll consider it a promise. You know what this means to me." *Everything.*

"You don't trust me?" she whispered, seemingly hurt.

It was on the tip of his tongue to state that he didn't. After her attempts to lure him with one carefully-constructed outfit and scene after another, her teasing, her hot and cold running emotions...

And that wasn't taking into account her dogged determination that his unwillingness to let her take him to climax was unfair. She hadn't even started with a hand job when he'd agreed. Memories of her taking him into her mouth nearly shook his resolve. He'd come too close to conceding when he'd agreed to let her play the same games with his pleasure that he played with hers.

Oh, but I do want to trust her. There was no denying it. He wanted Michelle to be serious, and if he intended to pursue her to mating, he'd have to trust that she was serious at some point in time. *The sooner, the better.* "I trust you."

"Then you'll—"

"No. Not until you state it when I haven't already aroused you."

"Devon," she pleaded, her voice cracking as if she might cry.

"It would be convincing you to willingness. Not willingness to make love but willingness to mate...or to consider mating."

"You're really going to turn me away?" she asked in misery.

Causing her unease ate at him, and yet he wouldn't risk even the appearance that he'd convinced her, even to himself. "For this... For this afternoon, yes."

Michelle pushed him away, then slid from the bed, pulling on her shirt in silence. He started to rise.

"Don't," she ordered. "It's light out. I'll get a cab."

"I can drive you—"

"I don't want you to!"

Devon winced. "I'm not refusing you, Michelle."

She paused, then straightened her underwear and reached for her jeans. "No. You're not. You just want me to say it in my right mind."

"Yes. I do. I need that. Can't you see?"

* * * *

"Yes, of course, I can." She pulled her jeans on, not daring to look at him.

Michelle could see. Unfortunately, she could also feel. She'd tried to tell him she'd consider his suit seriously a half dozen times, that she *was* considering it. Then she'd remember what that meant to a Warrior and choke on the words.

The reason was obvious. She cared for him. *Maybe, I more than care for him?*

As long as she made no promises to Devon, Michelle felt he could walk away. As long as she didn't, she wasn't really hurting him.

And there was no question that giving him hope would lead to hurting him. Accepting him wasn't like accepting a Hunter or Maher. Devon was a Kaufmann. If she became his mate, there'd be few visits home to see her family. *If any.*

Devon's range was half a world away. He'd be expected to stay there, and he wouldn't deal well with her globetrotting home at the drop of a hat.

Michelle couldn't deny that a life with Devon held appeal. It wasn't just that the man made her crazy sexually. He was solicitous, thoughtful, witty...

"Are you sure I can't drive you?" he asked.

Courteous, a little overprotective... "I'd rather you wouldn't."

He grumbled his agreement.

Michelle slid her feet into her heeled sandals and headed for the door, patting her front pocket though she didn't need keys to get into the manor. She turned the knob.

"Will you be coming back?" he asked calmly.

She glanced back, her mouth going dry at the sight of him. Devon sat in the bed, the sheets pooled low on his hips, one of the most powerful beings that hunted the night seeking a promise from her.

Releasing him now would be kindest.

Just the thought of it tore at her. They'd have little enough time together; how could she walk away before she had to?

To save him more pain.

Michelle wavered. It was the right thing to do, and she knew it, yet...

It came down to her wants versus his, her pain versus his. He needed her to say she wanted him when she was in her right mind. It seemed the only way she'd be able to say it would be if she wasn't.

She turned away, confused. "I... I need time." She left without giving him time to answer.

* * * *

"Michelle," Melissa shouted.

She managed a strained smile, hugging her twin.

Melissa didn't pause, exuberant as always. "Mack had four days off, and you know we just had to come. I thought I'd miss you. Tyler said—"

"Yeah. I know. Big sister is cock-teasing a Warrior." He'd hinted as much to her with more than a touch of disapproval.

"He did *not*!" She threaded her arm through Michelle's and pulled her along to the stairs. "Come on. You have to see Mickey."

That speeded Michelle's steps. She hadn't seen her nephew in more than a month. A few minutes with Mickey was just what she needed.

Michelle smiled widely at the sight of him playing in the bouncy seat set in the center of the smaller nursery, two of the toddler Warriors towering over him. She sat beside him, fingering his strawberry-blond curls.

"So," Melissa hedged, "are you planning to give this Warrior a dark-haired Mickey? Or are you really going to play house and leave him?"

"We're not playing house...precisely."

"You've been sleeping with the man for three—"

"No I haven't, and it's only been a little more than two—"

"So, you're not sleeping. Such nitpicking."

"We're not...really...um..." Michelle rubbed at the base of her skull, feeling a sick headache coming on.

Melissa appeared at her side, searching Michelle's face. "Not what?"

"Devon won't..." She glanced at the toddlers...then away. "He won't...consummate until I tell him I'm seriously considering more."

Her sister's mouth dropped open in shock. "You've got a Warrior so tied up he hasn't had release outside of self-release in almost three—"

"A little more than two!"

Melissa glared at her.

"Two and a half," she conceded.

"You've had this poor guy hanging on with nothing but self-release for that long? Are you nuts?"

"Of course not. He's...getting more than that."

"I thought he was serious about this?"

Michelle fumbled for words, her sister's twisted logic losing her. "He is...I guess. Okay, I know he is."

"He's taking other women to bed? Doesn't sound serious to—"

"No! Of course not. Not with other women. With me...well, once I convinced him to—"

"I don't think I follow you."

Michelle sighed and tried to order her thoughts. "We play around, but he's not... That's not the only thing there is, you know!

"Oh, I don't know what I'm doing anymore. What should I do, Melissa? Should I leave him? Should I stay with him? Should I—"

"Slow down. Do you want to leave him?"

She swallowed down a sob, shaking her head. Her eyes burned in the tears she blinked back.

"Then what's your malfunction?"

"He's not a Hunter or a Maher, Melissa. He's not even a Crossbearer."

She motioned for Michelle to continue, seemingly lost.

"If I do this, we'll never see each other. I won't see Mom and Dad or Mack and Mickey. I don't think I'd mind not seeing Tyler so much," she joked weakly. "I'll be on the other side of the world from everyone I love."

"Except Devon."

"That is the problem," she admitted. "If I have Devon..."

"You don't have everyone else," Melissa finished for her. "But if you stay here..."

Her stomach lurched at the thought. She nodded, feeling more than a little ill.

Her sister sighed. "I never said it was easy, Shell. When Mack and I had to relocate to San Diego—"

"There's still weekends at home," she argued. "No weekends, Melissa. No holidays."

"And if they moved us to Maine, there would be only holidays. If they moved us to China, would there be even that much?"

"And you'd go with him? You'd accept that being with Mack meant not being with us?"

"Either your love is strong enough or it isn't. If it's not, you need to figure that out soon and cut Devon loose while he has a chance."

"What if I don't know?"

"From what you've said, you still haven't given him a chance. How could you know?"

"But... If I do this, and it's not enough, what will I be doing to Devon?"

Melissa smiled. "The fact that you're afraid of that should tell you something."

A lead weight settled in her stomach. "That I'm going to hurt him, and I should let him go now," she replied woodenly.

"No. That you care enough about him to cut him loose, even if it hurts you. It just might be strong enough, after all."

Michelle nodded, thoughts crowding into her overloaded mind. "I think I have to go," she whispered.

"Is something wrong?"

"Yes. I walked away from him. I shouldn't have done that."

"Say 'hi' from me."

Michelle pushed to her feet, laying a kiss on Mickey's head and meandering toward the door. She snatched Tyler's Trans Am keys off the board and headed for the garage.

* * * *

Devon sat crossways on the hotel room love seat, his knees bent to facilitate his height. It seemed he spent more and more of the time Michelle wasn't with him here, brooding, biding his time, praying to Ani that she'd say what he needed to hear.

With her drives, he'd thought the game would be nearly over by now. Her stark interest in him coupled with her passionate nature had him convinced that he was right. Now it seemed he was wrong. Now...she might never come back.

I shouldn't have refused her. She said it, impassioned or not. I should have trusted her.

He considered his options. How long should he wait? How long should he give her before actively seeking to break printing?

Devon fought back the urge to scream. He couldn't choose to do it. Until Michelle spoke the words, until she refused him, he couldn't take that road...

Unless I pose a danger to her. If it came to that, he'd do whatever he had to. He would never hurt Michelle. It wouldn't come to that.

A knock at the door brought him back to the here and now. Devon ambled to it, his heart pounding, hoping it wasn't James Lord Armen with a cabin key in his hand and news that Michelle was calling it off.

He opened it, gaping at the sight of Michelle. Words deserted him.

"Am I welcome?" she asked, seemingly disconcerted.

He stepped back, nearly stumbling over his own bare feet. "Of course."

There were several long minutes of silence after he closed the door behind her. Michelle calmed herself visibly. "I was wrong to walk out that way. I was just...confused."

His heart sank. "I was afraid of that."

Her eyes widened. "No. I didn't mean..." She rubbed at her forehead, then the back of her neck. "I mean, I wasn't confused about what I said."

Devon stared at her. "You're certainly confusing me."

"I know. This...this isn't easy for me."

His heart stuttered. *This is where she calls it off.* Devon prepared himself to let her leave, then call her father to ask for a cabin to fight the madness.

"I've been seriously considering your suit for some time." She paused, darkening, biting her lower lip.

"But?" It was all he could do to force out that one word.

"I'm scared, Devon. I feel so...out of control."

She feels out of control? He bit back laughter at the irony of that statement.

"I don't know what will happen next. I'm confused. I can't promise to be your mate today—"

"I'm not demanding that."

"I don't want to hurt you. If I accept you and I'm wrong, I'll hurt you." Tears pooled in her eyes, threatening to fall.

Devon sighed. "I accepted being hurt when I asked your father's permission to pursue you."

Michelle stared at him, swallowing hard. Was she really that afraid of hurting him? If so, there was a chance.

"I don't understand, Michelle. Are you refusing me?"

"I want to know," she whispered.

"Know? Know what?" She wasn't making sense.

"If I love you enough to be the mate you need."

Devon crossed the space between them in two long strides, giddy in disbelief. He cupped his hands behind her head, raising her chin with his thumbs and claiming her mouth deeply, solemnly.

Michelle pressed her hands to his bare chest, sinking against him. She eased back from the kiss, breathing in quick gasps, trembling.

He nuzzled her lips. "Don't leave tonight."

She nodded, stammering out a reply that made no sense.

* * * *

Michelle couldn't have recounted how she got undressed. The only fact she was certain of was that she did none of it herself.

The little her mind acknowledged consciously was a montage of images.

Devon kissed her. He whispered his plans to her, though she scarcely heard them.

They were on the bed, her shirt off, his mouth providing an unhurried torture of her breasts, his palm pressed to the zipper of her jeans.

He was nude. Her jeans were open and ringing her thighs. His fingertips teased at her clit while she stroked him. He groaned, promising her all of him.

They were both nude. Michelle screamed as two fingers breached her body, aching for him. Devon whispered pleas, begging her not to come without him. She nodded.

He kissed her, his body rolling over hers, their limbs entwined. "Now, Michelle," he breathed into her lips, his fingers sliding free, then circling her clit again, using her own lubricant to arouse her.

"Yes, now."

She didn't question what 'now' meant. As long as it meant Devon was with her, 'now' was good. It turned out that 'now' meant he was going to replace his fingers with the much more substantial length and width of his cock.

Michelle tilted her hips up, unable to arch her body beneath his weight, moaning, grasping at his back.

He moved slowly, pushing the head of his cock through her, stretching her for the rest of him with painstaking care. It felt sublime, beyond all comprehension. She sobbed, and he stopped abruptly.

Devon stared at her, questioning her silently. Even now, she knew he'd stop if she asked him to. She nodded frantically, urging him on.

His advance resumed, heartbeat after heartbeat, until he nestled fully inside her. He slid back slightly, then returned, slowly building his speed and vigor until sweat coated their bodies.

Michelle whimpered in delight, teetering at the edge of climax.

"By Ani, yes. Give yourself to me," he pleaded.

As if invoking the goddess's name were the last straw, Michelle shattered, crying out harshly as her nails bit into his back and her body contracted around him.

Just when she thought Devon was going to ride her crest and push her further, he tensed, his heat playing sweet harmony to her climax. He pulsed inside her, massaging the clenched walls of her sheath.

Then it was over. Michelle let her hands slide away from his shoulders, her muscles aching from the strain of clenching them in the throes of passion. He pulsed inside her again, and she pressed up against him, aftershocks rocking her body.

"Baroo, give me strength," he growled.

She smiled at that.

His lips caressed hers, tracing them from one cheek to the other. "What are you thinking now?"

"I don't know whether to thank Syth as my house god, Baroo as yours, or Tes for granting wishes and blessings."

He chuckled. "I'm thanking them all. The whole lineup from Ani on."

"Even Fih and Zel?"

"Getting here wasn't easy."

"Ah. That's Fih, the god of battle. And Zel?"

"You've never heard of le petit morte?"

Michelle couldn't help it; she laughed long and hard, doubly so when Devon groaned at the sensation.

Chapter Fifteen

October 2, 2003

"Stop," Michelle pleaded, trying to push his hands away, giggling as he managed to tickle her again.

"I want to feel you laugh." Gods, but he seemed to love feeling her laugh while he was buried inside her.

"Stop playing and kiss me."

Devon's hands halted, then wound through hers. His voice was rough in arousal. "I love a woman who knows what she wants and demands it." His kiss was hot, hard, and full of promise.

He broke away, staring at her, abruptly serious. "Be my mate."

Ice settled in her stomach. The moment had arrived, the one she'd dreaded, the one she'd had nightmares about for the ten days since she'd accepted him.

She'd known it would come eventually. It had to, but she wished she had more time. How could this moment come before she'd made a decision?

Melissa had said that your love was either enough or it wasn't, but how could Michelle know if it was enough? The thought of losing him made her feel as if her heart were being ripped out. The thought of losing her family did the same.

He ground his teeth. "You're not going to," he guessed. "You're going to refuse me."

Tears she hadn't realized were pooling spilled over her lashes. "I don't... I need—"

"I have no more time," he roared. His hands fisted beside her head.

Michelle cringed, her heart pounding at the ferocity of his response.

Devon took a calming breath, closing his eyes, his hands unfisting. He left her body, then left the bed, pulling the sheet over her gently.

She watched him dress in dismay. "What are you doing?" He was leaving her?

"I need...space."

She winced at the monotone of his voice, wiping away the tears coursing down her cheeks.

He glanced at her, then away. "Promise me you won't leave. Not alone in the dark."

"I promise."

Devon nodded and strode away, locking the door behind him.

For a long moment, Michelle stared at nothing, her emotions rioting. It wasn't fair. There had to be a way to work this out. Maybe if she told Devon what her problem was, they could figure out a way together.

* * * *

Devon entered the Armen manor, defeat weighing on him heavily. He'd been sure she'd say 'yes.' For the last five days, she'd been so at ease that this outcome had ceased to exist for him.

He hesitated, then knocked on the Lord Armen's office door, knowing that someone would be there, likely James himself. He'd hunted the previous three nights, so he was due for down time.

"Come in," came the muffled reply.

Devon entered, still certain that this was the wrong course but uncertain what else he could do in his state.

The lord looked around his shoulder at the empty foyer, his smile morphing into a look of fury. "Where is she?"

"Safe. At the hotel and with a promise to stay there until morning."

"Why the hell would you—"

"She refused me."

James paled; he mumbled a curse, but he didn't comment.

"I need a cabin. I can't...trust myself anymore." *How close did I come to hurting her? Too close. Far too close.* "I beg this indulgence." *I won't hurt her. I'd rather die than do it.*

"You have it. Stay here while I get the keys and directions for you." He fairly bolted from the room.

Devon nodded stiffly, a knot of tears rising in his throat, pushed up by the urge to scream. Why did James have to be so accommodating? Part of him wished the lord would force him to try again, to ask Michelle one more time. Another part reasoned that he wouldn't survive her refusal again.

James returned, placing a set of keys on the desk between them. He started drawing the map that would lead Devon to the mad cabin he'd use.

Devon fisted them, his hand shaking in the effort not to punch something...or to scream. "My thanks," he rasped.

"The cabin is stocked."

I won't need it. The thought of eating makes me want to puke.

"Let me know if you need anything else."

"I do."

"Name it."

Devon unbuckled his weapons belt and set it on the desk. "Hold this for me."

James looked up at him, his eyes wide in horror.

"I can't trust myself," he repeated. "I'd rather die than use that weapon in madness."

"Syth protect you," he mumbled, going back to the map.

"Didn't seem to help last time," he whispered, wincing at the sacrilege he'd uttered.

James didn't call him on it, a sure sign that he believed Devon far gone.

Devon admitted to himself that he was. He recognized the emptiness eating at him, warring with his pain and loss. When push came to shove, it might be kindest if Syth led a beast to him and let him die.

Chapter Sixteen

October 3, 2003

Michelle groaned at the headache pounding behind her eyes. This was what too little sleep did to her, and crying probably hadn't helped. Now, she no doubt looked as horrible as she felt: red eyes, swollen cheeks and nose, upset stomach, and pounding head.

She blinked her eyes, cursing the gray light filtering around the drapes. Though it wasn't bright yet, it was brighter than her aching head wanted to deal with.

But, it was morning. She'd been awake half the night, waiting for Devon to come back so they could talk, but he hadn't. Michelle wasn't certain why she'd thought he'd come back in the night. He'd indicated that he might not, but she'd been keyed up and hopeful that he would.

When would he come back? Should she order breakfast for two and assume he'd be here soon or wait for him? Though her stomach rumbled in complaint, she knew eating wasn't on the agenda until she worked this out favorably.

The realization that she didn't know the time, and as such couldn't judge anything, assaulted her. That overcast light could be six o'clock in the morning or nine.

Michelle fumbled the bedside clock around, shaking her head in disbelief. It was wrong. It had to be wrong. She turned on the television, flipping through to the TV Guide Channel.

"Eleven-thirty," she choked.

Where was he? His belongings were still scattered around the room. Surely, he hadn't left for Kaufmann range.

Had he been in an accident? Fallen in battle? Decided to work off steam at training and stayed at the manor for lunch?

Yes. That one was likely. If he'd been in an accident or fallen in battle, someone would have come looking for her. He was just letting her sleep and getting the space he said he needed at the same time. She'd take a taxi to the manor. His car would be there, and she'd know he was all right.

* * * *

"Where is he?" Michelle demanded, her heart pounding in a mixture of anger and terror.

Her father sighed. "You've left him no choice, Michelle. A Warrior can only go so far. Devon has gone as far as he can. He had to go."

"Where?" she repeated, sick at the thought of Devon facing the madness.

"This isn't a game. If you don't intend on marrying him, let him go. Even now..." He ran a hand over his face, looking weary. "He could hurt you, Michelle. Devon has enough sanity left to know it and run like hell from it. Don't push him further unless you intend to seal...and don't go to him alone."

Memories of his fury when she'd tried to ask for more time to decide flitted in her mind. He'd startled her, but she hadn't considered that he might actually hurt her. "He'd really..." She stopped, annoyed with herself. Of course, Devon wouldn't hurt her. Why would she even ask it? Her father was just being overprotective.

"Yes. He would. Now, do you want me to take you to him?"

Yes! How could he ask that?

"Be sure, Michelle. If you're not sure, you could literally be the death of him."

Her head spun. She wanted him; there was no denying that she wanted him until it made her crazy, but did she want him enough to give up the life she treasured for him?

"Think about it, but be sure before you answer me. He deserves that, Princess."

"Yes. He does."

She wandered out of the office and across the foyer, trying desperately to sort her feelings. If only being with Devon didn't mean leaving her home and family, she'd agree in an instant, but it did. If only there was a way to talk to him alone, she was certain they'd be able to work this out somehow, but how could they do that with her father standing over them? Since he was playing the part of Warrior-father, he'd never tell her where Devon was.

The key board. Michelle looked at the closed office door, then around at the deserted foyer and stairs. She hurried to the key board, scanning the rows impatiently. For this to work, she'd have to figure out where he was and be gone before anyone was the wiser.

The keys on the board were spares used for only two reasons: making copies if someone lost a full set and to allow a visiting Warrior a place to track from. *And for me to change vehicles or have keys until I find the ones I've misplaced.* Wherever Devon was, he had to have keys, and unless James had sacrificed one of his own to keep her from doing precisely this...

Michelle noted the empty hook in satisfaction. *Typical!* Even her own father underestimated her abilities.

The cabin wasn't far at all, only an hour by car, less if she took her father's half-ton truck and used the back roads that were inaccessible to her Kia Sportage or Mazda Speed 6. She snatched the truck keys and left quietly, hoping her father wouldn't catch on. The miles passed in a dizzying rush, but there was no sign of pursuit.

She bit her lip lightly, remembering her father's warning about Devon's mental state. She pushed away the image of him as a raving lunatic. He wouldn't hurt her; she knew he couldn't. Michelle assured herself that Devon would only consider hurting her if she refused him again. Surely, if he knew she wanted to find a way to be his mate, he'd be able to control his madness. As a Warrior, he wouldn't want to cause her unease. If he knew that leaving her family was causing her unease, he'd work with her to solve this problem. That was what Warriors did for their mates.

A light rain started falling, and the mountain mist thickened. When the cabin finally came into view, she breathed a sigh of relief from the tension she hadn't realized she'd harbored. She slid out of the truck and followed the sound of splitting wood around to the back.

Devon didn't seem to note her approach. He swung the axe again and again, his muscles rippling smoothly, his hair slicked down in a mixture of sweat and rain, completely immersed in the physical labor though a full cord or more of wood was already stacked beside him. She wondered vaguely how much had already been there when he started.

He split another log and turned, dropping the axe at his feet and striding toward her, rain rolling down his bare chest, his eyes hard. His hands locked around her arms, and his mouth captured hers in a near-bruising kiss. For a moment, she stiffened in fear and pain, her gasp disappearing into his mouth as she opened hers to protest and he took advantage of it as if she'd invited his kiss. His mouth and hands gentled as the storm gathered steam.

Michelle moaned at the sensation of Devon over her, pressing her into the thick grass while he buried his face in her throat. She opened her fists, touching him, needing the connection of skin against skin. How could she lose this?

"You shouldn't have come here," he whispered.

She sobbed. "You don't want me here?" Wasn't that why she was here? She didn't want to lose Devon any more than she wanted to lose her family.

He pulled back so she could see his hopeful expression, brushing her hair off her cheek. "I want you here, but you know what I want from you."

"I do want it, Devon. But, we need—"

"Then you'll be my mate and go to my range and—"

She winced, trying to find the words to explain.

His face hardened and he pushed off of her, using his fists against the ground to lever himself up. Michelle grasped at his arm, stopping him at his knees, shaking her head.

He shook her off, growling. "Why are you here? What do you want?" he demanded.

"You. Devon, please—"

"I told you that release isn't enough for me," he shouted.

"It's not enough for me, either."

Confusion, hope, and fury warred in his expression.

"I want to be with you."

"But," he prodded.

She took a calming breath. "I have family here...my parents, brother, twin sister...and her family."

"I can't stay here. You know that."

Tears stung her eyes. "I know."

"And, you won't leave." His voice was bitter and cold.

"That's easy for you to say," she snapped. "You don't have the option. You can't be forced to give up—"

He vaulted to his feet, marching to the cabin, his posture stiff. The door slammed behind him.

Michelle wiped the tears from her cheeks, managing a weak laugh when more took their place, supplemented by the rain. She forced herself up and headed for the truck, feeling hollow. Devon wasn't willing to find a way. It was over. There was nothing left for them.

She stopped, patting down her pockets. *Good gods, now is not the time to lose keys.*

Retrace your steps. When did you have them last?

She'd had them in her hand when she'd approached Devon. Michelle plodded back to the spot where she'd lain, searching the grass for them as the rain became a downpour. They weren't there.

"I had them," she reasoned miserably. "Where could they go?"

Her heart stuttered. *Devon!* She looked at the cabin nervously, swallowing hard. She couldn't follow him now. Not when she'd just refused him.

Michelle slipped and slid her way to the truck, climbing inside, dripping wet, shivering, miserable in body and spirit. "I shouldn't have come."

* * * *

Devon paced the main room, fisting her keys in his hand. He wasn't sure why he took them. This situation was hopeless, but he couldn't let her leave until he had exhausted every possibility of making this work.

Michelle had come here to work something out. She *wanted* to be his mate. If he could meet her halfway, he had to do it.

But, she was right. He owed allegiance to his house. Even with two younger brothers, there was no chance his grandfather would release him to Armen range. He had no choice but to return.

"It's not fair," he grumbled. Certainly, Lord Armen wouldn't revel in the idea of having Michelle ripped from his side. She was his daughter; James loved her. She was also a tracker, as useful as any Warrior in that regard.

He went still, a mad idea taking shape. "Why not?" he half-laughed. It would be an equitable trade of resources...if his lord would go for it. Devon grabbed his cell phone, his hands shaking, praying to Dobler and Tes that he could strike a deal.

The phone rang three times before Kohl answered, and Devon's heart seemed to stop between each ring.

"Kaufmann," his brother intoned.

"I need Grandfather."

"Devon? I just heard. I'm sorry—"

"Max," he barked. "Now." The last thing Devon wanted was anyone's pity. At least the Lord Armen hadn't shown him that.

"Is this a good idea? I mean...the madness will explain away an awful lot, but—"

"Damn it, Kohl! Get me Max, or I'll come there and kill you with my bare hands. This is not the time to fuck with me."

"It's your funeral," he warned.

The line went quiet for several long moments. Devon ran a hand through his hair, trying desperately to rein in his frustration before his house lord came on the line. All too soon, Max's voice echoed over the connection.

"Devon, I realize you are in the grips of madness. I suggest highly that you turn off your phone for the duration."

"Wait! Hear me out. There is a possibility that I could still claim my mate."

"If she's refused you—"

"She hasn't. Not exactly...I mean—"

"I can't wait to hear this story." Max's voice dripped in sarcasm.

"Michelle's only problem with being my mate is leaving her family. She's been raised in Armen, insulated in a Warrior household. The idea of losing them is tearing her apart inside."

"You expect me to release you to Armen? Are you... Well, yes. You *are* insane right now. That's why you're asking."

"No. I'm not asking that. I want to meet Michelle halfway."

"Halfway? Devon, you're not making any sense. Maybe you should turn—"

"She's a tracker, Grandfather...cyber and foot. She's the best Armen has, bar none."

"Interesting." He hesitated. "Go on."

"I propose a trade. We're taking away one of Armen's best resources, a resource they raised and trained...or at least paid to have trained."

"If she agrees," he noted.

His gut twisted at that. Michelle could refuse this offer, even if he got permission to go forward. "My plan is a simple trade of resources. Six months in Kaufmann, during which we benefit from Michelle's expertise. Six months in Armen, during which they benefit from an additional Warrior. Any children would be Kaufmann, of course, and I would have to insist that Michelle be limited to cyber tracking when she carries or we have little ones."

Max didn't respond to that.

Devon nearly growled in irritation. "She's here, Grandfather. If you refuse me, you'll have to call in the Lord Armen and—"

"You've made this offer already?" he shouted. "Without consulting me first?"

"Of course not! I'd given up, but she's here, and she wants me. Any chance is better than none."

"You're the oldest of your generation, Devon. A lord can't oversee a range he's absent from half the year."

"I'll give my oath to Kohl when the time comes, if we're still traveling back and forth and not settled in Kaufmann. He'd make the better lord, anyway. I don't care if I'm ever lord. Would you have, if it came to a choice between your mate and being lord?"

"No," he admitted. "I wouldn't."

The silence stretched out between them, and Devon felt his nerves buzzing uncomfortably beneath his skin. "Will you support this?" he managed. "I have to know."

"On Michelle's word that she'll track for us, I'll accept this trade. She is excused from all tracking for three months after she has a child and cyber-tracking only for the first two years and her pregnancies, and that last portion is an order. She will accept my rule in this, just as any other Warrior would."

He laughed in relief. "Thank you, Grandfather. I should go now."

Devon vaguely heard Max saying something as he powered down, but he had far more important things to attend to. He had a woman waiting for him who wanted to be his mate...he hoped.

A steady beat made it through his refreshed senses, and he looked at the windows, his smile fading fast. Good gods! He'd left her stranded in a rainstorm. He wasn't even certain that she could seek shelter without the keys tucked in his pocket.

* * * *

Michelle wrapped the sleeping bag that had been stored behind the seat around her shoulders and shivered. If she had the keys, she'd turn on the heat. With the storm raging, she couldn't leave, even if she had them, and her father couldn't reach her, even if she had a cell phone to call him.

The cabin door flew open, and Devon marched out.

She felt the air catch in her lungs. She'd refused him again, and he was trapped in printing madness. The gods only knew what he'd do. Michelle locked the doors with numb fingers, then moved to the center of the seat, cursing herself for ignoring her father's warning and coming here.

He wrenched at the driver's side door, shooting her a look of disbelief.

Was she an idiot? He was a *Krieger der Nacht*. Even safety glass wouldn't stop him, if he wanted in. And, that was assuming he didn't have the truck keys. She sent up a prayer to Tes that he didn't have the keys.

Oh, so he'll use his hands or the axe? She bit back a groan.

"Open the door, Michelle," he ordered.

"Go inside, Devon. I was wrong to interfere in this and—"

"Open...the...door." His voice was edged in cold fury.

She shook her head, inching closer to the passenger-side door.

He pulled the keys from his pocket and inserted one in the lock. Michelle dove for the other door, pushing it open as the door behind her swung away. Devon's hands closed around her waist and dragged her back across the seat. She turned to face him, dropping the sleeping bag with a scream of fear. Rain plastered her half-dried hair back to her head in the space of a few heartbeats.

"Shhh," he soothed her, hugging her to his chest. "I won't hurt you." A weak smile curved up his mouth. "That's what you think. Isn't it?"

She felt her cheeks flush.

"I'm not that crazy. Now, will you come inside?"

She shook her head, fresh tears sliding down her cheeks between the raindrops. "You're right. What I want isn't possible."

He growled a curse and hefted her over his shoulder, striding back to the cabin.

Michelle tried to lever herself up against his slick skin, but the hand on her lower back stopped her. "Devon! The truck... We can't leave it—"

"You'll catch pneumonia. I don't give a damn about the truck."

She squeezed her eyes shut, seeing the next day play out. The truck was her father's favorite. She was never going to hear the end of destroying it this way, even if, as she suspected, Devon planned to pay Armen back for the damages.

Devon closed the door behind them and strode into the first room off the hall, setting her next to the bed. "Now, either you will take off your clothes in the bathroom and wrap up in a quilt, or I will do the same for you here."

She stared at him, stunned by that pronouncement. "You trust me not to...um..." What would his reaction be to the idea that she might run from him? Better not to chance it.

He scowled. "You have a point." He reached for her shirt.

Michelle sidestepped him. "Whoa. What are you doing?"

Devon chuckled. "Then you do it. Be reasonable, Michelle. You're freezing."

She hesitated, trying to unravel his strange mood.

His hands settled on the top button of his jeans. "Show me yours, and I'll show you mine." His voice was laced in sexual promise.

Michelle laughed in spite of herself, peeling away layer after layer of clothing. She looked up as she kicked away her jeans and panties, her heart stuttering at the sight of Devon's hungry eyes and rock-hard cock. She took a step back, reaching for the quilt as her thighs brushed the mattress.

Devon nodded. "Until we talk," he agreed.

She wrapped the quilt around her body and let him lead her close to the fireplace, settling onto the rag rug in the center of the floor. He built up the dying fire, his body rigid in strain.

"Do you want to be my mate?" he asked, still kneeling before the hearth.

"Devon... I didn't... I don't want to—"

He turned to her, his eyes pleading. "If your other concerns were met, would you still agree?"

It was unfair to give him hope. "They can't be met," she choked out. "I was dreaming to think—"

He dropped down on the rug, leaning toward her. It took Michelle a moment to realize that he wasn't at the edges of violence. She took a calming breath, shivering though she was warming nicely.

"I'm going to kiss you, Michelle."

No! "Yes." She needed this. She couldn't imagine life without it.

His kiss was slow and thorough, his hands caressing. Michelle was suddenly uncomfortably hot in the quilt. She released it, reaching for him.

Devon pulled back, closing the quilt around her again. "If you're needs were met—"

"In an instant," she breathed. It didn't matter what he meant. He'd decided to work this out with her, to find a way to save their relationship. Somehow, they'd manage that.

He sighed in seeming relief. "If I met you halfway... If I promised you half of every year here in Armen range, would that be enough for you?"

"What about you? You can't possibly go that much time without—"

"Both of us."

Her heart leapt, then sank again. "Your lord would never agree."

"He already has agreed to it. Now, if your father does—"

"He would, but... How? Why? I don't—" She wasn't making sense and she knew it.

Devon feathered another kiss over her lips. "Promise to track for Kaufmann when we're there and follow Max's orders on when you may not risk yourself, and we have the Lord Kaufmann's vow."

Michelle nodded, dumbstruck. "You did this for me? You asked your lord to allow this and willingly offered to give up your home the same amount of time I did...for me?"

"I would do anything for you. Don't you know that? I made this bargain for you. I vowed to swear allegiance to Kohl when the time comes for a lord in my generation for you. I'll swear allegiance to your father or any other lord of Armen when we reside here. Anything."

She nodded, shrugging the quilt off again.

His gaze followed it, and a strangled groan escaped his lips. "Say you'll be my mate."

"Yes...and your lord has my vow. I'll track for him."

* * * *

Yes! Devon drew Michelle to his chest and tossed the quilt out to cover the rug and floor behind her, easing her down beneath him to the cushioned surface.

She wiggled in his arms, untangling her legs from his and hooking them over his hips. He groaned, stroking deep inside her ready body. It was perfect: hot, soft, wet, throbbing in the precursors to climax already.

"Say you want me," he breathed.

"I want you. I need you." She started moving under him, urging him on.

"That's why you came here tonight?"

Michelle moaned, nodding frantically.

"Then I'm yours."

There was no need for words after that. Sighs and moans played sweet counterpoint to the crackling fire. Their bodies slid against each other, mouths tasting, hands pulling them closer, deeper.

Michelle cried out, her climax arching her body beneath his. Devon followed her gladly, closing his eyes to the strength-draining pulse of his orgasm within her. She guided his mouth to hers, gasping as his cock bucked against the walls of her sheath, seeking more of its mate.

My mate. That single phrase brought clarity and calm to his chaotic mind. He buried his face in her damp hair, drinking in the smells of mountain rain and their mixed musk. He was exhausted in body and mind, sated, surrendering to the lure of peace.

Michelle pulled the quilt around them, murmuring an invitation to sleep.

The darkness called, closing around their joined bodies until his entire world was Michelle.

Chapter Seventeen

James looked at the ringing phone in irritation, dropping his pen and scooping the receiver to his shoulder. It seemed it was a day for interruptions, and though he didn't mind Michelle, the rest he could have done without.

"Armen," he growled.

"James, you need to get to Devon," Max stated as if his grandson was the most urgent matter on the agenda.

While the idea of any Warrior facing the madness gave him chills, it was his own demon to best and interfering wouldn't help Devon. "You know I can't—"

"He has a plan to ease your daughter's reservations about mating. It's a good plan, and I've agreed to it, but he's riding the edges. If she refuses him again, I can't vouch for his control."

"What plan—"

"Later! He means to present it to her immediately."

James looked at the pouring rain pelting the windows, recalling the advance of the weather front from memory. "The weather will stop him temporarily. I don't think he's crazy enough to drive in—"

"*He's* not the one traveling, James. Unless Devon is hallucinating, your daughter is with him."

His heart seemed to stop beating at that pronouncement. Michelle would ignore his warnings. There was no question about it. If she wanted Devon, she'd find him. It was what she did.

"James! I said Michelle is with him. I tried to tell him to call you in and wait, but he shut down. James, are you there?"

"On my way out the door," he managed in a thick voice. He dropped the phone onto its base and stormed out into the foyer, shouting for Tyler.

His son appeared at the top of the stairs. "Here."

"Is Michelle in her room?"

"She left more than an hour ago in the half-ton. Let me guess. She didn't have permission to take your—"

James spat a series of curses. The half-ton would have been his first choice to reach the cabin in this weather.

"Problem?" his son asked nervously.

"Pull out Tim's mudder. We have to reach Devon."

His son stared at him in shock.

"And Michelle," he added with a note of warning. *Gods help him if he's gone too far.*

Tyler scrambled past him, already lit up for battle.

* * * *

"Damn this!" Tyler cursed, pulling himself up the washed-out slope.

James hauled him the last body length, scowling at the SUV in the gulch. "We won't be getting that out without the winch on the half-ton. We'll have to walk from here."

"At least we're close and the rain has stopped."

He nodded, fighting the tension in his muscles. Yes, they were almost there, but the usual forty-minute trip had taken them three hours of sliding along treacherous mountain trails in almost zero-visibility conditions.

It was only a few hundred yards further, and James wasn't about to waste another second. He fought his way up the slope, his heart hammering against his ribs.

The truck came into view first, both doors thrown wide and the sleeping bag dragged half into a mud puddle. He sprinted to it, pulling the keys from the door in dismay. Couldn't Michelle keep a key safe just once in her life? It had been too easy for Devon.

"Gods, no," Tyler breathed.

James's mind spun. They'd taken Devon's sacred weapon at his request. That was a bad sign in a Warrior facing the madness, because it marked his wish to die. If a beast met him unarmed, the Warrior would die.

Still, there were many other weapons at the cabin, starting with the Warrior himself. Michelle was human; Devon didn't need weapons to kill her.

He headed to the cabin on unsteady legs, praying the young Warrior hadn't gone too far. In the madness, his responses would be impossible to anticipate. Even if he hadn't killed her—or seriously injured her, he might have forced himself on her. That image proved too much for him. He couldn't allow it to form fully or he'd howl out his own madness.

James eased the cabin door open, stopping Tyler as he surged toward the couple on the floor. Michelle had to come first. Until they knew for certain, they had to assume that Devon would snap and kill her. That meant the utmost caution.

He motioned his son to Michelle, then gave him hand commands to wait for his move. They separated, moving to opposite sides of the quilt.

James sank to one knee, his eyes locking on a deep bruise marring Michelle's upper arm. He noted the tear tracks, much more enflamed than they'd been when he saw her that afternoon. The smell of sex assaulted him, and *Blutjagd* lit his fury like a bonfire.

* * * *

Devon opened his eyes in shock, reaching for the weapon that wasn't at his side. Reality hit him in a rush. He'd surrendered his weapon to Lord Armen. Now, he was unarmed at night with his mate to protect and something malevolent hovering over them. He had only an instant of realization that the danger wasn't a beast before there was a sacred weapon at his throat.

"Don't move," the Lord Armen ordered.

A second Warrior dragged Michelle from the quilt just as she started to stir, shushing her cry of fear and wrapping a leather coat around her. "It's okay," Tyler soothed her. "You're safe."

"I was *always* safe," she countered. "Let me go."

Devon sighed in relief at that, counting the seconds until James released him. The moment didn't come.

"Take Michelle to the back bedroom," the lord managed through clenched teeth.

"I'm sane," Devon grumbled. "We have sealed. Michelle is—"

"Sane?" James thundered. "You hurt her. What did you do? What rules of sanction did you break? As your judge, I demand to know."

"What? No. I never—"

Michelle shook her younger brother off, grasping at the jacket and shooting him a look of warning. In the faint firelight, the bruises on her arms stood out in stark contrast to her creamy skin.

"Oh, gods help me," he whispered. "I did." It must have been the moment he first touched her. *I didn't touch her; I grabbed her. Hard.* How hard had he grabbed her? Had she winced? How could he not have realized he was harming her?

Devon swallowed a tight knot of emotion. Michelle was his mate, and he'd injured her. The Lord Armen could kill him for this. By all rights, he *should* kill Devon for it.

She touched the bruises, shaking her head. "No. I surprised him. It was before—"

"He hurt you," her father growled.

"If you kill him, *you'll* hurt me."

James hesitated, meeting her eyes. "Princess, you cannot take this chance. He lacks control. If a dog bites once, it will bite again."

Devon forced back his anger at being called a dog. He was no better than one. How could he do this to her?

Tears rolled down her face. "Are you sane?"

The Lord Armen sputtered for a moment. "What? Of course, I'm sane."

"Are you? The bruises surprised you, and you're going to kill over them without even asking me what happened. Are you sane? Devon has never touched me in anger. Never."

"What about the truck?" he challenged.

Devon ground his teeth at the memory of dragging her out of the vehicle. She'd screamed, flailed, turned to him, wide-eyed. She'd been shaking in his arms, terrified of him. Had he bruised her then? No. He'd had her by the waist then, not the arms. It had to be when he first reached her.

No wonder, she was shaking. I'd hurt her once. Of course, she assumed I'd hurt her again.

"I didn't want to hurt Devon, so I refused to come inside," she explained. "It wasn't safe out there, and he knew it. He couldn't take the chance of me driving off into the storm...or being injured or taking ill. So, he brought me inside. You thanked him once for doing something similar, as I recall. You thanked him for protecting me. This was no different."

He looked to the bruises, his unspoken disagreement as clear as if he'd shouted it. This was different, and they all knew it. "Michelle, please go with Tyler."

"I love him, and Devon loves me. He's sane. I cannot let you do this, Dad. He's my husband. I won't let you take him from me."

"You'd really go off to Kaufmann with a potentially dangerous—"

"The six months in Armen," she pleaded. "To put your mind at ease, we'll take it now. His lord will agree, considering the circumstances. Give us that long." Her eyes brimmed with new tears, and she hugged herself tightly.

"What? What six months?"

She took a deep breath. "Devon made a deal with his house lord."

"Max mentioned it, but he didn't give me details."

"We'll spend six months of every year in Armen and six months in Kaufmann. Devon will swear allegiance to the Lord Armen and act as one of our Warriors while in our range. I'll track for Kaufmann when we're there, though they have limitations for me, because I'm a Warrior wife."

She pulled the jacket closer around her chest. "If we take our time in Armen first, you'll see that Devon is sane. Please... Please, promise me that time."

Devon's heart ached. He'd hurt her, but Michelle was pleading for his life. When this was over... If he survived to hold her again... There was no vow he could make that was worthy of this show of trust.

"On conditions," her father bargained.

"Anything," Devon vowed. *Anything for Michelle.*

"Anything within reason," she countered, her eyes flashing in challenge.

"You will swear your allegiance tonight," James demanded.

"Absolutely," Devon agreed.

"And the rest?" Michelle asked.

"You will not plant a child in her until the six months are up and I am convinced you're sane. I will not allow you to leave my daughter alone with a child that way, especially not the child of an unstable Warrior."

"I wouldn't dream of it," Devon assured him.

"If you ever bruise her again, I will kill you where you stand."

"If I ever come close to it, I'll hand you my blade to do it."

James pulled his weapon away from Devon's throat, rising to his feet. "Kneel and vow your allegiance...now."

"He's naked," Michelle protested.

"It's all right," Devon soothed her. He deserved less than they were giving him. He wouldn't complain about so trivial a thing.

"It's not all right!"

He pushed the quilt away and knelt before the Lord Armen. He'd stand nude before the Council of Lords and every house, as long as he had Michelle. She was all that mattered in his life.

Devon cleared his throat. "My blade is yours. My duty is at your whim. I stand as a Warrior of Armen, yours to order, My Lord."

"That wasn't necessary," she fumed.

James ignored her. "You return with us to the manor tomorrow. You will pay for the repairs to the truck."

"That was *my* fault," Michelle argued.

Devon motioned her to silence. "Agreed." Max would have a fit, but it was only right that he pay for his mistakes...all of his mistakes.

The Lord Armen seemed to consider something. He looked past Devon to his children. "You will have your blade when the bruises heal."

"Dad, you can't—"

"After that, you'll hunt like any Warrior of Armen. You'll check in until I release you from that burden, and Michelle will not be permitted to accompany you on trail until I approve it."

"Understood," Devon replied. "I am at your whim." *Gods help me, I am agreeing to walk back into Armen manor as a dishonored Warrior, stripped of my blade like a trainee.* But it didn't matter. None of it mattered.

"Tyler and I will take blows for every bruise on my daughter's body."

No doubt for imagined bruises as well. "Of course." *Anything for Michelle. Anything.*

"Very well. Tyler and I will be in the back bedroom, if you need us, Michelle."

"I won't," she snapped.

"She won't," Devon echoed, but it would be a long, hard road of being treated like a First Night pup until he proved that.

* * * *

Michelle glared at her brother as they closed the door to the bedroom. Devon bowed his head, and she bit back a sob.

"They had no right," she apologized.

"They had every right to do that and much more." He turned to her, touching one of the bruises with a wince. "I will never—"

"They aren't as bad as they look," she assured him. "I just have a pale complexion."

Devon kissed the spot, then moved to the other. He peeled the jacket away, scanning her body as if searching for more injuries. "He should have killed me for this," he whispered.

"No. That was before. You weren't responsible—"

"It's no excuse. A Warrior who can't control—"

"Please, don't. You didn't mean to. I know you didn't."

"I will never harm you again. You have my vow on that."

She pressed her lips to his, sighing as he responded.

Devon settled his hands in her hair, his cock hardening. "I love you."

"You know it will take a few weeks for the bruises to disappear."

His eyes filled with pain.

She spoke before he could. "You'll need a duty to perform until then."

"Your father will assign me duties that don't require—"

Michelle smiled, and he stopped speaking, smiling in return as her meaning became clear to him.

"You have a duty in mind?"

"One I trust you will enjoy. One that will prove your gentle touch."

Chapter Eighteen

March 15, 2004

Devon pushed through the doors into Armen manor. He smiled at the sight of Michelle hurtling down the staircase toward him, catching her and swinging her in his arms. She brought her mouth down on his, and the sweet joy of relief settled in his soul. There was nothing like holding her after a long track.

"Ahem," James interrupted them.

Michelle broke away, sighing. "I can't wait to get to Kaufmann," she grumbled.

Devon set her on her feet, at a loss to soothe her when he agreed completely with her.

Her father winced at her comment, looking hurt by her words. He offered his hand to Devon. "Good hunt."

Though he'd like to refuse, Michelle's words burned in his mind. It was rude to turn down a handshake. He clasped the offered hand. "Thanks," he replied uneasily.

It had been a long five and a half months. He'd been required to check in for the first two, and Michelle's freedom to follow him on trail still seemed at the lord's whim. It was maddening, being in a place where he wasn't trusted, where every moment with his mate was watched intently.

More than once, Michelle had promised not to return to Armen, but Devon had refused to accept that. He wouldn't cause a rift between Michelle and her family if he could avoid it, no matter the cost to him. He'd given his word on that, and he wasn't taking the easy road now.

"If you're done with my husband," she snapped.

Devon hugged her. "It's okay," he whispered. "Someday..." But, what could he promise? That James would accept him? That was unlikely. That they'd be free to leave Armen? That would only infuriate the Lord Armen.

Michelle shot her father a look that promised retribution. "You're never going to say it, are you? You're never going to admit you were wrong."

"Princess—"

"Don't Princess me." She turned without giving him a chance to answer and stalked back up the stairs.

Devon sighed, reining in his frustration. His homecoming was supposed to be a happy time, but James's reactions put the damper on it, as usual.

Their future together depended on this six months in Armen. Though his blood burned to stop the force causing his mate pain, any action or cross words might see Devon dead. They'd come too far and suffered too much to risk that now. Their best option... Their *only* option was putting up with it until they were free to return to Kaufmann.

"If I'm free to go, my Lord," he managed through clenched teeth.

"You're not free to go. Come with me."

Devon looked up the stairs, aching to hold Michelle. His discomfort meant nothing to Lord Armen. It never had. "As you wish."

They went to the office, and James took a seat behind the desk. Devon stood, needing a way to focus his raw nerves.

"Sit down," James ordered.

"If you don't mind—"

"I do mind."

Everything about me. Every move I make.

Devon forced his *Blutjagd* back and took a seat. More than ever, he was considering taking Michelle up on her offer to stay in Kaufmann permanently.

James stared at him, watching for something he couldn't comprehend. "The six months are nearly over," he commented coolly.

"Yes. They are."

"You're probably as anxious to get to Kaufmann as Michelle is." There was a bite of anger to his words.

"I miss my family, and I've promised to show Michelle Europe. She wants to ski in Czechoslovakia." He smiled at that, the plans they'd made in bed, the one place no one followed them. "Beautiful snow in the Czech Republic."

"And to get away from me."

Devon didn't answer that.

"You don't like me much, do you?"

"A Warrior doesn't have to like his lord. He just has to obey."

"Do you like your Lord Kaufmann?"

"Of course. Max is my grandfather, though he's one hell of a taskmaster." There would be hell to pay when he returned, trials for his lack of control and misdeeds, but once they got past that, Devon knew it would be business as usual in Kaufmann. *Nothing like it is here.*

"You still intend to come back to Armen in six months?"

"I gave Michelle my word that I would. As long as she wishes to return to Armen, we'll be coming back to Armen, and I will be acting as a Warrior of Armen when we do." Perhaps six months away from her sister and mother...and her nephew would convince Michelle that she really didn't want to leave for good.

"You always keep your word," he noted.

The silence stretched between them.

"You have nothing to say to me?"

Devon bit back a laugh at the irony of that question. "Are you inviting me to speak my mind? I'll be honest. I have no urge to lose my life so close to the end of my trial."

James seemed shocked into silence. "That's what you think this is?"

"A test. A punishment." He shrugged. "I don't deny your right to it. After what I did, I imagine vengeance will be long coming...if it ever does."

Despite all the blows James had dealt him in training, the long tracks Devon had taken on, his unceasing acceptance of every humiliation and injury... Despite everything that had been heaped on him in the last five and a half months, there had always been an edge of mistrust that the lord never lost. Even when his son and nephews had accepted Devon, their wives had stopped avoiding him, and the children flocked to him, James had never softened in the least.

Michelle is his child. If it were my daughter injured... No, he couldn't think of that. If it was his child, he'd never forgive the man in question, and he couldn't believe there was no hope of making peace.

"You think I'd kill you?" James asked, seemingly horrified.

"If I was unstable? Yes. You'd have to...and I'd welcome it. When I saw the bruises, some part of me wished you *would* kill me, because death would have been easier than knowing I'd hurt her, than seeing the proof of it every day for almost two weeks."

"Go on. I want to hear this."

Devon stared at the fireplace, searching for the words. "I can't remember it...not clearly, anyway. I try, endlessly some days. It's maddening to have half memories of an instant in time that is so vital."

He turned to James, hoping that he'd said enough, but the expression on the lord's face demanded more. Devon sighed and continued.

"I remember turning and seeing Michelle standing there. I needed to hold her. I needed to feel her in my arms and know she was real and not some hallucination the madness had conjured up for me. I was desperate for every sensory input I had that would prove her a solid reality.

"I didn't know I'd hurt her. I swear I didn't. I didn't mean to, not that it excuses me. I only meant to hold her. I had to ask Michelle, to be certain that moment was the one I hurt her. I suppose I knew it was when I saw the bruises, but... How could I not know I hurt her?"

The lord stared at him for a long moment, seemingly deep in thought. "And you put up with all of this, because you thought I'd kill you?"

"I'm no coward, Lord Armen. I don't want to die, but I put up with this..." He waved his hand in frustration. "Because the only way we will ever have peace between us is when I prove my self-control. I'm starting to think that will never happen, and it *has* to happen."

"Why?"

"Why?" Devon growled a curse.

"Tell me why," he barked.

"Michelle refused to be my mate until I made the agreement with Max. The agreement was my idea, but... Never mind that. She refused to lose her family for me, but she didn't want to lose me, either. She could have let me break printing, but she didn't. She begged me to allow her all of the people she loved, and I did that. I sacrificed my right to be Lord Kaufmann. I agreed to lose my family, just as she does, for half of every year...for her. All for Michelle. I would do anything for Michelle.

"If I don't find a way to appease you and learn to live in peace with you, I fail her. I gave my word not to be the breach between her and her family. So, you tell me, what else can I do to keep my vow to her?"

"You really would do anything I asked to keep Michelle happy."

"What do you think I've been trying to do these last five months? I gave my vow to do anything you requested of me."

"Anything within reason," James qualified.

"No. Michelle said that. I said 'anything' and I meant it."

"And you keep every vow."

"When I can." *If you let me.*

"What does Michelle want?" he asked honestly.

"It's not my place—"

"Tell me."

He nodded, recognizing the bark of an order well enough. "She wants your acceptance of our marriage. Not tolerance or grudging notice but respect for our union."

"And?"

Devon felt his face heat.

"And?" he repeated, less patient for a response.

"That will be enough for now."

"No. It won't. She hates me, and it's not just the way I've treated you. What have I done to make her loathe me this way? For the last four months, it's been getting worse. Tell me. What is it that I've done to her in particular?"

"A child."

James gaped at him.

"It's not unexpected. For months, she's held her sister's baby, knowing the new one is growing inside, and wanted one of her own. I assured her that, when the six months are up and we reach Kaufmann—"

"Tonight? I'm not blind, Devon. Some nights are worse than others, and I don't know why."

"She knows her cycle as well as I do," he replied simply.

"If I gave you my leave?"

"I wouldn't deny her. You know I wouldn't be able to."

"It's been maddening, hasn't it? You know she wants a child, and your drives demand you give her one, but you don't have leave to do it."

Devon ground his teeth. "I *am* sane, Lord Armen."

"Yes. You are."

His heart stuttered. "What did you say?"

"You're sane. We should probably have had this discussion long ago."

"What are you saying?"

"I'm saying you've proven yourself. You've more than proven it."

"Because, not giving her a child—"

"I know how hard that is, but... Do you know why I mistrusted you?"

"Well, that's obvious, isn't it?" he snapped. "I wouldn't have trusted me, either."

"I don't think so...that it's obvious, I mean. You are so stoic and controlled, I mistook it for a lack of remorse. Even in those first moments, I saw shock and resignation to punishment. I saw more misery in this interview than in the last six months combined, including when you asked me for a mad cabin."

Devon winced. "Controlled was what you wanted, what you demanded," he grumbled.

"Be careful what you ask for, I suppose. You're a good man, Devon, and I've done you both a disservice."

He waited, barely breathing, silently begging each god in order that this was really the end of his torture.

"Go to her. You are released from all restrictions."

"All?" he repeated, biting back relieved laughter.

"I trust you'll make a good husband and father, given the chance."

Devon took to his feet and offered James his hand, murmuring his thanks before sprinting for Michelle's—their bedroom.

* * * *

Michelle looked up at the sound of footsteps pounding down the hall, gaping as Devon charged in. He shut the door behind him and strode toward her, peeling off his leather jacket and dropping it to the floor.

She stood and wrapped her arms around him. "I'm sorry," she breathed.

He chuckled. "Don't be. Everything is—"

"Horrible," she sobbed. "It'll be different in Kaufmann—"

His mouth closed on hers, ravenous. Michelle wanted to scream in frustration at that. She pushed away the image of him pulling out the condom, of both of them pretending it wasn't there, dreaming of the child they'd conceive in Kaufmann range.

"I have so much to tell you," Devon breathed.

"Just love me," she pleaded. She didn't want to hear how her father had insulted Devon this time. She couldn't bear to hear it again.

He groaned at that, peeling off her clothes, then his own. "I'm going to make love to you all night, Michelle. Say you want me to. Say you want my son."

"You know I do." *More than anything.* If only her father would allow it.

It would be different in Kaufmann range. They'd be free to conceive a child next month. If Devon wanted to pretend as they always had until then, she wouldn't steal the illusion from him, though she ached for the reality.

Another ache soon overpowered that one, the insistent need to have him inside her, latex or no latex. Devon tasted and touched all of her, first leading her to the bed, then on it.

Michelle opened her eyes in shock as he entered her...without protection. "You can't," she whispered. If Devon broke the conditions placed on him, her father could—and likely would—kill him for it.

He chuckled, a dark sound of arousal. "I told you that I had a lot to tell you, but you didn't want to listen." He slid to the hilt, abruptly serious. "Now...are you sure you want this?"

She stared at him. "We actually have my father's blessing?"

"For anything our hearts desire, my love. What do you want?"

"He said it?" That seemed too good to be true.

Devon nodded, happier than she'd seen him since they'd sealed. "That I'm sane. That I've more than proven myself. That he's been mistaken all this time and has done us a disservice in it. That... That I'm released from all restrictions he'd placed on me."

Michelle threw her arms around his neck, laughing and crying at the same time.

"We're coming back to Armen," he whispered. "You know your father only wanted to protect you."

She scowled. "If he behaves," she decided. "Skipping a few months...or even the first year would do him a world of good, I think."

"Michelle," he reasoned.

She smiled at a wicked thought, arching against him purposefully.

Devon groaned, moving inside her, his eyes closed in pleasure. "Are you sure?" he repeated.

"We're spending the next year in Kaufmann," she insisted.

"Don't antagonize him," Devon pleaded. "Just make peace."

"I'm not antagonizing," she replied innocently. "Our son or daughter will be a Kaufmann. It's only right that he or she be born and blessed in Kaufmann."

He laughed heartily, opening deep brown eyes that glittered in mischief. "Anything for you."

Melissa:

Heart of A Warrior

A note from the author

The fun in Night Warriors books is usually watching a Warrior take a mate, but once in a while, a Warrior-raised daughter doesn't choose a Warrior to marry. Since "Devon's Price" centered on Michelle Armen, I thought I'd give a glimpse into her twin, Melissa, deciding to marry.

Of the two, Melissa is the more sedate in many ways, but while Michelle is the one who went into the 'family business,' Melissa is the one who can't seem to stay out of the line of fire.

I actually started writing "Heart of a Warrior," because Melissa heartily disagrees with Michelle's assertion that Mack couldn't be mistaken for a Warrior if he tried. I'll leave that determination up to you, fair reader.

Keep in mind that Mack isn't a Warrior. In fact, he has no idea what Warriors are. He's just some poor schmuck who has fallen in love with a beautiful woman, a woman unlike any he's met before.

In the original draft of "Heart of a Warrior," I started the piece with Melissa returning home after the first time she made love with Mack. Strangely enough, Mack and Melissa decided that wasn't early enough, and "Meet the Human Warrior" was born. In this re-release, I've worked "Meet the Human Warrior" into "Heart of a Warrior."

Happy reading!
Brenna

Chapter Nineteen

February 28, 2002

Melissa's lips left his, but they hovered close, nearly brushing over Mack's, offering promises of delights in some secluded place, if she were willing again.

"My place or yours?" Hell, questions like that hadn't worked so far, but at least they kept Melissa laughing, and Mack would fight fire to hear Melissa laugh. The best he could expect was some serious petting, but he hoped someday she'd allow him more. She was definitely in the mood for that petting tonight; her kisses and slumberous eyes announced that clearly.

She licked her lips, her voice a caress against his lips. "Yours."

Mack could hardly believe his ears. He had to be dreaming. "You actually said 'yours?'" he asked.

Melissa smiled against his lips. "Um. Yeah. I think I did."

He pressed her back against her car, urging her lips apart in a heated kiss that left them both breathing harshly. It was always easier to make himself clear in action than words where Melissa was concerned.

"We'll be doing more of that, I hope," she managed.

"Oh, yes. I'll pick up my car tomorrow, if you don't mind."

There was no question that she wouldn't spend the night. Melissa described her family as 'highly overprotective.' While he'd like to laugh at the concept of them sending bounty hunters to find her, she seemed sincere about the men she called 'Mayer Trackers,' and so he couldn't find it in him to chuckle at the mental image.

Melissa nodded and handed over her keys.

The trip to his apartment couldn't have been short enough. His body reacted fiercely to the knowledge that Melissa wouldn't have agreed unless she planned to take full advantage of the solitude with him.

Whether they ended up making love or just engaged in heavy petting in a more conducive environment for it, this was a major step for them. So far, she'd shied from visiting his place...or inviting him to hers. Petting, while enjoyable, had always been accomplished in cramped cars or on blankets in darkened parks and similar locales.

Mack pulled into a parking space and got settled without conscious thought about it. His consciousness was locked on Melissa's mouth caressing his jaw, her breasts pressed to his arm.

"Inside," he managed. He wasn't about to settle for his hands under her clothing in her car when he could get at least that much in a warm, lighted apartment.

She nodded and slid from the car.

He guided her inside, locked the door, then removed her suede jacket and hung it next to the door. Melissa did the same for him, then removed his tie and tossed it onto the hall table.

Mack scanned his apartment, trying not to presume too much. "Where do you want to...play?" Even if she said the couch, it was better than the back seat of one of their compact cars.

Her smile widened. "Apartments usually have beds."

He bit back a shiver of delight, leading her to the bedroom. Melissa didn't waste time. She kicked off her modest heels and lowered herself onto the spot he typically settled to sleep in. Mack toed off his own shoes and sat next to her, at a loss for how to proceed.

Michelle didn't appear lost, despite her lesser sexual experimentation. Her mouth brushed his, and her hands worked the buttons on his dress shirt open.

Their kiss was slow and deep, her touch drugging. She explored all of his exposed skin, seemingly mapping him as he inched her suede skirt up her thighs.

Her mouth left his. "Take it off," she breathed.

"My shirt?"

Michelle chuckled, stretching lazily. "That, too."

"Your skirt?" he asked, wanting to be certain. They were too close to miscommunicate now.

She licked her upper lip, her expression hungry. "For now."

Mack hiked his shirt over his head, tossed it in the general direction of the dresser, then worked the button and zipper on her skirt. Melissa raised her hips, aiding him in removing it. Then they were more undressed together than they'd ever been.

He stared at her lace-trimmed panties, his mouth watering to get past those as well. If her scent was any indication, she'd taste divine. She spread her legs, giving him a better view, baring a stray golden curl or two peeking through the lace.

"Do you like looking?" she asked.

"Very much. You're...beyond beautiful."

Melissa laid back, and he followed her down, nestling his cock to her heat, capturing her gasp in a kiss. She didn't back down, pressing further onto his rigid length.

Mack forced himself to slow, deep kisses, though his instincts demanded he pull the clothing between them away and thrust inside her as soon as possible. Her wandering hands and impassioned cries didn't help, and when her thighs wrapped around his waist, her calves nestled to his ass, he nearly gave in.

She broke away, staring at him, seemingly confused.

Maybe, I'm rushing her into this. "Should I open a bottle of wine?" he offered.

"Yes. That would be nice." Melissa eased her legs from around him, biting her lip as he retreated.

His cock ached, and he had to adjust the package before heading to the kitchen. Her flushed face darkened as he did it, and Mack hardened further, though moments before, he would have sworn under oath he could get no harder.

"Hurry back," she requested in a tremulous voice.

That statement was enough to convince Mack to make record time in opening the wine, grabbing two glasses and returning. He stopped in the bedroom doorway, rapt on the scene, nearly dropping the bottle in his inattention.

Melissa had unbuttoned her blouse, allowing him just a glimpse of the bra that matched the panties. She waited patiently for his reaction, her expression hopeful.

"Mack?" Her voice was uncertain, perhaps even a little fearful.

"Do you really want the wine?"

"Maybe later."

He nodded, setting his load awkwardly on the dresser to his right, one of the glasses toppling onto the towel he'd left there that morning. "Take it off. I want to look for a minute." And, this way, he wouldn't rip her clothes off of her body.

She shrugged the blouse off her shoulders, pulling it off the ends of her fingers and tossing it to the floor beyond the bed. There was only a momentary pause. Then her hands went to the bra clasp.

"If you do that, my trousers come off," he warned her.

Her hungry look proved to him that he'd never been fully-erect in his life.

"They're cutting off blood flow to my only working brain," he gasped, trying for humor instead of the pitiful plea that came out.

Melissa slid off the bed and strolled to him, stroking a hand over him that nearly brought him to his knees. Mack groaned, wrapping his hands around the back of her head.

"Remove it," she whispered.

"My trousers?" The thought of her watching him undress had him throbbing.

"No. My bra."

Before he could question that, Melissa had unbuttoned his trousers and was easing the zipper down. Mack hesitated only a moment, then unhooked her bra, trailing his fingertips down her arms as he slid it to her wrists. One hand at a time left her work at easing his trousers down, allowing the bra to fall away between them.

"English rose," he whispered, identifying the color of her nipples as a close match for the suede he'd removed. How many times in the last few weeks had he stroked those nipples—through her clothes or beneath them—and wondered what color they were?

"Boxers," Melissa noted, that same undertone of awe in her voice.

That did it. He kissed her, a hungry kiss, fondling her breasts, groaning as she pushed his trousers down his thighs. Stepping on the hems, he worked them the rest of the way off.

Mack guided her back to the bed, halting as the mattress forced them together. He slid his hands from the center of her back, down beneath the waistband of her panties, pulling her against his length. Her eyes closed on a moan.

"If you don't want me to finish, stop me now," he requested, using the last of his thinking mind to compose and issue the words.

Melissa eased to the side, and he released her, stepping back. Just as he opened his mouth to offer to walk her to her car, she moved again.

She stretched out on the bed, her hair fanned over his pillow, easing her panties down slowly. Inch by inch, her pinked skin and golden curls appeared, holding his undivided attention.

Melissa gasped, and Mack dragged his gaze to her face, closing the mouth he'd been too shocked to close earlier. Her eyes were locked on the length of him, currently tenting his boxers.

It took his muddled mind a full five seconds to register that she wanted to see him nude—or that she wanted him nude to facilitate sex. Mack hooked his fingers in the waistband and stretched it out around his aching cock. He eased them down slowly, watching her reaction as he uncovered the purpled head and finger-width after finger-width of the shaft.

Melissa raised her legs, and his gaze locked on the patch of curls between her slightly-parted thighs. She slid the panties off and started to lower her legs.

Mack knelt on the bed, trapping them against his body. She stared at him, questioning silently. He eased her knees further apart, feasting his eyes on her spreading body.

Without explanation, he sank his mouth to her weeping core, sampling her. Melissa cradled his head to her, begging for more with every tip of her hips and moan. She gasped his name, her hands tightening, pulling his hair and sending sweet twinges of pain through him in the process. She rolled her hips instinctively.

He groaned, picturing her making that move when he was inside her. Melissa froze, her back arched, and her moan morphed into a full-throated scream of pleasure.

Mack smiled, raising his head as her hands loosened. Her eyes were closed, her head thrown to the side. Her fingers stroked at his hair lazily. He laid a kiss on her clit, and her breathing hitched.

Melissa extended one leg and stroked his hip, seemingly seeking his cock, though it was buried beneath him.

"Yes?" he grumbled, fighting the urge to take her mindlessly.

"You're too low on the bed," she replied in invitation.

He crawled up between her thighs, planting his hands beside her head. "Too low for what?" If she was saying she wanted to lose her virginity tonight, in his bed, she'd have it.

Melissa raised her head from the pillow and sealed her mouth to his. Mack sank over her, deepening the kiss. In moments, they'd progressed from slow and deep to frantic. She wound her legs around him and pressed her hips up.

Mack pulled back slightly and thrust into her. Her ragged cry rumbled into his mouth, her hymen offering only minute resistance.

She didn't give him a chance to ask if she wanted time to recover. Her hips moved in that sinful roll, and her hands cupped his buttocks, encouraging him deeper.

He obliged her, thrusting deep, again and again. Melissa met him fully, her tight body and swiveling hips a slice of Heaven on Earth.

And then it washed over him. Mack shouted harshly, nestling his face in her hair as his climax went on and on, buried to the hilt in her still-circling body. Aftershocks wracked him, and Melissa gasped.

They lay together, fully entwined, chest to chest, lips brushing lips. It was perfect, and yet...

The niggling of unease coalesced into the solid reality that he'd screwed up. Mack raised his head, staring at her in guilty misery.

Her smile faded. "What is it?"

"We...uh..." *Not inside her, bonehead!* Mack rolled to the other side of the bed, sliding free of her body and drawing Melissa with him.

"Made love?" she asked, seemingly lost and confused.

"Well, yes. Of course, but we... I! I got carried away and didn't...um...use..." He looked toward his blood-streaked and semi-erect cock.

"Oh." Melissa bit her lip lightly. "We should have, I guess."

"I'm safe," he offered hastily. "AIDS-wise, I mean. It's been about nine months, and my work physical requires a test. The last one was just last month, so I'm not...you know...infected or anything."

She breathed a sigh of relief, laying her head onto his shoulder. "And, we know I'm safe, so that's okay."

"AIDS-wise, but—"

Her brow furrowed. "You have reason to believe you aren't in other ways?"

"No! Of course not, but... Oh, hell. I'm mangling this."

Melissa turned, folding her arms on his chest and planting her chin on them, her eyes assessing him. "Take it one step at a time."

Mack forced his mind to function as her golden hair cascaded over his stomach. "Even if neither of us... We've covered that. Let's move on."

"Agreed."

He took a deep breath, playing a curl between his fingertips. "Let's forget about disease for a minute."

She glanced at his cock, then back to his face, darkening. "Oh. You're worried about a baby," she deduced.

"You're not?" He couldn't picture Melissa taking birth control pills for no good reason, and she was smart enough not to jump blindly into something as important as motherhood.

"I...never really thought about it."

"Which is why I should have."

Melissa looked away, seemingly disconcerted.

Too late, he realized how that came out. "I mean, I don't want to rush you into anything you're not ready for."

She looked back at him, her mouth working as if she wanted to ask him something.

Mack cupped her cheek in his hand. "You've never had to think about it. I have. I should have protected you."

"Go back a step," she whispered.

He tried to retrace his steps. "I have?" He shifted uncomfortably. "You knew I'd been with—"

"No. Before that."

"What? What did I say?" The look on her face didn't tell him if it was very right or very wrong, but whatever it was had struck her hard. He prayed it was good and not bad.

"You don't want to rush me into having a baby?"

"I don't want to rush you into anything." He'd done his level best not to do that so far.

"But...you've thought about it already. About me having a baby with you." She didn't question it. Neither did the concept seem to scare her off.

"Oh, yeah." He'd thought of everything from the wedding and honeymoon to children and retirement, and there was no other woman he could picture sharing it with. "When you're ready."

Melissa kissed his chest as she'd done in his car a few nights earlier. Mack closed his eyes on a groan. That move cut through him, and she knew it. Her hand circled his cock, and she kissed again. He hardened with just that little provocation.

He opened his eyes, lost in pleasure and in her expression of awe. She stroked him, her breathing hitching in response to his.

"You're not rushing me into anything," she breathed. "I'm just where I want to be."

With that, she straddled him and took him in. Melissa rocked over him, crying out as he started bucking into her.

"Oh, God," he grumbled. *I'm doing it again. I'm letting her risk—*

"I can deal with that."

"Deal with..." He ground his teeth, holding back release, trying to make it last this time.

Melissa arched her back, fitting her body tight to his. "Making you see God."

Mack wrapped his hands around her hips, driving into her with a renewed sense of purpose. "Your turn," he promised.

Little cries of passion left her lips with each thrust into her, growing louder and less restrained. She ground against him, taking him to the root, forcing him to the limits of endurance.

The sweet contractions of her climax nearly sent him over again. Mack stared at her, drunk on her expression. "What does He look like?" he teased.

"Divine," she whispered.

That was the end of his control. He thrust up, releasing wave after wave of come into her, shivering as she screamed his name.

Mack pulled her down over him, parting her lips, tangling his fingers in her hair. She was right. It was divine...and she'd said this was just where she wanted to be.

* * * *

Melissa sauntered into the manor, swinging her arms at her sides, smiling at the memories of her evening. She bit back a giggle at how crazy she'd been, but somehow crazy seemed right with Mack. Gods, the man was hot. Of course, that wasn't the only reason she wanted him. He was funny, playful, considerate...and used the worst come-on lines to his best advantage.

"Hey, Baby Doll," Tyler called out.

She scowled at the pet name. Michelle had been Princess, and Melissa had been Baby Doll. It was probably the only thing she'd ever envied her big sister, the nickname their father had given Michelle within an hour of meeting them.

Her younger brother didn't seem to notice her irritation. He scooped Melissa up in a hug and twirled her around, planting a kiss on her cheek. He stopped short, his smile disappearing and his eyes narrowing.

Melissa's heart pounded in terror, but she feigned confusion, laughing lightly. "Let me down, Tyler. You're rumpling the suede."

"Who is he?" he asked through clenched teeth.

"Who is who?" *Oh, come on! That isn't going to work.*

"Whatever man took your maidenhead and gave you a good topping off tonight. Name, please." It wasn't really a request. More of a veiled threat, actually.

She felt her cheeks burn at his crass description of her beautiful evening. "I have autonomy, Tyler. That's none of your business."

"Fine. Then answer when Dad asks." He set her on her feet and turned Melissa toward James's office door.

"Little brother, you are going too far," she warned, but she marched to the door and knocked. The only way to knock Tyler on his arse was to have their father or Michelle do it, and she fully intended to.

"Come in."

Tyler opened the door for her and waved Melissa in. Their father's smile at seeing her faded, and he looked back and forth between them.

Melissa crossed the room and settled in one of the interview chairs, crossing one leg smoothly over the other, still acutely aware of the pleasurable ache of making love for the first time. "Well, go on then," she invited her brother.

"I believe I will. Melissa has..." He stopped, his face darkening as she'd known it would. Tyler was accustomed to censoring himself around Melissa, though he could vent any foul comment around Michelle.

"Made love? Taken release? Had sex?" she taunted him. She stopped short of 'fucked.' What she and Mack did wasn't fucking. "You're a Warrior, Tyler. You know the words. Just so you know, I prefer the first option. It has the right sound to me."

James chuckled, shooting a look that promised his sisters were about to best him again at Tyler. "And the problem is?" he asked, though he'd surely guessed closely enough to the fact.

"Your son."

"Ah... I see. You know Melissa has autonomy. We went through this with Michelle when she was eighteen, if you recall. I believe your oldest sister commented that she'd have taken care of her virginity before you'd started training if she'd realized how intolerable you'd be when she did." He picked up his pen, dismissing the complaint that simply, as she'd known he would. It was a good thing that Warriors were so predictable.

"Thank you, Daddy," she called out brightly. Her push to her feet was cut short when Tyler raised his protest of the matter.

"We *haven't* been through this before."

Melissa rolled her eyes and settled into the chair again with a sigh.

James glanced at him, then at the file on his desk. "How so? Michelle—"

"At least provided a name when asked."

Melissa snapped. "Michelle has never had a relationship that lasted longer than a week. She's never had to worry about you waltzing in and screwing up a good thing, and you would."

Too late, she realized she'd said too much. She grimaced as both Warriors' heads swung around to her. Release they could handle. If she planned to marry Mack, they'd want to do all the usual checks. There was too much chance of someone getting overzealous and ruining what she had developing with Mack. As it was, it was a miracle that she'd been seeing him for more than three months without Tyler barreling in.

They stared at her, waiting for her to continue.

Melissa groaned. "Blood in the water."

"You see?" Tyler asked.

Their father tapped his pen on the desk calendar. He didn't demand Mack's name; that was a surprise. Of course, as long as he wasn't demanding it, Melissa was free not to offer it. They stared at each other in silence.

"Aren't you going to tell us, Melissa?" Tyler asked.

"No. I'm not."

James raised an eyebrow.

"At least until I know if he's serious," she qualified, praying that would be enough to convince her father to wait.

"Fair enough," he decided. "Of course, if you don't prepare him for what we are, it may go badly when he learns it."

She sighed, voicing her greatest fear. "If I tell him too soon, he'll think I'm nuts."

"Maybe we should meet him," Tyler suggested.

James motioned for him to stand down. "When Melissa is ready."

Chapter Twenty

February 29, 2002

"What's your sign, baby?"

Melissa laughed in spite of herself, easing back into Mack's body. *Gods, but I wonder where he gets so many lame lines. Research. He has to do research on the subject to keep me laughing.* "Certainly not 'stop.'"

He groaned. "I was hoping you'd say that." His arms wrapped around her. "Dinner tonight?"

"Let's order in." She wiggled against his rising cock.

His voice went rough in response. "Pizza in bed? My favorite meal...besides you."

She turned to him, staring into his green eyes, her heart quickening. "Guess that means you can have both."

Mack lowered his face and kissed her, winding his hands in her hair. It was a slow kiss, patient, blooming into something more, a mirror of the way he'd taken her virginity.

He pulled away, his eyes opening, hot in need. "You know I—"

"So, this is him," Tyler drawled.

Melissa glared at him. "I am going to report you," she threatened. "You were warned off, if memory serves."

Her brother hopped up on the low walkway wall, making himself comfortable. "Aren't you going to introduce us?" he hinted.

"In a word, no!"

Mack recovered his senses and eased Melissa behind him. She snuggled to his back, taunting Tyler.

Tyler tensed slightly, most likely affected by the sight of another man, an outsider, protecting Melissa this way.

"Goth boy a problem?" Mack asked.

Tyler mouthed the 'Goth boy' back to her as a question, incredulous.

Melissa cracked a smile. "He's harmless," she stated with confidence.

"Harmless?" both men asked in unison.

"Mostly. More like a couple of flies than a swarm of bees."

"Are you calling me *annoying*?" Tyler demanded.

"If the boots fit..."

He scowled at her.

"I think I'd like that introduction," Mack hinted.

No time like the present. "This is my little brother, Tyler."

"Little? Yeah. I can see that." Mack eyed Tyler's six feet four warily.

"This is my *younger* brother, Tyler...the vampire hunter."

Mack didn't miss a beat. "Oh. I see. Dark clothes. Dyed black hair."

"That's natural, actually," she inserted.

Tyler looked up at the curls over his eyes in disbelief.

Mack shrugged. "How convenient for him. Type casting. Crosses and ash stakes are his thing, huh?"

"Not quite. Those stories aren't true. It actually takes a sacred weapon, sanctified and honed in the blue flame of the Stone, to kill one."

Tyler clenched his teeth, and she shrugged at him. This crash course wouldn't be necessary if she didn't need to cover for him in the first place.

Mack nodded. "Riiiight. Well, sure. Everyone knows that."

Tyler made a move as if to pull the weapon and show it to him.

Melissa shot him a look of warning. "Sorry, Tyler. We have a date to get to."

Mack nodded to him and turned, taking Melissa's arm and leaving her brother behind. He got her settled into his Protégé and headed away from campus.

She sighed at the sight of Tyler at the curb. He'd gotten the license plate number; that meant he'd know everything there was to know about Mack within hours.

* * * *

Mack breathed a sigh of relief. "Are you all right?" he asked.

"Just fine. As I said, my brother is annoying, but he won't hurt either of us."

"You're sure about that?" He didn't need to state that he wasn't. Melissa was quick enough to catch that without the explanation.

"I'm sure." She smiled brightly. "I should thank you for gallantly trying to save me, though."

Mack found himself smiling in return. "You know I love you."

Melissa gasped. "You mean that?"

"Hell, yes." After waiting for her for the last three months, how could she doubt it? He'd have waited twice as long...three times as long, at least.

"If you weren't driving, I'd kiss you."

Mack pulled into a parking space and slammed the car into park.

She knelt on the passenger seat and brought her mouth down on his. Her long, blonde hair cascaded around him, cool satin against his skin. Her mouth was a sweet promise that he desperately wanted to take her up on. Melissa backed away, breathing raggedly against his lips.

For once, even his pick-up lines deserted him. "I'm going to take you home and make love to you now," he whispered.

"That's a good idea. Yes." She eased back into the seat and put the seatbelt on.

Mack shook his head, trying to clear his mind enough to drive. It took a minute, but then they were on their way again.

At his apartment, the feast of touching started at the door. Clothing littered the floor from there to the bedroom.

He lowered her onto the bed, staring at her. Melissa was nude save the medallion at her throat—beautiful, trusting, in his bed, his for the taking. Mack couldn't begin to imagine how he'd gotten so lucky.

She reached for him, and Mack groaned. God, she made him crazy.

He joined her on the bed, searching for something to say, anything at all. She scattered him. It had always been like this, reducing an articulate man to lame come-ons that made her laugh.

"Come here often?" He had no clue where that one had come from; he hadn't used it before.

Melissa smiled, her chest shaking in silent laughter and her face darkening to deep pink. "Twice so far. I'd like to go for three, now."

"Definitely."

* * * *

Melissa trailed her fingers through the line of strawberry blond curls running down his chest, stroking his erect cock, spurring him to motion.

"Now," he rasped.

Mack settled over her, parting her labia and easing inside. She moaned, arching to invite him deeper.

He stopped, concerned. "Feel good?"

She nodded frantically. The pleasure of what he was doing overwhelmed the slight discomfort and made her throb for more.

As if in agreement, Mack filled her in one tender slide of his hips. The rest passed in a blur of moans and whispers, kisses and the glorious feeling of his body moving over and in hers.

He lasted only as long as she did, his heat exploding outward as she shattered, his shout mixing with hers. Then they lay entwined, stroking hands and lips reaffirming their bond.

Mack smiled, caressing the backs of his fingers over her cheek as he slid free of her body.

"What are you thinking?" she asked.

"That you really need to marry me...that I really need you to marry me."

Her heart stuttered at that pronouncement. "Are you asking?"

"Yes, I guess I am. I've wanted this practically since the night I met you, and..."

"And?" For his lack of inspiration at other intimate moments, he was certainly well-spoken when asking a woman to marry him.

He chuckled. "If we keep getting so caught up that we forget contraception, your father will be leading me to the altar with a shotgun. I'd rather get there before he has a chance and avoid the rumors."

He didn't question that she wanted a baby as much as he did. Gods, but they were going about this whole thing arse backwards. Until they made it to bed together, it had seemed to be a perfectly respectable dating situation, almost antiquated. Now, they were nearly planning to conceive a child out of wedlock.

But if they were going to do this, there were things he had to know. "The shotgun is unlikely." Since Melissa had autonomy, her father would leave this portion of her life to her to handle, even if she got pregnant and things fell apart with Mack. *Unless he hurts me, but Mack would never hurt me.* "And if he did make any threats, it would be with his bare hands or a sacred weapon. Most likely, it would be his bare hands." *Warriors don't need weapons to fight humans.*

Mack's smile disappeared; he stared at her, seemingly fishing for words again. "Sacred weapon? Your father thinks he's...uh...a...um..."

Melissa sighed. "If you're serious about marrying me, you need to know this, Mack. My family doesn't just think they're vampire hunters...*Krieger der Nacht*...Night Warriors. They are."

He didn't seem to know what to say to that. When he spoke, his voice cracked slightly. "A lot of money in that?"

Though she was sure he didn't really want an answer, Melissa resolved to answer every question, no matter how outrageous. Honesty was her only chance of salvaging a bad situation, and honesty was the only way she'd know if he could accept the truth of her life.

"A comfortable living. Fortunes have been amassed in the last fifteen hundred years. Some saved were wealthy, and they became powerful patrons. Houses are passed down through the families, owned *by* the families without individuals selling them off for a spending spree. Some of the old money is carefully invested to bring in new. Many necessities, like boots and medical care, are donated to—"

"Donated?"

Melissa nodded.

"Why?"

"The boot makers have been patrons for centuries, and they make a good living adapting new Warrior designs for Goth and cyclists. Doctors are protected, so they offer service for service."

"Protected from..."

"Beasts...what you would call vampires."

Mack took a calming breath. "You realize this sounds insane, don't you?"

"It sounds insane, but it isn't. I swear to you it's all true." She waited for his reaction, scared to death that he'd call it off.

He shifted his weight off of her, turning further to the side so that he was looking down on her, his head propped on one bent arm. "You actually believe this?"

"I'm not crazy, Mack. It's true. I've seen it."

"You... You've *seen* a vampire?"

Melissa nodded solemnly, then shuddered at the memory. He laid beside her, wrapping his arms around her, offering comfort as if they weren't discussing whether she was insane. For a moment, they didn't speak.

Mack fingered her amulet, studying it for the first time since they'd started seeing each other. "Interesting piece," he noted cautiously. "Old?"

"My father forged, etched, and sanctified my amulet himself when I was sixteen. It replaced the one I'd had since I was an infant."

"And how long ago was that?"

The urge to cry warred with the urge to hit him. She blinked back tears. "Seven years ago. I'm not a beast, Mack. Technically speaking, I'm not even a Warrior-born daughter. My father adopted us when he married my mother."

"Tyler?"

"Oh, he's a Warrior, all right. Born, bred, raised, and trained to be a cocky, overprotective..." She paused. "Everything I've told you about myself is true, Mack. I've never lied to you."

He stared at the amulet. "Swear... Shwear..."

"*Schwertträger.* It was the family name at the start of the second beast war. All but one of the house names have been changed over time to fit English sensibilities, but the amulets still bear the historical names, and they are used in formal ceremonies."

Mack didn't answer her.

She started to ease away from him. Obviously, this was all too much for him. "Maybe I should—"

His hands closed on her hips, and he shook his head. "I can't say I believe it, but I won't discount it until I'm sure one way or the other."

"Sure?" What would it take for him to be sure?

He floundered for a moment. "I do love you, Melissa. I won't throw that away lightly."

* * * *

She nodded, her expression pained.

"Tell me about the vampire you saw," Mack requested. He had to ask questions. So far, everything had been seamless. As long as it remained that way, he could hold onto hope that Melissa was sane and her family precisely what she claimed they were.

Melissa paled. The terror in her expression was so elemental that he started to ask her not to tell him.

"No," she managed. "I'll tell you. I was ten. My grandfather Ben had taken me for a ride on Cinnamon, a mare that belonged to my grandmother."

"Go on."

"The beast had a score to settle with my father and grandfather. It decided terrorizing the little girls of the household would bring it the Warriors it sought. Since Michelle was my father's princess, and I was my grandfather's baby doll, we were the obvious choices to take down the ones it wanted."

He nodded. It made sense in a twisted sort of way.

"It was dark. We'd watched the sunset over the water and were headed back in. We rode double, because I wasn't a good enough rider to ride at night, and Warriors have better eyesight." She stopped, seemingly deciding what to say next.

"Go on," he urged her.

"The beast unghosted in our path."

Mack wondered what 'unghosted' meant but decided to let her talk through and ask questions later.

"Animals are scattered by beasts. They sense the creature as foul, dangerous, evil...worse than a predator, probably worse than a carrion eater. Unghosting meant that my grandfather knew the beast was there, but so did Cinnamon.

"If it weren't for me, he'd have dismounted smoothly and fought. I was his handicap. When

Cinnamon reared, Grandfather wrapped me in his arms to cushion my fall." She paused, tears misting her eyes.

"You don't have to," he whispered. Whether it had been a vampire or a vagrant that night, the event had scarred her.

"No. I want to."

"*Only* if you want to. Not for me."

Melissa nodded. "Warriors heal quicker than humans, but they can still be hurt. The fall broke his left shoulder. Ben... He was a leftie, like you. Any Warrior can fight with the off-hand when he needs to, but it affects his skill, much as you wouldn't be able to write legibly with your right hand."

"Yes. I understand that."

"The beast made it clear that I was its target. I think it did it to enrage my grandfather, to put him even further off his usual prowess. Part of it was to terrify me. It did the full show: glowing red eyes, fangs extended, claws at the ends of its fingers..."

He shivered at the mental image.

"It kept trying to talk to me, but I was crying too hard to hear what it was saying. Not that it would have mattered; beasts always lie unless the truth will cause more pain. Grandfather...kept shouting at it to stop lying to me. I'm not certain that what it was saying was a lie, but..."

He wondered at that. What would she think the beast would want to tell her that would be painful to her?

"Their battle didn't last long. It couldn't, that close to the manor. The minute a beast unghosted on the property, every Warrior within the walls and a certain distance outside them would have felt it. Half of them were coming, and the beast knew it.

"It didn't have a lot of time, but it had enough. When it took off, I thought we were safe." She took a deep breath, closing her eyes, her face paling slightly.

"You weren't?"

"I was. The beast had taken a death blow on Grandfather. I didn't know it. He stood there, ordering me to stay at his back in case it was a trick, all the while bleeding out. When my father and uncles showed up, he finally gave up the pretense and collapsed. He...died later that night."

"I'm... I'm sorry sounds so lame."

She managed a weak smile. "You're trying, and I appreciate it."

"Yes. I am."

Melissa stared at him, waiting for his acceptance...or his condemnation.

"I'll try. I can't promise to believe it, but I will try."

* * * *

Melissa stopped in the library doorway, staring at the file in Tyler's hand in anger and exasperation mixed. "Well?" she challenged him.

Tyler darkened, looking somewhat sheepish. "Good job. Well-educated. Not in trouble with the law...now or in the past. No radical entanglements. No fluctuations of his bank account indicating...bad habits."

"Wonderful," she offered dryly.

"I didn't...um...screw this up for you, did I?"

"It's too early to tell."

He winced. "I'm—"

"I had to tell him everything. I didn't want to, but I had no choice, thanks to you."

"And?"

"He thinks you're insane; no change there. The jury is still out on me."

"What can I do, Baby Doll? I'll do anything you ask to make this up to you."

"Stop calling me Baby Doll! If you want to help, take my lead for once. Stay out of my way until I ask for your help."

"On my honor," he vowed.

"When you show some, I'll believe you." Melissa headed for the stairs, ignoring his groan.

Chapter Twenty-one

March 7, 2002

Melissa wound her fingers through Mack's, her back pressed to his chest, his face buried in her hair. She waited for the questions to start as they usually did, whispered in the afterglow of their loving.

She supposed she should be grateful that he was still asking questions, that he was still trying, though he'd been more attentive about birth control since she'd dropped the bomb on him. In fact, his cock, still buried inside her, was bare for the first time since then. She hoped that meant he was more at ease with the truth, more willing to tie himself to this crazy life.

"I want to meet them," Mack requested.

Her heart speeded. "My family?"

"Your father to start. But, yes. I think I should meet them all."

She glanced at the clock on his end table. "Okay. Get dressed, and we'll head to the manor."

"Now?"

Melissa slid off his length, smiling at his groan. She turned to him, biting back laughter. "He works nights, Mack. After dinner is the perfect time to meet him."

"What time does he...go to work? Shouldn't we call first?"

"My father made a kill last night. He'll be riding a desk tonight."

"Riding a desk? Vampire hunters have desks?"

She laughed heartily. "There's a lot of paperwork involved in hunting beasts."

"I'll take your word for it. Just...don't tell me who they file it with. I'm not ready for that."

Melissa planted a kiss on his cheek, then hopped from the bed and leaned to scoop up her blouse.

Mack hooked his hands around her hips and pulled her back into bed, rolling her beneath him. His mouth was urgent against hers, and he thrust into her again.

She tipped her hips to his, lost in the wild need that always drew them together. "What brought this on?" she managed.

"That pose was too tempting, Melissa. Don't you know how much I want you?"

Her eyes slid shut, and she held to him, giving herself fully to their loving. He wanted her. If he wanted her this badly and wanted to meet her family, maybe there was a chance for them.

* * * *

The man appeared out of thin air. One minute, there was open space in front of them, and the next, a six-foot man. Michelle gasped, dragging back on Mack's hand.

He didn't follow. He stared at the glowing red eyes in shock.

It's true. My God! Everything she said is true. Without hesitation, he dragged Michelle toward his back. If he died for her as her grandfather had, so be it. The vampire wasn't taking her.

She stumbled a step toward him, then planted her feet, releasing his hand and launching into the claws slashing toward them.

"No," they screamed together.

The vampire flew away, and Michelle hit Mack's chest, forcing him back as if he'd been tackled by a pro football player instead of a hundred plus change woman. The hit nearly knocked him off his feet, but he managed to right them both. Mack ran his hands over her shoulder and chest from his place behind her, searching frantically for blood that didn't seem to be there. Those claws should have skewered her, but they hadn't.

She turned toward him, making the same inventory for injuries on him.

Mack glanced at the vampire rising slowly from the ground, his mouth going dry. "Are you crazy?" he grumbled. "Get behind me."

"Back to the wall." She shoved at his chest, forcing him back.

"What? He's coming. Oh, Christ. He's coming. We should run while we have the chance." The wall was suddenly at his back.

"You can't outrun it," she stated calmly.

"Him," the vampire corrected her, behind her in the blink of an eye.

"Oh, God," Mack breathed. How the hell could you fight something that fast?

The vampire smiled, revealing lengthening canines.

Michelle turned, flattening her body to Mack's, face out toward their foe.

"No," Mack protested, reaching his arms around to lift her away. "You can't do this."

She grasped his hands and pinned them to the wall. "Use my amulet. If you stay behind me, the worst *it* can do is beat us up a little."

The vampire sneered at that, its head bobbing back and forth like a snake's.

"Melissa—"

"The amulet repels it. Please, stay at my back. Look at it this way... Without you there, I get the full force of the beast *and* a brick wall. This makes us even."

"That sucks," Mack grumbled. He was supposed to protect her, and the best he could do was 'even?'

"Now, he knows the game," the vampire taunted. "That will make it more enjoyable when I force him out."

Melissa nestled her head to Mack's face, covering as much of him as she could, but he was still uncovered from just below his eyes to the top of his head.

"Don't listen to it," she instructed. "Don't leave the wall. Don't give it your back. No matter what you do, don't put your body in front of mine and give it a target I can't protect."

The vampire took a step toward them, leaning until he was nearly face to face with her. "Him," it shouted.

Mack bit back a gag; the vampire's breath was nearly as foul as the garbage cans a few feet away.

"In a former life," she compromised.

"Thus the game begins. You cannot protect him any more than your grandfather could protect you, Baby Doll."

"*Don't* call me Baby Doll," she warned. "Go on then. Touch me. The Warriors are already on their way from the first time you tested the amulet. You'll only speed them up if you touch me again. And while we're at it, name yourself."

For his answer, the vampire struck her across the face. Her head rocked back, crashing into Mack's mouth hard enough to make him see stars and taste blood. His head spun. If this was the amount of force being exerted, what damage was this doing to Melissa? He calculated it out in a panic, then factored in his body acting as a buffer. She was right. As much as he loathed this arrangement, she'd be in worse shape without him.

She shook her head, taking a deep breath as the vampire pushed to its feet again. "Come on," Melissa whispered. "Where are you? There are always a half dozen Warriors or so in the city somewhere."

"Are you okay?" Mack asked, his heart pounding at the sight of the beast closing on them again.

"Fine. Here it comes again. Be ready."

Mack groaned, praying her family would arrive before the vampire managed to do her more harm.

"My name is Brandle. Release the boy to me, and you may leave without further injury," it offered. "Fight me, and I will see you dead before I'm through. You know it's not impossible."

"Never. My family will be here before you can do it, and you—"

"Unlikely. I know where they are. I checked."

She gasped. "You're lying."

Brandle smiled an unholy smile that made Mack's blood run cold. "You hope I am. Release him. This isn't your duty, Baby Doll. You aren't a Warrior. You aren't even trained like your twin is."

"And, you aren't much of a beast. At least the last one was less talk and more action, Brandle."

"What are you doing?" Mack choked. Egging him on didn't seem wise, but maybe she figured that keeping him talking meant less time getting hit. Or, maybe she hoped to keep him distracted long enough for her family to make it to them.

Melissa didn't answer him. "Who was it to you? A master? A lover?"

Brandle swiped at Mack's exposed face with a roar of fury. He ducked left; Michelle went right. In almost surreal slow motion—or so it seemed—the claws touched her face, retracted slightly, and the vampire flew away. Her rebound forced them both hard against the wall. She sagged slightly, groaning.

"Melissa?" he questioned frantically. He couldn't hold her up without becoming a target, and he wouldn't make her take more abuse than she could stand. Mack had never felt so helpless in his life.

She straightened, treading the fingers of her left hand through his and squeezing in reassurance. "Here," she gasped. Her hand shook slightly, but she seemed determined to hold on for reinforcements.

He couldn't let her do this. He couldn't hide behind her and let her get hurt. "Let it have me," he whispered. "Get out of here while you can, while it's still recovering."

"Never. I won't lose you to that damned beast."

"I won't lose *you* to it. It's going to kill you to get to me. The amulet isn't foolproof. You're getting hurt. I know you are."

"The Warriors will make it on time. They're close. Please, gods. They have to be close."

"If it comes down to a choice, you have to let it take me."

"It won't. Oh, shit."

Her choked whisper brought Mack's attention back to the beast.

Brandle was up and running. Mack calculated the damage this amount of force would do to Melissa in sick disbelief. He wrapped his right arm around her waist and started to lift her out of harm's way, moving sideways along the wall.

The ripping sensation through his forearm announced that he'd failed. Mack screamed in a mixture of pain and misery as the vampire rebounded and its claws ripped free.

They collapsed together, her hand loosening. Mack eased his left arm from under Melissa, smoothing her hair, whispering her name though he knew there would be no answer. She was unconscious.

The damned thing was getting back up, smiling widely at its victory already.

Mack forced himself to his feet, grasping a dented aluminum baseball bat that had fallen from one of the trash cans with his uninjured left hand. He stepped over Melissa, ignoring the blood running off the tips of his fingers and the blinding pain of the slashes. "If you want me, come and get me. You're not touching Melissa again while I live."

Brandle licked Mack's blood off its claws. "You think you can stop me?"

"I'll sure as hell try to."

"Little boy, you don't know what you're asking for. Killing you is going to be sweet pleasure."

Mack glanced at Melissa, then back to his foe. "I think I have a clue. If I had a sacred weapon, I'd shove it so far up your ass you'd taste shit, Brandle."

The vampire's eyes narrowed and then widened. It arched forward, jerked, and fell to a heap on the concrete.

Tyler appeared behind it. "Allow me to make him eat that..." His cocky smile faded, and he paled, his gaze moving past Mack to his sister. "Ani, no," he breathed.

Mack turned toward her, collapsing to his knees, abruptly dizzy. "It was a gut shot...hard." His voice was thick. He touched her blood-soaked sweater. "Blood's mine. I think it's mine."

Her brother was abruptly beside him, pulling up the sweater and running his hands over the unbroken line of her abdomen. He prodded at it, looking for signs of deeper injury, then checked her pupil response. "Can you walk?"

"Yes...I think. If not, take her."

Tyler pulled out a strip of black cloth, bound Mack's injuries tightly, then scooped up Melissa, dragging Mack up after them by his uninjured arm. "Follow me."

* * * *

James cradled the phone to his ear, pen in hand. It would be whatever Warrior had reached the protected under attack first. "Tell me," he ordered.

The move would have to be handled quickly and efficiently. When the beasts decided that the amulct wasn't reason enough to stay away, it was standard practice for the Warriors to protect their charges in any way they had to, and a move was essential to that.

"Dad?" Tyler called back, his voice strained to near panic.

He furrowed his brow. Tyler didn't call him 'Dad' when he was hunting. There were no relations in duty. Something had him rattled. "Here."

"Get to the clinic. Now."

His blood ran cold. "Who's hurt?" It couldn't be a Warrior, and an injured protected was bad news for everyone. It undermined the trust of every protected, and it hurt Warrior morale. Not to mention, no one liked to lose a protected.

There was a muttered curse from the other side of the connection. "Please, just do what—"

"Tyler," he barked, putting the demand of a house lord into it without speaking the words. Every Warrior recognized the tone promising pain for disobeying such an order.

"Mack and Melissa."

James felt faint.

"I've called in both George and Angela. Mack can't wait, but I don't want Melissa to."

He nodded stiffly, even as he reasoned that Tyler couldn't see it. Calling in both of their doctors at once was a bad sign. It meant that the injuries weren't minor, whatever they were.

"Dad? Are you still with me?"

"How bad are they?"

"I don't know. They'll survive, I guess."

"I'll make it there." He hung up and turned to find Beth in the doorway with Michelle just behind her. He didn't wonder at it. If Beth hadn't sensed that something was wrong, Michelle surely had. His wife and daughters were unusually close.

"It's Melissa," Beth stated. "Isn't it?"

James nodded numbly.

"Let's go."

"I'll drive," Michelle offered. "You're in no condition to."

He didn't remember much of the ride to the clinic. James supposed that Michelle drove much too fast, but in his near-madness, any speed would have felt too slow.

The next truly coherent moment for him was walking into the clinic room where Tyler sat next to Melissa and Angela stood across from him, a clipboard in hand. His daughter was pale, and there was a bruise on her cheek, but she wasn't hooked to machines as he'd feared she might be. The sight of her covered in a mass of tubes and wires would have been his end.

Angela cleared her throat. "Melissa is going to be okay, though the soreness is going to last several weeks," she assured him.

"You're sure?"

"Her blood is stable, and the tests show no soft tissue damage past the bruising."

Beth voiced his question for him. "What did the beast do to her?"

"Severe amulet bruising. Given enough time, the beast would have beaten her to death that way."

James fisted the lower bed rail, growling at the mental image.

Angela didn't seem to notice; she was busy consulting the file she'd had tucked under the clipboard. "It didn't have nearly enough time for that, of course. Her face, her shoulder... The one that put her out was to her abdomen. I think the pain was too much for her. I've given her something for it."

The rail bent, creaking as he tightened his grip. Angela gasped and moved a step away.

"James," Beth snapped. "You need to calm down. You're frightening the protected."

He nodded, forcing his *Blutjagd* back. "My apologies," he grumbled.

"None needed," the doctor managed calmly. "Now, the man brought in with her—"

James winced. "Mack. How bad is he?"

"He'll recover...maybe not to one-hundred percent of his original dexterity, though. George is piecing him back together at the moment. He'll need physical and occupational therapy for his injured arm. We agreed that it looked most like a mauling by a large dog. That's what we reported it as."

"I gave him protection," Tyler broke in. "When he was headed into surgery, I gave him an amulet and blessing."

"Without checking?" James asked. Tyler never skipped protocol; now he had twice in a day? There hadn't been a feeding. That meant protecting Mack hadn't been an emergency; beasts couldn't track him without a feeding. The house lord should have been consulted before protection was offered.

His son darkened. "He has the heart of a Warrior," he grumbled. "He deserved no less."

"He tried to fight the beast off Melissa?" Gods, but the man would have died trying without protection.

Tyler nodded. "With a baseball bat... He was injured, bleeding out. He knew what he was facing, but he didn't run, didn't panic, and didn't leave Melissa to the beast. He placed himself between it and Melissa and accepted death; he even threatened the beast with as much damage as he could do on the way to death."

James nodded. "I'm impressed. It takes a strong man to do something like that. I approve."

"There's more."

"What?" James caught the small box Tyler tossed his direction in one hand, without taking his gaze off Melissa.

"I think he planned to ask Baby Doll to marry him tonight. The ring was in his jacket pocket...and they were headed to the manor when they were attacked."

He stared at the blue velvet box, a lump rising in his throat. If he had to release a daughter to marriage, he could think of no better man to release her to. "Will Mack be able to travel when he comes out of surgery?"

Angela considered it for a moment. "I don't see why not."

"Good. We'll relocate him to the manor with Melissa. He's more than earned a place in the family."

Chapter Twenty-two

March 8, 2002

Mack opened his eyes, staring at the room around him in confusion. It wasn't a hospital room, and it wasn't his apartment. It was as big as the combination living and dining room at his apartment, and it was beautifully decorated: cool blue walls, nearly-matching high thread count sheets, a Battenberg lace quilt, and brocade drapes.

"Where the hell am I?" he grumbled. He forced himself up, wincing at the pain slicing through his right arm, panting as he cradled the braced and bandaged appendage to his chest. Mack glanced around at the room one more time, taking a deeper breath as the throbbing eased slightly. Maybe they'd taken him to what Melissa called 'the manor.'

"There's no way to know unless I ask." Since there was no one in the room, he'd have to get up to accomplish that.

Thankfully, he was still wearing his jeans. Heading out nude would have made him think twice. He would have done it, if for no other reason than to get information about Melissa, but he would have considered it first.

Mack ran his left hand over his chest, seeking out whatever was brushing over it. His fist closed on a metal disk on a leather thong that was undeniably an amulet. "That's good news," he muttered. At least if another vampire showed up, he'd have a better chance at protecting Melissa and himself.

He started out, making his way to the hall, then following the sound of voices to a wide staircase and down.

Children running through the foyer at the base stopped to stare at him, wide-mouthed. One of them bowed his head slightly and whispered something about 'the human Warrior.' Mack nodded to him, though he didn't understand what the greeting meant.

"What are you three up—" The familiar voice stopped abruptly as Mack whirled to her.

"Melissa..." He shook his head to clear his twitching vision. "No. You're not Melissa. You must be Michelle." He'd never met her sister, but the woman couldn't be anyone but Melissa's twin.

She smiled, striding to him, taking his uninjured arm. "Which means you're more intelligent and observant than my second boyfriend. He laid one hell of a kiss on Melissa before he got slapped and realized he had the wrong sister."

"Where is Melissa? Is she okay?"

"Sore but fine. Come with me. She's going to kick herself for not being there when you woke."

Michelle guided him across the floor to a closed door and opened it without knocking. She smiled, turned, and walked the other way, shooing the children ahead of her.

Everyone inside the room turned to Mack.

He stared at the Warriors, his gaze settling on one after another, feeling like a child amid giants. "Where's Melissa? Is she okay?" he repeated. Why had Michelle brought him here, if Melissa wasn't here? Was this some sort of interview or interrogation?

"Well done," Tyler called out. "A Warrior always thinks of his mate first."

"Heart of a Warrior," another added.

"Welcome to Armen manor, Mack," the one behind the desk offered. "Are you feeling all right?" He checked his watch. "You can have more meds now."

Mack didn't answer him. He was too busy watching Melissa make her way to him from behind the mass of male bodies. She moved quickly but tenderly, her face pale and her eyes wide.

He met her halfway, the need to touch her overwhelming any other concern. Her mouth was urgent against his, the silk-robed, lilac-scented solid reality of her in his arms the center of his senses.

"Heart of a Warrior," someone sighed.

Mack pressed his forehead to hers, holding her to his body. "You're never doing that again," he grumbled.

"Mack," she began.

"I have an amulet. I assume it does the same thing yours does?"

She nodded slightly. "It does."

"Then the next time I tell you to get behind me, you'll damned well do it."

She smiled, her blue eyes shining in tears. One spilled down her cheek.

"I can handle vampires, Warriors, and all the rest. *This* is the deal breaker, Melissa. I will never hold you in my arms, injured and unconscious, again."

Someone laughed lightly in the background.

"Agreed?" Mack demanded an answer. He needed to know she'd never try to risk herself for him again.

"Yeah. I think I can handle that."

Deep laughter brought his head around.

The Warrior who'd welcomed him offered his left hand in deference to Mack's injury. "James Armen," he stated.

Melissa's father. Mack released her and clasped the offered hand for a shake. He startled at the feeling of the ring box trapped between their palms.

"I believe you were coming to meet me last night," he answered the unanswered question between them.

"Yes. I was."

"I have a little work to do now. Lunch is in two hours. We'll talk then. Right now, it sounds as if you have a lot to discuss with Melissa."

Mack smiled in understanding. "I'll be there."

* * * *

Melissa led Mack back to her room, nodding to her mother's reminder of his meds.

He stopped in the center of the room, looking around in surprise. "They put me in your room?"

"Of course. I have autonomy, Mack." Michelle had brought a few men to her bed over the years. It wasn't as if no one knew they were sleeping together, after all.

He stared at her, seemingly confused by that.

"Autonomy," she repeated. "It means that I choose who I sleep with or marry without interference from or permission of my father."

He smiled. "Do you?" He glided toward her, his manner promising sensual delights.

"Can you? Your arm—"

"I won't need my arm for what I have planned."

That simply, she knew nothing would stop them. "If you say so."

"You should have told me about autonomy," he chided her.

She chuckled. "It didn't seem to stop you."

Mack raised his uninjured hand, flicking a ring box open with his thumb. "It slowed me down."

Melissa stared at the simple white gold band with a diamond, hardly daring to believe it wasn't a dream. "You're asking?"

"Oh, I am asking."

"Then I'm saying 'yes.'"

He smiled offering her the box. Melissa slipped the ring on and tucked the box into her robe pocket. Mack started to hug her, then grimaced.

"Your meds," she reminded herself.

"Not yet." He held to her lightly, shaking his head.

"I've agreed, Mack. You need to take care of yourself."

"Who said asking you was all I had planned?" He backed her toward the bed, his eyes hot as they always were before he made love to her.

"Your arm—"

"Do you feel up to being on top?"

"Tim was right. You have the heart of a Warrior."

"Is that good?"

"It's perfect."

"Is it a 'yes?'"

"Hell, yes." She smiled widely. "Come here often?"

Mack chuckled. "Not yet, but I intend to."

Scott:

The Blade Chaser's Son

Chapter Twenty-three

September 10, 2049

Scott Danvers surveyed the bar around him, hoping for a fight tonight. It wasn't that he wanted to prove he was needed. His boss wasn't about to fire him; with all the fights that broke out at Hanger Seven, an efficient bouncer like Scott was Jason's dream come true.

Nor did he want anyone to get hurt. Scott always stopped fights before anyone got hurt—except the instigators, if they fought him. Tonight, he hoped they'd fight him.

No. Some nights, working out with the bag and on mat wasn't enough. Sometimes, sparring just didn't cut it, and Scott itched for a knock down fight until his teeth ached, most likely from gritting them.

The fact that it was always him knocking someone else down didn't bother him. If there was one thing that his mother had taught him, it was that a man should always be in control of himself. When one of the bar patrons started throwing punches, he wasn't exercising control, and a lack of control was one thing Scott absolutely could not stand.

He made himself inconspicuous, hoping it would work as it had many times before.

Scott didn't really understand how it worked; it just did. At six feet three of muscle, it hardly seemed possible that anyone could miss him, but he'd proven that they could many times. Sometimes, they even walked into him, claiming later that they hadn't seen him standing there—if he concentrated hard enough on not being seen. As insane as it sounded, he'd wondered more than once if he was literally making himself invisible when he did it. It was so disconcerting that he didn't concentrate on it that hard very often.

He grinned. It was fun, however, to stride into the middle of a fist-fight and turn off whatever he was doing. From the looks on the combatants' faces, you'd think he suddenly sprouted six inches and seventy pounds before their eyes. When asked, they usually stammered something about not realizing he was *that* big.

Scott grumbled a curse, checking his watch. The bar would shut down in half an hour, and there'd been no sign of a fight in more than a week.

Maybe it was time to change jobs again. When the troublemakers moved on, so did Scott. Otherwise, he never had the opportunity to engage in a decent fight, and that wasn't acceptable. He had to restrain himself too much with his sparring partners to blow off the ever-rising tension in him adequately.

He showed the last of the patrons to the door with a grumbled curse. It would be another long day before he'd have a chance to release his tension. *Unless...*

It didn't seem sporting to go looking for a fight, though he'd resorted to it more than once in his life. Every city had areas where the crime rates were high, areas where a man who looked inconspicuous could count on being accosted. He didn't like stooping to that, but desperate times did call for desperate measures.

He ached for the simple times, back when he was a teenager and training was enough. No matter how little they had, his mother had sacrificed to make sure Scott had whatever self-defense and martial arts training was available. It was one of the truly selfless things the woman had done in her life, and he owed her for it.

But it wasn't enough now. It hadn't been since he was seventeen. "Sure you don't want me to stick around while you lock up, Jason?" he offered. Maybe someone would be stupid enough to try a robbery. It was unlikely, but at least the hope of it would carry him for another hour.

"No. Go on home." He raised an eyebrow with a knowing grin. "Or wherever you feel the need to."

Scott nodded, pocketing his offered pay, biting back a sigh. On another night, when he wasn't strung so tight, a good fuck might be enough. It wasn't tonight. He closed the side door behind him, considering the bad side of town as a serious possibility.

It was too quiet here. It was definitely time to move on.

He was halfway to his cycle when he felt it, a disconcerting sense of something wrong. It was a sensation he'd felt before, sometimes followed by a wrenching pain in his stomach. Scott didn't know what it was, only that following it guaranteed that it disappeared before he arrived.

Unless you make yourself really inconspicuous. He'd never tried that before. It was worth a shot. There had to be some way to find out what caused this sensation, and he wouldn't give up until he managed it.

Since he was already playing inconspicuous, forcing it further wasn't much of a stretch. Scott headed in the direction his senses led him, rounding the bar and moving silently toward the loading dock.

And then he saw it. The couple were all over each other, hands exploring bodies, his large frame pressing her to the wall while her sounds were muted into his mouth.

So? his mind argued. They certainly weren't the first couple to have drunken sex behind a bar. Scott had even indulged himself from time to time, though he preferred to make it to a bed...or at least shelter of some sort.

The feeling intensified, and Scott's heart started pounding. Little details stood out from the rest, the woman's trembling, the way her hand fisted on the man's jacket.

Not right!

Fury rose up fast and hard, more powerfully than he'd ever felt it before. His mother's commands to control the emotion seemed to fade into the background. Every thought but destroying the man in question fled.

In the blink of an eye, his commando knife was out and he was halfway across the distance that separated them, his attempts at hiding himself abandoned. Though he made not a sound, the woman's attacker moved swiftly aside.

Scott turned, placing himself between them, growling out a warning for the man to back off. The woman sobbing into his back kicked up his fury another notch.

The glowing red of the eyes facing him made his heart skip a beat. The—thing bared its fangs, and its fingers elongated into yellowed claws.

Was this what his mother meant? Was this the danger she'd warned him was lurking? The kind of beast she'd feared would find him? Maybe Mom wasn't quite so crazy after all. Who would have believed it?

Of course, Scott wasn't about to let Dr. James in on this one. If he didn't end up in the padded room next door to her, he'd still be releasing Lynne back into a world populated by the beasts she feared. She seemed calmer in the institution. If all of her stories were true, it was probably a blessing to be locked away from them.

"Armen," the beast rumbled, a sneer twisting its lips.

"What?" Scott demanded. What the hell did that mean?

"You think I can't smell your family's stench on you, Warrior?" The beast's nostrils flared. "One of the close-born ones. Matthew Armen. Yes, that is your sire, pup."

Oh, God! No one knew that. Even his mother wasn't sure if his father was Matt or Jordan. She'd planned to have a son from one of the brothers; she hadn't cared which.

It was one of the many reasons he'd never demanded his fathers' last name and tried to find them. They certainly hadn't asked to be saddled with a son. What would finding out about Scott do to their lives? Then there was the fact that their religion didn't account for children born out of wedlock.

"Big deal," Scott drawled. This was definitely a subject he didn't intend to discuss with a foul beast.

"What is an Armen doing in Maher range?" it continued. "And without his sacred weapon?"

He pretended not to be confused by the questions. "Are you fighting me or not?"

"If you wish."

He moved fast, faster than Scott had anticipated by far. Hampered by the woman he was protecting, the damned thing actually sliced his arm open before he managed to land his blade across its chest. A stench like a mixture of skunk spray, sewage, and noxious industrial waste filled the air around them, making Scott's lungs and eyes burn, and thick dark blood rolled down the beast's chest.

Scott didn't look at the damage to himself. No matter how long it had been since someone had managed to injure him, he knew it would heal quickly. The beast seemed as hardy as he was and more. That slice would have downed any human man, but it was still standing.

Knowing his adversary's strengths, the next two passes were a different matter. The beast sliced for his throat, and Scott turned, shouldering the woman away with him. The next swipe was aimed for his face. He blocked it and cut the beast's exposed throat neatly, spilling more of the foul blood.

To his surprise, the creature still didn't die. It stared at him, seething hate, the stomach-churning blood oozing from both wounds.

"Another night, Warrior," it growled.

Then it was gone, not quite vanished but insubstantial and moving away at incredible speed. Scott marveled at that. He could feel it moving. Was this why his mother thought they would kill him given the chance? Because he could track them? Or was there more?

Warrior... His mother had called his father and uncle Warriors, and so had the beast. He'd always assumed it was some romantic notion of hers, but what if it was more than that?

"Where is it?" the woman asked shakily.

"Gone." Too far away for Scott to sense anymore.

She remained silent, walking around him in seeming shock.

"Do you want me to call the police?" he asked, wincing at the thought. *What would we tell them if we did?*

She looked at the foul, black blood on his blade and hands. "Do you think they can find it? Do you think they even want to try?"

Scott turned, using the outside spigot to clean his burning hands and stained blade. As an afterthought, he cleaned his own blood from his arm, exposing the already-clotted wound that would be gone in days. *What am I?*

"No. I don't," he admitted. "What do you say I take you home and we both forget all about this?"

* * * *

Adam Lord Maher rounded the bar toward the site of the battle, determined to get to the bottom of this mess. Warriors did not hunt the range of other houses without leave. If one entered Maher on a track, he should have checked in with the manor by phone from the border.

Yet, there was no question that a Warrior was poaching his range. The border was three hundred miles away; there was no way this was an accident.

All of the Mahers had responded to his IM immediately, as had Curt and Erin. He'd even checked on his niece and nephew, but Kates and Bear were in Crossbearer on their way to Smith. With a Warrior injured in an area no one was reported in, no matter how mild the injury was or what house he hailed from, it was Adam's duty as lord to see to his health and safety. Once he'd exhausted all possible Warriors who might legitimately be hunting in Maher, he'd asked Curt to use the power of Lord *König* to find out from the houses who had a Warrior in or around Maher at the moment. So far, no one had responded positively to that query.

The smell of beast blood hung heavy in the air with a slight flavor of human—or Warrior blood beneath. That confirmed what he'd sensed of the battle: sloppy coercion of a victim, *Blutjagd*, a Warrior injured slightly and not hiding it, and a beast sent to ground.

Past that, there was little to go on—tracks of three shoes in a patch of dirt near the loading dock...a woman and two men, one in heavy tread boots and one in dress shoes. This track was going to be more difficult than most. He had no vehicle to trace, no name, nothing but the certainty that he was tracking a Warrior. Until someone admitted to culpability, there was little chance that he'd find his man.

"Smells like skunk scat out here," a man's voice complained, coming around the corner of the building.

Adam didn't ghost himself fully. Maybe this man had seen something of use.

The human stopped cold, a man about Adam's age, heavily grayed and lightly wrinkled though Adam didn't show much sign of his years yet. "What the hell are you—" He faltered, squinting into the area beyond the circles of light at Adam. His voice gentled into an almost apologetic tone. "Oh, sorry. Thought you were someone else."

So, he knew the Warrior. That could be useful. Adam stood, smiling warmly to put the man at ease. "Yes, my cousin and I do bear a bit of a resemblance."

"Well, if you're looking for Scott, I sent him home at closing time."

Adam searched his memories of the current houses. The only Scott was a Kaufmann, Devon's middle son. It was unlikely that he was in Maher range; more likely that the Warrior had assumed a fake name for some reason.

That alone was suspect. A rogue Warrior was bad news. He glanced at his watch, wincing. *Damn! He has almost an hour lead time.* "Don't know where I can find him, do you? I got into town late and missed him here, I guess."

"Ah, so that's why he was trying to hang around late." He ran a hand through his already-mussed, heavily salt and pepper hair. "Well, if he's not at his place, he's probably picked up some hot young thing for the night. Boy gets more pussy than a randy Tomcat."

Adam managed a heartfelt laugh at that one. That described most Warriors. Even if they weren't genetically predisposed to needing frequent sex by the curse, what young man could resist women throwing themselves at him because of his looks? "Yeah, well Scott was supposed to lead me to his place from here. Don't suppose you could give me directions, could you?"

The man looked uncomfortable for the first time, scanning Adam's six feet eight and swallowing hard. "Sorry, friend. Can't give out my employees' information. Privacy, you know."

Adam nodded, nearly laughing in relief. If the Warrior had an honest job here, Adam could have his information without help. The man had given him everything he needed and more. "I understand perfectly. Thanks for your help."

He returned to his truck, firing up his computer system behind the heavily tinted glass. The hack into Hanger Seven's state income records didn't take long. The backdoor they had into the DMV didn't take any longer. Within half an hour, he had Scott Danvers' name, picture, physical description, social security number—*It's going to be interesting finding out who he stole that from!*—address, phone number, vehicle description, and date of birth.

Within another half an hour, Adam was completely confused. Maybe this wasn't a Warrior, after all. He'd uncovered school records, tax forms, and even a juvenile police record. Unless 'Scott' was a master of computer forgery, he'd lived a human life for more than twenty-three years. There could be a Warrior, too, and it was happenstance that Scott Danvers resembled one. Maybe he'd just wasted two hours of tracking time on a false lead.

Maybe not. The only way to know for certain would be to pay Mr. Danvers a visit.

* * * *

Scott roared through the nearly-deserted streets with Melaina behind him, her arms wrapped around his waist. Since he never wore a helmet, he didn't have one to offer her. That made her nervous until he promised to stay off the main roads, though with his reaction time, he'd never had an accident and didn't anticipate one anytime soon.

He'd started thanking God for that promise about five minutes earlier, about the time Melaina's fear and shock gave way to arousal. Scott was hard as a gun barrel now, straining toward her teasing fingers. He sorely hoped he was going to see some action on the other end, or his cock was going to be mighty peeved at a simple beat-off.

No, even that wasn't an option. If she led him on, he'd have to find an after-hours joint to pick up a woman. Like fighting, there were some nights when close didn't cut it.

Melaina shouted the final directions over the road sounds, her busy fingers never pausing. Scott forced his mind to the road when he wanted to pull over and finish where they were. *Control*, he reminded himself.

But the call to sex was almost more than he could bear. How long had it been for him? He bit back a groan at the combination of Melaina popping the first two buttons on his jeans and his calculation that it had been two and a half weeks. She started massaging the aching head, popping a third button in the process, her fingers circling on the sensitive veins beneath the cap.

A week without a fight and two and a half without sex? It was a damned miracle that he wasn't stark raving mad. If there was one thing he needed as much as the physical test of fists, it was the feeling of a woman's body pulsing around his length.

His first woman had been when he was fifteen, a fact that hadn't surprised his mother in the least. In fact, she'd given him condoms on his birthday and started extending the mantra about self control to include the women she knew he would start bedding. Mom was definitely a strange bird all the way around. She always had been. His mother...

Scott pushed away the disturbing question of how much she told him was fact and not fantasy, concentrating instead on Melaina's body for a moment, using her skin to skin contact with him to his fullest advantage, sighing in relief that she was on some sort of hormone suppression of her periods. The last thing he needed was a woman pulling the same crap on him that his mother had pulled on Matt and Jordan.

His jaw tightened in anger at that, not quite the fury he'd felt when he moved out but the residual anger at the games she'd played with all of their lives. Still, Scott would never have known he had the power to avoid a similar trap had she not told him he could read a woman's body just by touching her and concentrating on it. Like the accelerated healing and the ability to make himself inconspicuous, it was something not every man could do. They were, she said, gifts from his father.

His musings about what that meant were cut off by some rather purposeful stroking ala Melaina. Scott gave up and groaned in pleasure. He made the last turn, cruising past the old farm house, over the hill, and stopping next to the smaller house as she'd instructed. Silence fell around them as he shut off the cycle.

Without missing a beat, Melaina slid off the seat, her skirt still hiked halfway up her thighs. She met his eyes with a coy little smile, brought her fingers to her mouth, and licked them with a look of pleasure.

"Here or inside?" he asked simply. There was no use beating around the bush. They wanted each other, and if she intended to back out, that was her cue.

"Ever done it on a swing?" she asked.

He didn't crack a smile. "Playground, porch, or erotic?" He'd done each several times. An erotic swing was his favorite by far, though a playground swing could be manipulated for height and was more comfortable than an old-fashioned porch swing.

"Sofa glider."

"Can't say as I have. Sounds interesting."

She purred and turned, stripping as she walked. Scott could take a hint as well as the next guy. His shirt landed over her skirt, about halfway to the door. He unbuckled his boots and dropped them on the porch, followed by his socks and jeans, with only a pit stop to snag a few condoms from the pocket on the way.

Melaina scanned his body with a look of appreciation. He'd seen looks like it on the faces of women since he'd been fifteen—and looked twenty. In fact, his first woman had been twenty. He strode through the door, closing the distance between them in two long strides.

The urge to have her beat at him, drowning out conscious thought. His arms circled her waist, and he lifted her to meet his mouth, carrying her toward the sofa as her lips parted beneath his. She matched his fervor, seemingly committed to going where he wished to go. That was good; Scott had no patience for games tonight.

She pulled back, running one hand through the close-cropped hair at the back of his head. "Why don't you sit down on the sofa," she suggested, pulling at his length with the other in promise.

"I intend to end up inside you," he warned, making his needs as clear as he could without demanding. His mother had always instructed that, with his sheer size and power, demanding anything with a woman would be setting himself up for repercussions.

"Oh, yeah," she breathed.

He set her on her feet, nodding as he settled on the soft cushions, spreading his legs to give her room to stand between them.

Melaina wasted no time. She sank to her knees, taking the head into the warmth of her mouth. Scott groaned, wrapping both fists in her hair, gliding the piece of furniture forward so that more of him slid into her mouth. It slid back, and she sucked hard at the tip.

God, but this game was good. He rocked the glider back and forth, forcing himself as deep as it would allow over and over. Still, it wasn't enough. Scott wanted to drag her closer, but that was something he'd always avoided. Any semblance of force was bad news. Any sign that he'd lost control was even worse than that.

"Deeper," he grumbled.

For one timeless moment, she buried her face in his body, taking his full length down. He didn't breathe. His heart hardly seemed to beat. Scott held back the urge to pour his load down her throat. If he wasted it that way, and she didn't give him another shot at her tonight, he'd be nearly as bad off as if he'd stroked it out himself.

Then she retreated, and he let out his breath in a harsh cry. His balls pulled tight to his body. He wasn't going to last if she did that again.

"Up," he ordered. "I want to be inside you." *I need to be there.*

Melaina looked up at him in surprise, but she rose. Too late, he realized that he'd barked it at her. Scott pulled her into his lap, kissing her, reassuring her with his actions that he wasn't out of control. She whimpered as he slid one finger inside her, rocking against him as if begging for more. He added another finger, and she gasped.

"That's right," he whispered. "You want all of me, don't you?"

"Yes."

"Then kneel on the sofa, facing the back, hands braced."

She scanned his full height again as if doing the mental math of whether or not he could make that work. Curiosity overcame her indecision, and she slid off him, doing what he asked as he stood behind her.

A fine tremor raced through her body as he ripped the condom open and rolled it down his length. Scott gripped her hips, smiling at her wide-spread legs and the curve of her ass pushed up to welcome him. He slid deep, closing his eyes for a moment to find his center as she whimpered again.

"Are you ready for me?" he asked. "Are you ready for the wildest ride of your life?"

Melaina nodded, gasping out her permission, begging for it.

"Just what I wanted to hear." He braced his hands next to hers, pushing the glider further away, sucking in his breath slowly as he slid nearly out of her. He held it there, savoring the moment of anticipation.

"Scott—"

"Don't move," he requested.

She held herself rigidly still save the mild quaking that announced her hunger for more. Just when she started to look over her shoulder to question him, he released the back, letting it rock toward him fully, driving him deeper than the first time. He caught it, stopping it again, the curve of her buttocks nestled to his hips.

"Scott," she pleaded, wriggling against him.

"I did promise you a wild ride," he noted.

Melaina nodded fiercely.

"Then I better deliver."

He pushed the glider out and pulled it back, rocking his hips in time with it, meeting her deeper and deeper until he gently brushed the os at every forward thrust. She cried out harshly at that, grinding against him every time their bodies joined tightly together. This was what he wanted, what he needed. She'd seek out the stimulation she needed to come hard, milking him over with her.

Scott ground his teeth. He needed that soon, or he'd come without it, and it was never as good when he didn't feel the woman come for him...with him. He moved one hand from the back of the glider to her stomach, sliding down until he was circling her clit in time with his continuing thrusts.

"Oh, God, Scott." It wasn't quite a shout—breathless, begging, a rough statement of pure need.

She was close. He could almost taste how close she was. Melaina just needed a little incentive to fire the mental side of the equation. "Come for me in the next thirty seconds, and I will show you every way I know to use this glider."

Her body clenched around him. She groaned deeply, her hips circling more purposefully.

"One wild ride after another, Melaina. Twenty seconds."

He held his breath, spurting precome into the condom as weak contractions of her muscles taunted him, holding the promise of what he needed.

"Ten. I'm going to enjoy eating you..."

One more clench, tighter than the last.

"Five. And watching you ride my cock—"

He roared as she gave him what he wanted, coming hard, pressing tight to him, screaming out in ecstasy. Scott joined her, his cock giving up wave after wave of repressed release into the condom between them. He rocked her slowly, sliding in and out of her still-spasming body.

"That was spectacular," he whispered, his body and mind at peace as it always was when he came with so willing a partner.

Melaina shivered. "You're not backing out now, are you?" she asked seriously.

Scott chuckled. "I never break my word."

She slid off his cock and turned, planting her ass on the edge of the glider and her heels close to her body. "Good. I believe this was what you promised next."

He dropped to his knees, blowing a gust of air over her sensitized body as he closed on her. "A woman's body tastes so good just after she comes." He buried his tongue inside her, smiling as her contractions started almost immediately.

* * * *

Adam watched the motorcycle intently, noting the make, color, and finally license plate number that marked it as Scott Danvers'. The young man had the look of a Warrior, though no Warrior Adam knew had blonde tips bleached onto the spiked hair on top of his head or tattoos decorating his muscular arms. Though many of the young Warriors adopted extreme personal appearances, this went beyond what any sane Warrior did; it was too easy to identify someone who stood out so markedly from the norm they kept. Nothing visible save hair styles was the rule of the houses.

He continued his perusal. Like most Warriors, Scott wore jeans and armored boots, though Scott's weren't in the Warrior style. They were a stunt cyclist's boots but functionally similar. His t-shirt was Navy blue instead of the typical black, and he wore no button-down shirt or leather jacket over it. It wasn't unusual for a Warrior to forego one of the two shirts on a warm night, but what Warrior didn't wear a leather jacket after nightfall? None he knew of besides Mikel of Crossbearer-*König*.

It didn't surprise Adam that Scott didn't wear a helmet or protective clothing for riding. That reckless disregard was typical of their pups.

But the weapon at Scott's back confused Adam more than the conflicted whole so far combined. He had no sacred weapon. The blade was a SEAL knife, no less deadly to a human but nearly useless against a high-level beast.

Scott parked and kicked over his cycle, ambling toward the door with the look of a man completely at ease. Adam considered that a Warrior who'd had successful battle—and from the smell of him, good sex—would be at the height of relaxation. It was Nirvana to the unmated man of their ranks.

No. I need to go into this with an unbiased eye. He may not be a Warrior.

That thought was banished only a moment later.

Scott caught sight of Adam lounging next to the door and tensed, *Blutjagd* burning lightly in his skin. The reaction was so unexpected that Adam found himself forcing back the urge to pull one of his weapons, to exact punishment as judge for his obvious lack of control.

"Which one are you?" the pup growled.

Again, his responses were off kilter. There was no recognition, no familiar address, not even a sign of respect for a house lord. "Who do you think I am?" Though there was no Warrior alive who could be mistaken for Adam, this youth was obviously having some difficulty.

"If you're here, I imagine you're either Matt or Jordan. I suppose you've come to fuck up my life a little more." There was a bite of sarcasm in that.

Armens. Though the last close Maher-Armen friendship was his grandfather Kord and James Armen, he'd met all of Tyler Lord Armen's sons, and none of them could be mistaken for Adam. No Armen could.

Scott's eyes narrowed and his jaw tightened; his *Blutjagd* stepping up another notch. "I see. I'm not in Armen—territory or whatever the hell that beast called it. Your name would probably be Maher, right?"

Dear Gods! The boy didn't even know what range he was in? Was he insane? Or maybe suffering some sort of head injury? Whatever the case may be, it was immaterial. Whether a Warrior was AWOL or otherwise misplaced, the other houses would need to know it.

"Hellooooo," Scott called out in apparent annoyance. "Look, if you're just going to stare at me all night, I have better things to do."

"I think we need to talk," Adam forced out. He had to find out what was going on here. Whatever it was, it didn't bode well for Armen.

Scott seemed surprised by the suggestion. It was a full thirty seconds before he answered, his brow furrowed, his fists unclenching, and his *Blutjagd* flickering, then dying slowly. "Sure. Come on in and have a beer."

Adam followed him inside the entryway, then into a large efficiency. It was roughly what he'd expect of a young Warrior alone: a stereo system, sleeper sofa, bureau, laptop, exercise mats, weights, a stationary bag, a kitchenette, and an apartment-style washer-dryer unit crammed into the main room with a three-quarter bath beyond. From the looks of it, his wheels were the most expensive thing Scott owned.

"Want one?" Scott called out from the kitchen arca.

"A beer? No alcohol, thanks." Was this kid insane or clueless?

"After the night I've had? It's a Beam night."

"The beast?" he prompted.

Scott turned, an open, half-empty bottle of Jim Beam in his hand, shrugging as he took a swallow and headed for the sofa. "Well, finding out my mother isn't quite as nuts as the state of North Dakota thinks she is probably didn't help." He flopped down on the threadbare piece of furniture, taking a long drag on the bottle that probably amounted to two full shots.

"Your—" An impossible scenario settled in his mind. Adam tried to reject it, but it stuck with him. "Your mother is in an asylum?" Gods! No house would allow it. The Stone wouldn't allow it. How would her mate survive? Or was he already dead?

He closed his eyes, a wry smile twisting his lips. "They call them institutions now. Well, when you believe some mysterious beasts are out to kill you and your son..." He laughed harshly. "Crazy bitch was right about that one. Stranger things have happened, I guess." He brought the bottle to his mouth again, his hand shaking lightly.

Adam stamped down the urge to leave scars for calling his mother such a foul thing.

The rest filtered in slowly. Scott had encountered his *first* beast tonight. He hadn't even known they really existed until he saw one. He was never trained and first nighted? Gods, he didn't even own a sacred weapon! "Where is your father?" *Your grandfather? Your uncles? Who is responsible for this pup, and how could this happen?*

Scott opened his eyes, murder in his expression though only the slightest edge of *Blutjagd* showed in him. "Why don't you tell me?" he challenged.

"What?" Oh, this sounded worse and worse with every exchange.

"I don't want it. I don't want these...damned gifts I've been given."

"And, killing your father is going to do what, precisely?" How unstable was this kid? And, how in the name of Ani could a Warrior walk away from his child? If Scott hadn't insinuated that the man was still alive somewhere, Adam would be back to the idea that he was dead.

He raised the bottle again, breathing his answer into the neck before he tipped it up. "Nothing." His *Blutjagd* faded. Scott swallowed the mouthful slowly. "Nothing at all. Forget it. I don't want to know where he is. I never did."

The birth certificate on file danced in Adam's mind. No father was named. What if it were true?

No, this wasn't possible. "Lynne never told him," he guessed, his stomach clenching at the idea of a young Warrior outside the framework of his house and family. How could he survive without going insane?

Scott downed the rest of the bottle and dropped the empty to the floor. For a moment, he was silent. "She didn't even know which one it was. No. A goddamn beast had to confirm which one was my father for me." He rubbed his eyes.

Her name *was* Lynne. The birth certificate was real. "Matt or Jordan?" he managed stiffly. Scott had assumed he was either Matt or Jordan. Those were the only names he knew. They must have been the names Lynne gave him for his 'fathers.'

"What does it matter? Think I want to ruin some poor schmuck's life? He probably has a wife and kids. Think he really wants to deal with this?"

Matt *did* have a mate and two sons, but either way, this wasn't something Adam could hide from them. Scott was a Warrior-born son. *A Warrior himself, Gods help him!* Any Warrior would want to know about a child.

What Lynne had done was criminal in their world, cruel to both the Warrior who'd sired her son and the son born of the union. Thank Ani that the child hadn't been female, or Lorian might have stolen her for his own use rather than pursuing Erin and meeting his end at Mikel's hands.

Scott was a Warrior. That meant he had a duty. More importantly, they had a duty to him; the entire Warrior world did. "He has a duty to—"

"I'm no one's duty!" Scott took a calming breath. "I don't need him, and I won't do this to him."

Adam recognized the lie for what it was. Scott needed his father more than any Warrior he'd ever met. He needed the knowledge and training that would make him sane and safe. He was simply afraid that he wouldn't be welcome for some reason. "He'll want to know."

Scott stared at him wearily. "Why?" His voice slurred slightly, the alcohol taking its toll. "Why would he care?"

"Because we're wired that way. Your mother probably hid you, because she knew your father would demand you. We can't be separated from our children—at least if we know they exist."

Frustration welled up in Adam. It was impossible to explain the soul-deep need to love and guide a child that their curse instilled in them. There was so much Scott didn't know about himself. They were blessed that the young man hadn't had a brush with printing and done damage in his madness, all for the stupidity of one woman. "Dear Ani! How could he make this mistake in the first place? It's common practice to—"

"Check a woman's cycle. I know."

Adam stared at him in shock. He hadn't even considered the possibility that Scott might have magnified the damage without knowledge of what another child out of printing would mean—or more than one. Did he even know how to check a cycle? How to ghost? Could he learn those things without training?

The young man blushed. "My mother imparted that rather useful bit of information to me along the way. Good thing, too. I have no intentions of playing the part of my dear old Dad, the sucker—or allowing some poor kid to live my life. Thanks but no thanks. I am quite capable of learning from someone else's mistakes, at least if they affect me."

"I don't think I understand." What was he saying? Either his father was sloppy, which would mean he'd have to answer for it to the Council of Lords, or Lynne had done something truly heinous. Adam wasn't sure which would be worse.

"It was no mistake. *I* was no accident. Mom set them up, played us all like a fine instrument." He grumbled several harsh curses under his breath, ending with a clear 'bitch.'

The term made a lot more sense this time around, but Adam's *Blutjagd* spiked anyway. This time, it spiked in sympathetic fury at the type of woman who'd plan something like this. If Lynne knew what thc Warriors were—enough to teach Scott a little about them, she knew why this was a bad idea and did it anyway.

Scott stiffened, shooting him a bleary look that was none-the-less dangerous, his hand creeping to his weapon as if gauging his need to draw it. Adam forced his rage back, rallying his calm. The pure instinct to fight when faced with *Blutjagd* was something his young charge hadn't learned to rein in yet. Scott wasn't his enemy, and Adam wouldn't give him reason to react. He nodded, and the young man relaxed, laying his hand on his thigh.

"How?" Adam asked. "How does a woman arrange something like this? Warriors aren't usually sloppy."

He snorted, a harsh sound of mirthless laughing. "You should learn to take your used condoms with you. You know, I carry mine out and dump them in a garbage can somewhere at random. Four or five loads over a few days from two of your finest was all it took." His smirk melted into a look of misery. "More than enough."

Adam winced. A single insemination would have been enough. If there was one thing they had to be mindful of it was how fertile they were, how easy it was to impregnate a woman at or even near high cycle. If anyone knew it, Adam did.

Scott closed his eyes, laying his head back, looking lost and lonely, worn beyond his years despite what he was—or maybe because of it. His arms went lax as sleep closed on him, a drugged sleep, but still sleep he needed.

"Which one?" Adam asked. "Which one is your father?" He had to know that. Calling in the Armens without a clue of which brother had sired him would end with two near-mad Warriors at each other's throats—and Scott's.

"Matthew Armen," he whispered.

Adam pulled out his cell phone and started dialing, watching Scott's breathing become deep and even while the phone rang three times.

The connection opened. "Armen manor. Jordan here," the voice on the other end intoned, a grim answer for a manor. Then again, a head-count summons from *König* wouldn't have put the houses in a good mood.

"It's Adam, Jordan."

"It's not one of ours," he replied immediately.

Adam ignored his statement. He'd expected that greeting, more or less. "I need to speak to Matt. It's—an emergency of sorts. Can you patch me through?" If Jordan refused, he'd have *König* order it. Damn it! He wasn't going to pass this message to Matt through anyone else.

"Don't have to. He's right here. Hang on."

"Thanks."

There was a long moment of fumbling before Matt came on the line. "It's not one of ours," he repeated.

Adam sighed. "There's no easy way to say this, Matt, so I'm going to come right out and say it. I'm standing here with your son."

"That's impossible," he exploded. "Antony is upstairs, and Tevin just walked out the door."

Other angry shouts echoed over the line, and Adam winced.

"You put this on speaker?"

"Of course, he did," Tyler Lord Armen shouted. "I don't know what game you're playing *Lord* Maher, but—"

"This is no game!"

Scott shifted uneasily, and Adam forced his *Blutjagd* back, unwilling to disturb him. He lowered his voice and began again.

"I am standing here with Matt's son. Not Tevin or Antony. His *oldest* son."

He paused. There was absolute silence over the line, most likely in shock.

"His name is Scott Danvers. Mother—Lynne. Born January the fifth, twenty-twenty-six."

"Dear Ani." Several curses followed close behind.

Adam couldn't tell who said it. He continued. "He's a smart-mouthed, bitter little punk who's been hurt by this as much as you have. He's also an honorable young man who faced his first beast tonight and sent the bastard to ground, with no training to do it and no sacred weapon to help him do the job. Now, if Armen is going to claim he's not one of theirs, Maher would be proud to give him a home." That wasn't really an option, and they all knew it, but Adam had a point to make, and he would make it in his typical style; they didn't call him Conan for nothing.

Matt's voice shook. He tried to say something several times, and he cleared his throat twice before he managed to force words to emerge. "I'll be there in three hours if I have to charter a jet to do it."

"I knew you would. Call me when you hit the tarmac, and I'll give you directions."

"We will," Jordan answered for him. Then they disconnected.

Adam flipped the phone shut and settled onto the weight bench, watching Scott sleep. In a few hours, his life would change forever. But whether being thrust into the Warrior world would bring him balance or grief remained to be seen.

Chapter Twenty-four

"Enough of this shit, Adam! Get the fuck out of my way and let me see my son."

The shout echoed through the apartment—and through Scott's head. He winced, opening his eyes. He rubbed at his forehead, memories of the previous night leaving him cold.

So, the old man actually showed up. "Big deal," he whispered. It wasn't like this was going to be a happy family reunion.

A chorus of voices rose, competing with each other.

"You can't go barreling in there like this," Maher replied calmly. "Not in this rage."

Scott pushed to his feet, heading for the door though his bladder demanded the bathroom.

"Damn you, Adam. If you don't step aside—" He stopped talking, his mouth dropping open in shock, his eyes tracking Scott from the moment he came into view.

The other three men turned to him, following the first man's line of sight. The silence in the room was absolute, so much so that Scott felt his muscles itch to fight. The shock on their faces said it all. Why had Maher bothered?

"Disappointed?" Scott asked, trying to convince himself that he didn't care if they were. "Well, that makes..." He swiveled his head as if conducting a head count. "Five of us, I guess, unless there are more of you hiding in the hall. You can get out of my apartment any time. I didn't ask Maher to call you in the first place."

He turned for the bathroom, pushing away the burning question of what they would do next. He'd taken them off the hook. No doubt, he'd come out to an empty room, and that would suit him just fine.

A spike of the same energy he'd felt from Maher the night before warned him that one of them was coming—but not Maher. The energy had a different feel to it than his.

Scott turned, sidestepping the attack at his back, backhanding the man to the floor smoothly, a different one than the one who'd been talking when he caught sight of them. The other three surged toward him, and Scott prepared to take them all on. He'd fought worse odds, though the fact that they were Warriors probably meant they were superior fighters. To his amazement, the two strangers took down the one rising from the floor. That left him even more unprepared for what Maher did.

The Warrior placed himself between Scott and the other three, offering his back to Scott much as Scott had with Melaina the night before. It was an undeniable move of protection. Maher pulled his blade, apparently ready to gut the first man if he escaped the other two. "Stay at my back," he grumbled.

"Stand down," the oldest of them ordered, pushing back on his attacker. "Stand down, or I will kill you myself."

The fight drained out of Armen immediately. He nodded, though he glared at Scott as if the reprieve would only last as long as they held him at bay.

Scott recovered his wits enough to be offended by this greeting. "I always knew I didn't want a father. Family sucks. Thanks for the reminder, Maher."

The younger of the two guarding his attacker looked at Scott in seeming dismay. He motioned to the glaring man. "This is not your father."

"Then, I guess *you* are." The ages would seem to indicate that.

He took a step toward Scott, his expression strangely—hopeful? No, it had to be something else. Why would he give a damn about a kid some groupie popped out?

"I guess I am. Gods alive, there is no question that I must be."

Scott turned for the bathroom, emotions he didn't want to feel pulling at him. Family was nothing special. They just let you down eventually. He had to remember that. "Thanks all the same, but I don't need you." He'd done without a father for twenty-three years. What did he need this shit for?

He closed the door before someone could decide to attack him again, forcing his breathing to even, panic making his head spin worse than the slight hangover he'd earned.

* * * *

Matt's stomach rolled at Scott's words. How could his son just walk away like that? The water turned on full-blast behind the door, and Matt's hopes sank. It was that simple for Scott? Just tell him to go away and wipe his own father out of his life? Matt couldn't. Now that he knew Scott existed, Matt couldn't let him shut him out like this.

"It's not what you think," Adam assured him, sheathing his sacred weapon again.

"Isn't it?" Fury welled up at the situation he'd been dealt. Even if Scott hadn't received him with open arms, he should have given Matt a chance. If Matt had known about him from birth or before, it was a chance he would have had. There might be too much damage now, and what would he do if it came to that? *Go insane.*

Lynne is insane. "Lynne is damned lucky she's in an asylum. I'd have to kill her for this if the opportunity arose."

"Matt," his father began, half in warning but half in seeming dismay at his lack of control.

"She hid my son from me," he thundered. "She turned him against me."

Adam winced.

"What?" Matt snapped at him.

"Maybe I should have told you the whole story up front, before you came here and met him. I counted on a different outcome." He waved off the many questions welling up in Matt. "Did you look at him, Matt?"

"Of course, I did. He's the image of Antony. How could anyone doubt that he's mine?"

"No. Did you *look* at him? Yes, he's angry; he has the right to be pissed off, but..."

"But?" Matt prompted him, his fury fading in light of his need to know his son. *Almost twenty-four years! She cost me a lifetime with one of my children.*

"He's scared. You have a life that doesn't include him. What if you want to keep it that way?"

"I don't," he snarled. "You know I could never want that."

"I do, but Scott doesn't. His understanding of Warriors is limited. His mother—"

Matt growled at the memory of the blade chaser that had carried his son.

Adam hurried on. "She didn't tell him much. Just enough, I suppose."

"Not enough," Jordan grumbled.

Matt turned to him, his rebuke dying in his throat at the sight of the empty Jim Beam bottle in his brother's hand.

"How much of this did he drink last night, Adam?" Jordan inquired. "I could still smell it on him when I took him on."

"Half of it."

Matt winced, fisting his hand that his son had come to this. It was Lynne's fault. He would have been stable if he'd been raised with the Warriors.

"He didn't have the best of moments," Adam admitted. "He battled his first beast, met his first Warrior and...found out who his father is. This is all new to him."

His *Blutjagd* blazed nearly out of control. "Lynne didn't tell him my name?"

Adam flicked a red-faced look at each of the Armens in turn. "She...didn't know which name to give him. This...Lynne wasn't so picky about who fathered her son—or how."

Jordan choked. He and Matt stared at each other. Memories of his farewell from Lynne when she'd announced that she was moving danced in Matt's mind. He'd found out later that she'd spent the following night with Jordan. They'd laughed about it at the time, at the true blade chaser she'd been, getting the most Warrior cock she could before she lost her supply. The implications of what Adam was saying were no doubt as clear to Jordan as they were to Matt.

"Oh, no. She wouldn't dare," Jordan managed.

"She did dare," Adam confirmed. "Before you attack him again, keep in mind that, until the beast last night, Scott had two candidates for the position. At best, he considers you both gullible."

"At worst..." Matt's mind refused to consider the rest. Lynne could have told him anything in the time she had.

The shower turned off, and Scott emerged, wrapped in a towel. His jaw tightened. "I thought I invited you to leave," he hinted, brushing past them to a battered bureau.

"I can't do that."

He snorted in seeming disgust. "You make a habit of staying where you're not wanted?"

"I make a habit of teaching, protecting, and nurturing my children, even those who hate me for it."

Scott turned with a Navy blue t-shirt in hand and a scowl on his face. "I'm past needing nurturing, I can protect myself, and there's nothing you can teach me that I want to learn." He pulled the shirt over his head, motioning pointedly to the door as he pushed his arm through.

Tyler raised a hand to still Matt's counterargument. "You've met your first beast. Whether you like it or not, that wound of yours is only the first. Unless you want the next one to be fatal, you will have to learn to do your duty—"

"I don't *have* a duty. Where do you get off, coming to my home and demanding anything of me?"

"Our laws—"

"Your laws! They are not mine. My laws fall under the penal code of whatever locality I hang my hat in. In case you missed this, I'm not part of your precious family, and I don't want to be. Live with it."

"You don't have a choice."

"Bet me."

"Scott's right," Jordan offered. "He does have a choice."

Matt turned on him, barely restraining the urge to gut his older brother by a year. "You know he doesn't."

"Sure he does. Every Warrior does. Do your duty or face the consequences."

Matt's *Blutjagd* burned fiercely at that, and he took a step closer to Scott, placing himself between Jordan and his son. His hand settled on his sacred weapon.

"Matt," Tyler warned.

"You're not killing my son," Matt managed in a low, dangerous voice.

"Matt—"

He turned to include his father in his arc radius, glancing at Scott out of the corner of his eye, nearly wincing at his son's pallor. "You're not. Either of you. He has the right to be angry. At me, if he wants to. At the situation. At the entire Warrior world. At—his mother, I surely hope. You're not killing him for it."

"He needs training. You know this life has to be driving him insane."

Scott pulled jeans out of another drawer. "You know what's driving me insane? All of you." But his hands shook, and his face was tense. He glanced toward the bathroom, probably laying odds on his chance of reaching the dagger he'd left with his dirty clothes.

Matt's heart ached. Though he knew what Jordan was doing, instinct honed in raising two sons told him that Scott wouldn't be driven to his family by fear of the consequences. "I want to talk to my son alone," he requested.

Jordan passed the empty liquor bottle into Matt's hands on the way out the door. Tyler followed him with a clap on his shoulder. Adam nodded his agreement and shut the door behind them.

Matt waited for Scott to finish dressing, heartened that he'd stopped glancing toward his weapon when no signs of attack came. He took his time, pulling on his jeans and socks...even a pair of hiking boots, but he didn't face Matt when he was done. Scott stared at the kitchenette, his fists clenched, seemingly waiting for the other shoe to drop.

Matt sighed. "Believe it or not, you're not just a duty to me. I really do want to get to know you."

"It'll pass. It's just the shock of finding out about me. It's fine, you know. I haven't had a father for twenty-three years. Don't put yourself out."

"That wasn't my choice. If I had known about you then—"

"What?" A bite of sarcasm crept into his voice. "You would have fought to keep me?"

"I would have done anything I had to just to be part of your life, and I probably would have gotten myself killed in the process."

"Riiiiight," he drawled, obviously convinced it wouldn't have passed that way.

"I don't get it. Why are you so sure that I wouldn't have? You obviously know nothing about our biological and psychological ties to our children, if you believe—"

"I know enough," he snapped.

Matt's head spun at the vehemence of his answer. "Like?" he prompted. What nonsense had Lynne told him to make him react this way?

Scott turned around him as if they were sparring, looking him up and down with a scowl. "I know you don't have kids that aren't from your marriage, and you only marry once. I know your religion doesn't recognize bastards, whatever religion that is. I guess I'm some embarrassment to you, huh?"

"No. You're not." A sick headache settled in the base of his skull. "You wanted to find me, didn't you?"

For a moment, Scott didn't answer him. "I was a stupid kid. I got over it quickly enough. Just like you'll get over me."

"She told you I wouldn't acknowledge you." He didn't question it, and Scott didn't reply to it. *Gods protect that woman if they ever release her.* "She told you a bunch of convenient half-truths. We do avoid children outside of mating, but you know why now that you've met a beast. That doesn't mean we can turn our backs on any child we sire."

"Why not?"

"We—can't." Who knew this would be so hard to explain? "Will you let me teach you?"

"Are you going to kill me, if I say 'no?'" he countered acidly.

"No. I'm not going to kill you."

"But they will." He tipped his head toward the door.

"Only if they kill me first. You have my vow."

He hesitated, his fists relaxing. "Fine. Teach me."

Matt pulled the sheath he'd stuck in the back of his belt out, noting Scott's instant tension. He offered it to him, nodding his head to let his son know he intended for him to take the weapon.

Scott watched him warily, pulling it from the sheath, examining it carefully, touching the Armen seal, even testing its weight and balance. "It's nice," he offered, "but I don't know what this means." He started to hand it back.

Matt shook his head, extending the sheath to him again. "It's yours."

"You're giving me this?"

"Yes, I am."

"Why?"

"We always give these to our sons. We all carry them. It's a little late...about eight years late, but..." He sighed. "The first thing I did when I heard about you, while your grandfather made the arrangements for our flight down here, was take one of my spare blades out for you."

Scott didn't seem to know what to say to that. He took the sheath and placed the blade back inside, staring at it. "I had a plastic commando dagger when I was a kid," he whispered. "It was one of my favorite toys."

Matt smiled at the lengths Lynne had gone to. At least, she did some things right. "We give our sons wooden weapons, usually at about the age of three."

"She called it... Oh, damn. This is what that beast meant."

"Scott?"

He looked up, scowling again. "You call these sacred weapons. That's what it said, that I was without my sacred weapon. It's also what my mother called that toy."

"It's the only thing that can kill them," Matt explained.

"Well, that's information I could have used," he commented wryly. "No wonder I couldn't kill it." Scott looked him up and down, seemingly considering something. "I guess there *are* some things I need you to teach me."

Matt nearly crowed in joy. "We'll pack you up and get you home to Armen range. I'm sure your brothers are already dying to meet you, and—"

Scott's hand fisted tight around the hilt of the sacred weapon. "Let's get this straight, *Matt.* I don't have a home, and I don't have brothers. I agreed to let you train me, because one way or the other, my life depends on knowing how to perform this damned duty of killing off beasts before they—or your family—kill me off."

Matt sighed. "You're an Armen, whether you acknowledge it or not."

"My name," he growled, "is Scott Danvers."

The urge to shake him was fierce. Matt forced it down, nearly growling in restraint. "You'll find that family is in your blood, Scott. Just as I can't ignore your existence, you can't ignore ours forever. For now, I'll train you."

Scott didn't answer that.

"How long will it take you to be ready to relocate?" he asked, changing the subject.

"A day or two. I don't have much, and bouncers are a nomadic lot, so quitting my job isn't that big a deal."

"Good. I'll make a few arrangements and be back for lunch."

He nodded.

Matt headed for the door, the arrangements that would need made coursing through his mind. Scott would need a small truck to transport his belongings, rooms—and a lot of space to himself.

An image of him reacting violently to attempts to welcome him filled Matt's mind. Until he was certain

Scott was stable, he'd have to keep Sarah at a distance. His big-hearted wife thought a loving embrace was the answer to all of life's problems, and Scott was certain to balk at that. The training house would be the best place to take him—for now.

His hand was on the door when he heard the muttered comment behind him.

"Big deal. Family sucks."

* * * *

JFK International Airport

"Kates? Earth to Katie *König*-Maher," her twin brother Corwyn, affectionately known as Bear, teased.

She looked up, managing a weak smile.

Her brother dropped into the seat next to her. "If you don't want to do this..." He let it hang between them, the offer to just head home and not look for a mate for her right now.

"No. I want to do this. I have to, really."

"But?"

"I don't know. I keep feeling like something's wrong, but I don't know what."

He looked around, on alert for any threat. "What is it that you feel?"

"I can't explain it. Like...I shouldn't be here, but where I should be, I don't know." She laughed nervously. "That doesn't make much sense, I know."

"I can call Mom," he offered.

"No! Oh, please, don't do that. The last thing I need is her thinking I've really lost it."

Bear wrapped his arms around her, holding her close. "Why would she think that?"

"I'm a mess, Bear. After my arguments that it was time to find my mate and all the arrangements for me to tour the ranges... Now, I feel like I shouldn't go, but the drive is still there. I think I've gone insane. Why wouldn't she?"

"Do you think it's cold feet?" he asked seriously.

"I guess so. Funny, huh? Me scared of a man I could probably slice and dice?"

"It will be okay," he soothed her. "They always say it's biology for us. When you meet the right one, it will all work out."

Katie closed her eyes, too tired to sleep. "I hope you're right."

Chapter Twenty-five

October 30, 2049

"I don't understand it," Katie complained. "I've met every Warrior in the world and zilch." She flopped down on the leather sofa in Cross manor and sighed, the urgency to find her mate eating at her as it had for the past four months.

"Maybe you're not ready yet," Bear suggested, trying to hide a smirk.

She shot him a look of warning. "Maybe I should gut you for that comment."

He chuckled, his eyes challenging her. "Whatever the *Blutjagdfrau* wishes."

Their Uncle Hunter laughed heartily. "She's ready."

Mikel smiled, raising his wife's hand to kiss it. "Yes. She most certainly is."

"But, I've met every Warrior," she repeated. "What the hell does the Stone want from me?"

"Well," her father began. "Actually..." He grimaced as if he found something highly distasteful.

The tension in the room kicked up several notches.

Katie shivered in response to the near-*Blutjagd*, laughing nervously. "What? You're not suggesting that I look for a human man, are you? I mean... *Blutjagdfrau* never go to bars trolling for..."

No one spoke, and several of the men shifted uneasily.

"What?" she demanded, reacting to their discomfort. She looked at Bear, but he seemed as confused as she was.

Hunter cleared his throat. "There...uh...there's actually one Warrior you haven't met yet."

"That's impossible. Every house I'm not closely related to trotted out every eligible Warrior. How could I miss one?"

Erin, her mother, rolled her eyes. "Men! After my mother, it amazes me that you are all so squeamish about this."

"That's different," Curt snapped, an uncharacteristic response to his mate that made Katie gasp at her father in surprise. "And, I hardly want my daughter marrying the James Dean of the Warrior world."

"It's hardly your choice," Erin countered smoothly. "It's his and Katie's. Or to be more precise, it's the Stone's will coming to fruition in them."

Mikel rubbed the back of his neck, smiling sheepishly. "He's not as bad as people make him out to be," he stated confidently. "I went to meet him pretty early on, when he was still circling everyone who approached him."

"I don't understand," Katie managed. "Who is this Warrior, and what does Grandma Jayde have to do with it?"

"Scott Armen," Curt grumbled.

"Danvers," Mikel corrected him. "His name is Scott Danvers."

Hunter muttered a series of curses in German. "He's still using that? Damn! Matt must be going insane."

"Dad?" Katie asked, swinging her gaze from her uncle to her father in confusion. "Why would a Warrior use an assumed name?"

Her mother cut in. "Because it's not an assumed name. Scott was the son of a rather overzealous blade chaser. She wanted a child, and she never told his father that Scott existed. Your uncle Adam found him, quite by accident, in his range."

"Oh, dear gods. How old is he?"

"Almost twenty-four." Erin smiled. "Just like your grandmother was."

A chill ran up Katie's spine. She tried to imagine what a trauma like that would do to a Warrior, but she kept coming back to Jayde, never comfortable in her life in their world, dying only days after her mate, unable to cope without him. Talon had been her only anchor, and without him, it was too much for her to bear.

"Katie," her father began.

"I want to meet him." *I have to meet him. No wonder I didn't want to leave the country. I knew I was headed the wrong direction. He's needed me, and I haven't been there.* She met her father's stricken look. "How soon can I get to Armen?"

Curt sighed. "Are you sure you won't wait—just for a bit, until he's more acclimated?"

"No. I really think... I know I have to go."

He nodded, grimacing. "As soon as you need to. You know that."

* * * *

October 31, 2049

"*König,*" Tyler called out, clasping Bear's hand then raising Katie's to kiss her knuckles.

She straightened her waist-length leather jacket and cast her eyes about for a Warrior she hadn't met yet. Her heart sank when she encountered only Jordan and a few children.

Tyler looked around, then back, his smile faltering. "Is there a reason for this visit?" He was understandably concerned. After all, an unannounced visit by *König*s was usually bad news.

Bear took over for her. "Can we talk in private?"

"Of course. Matt's in my office. Let's use the library." He led the way to the far door, stopping three steps into the room. "Oh, Scott. I didn't know you were in here. I need this room for a while. Can you study in your room or the den?"

"Sure. No problem."

Katie eased to one side, biting her lower lip at the sight of a broad back covered in a snug Navy blue t-shirt and a tight jean-covered backside. His hair was clipped thick but close in the back and spiked on top, tipped in blonde. He put one book back on the shelf and pulled another off, drawing her attention to the Celtic knotwork designs on his upper arms.

Scott turned with several of the ancient texts balanced on his left forearm. He looked up, his eyes locking with hers. He went still, his expression questioning. She smiled, but Scott didn't return it. He simply stared as if Katie confused him somehow.

Tyler cleared his throat. "Scott, these are our guests, Corwyn *König*-Maher and his sister—"

"The *Blutjagdfrau*," Scott noted. "Yes, I've heard of her." He exited the room without a backward glance, giving her a wide berth.

Katie watched him go, wondering at his strange reserve. When he'd turned, she'd felt certain something momentous was about to happen, but he didn't let it. Scott Danvers was an intriguing man, and she wasn't about to let him walk away that simply.

"Kaitlyn?" Tyler asked, using her legal name as everyone but her extensive family did. "Is something wrong?"

"No. I don't think so," she replied absently.

"I apologize for Scott's behavior. I'll speak to him about—"

"Why the apology?"

"He's not very personable, I know."

She nodded. "That's understandable."

"Are we leaving now?" Bear asked, a touch of anger in his tone.

"No. We're not," she informed him.

He groaned. "You are kidding. Please, for the love of Dobler and Jee, tell me you're kidding."

"I've never been more serious."

"Maybe you should explain," Tyler suggested. "I don't understand what's going on here, and as lord of this range, that is a little disconcerting."

Katie turned to him, smiling widely. "It's very simple, Lord Armen. There is one young Warrior I haven't gotten to know yet. Just one, in the entire world. I intend to correct that oversight."

He paled. "Perhaps, I should instruct—"

"No." She put the bark of an order in her response. "I forbid you to scare him into some unnatural response."

"He's still learning the rules of sanction," he warned.

"I'll keep that in mind and try not to take offense."

Tyler winced. "He's likely to offend. I'll be honest. He's likely to *try* to offend you, given the chance."

"I want his honest response, Lord Armen. If the Stone doesn't intend this, She doesn't."

"As you wish."

* * * *

Scott stopped walking, hopefully lost amidst the people milling about and taking their seats for the meal. He glanced at the *Blutjagdfrau* over the top of his book, then down at the page again, turning it though he wasn't done with the one before. He moved on, feigning ignorance of her presence.

"Scott," Matt called, a note of warning in his voice. "Dinner?"

How fatherly of the old man to be concerned. Tough shit. "Not hungry, Matt," he lied. In truth, he was famished, but the idea of staring into the *König* princess's bright blue eyes while he ate made his stomach squirm uncomfortably.

There was no question that he'd be looking at her. There was something mesmerizing in those eyes. Or, maybe he was just getting sick of brown-eyed carbon-copy Warriors. The tight, black jean number she was wearing was certainly like nothing he'd ever seen before.

He glanced toward the end of the table as he took another step, then down again. Tevin, the older of his 'younger brothers,' was preened to sickening perfection. Though there were four young Warriors—counting Jordan, who wasn't really young but still eligible—she could take to "mate" in Armen range, Tevin seemed convinced that she'd returned for him. In fact, all of them seemed convinced that was her aim, though they'd called Tom in from a track just to be certain her chosen was on hand.

Whichever one the princess wanted, Scott didn't intend to stand by and watch it happen. All of them, from Jordan to Tevin, were jerks in his opinion. Well, maybe not Antony, but Antony was pretty clueless and immature...and only seventeen, not a good match for the twenty-year-old *Blutjagdfrau*.

"Sit, Scott," Tyler commanded. "We have guests, remember?"

The Lord of the manor commands, he noted with a slight quickening of his pulse. Scott sighed, considering storming off in a show of defiance, but he loathed the idea of acting like a child. Instead, he turned and took his seat at his 'father's' right hand, setting the book beside his plate, staring at it, though he didn't see the words.

"Enough, Scott," Matt grumbled, closing *The Stone's Words* and taking it off the table.

Scott ground his teeth; there was no choice now but to play nice with the princes of their precious race. He looked up, intent on locking his eyes with Antony and keeping them there as long as possible, but it wasn't his youngest 'brother's' eyes across from him tonight but rather a startling blue in a smiling female face.

"You're very dedicated, Mr. Danvers," she commented.

Matt tensed at her use of his name, and several of the Warriors fought back low levels of *Blutjagd*.

Scott fought to keep a straight face. It was unusual to find someone who could get an entire room pissed off as quickly as he could, but the princess had it nailed. If there was a list of things that ticked off the Armens, his refusal of their name was in the top three, which was half the reason Scott still used it. He was born Danvers, and he'd go to his grave Danvers.

"It's the rule of the house—and I like learning." The more he knew, the sooner he could escape this house and roam as far as he would be permitted to go. "It always pays to know your enemies. Don't you think so?"

Tyler rolled his eyes skyward and seemed to be counting to a hundred as his mother often had. Scott noted the response in satisfaction. Apparently, his 'grandfather' didn't want to make a scene in front of the visiting royalty.

"And your adversaries," she commented, sipping the wine set beside her plate.

His smile faltered. "Is there a difference?"

"Of course. Enemies will cut your heart out. Adversaries want much less."

His humor fled, and memories of the morning he met his 'family' filled his mind. The threat had been stated clearly enough for even a hard-headed loner like Scott to get the picture. "I wouldn't know. I don't have any adversaries."

"Scott—" Matt began in warning.

"No," the princess ordered.

Several Warriors who'd begun talking fell silent at once, including Tyler. Scott marveled at the way they bent to her commands, perhaps even more than they did with her father, and he was 'The Lord of All Houses.'

She wasn't smiling now. Scott couldn't have named the expression on her face. It wasn't one he'd seen often enough to readily identify. It wasn't pity like the Warrior wives sent his way so often or curiosity like the children displayed. It wasn't fury like Jordan and Tevin were usually mired in. It wasn't the exasperation on

Tyler and Matt's faces. Whatever it was, it seemed open and honest. Scott wasn't sure how he felt about that.

"Go on," she invited. "I get the feeling this is something no one lets you talk about."

It wasn't, but it also wasn't something he intended to discuss with her, especially with Tevin and the rest listening in. "There's nothing to talk about. Between the rules of sanction and penalties... Well, you know them."

"Yes, I do. I imagine the idea of killing your own family for breaking them seems harsh to you."

"And, I *know* I don't need a shrink, especially not if that shrink is you."

The table erupted in sound and motion. Scott's eyes narrowed as her brother fisted his sacred weapon. The *Blutjagdfrau* silenced them all with a wave of her hand; Corwyn even released his blade though he placed his fists on the table in silent warning.

"If I was offended," she announced, "I would have challenged Scott myself. I fight my own battles, as did my mother and grandmother before me. Now... I believe I'd like to discuss this further with you, Mr. Danvers. Perhaps, after dinner?"

Scott pushed away from the table and stood. "Sorry, Princess. Not in my job description." He turned and strode for the kitchen door.

"You are bound to obey *König*," Jordan shouted after him.

"Lord and Lady *König*," he retorted, biting back laughter. "Last time I checked, she was still a generation off that title." He smiled all the way to the garage. At least, knowing their laws meant that he knew what they had the right to demand—and what they didn't.

* * * *

"May I apologize," Tevin began smoothly, making her skin crawl with his oily approach.

Katie managed not to snarl at him, though his voice made her want to rake her nails down his throat. "It isn't your apology to offer."

Several Warriors and their wives started speaking at once.

"Nor yours," she informed them, losing her patience.

"I'll speak to Scott about this," Tyler offered.

"No. I will." Katie rose from the table, motioning Bear not to follow her, and strode out the way Scott had.

The kitchen was empty, but the swinging sheers on the inset window of the back door announced his passage. She slid through the door, expecting Scott to be just outside. He wasn't, but his outline was clearly visible, retreating toward the garage.

She hoped he didn't intend to take off in a vehicle.

No. Tyler had reported that Scott typically lived to the letter of the law.

Of course, if he really believes his life is in danger in his family's sanctuary, he would take care not to break laws. Did he really believe that *any* infraction would mean his life? They'd show leniency for his inexperience, if for no other reason.

Katie debated the possibilities for a moment. If she ghosted and followed him, she could find out what Scott did to escape. She scrapped that idea almost immediately. It was obvious that Scott already felt he was under attack. Subterfuge would be the wrong answer. It would be better to approach him openly—and quietly.

Scott hadn't bothered to close the side door to the garage, probably in an attempt to get fresh air circulating. Harsh fluorescent light and the sound of metal on metal, but not blade on blade, escaped to the night outside. Taking a calming breath, she slipped inside.

His back was to her, his muscles more relaxed than he'd been inside. It took her only a few minutes to realize that he was working on a missing part to the motorcycle in front of her. It was a beautiful machine: sleek lines, leather that smelled of whatever oil he rubbed into it, and meticulously kept. Katie stepped toward it, running her hand along the soft, leather seat.

At the whisper of sound, Scott whipped around, his hand closing around the hilt of his weapon. His brow furrowed, his face morphing from a touch of panic to confusion so fast it made her dizzy.

Katie forced herself not to show emotion, stroking the seat again. "Nice bike," she commented, trying for a safe subject.

His muscles unwound slowly. He released his weapon and rolled his shoulder in what looked like a shrug. "Cycle," he corrected her, turning away and resuming his work.

"Beg your pardon?"

"It's a cycle. Bikes don't have engines. It's not exactly a Schwinn."

"Not remotely," she agreed.

Scott didn't answer her; he seemed intent on ignoring her presence.

"Do you always do that?" she asked.

"I always keep my cycle in good shape. The Great Lord Armen and Jordan added the other vehicles on—my chores, I guess. Have to be a contributing member somehow." There was an edge of sarcasm in his voice.

"I guess, but that's not really what I meant."

He didn't respond, didn't even acknowledge her comment.

"I see. Ignoring people is something you do a lot."

The slightest edge of *Blutjagd* lit in him and then faded. Still, he didn't comment.

She ground her teeth in frustration. "I'm not your enemy, Mr. Danvers."

"Why—why do you call me that?"

"It's your name."

He snorted as if in disgust. "Try telling... Never mind."

"*Schwertträger geboren,*" she whispered.

Scott tensed.

"Your name is your own. You know, my grandmother was separated from the Warriors for twenty-four years, from just after her birth."

"So?" he snapped.

"She didn't accept her birth name. I'd guess you didn't know that. She was born Erin Allison Hunter, but she was Jayde Marie Albright-Cross until the day she died."

"That's not what I've heard." But, his voice announced his uncertainty.

Katie crossed the room and hoisted herself up on the work table a yard away from him. "Jayde thought of the title *König* as a distinction—like *Blutjagdfrau* or protected." She crossed one leg over the other, leaning back on her arms so her chest pushed through the open front of her jacket. "If you want to get purely technical about it, I'm a Maher. Saying I'm *Blutjagdfrau* and *König* is redundant, since all female Warriors are from the *König* house."

Scott glanced her way, then back to his work, though he'd ceased doing any actual work at about the time she lifted her leg. "Makes sense." His jaw tensed slightly. "Now you know why I hit the books so hard."

"Oh, you won't find that in any book. The books are ancient writings. Corwyn—my great-grandfather Corwyn, that is— He kept journals of theories about the Stone, and my mother knows all the secrets, of course. I suppose there hasn't been time to write everything down that we've learned since the first *Blutjagdfrau* returned to the fold. I don't think any of the houses have kept a formal history since the late eighteen-hundreds."

"Armen's ends in nineteen-twenty-two."

She smiled at his offer of information. "Maybe, I should hit the books while I'm here."

His face flushed. "Why are you here? Obviously, you don't intend to punish me for being rude to you."

"Oh, were you being rude?" she asked coyly. "I thought you were hinting that you wanted a sparring partner."

Scott stared at her, his expression flickering through a myriad of emotions. Katie shifted to the side, twisting her torso so that the black pearl-buttoned sweater she wore under her jacket pulled tight over her chest. His gaze drifted down and back up sharply. His work sat by, forgotten for a moment.

"I...um...I'm probably not good enough to spar with you." His eyes flicked to her chest again. He looked away, seemingly discomfited.

"That's not what I've heard," she stated calmly.

Scott fisted the ratchet, swallowing slowly.

"Hungry?" she asked, dropping her leg so they sat side by side, slightly parted.

His head snapped around again, his gaze darting to the space between her thighs, then to her face. "What?"

"Are you hungry? I'm starving." She rolled the final statement out, adding just a hint of sexual innuendo to it.

He started to deny it, but his stomach grumbled, ruining his chances of lying.

"Chicken or burgers?" she offered.

His brow furrowed. "Excuse me?"

"You don't want to eat in there, and truth be told, neither do I. Why don't we take off and get something to eat?"

Scott looked at the ratchet in his hand, as if he was conferring with it for what answer to give her. "The cycle is out of commission," he reminded her.

"I have my F250." Katie motioned to the silver vehicle closest to the double sliders.

He paused as if he was considering it. "It's probably not a good idea."

"We both need to eat, and I'd still like to talk to you."

"I'll raid the kitchen later." He didn't answer the rest.

Katie bit back a sigh, easing to the floor. There was no question that Scott wanted her, but he wasn't going to make getting close to him easy.

"If you say so," she offered cordially. "I'll see you at training, Mr. Danvers." She started for the door.

"Scott," he whispered.

Her heart leapt at that.

"You'll only piss them off if you keep calling me Danvers."

"Okay, Scott. I'll see you at training." Katie headed back to the house with a smile on her face.

Step two. She had to learn more about Scott. Getting close to him meant learning about him—and not just what she could read in his file.

* * * *

Scott breathed a half dozen curses, forcing his attention back to the starter assembly. "You are undeniably the stupidest man alive," he berated himself.

The princess wanted inside his defenses, and she was damned good at using her body to get what she wanted. There was no mistaking that. Still, he'd almost fallen for it.

When she'd hoisted herself onto the work table, it had taken every ounce of his willpower not to drink in every curve, but she hadn't backed down, and before long, he'd been rapt on every delicious inch of her lush body.

Turning down her offer of dinner had stretched his control to dangerous levels. Trapped in the F250 with her, Scott felt certain that he'd have found himself all over her, pouring out his heart while he tried his best to get into her pants.

No! Sex was one area of his life where Scott had always been in charge. No *König* princess was going to change that. If they ended up taking release together, it wouldn't be in exchange for something she wanted—and he would be the one calling the shots.

He grumbled another curse. There was no way it would happen. Once she figured out he wasn't going to play it her way, it would be over before it started.

* * * *

"Come in," Katie called absently, not looking up from the file spread across the bed.

Bear strolled in, closing the door behind him. "Learning anything interesting?" he asked.

"Fascinating. How about you?"

Her twin settled on the bed beside her. "He's a felon, you know."

"No, he's not. It was a misdemeanor. That asshole was beating up on a woman, and Scott defended her."

"He sent that guy to the hospital for a week, Kates."

"And how long would the woman have spent in the hospital if he hadn't?" She sighed. "Yes, he went too far, which is why he ended up with a record, but look at the facts, Bear. He wasn't even sixteen yet. How long do we train to control our *Blutjagd*? Even you've had a serious slip in control—at about the same age, too. The only difference is that you were lucky enough to have Dad and Hunter with you at the time to take you down. Scott wasn't that lucky."

"But, that's my point. He's still not trained."

"Look at the line of work he was in. You can't seriously think he lacked control. He would have killed someone. He would have gone too far again."

"I just think..." He hesitated, a pained look on his face.

"Go on."

"When his training is complete—"

"You are *not* suggesting I wait a year for him."

"He's not exactly polished material, Kates."

"Neither was Dad, if memory serves. How many rules of sanction did he break the night we were conceived? Even he's not sure, but by my count, it was at least four, and he'd finished his training seven years before he and Mom mated."

He grimaced as he always did when she mentioned their parents' lack of control in mating.

"I won't last another year," she informed him miserably. Just being in the same house with Scott was driving her insane. "I won't, Bear, and you can't ask me to."

"Mom lasted four," he countered in as diplomatic a voice as he could muster.

"So have I—already. Self-release isn't enough anymore, just like it wasn't enough for her." She growled. "Like you men understand! If I didn't know for a fact that the Stone was female, I'd swear the damned thing was male. You men don't have to wait. No. You get to slake your hungers from the moment they hit."

"Okay. I get it. Waiting isn't an option."

"No. It isn't. I should have come when I felt the pull." Memories of her indecision made her stomach ache. Why hadn't she called her mother in and told her what she was feeling? By that time, her parents had to have known that Scott was found in Maher range. They were among the first to meet him, after all.

"Oh, yeah," he countered sarcastically. "That would have been grand. You'd have waltzed back to Maher—or to Armen to meet a borderline psychotic."

"Has it occurred to you that Grandma Jayde settled into Warrior life *because* Talon was there for her? Maybe I was meant to help Scott accept what he is. I missed him in Maher range by less than a day, you know. And, I almost got off the plane to Smith. You know I did."

"Then why didn't Mom order you back to Armen range when Scott was found? Why didn't the Stone lead you there?"

She faltered, feeling her cheeks heat. "I don't know. I'm not Stone Vessel yet, and the Stone doesn't always explain why it does things. Maybe it was a choice I had to make for myself."

"Or, maybe you're wrong."

Katie ground her teeth, trying not to snap at him. It was her printing driving her crazy, not Bear. Of the two of them, he was probably the more rational at the moment. "Maybe about that but not about Scott. Gods, just being in the same room with him makes me want—"

"This is way more information than I need from you."

She chuckled, enjoying his squeamish response to her sexual side. "So... I take it you talked to the other Warriors?"

His jaw tightened, and a touch of *Blutjagd* lit and then extinguished, all in the blink of an eye.

"Wow," she breathed. "Do I dare ask what that was all about?"

"I don't like the idea of you sleeping with that man," he stated bluntly.

"He's my mate, Bear. Having sex with him is part of the package, and I don't mind telling you, it's a part I don't intend to shy from."

Bear darkened, scrubbing a hand over his evening stubble.

"It can't possibly be that bad. Can it?"

Warriors weren't known for staid sexual practices. They were virile men, and they took every wild opportunity to indulge, as her parents more than proved. What could possibly make her brother so wary? She hoped it was just the idea of her budding sexuality, but his reactions didn't seem to support that. Of course, he didn't like Scott, so anything was possible.

"The women he picks up for release are..." He skated a quick look at her...then away.

Katie scowled at him. "What? Please, stop beating around the bush with me. I am an adult, you know."

"They're—not your type," he offered diplomatically.

"What? Blonde, green-eyed airheads?"

Bear turned to her, doing a slow perusal of her, head to toe. Katie stared at the mirror, taking stock of the steel-toed elf boots made especially for her, the skin-tight Lycra mix jeans, the black sweater with the gray pearl buttons, and the black curls pinned to her scalp and surrounding her face. She looked back to Bear, shrugging. Whatever he was looking at, it wasn't apparent to her.

He rolled his eyes. "He doesn't pick up the sweet sixteen and never been kissed type. He doesn't even go for the been around the block a time or two type. His chosen partners are usually...trashy." Bear shifted uncomfortably.

She considered her reflection again. Pulling the pins took a few minutes, but soon her curls were cascading over her shoulders.

"You're not trashy, Kates. Nothing you do to your hair is going to change that."

"Maybe not, but that's not the point. Is it?"

He groaned. "What are you planning this time?"

"Technically, all I have to do is get his attention, and Warrior biology will do the rest. Right?"

"Mom would not approve—"

"Of me going shopping and to a beauty shop? Puh-leeze! This is the same woman who seduced Dad."

"And just look how well *that* turned out," he grumbled.

"Oh, I don't know. You're not all that bad."

Bear cracked a smile at that. "Just do me a favor."

"Which is?" She wasn't making any promises about how she'd approach Scott. That was between the two of them.

"Meet me in the mall food court. I really don't want to know."

"Done."

Chapter Twenty-six

November 1, 2049

"So, when do you want to head to town?" Bear asked.

"After training and a shower." She turned toward the main training grounds.

It took him several seconds to catch up. "The Armen training?" he asked.

Katie chuckled. "Well, Scott's training, anyway."

"Gods give me strength," he growled.

"As long as they give me what I want, they can give you the patience you want."

"Just don't let him win. You'll insult his pride and intelligence if you do."

"Would I do that?" she replied, indignant at the suggestion. In truth, she only wanted to examine how Scott interacted with the other Warriors in training.

Bear cocked an eyebrow and snorted in disbelief.

"I'd do a lot of things to get laid, but that's not one of them."

"Good. Keep it that way."

Katie paused at the edge of the training area, watching Scott spar with Tevin, hand to hand. Warrior training or no Warrior training, Scott had the upper hand by just a hair.

Tevin noticed her at the fence first. A smile lit his face as he deflected one of his older brother's punches. His lips moved, some conversation obviously intended for Scott's ears only.

Scott's head jerked around, and Tevin struck a punch square in the cheek that knocked him flat. Scott didn't hesitate—he caught Tevin in the knees, bringing him down hard, coming up and surging over him with a murderous rage in his eyes, though he was hardly showing signs of bloodlust.

"Hold!" Tyler thundered.

Both combatants froze and then came to their feet, their hands fisted, glaring at each other across the two yards separating them.

"*This* is training, gentlemen. Street fighting won't work against a beast, and this isn't a challenge bout. Leave it at the fence."

"A beast wouldn't say something like that," Scott informed his brother.

Tevin smiled widely, entirely too cocky for his own good. "You've only met one of them. If you're sloppy enough to let them distract you, you're going to die."

Scott's face went red, his muscles strung tight in either embarrassment or anger. She couldn't tell which. Katie felt her temper simmer at that. There was no question in her mind that Tevin was baiting Scott, trying to make him look like a fool in front of her.

"This is not a good idea, Kates," Bear suggested.

Under normal circumstances, she might have considered that he was right. Printing was not normal circumstances.

In the field, Tyler shook his head, pointing to Scott. "He's right, Scott. You can't let a beast distract you. No matter what it says or does, you have to be in control and aware."

"It's a fabulous idea," she informed him. "Go ghost. You know what to do."

"How did I offend Tes and Fih this time?" he muttered.

"Just do it," she snapped.

Katie hoisted herself over the fence and strode toward the trio in the center of the field. Tevin and Scott both turned their heads to watch her progress, and Tyler stopped speaking, looking over his shoulder in apparent surprise.

"Can I help you, Kaitlyn?" he asked.

"I'd like to spar with them," she requested. "With your permission, of course."

"Granted. Together or separately?"

"I haven't had a warm-up, yet. I believe I'll start with Tevin." Though she was capable of fighting all three in unison from a cold start, her plan depended on splitting her time between them.

Tevin shot her a smile that announced his interest clearly, oblivious to the fact that she'd insulted him by naming him the least of her possible opponents. From his reaction, he considered himself favored by being chosen to face her first.

Scott turned and left the field, hiding his amusement rather unsuccessfully. Whether he suspected what she intended to do or not, he clearly recognized her intention to snub his brother.

"As you wish," Tyler conceded with a bow of his head. He waved Scott the final distance to the fence.

Tevin bowed as well, scanning her body. "You're looking lovely today, Kaitlyn," Tevin offered.

"This is training," she informed him.

His smile dimmed. "Of course." Staunch determination settled on his face. The fool had most likely postulated that she intended to test his strength in choosing a mate.

Katie widened her stance, brought her fists up and shifted her weight to the balls of her feet. To his credit, Tevin came in hard and fast, not pulling his punches or offering less than his best. She countered everything he threw at her, pushing him toward his endurance with barely a sheen of sweat to show for it. All the time, she waited patiently for Bear's move.

Her brother took his time, letting Tevin get fully engrossed in the match. By her opponent's reaction, Katie guessed that Bear touched his shoulder and faded away. Tevin spun toward the touch, exposing his back to her.

That was her cue. She drew both blades, pressing them to his back in position to take his lungs. He stiffened with a muttered curse.

"You're dead, Tevin," she announced, so all the Warriors assembled would be sure to hear it.

The older ones nodded or rolled their eyes at his mistake. The younger ones laughed heartily. Scott chuckled, an unholy smirk on his face at his painless revenge.

"I was supposed to be fighting *you*," Tevin protested, his cheeks a furious red.

Bear unghosted, his arms crossed over his chest, fighting back laughter.

Katie sheathed her weapons, allowing Tevin to turn to her. "I told you this is training, Tevin. Do you think beasts are going to announce themselves? If you sense one behind you, are you going to give the first your back?"

"Of course not!"

"Then you shouldn't have done it in training. You're dead, Tevin. You're dead, because you paid so much attention to one opponent that you forgot your surroundings. A beast may or may not *say* what you did to distract Scott, but one will come at your back. Count on it."

He bowed his head and brought his fists up again.

"I believe I've made my point, and I'm warmed-up." She dropped her voice so that only Tevin would hear it. "I'm ready to take on Scott now," she confided in him, swallowing a smile as he ground his teeth, the snub clearly stated this time. "Scott! You're up."

Tevin stormed off the field, followed by a chuckling Bear.

Scott ambled out, flicking his gaze along the fence line and nodding. He brought his fists up.

Katie did the same. "Taking a head count?" she asked, turning as he did.

His first punch came for her cheek, and she blocked it, sending one to his now-open face that he ducked expertly. They backed off a step and started circling.

"Any reason I shouldn't? As long as I can see all of the players, I know one's not sneaking up on me."

Katie tried a roundhouse, jerking her foot up and spinning away before his hands could lock around it fully. He counterattacked with a sweep at her knee that she sidestepped.

"You won't always know how many players there are," she noted conversationally.

"Of course." His gaze flicked down her body, then up again, but she couldn't tell if he was checking out her stance or her form.

She stifled the urge to look down at herself, suspecting an attempt at distraction. "What?"

"I thought *Blutjagdfrau* wore amulets under bracebands." He ended his statement with a barrage of punches.

Katie deflected them easily, giving her answer as she fought. "I was *en utero* when my mother became the Stone Vessel. It gives me the same protection without an amulet as my grandmother had with an amulet and no blessing. It was my choice to wear it or not, once I had autonomy."

They broke apart, circling again to a few claps and shouts of congratulations.

Scott did another quick head count. "Interesting. I thought they'd demand your protection, despite your autonomy."

"You think I can't protect myself?" She kept her tone conversational.

He chuckled. "I'm sure you can." His foot shot up.

Katie dropped, rolled, and flipped back to her feet before he could attempt to pin her. She smiled. "Smooth move. You're very good."

"Your bait and switch on Tevin was smooth, too. Though...I'm sure you could have taken him out without the distraction."

"You're right." She made a quick move to the side, aiming a punch for his left shoulder as he turned, missing by inches as he countered.

Scott smiled widely at the attempt, and cheers and whistles went up from the younger Warriors.

"So, what did Tevin say?" she inquired.

He scowled but didn't answer.

"Come on. It couldn't be *that* bad."

"Since it was about you—"

"Then you better tell me," she ordered.

"He said I had a chance of winning, because looking at you had him so hard he could barely think."

She faltered in mid-swing, her mind clouded in shock. *How dare he! The bastard is going to pay for that one.*

Scott took full advantage, grasping her arm and twisting around her, sweeping her feet. Katie swung herself face up and pulled back with her now-free arm, nearly throwing him off balance, forcing Scott to plant his feet rather than fall with her and complete the Maher maneuver—or pin her beneath his weight. He stumbled, coming down with her. She brought one knee up, missing her intended target by inches. They fell too quickly to get the steel toe into position, but the join of her foot and ankle slammed solidly into his balls.

Katie let her leg fall to the side, knowing the probability of injuring her knee when he landed was higher than the possibility of using her leg to throw him off without a proper foothold. And... *Dear gods, I want to feel his weight holding me down, even if it's only for a moment.*

Scott collapsed over her with a grunt of pain, a solid mass of man holding her to the hard-packed soil beneath her. He saved her the trouble of saving face and flipping him off by rolling away, cupping his battered privates. "Christ," he grumbled.

Older Warriors winced and shifted uncomfortably. The younger ones, as usual, laughed. Tevin joined them, nearly doubling over in mirth.

Katie eased to her feet, dusting off her jeans as he recovered. "I guess we can call a hold here. Excellent move. The Maher maneuver is usually a winner."

"But?" he croaked.

"I would guess no one warned you that my father created it. My mother went to great lengths to find a way to counter it."

His eyes opened, his color and breathing returning to normal slowly. "She taught you well, I see."

"Better that I nail you in training than a beast in battle."

"I'll remember that," he replied sarcastically, struggling to his feet.

"It's what Jayde told Talon when she nailed him," she offered by way of apology. "And he was her husband."

Scott stared at her for a moment and then nodded.

"Now... Is that really what Tevin said? Or was that a distraction?"

He smiled, chuckling darkly. "Would I lie about something like that?"

"I have no clue," she admitted.

Scott strolled away without answering.

* * * *

Scott headed for the library, his entire body alive to sensation. It seemed strange to react so intensely to a woman who'd kicked him in the nuts in front of half the Warriors of the house, but there was no denying it.

He'd rolled off her, because he'd hardened despite the pain he was in. He'd rolled off her, because the alternative had been lying over her with his cock pressed into her thigh, an ache unlike the screaming of his bruised balls driving him crazy. It was better not to touch her at that moment.

The line of leather-bound volumes beckoned, but Scott paused, not really seeing them. He shivered, memories of her face as she'd talked about Talon and Jayde arousing him all over again.

For just a moment, he'd been certain she was flirting with him again. The sidelong glance she'd shot him and her blush... But, she'd been talking about a mated couple, so that didn't add up.

Who said she was talking about mating? Maybe she's looking to sate her drive. Now, that made a lot more sense.

Scott turned at the sound of her laughter, heading for the foyer without conscious thought of what he intended. Tevin's voice brought him up short, halfway from his goal.

"Have a good day in town, Kaitlyn," he offered pleasantly.

"I'm sure I will."

"I would be honored to escort you."

She paused for a moment, and Scott's heart sank to his stomach. *Please, say 'no.'* But, he couldn't define why he cared what her answer was.

"No. It's— Well, it's woman's stuff. You'd just be bored."

"I could never be bored with you."

"Oh, gag me," Scott grumbled. He couldn't state categorically why he continued listening. Tevin's sickening show was raising the sour taste of bile into his mouth.

"Thank you, but Bear and I have family matters to discuss. And...there he is now."

Was he imagining it, or did the princess sound relieved? No, that had to be wishful thinking.

"Ready to go, Kates?" her brother asked, his voice cold.

Surely not for his sister. Maybe *König* was warning Tevin to back off. A smile curved Scott's mouth as footsteps faded away—one set toward the back of the house and the other two toward the front door.

He shook himself mentally. *Big deal.* So, Tevin was shot down? It wouldn't last long.

* * * *

"Are you sure about this?" Bear asked, looking as close to scared as she'd seen him in at least three years.

"Are *Blutjagdfrau* ever wrong when it comes to their mates?" she countered. And she certainly hadn't gone through the trouble of having herself waxed, primped, and dressed in this 'come fuck me' outfit to chicken out now. If Scott looked for this type of woman, Katie would give him what he wanted.

"They usually have better taste."

"I should take you to trial for daring to talk about my chosen mate that way." Despite her silent curses on the man when she was waxed! Only her overactive healing had allowed her to accept the punishment. How human women did it was a mystery.

A smiled pulled at his lips. "Whatever." He sighed, his smile disappearing. "Maybe I should talk to him before—"

"Don't you dare! This is between Scott and me." This was one thing Katie intended to do for herself. She straightened her skirt, then pulled her waist-length leather jacket on, feeling exposed but wickedly sexy.

"It doesn't have to be tonight," her twin suggested, his expression hopeful. "Maybe we should call in the troops for the usual fallout."

"They're not that stupid," she quipped. There were no elders left, after all. Even the highest levels didn't want to mess with her unless she made herself seem an easy kill, and the last thing she needed was a bunch of Warriors lurking outside the door, listening to them having sex.

"If you say so."

"I do." Katie squared her shoulders, steeling herself for what she had to do. "Wish me luck."

"You know I do."

She let herself into the hall and strode away from the central corridor. Scott lived as far from his family as he could. Katie found that sad; it was an anomaly she wanted to understand. But there was time to understand Scott later. Katie knocked on his door.

He opened it, drying his hands on a bath towel, a smudge of missed grease near his left elbow. His eyes narrowed, panning down her body inch by inch. His cock stiffened behind his jeans. "Yes?" he asked, his voice rough.

"Aren't you going to invite me in?" she asked.

"Sure." He moved aside and let her pass, hesitating before he shut the door.

Katie looked at his room curiously. It was very sparing, nothing but a queen bed, bureau, a weight bench set on an exercise mat, and work-out bag in the twenty-by-twenty space. There were few books and no pictures. It seemed Katie traveled with more than Scott lived with.

"Kates... Katl... *König*? Princess... Damn it! What *am* I supposed to call you, anyway?"

"Katie is fine."

"The other men don't call you that," he grumbled.

She chuckled, turning to him and surveying his bare chest hungrily. "The other men weren't invited to. No one calls me less than a formal name unless I invite them to."

He tossed the towel away, planting his arms across his chest, his muscles bunching. "And precisely what are you inviting?" he asked bluntly.

Good. He was cutting to the chase with her, just as she'd hoped. "I'll let you know if something is out of bounds. There isn't going to be much that—"

Scott fisted the edges of her jacket, dragging her against his body, his breath fanning over her upturned face, his mouth closing over hers. He pushed the jacket away, his tongue parting her lips as his hands pressed her closer by the meat of her buttocks. He explored her mouth completely, laying claim in the most primal way she could imagine possible. His palms slid up and forward, his fingertips tracing the side seams of her blouse. His thumbs stroked the hard points of her nipples through the single layer of black silk.

He pulled away, rapt on his still-circling thumbs. "Out of bounds?" he ventured.

Katie traced the outline of his erect length through his jeans. "Not remotely."

"Good." He looked over her shoulder in the direction of the bed.

"You want me to lie down?" she asked.

"You'll know it if I do." He stroked her nipples more purposefully, turning his hands to cup her breasts fully, kneading them. "Just how prepared did you come?"

"Why don't you find out," she offered.

"Why don't you show me." It was nothing less than an order.

Katie slid the skirt up her thighs, smiling as Scott took another step back to watch. His eyes widened at the sight of her waxed mound, exposed for him.

He smiled a purely male smile of sexual intent. "Mmmm. A regular Girl Scout."

"I hope not." Despite her best efforts, her breath came out as little more than a gasp. She arched into his hands, her drive maddening.

"I see," he whispered. "Bad girl."

The gravel in his voice made her heart pound. Scott kissed her again, a demanding interaction that made her want to be bad, as bad as he liked and more.

She started to unbutton her blouse, but he guided her hands away, nestling them to her back and pulling her tight to his body by the grip. Katie shifted against him, seeking pressure as her slit moistened, then seeped lubricant down her thighs.

His mouth retreated, and he stared at her, seemingly searching for answers in her eyes, but what the question was, she had no clue.

* * * *

Damn! She's beautiful.

Part of his mind reasoned that this was a bad idea. How would he handle her marrying Tevin if he did this? What problems would it cause? He'd have to stay at the furthest edges of the range. The alternative would be wanting her while that twerp fucked her every night.

It's not like it's never happened before. After all, Matt and Jordan both slept with his mother. Of course, neither of them married her, but the idea of two Warriors bedding the same woman did have precedence in Warrior history, the history of Armen range, no less.

Scott couldn't deny that he wanted it; he ached for it, and he'd take whatever she gave him. If Katie wanted him for a playmate before she took her mate, he'd count himself lucky—as long as she didn't try to pry his life's story out of him while they did it.

He dropped to one knee before her, laying a lick over a beaded nipple through the nearly-transparent silk. She jerked in his arms, arching against him with another gasp. Her arms tensed, and he tightened his grip minutely.

Scott didn't give her a chance to protest. He flicked his tongue over her nipples, back and forth until she was squirming against him. He suckled at her, and she went still, her breathing strangled.

"Scott," she managed weakly.

He closed his eyes, continuing his play. He'd be the best she'd ever had—the best she ever would have if it killed him.

"Scott, please..."

Katie moved her thighs against each other, and Scott released her and leaned back to watch, licking his lips. The wet silk molded to her breasts and her skirt was still hiked nearly to her hips. He reached between her thighs, stroking her clit, shivering at her low purr. *God!* She was the hottest woman he'd ever laid. Scott traced her seam, smiling at how ready she was for him, at how she trembled against him.

"You are such a bad girl," he growled, knowing it was the game she wanted to play with him. "Aren't you?" From the first time he saw her, he'd known this wasn't her style. Maybe that's why seeing her this way turned him on so much.

Katie's startling blue eyes opened, and she nodded shakily. Those eyes always cut through him, more so now that they were full of so much need—and so much trust in him.

Scott used her juices to stroke her clit again, wondering what the other men she'd been with were like in bed. From her reactions, it was a safe bet that they'd been nothing like him. "God, I am hard for you." And he was getting harder by the minute.

She tried to free her hands again, throwing her head back with a low cry of frustration when he restrained her. It was imperative that he keep charge. Scott didn't try to analyze that. He was afraid if he did, he'd find that he was striking back at the complete loss of control over his own life with the most powerful person he could, just another willful show.

No. There was a lot more to it than that. The certainty that Katie came here to be dominated, to slough off her authority for a little while, was in everything she did. He'd seen her in action at training. If she really wanted to escape him, she'd do it without breaking a sweat. If she didn't like what he was doing, she wouldn't be so wet or so responsive.

"Scott, please." Katie tipped back and forth against his fingertips, driving herself toward release.

He pulled his hand away, denying her. She'd come all right, but she'd come at his leisure and not her own. But, how to accomplish it?

Scott stood before her, lifting her slightly to grind his aching cock to her wickedly bare pussy. She started moving against him immediately, and he backed away.

"You want to come, and you will," he taunted. "Do what I say, and you'll have the ride of your life. You can do that, can't you?"

"Yes. Anything."

Her agreement sent a shiver of anticipation down his body. *Anything I say.* Ideas competed fiercely for attention, each more appealing than the one before. *There's time,* he assured himself. *I can keep her at the edges all night. But to start...*

He turned her toward the weight bench. "On your knees."

Katie complied, and he gauged her height for comfort. He'd have to improvise, or she'd be damned uncomfortable in just a few minutes.

Scott rose and strode to the bed, grabbing the two king-size pillows off and returning to her. He stripped the pillow case off of one, then stacked them next to her knees, lifting Katie onto them.

She braced her hands on the bench for balance. Scott grasped them and pulled them behind her back again, binding them snug with the pillow case. He eased her upper body down and forward, positioning her stomach across the bench, her breasts and mouth on one side and her wet slit on the other.

For a moment, he was breathless. Scott forced himself to speak through teeth clenched tight. "Now *that* is a pretty picture." It was more than pretty. His jeans suddenly felt a size or two too small, the pressure tempting him to enjoy other cozy places.

He pulled at his button fly with one hand, the other stroking at her clit until she was moving against him, soft cries of longing calling him inside. Her hot lubricant soaked his fingers, preparing them to thrust inside her. But Scott had no intentions of thrusting them into her. Watching her frenzy made him want one thing. He leaned over her, plundering her nipples with his free hand while he coaxed her to release.

"Come for me." His voice hardly seemed his own. "I want to feel it."

He would feel it, buried deep inside her, but he wouldn't come. He'd ride out her orgasm, bring his cock to her mouth for a taste, strip every stitch of clothing off her body, tie her to his bed, taste every inch of her body, then come deep inside her. Just the thought of it made his cock bob in search of her waiting body.

He didn't have long to wait. Katie's sounds and movements became more frantic. She whispered prayers begging patience from Dobler. At last, she stiffened, trembling, a choked cry catching in her throat.

Scott didn't waste a moment. He skated his hand back, spread her slit, and thrust deep inside her. His eyes, closed in anticipation of fighting back his release, flew open in shock.

Every sensation hit him at once, drowning his control. Her contracting body was the sweet torture he'd known it would be, but the unexpected stimuli did him in. The minute resistance of her hymen, coupled with the scent of blood and her sharply-indrawn breath, nearly stopped his heart in pleasure.

Her climax quickened, and he lost the battle silently, begging his God and all of hers for a reprieve that wouldn't come, his cock pouring wave after wave of come into her. He wrapped his hands around her waist, gripping tight, lost in the climax that seemed never-ending. Balance deserted him, and Scott slid to the mat, pulling Katie over him, still impaled on his length.

Then it was over. He lay on his side on the mat, his breathing quick and uneven, his heart racing. His grip faltered as his muscles went limp. His cock was anything but limp, still raging inside her, pulsing in aftershocks.

Katie wiggled her backside against him with a sigh of contentment. His body reacted fiercely to that provocation, ready to continue his plan for the evening despite his mind's rebellion.

What game was she playing? Scott tried to push away his uncertainty. He'd known Katie was playing with him when she came here. He'd known she was acting like the bad girl when every daily impression of her screamed that she wasn't one.

Yes, but I was in charge! How had she turned the tables on him so easily?

The tang of blood teased his nose. *That's how.* He'd known she wasn't a bad girl, but he hadn't known she was a virgin. The shock of discovery had given her the upper hand. She'd distracted him just as Tevin had distracted him in training, making him think with the wrong head at the right time.

His fingers fumbled at the twisted and knotted pillow case. Conflicting thoughts and feelings assaulted him. He needed to sort them out, and he needed time alone to do that.

Scott grimaced as he slipped out of her body, the urge to take her again nearly undoing his resolve to think before he acted. He turned to his back, scrubbing his hands over his face.

Katie turned toward him, nestling to his side, placing one hand on his stomach, too close to his cock for his sanity. "Scott?" she asked in a voice that renewed her promise of anything.

For an agonizing moment, he prayed she'd take the initiative and work her way down his body, sucking him into her mouth. If she did that, he wouldn't care about thinking anymore. *Gods, I need to stop this.* "I think you should leave," he whispered.

She retreated without question, taking her warmth with her so that he shivered in the sudden chill. Faint sounds announced her straightening her clothes and the click of her heels on the wood floor her departure. Katie paused, most likely to collect her jacket.

"Scott?" she called again, an unspoken plea not to send her away transmitted clearly in that single word.

"Go."

"If you wish." The door opened and then closed again.

He dropped his arms to the mat, opening his eyes and staring at the ceiling in numb disbelief. His cock still strained, chastising him for sending her away. Her scent surrounded him, making the hunger more acute.

Scott pushed to his feet. If he wanted to sleep tonight, he'd have to wash her musk from his body. He froze in the act of pulling his jeans shut, staring at the blood covering him wildly. It was a damn good thing that he did his own laundry.

He thought that in a vain effort to push another insistent, highly-disturbing thought away. He wished it worked...then called himself a liar.

She's mine. I'll make her belong to me.

* * * *

Katie hesitated before she entered her room, sure that Bear was still waiting for her. If she'd stayed with Scott all night, her brother would have been waiting for her to return.

He turned from the window, seemingly uncertain, not meeting her eyes. "It..." He cleared his throat.

"I'm fine, Bear."

His eyes closed and he nodded. His nostrils flared slightly, and he took a deep breath. "Is it bad?"

"Bad? Oh, you mean... Just twinges," she lied. It hurt, though she wondered if it would have hurt as much if it wasn't compounded by the aching emptiness she still wanted Scott to fill. "A hot bath will help, and with our healing, it should feel much better in the morning." *Except for wanting him.*

"Yeah." His voice was strained and his jaw tight in leashed anger. Katie crossed the room to him, touching his cheek, then sinking into his embrace when he reached for her blindly.

"There's a first time for everything," she soothed him. "No matter how gentle a man is, the first time is never easy."

She rationalized how hard this must be for Bear. He'd always been responsible for her, even starting his training three years early so he could 'protect her.' For the first time in his life, he couldn't protect her. Moreover, he shouldn't protect her from this. It had to happen.

His arms tightened around her as if he'd like to carry her away and put things back the way they were before the maddening call to her printing began. "He treated you well?" he managed.

She felt her face heat at how good he'd made her feel. "He's my mate, Bear."

"As Dad was with Mom?" he hinted.

He had her there. "Well, I certainly didn't make a point of advertising the fact that I'm a— Uh... I mean, that I *was*... Without warning him, you know he wouldn't take—"

He grumbled curses in seven languages. "I take it that's why you're back so soon?"

"Can you blame him for being upset? From what I hear, Dad practically ripped Mom's head off for pulling this on him."

"How upset was he, Kates?"

Katie eased away, straightening her jacket. "Not very." She tried to turn away, hoping her twin wouldn't see her upset at Scott's dismissal.

Bear caught her by the arms, dragging Katie back around to face him. "Spill it, Kate—" His eyes widened, and he scooped her wrist up, examining it. "I'll kill him for this."

"No!"

His *Blutjagd* burned brightly. "He bruised you, and—"

"It's not what you think. We were..." She groaned. Why was it so hard to talk to her brother about sex? It wasn't as if she was likely to do something he hadn't already—or he hadn't thought about already.

"Were? Were what?" He stroked the bruise, his eyes challenging her to explain them in a way that would keep him from killing Scott.

"Playing... Playing sex games," she forced out, only slightly uncomfortable with discussing the particulars of her deflowering with her brother.

"Bondage?" he asked in disbelief.

"Well, it wasn't as if I didn't like it," she defended herself hastily.

Corwyn flushed crimson, his *Blutjagd* fading fast. "I am *not* telling Mom and Dad this one. Not on a bet. Not for a million dollars."

"You better not!"

He scowled. "That's not going to heal for a few days. What are we going to tell everyone? Or are you going to make this public now that you've consummated it?"

"No. We're not ready for that yet." She bit her lip lightly. "We'll tell them they were training injuries."

Bear snorted, rolling his eyes. "Yeah. A new hold to subdue you. The Danvers maneuver."

Chapter Twenty-seven

November 2, 2049

Scott doused his head in water, shivering despite the heat of the shower. Visions of Katie danced in his mind, bringing randy fantasies of him striding to her room and finishing what he'd started the night before.

He'd been a fool. The previous night had likely been his only shot with her, and he hadn't even seen her nude. Now, he ached to, but from the glaring looks Corwyn had shot him every time he'd dared glance Katie's way, it was a safe bet that her brother was prepared to rebuff Scott quickly and quietly.

And who could blame Katie for asking him to? Scott had fucked her and then kicked her out of his room, not even offering her comfort or asking if she was okay once he'd learned she was a virgin. Worse...

He sighed, fisting his hand against the wall. No matter what he was before he knew he was a Warrior, now he was just what Tevin termed 'the bastard cursed.' Leave it to Tevin to lay it all on the line for him. The princess could choose to fuck whoever she wanted—human, Warrior, or bastard—but in the end, Katie would be marrying someone appropriate, and Scott was anything but.

A click interrupted his musings, followed by a second. Scott stepped back from the spray, listening for any telltale noise. He reached for the shower curtain...then hesitated. It was probably one of the children. There was no way it was Katie. Why would it be her?

But, I locked the door. Would one of the younger children, one young enough to sneak into a private bath, know how to disable the lock? How would one make it from the nurseries to his far corner of the house without being caught by a Warrior?

Curiosity overpowered his confusion, and he reached for the curtain again. It slid away from his fingers, and she appeared, a bulky terry-cloth robe open so that her body was framed by it, revealed to him.

"May I join you?" she asked seriously, though her eyes glittered in amusement.

Scott couldn't find his voice. He scanned every inch of her he could see, his semi-erect cock coming up hard and fast in response.

Katie stared at it, dropping the robe to the floor around her ankles. "I'll take that as a 'yes,'" she murmured, stepping into the shower and closing the curtain behind her.

She grasped the bar of soap and ducked her head under the spray of water, plastering her hair to her scalp and neck and sending droplets skittering over her skin. Scott hooked his hands on the safety bars in the shower and leaned back against the smooth surround, anticipating watching her soap herself up, her hands caressing her body.

It didn't happen. Katie closed the distance between them, bringing the soap to his chest. He forced his eyes open, savoring every sensation as she kneaded his muscles with the slick soap, memorizing her expression as she traced every line of his upper body. Her soaped hands cupped his balls, urging them to harden, then moved up his length, stroking slowly. Scott let out a hitching breath at that, thankfully managing not to beg her for more. She returned the soap to the dish, then took down the shower head and sprayed him down, watching the suds wash away.

My turn, he decided, but Katie had other ideas.

She sank to her knees, stroking her tongue along the underside of his cock, massaging the chorded veins, then sliding the tip through the cleft at the head. Scott fisted his hands on the bars as he released a shot of pre-come onto the pink expanse torturing him. Katie closed her mouth with a hum of satisfaction. She licked her lips, her gaze locked on his twitching length.

"God have mercy," he breathed.

Katie surged toward him, capturing the head between her lips and sucking hard on the knob.

"Oh, God," he repeated his plea, leaning toward her, seeking more.

She didn't disappoint him. The suction eased, and Katie slid most of his length into her mouth, stroking the sensitive underside with her tongue again.

Scott eased back, then forward again, setting the depth at a little less than she originally took him, allowing Katie to meet him shallower or deeper as she wished. Her eyes closed, and she moaned around his length.

The urge to drag her up and thrust inside her was intense, but he pushed it away. There was no knowing how long this affair would last, and he'd never forgive himself if the opportunity to have her mouth didn't come again.

Their pace increased, and their sounds of enjoyment deepened until he knew he'd passed the point of no return. His hands fisted the bars, and his muscles tensed until he felt certain he'd rip them off the walls before he came. It had to end soon. He couldn't take this much longer.

Scott watched her, his heart pounding, praying she wouldn't release him when he came. Pearl necklaces had never been his thing, though he imagined Katie could make even that appealing. No, Scott liked to come inside some hot, deep place in a woman. Even hand jobs only prepped him for more, which was why taking care of matters himself had never held his needs at bay for long.

The rushing sensation overpowered the building tension abruptly, coming without warning. Scott held his breath, letting it out in a groan as she swallowed, her mouth tightening around him. He laid his head back against the tub surround, closing his eyes, fighting the rising need to laugh in relief.

His lax hands tightened around the bars as Katie continued moving. His balls swelled almost painfully again. At last, his mind rebelled. He was in charge. Sexually, he had to be in charge.

* * * *

Katie closed her eyes again to Scott's shudder of pleasure. She'd intended to let him soften in her mouth, but he didn't seem to be softening. If he wanted more, she'd give him more until she was exhausted.

"Get up," he ordered.

She opened her eyes, laying a kiss on the tip of his erection as she released him. Then she met his eyes.

Scott still lounged in the corner of the tub enclosure, his muscles taut as if to strike, his expression fierce. "I said 'get up.'"

Katie smiled, pushing to her feet, running her hands and mouth up his body as she rose. Every muscle she touched tightened another notch. If Scott were anyone else, she'd be afraid he would snap and try to hurt her, but this was her mate. She pressed her body to his, chest to chest.

He grasped her face between his hands and captured her mouth with an animal growl. Katie took his lead, letting him sweep her away. Scott turned her and pressed her to the wall between the two safety bars, guiding her hands to them and forcing her fists closed within his. He didn't have to order her to keep them there. His meaning was unmistakable.

His mouth left hers, his tongue massaging her lips for an extra moment. "You love sucking my cock, don't you?" he grumbled.

The sound of his voice and the sheer audacity of the question made her already-prepared body dampen further. "Yes. I do."

His cock bobbed against her stomach, and her head spun. The vague realization that Scott was precisely what she'd always wanted in a man settled in her mind. This was a man who didn't walk on PC eggshells around her, scraping and apologizing at every turn. Scott was a man who dared to treat Katie like any other desirable woman and not a princess, a man who ordered the future Stone Vessel as he would any other female in the world.

"Are you planning to do it again?" There was a hint of challenge in that.

She licked her lips, and he stared at them hungrily. "Absolutely. Just say the word."

The soap appeared in his hands, making slick tracks from her throat and shoulders to her chest. His hands kneaded and pinched at her breasts until the sensations echoed in her womb and radiated down her thighs.

She didn't watch him bathe her. His eyes demanded she stay locked with them, and she did.

Scott trailed the soap down her ribs, then her stomach, pausing to circle it over her shaven mound. Katie circled her hips beneath it, begging him silently to stroke lower.

He smiled crookedly. "That's what you want, isn't it? Lower? Harder? Tell me."

"Yes." Her voice came out a whisper.

His expression was abruptly serious. "You want me to teach you how to be the bad girl." His lips brushed over hers. "Don't you?"

"Yes, Scott." *Now. Whatever you do, do it now.*

"Say it. Say you'll do what I say."

"Anything," she vowed again.

"Well then... I guess I should rinse this soap off." Scott moved back a few inches, dropped the soap back in the dish and grasped the shower head.

He took his time about it, patiently stroking away the soap, top to bottom. By the time he reached her mound again, Katie could barely stand independently.

His fingers traced circles, lower and lower, playing counterpoint to the moving water, finally reaching her clit. Katie cried out, but he captured the sound in his mouth. Their breaths mixed, ragged gusts of air that announced how close to release they each were.

"Spread wider," he instructed.

Katie did it, her sheath throbbing in time with her racing pulse, aching for his possession. Scott took his time, spreading her nether lips with two fingers. Her heart hammered so frantically that she was lightheaded. For a long moment, he did nothing more, as if he were deciding whether to finger her or skip straight to making love to her.

The change in sound was the first indication that he intended something else. A stunned plea to Tes for mercy was cut short when the slowly pulsing water surged up into her. It buffeted the walls, the feeling of a man's climax without benefit of his length buried inside her. The combination of feeling empty and full at the same time propelled her toward release.

His thumb massaged her clit, a lazy circling that closely matched the pulse of water. "You're close," he whispered.

She nodded, her mind seemingly disconnected from her mouth. Her body was connected just fine, though. Every touch wrenched inarticulate sounds that should have been pleas for him to fill her.

"I'm close, too. The pre-come is already running down my cock for you."

She licked her lips, savoring the flavor of that come in her mouth.

"The water is going to wash away some of your lubrication, so mine will have to be copious enough to ease the way." He hesitated only a moment. "Oh, baby, it's going to go in easy. Just watching you has me excited."

She attempted speech and failed, swallowing hard.

"Are you holding tight to the bars?" he asked.

Katie fisted them as the first whispers of approaching climax taunted her.

"You're on the edge."

She nodded, gasping out something that sounded remotely like 'yes.'

"Good." He released the shower head and lifted her, impaling her on his length, sealing his mouth to hers to mute her scream of climax.

She kissed him passionately, her body gripping him tight, starved for every sensation she could identify of him. His come swirled into her, so different than the water. Their cries came together, rumbling over dueling tongues.

Scott turned off the water, bringing his hand back to caress the curve of her ass, his expression no less intense than it had been when she'd pulled the shower curtain back. Maybe he felt it. She prayed he did, because all question of his place as her mate had fled long ago, and the itch to seal printing was already burning in her. According to her parents, it was always this way for *Blutjagdfrau* and their mates. He had to feel something.

At the very least, she'd make sure he felt something. Katie levered herself up by her grip on the bars, wrapping her legs around his waist. He shivered as he settled deeper within her.

"Scott?" she prodded him.

"I..." He buried his face in her wet hair, taking several deep breaths. "You don't keep very quiet," he teased.

Confusion cut through her arousal. "Why should I?" She had autonomy, after all. Who she bedded and when was her own business. *Okay, it's the Stone's business.*

He ignored her question, kissing the blood mark at the join of her upper arm and shoulder tenderly. "Did you mean anything, Katie?"

"Gods, yes." She'd never realized sex would be so addictive.

"I'm going to take you to my bed now. I think a proper introduction with my mouth is long overdue."

Aftershocks rocked her body at that pronouncement. "You're going to teach me to be a very bad girl," she managed. "I must be pretty bad, because I love it."

Scott groaned into her blood mark, his breathing abruptly ragged. "But, since you seem incapable of self-control, I'll have to keep your sweet mouth busy in return."

The image nearly sent her over again.

Chapter Twenty-eight

November 3, 2049

Scott ran his tongue around his mouth, savoring the taste of Katie. She'd only left for her own room a few hours earlier, and already he wanted to bring her back.

His smile faltered. He didn't just want to bring her back. He wanted to keep her there, and that wasn't going to happen. Her friendly but not intimate manner with him out of bed, coupled with Tevin's almost constant presence at her side, pointed to a very different future in store for her.

He closed his eyes to the memory of her in the shower. How close had he come to blurting out that he loved her? Too close...more than once. It was insanity. How did she get under his skin so fast? For that matter, how did she get under his skin, at all? But, telling her would be even more insane.

Why? I'm an eligible Warrior. I'm no different than Tevin and the others.

Scott forced his eyes open. Was he? Well, he was undeniably not the typical Warrior, but was he an eligible Warrior for her to take to mate? Pages upon pages of Rules of Sanction and mores poured through his mind, and he examined one after another.

"I'll be damned," he whispered.

Technically, he was an eligible Warrior, but he was an anomaly, untrained by their standards, not even blood sealed. He was barely tolerated, even when he wasn't going out of his way to be a pain in the ass.

By the Armens. Has Katie ever been less than gracious to me, even when I was an ass?

No. She hadn't been. Of course, she was probably trained in diplomacy. A future ruler would have to possess tact and...

Lacking many of them personally, Scott found himself at a loss for naming the skills. *Well, she'd have to possess people skills of all sorts.*

His cock ached in renewed arousal. Katie didn't just tolerate him. Scott didn't have a name for the way she came to him and gave him free rein to touch her.

He stretched out, breathing her scent deep into his lungs. What would Katie do if he admitted how he felt about her? Would she respond in kind? Laugh at him? End their affair? Did he really want to find out?

His stomach clenched in outright terror even as his heart ached in wanting to know. "Coward," he muttered. Scott couldn't even say why the thought of telling Katie he loved her scared him.

Maybe he was seeing something that wasn't there, and he was as crazy as Dear Old Mom. Was this the type of insanity that made Lynne decide to have a Warrior's child despite the risks? That thought was more than mildly distasteful.

What other options were there? Printing came immediately to mind. Maybe he was printing. According to the texts, that was supposed to make you nuts, too. Not to mention, he still would have no idea if she felt the same way, and if she didn't, the fallout wouldn't be pretty.

Well, if she did return his feelings... No. That was just too much to ask for.

Was it even possible to print this quickly? He hadn't asked anyone directly, but the books talked about Warriors printing over weeks or months. He'd only known Katie for four days. It hardly seemed possible to print that quickly, but asking someone would mean tipping his hand, and that wasn't an option.

A chilling thought occurred to him. What if he was using Katie to escape Armen? Her mate would be free to roam with her and free from this blasted family. They could settle somewhere of their choosing or simply travel and see the world. Did he want to escape this range badly enough to latch onto a mad scheme to get it? And if he did, could he do this to Katie?

No. I can't do this to her...if it isn't real, but how do I know if it's real?

Scott pushed from the bed and ambled to the shower to wash away Katie's scent. He needed time to think. He needed to get out of this house for a while and clear his head. Maybe time without Katie and without distractions would allow him to see clearly.

* * * *

Katie's heart skipped a beat. "Into town?"

Matt sighed. "I'd almost swear the young men got together and planned a walk-out, but I know Scott didn't go with the others. He never does."

"Yes. Of course." She managed a strained smile. "Warriors will be Warriors." Her heart ached at the realization that it was true.

"Did you need to see him? Is there something I can do for you?"

"No. Nothing really. It can wait until tomorrow." She turned to go, meeting Bear's eyes, then looking away, controlling her expression stoically. She was the *Blutjagdfrau*, the next Stone Vessel. The last thing she was about to do was cry in front of the Warriors.

Truth be told, she didn't really want to cry. The need to hurt someone rose up in her, eclipsing rational thought. Katie ran her hands over her weapons, taking inventory of the two sacred weapons at her hips and the four throwing blades her Uncle Adam had gifted her with at her back, all blessed in her mother's fire.

Bear followed her out into the night toward the garage. "Kates, you need to calm down. You don't want me to have to sit on you."

Usually, she'd make a witty comeback to his final statement, but wit was beyond her now. "Calm down? Are you fucking insane?"

He sighed. "Come on. I think you need a good workout to blow off steam."

"Only if you want to see the Warrior's Rest tonight. And don't you *dare* joke about it, because I will seriously hurt you tonight. If I don't kill a beast or three..."

"You'll kill him? Oh, you are far gone." There was just a flavor of humor in his comment.

The thought tore at her. "I wish I could," she grumbled.

"No, you don't."

"Stop being so damned rational. Damn him! How dare he..." She couldn't voice the rest; just the thought of him taking another woman to bed made her want to rip them both apart. *Okay, at least rip the little tramp he picks up apart. That man will beg before he touches me again.*

Though he was armed with a sacred weapon, Scott wasn't blood sealed; he wasn't permitted to hunt without a sealed Warrior of his house. He only lacked an amulet, because he was an adult and had refused it. If he wasn't allowed to hunt, there was only one reason for him to go to town.

"How dare he!"

"Kates," Bear sighed. "Has it occurred to you that Scott may have no clue what's happening to him? Printing is traumatic under the best of circumstances, but for him... It's probably freaking him out."

She turned on him. "So, now you're defending him? You're supposed to be on my side. Besides, I thought you hated Scott."

He turned her and wrapped an arm around her shoulders, leading her toward the garage, visibly fighting back a laugh. "He's not so bad for a clueless pup. I don't *like* him, but it's not my place to approve your choice of mate."

Katie wrapped her arms around him, burying her cheek in his side. "I don't know what I'd do without you, Bear."

His arm tightened, but he didn't comment. "Well," he changed the subject, "what do you have in mind?"

"I told you. There are always beasts stupid enough to want to expunge the next Stone Vessel. Let's go find them."

"You got it, little sister."

She punched him in the ribs, smiling at his release of breath. "By fifteen minutes, and I still say you cheated."

Bear's roar of laughter went a long way toward making her feel better, though it couldn't erase the dull ache Scott caused her. Tonight, she would do her best to forget about Scott and throw herself into the hunt. It had been too long since they'd enjoyed a hunt together.

* * * *

Scott rocked the empty shot glass back and forth with his fingertip, keeping himself lightly ghosted. *Oh, how the times have changed! The last time I spent an entire evening in a bar room, I didn't even know what ghosting was called.*

He'd had only the single shot in the three hours he'd been here, but he didn't want more. He didn't want to talk to anyone, didn't even want to look at the hot packages trolling for a man. He winced at that. If he relaxed his ghosting a bit, Scott could have any number of them all over him, but the thought of it did nothing to stir him. One thought of Katie, however...

Too late, he tried to push the images away. The force of his arousal hit him like one of Tyler's blows in training. Even Matt didn't hit this hard.

"What am I doing?" he whispered. Being away from the training house only made thinking harder. He wasn't even sure why he'd stayed here this long. He wasn't enjoying himself, and he wasn't accomplishing anything. What was the point?

Of course, if he went back to the house, the only thing he'd be able to think about would be Katie and how long it would take her to come to his bed once he got to his room. *How long will it take her?*

That thought put him in motion. He tossed a five on the bar and headed for the cycle.

Scott was more than a mile away and intent on reaching the training house when it hit him. *Blutjagd.* Someone was hunting. He tried to ignore it. Hunting wasn't his driving force. He had a lady waiting for him, and there would be punishment if he poached on someone else's hunt—even if he was allowed to hunt.

Realization hit him hard, shocking him out of his arousal. *Katie!* There were two Warriors battling, Katie and her brother. He'd only tasted their *Blutjagd* once, when they were training together, but there was no doubt it was theirs.

Anger coursed along his nerves, and he turned toward the battle without considering the consequences, the sanctions he would face for it later. Scott pulled his sacred weapon as he rounded the corner into the alleyway, taking the heart of one beast and the throat of another as they turned toward him. Beasts scattered, diving away or dematerializing as he roared toward the melee at the opposite end. Scott ignored them, making a beeline to Katie.

Somehow the damned things had separated Corwyn from his sister, breaking them from their normal back-to-back style of fighting. She didn't spare him a glance; Katie didn't have time to. It seemed she was in perpetual motion: taking a beast there, whipping around to drive off one at her back, wounding another without even looking his direction, throwing a small dagger at one trying to take Corwyn's back.

Scott ditched the cycle, took out a beast she'd driven back, and slid into place at her unprotected back. Working together, the beasts soon retreated. Katie turned toward Corwyn's continuing fight, but his shout brought her up short.

"Get her out of here, Danvers! Go...now! I'll catch up."

Scott nodded and pulled her through the minefield of beast bodies, hefting his cycle up and throwing a leg over.

To his surprise, Katie didn't argue with him. She hopped up behind him and held on tight. "I'm set," she informed him.

They were well outside town before either of them spoke again.

"How did you know?" she shouted.

Scott slowed to allow them to talk easier. "That it was you?"

"Yes. You—you knew it was me, didn't you?"

Her uncertainty tugged at some nameless place in his heart. He pulled the cycle over and stopped, searching for the words to explain it to her. It was another anomaly, and if he'd learned one thing it was that the Warriors didn't care for anomalous Warriors. He prayed this wouldn't be the final straw for Katie.

She slid off and circled him, touching his cheek, her expression hopeful. "Scott?"

"I'm a little odd, even for a Warrior," he admitted, not quite meeting her eyes. *That is the understatement of the millennium.* "I can—identify individual Warriors by the...the flavor of the *Blutjagd*."

Katie smiled. "Oh, that's wonderful," she breathed.

"Is it? I'm a freak in a race of weirdos."

Her brow furrowed and her smile faltered. "If you think that, you don't know much about the *König*s."

"I don't know much about anything."

Katie scanned his body slowly. "That's not true."

Scott laughed in spite of himself. "You don't have to be a Warrior to be good in bed."

She ran her fingertips through the beast blood splattered on his jacket. "I meant your skill at battle. You know, you'll have to trash this when we get back." She glanced down at his feet. "And the boots. The rest can be washed."

"That's no problem. I hate this jacket and these boots, anyway. I'd rather wear my own."

Katie lifted his hand away from the handlebars, urging him back by lifting her leg over the seat. She settled into his lap, her thighs over his, face to face with him. "Why don't you?"

Scott felt his cheeks heat. He trusted her. She hadn't asked much about him in the last few days; she'd respected his privacy. He had brought the subject up, and it was only to be expected that she'd ask.

She raised an eyebrow, her face contemplative. "They ordered you to wear the standard jacket and boots."

"It was all I could do to keep my blue shirts. Apparently, your cousin helped with that. As for the boots... Only the *Blutjagdfrau* wear something that varies."

"Hmmm... I thought you met my Uncle Adam."

Memories of Adam Lord Maher flitted in his mind. "Son of a bitch! He wore those high moccasins."

"Yes. I guarantee he did." She shifted against him, and her heat registered against his leg, making thinking difficult. "Feel free to inform them that a Warrior's personal appearance is not something they order."

Scott's shock dissipated into unease as she collected more of the beast blood from his jacket on her fingertips. She reached for his face, and he grasped her wrist, shaking his head.

"What do you think you're doing?" he asked.

Katie smiled a feminine smile that bordered on sensual. "You earned your seal tonight, Scott. Several times over, in fact. As the sealed Warrior in battle with you, I reserve the right to paint them in the blood of a beast you killed."

He released her, settling his hand on her thigh. The touch of her fingers was almost enough to make him forget that Katie was spreading the foul-smelling blood over his forehead in the glyph that represented Syth, the Stone. She dragged up at his shirt, painting the matching seal over his heart.

Her fingers trailed down his stomach, rubbing lightly at his cock. Scott leaned over her, closing his eyes as she tilted her head back and met his lips. She wrapped her legs around him, crossing her ankles on the seat behind him.

Scott pulled her into his lap, trying to argue his way out of peeling her out of her jeans right there. Visions of Katie on his lap, his full length inside her, danced in his mind. As he had the last few nights, he sensed her, making sure she wasn't approaching her fertile window.

At the word of the other Warriors, he hadn't bothered with condoms for women who weren't near ovulation since he'd reached their range; it seemed Warriors didn't have to worry about sexually-transmitted diseases, something his mother hadn't told him. In fact, he'd gone out of his way to pick women for the night who weren't 'high cycle' to capitalize on that fact, enjoying the freedom from latex.

For Katie, he'd make the exception. Realization that he'd not only use a condom just to make love to her but that he'd trust her enough to simply toss it in the trash can at his bedside shook him. He was definitely far gone, if he was considering that.

Katie isn't my mother. She isn't out to trick me.

But she *was* out to drive him over the edge. Her hand was under his shirt, baring his chest to her as she met his mouth, grinding her heat against his jean-covered cock. He groaned in surrender, reaching for her zipper.

The sound of an engine and a car horn broke him out of his daze. He looked up, scowling at Corwyn.

"Let's go, Kates," he ordered gruffly.

Scott grumbled a curse. There it was again. The princess couldn't be seen with the likes of him, and her family didn't approve, as he'd guessed they wouldn't.

Katie smiled and placed another quick kiss on his lips, unhooking her legs. "It's just to put my parents at ease," she said by way of assurance. "If I showed up—"

"Yeah."

She seemed confused by his curt response. "We can finish this later. This is not the place—"

"I'll see you then. Same time, same place."

He moved his arm and watched Katie climb into the truck with her brother, torn between his heartbreak and the mad need to have her again.

"You're going to do it," he berated himself. "You are the stupidest man on the face of the Earth, Scott Danvers." Scott headed for the house, his mind full of conflicting feelings about Katie.

* * * *

"Not smart, Kates," her brother admonished her, handing back the two throwing blades he'd collected for her.

Katie sighed. "Shut up, Bear. We'll see how easy it is for you to think when you're printing."

Gods help her, she needed to think, to analyze why Scott was angry with her. If she'd showed up back at the training house without Bear after they'd battled together, her parents would have heard about it, and there would have been more than a little discussion about it. Why was he upset about that?

Her brother interrupted her again. "You'd've really...made love to him right on the road, wouldn't you?"

At least Bear's frustration with her made sense. "May I remind you how we were conceived?"

Bear grimaced. "If you must."

"I think you get my point." She wondered if it was simply the fact that Scott ached for her and that stopping wasn't comfortable. It was a possibility, but the feeling that it was more than that plagued her.

A smile touched her mouth at her relief that Scott hadn't been with another woman. He didn't smell or taste of one, and with her Warrior senses, she'd know if he had so much as snuggled, beast blood masking it or not. A fervent hope that he hadn't been able to assaulted her. If he wasn't able to, he was printing, whether he recognized it for what it was or not.

He sighed and rolled the tension from his shoulders. "You have to keep your cool when we get back. If you blow, it's not going to go well."

Katie fought for clarity. "What are you talking about?"

"Scott is in a lot of trouble. You can't interfere in his judgment. You know you can't."

"He's not in any trouble," she stated. In fact, by the time he'd slid into place at her back, she'd worked out how to head that off.

Bear's look of disbelief was almost comical. "What are you saying? Do you have any clue what penalty Tyler is likely to take for his breach of conduct?"

"None. Just follow my lead, and Scott is off the hook."

He muttered a curse in Italian, then another in Gaelic, fisting his hands on the steering wheel. "I am not going to enjoy this."

"You don't have to enjoy it. You just have to do it. I'm—I'm asking you to do this for me."

He nodded, his jaw tight in anger. "Do you *Blutjagdfrau* ever do anything the right way?"

She smirked at him. "Never. That's why you *Soldat* find it more expedient to just agree with us."

Bear cracked a smile. "I was afraid of that."

The remaining miles passed in silence. They entered the house and came face to face with Tyler and Matt.

The Lord Armen panned his eyes down their befouled clothing and equipment. "That was quite a hunt," he noted carefully.

Katie didn't beat around the bush. "I owe you an apology," she stated calmly. "I overstepped my bounds tonight."

The two men looked at each other in confusion, then back at her.

"For hunting our range?" Matt asked. "You know you have leave to hunt wherever you wish, *König*."

"Not that, of course. I—" She paused, looking around as the front door opened again. She'd hoped to have more time to soften the blow, but it was head-on now.

Scott strode in, splattered in beast blood, his t-shirt untucked and bunched at the center of his belt, the seal standing out in stark contrast to the skin of his forehead. He came to a halt, his eyes darting from one person to another, his hands fisting and jaw tightening, most likely in the realization that he still had to face sanction.

"Scott," Tyler greeted him gruffly.

"You first nighted my son?" Matt growled.

Bear turned on him, his hand hovering at the hilt to his weapon in warning. There were formalities to be met, and Bear wouldn't allow him to simply attack in anger.

Scott opened his mouth to speak, but Katie cut him off, turning to face the Armens as she did. "Yes. I gave him permission to fight at my back," she lied. "Scott didn't know when he started following me that I was baiting beasts in. I could have sent him away, but I didn't." At least, that much was true.

She offered a quick dip of her head. "I take full responsibility for allowing this. It was a chance that wasn't mine to take. Despite his prior success in battle and his prowess in training, I might have gotten Scott killed tonight. I submit to my true judge."

"No," Scott protested. "You—"

"Quiet," Tyler barked. "Kaitlyn knows the laws she broke. You do her a disservice by interfering."

"It wasn't like that," Scott argued. "I—"

"Did she tell you to leave?" Bear interrupted him.

"No, but—I wouldn't have left if she had." His voice was laced in frustration, perhaps even desperation.

Katie managed not to wince. Scott wasn't helping himself by admitting that. "It doesn't matter what you *would* have done. A sealed Warrior not of your house allowed you to fight."

"Damn this, Katie! You cannot—"

"She's right," Tyler barked. "Stay out of this, Scott, or face me."

"I don't care if you—"

"Scott!" Katie cut him off, turning to face him. She mouthed a 'please' at him, praying he'd back off. Everything she was doing would be for nothing if he didn't stop.

Scott shook his head, *Blutjagd* flickering in his skin, grinding his teeth to keep from arguing with her. She turned back to her judge with a silent prayer of thanks to a handful of Gods that she'd silenced him.

Tyler turned to Matt. "He's your son. You are judge here."

Matt looked from one face to the next, fighting back a heavy dose of *Blutjagd.* Katie stiffened in response, then forced herself to relax. There was a very real possibility that she was about to face one hell of a beating in Scott's place.

From Matt's point of view, she'd endangered his son, a son he was only now getting to know, perhaps in its novelty a relationship he would view as he would a father with a new baby. This was one of the fiercest states a Warrior experienced, second only to a mate being lost or endangered, and there was no telling what a Warrior in the grips of this particular madness would do.

Matt stepped forward, his hand fisted, his eyes crazed.

Katie waved her brother away as he stiffened. This wasn't something he could interfere in. Whatever price Matt took, within reason, it was his right to take it.

The room went silent, her heartbeat the loudest thing she could hear.

Matt hesitated, looking at his fist as if in indecision. Was he assuring himself that what he intended was rational and reasonable under the rules of sanction? Was he reasoning his way out of harming her simply because she was *Blutjagdfrau*?

"I am not above the rules of sanction," she stated proudly. "I accept your blow, if that's what it takes."

"No." Scott's voice was the deadly calm that comes before the storm of bloodlust.

Katie motioned him to silence.

"Are you injured, Scott?" Matt managed.

She considered that. Matt was beyond thinking. If any of them had been injured, every Warrior in range of them would have felt it. But, he was trying to be rational, trying to gauge the appropriate response to the offense to his family. That meant he wouldn't go too far, not that she would have taken him to judge if he had.

"No. I'm fine."

He nodded, unfisting his hand. Matt met her eyes, looking pained—and slapped her backhand across the face. Bear grasped her shoulders, steadying Katie for the few moments until her bearings righted themselves.

Matt swallowed hard, looking like he was on the verge of tears. "Repayment in kind," he muttered.

Katie dipped her head again. "My apologies, Matt." She turned and headed up the stairs with Bear a few steps behind, praying that her sacrifice would head off any further violence.

* * * *

Scott glared at his 'father and grandfather,' cursing them to their version of hell for this. "This is how you revere your women? This is how you protect them?" he spat.

"Kaitlyn is a Warrior," Tyler began.

"She's innocent," he countered. "I shouldn't have followed her into a battle. Even though she was penned in, I shouldn't have barged into her fight. But even if she'd ordered me away *and* I chose to obey her, I would have had to kill beasts to leave the area.

"It's only common sense. I don't wear an amulet. What the hell would you have done if a beast had confronted me in town? It's happened before, you recall, which is why I'm in this mess in the first place. Would you have punished me for defending myself?"

"Of course not!"

"Then why the hell did you do this? That's all it was, defending myself. And her. I won't lie about that. I saw—a Warrior in trouble, and I was already in the thick of it, too late to back out without battle." He tried not to contradict her. If they had even the slightest inkling that Katie had lied to them, she'd face a lot worse than she already had.

He almost groaned at the idea that he was lying to them, too. *All that time of keeping to the letter of the law, and now I'm blowing it. Well, what they don't know can't hurt me.*

Matt sighed, rubbing a hand over the stubble on his chin. "She broke the rules of sanction, Scott. Whether you had to fight your way out or not, she should have ordered you back. You weren't hurt, by the grace of Fih, and that's why she only faced a single open-handed blow."

"She shouldn't have *faced* anything," he thundered.

"You don't understand the rules of—"

"I understand them just fine." *I also understand that the people enforcing them are completely without common sense.* "In fact... Since I'm a sealed Warrior now, I request permission to roam."

The older men shot each other a calculating look.

"Denied," Tyler stated.

"What?" Scott forced his voice to a conversational tone and his hands not to fist. "Why not?" Though he knew they still had the right to order his movement, he'd counted on their willingness to give him space.

"It's obvious that you still lack the proper respect for our laws."

"I respect the laws just fine," he managed through gritted teeth. "It's you I find hard to respect."

For a moment, they simply stared at him. Scott prepared for the beating he'd take for that. Whatever they did to him, it would be worth it for admitting how he felt about them.

"Well then," Tyler responded in an even voice. "I suppose you'll have to stay here until you learn the proper respect for both the laws *and* the lord of your house."

Scott nodded stiffly and headed for the stairs.

"Scott," Matt called after him.

He stopped on the third riser. "Yes, Matt?" *Here it comes.* Tyler didn't intend to take him to trial, but the old man did as a show of his control.

There was a moment of silence. "I'm proud of you. You battled well. I want you to know I'm truly proud of you for it."

"It's my duty. I don't have much of a choice in that."

He took the rest of the stairs two at a time and closed himself into his bathroom, noting the trash bags that had been stored on the shelves since his arrival and the chute to the furnace in new appreciation. He started undressing, his movements measured and his mind busy.

Down the hall, the shower between Katie and Corwyn's rooms was already going. He vaguely wondered which of them would bathe first, then decided that Corwyn would defer to his sister.

At a loss for something to distract him, Scott started analyzing the interactions downstairs. Conflicting emotions washed over him. The more he tried to understand Katie and Matt, the less he did.

* * * *

Katie planned her presentation carefully. She sat at the head of Scott's bed, her robe opened around her body, her legs spread, one knee bent and the other crooked behind it, so she was on display for him.

The shower turned off, and her heart rate stepped up in anticipation. There were a few torturous moments before Scott slipped into the bedroom. He went still, closing the door behind him, scanning her body, the towel around his lower body tenting as he hardened. Scott crossed the room, pulling off the towel and throwing it over the footboard, his expression intense.

She forced a breath, noting her spinning head. Scott paused, then sat beside her, his eyes locked on her face. She reached for him, but he gripped her hand before she could connect.

"You shouldn't have..." He took a calming breath. "You lied to them."

"I didn't stop you. If I didn't, it was as good as giving you permission."

Scott ground his teeth. He moved abruptly, wrapping one arm around her back and the other around her cheek. Katie gasped as he dragged her down the bed, around his body, and lay over her.

His fingertips brushed the tender spot on her cheek. "I take my own blows. What was it that Tyler said? You do me a disservice by interfering."

Katie felt her cheeks flush. "You had no choice in what you did. You felt that. You had to feel it."

The desperate need to know that Scott was printing settled in her. When she'd seen him under attack, it had affected her. What would it have been like for him? Scott would have known his mate was threatened from miles away.

"A Warrior masters his curse," he quoted. "If I lack self-control, I deserve my punishment."

"They couldn't know..."

She stopped herself, uncertain for the first time. What if he really didn't feel it? What if she was pursuing the wrong man? There had only been two *Blutjagdfrau* before her. The fact that they had both known their mates immediately, at least once they were cursed, might have been a fluke. If he wasn't the right one, she'd have to face the madness when she broke printing. Just the thought of it sent an unwelcome and atypical shaft of fear through her.

No! Blutjagdfrau don't pursue the wrong men. They don't. They always go to their mates virginal.

There's a first time for everything. Look at your birth. Look at his.

"They know," he grumbled, snapping her out of her internal argument. "They know all about my little—gift." His tone made it seem that he didn't consider it a gift, at all.

"Yes, I guess they would." Why couldn't he say it? Was she wrong?

"I fight my own fights and take my own punishments. Understood?"

Katie grimaced, forcing back the need to tell him how her printing demanded she protect him. Mate or not, he was a Warrior and not a child. His pride alone would dictate that he stand on his own feet. "Yes. I understand. You're right."

Scott hesitated, touching the bruise again.

"It wasn't all that hard," she assured him. "It will be gone in a day or two." It would have been much worse for him, though.

"Yes. I know." Still, he didn't move.

"Scott?"

He met her eyes, seemingly deep in thought.

"What is it?"

His smile erupted. He cupped her buttocks in his hands, pulling her to his body so that his cock nestled between her thighs. Katie pushed against his shoulders, forcing his body up a few inches and herself down until he settled a fraction of an inch inside her.

Scott grasped her hips and stopped her cold. "Oh no, you don't. You don't tease me and not pay off," he informed her.

"Tease you?" Katie asked incredulously. "When have I failed to pay off?" Dear gods, given the chance, she'd drag him to bed for as much of the day and night as their duties would excuse them.

"You haven't, and I intend to keep it that way."

"Mind telling me what I promised then?" *And quickly.* His cock pulsing lightly at her labia was making her crazy.

Scott sat up, leaving her body, lifting her with him until she sat across his lap with his legs on the floor beside the bed. "You said we'd finish later. You left me aching on the cycle, you know."

She smiled widely, standing and straddling his legs, shedding her robe onto the floor. "Can't have that," she purred. Katie stroked his cock slowly, shivering at his gasp of delight. "Are you aching?"

He scooped her legs behind him as she was on the cycle. Without missing a beat, he pushed her hand away and guided Katie onto him. She gripped at the tattooed bands on his arms, fighting for breath as he stretched her around his length.

"Are you?" he taunted.

Katie nodded frantically, shifting further onto him.

"Yes, you are. I feel it." Scott started lifting her and forcing her down, thrusting up into her over and over. "Oh, God," he breathed. "I feel it."

She buried her face at the base of his throat, kissing along his collarbone. Scott stiffened as she nibbled on him, marking his shoulder. His thrusts slowed.

Katie looked up, meeting his questioning eyes, embarrassed at having done something so juvenile. One hand left her hip and cupped her mouth back to the spot.

"You want me to mark you?" she whispered.

"I want to feel it burning all day. Leave scratches. Leave love bites."

She didn't waste time. Katie sucked at his shoulder, biting lightly, raking her nails along his back, growing rougher as her climax loomed.

Then it crashed over her. She pulled her head back, a groan of pleasure building to a scream. Scott captured the sound as he always had, his mouth ravenous, his thrusts stilling as waves of come flooded her body.

He cradled her against him, his kisses becoming less frenzied, his lips feathering over her face, then returning to drink deeply from her again, his eyes closed, his cock still pulsing in aftershocks. "Someday," he breathed.

Her heart pounded in anticipation, her fingers pausing in their investigation of the furrows she'd left on his back. "Someday, what?"

His eyes opened, and he stared at her, seemingly speechless. "It's nothing," he denied.

"Scott," she warned.

He pulled her closer, as if he expected her to walk away from him. "Someday..." His expression was abruptly pained. "I want to do that on the cycle," he admitted sheepishly.

"Oh. As long as it's not dark, I can't see why not." Why did she keep hoping for more? *Because, you're my mate!* But he treated her like a mistress, a sordid little secret.

Katie forced a smile to her face and traced his lower lip with her fingertip. "Why do you always do that?"

"Do what?"

"Mute the sound of my release. I do have autonomy, you know."

* * * *

Scott tensed involuntarily. And what would happen if someone did hear her?

According to the rules of sanction, she was allowed to sleep with whoever she wanted to, as long as she didn't conceive a child outside of printing, but he wasn't stupid enough to think that the Lord *König* would approve of Scott. The Lady *König* was gracious, as were most of the Warrior wives he'd met, but Curtis Lord *König* had the look of a man who'd like to beat Scott into obedience and respect.

The scene played out in his mind in startling detail. The other Warriors of Armen would hear her, and one of them would, in all due concern, let her parents know who was 'fucking' their precious daughter. It was a damned miracle that Corwyn hadn't informed them already, but someone in the Armen household was sure to, most likely Tevin. There was little doubt that that particular shithead would do it just to spite Scott.

Though Katie had the autonomy to fuck—or even to marry—whomever she wanted, her parents had the right to place her in any range they wanted to. If they knew she was screwing Scott, she'd be shipped off to Cross, Hunter, or Maher range so fast it would make her pretty little head spin, surrounded by relatives and far from Scott. Or, conversely, Tyler would strand Scott as far into the Canadian ice as he could for the duration.

The thought of it made him ill. Anything he had to do to keep it from ending, Scott would do. Keeping their relationship quiet ranked high on that list, as far as he was concerned.

"Scott?" Katie prodded him, something that resembled uncertainty in her eyes.

He kissed her, groaning into her mouth as her Warrior-strength passion took off again. Scott thrust inside her, pulling his mouth away at her whimper.

"Your sounds are for me alone," he informed her. "Not for your brother. Not for the Armens. For me."

A smile lit her eyes, warming his heart. Scott had no idea what he'd said right, but her expression promised the ride of *his* life.

* * * *

Katie slipped back into her room, too excited to sleep though not doing so would give Bear the upper hand in training, a rare event in their lives. She stretched out on her bed, parting her robe and trailing her fingertips over the love bite Scott had left on the upper swell of her breast.

He was getting possessive—and protective of her. That was a good sign. It wouldn't be long until he'd ask her to marry him. Katie smiled. Knowing Scott, he wouldn't ask; he'd demand it, probably while he was buried inside her body. If her great-grandfather Corwyn Lord Hunter was right, that day was coming soon.

Theoretically, as she neared high cycle, their drive to print should become more urgent. She was approaching cusp. Soon, they'd have to either seal and conceive a baby or not seal and start using protection—or seal and choose to wait to conceive, though Katie wasn't certain that was possible.

The urge to mate was usually kept in check by a rational, human mate—or the Stone's schedule-making. With two Warriors the Stone wanted to reproduce, the drive to do so should be nearly impossible to ignore.

Katie sighed wistfully, running her hands down to the soft expanse below her navel. What would it be like to feel Scott's child growing in her? She smiled even wider at the thought of sealing printing.

The only thing that troubled her was his insistence on secrecy. There was no reason she could understand for it.

One of the rules of sanction was that no Warrior could interfere with the mating of another, unless the woman was a freed daughter. That precedent had been tested and set in stone by her grandmother Jayde and grandfather Talon. Maybe Scott didn't know it.

Or, maybe he does! Katie bit back a peel of laughter. Jayde and Talon had kept their mating secret until the lords came upon them in a heated embrace in hopes that Jayde would be trained enough to defend their union, if it came to that. Did Scott think he'd be called to defend their choice? Did he fear he'd fail that challenge?

Memories of how he'd mastered her sexually sent shivers down her spine. No man was more worthy to be her mate. All she had to do was prove it to Scott—and perhaps bring their relationship more into the public eye.

Chapter Twenty-nine

November 4, 2049

Matt paused at the edge of the training field, swiveling his wrist, making his weapon dance to limber his wrists and arms. His brow furrowed as he catalogued the Warriors present. He strode to Antony, glancing at the ferocity with which Tevin was training in unease. Had he and Scott tangled verbally again? Or worse...physically?

"Morning, Dad," Antony greeted him.

"Morning. Uh... Where is Scott? Early workout?"

Though he'd tried to discourage it, this wouldn't be the first time—or the last that Scott chose to catch an early training with one Warrior instead of the main workout with the bulk of the household. It seemed that his eldest son used any opportunity to isolate himself to the fullest: living in a private corner of the house, working in the garage, even disappearing for hours with armloads of texts to Gods knew where.

"*König* invited him for some special instruction." His youngest son's smile spread in apparent glee. "Tevin's really hacked about it, too."

"Corwyn?" he asked. Though Matt anticipated a negative response, he wasn't certain why he did. There'd been little sign that either of the *König*s had taken more than a scientific interest in Scott—save the fact that he'd obviously been invited to call the princess 'Katie.'

"Nope. Kaitlyn." He chuckled and then continued. "A very *innocent* little invitation it was, too. Buuut...you know Tevin. He looked as if Scott planned to seal printing tonight or something."

Matt managed not to grimace at the idea of his sons going head to head over a woman...barely. Gods, but some days he really wished he knew what was going on in his family before it turned to fists.

"Well then..." What excuse could he give? "Maybe I should go see what fault Kaitlyn found to correct in his battle style." He winced at the blow Tevin dealt Jordan. "Make sure your brother doesn't kill anyone."

"Am I my brother's keeper, now?"

Matt glared at him.

Antony put up his hands in mock apology. "The humans say it. It comes from one of their holy texts."

"The Bible, Antony. Your mother owns one."

Sincere interest lit his eyes. "Does she, really?"

"It's not that surprising. Just remember what happened to the man who said it."

His smile disappeared. "I don't know what happened to him," he admitted.

"Ask your mother to tell you the tale." He looked to Tevin pointedly. "After training."

Antony nodded, and Matt left him with a clap on the shoulder. Though the Bible wasn't their text, it often had important lessons to teach.

The distance to *König*'s chosen training ground gave him more than enough time to think. This rivalry between his older sons had to end, but as much as Matt would love to call a halt, his sons were grown men and not errant children. They were Warriors and had to learn to work together.

Kaitlyn's laughter reached him before he topped the hill, then the sound of blade on blade. Matt scowled in the realization that Scott was just the type of careless pup who would agree to train that way.

He was good—a damned sight better than most of the other young Warriors his age, despite his lack of Warrior training. His first battle had proven that, the fact that he'd sent a beast to ground without a sacred weapon. Still, he took too many wild chances, crazy stunts that no other Warrior alive took—which probably kept him alive that night in Maher range. When fighting beasts, a certain level of being different was good.

Matt topped the hill and dropped to one knee, watching Kaitlyn and Scott train together. They went at each other hard but smiling and laughing. That was unusual. Scott was typically focused and serious in training. This relaxed stance was something Matt had never seen from him. Of course, he wasn't at ease with his family, in general.

Scott sliced at her head, and Kaitlyn ducked and danced away with another tinkling laugh. She responded with a side snap kick that he deflected easily. Scott wagged his finger at her, clucking his tongue as if in reproach, a move sure to infuriate her.

Kaitlyn kicked it up a notch, swinging blades that Scott avoided or deflected, spinning away from his attack, then back-fisting his shoulder without warning. He took a step back, looking from his shoulder to her smirk.

"I see," Scott mused, sheathing his weapon.

Matt furrowed his brow. *What* did Scott see? That he'd left a hole? He hadn't really left one. It was impossible to cover his entire body at once, and Kaitlyn moved faster than any Warrior and some beasts.

His son stalked around his opponent, unarmed, a speculative look on his face. She glided with him, sheathing her own weapons, her hands loose at her sides as if waiting to grapple instead of laying fists.

Kaitlyn moved first, a punch to his face that came to a screeching halt with his hand wrapped around her wrist. She drew in a shaky breath, her smile fading fast.

"You want to use my weakest point?" he taunted. "Two can play that game."

Matt bit back a laugh at his son's balls of steel. Insinuating that a *König had* a weak spot was a death sentence in the making.

At least, it typically was. Kaitlyn stared at him in seeming shock, making no move against him as Scott nestled her captured hand to her back and pulled her against his body.

A flicker of movement caught Matt's attention, and he snapped his head around, noting Corwyn turning away from the field. The young prince went still, his jaw tensing as their eyes locked.

"Hey, Matt!" he yelled in a cheery voice that was completely at odds with his look of warning.

His reaction gave Matt a moment's pause. Suddenly, nothing made sense. What was going on here? Tyler had confided that the *König*s had come to Armen to meet his son, but there'd been no sign of a relationship forming. If that was what was going on, why would anyone hide it from him? He looked back at the couple on the field, hoping for anything that would make this interaction clear to him.

Scott had already released Kaitlyn. Gone was the relaxed young Warrior, happier than Matt had ever seen him. His son was tense, more pissed than Tevin had been by far.

A sudden flash of comprehension made Matt wince. Hadn't he considered that his sons were going head to head over a woman on the way here?

Please, for the love of Ani and Dobler, don't let this be a game to him. Matt knew for a fact that Kaitlyn had never permitted Tevin such intimacy. If she did with Scott, she was playing for keeps. If Scott wasn't... If he was pursuing Kaitlyn just to spin Tevin tight, the results would be catastrophic.

"Matt?" Kaitlyn asked calmly. "Did you need something?"

He hesitated. By the rules of sanction, Matt had no right to interfere in Scott's mating or release...

Release! It was a safe bet Scott didn't know that *Blutjagdfrau* took no release but self-release until they intended to mate. "I—need to speak to Scott. Later. When you're done." Matt turned abruptly and started back to the main training area.

"We're done," Scott grumbled. Before Matt could turn back to protest, his son had crossed the distance of the field and started up the hillside.

The twins each shot him a look that promised his early end, and Kaitlyn's *Blutjagd* flared for a moment.

One look at Scott convinced him that it was too late to call it off now. Once his son made up his mind about something, you needed to knock it loose with a sledge. He nodded and fell into step beside Scott. Finding the words he needed was painful—in the extreme.

Scott sighed. "Let's get this over with."

Matt faltered. "Get what over with?"

"Whatever you're about to lecture me about. What? You think I don't know when you're about to do it?" The sarcasm Matt loathed settled in his voice again.

"I didn't tell you to leave training. I said I wanted to talk to you later, at a time convenient to you. This isn't a lecture."

"Then what is it? People don't go out of their way just to talk to me."

Matt swallowed the urge to snap back at him. Scott's attitude was the reason no one talked to him. Given the chance, Matt would spend hours filling the void Lynne had left him with, getting to know the relative stranger that was his oldest son. Scott wanted a fight, and Matt wasn't about to give it to him this time.

"I just wanted to warn you about—"

Scott scowled at him, *Blutjagd* burning lightly in his skin.

"It's not what you think," Matt protested, frustrated that he hadn't even gotten an entire sentence out before Scott jumped to the conclusion that he was being sanctioned for something. "It's just..." Matt growled a curse on Lynne. "There's something you need to know about *Blutjagdfrau.*"

Scott turned away, running a hand through his hair, his muscles tensing.

"When a *Blutjagdfrau* chooses a mate—"

"Don't sweat it."

The offhand comment stopped Matt cold. "Scott?"

He turned, not angry, not frustrated, deadly cold as if preparing for judgment. "I won't embarrass your precious family, Matt. Don't worry about that." Scott strode toward the garage as if the conversation was over.

Matt ground his teeth, fighting the drive to shake some sense into him—or knock it into him. "After lunch," he ordered. "We will finish this discussion. No ducking it."

Scott stopped walking. He took a deep breath, visibly calming himself. "It's your game, Matt. It always has been." He continued on, a plodding pace as if he had to force one foot in front of the other.

"And you'll never forgive that," he whispered.

They were both trapped, and there was no way out. Until Kaitlyn released him, Tyler would never give Scott permission to roam. Until Scott felt in control of his own life again, there was no chance his son would allow Matt to attempt any sort of reconciliation.

* * * *

Scott sighed at the feeling of someone behind him. He didn't have to look over his shoulder to know it was Tevin; the tang of his *Blutjagd* announced it clearly enough. Over the months in Armen range, he'd come to regret his ability to recognize people this way. It was different, and it was the final strike with many of the Warriors.

Great! First Matt and now Tevin. It was probably another friendly warning to cool it with Katie. Just what he needed.

When he didn't address his 'brother,' Tevin spoke. "I wouldn't get my hopes up, if I were you."

"About?" Though he knew what Tevin meant, playing dumb with him had its own rewards.

"She considers you an anomaly, a science experiment to study for a while. She may even consider it her duty to help you adjust to life as a Warrior. She's not going to marry a bastard, you know."

"She was conceived before printing, you know."

He refused to acknowledge the rest. Tevin was probably right about it. After all, Katie certainly wasn't making their affair public. Not that Scott was stupid enough to want her to. It all boiled down to late-night fucks between a princess and a bad boy, an itch she probably wanted to scratch before she married, her version of sowing wild oats like any other Warrior did.

He'd argued many times that he was little better than the blade chasers that got off on bedding Warriors in that respect. Only the fact that he felt more for her separated him from the rest of the thrill-seekers.

"At least *her* parents did print."

Scott didn't bother to answer that. It had always been like this with Tevin, as if he believed Scott existed for no other reason than to annoy him, to steal his place in the family. One of the reasons Scott was so dedicated to learning all facets of the Warrior ways was that he lived for the day he'd be able to roam the farthest edges of Armen. The farther from Tevin, the better.

"I'm the only Warrior in Armen she's taken a sincere interest in."

More like she's courteous enough not to slit your throat in your own home.

Scott had watched her interactions with the other Warriors for days; he hardly seemed able to take his eyes off her whenever anyone approached her, though he could barely stand watching her make nice with the other Warriors. More than ever, he was convinced that Tevin was deluding himself. Of course, Scott had questioned his sanity and rationality more than once in the past few days, and pointing out what he believed was true to Tevin would be a waste of time.

In all honesty, Scott had taken off to his rooms many times, unable to watch her with the others any longer. Perhaps he'd even been hoping she'd come to him all that much sooner if he made an early exit.

What did he know about how she spent the time he wasn't with her? For all Scott knew, Katie was making wedding plans with Tevin before she had sex with Scott every night. For that matter, she could be in both beds.

His hand fisted around the carb he was cleaning at that thought. Scott capped his *Blutjagd* and forced it back before it could blow, unwilling to let Tevin know he'd struck deep.

"I'll have her maidenhead and her agreement to be my mate," Tevin gloated.

Relief coursed through Scott so abruptly that he chuckled. Tevin wasn't sleeping with her, if he believed that.

"What's so damned funny?" Tevin demanded.

"You're awfully damned intent on being her first," he noted.

"Of course."

He laughed harder. Oh, it was going to be so sweet when his 'dear little brother' learned that her hand in marriage was the only prize he had a shot at—if he even learned that before they'd sealed. Tevin may end up a *König*, but he'd already lost half of the prize he sought to his greatest adversary. The laughter continued at that thought.

"What the hell is the matter with you?" Tevin shouted.

"She's a Warrior. What makes you think she's going to come to you a virgin?" he taunted.

"Don't you know anything about *Blutjagdfrau*? They don't have sex until they choose a mate—ever."

Scott's smile faded, and his head spun. "Really?"

"That's how *Blutjagdfrau* mark their mates, and once they latch on, they don't take 'no' for an answer. I hear they're insatiable."

If his mind would have cleared, Scott would have made Tevin swallow teeth. As it was, he couldn't reconcile anything.

If Katie slept with Scott, she wanted to marry him.

No! She intended to marry him. This wasn't an option plan. Like everyone else, she'd walked into his life and demanded something from Scott. He'd trusted her, believed she didn't just want something from him, believed she was honestly giving herself to him.

God, I am the world's biggest fool. Katie hadn't even had the decency to tell him what sleeping with her meant. She'd used Scott's ignorance of the rules against him.

His grip on his *Blutjagd* slipped. Scott turned abruptly and stormed toward the house.

Tevin backed off, his eyes wide in shock, his hand fisting the grip of his sacred weapon, probably believing Scott meant to kill him. Scott ignored him, rounding him without a word. The little twerp was the least of his problems.

He spied Katie heading for the garage, and his *Blutjagd* stepped up another notch. How nice of his 'problem' to come to him.

She slowed, then stopped, her smile melting into a look of concern. "Scott?"

He didn't give her a chance to question him. "I just came to say goodbye, princess."

"Wh—Good—goodbye?" Her eyes pleaded with him for an explanation.

His gut twisted, and the urge to comfort her assaulted him. Scott pushed it away angrily. "It's over. You've had your fun. Hope you enjoyed it." He started to turn away.

Katie grasped his arm, shaking her head. "You can't just..." she stammered out.

"Walk away from my precious *family*? I'm not. I'm going roving like any other Night Warrior. That's my duty. Do it or die, right?" His head supplied the truth that they still controlled his movements, but for what he intended, he needed solitude. They couldn't deny him that.

"But...you—"

"Or maybe you think I can't walk away from you? I can and I will."

Tears pooled in her eyes, setting off that mad need to hold her again. Scott pulled from her hand with a growl of self-loathing. He was hurting her, and he knew it.

She hurt me! "I trusted you, and you betrayed me, just like everyone else. You— You should have told me instead of playing with my life."

He stormed back to the garage, half-praying she'd let him go and half-praying that she'd come after him, tell him she was wrong, ask him to stay. He nearly roared in frustration as his heart leapt at the idea that she might, because he knew he'd stay. He knew he'd forgive her anything if he didn't get away and get his head straight.

Tevin ducked out of his way. Scott didn't spare him a glance. He hit the door controls, starting the sliders moving along their tracks, and slid onto his cycle. He cleared the doors and laid on speed, putting as much distance between Katie and himself as possible.

With every mile, he felt as if his heart was being shredded. It was printing, and printing could be broken. If there was one thing Scott had, it was self-control. It was one of the few things his mother had taught him well.

The rage and despair built inside him until he felt as if he'd explode if something didn't give. Scott screamed, venting his grief until his lungs and throat ached—and still he felt no better. It was the madness, his punishment for playing the fool.

I can beat it. He had money in his pocket and in his account. All he needed were supplies and a quiet place. Nothing else. No one else.

* * * *

Katie stood, watching him walk away, her feet rooted to the ground though she ached to follow him.

His words echoed in her mind. How had she betrayed him? How had she played with his life? What did he think she should have told him?

Scott left on his cycle, racing away at break-neck speed. She ran a shaking hand through her hair, left loose just for him, her heart hollow and emotions disconnected.

Fury gathered speed, eclipsing all the scattered emotions vying for her attention. Katie stomped back toward the house, muttering curses in every language she could remember, and since she knew ten of them, she would have enough to reach the house, easily.

"I don't know what he said," Tevin started in.

"This isn't a good time," she snapped, going for the direct route with him instead of being gracious for once. Gracious was about a mile past her limit at the moment.

"But—"

"Back off," she warned him. Katie broke into a trot, slowing to a walk again as she pushed through the doors, not bothering to close them behind her.

Matt looked up from the phone, his face pale.

Katie didn't give him time to tell her what she already knew. Of everyone she could conceive, she wanted to talk to her mother and the Stone entity in her head least of all. "Tell my mother to fuck off," she informed him, knowing full well that nothing resembling that would be passed along. That was fine with her.

She kept moving, not entirely certain where she was going and why anymore. She'd pack. She'd leave. As long as she was on the road and not here, she had to feel better.

Her heart ached at the memory of Scott on that same road, headed anywhere she wasn't, just as she was forced to do now. She wanted to cry—or to scream.

"Kaitlyn, wait," Tevin called out, his hand closing on her shoulder.

Or to hurt someone! She whirled around, drawing her right blade with a scream of frustration, knocking his hand away and planting the killing edge at his throat.

The room went silent, and the tension forced her fury higher. Her hands shook. Tevin ground his teeth, his eyes narrowed, barely breathing.

"Do not touch me," she ordered.

He pulled his hands up and back in a sign of surrender.

She tried to force her hand back, but the need to hurt him wasn't abating. He had no right to touch her. He wasn't her mate. He had no right...

Bear's attack came without warning. His left arm circled her body and his right hand closed around her wrist. She thrust her elbow toward his head an instant too late. Bear was already in motion. Her feet left the floor, and her twin twisted behind her. The air left her lungs in a rush as she crashed to the floor beneath him, leaving her momentarily unable to push him off.

She closed her eyes to the chorus of angry shouts surrounding her, pushing in on her until all she wanted was silence and darkness.

"What the hell have you done, Tevin?" Tyler roared.

"It wasn't me, grandfather! Scott—"

Katie pulled against Bear's hold with a scream of rage made ragged by her brother's weight pinning her down. She let the full depth of her *Blutjagd* light, frantic to end Tevin's comments any way it took. *How dare he speak Scott's name!*

Corwyn was ready for her reaction. His grip tightened, and he drove his body onto her with the lesser, but still formidable, force of his own *Blutjagd.*

It suddenly seemed that every Warrior of Armen was around her, some lit, some not, all shouting.

"Shut up," Bear thundered over them. "All of you, shut up."

Silence reigned, only the ragged breathing of a dozen or so people breaking the stillness.

His voice gentled. "I'm here, Kates. Let it go, now. By Dobler, let it go."

She forced it back, realizing the futility of fighting her twin. He had the upper hand, he knew her style better than anyone in the world, and she didn't want to hurt Bear. Tevin was the one she wanted to kill.

"Better," he soothed her, not relaxing his hold or his bloodlust, though she gasped for breath beneath him, her ribs aching. "Now the blade."

Katie dropped her weapon, sobbing as someone eased it from her reach, then unsheathed the other. For the first time in her life, she didn't care if she ever saw them again.

Bear released her wrist, stroking her hair, easing off her slightly to let her breathe, his longer body half over and half beside hers. His *Blutjagd* faded. "Where is he?" he asked, not raising his voice despite the tension he transmitted in his tone.

"Scott?" Tevin asked in seeming shock.

"Gone," Katie gasped out, drained by her *Blutjagd*, possibly poisoned with adrenaline as her mother once was, her muscles going lax in exhaustion. "He's not coming back."

Bear pressed his forehead to the back of her head, taking several deep breaths. "It will be okay," he whispered. "No one will touch you. We'll go away. I promise. Just you and me, Kates."

She closed her eyes, imagining she could hear Scott's cycle, praying he would come back to her.

"Tyler," he called, his voice only a fraction louder than before. "We need a cabin. Now."

"Matt, get the keys to cabin number five," Tyler ordered in a voice no louder than Bear's.

A mad cabin. Katie gave up all pretenses and started crying, letting her brother hug her to his chest.

Chapter Thirty

November 9, 2049

Scott ground his teeth at the knock on the door. He'd known the Warriors would find him eventually. It simply annoyed him that they wouldn't leave him alone—and amazed him that they'd bothered to knock.

He didn't answer. *Let them come or let them leave.* It made no difference to Scott. It was unlikely that they'd go away, but the last thing he wanted was to invite their interference.

The lock clicked, and the door swung open. Matt strode in. He scanned the room with a scowl, then stared at Scott, sighing deeply. "Something you want to talk about?" he asked in a conversational tone, as if they were discussing the weather or stocks instead of Scott taking off on the princess.

Scott stretched his bare feet out on the bed, scratching at the four-day's growth of beard on his chin. "There's nothing to talk about. Once I break printing, I'll start doing my job."

Matt pulled a chair from the table and settled in it. "Why are you doing this? If you're printing, you love her. Why would you throw that away?"

"Other Warriors have broken printing."

"When a woman refuses him. Kaitlyn hasn't refused you. Right now, she's off in a cabin, stripped of her weapons, under her brother's care—suffering because of *your* choice. Doesn't that mean anything to you?"

Scott rubbed at the constriction in his chest, fighting the need to scream again, forcing slow, deep breaths when his body fought him. He didn't want to scream again. He didn't want to cry. When he did indulge in either of those things, it only left him feeling weaker and more miserable, so why would he?

"It does make a difference. Why are you doing this? Why are you hurting her, if you love her? Why are you hurting yourself? Explain it to me, because it makes no sense."

Scott couldn't find his voice. The only clear thing to him was a mindless rage. Scott didn't want the confusion. He didn't want the pain. He wanted to be numb. The bottle of Beam beckoned.

Matt was in motion before it was halfway from the bed to Scott's mouth. He snatched it away, pitching it against the far wall of the cabin before the chair he'd been using hit the floor.

"It's not against your precious laws to drink," Scott grumbled. "I checked."

"A Warrior never hides in a bottle. Even when his mate dies, he doesn't. You are at your lowest point when you battle the madness. The beasts know it. If you meet them in that state, it's a death sentence."

The thought was strangely appealing. Dying would solve all of his problems from breaking printing to escaping the Armens.

"Scott, you need—"

"I don't care."

"What?" Matt's anger faded.

He laughed, though it felt like his heart was being ripped out. "Enemies cut your heart out," Scott whispered. That was family for you. That described anyone you let close in life.

Matt fisted his hands. "That probably sounds pretty damned appealing to you right now. Cut out your heart so you don't have to feel. Just wait for a beast to—"

"Why wait? Just call Jordan and Tevin. They want to kill me, anyway. Let's get this over with."

"No one wants to kill you," he snapped.

"You're not that stupid."

Scott closed his eyes, too tired to argue, but visions of Katie were waiting to torment him. He opened them with a sigh. Lack of sleep was going to drive him insane before the rest had a chance to. Every time he nodded off, he woke hard and wanting, on the brink of release he couldn't claim.

Matt stared at him, seemingly shocked. "Even if it's true, there are plenty of people who want to accept you, if you let us."

"You? It's so simple for you, isn't it?"

"You certainly don't make it simple to love you, but...yes. Me, Sarah, Antony, Jacob, Stephanie, Elise, the children... My Gods! Kaitlyn would give you the most unconditional love that—"

"Nothing is without conditions."

"Did she ever ask anything of you that you didn't want to give?"

Scott didn't answer that. He couldn't find it in himself to answer it, because he couldn't refute it. He'd wanted her before she came to his bed. He'd wanted to marry her, and she hadn't actually asked—or demanded it. If anything, Katie had been waiting for him to acknowledge what he wanted, to stake a claim on her. Wasn't that how most people—human people—married?

"Did she?" Matt prodded.

"No." But she hadn't been honest with him, either.

He nodded. "I thought not."

Scott rubbed a hand across his eyes. "She'll forget me." He could hardly say it and didn't want to think about it.

Matt darkened. "Will you forget her?" he challenged.

Not if I live to be a thousand.

"Will you go on and marry someone else and wipe her out of your life? Do you want her to?"

Scott swallowed down the urge to puke. "Stop," he requested weakly. Just the thought of it was too much for him, and the idea that he could force Katie to it made him feel worse.

"Then stop this, before you cause any more harm." He didn't give Scott time to answer. Matt walked away, shutting the door behind him.

"Leaving me alone to sink or swim," he grumbled. Well, wasn't that what he'd wanted? If Scott could just figure out why it wasn't a relief, he might stay sane another day.

* * * *

Matt ambled into the training house, feeling twice his fifty years.

"You found him?" a rather tense voice inquired.

He winced in the realization that *König* had come to bear, turning toward the library though he didn't meet Curt's eyes. "He didn't go far, just holed up to weather it out."

And was damned ingenious about it, too. Scott had taken only a single cash withdrawal as he rode, done everything in cash, stayed off the beaten path, and stayed put. It had taken Matt five days to track the crafty young Warrior. It probably would have taken the

Mahers three or less, but the last thing he'd agree to was putting Kaitlyn's relatives on his son's trail, so he went himself.

Curt sighed. "How's he look?"

"Like shit."

Scott had lost weight, so much that Matt hoped his son hadn't been subsisting on the bottle he'd smashed. It was unlikely that he had. Besides the fact that Scott seemed fairly lucid, he seemed to have stayed put after his single stock-up run. It was more likely that he'd not been able to stomach food—or that he had no drive to eat. Warriors who had broken printing had reported both.

The young lord sighed, visibly fighting something he wanted to say, most likely that it was good that Scott was in pain for doing something so hurtful to his daughter. Curt leaned back against the bookshelves, looking lost.

"And yours?" Matt inquired.

"She won't eat. She's not sleeping. She won't even talk to Corwyn. All she does is wander around and stare into space—and cry."

"Yeah." Matt wanted to say more, but what could he say that would make a father feel better? Nothing of use.

Maybe if Scott knew how dire it was, he'd go to her.

No. He knew. The dark circles under his eyes attested to his lack of sleep, and his raw voice attested to the rest.

"What are the chances he'll change his mind?" Curt asked.

Matt shook his head. "I don't know. Not good, I guess. What are the chances that she'll choose someone else eventually? She hasn't sealed yet, after all."

Curt's face went a vivid red, tightening in anger. "Off hand, I'd say it might be too late for that."

A spike of pain cut through Matt's weary mind, the beginnings of one hell of a headache. "How late is it, Curt?"

"Well, she wasn't high cycle, if that's what you mean."

"He slept with her." There was no question in his mind that it had gone that far now.

"Scott didn't pursue her. Katie... Well, she's a lot like the other *Blutjagdfrau*. She knows what she wants." Curt shoved his fists in his pockets, offering a weak smile.

"Oh, hell."

"Yeah." Curt wandered away, rounding Matt without another word. After that revelation, there hardly seemed the need for more bad news.

Chapter Thirty-one

November 11, 2049

Scott watched her from the treeline, ghosted, tucking his switchblade back into his boot.

It had taken him only two hours after Matt left to decide to clean up and find her. Scott had to know for certain what was between them.

Of course, since he didn't want to start a war or court interference, he'd had to track her rather than asking where she was. That meant checking every Armen stronghold on record, one at a time, and praying she hadn't been transported all the way back to Maher range. The two days that it had taken to find her had been nerve wracking, only slightly less maddening than sitting at the cabin he'd rented because he was doing something positive toward salvaging their printing.

Katie wandered the clearing aimlessly, her arms crossed over her stomach, shivering. She laid her head back, closing her eyes to the sunlight, stumbling in exhaustion.

He rubbed at the dull ache in his gut. Just seeing her was painful, but he couldn't live without her. Scott cursed his printing. He'd tried to break it. The damned texts said he could, but he couldn't. Maybe it was because Katie had never refused him.

Panic nearly drowned his thinking mind. He had refused her. She'd had more than a week to put him out of her system, and she didn't look like a madwoman. What would he do if she refused him?

Convincing her to take him back was probably against their precious rules, just as convincing a woman to have sex with you was. Worse, what if she couldn't take him back? What if breaking printing was a permanent step? He wasn't too proud to admit that losing her now would kill him.

There was no way to know but to try. He'd taken care of her brother, as well as he dared and without breaking any rules of sanction. Now, he had to convince Katie to give him another chance.

Scott made his way back to his cycle, wiping his shaking hands on his jeans. He wouldn't touch her. He couldn't risk hurting Katie if she refused him.

Resolved, he fired up the cycle and raced up the path to the cabin and the clearing beyond. Katie turned, watching him come in seeming shock, shaking her head, her eyes wide. She took a few shuffling steps back as if she were ready to bolt.

He came to a stop between her and the cabin. "Get on, Katie." He wanted it to sound self-assured, but it came out as a plea.

"I—I can't," she stammered. "I—"

A scream of rage crossed the distance between the cabin and their position. Katie glanced up, confusion warring with amusement. Corwyn lit up hard, a white-hot tang that scorched Scott's senses, second only to the feeling of Katie lighting after he'd left her.

"Your brother is going to kill me when he gets out of there," he confided, trying to lighten the mood. "Please, get on. I need to talk to you."

She backed off a step, terror in her expression.

Glass broke at the cabin, probably a window.

It was time to lay it all on the table and hope for the best. "I have never felt like I belonged anywhere," Scott whispered. "I've never been part of anything. Not with my mother. Not at school, and not with the

Armens...until you. If you feel like you belong with me, get on the cycle. If you don't...I don't care what Corwyn does to me."

Katie flicked a startled look at the furious Warrior sprinting toward them.

"Should I turn off the cycle and wait for him to kill me?" he offered.

She threw her leg over the seat, grasped handfuls of his jacket, and pressed to his back. "Go," she shouted.

Scott turned a doughnut, spraying dirt and grass in Corwyn's general direction, then picked up speed as he raced back to the main road. He fought the urge to laugh aloud, simply for having Katie on the cycle with him, but a kernel of rational thought informed him that the work had only just begun. Katie had come with him to save his life. Now, Scott had to convince her to stay.

Katie's hands loosened, and she shifted closer to him. He hardened painfully in response.

"There's an access road a mile ahead on the right. Take it," she ordered him.

"I sabotaged Corwyn's truck. He can't follow us."

"It's coming up. Take it."

Scott turned onto the access road, not slowing. "Okay. Why are we doing this?"

"By now, the Maher trackers are looking for us. If you want to beat a Maher tracker, ask a Maher tracker."

He nodded. Katie may be a *König*, but she was a *König*-Maher.

* * * *

Erin went still, the Armen history she was reading slipping from her fingers and thumping on the carpet. Her heart pounded in warning, and snippets of images filtered through her mind. Corwyn's *Blutjagd* joined it.

Curt enveloped her hands in his own. "Erin, what is it?"

The words stuck in her throat. She searched the Stone for insight, but the damned thing wouldn't let her see into Scott to gauge his intentions. *Or, he's over the edge of madness and doesn't know what he intends any more than I do.*

No, thinking that would drive her mad.

The cell phone at Curt's hip rang, and he looked at it in unease.

She forced herself to speak. "Tell Bear we'll have a car to him within the hour. Then call Adam. We need him to start tracking from his end...Scott and Katie."

Curt snatched his phone up, flipping it open with a look of pure fury. "Corwyn?"

Her son's voice barked over the phone, panicked, angry, barely leashed.

Erin closed her eyes, pyramiding her hands in an attempt to focus her attention on any information the Stone *could*—or maybe, would—give her. Anything that helped with tracking or even clarity of the situation would be welcome. She blocked out the rest of the Warriors, then the rest of her family, concentrating solely on Katie.

Vertigo played havoc with her senses. A turn. The sound of the motorcycle and rushing air drowned out everything else of note. The smell of leather teased her nose, and the buttery material brushed the palms of her hands and cheek. Katie was traveling blind, her eyes squeezed shut, as if keeping her mother from tracking her on purpose.

"Okay. Why are we doing this?" Scott shouted to make himself heard.

"By now, the Maher trackers are looking for us. If you want to beat a Maher tracker, ask a Maher tracker."

Then it was gone. Erin tried again, but the Stone had blacked out the scene for some reason. She opened her eyes with a series of vicious curses.

Curt looked up, wincing. "Something I should tell Adam while I have him?" he asked, his entire body tensing.

"Yes. She's working against us—and the Stone is helping her."

* * * *

Katie fit her body tight to Scott's back. The urge to seal printing beat at her nerves, untouched by the week of hell she'd been through. Her hand strayed south, the need to touch all of him as strong as it had ever been.

His groan returned some semblance of sanity to her. She couldn't do this yet. Until they'd had a long talk, it couldn't go further.

"Pull over," she shouted.

"Here?"

"Anywhere. We need to talk."

Scott nodded, turning cross-country to get them away from the road and the higher probability of detection. Her ears buzzed in the near-silence when he turned the cycle off.

Katie eased her hands from his body, praying he hadn't noted her trembling. She'd gone with him for reasons even she couldn't fathom. Now that they were stopped, she couldn't find the words to question him.

He stood and slid off the cycle, turning and dropping to one knee before her. His eyes pleaded with her. Her breathing hitched as Scott scooped her hand up and kissed her knuckles.

"Scott... I..." Gods, how Katie ached to believe he was sincere.

"I was wrong, Katie. I have no right to ask your forgiveness, but if I don't try, I have nothing to live for." His fingers massaged her hand, finding tension and relieving it patiently.

"Why?" It was a weak response at best. "Why the change?"

He blushed deeply. "There was no change, except... I was angry. I was scared. I thought— I thought, if I tried hard enough—"

"You could prove something."

He winced. "Yes. I did."

"But, you couldn't."

Scott shook his head.

Katie eased her hand away, fighting back tears. "So, you're back. You failed, and the pain is enough to force you to—"

"No," he protested. His face went ashen. "I'm risking my life, because..."

"Because?" she prompted him, her heart skipping at what he might say.

Scott's hands closed around her hips, massaging lightly, his eyes half-closed in pleasure.

Her arousal was immediate and intense. As much as Katie wanted him to continue, this was a bad idea. "Scott," she begged. "We can't—"

He surged up, cocking his head to one side to seal his mouth to hers. His tongue teased just inside her still-parted lips. Katie groaned as she admitted him.

Suddenly, they were moving. She couldn't seem to figure out if she dove at Scott or he dragged her toward him. Katie didn't care which it was. She landed over him, slowed slightly by his grip on her, their mouths meshing, legs tangling as he laid back, then rolled her beneath him. His solid length pressed into her thigh.

Katie fumbled at the buttons on her sweater, finally grasping the material in both hands and yanking it apart. Some of the buttons slid from their buttonholes without catching; those that didn't, popped off.

Scott's mouth left hers. His gaze trailed down her body, his breathing harsh. A wicked smile curved his lips. "You'll be going back in one of my shirts," he informed her, his voice rough.

She nodded, easing the sweater aside so he could feast his eyes on her breasts—or anything else he wanted to feast on them. Katie wanted him to feast, slowly, completely, until she begged for more of him.

His eyes glazed over, his hand cupping one bare mound, his thumb feathering back and forth over the beaded nipple. She arched to him, gasping out a request for more.

He closed his eyes, taking a deep breath. "Talk first," he managed.

"Talk? How can you think about talking at a time like this?"

"Because, I should have spent more time talking to you from the beginning."

Katie nodded, encouraging him.

"I love you. I've wanted to marry you since the first time you met my eyes, I think. I couldn't think of anything but you. I can't, I mean."

Katie fought for a decent breath.

"I said—"

"I heard you."

He waited for an answer she couldn't seem to formulate. "Katie?"

"If that's true, why did you push me away? Why did you act like it was just sex? Why—"

"Everyone seemed so sure..." A look of misery settled on his face.

She cupped his cheek, needing to understand. "Please, tell me."

Scott turned his head, pressing a kiss into her palm. "When you returned to Armen, everyone assumed you'd made your decision and chosen Tevin. I couldn't stand to watch it. It was killing me. And then when I found out—"

A sour taste rose up from her stomach. "That self-important, self-absorbed creep? You have to be kidding. How could you ever think—"

Scott kissed her, a hard, fast kiss, then laughed heartily. "I'm glad to hear it."

"He was the one who convinced you to leave. Wasn't he?" She corked her *Blutjagd*, unwilling to give the Warriors anything to track.

"I think that was his aim—that or goading me again. I'm sorry. I played right into his hands."

"I'm not," she snapped, visions of her blade against Tevin's throat in her mind.

He looked away, his smile disappearing, swallowing hard. His hand retreated. "I should take you back," he choked out.

Realization chilled her. "No. Oh, gods, Scott! I meant—"

He trained hopeful eyes on her.

"When you left me, I ended up with my blade to Tevin's throat. My only regret is that Corwyn stopped me before I killed him or left scars."

His eyes widened. A smile lit his face, and he was abruptly laughing hysterically.

"I love you, Scott. I've hoped that you'd come to me every hour since you left me. That's a lot of hours."

His laughter died out. "Yes it is. We have so much to discuss," he whispered.

Katie nodded slowly. "Do you have sacred weapons?" she asked.

"One in my saddle bag. Why?"

"Then I suggest that we seal printing now and report back to Armen before nightfall. We can talk later, but meeting dark without weapons isn't a smart move." She managed a wry smile. "And facing our families without sealing might be even more dangerous than that."

Scott barely breathed. "You still want me?"

"Gods, yes. There's no one else for me."

"If I make love to you, it's forever. You won't be getting rid of me."

"I don't want to get rid of you."

He nodded, pushing to kneeling between her knees. Scott peeled off his jacket and hung it over the seat of his cycle, then did the same with his t-shirt. Katie slipped her arms out of her sweater and trailed her hands down to her jeans.

"Yes," he urged her. His movements mirrored her own right down to his rapt attention on her slit and hers on his ram-rod cock as their jeans slid away.

Scott scooped his hands under her knees and lifted slightly, smiling as she fought the jeans at her calves and succeeded in binding her ankles together in the cloth. There was no way out; her jeans were trapped on her boots, lace-up style, so she couldn't slip them off—and her legs were braced out on his arms.

He lowered his head, stroking his tongue up the sensitive span between her legs. Katie cried out, thrusting her hips up in shock and pleasure. He didn't explain himself; he hardly needed to. Scott wanted Katie at his mercy, her release in his hands and no one else's.

He had no mercy. When she grasped at his hair, Scott captured her wrists in his hands and pinned them to her knees. She was trapped, fully open to his ministrations. He brought her up fast and hard, nipping at her outer lips, sucking and licking at her clit, thrusting his tongue inside her. Katie screamed, arching her back so that she all but left the ground.

Scott eased her down, releasing her legs and grasping her wrists again, pinning them to the ground above her head, then winding his fingers through hers as he rose up over her. "Oh, so very bad," he breathed, taking her breast in his mouth.

His flicking tongue sent reminder notices that she was still empty and wanting. Katie rolled her head side to side, licking her lips, trying unsuccessfully to shift against him.

He released her and moved to the other, his breath making promises. "We're going shopping tomorrow."

"For?" she managed in a thick voice.

His lips brushed back and forth over the rigid tip of her nipple. "Sex toys. Lingerie. I promised to make you a bad girl, and I intend to do it." His mouth closed over her breast, nipping, sucking, ravenous.

She whimpered, trying to force it deeper, though she could barely move. He eased further up her body, his breath fanning over her lips as if he couldn't decide whether or not to kiss her. His body pressed hard to hers, his cock leaving a damp trail across her inner thigh.

The solid fact that beads of pre-come caused the wetness brought her mind into focus. She couldn't allow Scott to undermine his position by forgetting the rules of sanction.

"Scott," she whispered, waiting for him to make eye contact before continuing. "You know I'm high cycle."

A fresh spurt of his seed wet her leg, announcing his tenuous control. "I want to do this right," he assured her.

"So which—"

"Give me permission, Katie. I'm—begging you to let me have everything."

She seemed to forget how to breathe for a moment. Despite their Warrior inclinations, she'd felt sure he would want to wait.

Misery touched his face. "Let me be a father. Let me raise our children right. I can't promise I'll be perfect, but—"

"Yes."

He stared at her, his expression cycling between disbelief and hope.

"I'll help you," she promised. If there was one thing Katie knew, it was family.

His mouth closed over hers, thanking her without words. Then he released her and slid home. She gasped at the feeling of a single spurt inside of her.

Scott grimaced, trembling, no doubt reining in the urge to spill immediately in his excitement. He thrust into her again and again, his groans and whispers mixing with her cries of pleasure.

"I'm asking," he began seriously.

"Yes," Katie pleaded.

"Forever. Say you'll give me everything, Katie, and I'll never leave you again."

"I'm all yours," she panted, her body reaching for another release. She tightened her grip on his hands, pressing her hips hard against his and forcing him deeper.

He shouted her name, his seed swirling inside her. Katie screamed, her body pulsing in time with his continuing thrusts. Heat enveloped them, imprinting the moment in her memory, imprinting his now-still cock to her gripping sheath until she knew no other would feel right filling her.

"Oh, God," he breathed. "I never dreamed it would be this good." His lips caressed her forehead.

* * * *

"How can you be so calm?" Curt grumbled.

Erin smiled, touching his cheek. "She's perfectly safe."

Corwyn snorted. "If that's true, why haven't you called the Mahers in?"

"The *only* reason I'm letting his search continue is the fact that your sister is unarmed. I hope they have enough sense to come in on their own, before night falls. If not—"

"Of course we do," Katie stated calmly.

Erin spun to greet her, raising a hand to still her husband and son. The last thing they needed was some hothead killing Scott in the heat of the moment, when they'd just sealed printing.

Scott tensed at Katie's shoulder, but there was no other sign of aggression from the young Warrior. Not that Erin had expected there would be.

She scanned her daughter, making note of the mussed hair, crumpled jeans, oversized Navy blue t-shirt, and men's leather jacket Katie wore. The distinct smell of sex lingered on them, as well, confirming what the Stone had finally told Erin an hour before.

"You bastard," Corwyn growled, his *Blutjagd* spiking. Before Erin could call him back, her son lunged for Scott.

Katie didn't waste a moment. She drew Scott's weapon and took a defensive stance in front of him, ready to take down even her twin if he posed a threat to her mate. Corwyn came to a halt a little less than an arm's length outside her arc radius, shooting a look requesting aid at his parents.

Scott stepped forward, grasping the hilt of his weapon just below the blade and yanking it from her fingers. "Another subject to discuss," he informed her.

"Even if I do conceive, I haven't yet," she argued.

Corwyn choked on that.

"Katie," Curt began.

She ignored him, focusing on Scott. "I *am* a Warrior, you know. It's ingrained in me to protect my mate."

He chuckled, wrapping a hand around her waist and drawing her to his body. His eyes gleamed in challenge. "Do you want to be a Warrior right now? I can think of better things to be." He mouthed something at her, then smiled widely.

Erin replayed that silent message several times, but all she could come up with was the word 'bad.'

Katie seemed to have problems forming a sentence, and she blushed crimson. "I think we should discuss this upstairs," she finally managed.

"Yes. Discussing is definitely on the list of priorities," he said, though his tone clearly announced that it wasn't the highest priority. Scott glanced their way, bowing his head slightly. "By your leave?"

Erin bit back laughter. "House lords and Stone Vessels do not interfere in the relationships between Warriors and their spouses."

He smiled and turned Katie toward the doorway to the foyer and the stairs beyond. Corwyn stared at the bulge in Scott's jeans, an indicator of their highest priority, and rolled his eyes as they turned away.

"Well, what now?" Curt asked.

"Call the Mahers and Armens in—and make the announcement that we'll have a *König*-Armen baby before Labor Day."

"You can't know that," Corwyn snapped.

Erin raised an eyebrow and waited for him to catch up with the fact that she knew a lot more than he counted on.

He sighed. "Damn it."

Chapter Thirty-two

November 19, 2049

Katie groaned into Scott's mouth, noting his fingers inching up the t-shirt she'd donned. She pulled away, her mind muddled. "Dinner, Scott," she gasped. "They won't send it up like they did the first night." As it was, they'd barely emerged for meals and the occasional training session in the last eight days.

"We'll raid the kitchen later," he promised absently.

"I'm starving. We missed lunch."

He lifted her, grinding Katie against his still-ready length. "I'm starving, too."

She bit her lip as the force of her arousal swamped reason. "How do they do it?" she wondered aloud.

"They who?" His voice was rough, but in jealousy or arousal, she couldn't tell.

"Warriors. How do they survive conceiving a child without dying of starvation or dehydration?"

Scott's head came back, his eyes wide. His hand dipped inside her jeans, caressing her lower abdomen. "Oh, God."

Katie didn't ask if he'd sensed her. She simply waited for his reaction. She didn't have long to wait.

He settled her back on her feet, dropping to one knee before her as he had in the field they'd sealed in. The press of his lips through her jeans made her heart stutter. Scott kissed her over and over, a silent testament to his feelings.

She forced his name past her lips, her knees quaking.

"Food," Scott decided, standing and scooping Katie up so abruptly that it stole her breath. He wrenched the door open and headed for the stairs.

"Scott," she protested weakly. "I can walk."

"You're lightheaded. Once we're downstairs..."

Katie nodded, sinking into his chest, breathing his musk deep into her lungs and smiling in response. At the foot of the stairs, Scott eased her to her feet, keeping a hand on her lower back, presumably ready to catch Katie if her balance deserted her.

Conversations quieted somewhat as they entered the dining room. It was a smaller company than they'd come to expect.

Tevin, Jordan, and Antony had been sent away when Katie went to the mad cabin on the assumption that neither of them would be up for facing the other eligible Warriors just after breaking printing. Tom had asked to leave on his own, apparently interested in a permanent arrangement that had nothing to do with Katie.

Still, the house had been filled again by dinner the day after they'd sealed. Between Katie's Uncle Adam Lord Maher, his wife Jo, and their son Joseph, her cousin Mikel of Crossbearer-*König* and his wife Holly, and her distant cousin Brandon Lord Hunter, the table had been more overloaded than it had ever been.

It had taken three days for her assorted relatives to start clearing out. Katie's immediate family had lasted the longest, a full week before Bear had reluctantly taken his leave along with their parents. But, while they'd headed for Maher range, Bear had headed for Hunter.

That had left the skeleton crew of Armens behind at the training house with them.

Scott guided Katie to her chair and saw her settled before he sat next to her. Katie dug in, filling her plate from the platters without delay, but Scott didn't move to fill his own. She stopped, staring at his speculative look in confusion. Before she could speak, he did.

"Matt? I wanted to say I was sorry."

The room went silent and still; forks stopped halfway to mouths.

Matt swallowed his mouthful of food slowly. "For?" He managed an even tone, though his heart had to be racing.

"I've thought about the conversation we had before I left, over and over again. You were trying to keep me from hurting Katie. Weren't you?"

"Yes. I was."

"Then I owe you an apology. You see... I've never had a father. I know that's not your fault, but..." He sighed. "I don't understand how a father thinks. I don't understand why you do the things you do."

Matt started to speak, but Scott motioned him for patience. He raised Katie's hand to his mouth and kissed her knuckles tenderly. Scott didn't look at his father when he continued.

"I need to know these things now. I'm...asking...for your help, because you're good at this. You offered to teach me, once."

Katie looked back and forth between them.

Scott didn't meet her eyes or Matt's. He breathed in shallow streams of air. She could almost taste his fear. Scott had laid himself open in a rare show of trust, extended the olive branch, knowing it might be refused.

Matt had gone pale, his eyes wide, his fists set at either side of his plate. "That's what fathers do, Scott." His voice was strained.

Sarah, his wife, squeezed his arm in reassurance. For a long moment, no one spoke.

Scott turned to him, nodding. "Lesson one."

"Lesson two," Matt countered. "You never stop learning. Your children teach you as much as you teach them."

Scott chuckled, most probably in relief. "I guess I'm a little behind on teaching you."

Matt joined him, laughing heartily. "Me, too. If you're willing, I'd like to catch up, though."

Scott met Katie's eyes and brushed his fingertips along her cheek. "This is a *König*-Armen baby. He or she is going to have everything I never did, especially family."

Alyssa:

The Warrior's Widow

A note from the author

In *The Blade Chaser's Son*, I introduced Corwyn, otherwise known as Bear, Katie's twin brother. At the end of the story, I made it clear that he left Armen range and headed to Hunter, while his parents headed off in another direction, but I didn't say why. Bear is a man looking for home, tired of the wandering life. He's about to find what he's always wanted...in spades!

In *Blade Chaser*, I also mentioned Tom Armen. I stated specifically that Tom asked to withdraw from Katie's match pool in Armen to pursue printing of his own. That he did, and in doing so, he set off a chain of events that was to bring together two houses and provide a home for Corwyn in the bargain.

It all started with Tom, but it will end in Hunter range, the night when Corwyn enters El Oso Oro, which fates would have it means "The Golden Bear." It's a quaint little bar, primarily run by a family of women and friends, but it's about to become more to Corwyn and his Hunter cousins.

You can look forward to reading more about the women of El Oso Oro in Bear's Women. In the meantime, it all stared with Tom Armen...

Happy reading!
Brenna

Chapter Thirty-three

December 8, 2049

Tom winced at the sound of his cell phone, pausing with one hand extended into his truck, the shopping bag dangling over the plush woven seats.

Answer it. You've refused to answer it since you turned the damned thing back on early this evening.

Gods only knew how long they'd tried to reach him before that. How long had he been out of contact before they started to worry about him? A week? Ten days? Tom certainly hadn't left them a trail to follow.

It rang again, accusing him.

As well it should. Answer it, you coward. He dropped the bag but still didn't lift the damned bit of machinery to his ear.

Coward! If you don't answer it, they'll get a Maher to GPS track the signal. They won't wait to do that much later than tonight.

He raised it to his ear and opened the connection. "Here," he forced out.

"Damn it, Tom," his father shouted. "Where have you been?"

"I've been...preoccupied."

That much was true. He'd been preoccupied with breaking nearly every sanction dealing with release and printing in less than a month's time. It had to be a new record.

All for Alyssa. He'd do anything to have her. *I have done everything, every dirty trick in my arsenal and more.*

His father stuttered for a few moments. "Pr...pre...pre*occupied*? For...god's alive! How many weeks?" His voice got steadily louder with each word.

Tom sighed. "Yeah." What else was there to say to it? He'd been single-minded in his pursuit of her.

His father's voice went to a deadly calm that marked his intention to battle. Tom imagined...or perhaps it wasn't imagination...that he could feel his father's *Blutjagd* across all the miles separating them.

"Where are you?"

"Cabin twenty-two. About five miles from it at the moment." *Buying milk to support my son, to be precise.*

"Twenty-two is in Utah."

Tom winced again, picturing the beating he was due for this. *I'm due for a hell of a lot more than a beating.* But, he wouldn't consider that at the moment. "Yeah. It is."

"You're supposed to be in Idaho!"

"Yeah. I know." But, he'd be too easy to find in Idaho...and too close to home. They'd have been interrupted in Idaho; he'd needed time alone with Alyssa. *I still need time, but time has run out.*

"Are you going to return here to face trial, or do I have to track you down myself?"

Tom rubbed his eyes roughly. "Be there in a day," he vowed.

"Unless you're going to tell me you were busy breaking printing, you're going to face some serious sanctions for this."

"Can't do that," he admitted.

"If I have anything to say about it, you'll be tethered to the manor for the next year."

"I'll accept my punishment." *Any punishment I deserve. I must have been mad to do this.*

"You're damned right, you will. You've driven your mother near mad with worry."

So, that's why he's so angry with me. Seeing his mate in pain must have had him on the edges.

"You've driven *me* near mad. Now, you tell me what the hell you've been doing," he thundered.

"Sealing printing, and... Well, Alyssa was high cycle, so we..." *And, boy did I do it! What is it the Christians say? To hell in a hand basket?*

"This doesn't excuse you." But, Tim's voice softened at the news that Tom had a mate and child to consider.

"I don't ask to be excused." *For anything. Ani help me! What have I done?*

"Good, because a Warrior who can't control his drives is no better than a beast."

Tears stung at Tom's eyes. "I know." *That's what I am. I'm a beast. What have I done to her?*

But he knew full well what he'd done to Alyssa, from getting her drunk to get between her thighs the first time to pursuing her though he knew it made her nervous that he did. From convincing her to willingness to tricking her into the seal in the heat of passion. And from playing on her sympathies to win his son to lying to her about the rules of sanction.

And now she'd find out what he'd done to her. *Everyone* would learn what crimes he'd committed. In all too short a time, his father or Tyler would kill Tom, and Alyssa would abort his son.

He swallowed a sob at the thought of his son paying for his crimes. If he could keep Alyssa ignorant until it was too late to abort...

Five months!

I have to do it.

But, could he live with himself for perpetuating this fraud on her for that long?

I must! My son's life depends on it. At least, this way, his son would live. Whether Alyssa decided to keep him until fifteen or she left the baby with his parents, his son would live.

"Tom," his father barked.

"Sorry. What did you say?"

"When will you know?"

He'd really lost track of the conversation. "Know?"

"Her cycle," he hinted in annoyance.

Tom couldn't help himself. He smiled, fingering the gallon of milk on the seat. "She carries my son."

There was a moment of silence. "I assume I'll get to meet her tomorrow?" The unspoken "finally" was impossible to miss.

"Of course."

"I meant what I said. I intend to have Tyler tether you to the manor, especially now that my grandson is involved."

His stomach lurched. At the manor, it would be nearly impossible to keep Alyssa and his family from trading too much information long enough to save his son's life.

"Tom! Do you understand me?"

"Perfectly," he breathed. "Whatever happens to me, I deserve it." *But, not my son. Ani, if you have any mercy, protect my son...and Alyssa.*

* * * *

December 9, 2049

"You said they'd expect nothing less from you," Alyssa complained, a touch off of hysterical.

Tom fought to keep a neutral expression, as she repeated his lies back to him. "They'd expect it. That doesn't mean they'll excuse it. I broke laws, and I have to pay for that."

Her hand closed on his arm and her cheek nestled to his shoulder. "What will they do?"

"It's called trial."

"Not the trial. What will your punishment be?"

"There is no trial as you know it. It's a trial of battle. Usually, the older Warriors are better fighters. If they weren't, they wouldn't have survived this long. *If I even get the opportunity to defend myself.*

No. He hadn't injured anyone physically. *That they know about, anyway.* It wouldn't be blows he had to take without a fair fight.

"And?"

He turned to her. "I'll face them, as many of them as they deem injured by my actions. Then they'll put on other sanctions like being unable to roam freely, being paired with another Warrior like a first night... I'll have to prove myself again."

She paled. "They're going to batter you?"

"Yes, but I'll heal from that quickly enough," he assured her. "Our healing is accelerated."

Alyssa shook her head, seemingly horrified. "No. You—"

"I have to face my punishment. It's a matter of honor that I do this."

"But... It's not right." Tears made her eyes bright.

"Our laws are absolute." Finally, he was telling her the truth. *Where was that kernel of wisdom when I was breaking those laws to lay claim to her? Strangely silent.*

Or drowned out by my madness.

The tears pooled on her eyelashes. "I'll explain," she offered desperately. "I'll ask them... I'll explain."

Tom wound his hand in her long, blonde hair, brushing his lips over hers, fighting the urge to shout out in triumph. Alyssa loved him; she wanted to protect him from harm.

He sobered, deepening the kiss, fisting his hand in her hair reflexively. If Alyssa tried to defend him, she'd damn him further. As it was, her innocent answer of where she lived had added fuel to the fire. It was only by pure luck that they hadn't decided to question her further upon learning he'd left Armen range without permission to pursue her in Hunter. He would certainly face several additional blows for it.

"Thank you, but it's a matter of honor that I take my blows without such a show."

He was lying to her again. He'd face no ribbing or sanction for Alyssa's heartfelt concern; his family would envy Tom her solicitude. They might even ease off the physical blows in deference to her naivety and pain. But, the price of her intervention would be too high to allow her to attempt it.

She sobbed.

"I don't want you to go with me." If she spoke out at the wrong moment— "I don't want you to see what they'll do."

Alyssa paled further, weaving on her feet. Tom scooped her up, laying her on the bed, berating himself for scaring her. It wasn't right to make her fear his family, even if it served his purpose to cause a rift between them.

"Promise me you'll stay here. I can bear this, if I know you're here...waiting for me." *Now, I'm playing on her emotions again. When did I become such a beast?*

She nodded, a single-tear tracking down her cheek. "I'll take care of you."

He groaned, hardening. "If you do that, I'll have to thank you properly."

She smiled, darkening, most likely in memories of how he usually thanked her.

"I have to go down now." As it was, he'd lingered too long.

Alyssa sighed, closing her eyes.

Tom pulled the blanket over her. "Rest. I'll be back soon." But, first he'd wash up and change clothes. He wouldn't let her see the worst of it. He couldn't do that to her.

He watched her for a moment, memorizing the lines of her face that he'd surely know for too short a time. Tom turned away and headed down to the training room with a heavy heart.

All of the close Warriors had been assembled, as well as the trainees and a few of the older women who'd no doubt come to comfort Alyssa.

His father looked around Tom's shoulder, his eyebrow rising in surprise. The question remained unspoken. Of course, they expected Tom to bring Alyssa. By breaking the rules they knew of alone, he'd committed an offense against her, and she was expected to watch him pay the price for it.

Tom cleared his throat. "Alyssa knows what will happen here and why. I asked her not to come."

"Tom," Tyler began.

He didn't give the house lord a chance to finish his thought. "She carries my son. I will pay for my crimes. You cannot demand that my mate and son pay for them. As it is, this has her upset. She's lying in my bed, crying, as we speak. Don't make me add to that.

Being upset while she carries isn't good. You know that."

Tim winced.

Tyler seemed to consider that carefully. "Because she carries," he conceded.

The women filed out, confirming his suspicions about why they came here.

"Because she carries," Tom parroted. *When they kill me, I will hold him to that pledge.*

"You know the rules of sanction you broke."

"Yes, I do. I take full responsibility for my actions."

"Is there anything else you want to tell us?"

They cannot know. "No. Nothing." They hadn't asked if there was anything else he'd done wrong. They'd asked if there was anything else he wanted to tell them. He certainly didn't *want* to tell them the other rules of sanction he'd tossed when his son's life hung in the balance.

They implied it.

My son! "Nothing," he repeated quietly.

Tyler nodded, his jaw tight in anger. "Tim."

His father stepped forward, and Tom steeled himself for one hell of an opening blow. It was actually two blows: one to the gut and the other to his face.

Tom knelt on the floor, recovering slowly, fingering his cracked rib with one hand while he pressed the other to the floor to steady himself. Colors danced before his eyes, starbursts that appeared and disappeared without plan.

"The first was for the eleven days of grief you caused your mother," Tim growled. "The second is because you have yet to beg her forgiveness for it."

Tom nodded, gasping out a vow to do so at his earliest convenience. *As soon as I can move from bed.* If those first two blows were any indication, he might not be getting back up for three days, and with Warrior healing, that said a lot.

"Then do it now," Tyler suggested. "You won't be in any condition to do it later. While you recover, let me lay out your other sanctions. First, you'll face your father, then me, and finally your brother. When you recover from that, you'll hunt with another Warrior for six months."

I won't live to hunt alone again.

"You will not be trusted to roam more than two hundred miles from the manor for at least a year. You'll check in like a first night until that time." He hesitated. "Am I understood?"

"Yes. I understand and accept." Tim managed an even breath, his chest easing.

"Tyler," his father hinted.

"Oh, yes. Until your six months are up, you are required to live at the manor."

Tom's stomach turned to a block of ice. It was over. In such close proximity, he'd never make it to five months.

You have to. Your son's life depends on this. "I understand."

* * * *

December 17, 2049

Alyssa smiled her thanks as Debra handed her a glass of warm milk. Tom's mother waited until she'd taken a sip before she turned away. His parents pampered her horribly, and that was disconcerting, but Alyssa was at a loss for a polite way to tell them not to, so it went on endlessly.

She glanced toward the two Warriors in the corner nervously, considering disappearing to Tom's room yet again, though she loved the library at the manor house.

Tim and Tyler weren't themselves. There were no smiles, no jokes, not even discussion between them. Their grim dispositions and intensity unnerved her, but she couldn't state why.

She'd always known Warriors were unbalanced. Tom had told her that often enough. He'd been crazy for her: crazy to get her into bed, crazy to marry her, crazy to have a son, crazy because of what he was.

But, this went beyond the typical edge of violence inherent in the breed. There was something brewing, seething beneath the surface.

Alyssa opened her mouth to ask what was wrong, then shut it, lifting the glass to her mouth. If they were this close to the edge, she wasn't going to risk pushing them over. Like the wolves they compared themselves to, Warriors snapped. She shivered at the memory of their tenuous control.

The smell caught her attention first. Alyssa coughed, her eyes watering. Beast blood was foul stuff, the type of odor you never got used to.

She looked at the doorway, screwing her face up in disgust. Chad was splattered in the tar-like substance. He held one of their weapons, his hands cupped under the hilt and the blade.

"Tim, no," Tyler ordered.

Alyssa didn't look at them. Something in Chad's expression made her heart pound. He lurched toward her, and she scrambled back to the far end of the couch, upsetting the milk onto the hardwood floor. She didn't know what Chad was doing, but instinct told her she wanted no part of it.

"No," Tim growled.

"Stand down," Tyler ordered.

Chad reached her and dropped to his knees. He lowered his face and raised the weapon as if offering it to her. Alyssa glanced at Tyler, hoping for guidance...and gaped at the scene.

Tyler had Tim in a bear hug and was struggling to force him to the floor. She shook her head, gasping out a plea to God as Tim howled.

"I'm sorry for your loss," Chad choked out. "If I could have—"

Tim roared, eclipsing the rest.

Alyssa recoiled from the feeling of the hilt of the weapon Chad held, tacky in beast blood, touching her hand. Still, Chad extended the weapon to her, forcing her back.

"It's over," he pleaded. "I killed the beast. I swear I have."

"I don't understand," she managed, jumping as Tim cursed at Tyler and nearly broke the hold on him. Her heart pounded in terror.

Chad's head swung up, and he stared at her, tears fresh on his cheeks. "Tom is dead," he whispered. He nodded toward the blade. "The beast who killed him. This is yours...for the son you carry."

Tim threw Tyler off, launching to his feet. He swept the antique lanterns off the mantle. They shattered on the floor, sending up a shower of glass. He picked up a chair and chucked it into the floor-to-ceiling mirror.

Alyssa flipped over the back of the couch and ran. Warriors streamed into the room, parting for her, then closing ranks between Alyssa and hell itself. The women at the stairs were less accommodating. More than once, she had to shake off a hand grasping at her or push past the mass of bodies.

The sounds of destruction followed her. Furniture splintered. Glass shattered. Heavy objects fell. Tim screamed out his fury, again and again.

"Let him vent the madness," Tyler shouted. "Let him destroy the room. Get the women and trainees away."

Alyssa bolted into Tom's room and slammed the door, locking it behind her. She stumbled to the bed, shaking, sobbing, jumping every time Tim's anguished cries reached her.

The bed seemed too open, too exposed. She dragged a quilt from it and sank into the corner of the closet, pulling it around her, chilled.

* * * *

The snap of the lock brought Alyssa to a hazy half-awareness. She'd known they'd come in eventually.

The knocking had started within minutes of her locking herself into the room. Their pleas to open the door had gone unanswered. Finally, Sammi, Tyler's wife, had ordered them to give Alyssa time to compose herself.

"Alyssa?" Tonya called. "Where could she go?"

"Nowhere," Sammi answered. "We saw her come in here. She's here, somewhere."

"But, where?"

There was a moment of silence, and Alyssa allowed herself to slip closer to the sleep they'd interrupted.

"Oh, God," Sammi breathed.

The closet door opened, and the clothing overhead slid away. Alyssa turned her face from the light streaming in.

"Oh, God," Sammi repeated, touching a sore spot on Alyssa's hand.

She yanked it away with a whimper of pain, burying herself under the quilt more fully.

"Alyssa, honey... Come with me. You have to come with me."

"Go away." Her voice was rough in a combination of thirst and crying.

Sammi touched her cheek, and Alyssa shied away, choking on a sob.

"Get Tyler," the Lady Armen ordered.

"Sammi?" Tonya questioned.

"Get him, now."

Alyssa squeezed her eyes shut, seeking sleep. Whispers intruded on her respite.

Arms slid behind and beneath her, and she twisted, trying to escape them. The arms tightened, denying her. Alyssa cried out in fear and dismay as she collided with a male chest.

"Shhh," Tyler soothed her. "Let us help you."

She sank into the bed, shivering at the feeling of his hand smoothing her hair. Warm milk touched her lips, and Alyssa swallowed a mouthful of it. Heated, soft cloths bathed her face. Another trailed over the sore spot on her hand, and the injury throbbed. Alyssa sighed, nearly numb in exhaustion. Someone removed her Keds, then her socks.

"How is she?" Tim asked in a hoarse voice.

"Facing her own madness," Tyler replied.

Alyssa opened her eyes, staring at the cuts and bruises on Tim's hands in a detached sort of understanding. She wasn't capable of fear, of anger, or of pain. She wasn't even certain which of those she should feel. There was nothing. She was empty. Her eyes slid shut.

"We'll make her comfortable," Sammi promised.

* * * *

The house was quiet, dark, unnaturally still. Alyssa had no idea how late it was...or how early, but she had to move.

She pulled on a pair of black jeans and a black turtleneck over her jockey shorts and spaghetti-strap t-shirt. Black felt right. Widows should wear black. Shouldn't they?

The bathroom beckoned, and Alyssa headed in, relieving herself and washing her face. She stared at her reflection, noting the blotched cheeks and reddened eyes. Her hair caught her attention, the halo of mussed gold like a beacon on a dark night.

Memories of Tom flooded her mind. He'd noticed her hair first, buried his hands in it moments after he'd cleaned his blade on the beast who'd attacked her. He'd nuzzled his face in it as he made love to her, combed his fingers through it, fisted it in his hands.

Would Tom have given her a second look if it weren't for her hair? Would she be here now? Pregnant? Widowed? *Not even widowed. We never made it to the altar.* Trapped in a world full of madmen?

"Why did you leave me?" she whispered. "Why did you...notice me?"

Alyssa dragged the medicine cabinet open and pulled a pair of scissors from the first aid kit. She grasped handfuls of her hair and cut it off, dropping it to the floor around her bare feet. Her hands shook, and she swallowed hard, staring at the jagged mess left on her head. Alyssa shoved the scissors back into the kit, turning away from the mirror and trudging toward the kitchen.

She kept her gaze to the floor, all too aware that she didn't belong there. She was an interloper in this world, an imposter.

She wasn't really hungry, but common sense dictated that she had to eat something. It was routine. It was normal. She needed normal.

The few Warriors in the hallways cleared the way for her with gasps and muttered curses. Conversation died out as she entered the kitchen.

"Alyssa?" a woman's voice intoned.

She looked up, panning her gaze over the bulk of the Armens in the room, pausing only momentarily on Tim, then nodding to Kaitlyn, acknowledging that she was the one who'd spoken.

The *König* princess sat at the table with her Armen mate at her side. "What do you need, Alyssa?" she asked solemnly. "What is it you want?"

Her head spun. They'd actually asked. Kaitlyn was *König*. If Alyssa requested it... This woman could grant her nearly anything.

"Alyssa, do you understand—"

"Home," she pleaded.

"You are home," Tim growled.

Kaitlyn motioned to him, ordering silence. Alyssa didn't look at him, terrified of what she'd see if she met his eyes.

"I want to go home," she repeated in a stronger voice. "I can't stay here."

"We're your family," Tim protested.

Scott winced, shooting a pained look in his direction.

Alyssa shook her head, fighting back tears. She wasn't family. This was a lie, a mistake. She never should have agreed to it.

Kaitlyn sighed. "A month," she decided. "Stay here for a month. If you still feel this way—"

"I will."

"*If* you do, I'll petition my parents for you, personally. You have my vow that I will."

Alyssa stammered out her thanks, abandoning food for the oblivion of sleep.

Chapter Thirty-four

February 11, 2050

Corwyn scanned the barroom slowly, biting back a sigh of relief. It wasn't nearly as bad as he'd feared. It was a homey little place with an etched mahogany bar along the left wall and two pool tables at the far side. It was a nice family establishment. That meant he could report favorably to the Armens.

"See her yet?" his distant cousin, Daniel Hunter, asked.

A negative response was on the tip of his tongue when he spied a crop of startling blond hair. "I've got her."

"What now?"

By the tension in his voice, Corwyn could tell Daniel hoped he intended to throw Alyssa Bradley over his shoulder and carry her out while her hand-shorn hair bounced with each step.

The fact that Corwyn intended nothing of the sort was sure to send his cousin to the edges of *Blutjagd*, but this situation required kid gloves. Alyssa was a young bride, shattered and grieving the loss of her mate. She'd barely settled into Tom's home and met all his family when she'd found herself alone with strangers who wanted her to act the part of loving daughter.

As when Scott, Corwyn's brother-in-law, had returned to the Armen fold, force would be the wrong way to engender the family spirit. Alyssa had to accept the Warriors willingly. As it was, she kept the amulet out of fear. At *König*'s order and Hunter's agreement, she'd been allowed to return home to the life she'd known and the friends she'd left behind—*until it becomes necessary to change that situation.* There was no 'unless' about it; eventually, the decision would have to be reversed.

"Bear? What now?" Daniel repeated.

"Now...we have a beer."

They started toward an open table at the rear of the room, but their plans changed abruptly.

Two men, playing pool at the table nearer the bar, took stock of Alyssa, whispering between themselves and chuckling. Corwyn pushed his jacket back over his hip, preparing for a fight that simply. Whatever they were planning, it didn't look good, and young men like these rarely thought clearly with a few beers in them.

Alyssa reached for the empty bottle on the edge of their table, and the larger man moved. In a heartbeat, he had her by the arm. Her empty tray clattered to the floor as he dragged her to his chest. She gasped, pulling at his hold with a wide-eyed look of fear.

A flash of motion between the Warriors and their prey brought Corwyn up short, startled at *her* vault over the bar. The woman stood in his path, her back to him, short black hair with undertones of purple catching his eye. She was a Bohemian of sorts; graduated gold tribal hoops adorned her ears, a goddess hanging from the lowest on her left ear, and a woven belt decorated her black stretch jeans, adding color to the uniform white and black of a barmaid.

"Let her go," the woman growled.

She hardly seemed a threat to the two men. At roughly five feet two or three and a little over an even hundred pounds, the bartender couldn't possibly back up that order...he believed.

The punk scowled at her, and Corwyn reached out to move the well-intentioned woman out of his way. He had a duty to attend to, and it was a duty he'd be more than happy to carry out. His blood burned to teach the two barely-legal idiots the proper way to treat a lady.

The bartender moved like lightning. The baseball bat Corwyn hadn't realized she was holding came up into her opponent's arm, and he released Alyssa with a shout of pain.

The young widow pushed from him, ducking the second man's hands, and raced past her co-worker into Corwyn's arms.

He passed her off to Daniel with a grumbled, "At my back," turning back in time to see the bartender swing the bat into the second man's ribs. Corwyn winced at the crack of bones. While the first would only be bruised, the second wouldn't breathe without pain for several weeks.

She brought the weapon up in warning. "Not in my place," she informed them. "I suggest you leave, before the doctors who patch you up are called to County lockup."

They glowered at her, then at Corwyn, shambling down the next aisle over. She turned to watch them leave, her attention fixed on her foes until the door closed behind them, despite the cheers and shouts of encouragement some of the other patrons let loose.

"That's the way, Jessica!"

"You picked the wrong place, losers."

"That's why I come here, baby."

"You tell them, sister."

Jessica nodded to that last speaker, then turned on Corwyn, motioning to him with the bat. "You want to be next?"

He smiled, managing not to laugh outright at the threat. "Thank you. No."

"Then tell your friend to take his hands off the lady."

The edge of *Blutjagd* spiked behind him.

"Stand down, Daniel," Corwyn ordered calmly.

* * * *

Alyssa tried to force her mind to work. Ever since the *König* prince had passed her to the other Warrior, she'd had a problem in that department.

"You're safe now," he whispered again.

She closed her eyes, shivering in delight. How many times had Tom said that to her in their few weeks together? *Every time the nightmares started.*

"Are you okay?" His voice was rough in the promise of retribution.

She nodded, burying her face in his intoxicating scent.

His hand caressed the nearly-flat plane of her womb. "And the baby?"

Her breath caught at his tenderness, his hesitancy. "Fine," she managed.

The whisper of heat from his breath bathed her face, and she trembled in anticipation, though in anticipation of what she couldn't say.

Jessica's voice registered in her mind, but no meaning came assigned to the words. Corwyn's voice followed. Still, she nestled into the offered embrace.

"Then tell your friend to take his hands off the lady," Jessica barked.

Alyssa stiffened, and the Warrior holding her did likewise. His head turned toward the prince and her boss, and his muscles tightened down another notch.

"Stand down, Daniel."

She took a calming breath as Daniel Hunter relaxed, obeying Corwyn absolutely.

"Look, Ms—" Corwyn continued.

"I am giving you until the count of three to release her, or you're going to look worse than the two losers who just stumbled out of here."

"It's not what you think."

Corwyn was calm, which was more than Alyssa could say for anyone else in the room. Her heart was abruptly pounding, and she winced at the escalating scene.

"One."

Jessica didn't bluff. This was about to get ugly very quickly, considering both sides thought they were protecting her and neither would hesitate to do it with force.

"It's okay, Jessica. They're...uh...friends of the family." Alyssa extricated herself from Daniel's arms and smoothed her apron self-consciously. She tapped Corwyn's arm and rounded him when he turned to let her pass.

Jessica scanned each man in turn, seemingly weighing their threat level. Her gaze settled on Alyssa, and she smiled weakly. "You okay?"

"Fine," she lied. Alyssa's nerves were jumping from a combination of the shock of her attack and the disconcerting emotions Daniel unleashed in her.

Her boss's face announced clearly that she knew better. "We're light. Mel and I can handle it until closing. Go home." She raised a hand to still Alyssa's protest. "My dime. I said you'd be safe here, and I won't lose you after a week."

"I'll be back tomorrow," Alyssa promised, as much for the information of the Warriors at her back as for Jessica.

Jessica smiled. "You better be. Saturday is always our busiest, and this is the first Saturday night Tia has had off in three months. She'll throttle me if I try to play the 'I need just this one favor' routine on her."

"Well, you won't have to."

"And, you get some rest tonight."

"Deal."

Corwyn placed a hand on her shoulder. "Daniel will see you home," he stated in what sounded like an offer, but Alyssa guessed that it wasn't.

She turned to him, pleading silently for discretion and understanding. If he caused a scene, she'd lose her job. Jessica's love for Gi, Alyssa's grandmother, would only stretch so far. Of course, if Jessica perceived Alyssa as threatened, nothing Corwyn could do, even as *König*, would force Jessica to cut her loose.

But, he could still side with Armen against her. If he did that, there was no saying which way *König* would swing in the battle. God only knew what Tom's family would do then. Job or no job, Alyssa was afraid she would find herself carted back to Armen range against her will.

He touched her cheek, smiling warmly. "Those idiots interrupted me ordering a beer. I'll be along later."

"And you let them live?" she quipped. Alyssa bit her lower lip, nearly groaning at her stupidity in egging him on.

"Well, they might come back. I have high hopes," he joked in return.

Alyssa swallowed a sigh of relief, leaving her apron on the bar and following Daniel to the door. If Corwyn said it was nothing, it was nothing. If there was one thing she'd learned it was that Warriors didn't lie.

* * * *

Daniel followed Alyssa into her townhouse, instantly at home in the slightly-cramped comfort of the place.

"Not exactly a manor house, I know," she noted nervously.

"I hate the manor house," he replied without hesitation.

"Really?" She seemed surprised by that. "I did, too. Not yours, of course. I've never been to the Hunter manor."

"They're not much different." He'd been to the Armen and Maher manors. For the most part, manors were manors and cabins were cabins, regardless of range.

A row of leather-bound books on the shelves caught his eye, and Daniel ambled over to them. It was a force of habit, he knew. 'Leather-bound' was usually synonymous with 'important' in the Warrior world.

"Hardy Boys, Nancy Drew, Trixie Belden, The Bobsey Twins, and a bunch of classics," Alyssa offered. "Gi was a collector."

He smiled. "Now those are some books I wish I'd read more of."

Alyssa turned from the window, her brow furrowed. "Really?"

"Really. My uncle had an odd sense of humor. He gave me Brahm Stoker and Mary Shelley to read when I was about eight or nine. Said they were training manuals."

She snickered, then laughed outright. The color she'd been missing all evening seeped into her cheeks and lit her eyes. She was beautiful.

And, here I am, staring at her like a horny trainee. What in the gods' names is wrong with me?

Alyssa was a widow, newly pregnant with her dead husband's son. The hunger he felt was completely inappropriate.

"Can I get you anything?" she offered. "Since it seems that you're stuck here until Corwyn shows..."

"Anything you have handy will do."

Daniel turned back to the books, hiding his wince. If his throbbing cock was any indication, he wanted everything she had to offer.

Fih! Bear would kill me, if my father didn't get to me first. Then Tim and Jason Armen would finish any scrap of him that remained. Tyler Lord Armen wouldn't get within ten yards of his sorry hide while he still breathed. Alyssa Armen was the last woman on the face of the Earth he should consider bedding.

Alyssa Bradley. They never actually married. She's not really an Armen.

But, she was. She'd sealed printing with Tom. She carried the Warrior's son. She was an Armen, and they wouldn't hesitate to protect her with all they had.

With that in mind, he pulled a book off the shelves and turned to face Alyssa. He took the glass of Pepsi from her hand with a nod of thanks.

* * * *

They sat, side-by-side, each of them with a book in hand. Alyssa found it nearly impossible to concentrate on the words on the page. There was something disconcerting about sitting here with a Warrior.

She'd like to pretend it was fear she felt, but it wasn't. Daniel was comforting, a calming influence...and yet not.

Her body was reacting to frissions of sexual awareness. She tried to shake them off, arguing with herself that it was just biology talking, the crazy roller coaster of pregnancy hormones.

Daniel chuckled, bringing her back to reality.

Alyssa smiled at his expression of wonder. "What is it?" She slid to her left, nestling her head to his shoulder to read the page he was on. "Oh, yes. One of my favorites." It was a Hardy Boys first edition, signed by the author, light years away from Sherrilyn Kenyon's latest that she'd jokingly told him was a 'training manual.' "You know. They changed that scene in the second edition. It's a collector's item."

"What did they change?" His voice had gone rough.

She avoided looking at him, swallowing slowly. "They decided it was too rough...I mean, intense..." *Give it up and move on!* "for kids. They changed the location and—"

He shifted, giving her a better pillow of his shoulder. "And?"

Alyssa looked up at him, her breath catching at the intensity in his eyes, directed entirely at her.

"And?" he repeated.

"Made it...um..." *What were we talking about? The first edition!* "Less violent."

"Yeah. Makes sense." He looked back at the book, his eyes widening, clearing his throat. "Wonder where Bear is."

"Bear?"

"Corwyn. His blood mark is Kor, the strength of the bear. The story is that Kates' first word was 'Bear.' Close family has called him that ever since."

"You're close family to the *König*s?"

"Now that Kates has married Scott, all of the North American ranges are. Hunter Crossbearer-*König*'s line runs Cross range. *König* was founded by Talon Cross and Jayde...a Hunter. My father is Jayde's first cousin, and the current Lord *König* is—"

"A Maher," she remembered. She'd heard Tom call Kaitlyn 'a Maher tracker' more than once.

"Yes. He's the youngest brother of the current Lord Maher."

Alyssa suddenly realized how little she knew about the Warrior world. She straightened, contemplating that. Considering her situation, she should probably know more.

"Is something wrong?" Daniel asked.

"No. I..." *Chicken!* She forced a smile. "I guess marrying more houses in is going to be difficult."

"Not really. The Stone Vessels tour to meet the eligible Warriors from every house that isn't closely related to them. They'll just have to look to Europe for the next few generations. By the time they run out of houses, they'll be far enough removed from Hunter and Crossbearer to start over again." He hesitated. "Though, Jee willing, by then, the last beast will be dead, and we'll all be free."

Alyssa stared at him, at a loss for words. "You want the curse to end?" Tom had always talked about the glory of being a Warrior.

Daniel nodded, seemingly confused. "Of course. Who *wants* to fight beasts? No one sane."

Tom had. He'd loved everything about his life, from the thrill of the hunt and the rush of the kill to the power and respect he got for being a *Krieger der Nacht*.

"We do it for duty, because we're driven to, because the alternative is watching people hurting and dying...and hurting ourselves, because we know we can do something about it. We're given the gifts to make a difference, and we do. If we don't, who else can?"

It was a lovely description of their life, much nicer than Tom's had been. "But?"

"If I could kill the last beast tonight, I'd die doing it to free every Warrior in the world. Given the right woman, I'll have sons, and I'll train those sons to this life, but I don't want them to be cursed. I'd die to—" He choked. "Dear Ani, forgive me."

She shook her head in confusion. "I want to hear this. I want to hear everything."

"I shouldn't talk about Warriors falling in battle so lightly. You have my apologies."

Her face heated. She hadn't even considered Tom, while he'd been talking about Warriors dying, fighting beasts. It was if the entire world had been reduced to Daniel Hunter and herself. "No apologies needed," she managed in an even voice. "It's the Warrior world, the lives you lead."

He bowed his head slightly. "I got carried away."

This is your chance. "So did I." *Go on.* "I meant what I said. I want to learn everything. I didn't have much time with Tom. There's so much I don't know."

Daniel took a calming breath. "What do you want to start with?"

"My...my standing, I guess."

"You're a widow." He seemed to consider it. "Widows usually choose to stay with their husbands' families, but like any general protected, you have autonomy."

"I thought wives were..."

He shifted closer. "What?"

"I thought wives had to obey the Warriors of their house, to go wherever they ordered them to go."

"Only when it comes to your safety. You have to listen to any Warrior then, of your range or not. If your safety is compromised, the Warriors will do everything in our power to protect you, but you have to let us do that. As long as you're safe in this house, you cannot be forced to leave it."

"Then why was I held in Armen range for more than a month?"

Daniel shrugged, clearing his throat again. "I imagine they felt you were a danger to yourself and your child in your grief. If you weren't stable, they would have waited until you were to allow you to make choices for yourself."

Alyssa nodded. "I wasn't making good choices the first few days." For one thing, she would probably always have the faint scar on her hand from the smear of beast blood she hadn't had the sense of self-preservation to wash off. By the time Sammi had done it for her, it had eaten away her skin entirely.

He glanced at her hair, then away, but he didn't comment.

She smoothed down the spikes, swallowing a lump that would bring tears. "Yeah. That was one of them. It's growing back in." Not nearly fast enough for her tastes, though.

"Why did you—" He grimaced. "Never mind. I shouldn't ask such personal questions."

"It's okay." Alyssa stared at her hands, currently white-knuckling the book in her lap. "I wasn't thinking straight." She still wasn't. Putting it into words was difficult. No one had ever asked her why she'd done it. She'd never tried to explain it. "Tom noticed me because of my hair."

"And cutting it off meant what to you?"

The moments before she grabbed the scissors coursed through her mind. It was so complex, and yet it was deceptively simple. "A wish that I could change history." Alyssa met his questioning eyes. "I... I was wishing I'd never met him...or that he'd never noticed me. Anything that would have meant I wasn't where I was at that moment...how I was at that moment."

It took him only a moment to answer. "That seems perfectly sane to me."

Alyssa managed a shaky smile. "Does it?"

* * * *

How could she ask that? "Of course, it does. How long did you have with Tom?"

"Total? Or after we... We never actually married. We'd talked about coming here to do it, but...we only..." She faltered, her brow furrowing over her deep blue eyes.

"Sealed printing?" he supplied. Alyssa really didn't know much. It wasn't natural for a wife to know so little. "Both."

"We'd been married..."

"Sealed," he reminded her. For some reason, he found himself adamant, yet again, that there was a tremendous difference between the two. Tom hadn't married her, but that didn't make her any less his widow.

"Sealed, I mean. We'd been sealed for less than a month when he died."

Daniel tried desperately to hide his shock.

"He saved me about three weeks before we...sealed."

Dear Ani! And, he'd already saddled her with... "How far along were you when he died?"

Alyssa blushed deeply. "I was just before ovulation when we... At the time, having a baby right away didn't seem... Most Warriors do. Don't they?"

"Many of them," he forced out. "So, you hadn't even known for long."

She shook her head. "Only a week and a half or so."

Daniel tried to grasp the depth of her trauma. She'd only known her husband for a month and a half when he left her, alone and pregnant. How could the gods have allowed something so horrible?

Alyssa changed the subject again. "What does it mean to have autonomy? I mean, besides being allowed to stay here as long as I'm safe?"

Didn't Tom teach her anything outside the bedroom? That was one question he wouldn't ask her. "Autonomy means you make your own decisions."

"What kind of decisions?"

"Where you live and travel...and work, unless your safety is compromised." He felt his cheeks heating at the rest, all too aware of what it meant. "And your sexuality. You're a widow, not a daughter born of a house."

She stared at him, apparently lost again.

"Unlike a daughter of a house, you're free to choose lovers or another husband without interference of the house you married into...or were born into."

"I see," she replied cryptically. Alyssa seemed lost in contemplation. "So... I could remarry, like any other widow in the world?"

"Of course." Had someone told her she couldn't, or was this some misunderstanding?

Alyssa remained quiet for several minutes, and Daniel's nerves jangled in the certainty that something was very wrong. Why would she know so little? And, why was she so certain that she had no rights outside of what was specifically granted to her?

"I will answer all of your questions," he vowed. Daniel pulled out a pen and a pocket notebook, writing down his cell phone number. "You can call me any time, day or night. You... You have the right to know everything about our world. You've always had that right."

She took it, reading the number as if she couldn't believe what she held. "Thank you, Daniel. You don't have to do this."

"I do...and I want to. Someone should have done this long ago. Before you sealed with Tom, to be sure."

Her cheeks went scarlet. "Who?"

"I don't think I understand."

"Who, besides Tom, would tell me these things?"

His frustration spiked. "Tom *should* have, but barring that, his family should have—"

"But, I never met them before we sealed."

Daniel fought for clarity. "He never introduced you to his family?"

"After, of course. Tom made a point of moving me to the manor when he found out I was pregnant."

He was ordered to. Didn't she know that? Or, did she think she was protecting Tom somehow by glossing over that point? But, that wasn't the most startling thing. "You met his family for the first time the week before he died?"

Alyssa nodded, her expression pained. "More or less."

"What was his reason for that?" What Warrior didn't show off his mate? What one didn't impress family on her from the moment he started printing? *Tom Armen, apparently.*

"He was assigned pretty far out. It took us all night to reach the manor. I guess he didn't visit often."

Daniel forced his jaw shut. There was something very wrong here, but he wasn't sure what it was yet.

It had taken them all night to reach the *manor.* There were other cabins and houses that would have been closer, no matter where they were coming from. The ideal was to have a haven no further than every four hours by car.

Armen was a Warrior-rich range, much more so than either Cross or Maher was, even more rich in manpower than Hunter currently was, despite how low Hunter had been in the days before Corwyn Lord Hunter had taken control of the range. There had to have been another Warrior or three close enough to their location to introduce her to; Tom hadn't done that...until she was pregnant to him. It was almost as if he'd wanted to keep Alyssa isolated and ignorant, but there was no reason Daniel could fathom to do that.

Alyssa shot him a nervous look. "Something wrong?"

Yes! Hell, yes! "No. Nothing at all." He needed information...a lot more information.

A brisk knock brought his head around. It was Bear, and it was far too early.

Alyssa paused in getting to her feet, yawning widely.

"Let me," he offered.

She nodded, sinking back into the couch with a sigh of relief.

Daniel's mind worked fast. He'd won a measure of Alyssa's trust. Losing that now wasn't acceptable. "Would you like me to come here again...to discuss more of our laws?"

That seemed to wake her. Alyssa shot him a wary look, distancing herself on the couch.

Daniel couldn't help wondering why that would concern her. *No time. I'm losing her.* He affected a sheepish smile. "Actually... I'd also be interested in raiding your library a bit."

She smiled, then chuckled. "A lover of fine literature is always welcome. That was Gi's law of the house. It would be an affront to her not to live to that now."

"You're off on Sunday, right?"

Her smile disappeared.

Bear knocked again, less patient than the first time he had.

Damn this! I am running out of time and luck here. "I saw the bar's hours of operation posted in the window," he explained hurriedly.

Alyssa nodded, still grave. "I guess Sunday would be okay."

He headed for the door. "Five o'clock? I'll bring dinner."

"You don't have to," she assured him.

"Just take-out. It won't be gourmet. The Colonel good for you?"

She hesitated, then nodded.

"Night, Alyssa. Oh, don't forget to lock this behind me."

He didn't wait for her reply.

Bear shot him a look of annoyance, as he stepped outside. "Took you long enough."

"Yeah. You, too." Actually, he'd shown up too soon. Daniel would have seriously considered bargaining with the enemy for another hour to get to the bottom of Tom Armen.

"Is she—"

The door locked behind Daniel, and Corwyn stopped to listen.

"Off to bed," Daniel replied. *Alone.* Why did that bother him so much? He tried to argue that it bothered him because of the way she ended up alone. *How could the gods allow it?*

Bear's eyes narrowed. "Problem?" he inquired.

Daniel hesitated, rounding him and heading down the three steps to the street.

"Danny Boy, this better be good," he growled.

Daniel bristled at the reminder of his childhood nickname. "There's something wrong here, Bear. Something *very* wrong with this whole thing."

"Of course there is," Bear dismissed him. "Alyssa became a widow when she was barely a bri—"

"No!" He turned to face his cousin, barely controlling the need to vent *Blutjagd.* Daniel forced his voice to a conversational tone again. "There is something else. My gut tells me...something worse."

Bear shifted uncomfortably. "What else?"

"I don't know that yet. The facts just don't add up. I mean... They *seriously* don't add up."

"Maybe we better have a talk."

Daniel nodded. "Maybe we should."

Chapter Thirty-five

February 12, 2050

"Find out anything, Kates?" Corwyn asked.

"A lot, and not much of it makes sense," his twin replied.

That niggling sense of unease returned like a blow to the gut. "Hit me." *Why not? I feel like you already have.*

"Everything Daniel reported is accurate. It's spooky, Bear. I'm talking surreal."

"How so?" What Daniel had supplied looked bad enough. Corwyn had the sinking feeling that Kates' information wasn't going to make it any better.

"His gut feeling that it seemed as if Tom was isolating Alyssa?" She paused.

"Yes?"

"Well, I didn't phrase it that way, obviously. I asked how much time Alyssa spent with the family between when she was introduced to them and when Tom died. I...uh...made it seem I was trying to figure out if she'd never formed a bond with them or if her distance was grief-related."

"And they said?" he hinted.

"Tom was head over heels for her, that initial rush where a Warrior is endlessly horny."

"Yeah. I know it." *A little too well of late.*

"Or so they thought."

"You don't think so." He refrained from saying 'either' but only just. If there was one thing he didn't want to do it was lead the investigation into this mess with geared questions and comments.

"There are too many oversights to ignore. They wrote them off, but I can't.

"Tom didn't introduce Alyssa to his family until he was forced to. He monopolized her time once he did. She never formed a bond with them, because Tom was always whisking her away to their room.

"He didn't encourage her to embrace his family...and vice versa, as Warriors typically do. He didn't... He didn't tell stories about their printing. He didn't tell her stories about people sitting in the room with them. They rarely ate at the family table, even after he recovered. When they did, they were typically huddled together and off to some far corner of the house as soon as they'd finished eating.

"Alyssa always spoke to them in monosyllables. At least, she did after the first time she opened her mouth increased Tom's sanctions. They—"

"Wait," Corwyn interrupted her. "Back up, and run that one past me again. I don't think I understand what you're saying."

"Tom hadn't told his father that he'd left Armen range without permission, and without notifying Hunter that he was visiting their range, to pursue Alyssa. They found that delightful little truth out when Debra and Tim asked Alyssa where she'd lived before they printed."

Silence fell between them for a moment, as Kates let him digest that fact.

"You think Alyssa felt responsible for the beating Tom took for it?" It would certainly explain a lot about her reactions.

"I don't have a clue. I do, however, think that the trial scared the crap out of her."

"But, she didn't watch it."

Kates huffed and waited for him to catch up.

"But, she saw the aftermath," he finished.

"Yes. I saw her after Tom died. I watched her jumping at every shout, paling at every tense moment... Not that anyone did that to her, but... You know Warriors."

"Warriors snap," he agreed. "She was traumatized, Kates."

"I thought so, too, but they said she was like that before. They had been giving her time, letting her relax. They'd thought it was the reaction some saved have after an attack, a sort of post-traumatic. The problem was—"

"She was with them too short a time before Tom died to find out what really caused it," he surmised.

"Yes. I can't write all of this off, Bear. I can't. Tom was undeniably not acting like a normal Warrior."

"It doesn't add up," he agreed.

"Worse than you can know," Kates sighed.

His heart pounded in an adrenaline rush. "What else did you find out?"

"I spoke to Chad."

"He was with Tom when he died," Corwyn recalled. "How is he?" Losing a Warrior you were hunting with was shattering, nearly as bad for a Warrior as losing a protected or an innocent victim was.

"Yes, he was. Better but still shaky, and..." She groaned, whispering her thanks through the covered receiver, probably to Scott for rubbing her shoulders or back. Her hand moved away and she started talking again. "Chad says Tom was off his game the night he died."

"Worse than usual, considering he's dead," he grumbled.

"Much. Tom was all nerves, sloppy. He gave the beast his back."

Silence fell between them again. Corwyn found it hard to speak in light of that revelation. "You think he wanted to die." *So much for not leading anyone to conclusions.*

"Hell, yes! I do think it. Now, you tell me why he would. I don't think a Warrior could or would fake printing. By all accounts, Tom doted on Alyssa. He had a son on the way. It must have been like the Christian Heaven to him. Why the hell would he want to die?"

"Good question."

"Think you can get an answer to it from Alyssa?"

Corwyn considered the young widow's nearly-tangible fear of him. "Not me, but maybe someone else can."

"What's up, Bear?"

"If it pans out, I'll let you know."

Corwyn hung up, then went in search of Daniel. He found his cousin pouring over *The Stone's Words.*

"What are you doing?" he asked. That was a basic text, the sort of thing a trainee would be reading.

Daniel sighed. "Looking for something I'm never going to find."

Corwyn leaned against the doorframe. "For instance?"

"What the hell Tom Armen was thinking."

He smiled. "Great minds think alike, I see. How interesting that we're on the same wavelength."

Daniel didn't look up from the book. "Then you agree that something is wrong here?"

"Yes. And I have to ask you something."

He looked up, seemingly still lost in the book. "What?"

Corwyn ambled across the room and settled on the couch across from him. "How did it go last night?"

"Fine. Alyssa's responses are off, but I told you that. She's great, otherwise. She's friendly, a little lonely. Confused sometimes, but surprisingly together, all things considered. I...like her." That seemed to disconcert him.

"I want you to see her again."

Daniel blushed deeply.

"I'm not asking you to spy on her or anything dishonorable like that," Corwyn hastened to assure him.

"It's not that, Bear." He looked away toward the window, his hand fisting on the edge of the book.

"Then what is it?"

"I'm already seeing her again. Tomorrow evening, to be precise." Daniel glanced at him out of the corner of his eye.

Corwyn fought back shock. "Why?"

"We share...an interest in books."

"Books?"

Daniel nodded, sheepish. "Fine literature."

Corwyn smiled. "I never knew that about you."

He scowled. "Can it, Bear. Tell me what you have in mind."

Chapter Thirty-six

February 13, 2050

"So... Tell me about Tom."

The question came from nowhere. Alyssa froze, berating herself yet again for telling Daniel anything that might undermine her rights.

She'd asked him about herself the other night, but she hadn't asked about the baby. She had autonomy, but she'd heard Warriors didn't have that until they were sixteen. Even then, it wouldn't be full autonomy. Warriors weren't allowed to choose where they lived and traveled. Tom said a Warrior belonged to his family, that he was, more or less, a piece of equipment, and that ownership started at birth.

At the moment, Tim Armen was being kind, for whatever reason. What if he wasn't being kind anymore? Could he take the baby from her? Could he demand his grandson live in Armen range, with or without his mother?

"Alyssa? Are you all right?"

"Fine," she lied.

"You're trembling." His hands covered hers.

She pulled away and rose, striding to the coat rack. Alyssa pulled Gi's old sweater coat on and held the collar to her cheeks.

"Alyssa?" He was a few feet behind her. "Are you all right?"

"Just cold." It seemed she was full of lies tonight.

Far from rebuffing him, the complaint shot Daniel to her side. He pressed a hand to her forehead. "Are you sick?"

Alyssa shook it off. "No. Just a chill."

His eyes narrowed. "No."

She stared at him, barely breathing. "No what?"

"You're not cold. Your hands are warm. What did I say to upset you?"

Her mouth went dry. "Nothing. I..."

"What was it?" He waited patiently, his hands caressing hers.

"I don't...want to talk about Tom," she managed. That wasn't a lie. She'd talk about anything he wanted to, except Tom Armen.

"Why?" It wasn't a demand. He almost seemed to be pleading with her.

"I told you. You...you said you understood that I wish he'd never noticed me." With every breath she took some nights. Strange how she'd never lived in fear until the man who was supposed to take her fear away made her his own and then left her.

* * * *

Daniel cupped her cheek, his heart aching. "I do understand. You're not alone. Do you understand that? I'll protect you."

Alyssa looked up at him, pleading for something he couldn't comprehend, tears pooled on her lashes.

"Any threat," he whispered. "Just tell me what it is. Any...wrong or hurt. I'll fix it, if I can."

For a moment, he thought she was going to speak. Then she pulled away, wiping her eyes on the sweater cuffs, laughing nervously.

"I guess I'm more tired than I thought."

Daniel nodded, forcing his jaw to unclench. "You should sleep. If you don't mind, I'd like to borrow a book or two." At the very least, he'd get to see her when he returned them.

"Sure. Anything you want."

Not remotely. "Thanks, Alyssa." He didn't try to fake a smile for her. Daniel headed to the book he'd dropped in the living room.

"Daniel?" Her voice was tremulous.

His heart rhythm faltered. "Yes?"

She started to speak, stopped, then started again. "Do you like burgers?"

"Love them." But, what the hell was she talking about?

"I have tomorrow night off, too. I could cook some burgers. I'm not much of a cook, but simple things come out okay."

Daniel stood with the book in hand, noting her attack of nerves. "I'd like that." It was downright uncomfortable that he looked forward so much to it.

Alyssa nodded, relaxing slightly. "Until then?"

He took two steps, bringing him nearly body-to-body with her. As always when they were this close, the need to touch her was maddening. Daniel brushed a kiss onto her forehead. "Until then."

Her stunned look nearly brought him up short. He forced himself onward, reminding her to lock the door behind him on the way out.

Chapter Thirty-seven

February 23, 2050

Daniel itched to find a way to get Alyssa to talk to him about Tom. Every time he mentioned her dead husband's name, she closed herself off, so much so that he hesitated to bring the subject up, despite his promise to Bear.

Of course, he also burned to touch her. Every night she'd had off for more than a week and two afternoons, he'd sat with her, reading, talking about nothing important, eating a few meals.

He fought to focus on the page in front of him, a classic this time. Daniel's first few attempts at the 'classics' had led him to decide that the classics fell into two categories: those that he couldn't understand anyone considering classic and those he could. Nicholas Nickelby was definitely the former.

"Fantasy is one thing, but no offense..." he stated.

"Ridiculous," Alyssa agreed without looking up from her own book.

Daniel stared at her. "Why didn't you warn me?"

A smile curved her lips up. "You didn't ask my opinion."

He closed the novel and set it aside. "Fair enough. I'm asking."

Alyssa slipped a bookmark in her book, closed it and turned toward him, folding her left leg under her. "Okay. What do you like?"

He was hard in less than a heartbeat. With her lips so close to his own, the only thing his mind could identify that he'd like was to taste them.

Her smile faltered and her breathing quickened, but she didn't shy from him. Daniel held his ground, too caught up in the moment to care that what he wanted was wrong on so many levels.

Alyssa tipped her head to the right and closed the distance between them. Her lips parted for him, inviting him inside. Daniel accepted, stroking inside her mouth with increasing vigor. Her hand cupped him, and he groaned.

She pulled away, breaking the kiss. Her eyes opened slowly, and her gaze panned from his face to her hand in his lap. "Pregnancy hormones," she whispered in what sounded like an apology.

"I don't believe that." Daniel needed to believe there was more in that kiss than a biological drive for sex. Whatever her reason, she wanted him, and he wanted her. The only question was whether she was using him to hide from Tom...or to pretend he *was* Tom.

Her fingers trailed along his length, and he realized that he wasn't nearly as concerned with her reasons as he should have been.

"No. It's not," she admitted.

Daniel tipped her chin back up. "Then I'm going to kiss you again. All right?"

Her nod was cut short when he captured her mouth. They picked up roughly where they'd left off, mouths closely meshed, hands cupping heads closer, frantically seeking more. She stroked his cock purposefully, moaning into his mouth as he twitched against her hand.

He pulled Alyssa astride his lap, using his aching cock to return the favor. She broke off the kiss again, not stopping but riding hard on his length.

"Do you want me to touch you?" he asked.

Alyssa nodded, gasping out her agreement.

Daniel had only a momentary qualm about it. She had autonomy; he had autonomy. No one had the right to tell them not to follow through with this.

He stroked the rock-hard nipples through her blouse, swallowing a curse that she wasn't wearing a bra. She arched into his hands, filling his palms with her breasts, seemingly begging for more.

Screw it! As long as she wasn't stopping him, they were both going to enjoy themselves.

He silenced a niggling voice that argued that she might open up to him about Tom if she let him close in other ways. This wasn't for Bear or any other Warrior. This was between himself and Alyssa, and it wasn't about Tom Armen.

At least for me.

Shut up!

Daniel slid to the floor, laying her on the rug and following her down. He held himself up on his forearms, his cock pressed to her, watching in fascination as she writhed against him. She arched against him, and Daniel closed his mouth on her breast through the thin cotton of her blouse, pushing back on his knees to accomplish the task. Alyssa cried out harshly, though at the loss of his cock or the gain of his mouth, he couldn't say.

The shock of his trilling cell phone jangled his nerves. He pulled back, grumbling a series of curses. Daniel closed his eyes, his jaw tightening as the phone rang again.

Not now. Damn this! My curse can wait for an hour or two.

"You have to answer," Alyssa whispered.

No, I don't. But, he did have to, and they both knew it. Daniel pushed to his knees, fishing the phone out as it rang a third time. He flipped it open and pressed it to his ear. "Daniel here." He tried not to growl it, but that was a lost cause.

"Outside," Bear ordered. "Now."

He fought back *Blutjagd.* Bear had no right to...

"I don't suggest you try it. I imagine you'll need a few minutes. You have five."

"And then?" It wasn't quite a challenge, but it was close enough to make his meaning clear.

"Then you face a lot worse than a discussion with me."

"Yeah. Got it." *But there had better be a damned good reason for this.* Somehow, he suspected there wasn't one.

"The clock is ticking." Bear disconnected.

Daniel closed the phone and tucked it into his back pocket.

Alyssa slid back, her legs drawing up between them. "What is it?"

He opened his eyes, staring at her in misery. She took his breath away. Alyssa was mussed, thoroughly kissed, flushed. Her nipple was clearly visible through the damp fabric of her blouse.

"Daniel?" She smoothed her hair down self-consciously.

"Tes, you're beautiful." He traced his fingertip along her kiss-swollen lips.

"Something's wrong. Isn't it?"

"I have to go. Duty calls. Tell me I can come back another day?" His heart pounded in preparation for her refusal. The reminder that he was a Warrior was likely to make her turn from him completely. *There better be a good reason for this!*

She hesitated, then nodded.

Daniel leaned across her legs. "One more for the road?"

That kiss was slower, his solemn oath that he'd return. He pulled away, his gaze gravitating to the exposed nipple. Alyssa arched her back, and he dipped his head, laying a lick across it in parting.

He pushed to his feet, lifting her after him. Daniel held her to his body for a moment, seriously considering calling Bear's bluff. It had to be a bluff. He wasn't breaking any laws by sleeping with Alyssa.

That meant there was no way they could keep him from returning. "I'll be back soon," he vowed.

Alyssa nodded, watching him walk away as if something fascinated her. She was still standing there when he'd pulled on his weapons belt and jacket.

Daniel offered her a strained smile and headed out the door for his head-to-head with Bear.

His cousin didn't disappoint him; Bear leaned against the passenger door to his truck, his expression grim. He glanced at his watch, nodded, then started to round the vehicle. "Get in."

"My car—"

"We'll pick it up later."

Daniel ground his teeth in frustration, but he climbed in. They were a block away before he trusted himself to speak. "What the hell do you think you're doing, Bear?"

"Making sure you're thinking with the right head, so you continue to keep both of them."

His temper uncorked. "There is no law that says you—"

"On the floor, Daniel? You were...were... On the floor?"

He glared at Bear, noting his cousin's white-knuckled grip on the wheel in surprise that did nothing to reduce his fury.

"I saw the two of you getting up off the floor through the front window." He had the courtesy to look ashamed of that.

Okay... Maybe the floor was a bad choice. Alyssa does deserve better, and the baby... But, still. "I don't have to justify my actions to you. Not about this. I have autonomy. She has—"

"Alyssa is a widow. A Warrior's widow."

"They've remarried before, sometimes to other Warriors."

"Is that what you want?" Bear didn't give him time to answer. "Is that what *she* wants?"

"You think I've asked her to seal? Ani! I am not Tom Armen."

"Are you prepared to find out that she's not serious? Chances are, she's confused as hell right now, and she's going to decide this was a mistake later. Even if she falls for you, what are the odds that she'll let another Warrior seal after Tom? Are you prepared—"

"Of course, I am. Every Warrior has to be prepared for it. If I fall, and she doesn't, I'll go to the mad cabin and pay the price."

"That easy?" he taunted.

"Is it ever easy? Is it, Bear?"

"Fine. Consider the other alternatives for a minute."

"What alternatives?" Daniel snapped. "You really are stretching it."

"Am I? Well, then, let's stretch it all the way. What if Tom screwed her up completely? What if she commits to you and then gets her head straight and pulls on you after you've sealed?"

Daniel found it hard to breathe. He couldn't believe Alyssa would do it to him, and yet it was a chilling thought.

"What if..." Bear sighed.

"What?" Daniel managed weakly.

"What if Alyssa feels responsible for Tom's death? If they had an argument or something before he died, and that's what threw him?"

"I don't follow you."

"What if she believes she can get it right this time? That she has an obligation to?"

"Inserting me in Tom's place?" Hadn't he considered that?

Bear shrugged.

"Are..." Daniel could hardly force the words past his lips. "Are you ordering me to stand down?"

"You know I can't."

"Are you doing it anyway?"

"No. As much as I want to, I won't do that. Just watch your back and be sure you've thought it out before you go there with her."

Daniel nodded.

"One more thing," Bear added.

"Yeah?"

"Be gentle with her."

"I would never—"

"I'm serious. You said it. Something went wrong between Tom and Alyssa. We don't even know what went wrong, which makes this a minefield."

"Whatever it was, I cannot believe it was Alyssa's fault."

"Probably not, but she's still explosive. If you hurt her, even accidentally cause her more pain and grief, three houses are going to land on you."

"No pressure, though," Daniel quipped.

Bear chuckled. "None at all."

"Out of curiosity..."

"You want to know how I knew you and Alyssa were...intimate?"

"It crossed my mind." Actually, it was eating him alive.

"I got a phone call."

Someone was spying on them? "From?"

Corwyn smiled and raised an eyebrow.

"Your *mother*? No fucking way! Why would the Stone interfere in this?"

"It doesn't interfere, but it does thrust situations it finds noteworthy on her."

"So, what is it saying?"

Bear's smile disappeared. "Nothing. It's not committing to a damned thing."

Daniel groaned. "You are shitting me. Right?" It was always bad news when the Stone withdrew.

"I wish I was...about the Stone. As for my mother... Let's put it this way. She said to tell you that she considered taking a blade to you herself for the thought about using sex to crack the mystery of Tom."

He winced. "It didn't last long," he admitted.

"She was impressed at your ultimate determination on the subject. Good thing for you. She'd have left some decent scars."

"She heard all of that, but she doesn't know a damned thing useful?"

Bear sighed. "The Stone loves Her jokes and riddles. What's funny this time?"

"Ha. Ha. Ha."

* * * *

Alyssa stood, staring at the empty entryway for several minutes, her body and mind rioting. She lurched toward the door, locking the chain with numb fingers.

Gi's hat mirror caught her attention, and Alyssa gasped. Her lips were swollen and sensitive, her face flushed and her blouse rumpled. It was also nearly-transparent, at least where Daniel had sucked through the fabric, her nipple rubbing the damp cotton as if seeking his mouth again.

She feathered her thumb across it, her vaginal muscles clenching in arousal. Every nerve was alive and aware of him, even after he'd left her. It would be a long evening with the battery operated boyfriend now, and she hadn't resorted to that in a long, long time.

Alyssa sobered. It was all too easy to remember the last time she'd resorted to it. The three days between when Tom Armen had saved her and when he'd shown up on her doorstep, intent on making good on his vow to make her his wife, had marked the last time she'd used the jelly vibrator...and the last time she'd felt the need to.

I should have turned him away when he came here.

But, she hadn't. Whatever else Tom Armen was, he was the best lay she'd ever had. Not that she'd had many to compare him to.

Not to mention, there was something captivating about a man who announces he's going to make you his bride on the first kiss. It was all too easy to imagine Tom getting into her house somehow and convincing her, if she did turn him away. He'd known no boundaries in pursuing her.

He'd seduced her within hours of killing the beast that had attacked her, claiming first his concern with her well-being, plying her with fine wine and taking her back to her room. His kiss, coupled with the tales of his sexual needs and hungers, had played at her wine-soaked mind and made her head spin. Before she knew it, Alyssa had been bent over a hotel chair with Tom's cock working her hard...in the chair, on the balcony, in the bed.

In the morning, he'd calmly stated again what he'd vowed the night before: he'd do anything he had to do to make Alyssa his. She'd found it disconcerting, and it had been something of a relief that he'd left when she'd asked him to. Returning home had rarely felt so soothing.

But, Tom hadn't stopped there. He'd followed her, he claimed, without permission of his family to leave his own range and enter Hunter. Tom had described Warriors as nearly-feral when taking a mate; he'd stated that the other Warriors would expect nothing less of him. Then he'd made his needs clear to her—his need to have her as his lover, wife, and the mother of his sons.

The combination of lingering arousal and the passion of his pursuit had led her to agree to let him into her life. She hadn't made it to work that day...or for three days after. When Alyssa was fired, Tom had convinced her to go back to Armen with him. A little over two weeks and a sensual haze later, he'd managed to convince her.

She didn't actually remember agreeing to allow him to seal printing. Alyssa imagined that it happened in the heat of the moment. Her only clear memories of the event came down to Tom's pleading with her to save his sanity and his—*bliss, relief, gratitude?*—at the moment it was done.

Though it had been a frightening concept that the only way out of their union would be killing Tom, it hadn't been an awful place to be. He'd still been loving, attentive, committed to keeping her mired in pleasure...until she got pregnant.

At that point, Tom had become restive. Alyssa had assumed he was simply settling into the changes her pregnancy had forced on them: the move to the manor house, introducing her to his family, and settling into hunting with other Warriors again when he'd been solitary for so long.

Added to that had been the tension between them over her grandmother's house. Tom had been incredibly insecure; he'd seen her refusal to part with her home as an indication that she'd leave him someday. Considering the consequences to him if she chose that, Alyssa understood his fear.

More than once, she'd wondered if his upset with her had caused his inattention. No one had ever accused it, but everyone agreed that Tom had made a mistake he never should have made.

And, I'm playing with that fire again?

But she wasn't. Daniel wasn't Tom. He hadn't touched her until she'd touched him, though he'd clearly wanted to. He hadn't stated his need to make her his mate. He'd requested to kiss her, to touch her, to make love to her. Tom hadn't been a fan of requesting anything. He'd been printing; he'd *needed*, not wanted.

Alyssa had heard about Warriors' sexual appetites. They had sex often, with just about any willing, adult woman that crossed their paths. They met them in barrooms, loved them, and left them quickly.

How appropriate.

She deserved a little fun, and there was no reason not to get it, with Daniel or any other Warrior who appealed to her. Maybe she'd become one of their blade chasers.

Her heart stuttered at the thought of Warriors parading through her bed. Maybe not a blade chaser, but if Daniel showed up again, she wasn't going to balk at a flesh and blood cock taking the place of her vibrator.

Chapter Thirty-eight

February 26, 2050

Alyssa turned at the sound of a brisk knock at her door, crossed the room, and checked the peep hole. Her heart pounded at the sight of Daniel Hunter, memories of his hands and mouth making her weak-kneed. She unlocked the door and pulled it open.

He held up a bag from The Book Swap, a local used book store that Gi had frequented, bulging with books. He met her eyes, looking sheepish. "I thought we might discuss some fine literature."

The urge to laugh bubbled up, followed by another urge. Alyssa wrapped her hand over his shoulder and rose up on her toes, silencing Daniel with a brush of her lips over his. For a moment, he stared at her, his eyes so hungry she felt her stomach flutter nervously.

"May I come in?" he asked.

Her stomach gave another twinge as Daniel guided her inside, only then realizing that she'd nodded in answer to his question. He swung the door shut, dropped the books on the foyer table and locked the door without looking at it.

"I shouldn't do this," he whispered, his hand cupping her jawline and tipping her head up. "Ani knows I want to, but I shouldn't." His lips closed on hers.

Alyssa didn't argue that. She didn't ask what he meant, but her gut told her he was wrong. Neither of them had any reason not to do this, and despite his comment, he wasn't leaving.

By the time they came up for air, they were at the foot of the stairs. Her entire body was alive in sensation, more alive than she'd ever felt.

"Are you thinking of Tom?"

She couldn't follow the logic of that question fully. "No. I'm not." It wasn't a lie. The furthest thing from her mind was Tom Armen.

Daniel scooped her up in his arms, then hesitated. "If you don't want this..."

"I do."

The stairs fell behind them in a whirlwind of motion. Alyssa gasped as he deposited her in the middle of her bed, as gentle as blown glass on a pillow. The anticipated press of his body didn't come.

She opened her eyes, watching breathlessly as one shirt button after another slid open behind his nimble fingers. Then both layers of black glided off over his shoulders, skimmed down his side and dropped to the floor. The sudden realization that she was straining to follow the shirts' progress sent her gaze back to his chest.

God, he's beautiful.

Daniel's chest was broader than Tom's had been, smooth save the thin T of curls, nearly devoid of scars.

"Alyssa?"

She untied her short robe and slid it off her shoulders. Her nightshirt followed, and she tossed them both off the bed, focusing on Daniel again.

He hadn't wasted the time. His running shoes had been kicked away, and he pulled his socks and jeans off his feet together, the twin weapons hooked directly to a mundane belt sliding with them.

Her eyes locked on the thick length of his cock straining up in readiness. The empty ache took up the cadence of her heart, and she arched her back clumsily, offering herself to him.

Daniel groaned, sinking to the bed beside her, but the urgency didn't materialize. His mouth parted hers slowly, his hands tracing her curves like a blind man reading Braille. Her body obliged him; her tightening nipples, rising goose bumps, and slick core giving him plenty to explore. And he did, until she thought she might explode from his hands alone.

Alyssa stroked his length, trying desperately to entice Daniel inside. Still, he denied her. She ripped her mouth from his and slid further down his body, guiding the head of his cock inside...then further as he moaned softly, ruffling her hair.

Her muscles gripped him, her numb confusion about whether he was much larger than Tom or she was simply out of practice washed away by waves of delight as he turned her beneath him and surged inside. For a moment, he lay still, probably allowing her time to adjust. Alyssa had heard of men doing it, though she didn't really understand why they would. Her body was screaming for more.

"Daniel." She begged him with that one word for what she wanted.

He shivered at something she couldn't name. "Are you ready for me?" His voice was rough, sending tremors of sexual energy through her.

Alyssa nodded frantically.

His hips slid back, then forward...again and again, forcing her to climax that quickly. Her scream of pleasure had him groaning, his hands gripping low on her hips, his cock working her tirelessly until her lessening climax ignited a second time.

"Dobler help me," he pleaded, as she pulled at his buttocks, forcing him deeper. "Again. Let me feel it again."

She started stuttering out her denial. She'd never come twice with Tom. How could she a third time?

Daniel's control seemed to shatter; his hips thrust hard and fast, and she bowed with a howl, as he brought her over again.

"Oh, yes," he growled, his come pumping in time with her renewed contractions.

They lay together in a comfortable silence, Daniel's body wrapped around hers, his sweat-slicked chest a delicious assurance that he wasn't a dream. Alyssa wrapped her arms around him, closing her eyes to the whisper of his beating heart.

* * * *

Daniel chuckled at her even breathing, turning gingerly to remove his weight from her. Alyssa followed, her body conforming to the lines of his, her hand laid across his lower abdomen, her little finger teasing at the nest of curls and firing his cock to life again. It brushed over the soft skin of her hand as if seeking more of her, any of her it could reach.

He took a deep breath, arguing his way out of the urge to wake her. He examined her pale face and lush body. She was so responsive, beautiful, intelligent... She was everything a man could want in a woman.

A spike of jealousy took arousal's place. Gods, what he wouldn't do to have the months with her that Tom had!

Tom... Anger flashed out, shoving jealousy aside. Tom had always been sloppy, but this went beyond any stupidity he'd shown before. The fool had every Warriors' dream life: the trust and love of a passionate wife, a son on the way... And, he'd thrown it all away in one of his signature moments of inattention. Worse, he'd left Alyssa in a new and frightening world, carrying a child, a widow when she should have been protected and loved by a responsible husband.

Alyssa shifted against him, murmuring Daniel's name in her sleep. He stroked her cheek, the need to be the one who protected and loved her rising up as it had every time he'd touched her, from that first night in El Oso Oro on.

Daniel ground his teeth in frustration. Was it possible that she would allow such a thing after losing Tom as she had?

Facts poured into his mind, bringing confusion with them. Alyssa never called for Tom, even unconsciously. She never mentioned her dead husband. It wasn't simply that she didn't want to talk about him. It seemed she rarely thought about him at all, even when faced intimately with another Warrior less than three months after his death.

"Why?" he whispered. Daniel had no doubt that the fault wasn't Alyssa's, but why wouldn't she think of him?

Had Tom been sloppy and inattentive in other areas of their lives together?

I can't, Daniel. I've never... Never more than once...

Daniel shivered in renewed arousal. He'd nearly come from that pronouncement alone. Tom had been her first, but Daniel had given her an experience she'd never had with her husband.

"Now, I just have to prove that I'm better for you in other ways."

And, I have to find out what went wrong with Tom.

Chapter Thirty-nine

March 17, 2050

Alyssa sighed at the feeling of Daniel's lips against her neck, tipping her head to the side as he trailed them toward her shoulder blade. His hands traced the lines of her body, making her knees tremble in a sudden weakness. She closed her eyes, drinking in his gentle touch.

"Tell me about Tom," he whispered.

Those words were like ice water in her veins.

Daniel raised his head, his muscles tensing. "Alyssa, please. I have to know."

"Know what?" she managed.

"What went wrong between you? I know something did."

She forced herself not to shudder, though she did tremble. "What do you mean?" Was he going to accuse that the stress of her refusal to give up this house had caused it, after all? *Please, God. Not that. I don't think I can stand it.*

"Why don't you talk about him?"

He'd tried several times. Never this directly since the first time, before they'd made love, but he'd tried to get her to talk about Tom.

"The memories aren't that great," she offered in half-truth. "And...there isn't much, is there? Just a few weeks."

"I guessed that. Why do you tremble every time I bring him up?"

Alyssa pulled from Daniel's arms, turning to face him, her back to the sink. Her heart beat double-time.

His eyes narrowed, and he cocked his head. "You're honestly afraid of him."

"No." On some level, she knew she was lying.

"Then you're afraid of me."

"No!" Oh, but he was even more dangerous to her in some ways.

Daniel reached out to pull her into his arms; Alyssa hesitated for a moment but let him. Part of her argued that it was stupid to get this close to someone who had the power to destroy her. Another part argued that a man so tender could never destroy her.

But, their laws... She wished she knew what those laws said. What little she did know would damn her in ways she could only imagine in nightmares. Alyssa didn't know the precise wording, but it was something about hunting: poaching a Warrior...or maybe baiting one? A woman who made promises she might break was against their laws. She knew that. Since she knew her entire marriage to Tom had been a sham, had she been poaching? *Baiting?*

"Is it me or all Warriors?" he asked.

Maybe this was her chance. "You're not exactly stable men," she reasoned. "That's why your punishments are so harsh."

"You've seen unstable Warriors." He seemed to consider that, repeating it under his breath a second time.

"Of...of course. I mean, all Warriors are—"

"No. We're not. Not all of us. Not nearly all of us. Was Tom unstable?"

"Tom was..." She swallowed a lump. "He was a Warrior," she offered weakly.

Daniel eased away, staring down at her in confusion. "I don't know what that means to you."

"Your needs... You don't just want things like...like children. You need them."

His gaze went to the rounding landscape of her womb, his breathing going ragged. "My gods, what did he do?"

Her face heated at his assumption. "He just explained his needs to me."

"No. It's not like that, Alyssa."

"But, you go crazy if—"

"No," he thundered.

Alyssa jerked away two steps.

Daniel winced, motioning for peace. "I'm sorry. It's just... This isn't your fault."

"What isn't?" she breathed, avoiding his offered hand, wary though she hated herself for the reaction.

"Tom told you he'd go mad, if you didn't give him a son?" His words were slow and measured, as if he had tenuous control of himself.

Alyssa nodded, backing off another step in case he lost that control, her heart pounding so hard she felt faint.

Daniel ambled to a chair at the table and dropped into it, his expression passing from pain to anger to misery over and over. He glanced at her, settling on worry. "Sit down, Alyssa," he invited.

She hesitated, anticipating the calm before the explosion.

"Please. You have nothing to fear from me." He motioned to the seat across from him, indicating that she could have all the space she felt necessary.

Alyssa settled into the chair, bracing her hands on the edges. "Tom...did something wrong," she guessed. "Something worse than being out of contact and leaving Armen range to see me again."

"Wrong? Criminal is more like it."

Her head spun. Alyssa buried her face in her hands. *Criminal? What other laws had he broken? What would they have done to him if they'd known it?*

She vaguely noted water running in the refrigerator dispenser. A cold glass brushed her hand.

"Drink this. It will help."

The icy water revived her, though she still felt numb inside. There were so many questions she should ask, and she couldn't find the words to ask a single one.

Daniel squatted next to her, brushing the hair from her forehead tenderly. It was so at odds with what she knew of Warriors that it seemed all the more soothing for the novelty.

"If the other Warriors had known, his punishment would have been harsh." He traced the line of her ear, then her jaw. "He might have been killed for it. I won't lie to you. This isn't a little thing we're talking about."

"Killed?" she murmured. It hardly seemed possible that he could have done something that warranted that.

"Do you want this child?"

"Want?" Daniel wasn't making sense. "Of course, I do." It was the only good thing to come of her marriage to Tom.

He drew her toward him, kneeling up so she nestled to his bare chest. "Be sure. Don't just say it. Our laws say we may not create life without our mates' permission to do it."

"He had permission."

"Which he lied to get. Tom convinced you. He was dishonorable. If you don't want the baby, our laws will allow you to terminate. It's not right to force you to this."

Alyssa sat back, her hand laid on his chest, her thoughts and emotions in a riot. "All because he lied?"

Daniel covered her hand with his own, nodding. "A woman's choice is paramount in every move a Warrior makes. It's essential to our laws. We can't create life without her permission, freely given, and lying to get it means the permission wasn't freely given. Nor is convincing her to it allowed. She isn't free, if she's coerced."

She tried to digest that revelation, while Daniel continued.

"We can't seal printing without her free consent to it. We can't even—"

Daniel choked, staring at her in apparent horror. Too late, Alyssa realized that her shock must have told him more than she'd wanted to.

"Gods, no," he pleaded.

She looked away, tears pooling in her eyes.

"He convinced you to let him seal?"

Alyssa didn't answer. Though his reaction indicated that she was safe, there was no way to know for certain.

"He rushed you to it." That wasn't a question.

Refusing to answer was easier.

"Did he convince you to bed, as well?" Daniel growled.

She found it impossible to meet his eyes. A knot of tears rose in her throat, and she fought for breath.

"Jee, how could you allow this?"

Alyssa sobbed. The blame was going to fall on her, after all. "I th-thought..." she stammered.

Daniel pulled her into his lap, rocking her against his chest. His voice cracked. "Understand this. What Tom did was beneath contempt, Alyssa. He would have been killed for it. There is no question of that.

"A warrior who cannot control his curse is no better than a beast. A warrior may not take an unwilling woman, even if she is the woman of an enemy or an enemy herself. Neither shall a warrior use his whiles to sway an unwilling woman to some form of willingness to bed her. Such a move is dishonorable in that it exploits her innocence and does her injustice.

"That's what the rules of sanction say. No better than a beast, and if he were here, any Warrior would kill him as a beast for this."

She wrapped her arms around his neck, nodding in relief.

"Tell me. You have to tell me everything. After that, we'll call Corwyn."

She shook her head. "No. He'll...he'll..." Alyssa didn't know what he'd do, and she didn't want to find out.

"He'll protect you as you *should* have been protected in our world."

"Promise me. I don't know much, but I know you're supposed to keep your vows."

"I'll take a blood oath on it, if you want me to. Bear will protect your rights, and so will I." His eyes widened. "Tell me when he's here."

"I don't—"

"I will not make you do this twice."

"All...all right."

"You'll tell us?" he asked.

"Yes. I'll tell you."

* * * *

Daniel resisted the urge to pace the floor. Alyssa's nerves were strung tight enough; he wouldn't make it worse if he could help it.

When the knock came at the door, he didn't jump up. Instead, he kissed Alyssa's hair and rose slowly, padding to it on bare feet.

Bear looked grim, more serious than Daniel had seen him in months, hunting or playing. "She's told you?"

"Enough. I waited for you to get the full story. I...don't want to make her do this twice. Not for me."

"Good choice. May I?"

Daniel waved him in, locking the door behind them.

Alyssa's eyes darted from Bear to the kitchen, and she looked ready to bolt.

Daniel returned to her side, drawing her to his chest and offering the comfort of his arms. "I told you. You have nothing to fear from us. You should *never* have had to fear Warriors."

Bear's eyebrows rose at that. "Fear? Who did you fear?"

Alyssa took a deep breath and began calmly. "Tim Ar—"

"No," Daniel interrupted her. "Start at the beginning. Start with Tom."

"But, I didn't—" She halted, swallowing hard. "I guess I did, at first. Warriors aren't... But, that's not true of all of you, is it?"

Bear looked to Daniel in confusion. "Aren't what?"

Daniel forced the words out through gritted teeth. "Stable men."

His cousin settled into the easy chair, leaning forward, his elbows on his knees. "Go on. Tom saved you."

Daniel grimaced at the false calm Bear was offering. He was simmering beneath the surface, his *Blutjagd* burning lightly.

Alyssa took a calming breath. "He escorted me back to my hotel. Said I shouldn't be alone while I was so upset. On the way, we stopped for drinks. I probably drank too much, but when you've just been attacked by a mythical creature..." She darkened considerably.

"Perfectly reasonable choice, actually," Bear inserted. "Scott drank half a bottle of Beam after his first beast."

"Ouch," Daniel commented, visualizing a hung-over Warrior. It wasn't a pretty visualization.

"Anyway," she hedged. "He took me to my room and..."

"You had sex," Bear interjected, probably hoping to save her embarrassment.

"Slow down, Bear," Daniel requested. "You forgot a step."

His cousin shot him a look of confusion that melted into horror.

Daniel nodded once. "Tell us, Alyssa."

"He started touching my hair, leaning close to me, telling me about your...drives."

"What about our drives?" Bear asked, red-faced.

"How you need sex to stay sane and—"

Bear shot to his feet, and Alyssa pulled her legs up, all but vaulting from Daniel's arms. Daniel shot a look that he hoped promised death at him, soothing her. Dear Ani, didn't Bear have more sense than that?

Bear stared at her, his fists unclenching. "She really fears us, doesn't she?"

"Acutely."

"My apologies," Bear stated, regaining his calm. It seemed he was too disconcerted to maintain a *Blutjagd* anymore.

"Do you want me to do this alone and give you the highlights?" Daniel offered. "If you're going to do that every time she—"

"There's more? Like that, I mean?"

Daniel nodded. Alyssa sank further into his embrace, holding her breath.

Bear dropped into the chair again, shaking his head. "No. I better hear this from the source."

"Go on," Daniel instructed.

Alyssa didn't relax her position. "He started to kiss me, and..." Her brow furrowed. "And he kept saying I was made to be his mate. I thought it was an inventive come-on line, and it worked."

"So, he asked you to...go to bed with him?" Bear asked delicately.

"No. It just sort of happened. We were kissing and then we were... Well, you know what I mean."

Bear met Daniel's eyes. "And you were drunk. Tom got you drunk first?"

"Yes."

Bear didn't need to state the obvious. Tom had convinced her to willingness. "Go on."

"I woke up in the morning: hung-over, aching, and—"

"Aching?" they asked together.

A lover must always be treated kindly and with respect. What did Tom do?

"He... He was rather vigorous, much more than I was used to at the time." She cleared her throat. "Tom was still there, and he was still telling me that he'd do anything to make me his bride."

Bear winced. "He told you that you would be? He didn't ask you to be?"

"Not then. He was adamant that it was going to happen, though he conceded that it wouldn't be that day."

"Why did he concede?"

"It may have had something to do with me telling him to leave. He... It's safe to say that he made me really uncomfortable. It just sounded..."

"Insane?" Bear offered.

"Yes. Insane. So, I asked him to leave. He scowled, but he left."

Daniel couldn't bear it; he had to say something or he'd lose his mind. "You told him to leave you alone? That you had no intention of sealing printing with him? And he pursued you further?"

She tipped her head back and nodded, her eyes pleading with him. "Three days later, he showed up here to—"

"Here? At this house?"

Bear motioned for him to calm down. "We already knew he came here," he reasoned.

"I know. I just..." *Hadn't realized he'd shared that bed with her?* Why the hell did that hurt so much? It shouldn't.

Alyssa shifted, looking toward Bear again. "He told me that he needed me, that having me would keep him sane and—"

"He wasn't sane then," Daniel grumbled.

Bear sighed. "Do you want *me* to do this and give *you* the highlights?" he asked pointedly.

"Hell, no."

"Then shut up. Go on, Alyssa."

"Well... Um... I admit I was unsure. The idea that he needed me to—"

Daniel's *Blutjagd* ignited and Bear shot him a look of warning.

"—stay sane bothered me on a lot of levels, but there was something sad and poignant about the situation. I told him we'd discuss it. I didn't want to dismiss him without giving him a chance to explain. It was so vital to him. I should... I felt I should at least hear him out."

"Did you?" Bear asked. "Did you discuss it?"

"No. We didn't."

"Why not?"

"Tom... He had a way of avoiding discussing it with me by seducing me. He was so good at it, I was fired for missing work."

Silence fell so completely that Alyssa's nervous wiggling was the loudest noise in the room.

Bear cleared his throat. "How long did Tom Armen spend in your home?"

"Three days. When I got fired, he convinced me to head off to the country with him for a few weeks."

"Convinced?" Daniel croaked.

"He...um...did have a way about him." She looked away, biting her lower lip.

Daniel pressed her cheek to his chest, offering the circle of his body as protection. "You have nothing to be ashamed of," he assured her. "I told you that we consider convincing a woman taking away her right to choose freely." He found he couldn't continue.

Bear steered the conversation back on course. "Tom took you to the cabin in Utah, and you sealed." His cousin's eyes narrowed as Daniel's *Blutjagd* spiked. "On second thought, tell me about the seal."

Alyssa fisted her hand against Daniel's chest. "I don't really remember it. I mean... I know when it happened, but I don't really..."

"Don't what, Alyssa?" Bear prodded her.

"Remember...agreeing to it."

Daniel fought back the urge to put his fists through something. This house meant too much to her to destroy it in anger, and he would show her self-control if it killed him. She'd had too little of that from Warriors so far.

"Did Tom ask you?" Bear continued, trying to dissect precisely what his crime had been.

"I imagine so. He asked every time. He pleaded with me, actually."

"Every time? Every time, what, Alyssa?"

"We... Every time we made love. We'd start and... He'd tell me how much he needed me to agree, how his sanity was only in check—"

Daniel tensed, and she snapped her eyes to him.

"For me," she gasped.

He loosened his grip, chastising himself for frightening her. Gods, but she'd never known a moment of sanity from Tom. Daniel pressed a kiss to her forehead. "Go on."

"He'd ask me to seal while we...we were..."

"Intimate," Daniel offered.

Alyssa nodded.

Bear rubbed at his forehead, no doubt suffering the same sort of tension headache building steam in

Daniel. "He'd ask you when you were aroused? While you were at the edges of climax?"

She paled.

"Gods, no," Daniel pleaded.

Bear cut in. "When he sealed, what do you remember about it?"

"It was like any other time...at first. He was whispering to me, and I came. The most incredible look came over him, and he came after me. He was so—"

Daniel snapped. "Can't you see, Bear?" he growled.

"Yes. I do."

"Dear Ani! She probably screamed out as she came, and he—"

"I know!" Bear looked completely rattled.

That settled Daniel. The last thing Alyssa needed was two furious Warriors. "Tell us. Please, Alyssa." He had to hear the rest.

"Tom told me that I'd agreed, that the biological tie had been forged between us."

Bear groaned. "He told you that you had no choice?"

She stammered for a moment, stopped, and began again. "Killing him? Oh, that's a wonderful choice."

Daniel was relieved to hear the sarcasm in her tone, though he disagreed with her determination. In Tom's case, killing him then would have been best for all involved.

"I did li—No, I did love him. I just wasn't ready to commit to something lifelong with him yet. But, killing him because I wasn't sure?"

Daniel stared at Bear, at a loss for words. Surprisingly, Daniel recovered first. "He offered to have his family kill him to play on your emotions?" *He probably handed her the phone to do it.*

"His family? No. He handed me his...sacred weapon and—"

"Dear Gods." His stomach lurched, threatening to empty.

"But, baiting... Do you call it baiting?"

"You were *not* baiting," Daniel started in, at the edges of control. "He actually accused you of—"

"Daniel," Bear warned. He sighed. "Now, Alyssa. You were not baiting. If Tom told you that you were, he lied to you. Did he tell you that?"

"He... No. He said something about making promises you don't intend to keep...or might not keep. It was more inferred, I guess."

"He probably did say it with that in mind. I can't fathom what he was thinking. But, you have to see how wrong it was of him to ask you to kill him, Alyssa. We'd never ask a woman to do that, especially not to her own lover."

Daniel sighed in gratitude that Bear hadn't called Tom her husband.

"I thought it was overly harsh, but your lives are harsh. Your punishments—"

"Are supposed to prevent things like this from happening." Bear visibly calmed himself. "If you'd have mentioned any of this to his family, they would have killed him without question. No wonder Tom was off his game. It must have been increasingly clear to him that he couldn't hide what he'd done in close proximity to his family."

Daniel contained the explosion, but he couldn't control the tremor in his voice. "Tom deserved to die. What reason could he possibly have to..." He choked, touching her womb tenderly, the answer all too clear to him.

"His son," Bear agreed solemnly. "It had to come down to a choice between Alyssa and his son."

She sobbed, burying her face in Daniel's chest. "After everything, he didn't choose me."

Daniel grumbled several harsh curses. He suspected that it had never been Alyssa and had always been about Tom's son, but he couldn't prove it.

But, more than that, it was better to remain silent and let Alyssa hold to whatever thin threads of trust remained that Tom had harbored kind feelings for her but loved his son more. She deserved to believe he'd loved her; she deserved that love.

In the meantime, there was something he had to ask, the choice Tom hadn't wanted her to have. "You still have the choice, Alyssa. Tom lied and schemed to get into your bed, to seal, and to plant his son."

Bear started to protest, but Daniel cut him off.

"It's not too late, if you want to terminate. Honor demands that we allow you to."

For a long moment, she didn't answer. To his surprise, Daniel found the thought of her choosing to abort painful, but he had told the truth. Honor and duty demanded he offer it in light of Tom's crimes.

"No," she whispered. "I don't want that. I want to keep my baby."

Daniel let out a breath he hadn't realized he'd been holding. "I'm glad."

Alyssa met his eyes, seemingly fascinated. "You are?"

"I am," he replied. "More than I can say."

Bear cleared his throat. "I can see how stressful this is for you, Alyssa. I do have to ask you about how your baby was conceived, about your life with

Tom...and about Tim Armen. After that, I'll let you rest."

Chapter Forty

April 1, 2050

Daniel chuckled, wrapping his arms around her. "Tease me much more, and we'll both be late to work," he vowed.

"Promises. Promises," she sighed but with a look that announced she wouldn't be sorry in the least to be late.

He kissed her, testing her resolve. As he guessed, Alyssa didn't draw away and protest the lack of time.

Warriors don't punch time clocks. Who would really care if he hit the streets a little after sunset?

Alyssa pressed to him, pulling at his clothes.

Screw it. Daniel raked one hand through her hair, nearly groaning that it had grown long enough to wind his fingers in.

A knock at the door broke them apart. Alyssa looked past him, frowning, most likely doing the mental math that all of her friends were already at work.

"Bear," he grumbled, coming to the obvious conclusion.

"Corwyn? Why would Corwyn be here?" Her eyes narrowed, and she smoothed the white men's shirt she wore self-consciously.

"He wants to talk to me. He sent an IM to my phone earlier, saying he would contact me this evening. I'd forgotten about it. I thought he was going to call, but..." Daniel headed for the door, buttoning his shirt.

"What does he need to talk to you about?" she asked nervously.

He shrugged. "No big deal." If it were, Bear would have said so. "I'll get it. Grab your stuff, and I'll drive you to work."

Daniel opened the door, tucking his shirt tails back into his jeans hastily. "Be just a—" *Oh, gods!*

Tim Armen's shock was unmistakable. He ranged his eyes over Daniel's rumpled appearance, his jaw tightening and eyes hardening in preparation for a knock-down fight; his *Blutjagd* rose steadily in confirmation of that assumption.

Daniel's rose in response. If it wasn't for Tim's mishandling, Tom might have been a decent husband to Alyssa. If not for his intemperate response to Tom's death, Alyssa might not be terrified of every Warrior on Earth save Daniel. If any single member of their household, especially Tom's father, had taken the time to explain their world to Alyssa in her two months with them, she might have trusted them enough to report Tom's crimes to them. At the very least, she wouldn't have felt isolated, inadequate, responsible for her own fate, trapped, and threatened.

"Tim," he forced out, reminding himself to leash his temper.

"I'm looking for Alyssa."

"She'll be out in a minute."

"So, I gathered," he growled, shooting another look at the sloppy tuck job.

Daniel smoothed his shirt without looking at it, daring Armen to make a comment about the situation.

Armen made as if to barge into the house, and Daniel blocked him.

Tim's *Blutjagd* hiked up another notch. "What the hell do you think you're—"

"Alyssa hasn't invited you into her house."

"She's family," he protested.

Daniel ground his teeth at that. How dare Armen claim her as family, after the way she was treated!

"She *is* my daughter-in-law, Hunter."

All that reminder did was fuel Daniel's hatred of the man...of both men. "Some husband," he grumbled. "And, last time I checked, Tom was—"

Armen fisted his hands, lit up as if for serious battle. "You dare insult—"

"Oh, that's right," he snapped. "You've always thought Tom could do no—"

The crash of glass brought them both around. Alyssa stood, surrounded by a puddle of juice and the fragments of one of her grandmother's glasses. Her shoes and maternity jeans were liberally dotted. Her eyes were wide and locked on Armen. She paled, her mouth opening as if she meant to speak, then closing again.

Daniel strode to her, lifting Alyssa out of harm's way and setting her on the lowest riser. "Go get changed. I'll wait for you."

She smoothed her hair, looking at Armen out of the corner of her eye. "Maybe... I think you should just pick me up tonight," she breathed.

"If you're sure." He wasn't sure about it. Daniel still wanted to spill blood for the wrongs done to Alyssa, and Tim Armen was nearly as guilty as Tom in the grand scheme of things.

She nodded, smoothing the back of her hair again.

"I'll clean this up before I—"

"No. It's okay. I'll get it."

"*I* will," Armen growled, halfway across the entryway, his shoulders hunched, his feet planted for a fight, and his fists shoved into his jacket pockets.

Daniel turned to place Alyssa at his back, prepared to make Armen keep his distance.

Alyssa's hand closed on his shoulder. "Don't, Daniel. Go to work. I'll see you...later."

He nodded stiffly, giving Armen a wide berth, their gazes locked. "Until next time, Tim." It was a veiled threat, at best.

"I look forward to it." As was his response.

Daniel sat in his car and considered staying to make sure Alyssa was safe, but she'd asked him to go. And he still had to hook up with Bear.

He was half a block away when his cell phone rang. Daniel answered it in a rougher voice than he would have liked, a crisp "Yeah?" that made him wince.

"Hey, Daniel," Bear offered cheerfully. "You okay?"

"Stellar," he grumbled.

"Oh, that's nice. As long as I'm not ruining a *good* mood."

Daniel groaned. "What now?"

"Just a heads-up for you. Tim Armen will be hitting town sometime soon."

"A little late, Bear. He's here."

"Ah, hell. Sorry I didn't get to you sooner. I was...delayed." Sounds of him shifting the phone filtered through. "How bad was it?"

"We didn't come to blows, if that's what you mean."

"He knows about the two of you?"

"That's a safe bet. He damned near caught me with my pants down."

"At this time of night?" he asked, seemingly incredulous.

"Lay off."

A woman's voice sounded in the background. Bear covered the mouthpiece and replied.

Daniel smirked. "And, how were you delayed, cousin?"

"Lay off," he warned.

"I think you get my point."

"Lay off, or you'll taste mine."

"Ooooh, I'm scared," he taunted.

Sounds of Bear dressing were unmistakable. "Lay off, or I won't make Tim back down."

Daniel sobered. "If you do that, I'll never mention your love life again."

"Consider it done."

* * * *

Alyssa came down the stairs in a fresh pair of jeans and her black Keds, watching Tim in amazement.

He mopped the juice spot on the floor, his face lowered, paying painstaking attention to the task. There was something serene about him, something she'd never seen in him before.

No, that wasn't quite right. Alyssa had never seen a Warrior so at ease except with a sacred weapon in hand or while throwing punches...until Daniel. But, she'd already decided that Daniel was unlike any Warrior she'd met before.

Tim didn't look up, but he spoke softly to her. "I'm sorry. I didn't mean to startle you."

Alyssa shook her head in disbelief. Tim sounded genuinely remorseful. She reached to scoop her hair behind her ear, encountered the short style, and smoothed it down.

"It's okay," she replied. "I didn't expect to see you." And fighting about Tom, to boot. That had nearly stopped her heart.

"I imagine that's true." There was no bite of sarcasm or anger in that. Tim was worn, perhaps sad. Was he disappointed to find her with Daniel?

An uncomfortable silence fell between them. Alyssa settled on the stairs, watching the mop move to avoid meeting his eyes. "Why did you come here, Tim?"

"To ask you to come home."

Her mouth went dry. "I am home."

He sighed. "Then I came to bring you some things for the baby."

"I shouldn't—"

"They're just old furniture and toys of Tom's."

Then I really shouldn't. "Old? Even the antiques at the Armen manor house are immaculate," she joked weakly.

"Is that why you're uncomfortable there?" he asked, seemingly grasping for straws.

She shook her head. "It's just not..."

"Home," he finished for her.

"Yes. Home," she agreed.

"It could be. You have no family here. We're—"

She couldn't let him say it. It was a lie. "I have this house. I've lived here all my life...well, for as long as I can remember anyway."

"Alone," he reasoned. "You're alone and you don't have to be."

"I have friends."

"And Daniel Hunter."

Alyssa fought for a decent breath. "I don't think it's fair to say I *have* Daniel. It's..." *What is it? An affair? More than that?* Even she didn't know for sure what Daniel was to her or what she wanted him to be. "It's not like that." Not yet, if it ever would be.

Tim knelt before her, meeting her eyes. "Promise me you'll think about it," he pleaded.

She nodded, though she knew she didn't belong in Armen manor. She'd never belonged there; that's why she'd kept this house intact when Tom wanted—

"I'll bring the furniture in. Just tell me where you want it and I'll set it—"

"I can't accept it," she whispered.

"You're not accepting it. It already belongs to the baby," he argued.

"I've already bought a nursery set." It probably wasn't as nice as the one Tim had bought for his son, but it was something she was entitled to, something she'd earned.

"Did Hunter help with that, too?" he snapped.

"It's not like that. It's...really not."

Tim stood, pacing the entryway, his face a vivid red. "That baby is an Armen. Just come home until he's born. After that—"

"I'd lose my job."

"You can't keep it once he's born anyway, and if you'd draw on your account, you wouldn't have to—"

"Who says I can't work with a baby?" she fumed. Was he telling her how to live already? "Jessica and I have already figured it out. And that is Tom's money."

"You're Tom's widow," he barked. "What was his is yours."

"No. I can't accept it. I didn't marry Tom for his money. Save it for the baby."

"I'd rather you *use* it for the baby. No, I'd rather you come home until he's born."

"My life is here."

"His life is in Armen."

Her stomach lurched at that. "Not until he's fifteen," she managed.

Tim stopped, staring at her. "He's my grandson. How am I supposed to give him an amulet and blessing when he's born?"

"Corwyn has already promised—"

"He's not an Armen."

"Then I'll call Scott and Kaitlyn—"

"Do you want him to come to Armen as lost as Scott was?"

"He'll know Warriors. I'm not stopping him from becoming a Warrior. Not that I could stop it."

"But, you would if you could?"

Alyssa took a calming breath. "You know that's impossible. He's a Warrior. He'll be raised a Warrior and trained a Warrior...hopefully a good enough one to live a long, long life." *And, knowing I intend to see to it may convince him not to try and take what he really wants.* "He's going to live a really long time, Tim. I won't stand for less."

Tim sighed, the tension in his shoulders easing. "He won't know his family."

"We'll work that out."

"What? Weekends in Armen when he's old enough to travel? Weekends here until then, any time I can get free to do it? Maybe a summer vacation, once in a while? He won't *know* us, Alyssa."

She didn't answer that. It was too dangerous until she knew what their laws said their respective rights were. Daniel would tell her that. Until then, it wasn't safe to comment.

"Promise me—"

"I'll consider it." But, she wouldn't. Armen wasn't her home.

"I'll drive you to work."

"I'd appreciate that. I'm late."

"You're family."

She faltered, at a loss for a way to answer his insistence that she was family to him, when she couldn't say the same. "Maybe... Maybe you could put the toys in the nursery. I haven't bought many toys yet."

He smiled faintly. "I'd be glad to."

"I'll show you where it is." Alyssa started to push to her feet.

Tim took her elbows, steadying her. He looked around uncertainly. "You'll want to be careful. I think I got all the glass, but I can't be sure."

"I will," she promised.

* * * *

Their voices reached Corwyn before he reached the door, passing through the hardwood in a manner that told him, without the proof of Tim Armen's *Blutjagd*, that the other man had no calm left about him.

"She's fragile, Brandon. This will kill her."

He sighed at the scene ahead, pushed through the office door, dropped into a chair, and offered Tim and his cousin each a weary smile and a nod.

Brandon recovered first. "If you don't mind, Bear..."

"Actually, you're going to want my input," he countered.

Tim's *Blutjagd* stepped up another notch at that pronouncement, then was forced back by the Warrior in question. "This hardly needs *König* intervention."

"If you're considering having Brandon order Daniel away from Alyssa, it *will* go before *König* when Daniel appeals. It's only expedient leadership for me to inform you what advice I will give my parents when they ask for it."

His *Blutjagd* went up and didn't come immediately down. His muscles tensed. "You'd recommend I lose?"

Corwyn didn't hesitate. "Hell, yes, I will."

"Bear," Brandon warned.

"I think it's safe to say I know more about this situation than either of you do."

Tim leaned forward in his chair, his expression fierce. "You knew he was fucking Alyssa?"

"I *don't* suggest you accuse Daniel of something so crass."

"Alyssa is newly widowed," he thundered.

"Yes. She is that," Corwyn admitted.

"He cannot believe she's serious. She's rebounding. She's confused."

"I don't think so, but that's a chance Daniel is willing to take."

"She can't heal this way!"

Corwyn didn't answer that. In truth, he didn't know that Tim was wrong. The only thing he could operate on was his gut instinct. Since Alyssa and Daniel had...well, whatever they had formed together... She was happier, calmer, more whole than he'd ever seen her.

"This is insane. What can he possibly offer her?"

"A positive experience with a Warrior." He hadn't meant to blurt it out that way, but it was the honest truth. No matter what came of this, Alyssa would know she didn't have to fear every Warrior on the face of the planet.

Tim was abruptly on his feet, his hand fisted on the hilt of his sacred weapon. Corwyn waved Brandon back, regarding Tim calmly, one eyebrow raised in disbelief.

His opponent backed off slowly. "Alyssa loves Tom."

"Loved Tom," he corrected. "She did love Tom, but Tom is gone, Tim. He's gone."

Tim floundered for words. "A pos... You actually believe whatever insane lies Daniel is—"

"Again, I don't suggest you call Alyssa a liar. Not to Daniel...and certainly not to me."

He looked toward the door, murder in his eyes.

"Sit down, Tim."

"You have no right—"

Corwyn pushed to his feet, staring his opponent down. "I said 'sit,' and I mean now," he ordered.

Tim scowled at him, then sank into his chair. "Afraid I'll find out the truth?" he challenged.

Corwyn sighed. "If Alyssa was afraid to talk to you before, do you honestly think that scaring it out of her or shaking it out of her is going to work?"

There was no sign that he would relent from his course so easily.

"Explain," Brandon requested, looking annoyed at being usurped in his own office.

"Tom was everything to you," Corwyn addressed Tim.

"He was my son, *König*. I pray you never know what it's like to lose your son."

"And, when you lost him?"

Misery replaced fury in his expression, and he seemed to age a decade before Corwyn's eyes.

"You destroyed everything in your sight," he repeated what Alyssa had told him about that night. "Alyssa shudders when she recounts it."

Tim winced.

"And you question why she'd be afraid to tell you that your son wasn't as perfect as you'd like to believe he was?"

"I never would have hurt Alyssa."

"She was new to our world. She couldn't have known that, and no one had bothered to explain it to her."

"I can't believe Tom was abusive. I won't believe that of him," he whispered. "You didn't see them together. I did."

Corwyn settled back in his seat. "He wasn't."

Tim nodded. "Then what? What is he accused of?"

"Tom was...Tom. He was impatient, impetuous, and sloppy."

"I don't think I understand that."

Corwyn ran a hand over his eyes, searching for a tactful way to begin tearing a man's image of his older son apart at the seams.

"*König*?" Tim prodded him.

"You've come this far, Bear," Brandon added.

"I know it." He met Tim's eyes. "Alyssa really did love Tom. I don't doubt that she did." *Though I'm not certain how much he loved her. Enough to seal printing, though as unbalanced as he was, only the gods know if it was real.*

"But?" Tim asked. "There has to be more."

"She wasn't sure yet. She needed time that Tom wouldn't give her. She probably would have been ready to accept him soon, but..."

Tim paled, swallowing hard, a sour look on his face.

"Every time he wanted something from her, he..." Gods, how do you say it to a man's father?

"What?" His voice was tremulous.

"Tom convinced Alyssa that he couldn't wait, that being a Warrior meant he couldn't wait for anything he wanted. Once it had worked on her once, he kept—"

"No."

"Either she sealed with him immediately, or she'd lose him to madness. Either—"

"He told her that?" Tim croaked, understandably repulsed by the thought of it, as any normal Warrior would be.

"Either she let him produce an heir, or he'd go mad in wanting one."

He buried his face in his hands. "Dear gods? How could he?"

"I won't even go into how he got her into bed the first time...or the second or third. That alone would have seen him dead. I hate to tell you this, Tim, but you have to know it. It's only fair to Alyssa that you do." Now that he was on a roll, the words were coming easier, though the trauma they'd do a grieving father was incalculable.

"Once it worked the first time," Tim whispered hoarsely.

"And once he'd, from her point of view, trapped her in our world, he got himself killed. She never had a chance to accept that she was an Armen, Tim. Alyssa wasn't ready for any of it, but she was afraid to lose him to madness, so she agreed. Knowing what she'd done...that she'd agreed just to save him and not because she was sure... She felt even less worthy to be an Armen. She felt like an imposter, masquerading as your dead son's wife. Then—"

Tim looked up, grief-stricken. "She really lost him, and I... Oh, gods. Why didn't she tell me? I would have killed him myself. You know I would."

"Until Daniel, Alyssa didn't realize the failing was Tom's. She didn't know he'd been dishonorable. She was afraid to admit the story, even to a Hunter. If weren't for her son, she was afraid you'd strip away her amulet for it. Trusting Daniel with her story was a monumental step for her. From Alyssa's limited knowledge about our laws, she was risking everything on the slim hope that he'd understand why she did what she did."

"I would never—"

"Did anyone ever explain that to her? Armen has a long history of failing in this respect...even as far back as Sharon and Jannelle. It is a weakness of your house, 'claiming' family members without considering the consequences of your words."

Tim winced, but he didn't deny it.

"I want to make my intentions clear, Tim."

"Are you threatening me?" His *Blutjagd* didn't even twitch at that. He seemed weary, defeated.

"No. I am trying to right a wrong as best I can. Alyssa wasn't given the proper consideration."

"How can I possibly right that? I wasn't even... Well, a portion of it was my fault, but I didn't know. I'd just lost my son, and within a day, your sister agreed to take away his bride and son."

Corwyn leaned forward, bracing himself for an argument. "I want her son to have a choice, and I want Armen to support it. This isn't about you anymore. This is about Alyssa and what's right."

"You want him to be a Warrior of Hunter." He didn't question it.

"I want him to have that choice. He will be raised by his mother in Hunter range. His only close relationships will be with Hunter Warriors. Knowing what you do, do you think it's appropriate to force him to Armen and away from his mother at fifteen?"

Tim started to speak, but Corwyn cut him off.

"Do you think it's appropriate to force Alyssa to return to Armen to be with her son?"

"No," he admitted. "I don't."

"Then present it to Tyler. Don't make me force this on you."

"But...he's my grandson," he pleaded.

"And he's only alive now, because Alyssa chose it. When I learned of Tom's crimes, she was given the choice of aborting."

Tim stared at him, his skin going a sickly gray color.

"She chose to carry him. She chose it, believing he'd be taken from her somehow. Give Alyssa this. It's right." Corwyn didn't wait for his response. Something like this wouldn't come easily. He stood and left with a nod to Brandon.

* * * *

Daniel strode through the doors to El Oso Oro, feeling on top of the world. He'd had a successful hunt, a hot shower, and a meal, but that wasn't the lion's share of his elation.

Corwyn had called earlier, letting him know that the matter of Tim Armen had been settled. The Armens had been informed of Tom's crimes against Alyssa, and they didn't argue her position.

Speaking of the lady, she looked up, smiling weakly. She set her tray on the bar, then hoisted herself onto a stool.

The bar was empty and the work nearly done. From the looks of things, Jessica had closing. That was good; Daniel would hate to make a scene by insisting Alyssa leave with him to rest.

He planted a kiss on her forehead, narrowly stopping himself from laughing out loud. "Ready to go?" he asked.

"Oh, boy, yeah."

Daniel helped her down, wrapping an arm around her shoulder and leading her to the door.

She glanced at him out of the corner of her eye. "Was there any trouble?"

"About?"

She darkened.

"No, and there won't be."

Alyssa stopped five feet from his car, turning to him. "What do you mean?"

"The Lords Hunter and Armen have been informed of Tom's crimes. Bear also filled in his family. No one will forcibly remove you from Hunter range...ever."

She took two more steps toward the car, fisting her hands in her shirt. "Until he's fifteen, you mean."

"That remains to be seen." It was the one thing Armen hadn't agreed to...yet. He hoped they'd be reasonable about it, but Daniel doubted *König* and the Council of Lords would allow Armen custody, even at fifteen.

"I don't understand."

"Bear has requested that your son be permitted to train and serve Hunter. I can't make any promises, but it's likely that—"

The rest was knocked out of him when Alyssa dove into his arms, a sob echoing against the buildings.

"It's okay," he soothed her. Daniel laid a kiss in her hair, rocking from side to side slightly.

Alyssa nodded, her grip easing and her breathing slowing. She backed away, revealing a single track of tears.

Daniel stroked it away on his fingertips. "I promised to protect you."

He laid a kiss over the streak, and Alyssa turned her mouth to his, trembling. It was a solemn kiss, a vow, his oath unspoken.

When it ended, Daniel looked toward his car, freezing at the sight of Tim Armen. Tom's father hesitated, then nodded and turned away, moving silently toward the alley.

"Is something wrong?" Alyssa asked. She turned to look a heartbeat after Tim turned the corner and disappeared from view.

"Nothing," he assured her. "Nothing at all."

Chapter Forty-one

April 13, 2050

Alyssa laughed heartily, setting a beer on the bar in front of Corwyn. "You are all nuts," she accused.

He smiled. "I'll take that as a compliment."

She smoothed Daniel's button-down shirt over her son, then rubbed the ache in her lower back.

Corwyn's eyes narrowed. "Maybe Jessica should relieve you for a while," he mused.

"Don't be ridiculous. I can—"

Alyssa stopped speaking at the look on Corwyn's face. It made her blood run cold. She took a step back, watching his hand tighten around the beer, a knot forming in the pit of her stomach. The glass shattered, and beer rained down over the bar. He was little more than a breathing statue, his face cold and eyes hard.

But he wasn't looking at her. He didn't appear to be looking at anything in particular.

She glanced from one Warrior to another, noting the rising tension in sick disbelief, dizzy, her stomach rolling. "No," she pleaded. "Not again."

Corwyn's eyes snapped to her, and he stood, shaking his head. "No. It's not like that, Alyssa."

"It is," she insisted, forcing back near-hysteria. Visions of Daniel... *No, don't go there!*

"No one is dead, except a beast. No one is dying," he reasoned in a whisper across the bar. "It's nothing—"

"I've seen 'nothing serious' and I've seen... This isn't a scratch that requires a dozen stitches. Is it?"

He ground his teeth, a sure sign that he'd like to lie to her. "No. It's not fatal, but it's not minor, either," he admitted. "But, no one—"

"Is it Daniel?" The question was out before she could stop herself. Alyssa didn't want the answer to that; she was terrified of what answer she might get. She clapped her hand over her mouth, shaking her head as if to plead with him to disregard it.

Corwyn pulled out his cell phone and started dialing, seemingly pained.

"Alyssa?" Jessica asked. She pushed Alyssa's hair back from her forehead. "What is it?"

"Daniel," Corwyn grumbled. "Are you free?"

Alyssa held her breath, hardly daring to trust that it was really Daniel on the other end, well enough to talk, maybe without a scratch on him.

"What's going on? You're shaking like a leaf."

Several Warriors started to speak, but Corwyn motioned them to silence.

"That can wait. I need you at El Oso."

"Alyssa?" Jessica called again. "You're scaring me, hon."

"The *highest* priority.

"No. Nothing like that.

"You're wasting time. Just get in the damned car and leave him to Charlie.

"Yes, you *can* do that. I'm ordering you to.

"Not now, Daniel.

"Okay. See you in a few."

He disconnected and raised the phone to her, then dropped it in his jacket pocket.

"What the hell is going on?" Jessica demanded.

Alyssa didn't answer. She realized that she still had her hand pressed to her mouth and forced it down, fisting it in Daniel's shirt, staring at the door, her heart pounding and her head following suit.

He's okay. Corwyn said he's okay, and no matter what Tom did, Königs don't make empty promises.

Corwyn appeared at her side, his hands closing on her shoulders and turning her toward the pass-through. "Come sit down, Alyssa," he whispered, guiding her out to a stool. "Ice water, please, Jessica."

Alyssa looked back toward the door, straining her neck to keep it in her line of sight, bobbing her head to see around the wall of concerned Warriors. Corwyn lifted her onto a bar stool, and Jessica pressed a glass into her hand.

"Now, what the hell—"

Corwyn pulled her a few feet away from Alyssa, dropping his voice slightly. "One of the Warriors got hurt...Cole."

"And?"

There was a moment of silence.

"Oh!" She wrapped her arms around Alyssa. "He's okay, baby. You'll see. Drink the water and relax. He's just fine."

Alyssa managed a mouthful. Her stomach clenched on that, threatening to bring it and dinner back up. She settled the glass on the beer-splattered bar, giving up on the thought of more.

No one spoke. Jessica served up drinks to Brad, who took on the part of barmaid with surprising ease, though few customers remained at the tables. Corwyn stood at her side, looking every inch the prince he was.

The door opened, and Alyssa looked around, closing her eyes to the sight of Daniel crossing the room. He was alive and seemingly uninjured.

"Thanks for coming out," Corwyn stated.

"Alyssa?" Daniel touched her cheek.

She buried her face in his chest, too exhausted to do more than sob.

"I'll take her home."

* * * *

Daniel glanced at Alyssa, then turned his attention back to the road. She'd given in to sleep within a few minutes of settling into his car, curling in on herself in the passenger seat.

Gods, she'd scared the shit out of him! When Corwyn called and ordered him to leave a downed Warrior to someone else and high-tail it to the bar, Daniel had been sure there was some problem with Alyssa, that she'd collapsed or been hurt. Bear's reassurances had only calmed him until the answers had stopped flowing. The drive to El Oso Oro had been nerve wracking, but feeding elders couldn't have driven him there faster.

And then he'd seen her. Daniel hadn't questioned why Bear had called him in. Alyssa had been pale, jittery, a bundle of raw nerves and little more. She knew Warriors well enough, it seemed, to guess that someone was down.

"It must have been a living nightmare for her," he breathed. "A repeat of Tom."

His hands fisted on the wheel. Daniel wasn't Tom. Corwyn Lord Hunter, Bear's great-grandfather, had been reported as saying sealing printing with the right woman made a Warrior determined to survive the night for her alone. That was printing as it should be, printing as Daniel was experiencing it. He was faster, more alert... He'd do anything to come back to Alyssa.

At her house, he parked, retrieved the key from his pocket, and carried her inside. Alyssa woke as he locked the door behind them, stiffening on the curve of his arm so that he had to shift abruptly to hold onto her. Her breathing caught at the move.

"What—" he started to ask.

"Let me down," she whispered hoarsely.

"It's me, Alyssa...Daniel." Was she thinking about Tom now? He certainly didn't want her to be.

"I...I know." She didn't meet his eyes.

Daniel crossed to the couch and put her down, confused by her withdrawl. Had Cole's injury shaken her that much? She liked Cole, but they weren't that close. Or maybe... "It's okay," he soothed her. "I'm okay."

"This time. What about next time?"

He floundered, at a loss to give her assurances. Chances were, he *would* die at a beast's hand someday. He knew it, and she knew it. Anything else he said would be a lie. Finally, he settled on the only assurance he could give her.

"I love you."

Alyssa didn't answer.

"I will always do my best to come back to you." That was all he could offer, all any Warrior could.

Tears pooled in her eyes. "Like Tom did?"

Daniel fought the urge to scream in fury. "I'm not Tom, and Tom's best was pretty shitty...in every conceivable department."

She didn't seem to know what to say to that. The tears escaped, pinking her pale face.

Daniel sighed. "You're tired. I shouldn't...shouldn't snap at you that way. Maybe we should discuss this tomorrow."

"You'll still be a Warrior tomorrow," she managed. "You can't stop being a Warrior."

"Did you expect me to?"

Alyssa closed her eyes, laying her head back. Her voice was thick in near-sleep. "Being a Warrior means someone bringing me a blade...tomorrow or next week or next year."

Daniel's heart ached. "My best isn't enough," he choked. *It's never going to be enough, because of Tom. Damn him for this!* He could hardly force himself to ask the question that needed asked. "Do you want me to leave?"

For a handful of heartbeats, he was sure she wasn't going to answer him.

"Yes."

He stood, taking one last look at her. Daniel marched to the door, hesitating with the key in his hand.

I can't stop being a Warrior.

And, you can't accept a Warrior after that bastard, Tom. I have no right to stay here. I have no right to hurt you again.

The laws of sanction stated it clearly and repeatedly. Nearly everything was the lady's choice. There was no force and no convincing them—not to bed, not to sealing printing, not to children. The fact that Tom had done all of that had ruined Alyssa for any decent Warrior.

Do you want me to leave?

She'd said 'yes' to that. As always, her choice was law. Daniel placed the key on the table and let himself out quietly.

He was a block away, before he gave in to the urge to scream out loud. Alyssa was the only thing in his life that mattered, and he was losing her thanks to the poorest excuse for a Warrior to walk the Earth since Veriel had gone beast. If Tom was still alive, Daniel would kill him with his bare hands.

* * * *

Corwyn groaned at the sight of Daniel heading across the manor foyer, red-faced, his *Blutjagd* burning merrily. He'd been afraid of this. There was only one thing to do now. He intercepted Daniel and prepared for the argument to come.

"I'm not in the mood, Bear," he growled, his hands fisting.

Oh, hell! He's further gone than I realized. That would complicate things. "What are you doing?"

"Your mother and sister know everything. Get on the cell phone and call them. Ask them how screwed I am, all because I was born to this shit."

Brandon came from upstairs at a run, seemingly ready to take his older son down.

Corwyn waved him off. He didn't need anyone's protection, and he had to take Daniel head-on. It was the only way. "So, you're giving up on her? She has one bad night, and you're—"

"She told me to leave."

He winced at that. "Did she tell you she wouldn't marry you?"

"She told me she didn't want to get handed another blade. Not tomorrow. Not next week or month or year." His voice rose steadily and his rage with it. "I'm a Warrior. Someday..." He swallowed hard, probably a scream of loss.

"Someday a beast will take you."

Daniel nodded, a tense jerk of his head.

"She's upset, Daniel. Alyssa loves you; she'll reconsider when she calms down."

He ground his teeth, shaking his head.

Brandon pushed a hand through his hair, pained because his son was suffering, no doubt.

It was time to lay it out. "You love her. You'd do anything for her."

"Which is why I will never hurt her. If someone offering her the blade..." He looked away, suddenly weary. "It's her choice. You know that."

"I know that choices made in anger or fear aren't choices."

Daniel started to protest, and Corwyn cut him off cleanly.

"People change their minds once they think things through. Scott—"

"Anecdotes aren't going to cut it," he shouted.

"Scott couldn't break printing, you know. My mother believes it was because Kates never *chose* to leave him."

"Alyssa chose."

"No. Alyssa is running scared."

"And what am I supposed to do to change that?" he snapped.

"Nothing."

"Then what the hell are you doing this for? Let me go to the cabin and..." His face screwed up, and he swallowed again, definitely a scream of loss this time. "Damn you!"

"You don't want to do that," Corwyn stated confidently.

"Of course, I don't, but it's not my choice."

Corwyn glanced at Brandon, taking his calculating expression to mean that he'd caught up, at least. "Your son doesn't listen worth a damn. You know that, don't you?"

Brandon nodded wearily.

"Oh, this makes sense to you?" Daniel shouted at his father.

"Yes," Brandon answered, "but I'm thinking with the right head."

Corwyn motioned to Daniel, inviting Brandon to give it a try.

The lord took a deep breath. "Give her time to make a calm, rational decision. What if... Just consider this."

Daniel looked at the ceiling, seemingly seeking patience.

"Don't make me take you to trial."

"As you wish," he grumbled.

"What if you go to the cabin and get over this—"

"That's the general plan."

"But, what if she *does* want you? What will it do to Alyssa, if she comes to her senses, and you're not there for her, as you promised you would be? What if breaking printing means you can't be there for her ever again? What if it kills that part of you?"

Daniel's expression shifted from pain to horror and back again. Now, he was thinking. "But, what happens next time someone gets hurt? Next time someone gets killed? If she's not sure, and I do commit to her..."

Corwyn forced his hands not to fist. If he made a fist, he wouldn't be able to stop until Daniel was unconscious. *At least.* "I think you need trial with *me*," he warned.

Brandon nodded. "Count me in."

"There won't be enough left for you."

"Then I get him first."

"It is your range and your son," Corwyn conceded.

"Maybe I should have done this sooner."

Corwyn shrugged.

Daniel paled, stammering out something that made no sense.

Brandon took an aggressive step toward his son, his 'lord face' firmly in place. "Either you're serious about printing, and you're willing to give her that chance..."

Corwyn took over there. "Or you're not, and you need to slink off to that cabin like a kicked dog before you hurt her any more. But, if she's willing to chance everything on your sorry hide after Tom, you're no cousin of mine if you won't do the same for her."

Daniel took several deep breaths, regaining some semblance of calm. He nodded. "I won't rush her," he vowed.

Brandon sighed, releasing the tension in his shoulders. "Then we'll help you survive it however we can."

Chapter Forty-two

April 14, 2050

Alyssa groaned, her muscles protesting movement. Realization that she'd slept on the couch came abruptly, at about the time she tried to roll over and landed on her knees on the floor, emitting a squeak of surprise.

She rubbed at her lower back, wincing from the stiffness that stretched from her hips to her shoulders and neck. Her head pounded, and her eyes felt raw.

"What a mess," she grumbled. If she looked as bad as she felt, Alyssa could moonlight...*daylight* as a scarecrow. "A really pregnant scarecrow."

Her memories of the night were as fuzzy as her vision. Piecing it together made her headache spike, and she groaned in response.

Alyssa pushed to her feet and headed for the stairs and, more importantly, the Tylenol in the medicine cabinet. She paused in the entryway, staring at the door in confusion. The knob and top lock were both thrown, but the chain was undone.

Daniel... A chill coursed over her nerves. The yo-yo effect of her memories returning had her grasping the table, lightheaded.

A key bit into her hand, and Alyssa picked it up, staring at it in disbelief. She sobbed. He left her; Daniel had walked away and had no intention of returning.

I told him to. Unlike Tom, Daniel follows their laws to the letter.

But, she hadn't wanted him to leave permanently. She'd been upset, confused. Alyssa had just wanted to think.

She headed for the phone, then faltered. Her reason for sending him away still stood. Could she accept a man who would eventually die fighting beasts?

Everyone dies.

Not that way.

Did it really matter how someone died? Dead was dead, no matter how it happened. Everyone died somehow.

Many of the better Warriors outlived their wives, and Daniel was undeniably a good Warrior. It was said that the madness of losing a mate was worse even than the madness of losing a son, worse than Tim losing Tom, and she'd seen that. Daniel was willing to take that risk for her. Was she willing to do the same for him?

Guilt that she couldn't immediately say 'yes' seared her. Alyssa had accepted one Warrior when she wasn't sure of her feelings. She wouldn't make that mistake again. Until she could commit to him, wholeheartedly and without reservations, it wasn't fair to Daniel. She'd only be leading him on.

But, what if he breaks printing?

Alyssa ambled to the couch and sank into it, torn. If she waited, she might lose him. If she didn't wait...

She gasped. "I've been here before." And, she'd chosen wrong that time. "In the extreme."

But, which choice was wrong this time?

Alyssa stared at the key in misery. *I can't call him until I know which is right, but maybe I can call someone else.*

* * * *

"Oh, baby," Jessica gushed. "Are you okay?"

Alyssa smiled weakly. *Okay?* She felt as if she'd never be okay again.

"Have you had lunch yet? You haven't. Have you?"

"Guilty." In truth, she hadn't managed more than half a slice of toast with jam and half a glass of milk in all the time she'd been trying to convince herself to call Corwyn.

Jessica slid half of an Anthony's roast beef sub in front of her. "Eat."

"I can't take your lunch," she protested.

"I've eaten the other half. This was the half I was saving for tomorrow. It's never as good the second day."

Alyssa mumbled her thanks, managing a single bite.

Jessica served a regular at the far end of the bar, then returned, leaning across with her arms folded on the top. "So, why are you here? I know you didn't come to bum lunch."

"You... You spend a lot of time with Corwyn," she hinted.

To her amazement, Jessica blushed. "A fair amount," she admitted.

"You two are..." Alyssa bit her lip. "Never mind. That's none of my business." She took another bite of the sandwich.

"I don't know what we are to each other," Jessica sighed.

"That makes two of us," Alyssa grumbled through a mouthful of roast beef and cheddar.

"You and Daniel? Yeah, I heard."

Alyssa choked, swallowing painfully, her eyes watering. "You heard what?"

"That you need time to decide what you want. Daniel's okay, by the way. His Uncle Nick is keeping an eye on him."

She sobbed in relief. "Then he hasn't decided to...um..." She couldn't say it.

"Break printing? No. He told Corwyn that he'd give you the time you need."

Her heart warmed at that. Time was one thing Tom hadn't given her. It was the one thing she wished he had.

"Better?" Jessica asked.

Alyssa sobered. "Where exactly did you hear all of this?"

"Corwyn. He figured you wouldn't want his company, but he wanted to make sure you were okay. It was a solid bet you'd show up here...eventually."

She took another bite, struggling to digest more than the sandwich.

Jessica set a glass of orange juice in front of her. "You'd have to show up here. Hell! Tia, Mel, and I are the only family you have left. Well, except for your little one."

That was the last reminder Alyssa needed, that she was alone, as Tim had accused she was. She sipped the juice.

"You want him. Don't you?"

"You know I do." There went her appetite, right down the drain. Just the thought of turning down Daniel willingly killed it.

"And you're going to let the ghost of Tom ruin that?" It wasn't an accusation. Jessica seemed genuinely interested in the answer.

"I...don't know. It's not about Tom."

Jessica shot her a look that proclaimed she knew better.

"Okay. It is, in a way, but... If Tom had been a cop in a neighborhood with a ninety-nine percent mortality rate for cops, and Daniel worked in the same neighborhood—"

Jessica scrunched up her nose. "That is really morbid, Alyssa."

"That's reality, and it scares the hell out of me."

"Yeah," she sighed. "Sooner or later, we all have to face our demons."

The door opened, and Jessica looked around at it. "Break's over," she announced. "Here comes the demolition crew from down the street."

Chapter Forty-three

April 23, 2050

Alyssa opened Tom's toy box, a heavy wooden monstrosity that would look at home in a log cabin, smiling at the earmarks of a lost era tied to the members of an ancient race.

There was a wooden sacred weapon on top that looked as if it had seen many loving years and more than one owner, maybe even before Tim's years with it. On close inspection, it almost appeared that it had been used by a teething baby. She gave it a place of honor on the top shelf.

There were toy soldiers, action figures, superheroes, and more than a few toy weapons. The theme of protectors, those who took an oath to safeguard others, and the means they used to do it, wasn't lost on her. This was what her son's life would be, whether he chose to do that duty in Armen or Hunter.

She laughed at the antique toy garage with the working elevator, accompanied by the collector's case of vintage Matchbox sports cars. Yet again, her son's life was being shaped by the playthings representing the tools of the Warrior trade.

"Boys with toys. Cars and blades, even as toddlers."

The vampire dolls brought a new peal of laughter. Tim or Deb had a wicked sense of humor. She suspected that it was Tim.

Alyssa pulled out a hand-carved music box, marveling at the workmanship put into it. It was gorgeous, precious. Few things were so beautifully crafted. She opened it, interested to hear what music had been chosen for it, rolling her eyes at the computer chip recording of *Don't Let The Sun Go Down On Me.* "Definitely Tim," she decided, placing it on another high shelf.

The cardboard box at the bottom held the most amazing treasures, the beloved belongings of an infant Tom. There were teething rings with puppies on them that made her seriously consider getting a dog that would grow up with her son. A Peanuts character mobile with Snoopy, The Flying Ace as a centerpiece followed and then a fuzzy beige teddy bear that felt soft as mink. She set the mobile in the crib and placed the other items on the high shelves

She lifted a paper bag from the box, opening it, laughing and crying at the same time. Tim had bought his son a miniature Warrior outfit, complete with jeans, black shirts, and soft black baby boots. Alyssa would have to send them a picture of the baby dressed in it. She smiled wickedly. He'd be holding Tom's wooden weapon, chewing on it, if she could arrange it.

The empty toy box was easy enough to move to the far wall. Alyssa placed the toddler toys back into it and closed the lid, wiping her dusty hands on her jeans. She looked around, noting a job well done. She'd hang the mobile after lunch, then clean the kitchen.

The phone seemed to beckon her, and Alyssa reached for it, punching the number from memory. It seemed inconceivable that she still remembered it. She'd never used it before she and Tom sealed printing, though he'd left it, along with his cell phone number, with her the morning after he'd saved her, and she hadn't called it once since he'd died. In fact, she'd only used it once that she could remember.

It was answered on the second ring with a cheery, "Armen Manor."

Her voice seemed to desert her. She'd called to speak to Deb, but Alyssa hadn't expected her to answer the phone.

"Hello?"

"Hi, Deb," she managed. "It's me...Alyssa, I mean." Just saying that made her feel like an idiot.

"Alyssa? Are you okay? Is anything wrong?"

"No. I...I mean, yes, I'm fine. No, nothing is wrong." *I can't even talk to her without falling all over myself.* "I just...called to thank you for the toys...Tom's toys. They're wonderful, and I wanted to let you know."

"You're welcome." There was a moment of silence. "Are you sure you're okay?"

"Yes. I..." She cleared her throat. "It's just being pregnant. You know. You've done it a couple of times."

"If you're sure..."

The punch or kick from inside stole Alyssa's breath. She'd always heard that babies started with flutters. Or maybe she'd been so preoccupied, she'd missed those movements.

Deb said something about Tim.

"Yeah," Alyssa replied automatically.

The kicking came again, harder. Alyssa gasped in response to it. She'd known Warrior babies were larger than other babies, more vigorous and hearty, but this was beyond anything she'd expected.

"Alyssa?" Tim asked worriedly. "Do you need something? Anything?"

Yes! She wanted to scream out her news, share it with the world.

Her smile faded. No. She wanted to share it with Daniel. Daniel first, and then the world.

"Alyssa, are you all right?"

"Yes. I'm fine. Sorry. I just realized that I'm late getting somewhere." That wasn't a lie. She was more than a week late getting there. "Pregnancy-induced senility, I guess."

He sighed. "If you want or need anything—"

"I do...sort of. I'd like some pictures of Tom for the baby. Actually, pictures of you all. Could you... Would you do that for me?"

There was a moment of silence on the other end. "You know I will. I'll send them—"

"No need to. You...you'll be coming to see the baby when he's born. Won't you? You and Deb?"

There was a sound as if he'd been gut punched. "Call when labor starts. Ani willing, I'd like to give him my blessing."

"I will, and I'll call again soon. Right now..." Her son kicked again. "I have to go."

"We'll be waiting," he promised.

Alyssa disconnected, her head spinning. She had to find Daniel and find out if there was still a chance for them. That meant heading to the Hunter manor house. Though she hated manors with a passion, there were some things more important than that. Not screwing up her second chance was one of them. If she wanted a future and a family, she had to settle with the past.

* * * *

Corwyn headed toward the sound of Alyssa's voice, certain he was hearing things. It had been more than a week. Even Daniel had all but given up hope.

"I need to reach Daniel," she repeated, more upset than she'd been the first time she'd asked.

Brad rubbed a hand over the back of his neck. "I'll have to call Brandon. I don't have permission to—"

"I've got this one," Corwyn ordered.

Alyssa turned to him, managing a weak smile. "Has *König* decided that I'm a jinx for the Warriors? Or will you take me to Daniel?"

Brad retreated, seemingly mortified at her tone.

Corwyn took her hand. "He's waiting for you. No matter what you have to say, Daniel needs to hear it."

"You're not going to ask me what my answer is?"

He sighed. "That's between you and Daniel. It's really none of my business."

"None of your business?" Her tone was one of supreme disbelief.

"None."

"But, you—"

"I'm a Warrior, Alyssa. I'll never be lord of a range. I'm not allowed to be one. Cross will be knee-deep in heirs, and as a *König*, that's the only range I might have someday claimed. I'll never be Lord *König*, because that passes to the mates of the Stone Vessels. I don't belong anywhere, so if I use my misplaced notoriety to stick my nose where it doesn't belong, once in a while... Well, that's a failing of mine, and everyone tolerates it, because the only hierarchy in my life is one I can never rise higher in. In short, it's none of my business what you've chosen."

"But, you'll help me get to Daniel, when Brad said—"

"Ah, but I know something Brad doesn't." He guided her toward the door.

"For instance?"

"Brandon would take you to Daniel himself, if he were here to do it, though he *might* ask what your decision is first. He's a father, so he worries."

She slipped through the open door ahead of him. "And you don't? I don't believe that."

He smiled. She had him dead to rights, when so few did. "Of course, I do. But, Daniel is a Warrior. He's not my son to coddle." *Would that I had a son to coddle someday.*

Alyssa seemed to consider that for a moment. "Thanks, Corwyn."

"For what?"

"For not making me tell you first. Daniel deserves to hear it from me."

"You're welcome." Corwyn paused at the door to his car, feeling oddly at home as he hadn't since leaving Katie. "Do me a favor." Gods, but this felt right.

She stared at him, confused by that request. "You want a favor from me?"

He nodded, at a loss to explain why this mattered so much to him.

"Okay," she stammered. "If I can."

"Call me 'Bear.'"

"Bear?"

He smiled. "Corwyn is a tall order to have to live up to. I prefer to be called 'Bear,' and all my friends call me that."

"Okay. I can handle that."

That simply, Corwyn decided that Hunter would probably be his home...as long as Alyssa was about to accept Daniel. If she didn't, this home would be as broken as any other in the Warrior world.

* * * *

"Hey, Daniel," his Uncle Nicky called out. "It's for you."

He nodded his thanks, plodding barefoot down the stairs toward the living room with a grumbled curse, wondering yet again if tomorrow should be the day he gave up, headed to the mad cabin, and let breaking printing take its course.

Screw it. Screw Bear and Dad. I can't live this way much longer.

No! Doing that would be too close to walking away. I can't—

Daniel stopped in the living room doorway, stunned by the sight of her. Alyssa stood at Bear's side, her hands clasped nervously under the already-larger mound of her son.

Warrior babies grow so quickly. In a few months, she'll be huge.

He itched to touch her, but he had no right to do that. "Alyssa," he greeted her, his voice rough, acutely aware that his cock was already erect. *Gods, I need that mad cabin.* "Was there a reason—"

She strode to him, grasping his wrist and drawing his palm to her womb. His question died in his throat. For a long moment, he stood absolutely still, breathing in the coconut scent of her shampoo like a man starved.

Then he felt it.

Daniel laughed aloud, giddy in joy. "He's kicking. Dear Ani, he's kicking. Bear, you have to feel this. He's so strong."

"When I felt it..." Alyssa faltered, her hand cupping his cheek. "There was no one else I wanted to share it with. You had to be first.

"I was wrong, Daniel. I shouldn't—" She bit back a sob. "I couldn't stand it if... When I saw their faces, I knew one of you was hurt or dead. I was so afraid it was you."

His heart pounded in a mixture of hope and terror. "And the next time?" he asked. "The next time someone gets hurt?" He held his breath, panning his gaze up to her face, to the tear escaping the corner of her eye and winding down the line of her cheekbone.

"You're not Tom," she whispered.

"No. I'm not Tom." He'd tried to tell her that.

"You'll...try your best to always come home to me?"

"If you're offering a home to come to," Daniel countered, pouring every ounce of prayer into that near-plea.

"What... What are you offering?" She seemed painfully unsure.

Daniel tilted his head and brushed her lips with his own. "I want you to be my wife, my lover..." He stroked her womb. "The mother of my sons."

Her eyes widened, and she looked to her womb miserably.

"You know I love him as my own."

"But, Armen still hasn't agreed to—"

Bear cleared his throat. "Do you want Daniel to raise your son as his own, Alyssa?"

She darkened, nodding. "They're still the baby's family, though, and I told Tim he could bless... I promised him, Bear. They have a place, but..."

"Then give me ten minutes."

"But, Armen will never agree to—"

"Tom isn't alive to be driven mad by the idea of someone else raising his son. Tim will want to see you happy. He'll want to see his grandson from time to time, and he'll want the baby to know who his biological father is, have him carry his true family name and amulet. But, he'll let your son stay here, no matter what happens to you. You have my vow on that."

Daniel stepped closer to her, tracing the lines of her womb, unable to stop touching her after waiting so long to.

Alyssa closed her eyes in a look of rapture. "Daniel?" she asked.

"As long as Armen acknowledges that he is my son, that the bond is mine. I won't survive losing him."

"I'm sure he will," Bear assured them. "Now, go seal printing, already."

"No," Daniel whispered.

Her eyes opened, uncertain and pained.

"You haven't said 'yes,'" he reminded her.

Alyssa laughed nervously. "Oh, yes."

Daniel scooped her up with a grumbled curse and headed for the stairs.

* * * *

Alyssa didn't question where he was taking her. She knew Daniel wouldn't stop until whatever chemical bond tied them together was forged tight. Memories of the bliss on Tom's face when he sealed made her shiver. What would Daniel look like at that moment?

He set her on her feet, and a door closed. For a moment, he stood, cradling her to his body. Daniel tipped her chin up, his expression strangely devoid of emotion.

"I can wait, Alyssa. It doesn't have to be today. If you're unsure in the least, I want you to tell me."

She smiled, tears pooling in her eyes again, though she felt the need to laugh out loud in joy. "You really mean that, don't you? You'd wait for me?"

"As long as you need. Knowing you're willing is a gift."

If she'd had any remaining doubts, that was all it would have taken to convince her. As it was, she was already convinced that it was right this time, that Daniel was right for her. "I'm sure. I've never been surer."

Daniel didn't reply. His fingers trailed down her throat to the buttons on the men's-style dress shirt she wore. One by one, he undid them, his breath catching as he spread it wide around her body, his gaze ranging over her hungrily.

Alyssa bit her lip, closing her eyes as he slid the shirt off. His fingers followed the fabric, then returned and unclasped her bra, pulling it away.

Tom had been crazy, nearly frantic when they'd sealed. It seemed Daniel was going to make her crazy instead.

His mouth trailed lazily over her face, neck and shoulders, seemingly committing every inch of her body to memory. "By Tes, I missed you."

Alyssa pulled his t-shirt up his stomach, mapping him with her fingertips. "I've been thinking of you. Nearly every minute, awake and asleep."

"Are you sure about this?"

She nodded. "I told you I want—"

"Here, I mean. We can seal at your house, if you'd prefer. In your bed."

"You'd really put this off just for that?"

Daniel raised his head, his expression earnest. "Anything you need from me," he vowed. "That house is your home. Given half a chance, I'll introduce you to mine, but I'd never take you from home."

"But you're a Warrior. If you're ordered to go, we have to go, you and, as your mate, me."

He shook his head, smiling. "I'll go on trail, from time to time. They won't be reassigning me."

"Why?"

"I'm giving you my vow that I won't ask you to leave your home. Even my house lord cannot force me to break an oath to my mate. No one can."

"God, the things he never told me!"

"Hunter would have been a little far... Never mind. Now, do you want to seal at home?"

"No." Alyssa eased his t-shirt further up his chest, laying a kiss over his right nipple.

The shirt jerked up and away. Then his hands were on her waist, lifting her, lowering her onto the bed. To her surprise, he still wasn't rushed.

Daniel removed her shoes and every stitch of clothing, his mouth caressing her bare skin. Then he entered her, freezing at the pinnacle as he had the first few times.

Alyssa gasped his name, all but begging him not to stop.

"Marry me," Daniel requested.

"I already said I'd... Oh, Daniel." He'd asked while her mind was still fairly clear and uncluttered.

"You've accepted printing." His mouth trailed along her hairline. "I want to marry you."

Visions of the wedding they'd have coursed through her mind. "Yes."

Daniel pulled back and thrust again. "Yes, you'll marry me?"

"White dress and all."

She expected him to laugh at the idea of her wearing white, but he didn't. "With pink roses and sparkling cider instead of champagne."

Alyssa didn't answer with more than a groan of acceptance. Everything spiraled in to the feeling of Daniel's body in hers, over hers, around hers.

He waited for her to come, but only just. Alyssa made a point of watching Daniel during climax.

Tom had closed his eyes, but Daniel kept his open and locked on hers, his love shining brightly. A look of wonder softened his face, and his cock spasmed in continuing spurts of release.

"Oh, gods... It's beautiful," he whispered.

Alyssa laughed. "You're not weaseling out of the wedding now," she teased.

"I wouldn't dream of it."

Chapter Forty-four

August 10, 2050

"One more, Alyssa," Daniel encouraged her.

She bore down, fighting every inch as hard as Daniel ever had in battle with beasts, panting as her contraction waned, trembling wildly, exhausted.

Dear Tes! She was beautiful, and if the dark crop of hair was any indication, their baby would be beautiful, as well.

"The head is out," he offered, massaging the leg he braced for her, nodding to Melanie to do the same with the other. The books said massage would help, and he wouldn't fail on the subject of anything that would ease this for her.

"Good," she whispered. Alyssa reached her hand out, smiling weakly as Daniel caught it in his and rocked her wedding band beneath his thumb.

"I'm here for you."

"Just the shoulders, Alyssa," Tabitha informed her. "The neck is clear, and the next contraction is coming up."

Alyssa nodded, her hand tightening on Daniel's, her foot pressing hard against his chest. She pulled up, using his hand to assist her, curling into the contraction, grimacing.

Tabitha rocked the baby this way and that, freeing one shoulder from her straining opening. Alyssa cried out, and Daniel snapped his gaze to her, murmuring assurances that it was nearly over.

A furious squall brought his head back around. Daniel laughed in delight at the sight of the two nurses crowded around their son, doing all the things a modern medical center deemed necessary for a newborn baby.

"He's here," Daniel crowed. "Oh, Alyssa! He's beautiful." He set her leg on the bed and stepped up to kiss her.

Tabitha chuckled. "Strike that 'he' stuff, Daddy. This 'young Warrior' happens to be a girl."

Daniel's heart pounded in a combination of disbelief and unbearable joy. They'd discussed a girl, but neither one of them had dared hope for it.

He met the doctor's eyes, nodding. Tabitha was protected, and she knew what he had to do. While an amulet could be given with others in the room, the blood oath to free a daughter couldn't. It had to be done quickly, and she'd know that.

Tabitha was abruptly serious. "Jackie, Dweena... There are religious observances. Please, withdraw and send in the baby's grandfather."

They seemed confused by that announcement, but they left as instructed. Tabitha set their daughter at the edge of the bed and started tending to Alyssa's afterbirth, while Mel bathed her face.

Daniel drew his sacred weapon and sliced his left palm, savoring the sweet pain that would tie them together. In a matter of heartbeats, the seal was drawn over her forehead and chest in his blood and the words spoken. As the final line of the freeing passed his lips, the door opened and Tim stepped in.

His smile faltered. "When I heard it was a girl, I'd hoped... But, you're right. You'll be her father."

Daniel smiled, laying a kiss over his daughter's forehead and accepting a strip of gauze from Tabitha. He stood, wrapping it slowly. "Thank you for understanding. Alyssa promised you the *Schutzes*." He stepped back and waved Tim over, tying the field bandage tight around his hand.

The older Warrior hesitated, touching the baby's face tenderly. "You've got a good Daddy, little one."

"And a good grandfather," Daniel replied. He sat on the edge of the bed, waiting for Tim to begin the blessing.

Armen's hand swung out toward them, and Daniel stared at it in confusion.

"What is it?" Daniel asked.

A muscle twitched in Tim's jaw, and his voice was rough in emotion. "She's my granddaughter, and she'll have my blessing, but as your daughter, she should wear your amulet."

Daniel didn't argue it. It was an incredible show of trust and solidarity that Armen was offering. "For now." He pulled one out of his jacket pocket and handed it over. "Have one of yours make an amulet with both seals on it."

Tim smiled widely. "I'll forge it myself. Now, what is my granddaughter's name?"

Daniel looked at Alyssa, ruffling her hair affectionately. "We got down to three. The final choice is yours."

"Crystal," she decided. "Crystal Arielle Armen-Hunter." Alyssa bit her lip, gauging Tim's reaction to her solution for their daughter's last name.

Tim nodded. "A beautiful name for a beautiful baby."

Crystal:

Daddy's Little Girl

A note from the author

Sometimes, a character or situation sticks with you after the end of the story. In the case of "The Warrior's Widow," I was left with the dichotomy of an Armen daughter being raised as a daughter of Hunter. What kinds of problems would that cause? Well, not many, because Tim and Daniel had so obligingly come to an understanding at her birth. I envisioned years of visits, a properly spoiled Warrior daughter/granddaughter, and a lot of love on all sides.

But, there was still one more problem that might rear its head, and it did.

Happy reading!
Brenna

Chapter Forty-five

November 5, 2072

"Hello, Daddy."

Daniel chuckled, as Crystal wrapped her arms around his neck and kissed his cheek, leaping into his circling arms. "Oh, no. What's it going to cost me this time?"

Her nose wrinkled. "Not everything I ask you costs you money."

He set her down, crossing his arms over his chest. "True, but 'Daddy' usually implies it. Any other time, I'm 'Dad.'"

Crystal bit her lower lip, as her mother often did. "I never realized I'd left such an overt tell." She smiled brightly. "Guess I'll have to fix that."

"I'll just bet you will." He fought back laughter at their verbal sparring. "Now, why don't you tell me how much this is going to cost me and why I just have to agree?"

"Not a dime, and because you love me."

"Oh, no. Then it's even more expensive than I thought it would be."

Her expression was heartbreakingly hopeful.

Daniel sighed, wrapped an arm around her, and led her to the couch. "I think I'll need to sit down for this."

She settled beside him, looking decidedly nervous. "Most likely."

"Not what I needed."

"Sorry." Crystal honestly did sound contrite.

"Hit me."

She smiled, elbowing him in the stomach lightly. It was an old joke between them, and they both started laughing.

Daniel pulled her into his lap, his heart aching that she was twenty-two and would leave him someday soon. "Now, what do I love you so much I'll agree to?"

"I love someone."

He buried his face in her hair, cursing himself for hating those words. Crystal deserved love in her life, and he couldn't begrudge her that. *If Tim Armen released her into my care, I can release her into the care of another...if it's the right other.*

"Does he love you?" he managed.

"I think so."

"He hasn't said it?" That was one strike against him.

"A hundred times, at least."

Daniel leaned back, turning her face to his. "Then why aren't you sure? If you have any qualms—"

"I don't," she assured him, her expression earnest.

"If he does—"

Crystal darkened and shifted her eyes away.

"Something you need to tell me?" he asked.

"Well..."

"Maybe, we should start with his name. I'll start all of the usual checks."

"That...um...that won't be necessary."

"Like hell it won't," he growled.

"You already know each other." She peeked up at him.

"I already... A Warrior?"

Crystal nodded. "So, you see... He wouldn't dare—"

"But, you said he's told you he loves you a hundred times." If this was another Tom Armen, there would be hell to pay.

She winced. "It's not what you think."

"Then what?" His mind clasped on the only possible answer. "He's a Hunter?"

"I'm not related by blood to anyone but my brothers," she defended herself hotly. "There's nothing wrong with it."

Daniel picked that logic apart and found it sound. "Okay. I can't argue that, but—"

"Look at it this way. If I marry a Hunter, I'll always be nearby."

He groaned. "Which one?"

"Kyle."

His mind kicked into gear. "Kyle is requesting— Oh, hell!"

Daniel set Crystal on her feet and bolted out of the room. She pounded after him, but he reached Nick's office a full hallway before she did. He knocked and entered without waiting for an answer.

Nick looked up, raising an eyebrow. "Daniel, this isn't—"

Crystal loped in after him, gasping from the mad dash up the stairs and out into the lord's wing. "What is it?"

Kyle turned to her in apparent shock. He snapped his mouth shut, darkening to crimson, choosing to stare a hole in the desk rather than looking at Crystal.

"I'll be damned," Daniel breathed. Why had he never seen this?

Nick cleared his throat. "If you don't mind, Daniel, I was just about to—"

"Don't approve his request. Not yet."

"What request?" Crystal asked.

* * * *

Kyle bit back a groan. Who knew life could suck so badly? He chanced a glance at her, knowing he shouldn't. *I'm printing, and I can't help it.* Breaking printing was going to be the hardest thing he'd ever do.

"What request?" she repeated.

"Crystal, let me ex—" Daniel began.

"A transfer," Nick replied simply.

All color drained from her face, and Kyle ached to comfort her.

Knock it off! She's your cousin.

But she wasn't really his cousin, and his libido knew that all too well, even if his mind argued it.

She's a woman of my house.

I want her to be my woman, my mate.

It was the argument that had driven him mad for months.

"Crystal," her father soothed her.

"You were asking to leave? You weren't even going to tell me?"

Kyle ground his teeth. Ani knew he didn't want to leave her, but staying was going to drive him completely insane. He dreamed of her every night, waking hard and wanting. He couldn't even take solace in other women anymore. "Yes."

She stomped toward him, her fist raised to punch him. Kyle stood his ground. Whatever she did couldn't hurt worse than he already did, and he'd rather die than raise a hand to her.

Daniel grasped her in a bear-hug, shaking his head. "None of that."

She sobbed, then swallowed hard and steeled her expression.

"Better," her father decided. "Now, Kyle—"

"Don't bother," she snapped. "Let him leave, if that's what he wants." Crystal fought her father's hold.

He didn't release her. "Stop that," he ordered. "Now, Kyle."

"Yes, sir?" he grumbled.

"Why did you request a transfer?"

"I respectfully decline—"

"Don't try that with me. I have a pretty clear picture already, so you might as well—"

Nick rapped his knuckles on the desk to get attention. "Since you've obviously lied to me about your reason, I suggest you answer that question honestly."

Kyle fought the tension in his jaw. "I'm printing. I'm pretty damned far gone, to tell the truth, and since she's not a woman I can have, I can't look at her every day and stay sane."

Crystal stared at him, tears glittering on her dark lashes. "You dope. You weren't even going to ask? I asked. I believed in you that much."

His heart stuttered. Kyle couldn't seem to form words. He was two steps closer to her when coherent thought intruded.

The fact that Daniel had stopped Crystal from belting him one across the mouth didn't mean that her father didn't intend to do it himself. Kyle met Daniel's eyes, seeking out his intent.

"You're printing on Crystal, and you asked to leave?" he asked.

"I didn't think you'd approve," Kyle admitted.

"Why?"

"She's my... Well, she's not my cousin, but she's... She's a woman of my own house. We were raised together."

"Dope," Crystal repeated, though her expression was one of hurt and not anger.

"Crystal, you have to understand—"

"I don't have to understand anything," she shouted. "Just take your damned transfer and good riddance."

Kyle forced slow even breaths. He'd blown it; she'd never accept him now.

Nick looked from Kyle to Crystal, then settled his gaze on Daniel. "Do you intend to let them work this out?" he asked.

"Oh, hell, yes." Daniel pushed his daughter at Kyle.

Crystal stumbled, and Kyle caught her, his body reacting to her in his arms though it wasn't prudent that he do so. She gasped, straightening and pushing at his chest, putting a step between them.

"Go on," Daniel ordered. "Don't come back until you find something to agree on."

"And no storming off in different directions," Nick added. "Go together and work this out. Until the two of you agree on what I'm going to do next, I don't want to see either one of you. Got it?"

Kyle fought for clarity. "You're actually giving me permission?" he asked.

Daniel crossed his arms over his chest. "I've already done that. It's not my permission you need now."

Crystal turned away. "Then he can forget it."

Kyle cursed fluently in German and French, then in Gaelic for good measure.

Her father glared at her. "Are you really that fickle?"

She turned to him, seemingly horrified. "Me? He's the one who—"

"Then stop letting your anger and hurt talk for you, and talk to Kyle in the same terms you talked to me downstairs."

Crystal blushed. "If you insist, though I don't see what good it's going to do."

"A closed mind is a wonderful thing, isn't it?" he replied sarcastically.

Nick nodded. "It's going to take a long time to work this out with that attitude."

To Kyle's surprise, Crystal didn't rise to their bait. She rounded her father and looked back to see if Kyle was following.

He nodded, offering her his hand. She pivoted and marched through the open office door, turning toward the center staircase and the Warriors' wing.

Kyle followed, his head reeling. Fifteen minutes ago, he'd been well on his way to never seeing Crystal again, devoid of hope and miserable. Well, the only things that had changed in that time were that he had permission to take her as his mate, if she were willing to, and he was being forced into her company. Hopelessness and misery were still his companions.

He'd hurt her and angered her. Kyle hadn't even realized how serious she was about his interest in her, how aware and eager she'd been. *And, now I've thrown it all away.*

Crystal headed down the stairs to the garage.

"What are you doing?" he asked.

"We were ordered to go somewhere and talk this out."

"And?"

"If we stick around here, we'll have people listening at keyholes and offering input I don't want." She stopped at his truck, pulling the door open. "And it's not as if I'll be rushing to your room with you."

Kyle hardened at the mental image of Crystal in his bed. He strode toward her, needing the connection they'd always shared desperately.

She backed into the truck, her eyes widening as he lifted her onto the seat. "Wh...What are you doing?"

"Finishing what we started earlier." He planted his hands on either side of her hips and leaned toward her, giving her every chance to stop him.

That moment had been the last straw for Kyle. Crystal had been backed to the wall in the corridor outside the library, laughing at a joke he'd told her. Kyle had found himself a hand-width from her lips, fighting back the urge to kiss her. Forcing his mind to work had been nearly impossible, and walking to his room had been all the time he'd needed to decide that he was going to break some serious sanctions if he didn't get away from her quickly.

This time, there was no reason to stop...unless she told him to, and there was no more indication that Crystal wanted him to stop than there'd been the last time. Kyle bit back a groan as her eyes closed, her face tipped up to his and off to one side, and their lips met.

His mind fractured, coherent thought scattered in waves of sensation. Her scent and taste had him dizzy and aching.

Her lips parted beneath his, and her arms circled him, her fingers tunneling through his hair. Kyle couldn't rein in his hunger any longer. He dragged her to his body, muting her gasp in his mouth. Her legs wrapped around his hips.

Kyle stepped back, lifting her off the seat by her grip and his hands under her buttocks. The cab of the truck provided the hard surface he needed to grind himself against her.

Crystal broke off the kiss and looked around, her eyes slumberous, her center hot and damp, even through two layers of blue jeans and whatever lay beneath. She licked her upper lip. "This doesn't excuse you," she stated in a slightly slurred voice.

Kyle smiled. "I didn't think that it would."

She extricated herself from his hold, sliding onto the seat, smoothing her hair. "Good. Then let's go."

"Where do you propose?"

"Far away. Out of the city. Somewhere we won't run into Warriors."

"As my lady wishes." He shut her door and rounded the truck.

"I'm not your lady," she snapped. The rest was mumbled under her breath, almost inaudible, even to him. "Yet."

* * * *

Crystal watched Kyle out of the corner of her eye. They'd been driving for almost an hour, and he'd tried to apologize three times...badly.

That annoyed her further. Not that he was so bad at it, but that he wanted to talk. Gods, all she wanted was more of him.

"So, where do you want to go? We'll run out of fuel...or at least have to ask permission to enter another range, eventually."

Bed!

Oh, no. You don't get off the hook that easily.

"How could you walk away without even asking?" she countered. *You want to talk? Let's talk.*

His smile disappeared. "Contrary to what you think of me, I don't want to leave you."

"Now." How could he choose to leave her?

"I never *wanted* to leave you. Hell, if I'd known getting your father's permission would be this easy, I'd have asked two years ago."

"Because it wasn't easy, it wasn't worth—"

"No! You're worth everything and more, but..."

Her heart pounded in anticipation. "But?"

"If I'd asked him and been turned down, I'd have been shipped off to the furthest reaches of Hunter."

"So, you asked to be shipped off? Well, that makes perfect sense," she offered sarcastically.

"It was a catch twenty-two. To feel comfortable asking your father's permission, I'd have to approach you first...formally. I'd have to know you wanted me to do it."

"You were afraid of me?"

"No, but... If I'd asked you and knew you wanted me to ask permission..." He sighed.

"This is one of those Warrior-things, isn't it?"

He shot her a long-suffering look. "Yes. It is."

"Go on, then."

"If I got your hopes up, and your father said 'no,' could I live with myself for giving you hope of something I couldn't provide for you? I never expected... I mean I really never expected him to—"

"I softened him up for you," she admitted. "Coming from me, he was unlikely to decide against you."

Kyle nodded. His hands fisted on the steering wheel. "I've ruined it, haven't I?"

Crystal considered that. "If you had, would I have been all over you in the garage?"

He groaned. "Unless you want more of the same, we should change the subject."

Now, that was the Kyle she wanted. She slid across the seat to him, laying a hand on his thigh. "How far is it to cabin three?"

"Crystal," he warned, his thigh muscles tensing.

The temptation was too much for her. Crystal trailed her fingertips up his inner thigh, her breath catching as he hardened again. She'd felt it in the garage, but she hadn't realized how mesmerizing watching it happen would be. "Cabin three?" she suggested. *As if you aren't heading for it, at least subconsciously.*

Kyle hit the turn signal. "Ten miles."

She traced the growing bulge, and he snagged her hand, wide-eyed.

"We have permission," she reminded him.

His grip faltered, then tightened.

"How long have we wanted this?"

"I want more than this, better for your first time."

"Most people touch in cars before they—"

Kyle pressed her hand to his length, gasping out a curse. Crystal rubbed him, feeling him thicken further, then pulled at the buttons on his jeans. He jerked the wheel to the right and left the pavement, pouring on steam up the dirt track.

He was hard and heavy in her hand, and Crystal felt her breathing going as ragged as his. A trickle of moisture ran down her perineum, and she rubbed her thighs together, needing the friction.

Kyle thrust his hand between her thighs, forcing them apart. "Not by yourself," he grumbled.

She swiveled her hips, shivering as he touched her. "Only for you," she gasped. Oh, yes. She'd come for him. If he touched the seam over her crotch once more, even lightly, she'd likely come apart.

"Not at all, until we stop, or we won't make it to a bed. I refuse to take your maidenhead in the truck or against a tree."

Humor was all she had left. "Picking out the splinters could be fun."

His smile returned. "What I intend to do is going to be a lot more fun."

Crystal nodded, crying out as they hit a bump, and his hand cupped her center.

He didn't move it. "You are so hot and wet." His come trailed over her fingers.

"Speaking of wet," she hinted.

He slammed the truck into park. "Make me come."

She glanced at the cabin, her heart pounding.

"Here."

Crystal stared at him in confusion. "What?"

"I intend to take your maidenhead slowly. This isn't going to be slow. Make me come." His fingertips traced her seam. "And, I'll make you come. Then we'll go inside and do whatever you want to."

"You promise?" she asked.

Kyle shot her a hungry look. "Make me come, Crystal. See what you do to me."

"How can I resist?" She looked to his hand pointedly, smiling as he guided it away from her body.

She collected his come on the pad of her thumb and massaged the cleft of his cock with it. Kyle groaned, tipping his hips up.

"I've heard men like that," she mused. "And..." Crystal made circles over the thick veins beneath the head.

He laid his head back, his eyes closing. "Damn right, they do. Tes, that's good."

"You're seeing stars?" she teased.

"Let me touch you, and you'll see them."

"You first."

Kyle wrapped his hand around hers, guiding her, showing her how to bring him over. His hips thrust faster and harder, and Crystal watched in fascination.

As if he'd picked the emotion out of her mind, he played on it. "Watch it, Crystal. The next time will be inside you. Do you want it hard..." He slowed his thrusts. "Or soft?"

"Hard. Most definitely hard." Her dreams of this certainly hadn't included slow, soft lovemaking. In them, Kyle hadn't done anything gently, and she'd loved every moment of it.

Kyle resumed his frantic pace. "Oh, yeah. Like that. Every inch inside you."

She moaned.

"Are you rubbing those thighs together?"

Her face heated. She hadn't intended to, but she was.

His hand returned to her, stroking back and forth, then in a concentrated effort against her clit.

"Kyle," she begged. "I'm going to..."

"Yes. We both are. Watch, Crystal."

She felt the pumping sensation beneath her fingers a moment before he erupted. A fountain of milky semen followed, coating their hands and dotting his clothing heavily.

And she'd feel that inside her. "Oh, gods," she breathed. It was going to feel so good.

Kyle peeled her hand away, turning toward her, pressing her semen-coated fingertips to her clit through her jeans. "Show me how to touch you."

Crystal didn't question it. There was something inherently wicked about rubbing his come into herself while he watched. She bit her lip, her breathing coming in gasps.

"What is it?" he asked.

"Take me inside."

"I want you to come first."

"I want to touch myself, and I want you to see it."

He opened her jeans, peeling them down her thighs. Her panties followed.

Kyle spread her knees to the extent the fabric allowed, his eyes dilated. "Not here," he whispered. "I won't take you here."

We'll see about that. Crystal slid her fingers between her thighs, circling her clit slowly. She'd had plenty of practice pleasuring herself and thinking of Kyle, so much so that she'd wondered if freed Warrior daughters shared that portion of the curse.

She separated her outer labia, spreading the drying slick of his fluids inside.

He groaned. "You want my seed inside you that badly?"

"Oh, yeah."

Kyle turned her toward him, kneeling between her knees so she was all but immobilized from the hips down. He leaned across her, kissing her passionately.

He's going to do it. I've pushed him too far. God's, but that thought was exciting.

"You want more?" he asked.

Crystal nodded, her body in a riot for him. The expected piercing sensation didn't materialize. The head of his cock stroked through her parted folds, teasing her. She cried out, begging without words for more.

He moved her hand away, using the silky, come-coated head to explore her, his breathing ragged. "It's all for you, Crystal."

The first whispers of her climax made her groan weakly. She closed her eyes.

"Ride it out. I'll be inside you soon."

A trickle of warmth ran down her seam.

"More for you," he informed her. "Gods help me, you're going to have it all again."

Crystal opened her eyes in surprise. Judging by the intensity of his expression, she was going to feel precisely that. The knowledge that he was so close sent her over.

Kyle breathed a series of curses, bathing her in waves of come. Crystal screamed in pleasure...then again as he parted her labia and buffeted her sensitive inner tissues.

"Gods, I'm depraved," he gasped.

She shivered in aftershocks. "Then I'm worse."

"You don't know what I want." He darkened.

"Let's go inside and find out."

He pulled back with a growl, backing out of the truck and pulling her after him. Before she'd figured out how she was supposed to walk with her jeans around her calves, she had been tossed over his shoulder, her bare bottom warmed by the afternoon sunshine.

Crystal wiggled against him, feeling exposed. His hand trailed up her thigh, his fingers massaging the slick of come into her. She stilled with a sigh. She'd always known Kyle would feel this wonderful...and he hadn't even made it inside her yet.

Chapter Forty-six

Kyle forced his mind to function. He'd come damned close to taking her on the truck seat, and the urge to take her over the porch rail was equally intense.

Like what I want to do is so much better? He grimaced at that, at visions from a few movies he'd seen set in the very decadent ancient Rome.

He never would have considered it if Crystal hadn't been so turned on by having his come on her...and he hadn't been so aroused by seeing it on her. *At least, be honest about it.* He loved it, probably because he never thought he'd see it.

Taking her maidenhead comes first. We've both waited too long for that.

Kyle punched the code into the keypad and kicked the door open, praising whoever decided this was more efficient than two pounds of keys. He shut the door and pressed the lock button, heading for the bed without a word.

Ani help him! He was hard again. With months of fantasies fueling him, Kyle had no doubt that he'd be hard quite a bit in the near future. He laid her on the bed, prepared to enact as many of them as he could in short order.

Crystal started to slide her shirt up. He stopped her, shaking his head. She hesitated, looking at his throbbing cock, then lying back as if she expected him to finish as he nearly had in the truck.

"Not on your life," he whispered, following her down.

Anticipating his intent, she met him in a hard, hot kiss. If Crystal wanted a crash course in heavy petting, she'd get it in spades, followed by a full education in sex.

Kyle cupped one hand around the back of her neck, rolling to his side and drawing her along without losing her mouth. Free to touch her, he palmed a breast with his opposite hand. The already-taut nipple pressed to him as she arched, and he groaned in the realization that she wasn't wearing a bra.

The invitation couldn't have been stated more clearly...at least not while their tongues were dancing against each other. He slid his hand beneath her shirt, fondling her, exploring her body.

Crystal pressed hard against him, pulling at his shoulders in a vain attempt to coax him over...then inside her. She broke off the kiss and started to protest his refusal.

Kyle dragged her shirt up and off, lifting her and latching onto first one and then the other nipple. Visions of her pert breasts coated in milky come had him silently cursing himself a degenerate again.

"Were you planning to take me after you got your father's permission?" he asked.

"What?" It was a gasp, escaping her lips as he licked at a ready peak.

He laid a lick over the other. "You usually wear a bra."

"I hoped you'd notice that earlier."

"This morning?"

"Um...yes."

"I was too busy looking at your mouth," he admitted. "If I'd noticed I would have paid one hell of a penalty for breaking the rules of sanction." *I certainly wouldn't have been able to walk away from her then.* Kyle trailed his lips down her stomach, inching her pants further down her calves.

She wound her fingers in his hair. "Mmmm... What are you doing?"

"It's called foreplay," he teased. "It's what most people do in cars and beds before they advance to sex."

"Oh, yeah. I should be doing some of that. Shouldn't I?"

"What did you have in mind?" Gods, the discussion was driving him crazy. Whatever she requested of him, he'd give her.

"Tasting you."

That simply, his cock was weeping pre-come again. "Fuck this." He dragged off his shirts, then his boots, socks, and pants.

"Finally," she breathed, panning wide eyes down his body. "Common sense."

Kyle knelt up beside her. "You want to taste it?"

"Oh, yes."

"Don't move."

Crystal held very still, her eyes widening further as he painted her lips. Her nostrils flared, and she drew in his scent. He locked down on his control, narrowly avoiding the vision of her in his mind.

Kyle pulled back slightly, staring at a milk-white drop on her lower lip. "Taste it," he rasped.

She licked her lips, purring, her eyes promising delights he hadn't even dared dream of. Without conscious plan, Kyle brought his cock back to her lips, then teased it between. He shuddered at the silken tip of her tongue on the head. She let him play inside her as if he'd ordered her to be still again. It was too much.

"Suck it, then name what you want."

Crystal lunged up, turning and burying her mouth in his lap. He cried out harshly, stamping down on his self-control as she bobbed up and down on his length.

"Do you want it this way, Crystal?" He sought out her clit with his fingertips, gasping as she spread her legs for him and groaned around his length. "Or do you want me inside you? We can come back to this later. What I plan to do—"

She released him, turning to her back to open fully to him. "Tell me about your plan."

His face heated.

"Tell me."

Kyle prayed that she wouldn't think he was completely demented. "You like having my come on you," he stated.

She nodded frantically at that.

"You like having it massaged into your body." He stroked her seam, spreading the mixture of their fluids over her again.

Crystal bowed up to his fingers. "You know I do. When you came on me, it felt so good."

"I'm going to do it again...and again...and again." He punctuated each 'again' with a stroke of his fingers.

She nodded, writhing against his hand.

Moment of truth. Either you're as turned on by this idea as I am or not. "I'm going to spray come on your pretty breasts and stomach, your thighs, your backside and your lips. I'm going to massage it into you, until you're covered in it. Then I'm going to take you to the shower and wash my seed off while I plant a second load deep inside you."

"S-second? I still need the first, Kyle." She screamed, trembling, her thighs clamping tight on his fingers, the pulse beat of her climax resonating in the pads of his fingers.

Kyle dragged her legs apart, numbly noting that her jeans were still around her ankles. He knelt between her calves, then laid out over her, piercing her body in one long slide.

Crystal screamed again but in pleasure rather than the pain he'd expected. Her contracting muscles welcomed him in. He didn't pause; it hardly seemed possible to. Rather, he pounded hard and fast, as she'd requested.

Her climax quickened. Her nails bit into his back, and she shouted out his name, over and over.

It was over all too quickly, Kyle buried to the hilt in her, his body releasing in sweet waves played harmony to her continuing climax. Crystal held to him, her bent knees cradling his thighs while her bound ankles were trapped beneath his legs. The things he wanted to do to her...

"Oh, gods. I am depraved," he whispered.

She laughed. "What is it, now?"

"Your father is going to kill me if he ever finds out the things I plan to do to you."

"We have permission to do anything I agree to." She shifted her legs, caressing her knees back and forth. "You can keep making promises."

"I want to tie you to the bed while I anoint you with my come." He blurted it out, seemingly without a care to what she might think of him.

Crystal seemed to consider that carefully.

Maybe that was too far for her. "If you—"

"On one condition."

"And that is?" Did he care? If she'd give him that, Kyle would promise her almost anything.

"When we set out to conceive your son..."

Aftershocks wracked him. She moaned and moved against him, a sure sign that he'd released more come into her at that statement of fact.

Gods, he was far gone. If just the thought of her allowing that... "Tell me about it, Crystal," he begged.

"How many times do you think you can release on me like you did in the truck before you have to be inside me?"

He tipped her chin up, capturing her lips in a near-brutal kiss. "A lot. Ani and Tes help me. And every one will carry the chance without the soreness of a sexual marathon for you."

Crystal bit lightly at his earlobe. "You're getting hard again, just thinking about your son," she whispered. "You are far gone."

Kyle sought her lips, sampling them in nips and feathering touches. "Very. I was serious. If I'd have kissed you this morning, the rest of the day would have passed with me inside you."

"Good. Then you should tie me down."

Her lips still fascinated him. They were warm, soft and tasted faintly of sex. "I agree. I should."

"Don't."

"Don't what?"

"Don't agree with me about anything."

He met her eyes, mired in confusion. "Why not?"

Crystal smiled a little too sweetly. "We were ordered not to come back until we agree on something."

"You really think that will work?"

"Do you really care?"

"Not at all," he admitted.

* * * *

November 8, 2072

Daniel strolled into the kitchen at the manor, smiling faintly as Nick chuckled. "Shut up. Will you?" he grumbled.

"She's your daughter, but I remind you that *you're* the one who ordered them not to return until they'd come to an agreement. I didn't do that. I just backed you on it."

"How hard can it be to reach an agreement? They agree to sleep together and consider printing. Done."

"I guess that depends on how hard they are trying to agree. Doesn't it?"

Daniel stared at him, incredulous. "You don't honestly think she's still refusing him." He pushed that thought away. If he thought for a moment that Kyle was busy breaking sanctions by convincing her, he'd track him down and gut his cousin personally.

Nick erupted in gales of laughter. "It's a damned safe bet that she hasn't refused him. In fact..." He slid a look at his youngest son, Warren. "It's a safe bet that her refusal didn't last an hour after her protestations in my office."

Warren darkened, staring into his cup a little too intently.

Daniel felt his muscles tensing. "Something I should know?" he challenged.

Warren didn't answer.

Nick laughed harder. "Warren got a bit of a surprise when Kyle and Crystal left here."

"In the garage?" Daniel barked, locking on the truth that Warren was in charge of routine maintenance on the vehicles and would likely have been working down there. "Has he no respect for her, at all?"

Warren rubbed a hand across the back of his neck. "They weren't having sex," he supplied hastily. "They were just...um..."

Nick snickered. "All over each other will do. Still clothed but obviously well on their way to working things out."

"Yeah. That will do, all right."

Daniel pulled out a chair and settled in. "Any reason you decided not to share this?"

"Any reason I should have?" Warren countered acidly. "None of *my* business, if you gave your permission."

Nick sighed. "Warren did come to me."

Daniel pounced on that. "To you and not to me? I would have been Kyle's judge."

"Would you tell another Warrior that your cousin was sleeping with his daughter without back-up?"

He started to deny that he'd lose control, then thought better of it. "I see your point. If I hadn't known about Kyle, it wouldn't have been pretty." Daniel fingered the cell phone in his jacket pocket, dreading the coming call. "Did Kyle take his cell with him, by the way?"

Nick snorted. "Hell, no. He wasn't wearing his jacket when they lit out of here. Probably didn't want to have Crystal take off on him while he grabbed it... Or, he wasn't thinking straight."

Daniel winced.

Nick mirrored it. "Problem?"

"Crystal left hers on the car charger."

"And?" His expression announced that he'd finally scented circling danger.

"Oh, just that Tim Armen is looking for Crystal."

Nick groaned in understanding. "And, for the first time in twenty-two years, you can't account for her."

"Yes. So, if you have any idea how to narrow my search, I'd love to hear it."

"Checked Crystal's cards?"

"Of course. Not a thing."

"Warren, check Kyle's," he ordered.

The younger Warrior pushed to his feet and grabbed his coffee cup. "Will do."

It was a tense ten minutes of waiting. Nick offered coffee and food that Daniel refused. Attempts at small talk failed or turned into tentative plans to hook the electronic locks at the cabins in to a system that would show them entries, like the Mahers had instituted half a century earlier.

By the time Warren cleared his throat, Daniel's nerves were frayed.

"Found something?" Nick asked.

"Uh...you could say that," his son replied carefully.

Daniel snatched the sheet of paper from Warren's hand.

"You don't want to—" Warren groaned, shooting his father a pained look.

Daniel read the last two entries twice, his jaw tightening. "A lingerie store and a sex shop. Right." What else had he expected? Well, a hotel would have been more acceptable than a sex shop. "You looked up the addresses for these?"

Warren shook his head. "I know them well enough."

"Not germane to the discussion."

He darkened considerably.

"Well?" Daniel prompted him.

"About fifteen miles from cabin three," he reported.

"Then let's move."

A new voice made his heart stutter. "Not without me, you won't."

Daniel winced, turning to face Tim Armen. "You said you'd call."

"You said everything was under control," he countered.

"It is." *More or less.*

"A lingerie store and a sex shop? And, she's hiding out in a Hunter cabin? You're not making good on the confidence I placed in you, Daniel."

"She's not hiding out. Crystal had permission to pursue a relationship. She just got a little carried away and left her cell phone behind."

Tim's eyebrows rose. "So, you've checked this man out? He's clean?"

Warren coughed harshly. "As clean as they come," he muttered. He paled under Armen's scrutiny.

Tim plucked the printout from Daniel's fingers. "As clean as they come?" he challenged. "With charges for—" His eyes widened, and he stared at the top of the sheet.

Daniel adjusted his weapons belt. "As clean as a Warrior comes," he affirmed.

"A Hunter?" Tim choked.

"Better than an Armen. Crystal isn't related to her Hunter cousins by blood. She knows it. Kyle knows it. We all know it. Try as Kyle did not to print, when it's the right woman, there's no stopping it."

Tim nodded solemnly. "He's serious about this?"

"If he wasn't, I never would have given my blessing to it. The *only* reason I decided to track her was—"

"To put me at ease," he finished.

Daniel sighed. "Do you still insist on this?"

"I...well..."

"You do?" Damn, he'd been hoping that Tim would back down, given the circumstances.

"Just to put Deb at ease."

Nick snorted.

Tim offered a sheepish look. "And me."

Daniel nodded. "Okay. We'll do it." In truth, it would put Daniel at ease, as well, though he wasn't about to admit that aloud.

* * * *

Crystal heard his voice through a haze of pleasure, licking her lip before she attempted to answer. "Oh, gods. How can you ask that?"

Kyle chuckled. "I knew you'd like it."

Like it? She moaned as his cock slid deeper, the band at the base lodging between her labia, the nubs massaging inside her. Her nails raked at his shoulders, drawing a startled gasp from him.

"Come again," he whispered, retreating.

Gods, the man loved making her come, but this torture was beyond any he'd devised for her yet. The Body Candy massaged into both of their bodies provided a tantalizing slick that brought every inch of flesh to screaming awareness. As if every touch weren't orgasmic enough, the sex wrap and cock ring combination strapped onto him had sent her over again and again while he was still going strong.

The silken skin of the head returned, followed by the heavy textured latex and the thick nub-covered band that was such a slice of the Christian heaven to her.

"Again," he pleaded.

The sex toys he'd introduced her to were pure decadence, and Kyle had decreed several times that they'd have to live at the manor house, so her father wouldn't find out how depraved he was and kill him for it. Though she'd never really cared for the manor, the idea of moving into Kyle's rooms was strangely appealing to her.

The need to make him lose control was fierce. Crystal considered her best course of action carefully, biting her lip.

It wasn't a snap decision. She'd known what she wanted when she'd asked her father's permission. They hadn't pussyfooted around the subject in their time together. They'd already discussed their future sons several times; how much more direct could they get?

But, what if Kyle wasn't ready? What if he hadn't reached *Endspiel* yet? He'd said he was far gone, not that he was at the edges of terminal madness for her.

If he isn't ready, he'll just say so. I can't demand he become ready for something so momentous at the snap of a finger. Crystal resolved to not take rejection personally. *Endspiel* came to a Warrior when it came to him. No sooner and no later.

Kyle traced the indent of her lip with the tip of his tongue, making her shiver. "You're thinking hard when you should be feeling," he chided. "What's on your mind?"

There was no time like the present. "You want me to come," she stated.

His eyes went hot in promise. "You know I do."

"I want you to seal."

He faltered, his cock pulsing inside her, a strangled groan escaping his lips. Kyle squeezed his eyes closed, grumbling a curse, his muscles tensing.

Crystal steeled her expression. He couldn't do it. Not yet. How long would it be? A day? A week? A month or more? She had to let him find the time on his own. "I'm sorry," she managed. It hadn't been fair to put him on the spot that way.

"You shouldn't do that to a Warrior," he gasped, his pace increasing.

"I asked too much, too soon," she agreed.

His eyes opened, and he stared at her in stunned fascination. "You're sure?"

"I don't—"

"If I allow this, it can't be undone, you know. It would be irresponsible of me to take you at your word, if you were speaking out of passion, if you were lost in the moment."

Her heart ached. "Like my...my mother's first mate?" Her birth father hadn't been a stable Warrior, and he'd broken a lot of laws to win his bride and child.

The expression on his face was tender, completely at odds with his lovemaking. "I would never do that to you, Crystal. Never."

He confused her. "Then you want to?" she asked. "You want to seal?"

Again he cursed, cupping her buttocks to force her closer to him. Kyle panted, his jaw so tight there was a white line where his bones met. He relaxed slowly. "I don't know how many times I can hear you ask it and not do it," he warned. "Gods, please be sure."

Crystal smiled, moving against him, a wicked plan taking shape. "If you don't seal, we won't ever get on with making your son a reality, Kyle."

His cock pulsed, and he thrust harder into her, his breathing ragged. Even with the cock ring in place, she was going to force him over.

She cradled his thighs with her knees, as he liked. "When will I be fertile?" she inquired, playing coy.

His voice was rough, deep, gravelly. "Two weeks. Cusp in about eleven days or so." He swallowed hard. "You already want—"

"I wanted it in the truck. I wanted it in the garage." She nipped at his jawline. "I wanted it in the hallway."

He cried out harshly.

"It's so close, Kyle. I'm asking you to take me as your mate. Seal to me. Promise me forever...then give me your son."

Kyle's seed coursed into her, and she arched up, whispering her encouragement. He roared, his climax increasing, the waves of come filling her and running over. His lips captured hers, parting them, claiming her.

His eyes opened, and he froze, his lips a fraction of an inch from hers. "Oh, shit."

Crystal stroked his cheek with her folded hand, laughing in joy. "You didn't take advantage of me," she assured him.

"It's not that."

* * * *

Daniel looked around the main room in disbelief. Clothes had been hastily shed and the plush rug set before the hearth was crushed down and mussed. The scent of sex was heavy, leaving little room for speculation that most of the three days they'd been gone had been invested in his daughter's sexual education.

The sounds originating from behind the closed bedroom door left no doubt as to what was going on inside. *Again.* Whispers and ragged breathing were punctuated by moans and the vigorous creaking of the bed.

Kyle cried out, and Crystal seemed to soothe him. His roar shook the walls, and his thrusts slowed. There was a moment of near silence, more whispers, Crystal's laugh of delight and...

"What?" she demanded.

Tim took a step toward the closed door, and Daniel grasped his arm, wrenching him to a stop. They wouldn't barge in, unless it sounded as if Crystal needed them.

"Crystal..." Kyle's voice was one of half-soothing and half-warning.

"I'll be damned if..." The rest was muffled, most likely in a kiss.

Tim and Daniel looked to each other, nodded, and stepped forward together, prepared to judge Kyle for whatever was going on behind that door.

The door in question flew open an instant before they reached it, bringing them to a halt.

Crystal stood in the doorway, dressed in a rumpled silk spaghetti-strap nightgown that nearly reached her knees. Her lips were kiss swollen, her breasts full and lush and her hair in disarray. A fragrant lotion of some sort made her skin glow. Her fists were planted on her hips, and her eyes flashed in seeming fury.

Daniel abruptly felt chastised. *As well I should. What was I thinking, coming here?*

Kyle appeared behind her, holding a sheet around himself at the hips, looking decidedly tense. He pulled a light blanket around her shoulders with his free hand. "Crystal, please," he hinted.

"I put on a gown," she challenged. "It's more than they deserve."

Kyle didn't argue it. He pulled the blanket shut, then raised her right hand to the overlap. She complied, holding it shut, as he wished.

"Well, I guess we should return home." Her voice shook in fury.

Daniel started to offer apologies, but she cut him off.

"After all, Kyle and I finally agree on several things."

The young Warrior's eyes went wide and wild. "No, Crystal. Never make decisions like this in anger."

"If his vow means—"

"No," Tim shouted. "I demanded this. I was worried. Your father tried to talk me out of it. On my honor, he did. Whatever you're planning—"

"Do you want to spend every generation at a disadvantage with your relatives?" Crystal snapped at him.

Tim managed a sheepish smile. "You know I don't."

Crystal nodded, then glared at Daniel. "And you..." She faltered. "I think it would be better if Kyle and I lived at the manor house."

Daniel sighed in relief. "If you'll be happy there, by all means."

"Happy? If you wanted me happy, why didn't you tell him—" She jerked her head at Tim. "—to go home and let me call when I was good and ready to?"

"Well, you see—"

"Oh, I see very well, thanks. You just couldn't let us seal in peace. You didn't trust Kyle, or you didn't trust me. Checking up on me meant more to you than your word to let us work this out for ourselves."

Daniel felt his cheeks heat, and he fumbled for words. How could he argue it? She had nailed his dishonor perfectly.

"Go on. Deny it," she invited acidly.

"I...can't. You know I can't."

Kyle wrapped his free arm around her, laying a kiss on top of her head. "Misguided but protecting you," he soothed her.

Crystal nodded, easing into his chest. "If you'll excuse us, I'd like to enjoy our first time as a mated couple with *some* semblance of privacy."

Daniel met Kyle's eyes in disbelief. He'd reached *Endspiel* already? He must have waited until he was near mad before asking for that transfer.

Kyle smiled crookedly, drawing her back into the bedroom and shutting the door, his sheet sliding away as he accomplished the task.

Tim shook his head. "I think we've been dismissed."

A creak announced them flopping to the waiting bed.

"I think we have. Come on. I'll buy you a beer on the way back."

Terry:

The Warrior's Man

Chapter Forty-seven

Terry Armen cursed under his breath, cleaning the cut on the other man's neck with an alcohol pad to get a better look at it. Thankfully, it was little more than a scratch. The beast had been going for the kill when Terry reached them, and as a result, the damned thing got the tip of a fang in.

Gods damn it! A minute earlier... Ten gods' damned seconds earlier, and this wouldn't be necessary.

The victim was a young man. Terry would guess his age at twenty or so, a little more than half Terry's thirty-six years. In human terms, he was little more than a boy, and he looked it.

Right now, that boy was trembling hard, using the brick wall behind him for support. There was something endearing in that, something that called to Terry's base instincts as a Warrior. He wanted to protect him.

I have *to offer protection.* Even the tip of a beast's fang was too much. It marked the prey for other beasts, making him nothing short of a beacon, screaming out: *"Come eat me. Easy meal."*

"That was..." The kid took an unsteady breath. "That was a vampire. Wasn't it? I'm not hallucinating? Someone didn't slip something in my drink?"

He was calmer than most victims of attacks were. That was good, considering the news Terry had to impart to him.

"Yes. We call them beasts."

The kid swallowed what sounded like a lump in his throat. "And you...hunt them? I mean... I'm sure you don't just walk around with that hardware for fun."

"Yes, I do." He tossed the alcohol pad at the nearest trash can and stepped back to meet the young man's eyes. "And now I have to protect you." Terry didn't make it a question, as he should have. A rebellious corner of his mind insisted that he wasn't taking 'no' for an answer.

"Protect me? Isn't that..." The kid motioned to the dead beast lying ten yards away. "Isn't that what you've already done? Thank you, by the way."

Terry sighed. "The beast got his teeth into you." He put up a hand for calm, before the kid could get the wrong idea. "It's not going to turn you into one or anything like that, but it makes it easier for others to find you."

His mouth worked as if to form words, but nothing emerged. His blue eyes went wide and wild, and he pushed a quaking hand through his rust-colored curls.

"Yeah. I know. If one had a meal, the others want a bite too. But that's my job. To make it impossible for any of them to get a bite out of you." *If I can. I haven't done a bang up job of it so far.*

"Whatever it takes," the kid vowed. "I'd rather not be some vampire's juice box. Thanks but no thanks."

"It's fairly simple. I give you this." Terry pulled out an amulet and held it up in the dim light from the street. "I speak a few magic words. I take some information, so the others like me know who you are to protect you better. All done, save that you obey when one of us gives you orders for your own protection."

"Magic words? Seriously? Will that work?"

"Did I kill it?"

The kid glanced toward the downed beast again, nodded, then turned his gaze back to Terry. "Good deal. I'm in."

Thank the gods!

Terry eased the amulet over the kid's ears and let it fall to his chest. "Never remove this. It only works while it's on your body somewhere. Put it under your shirt or looped around your belt loop and shoved inside your pants, but keep it on and preferably covered, so the cord can't be severed."

He fingered the leather cord. "Can I replace this?"

"With a chain or something, so it's sturdier?"

He nodded.

"Yes, but still...keep it next to your skin. No further than a shirt between you and the amulet."

"Got it."

Terry leaned closer to him and started reciting the Zeremonie des Schutzes. He chose Gaelic, because it had always been his favorite language.

The kid's eyes slid shut, and Terry thanked the gods for it. Most men balked at the idea of a kiss being part of the blessing, fed on or not. It was always easier to do it quickly, while the other man was unaware, then offer apologies for the 'oversight' of not mentioning it, than make a big deal out of it and end up in an argument while beasts might be closing on their position.

The final syllable left his lips and Terry leaned down to lay a quick peck on the kid's forehead. He jerked his head up, probably at the sensation of Terry moving. Their lips brushed, and Terry went still. A whisper of sound escaped the kid's lips, and Terry savored it.

Common sense kicked in, and Terry moved to plant the kiss on the kid's forehead. *Where I should.* He stepped back, acutely aware of his cock battling with his jeans for land rights on the now-too-tight fabric.

The kid's eyes opened and he took a step back, colliding with the wall. He shot a panicked look at Terry, his hand raised, seemingly waiting to take blows. He launched into a hasty apology. "I'm...sorry. Didn't mean to."

The urge to reassure him was more powerful than ever. "No problem. I should have warned you. The...uh...kiss on the forehead? Sort of part of the magic."

He breathed what looked like a sigh of relief. Terry tried to reason his way out of his disappointment. The kid wasn't arguing with him. Wasn't that good news?

The kid leaned against the wall, scrubbing a hand over his sweat-coated face. The movement drew Terry's gaze down his slim body to the unmistakable outline of his erection.

Terry's heart thundered, and his curse started demanding sex. Hard sex. Now. With the kid, of all people.

He'd noticed men before, but Terry had chalked it up to the curse making an unmated man indiscriminate. As such, he'd never followed through on it and had funneled it toward the next available willing female. He'd never felt himself driven to any sexual partner this way before, not even a female.

The kid looked up at him, his eyes narrowing. "What now?" he asked, seemingly wary.

Terry tipped his head. "What's your name?"

"Why?"

"Paperwork," he reminded him.

"Oh...yeah. You did say that. Steve Cole. My friends call me Stevie."

Terry forced a smile to his face. "Well, Stevie. Next, I drive you home, so I'm sure you make it there alive. It will be easier to get the information I need there, and I'll tell you how to reach us in an emergency."

Stevie hesitated a moment and then nodded. "Sure. Sounds good."

* * * *

Stevie unlocked the door to his apartment and led the way inside, hitting light switches at the door, then the next set at the entrance to the living room. His nerves were strung tight, and it wasn't just being attacked by a vampire talking.

The sound of the door closing and locking behind him reinforced what had him on edge. *Terry.* The man was sex in leather and jeans, and he'd had Stevie scrambled since he appeared over him and dragged Stevie away from the vampire who'd been trying to make him a late dinner.

I can't believe I almost kissed him. What am I? Stupid? He'd like to claim it had been some sort of post traumatic reaction speaking, but it wasn't, and he knew it. He wanted Terry, and there was no denying it.

"Nice place," Terry complimented him.

Stevie nodded. "I've been working on it."

"Very...calming."

Translation. It's screams 'Gaaa-aay.' "Yeah. I think so." Common courtesy kicked Stevie in the head. "Can I get you something? A beer? Soda?" *A nice white wine?* He bit back a wince at Terry's reaction to that.

"Got any coffee?"

"Sure." Stevie made his way into the kitchen, forcing his gaze to pass by Terry when he wanted to linger. *And drool.* Terry was eye candy supreme.

He pushed away the thought and set to work grinding beans. He was halfway through the preheat on the machine when Terry's voice stopped him cold.

"Not bad. A Barista Express."

Stevie swallowed hard. "Yeah. I bought it refurbished." The six hundred dollar price tag for a new one had been a little out of his range. He glanced at Terry over his shoulder, packing the grounds down. "You're familiar with it?"

Terry laughed. "Warriors *live* on coffee, espresso, cappuccino...anything made from roasted coffee beans. I don't think I've met a Warrior who doesn't drink the stuff." His brow furrowed. "Well, maybe the young *Blutjagdfrau*," he amended. "Last time I saw her, it was soda or chocolate milk."

"What's a...um...?" Stevie gave up. It was a safe bet he'd massacre the word if he tried to repeat it.

"Female Warrior. We have a couple of them...not many."

His heart sank. "Oh. Okay." *Stop dreaming. It's fairly certain Terry is into women.*

"We have the same model at one of the cabins," he switched subjects back to coffee. "We just replaced the Portofino Exec Two at the main house."

"Replaced? That's a new model."

"It gets a lot of use."

"But..." Stevie's head spun at the expense. "That's a five-thousand dollar unit. I know coffee shops that don't use one that expensive."

"Six, actually."

Stevie gaped at him. "What did you replace it with?" Something told him he *had* to ask.

Terry went red-faced, and he cleared his throat.

"Oh, come on. I have to know. One coffee lover to another."

"Uh...a couple of TopBrewer Coffee Faucets."

Stevie gaped at him. "Couple of?" He couldn't afford one of those on a good day.

"Three. I think. I'm usually too tired to pay attention."

"Hence the coffee," he quipped.

"Pretty much. I'm shit before my second cup."

* * * *

Terry tucked the notebook back into his pocket, resigning himself to the fact that it was time to leave. He couldn't state with certainty why he'd stayed this long. Sure, he liked talking to Stevie. They shared some common interests, but he expected that he'd stayed because his damned libido was still playing havoc with him.

As if reinforcing that fact, Stevie stretched and yawned, and Terry's cock hardened against his zipper again. He opened his mouth to suggest that it was time to leave.

The sound never emerged. Stevie glanced at Terry's lap, started to turn his head, and his gaze returned. The silence around them was potent, and Terry swore he could detect musk rising from the younger man.

He stared, swallowing audibly, his expression unreadable.

I should give him an out. Explain it. "Warriors... We are a pretty sexual bunch. Need it often. You know."

"I...don't mind."

Terry ground his teeth, frustrated by the answer. Part of him wished Stevie would suggest they find a bed. The other part wished he'd tell Terry he wasn't interested. Not knowing made wanting the kid this way worse. Whether he was interested or not, Terry had to find someone to sate this need.

Neither of them broke the silence. It seemed they were at an impasse.

Time to go. Definitely time to go. "I probably should..."

"I mean... I *really* don't mind." Stevie met Terry's eyes, a slight smile curving his lips, one brow cocked.

No one could mistake the implied invitation. "What are you offering?"

"What are you asking for?"

Terry's mind rioted, and his cock added all sorts of demands to the mix. "I've never been with a guy before, so... Honestly, I don't know what I want." That was a first. Even his first time with a woman, Terry had known what he wanted.

"How about something you're comfortable with, then?"

Terry nodded dumbly, as Stevie stood and crossed the room toward him. He faltered and looked toward the hallway.

Please let him suggest a bed. Why it was so important to make it to a bed was beyond Terry.

"I have condoms in the bathroom. I should—"

"They aren't necessary."

Stevie shot him a startled look.

"Warriors don't carry STDs. We can't get them if someone else does carry them. We're immune, on all levels." *And we don't have to worry about pregnancy.* That went without saying, so he didn't offer it.

He stared, open-mouthed.

He doesn't believe me. "But if you're more comfortable with—"

"Part of your magic?"

"Yes. We also heal quicker than most people do." *A lot faster.* But there was no sense in scaring Stevie with that.

"Okay then." Stevie took the last step and sank to his knees between Terry's spread legs.

When did I widen my stance? His mind refused to provide an answer.

Stevie unbuttoned Terry's jeans and slipped the zipper down. Terry savored every moment, committing it to memory. When Stevie untucked the two layers of shirt, Terry peeled them up and off, tossing them on top of the leather jacket he'd already removed.

There was a moment of dead silence. Terry realized Stevie was holding his breath. His gaze trailed up and down Terry's chest, and color bloomed in his cheeks.

"Like what you see?" Terry asked, trying to lighten the mood.

"Yes is an understatement."

Terry's cock jerked in response, drawing Stevie's gaze down to it. He went back to spreading the jeans and easing them down. Terry tipped his hips up, allowing him to pull the fabric down to the tops of his armored boots.

Stevie closed a hand around Terry's length and started stroking. His hand was softer than Terry's was, lacking the calluses a Warrior built up. But not a woman's hand either. Stevie's hand was stronger, more knowing, and his grip harder and more demanding.

It would be far too easy to come this way, but Terry wanted more. He opened his mouth, intent on asking for it. Stevie's mouth closing on the head of his cock wrenched a groan from him.

There was nothing sweet in that move, nothing tentative. Stevie knew what Terry wanted and offered it with ruthless efficiency.

There was no play at Terry pretending it was a woman sucking him off. He didn't close his eyes and daydream of one of the women who'd done this for him. He kept his eyes wide open, enthralled by the red-brown curls, rising and sinking over his cock, the suction on the withdrawals.

I'm letting a guy suck me off, and damn it's good.

Terry wrapped his hand around the back of Stevie's head, and Stevie faltered for a moment. He wondered at that, but before Terry could ask, Stevie was back at it full steam.

His balls pulled up tight to his body, and Terry managed to gasp out a warning that he was close. It was always a fifty-fifty proposition, whether or not his partner would choose to swallow.

Stevie didn't hesitate. He took Terry to the root. The sweet suction along the full length forced him to climax. Terry closed his fist in Stevie's hair, the cum rushing up his length, a shout echoing off the walls.

He sat there for a moment, spent, stunned by his reaction to Stevie. *And wanting more.* Like most Warriors, a blow job didn't fully relieve him.

I should return the favor. At least give him a hand job. The Rules of Sanction were pretty specific about returning the kindness of a lover.

"Come up here, Stevie."

* * * *

Stevie pushed to his feet, watching for signs that Terry might snap. He'd said he'd never been with a man before. That, in itself, could be a warning sign. Terry lived a violent life; he was *über*-alpha male. That kind sometimes experimented and then got scared or pissed off when they found they enjoyed sex with a guy.

Terry wrapped his hands around Stevie's hips and pulled him down to the couch. Stevie's tensing muscles relaxed at the fingers working his jeans open.

"What are you doing?" Stevie's question came out a gasp.

The tug at Stevie's jeans and the hum of appreciation from Terry was the only answer. In the next instant, Terry's hand was wrapped around Stevie's cock, milking him hard.

The first stroke up his length had Stevie arching toward him with a gasp of delight. The second wrenched a groan from him.

"Softer?" Terry offered.

Stevie shook his head, incapable of making a verbal response.

Terry squeezed and stroked, jerking Stevie toward orgasm with brutal efficiency. Stevie's breathing went harsh, and his legs shook.

Terry's hand retreated, and Stevie looked up at him, stuttering out a plea for more.

"Lay down. Wrap your legs around me."

I'm opening myself to him. Visions of Terry working him up and sliding home made him dizzy in pleasure, and Stevie complied.

Terry didn't do anything of the sort. He knelt between Stevie's legs and looked down at him with a potent expression that made Stevie's heart race.

Then he started stroking again. It was all Stevie could do to keep his eyes open and to force enough oxygen into his body to stay conscious.

That didn't mean Stevie was capable of stringing two words together. He could barely get out one at a time, pathetic pleas for more.

Terry growled out a series of curses, then brought his mouth down on Stevie's. The kiss was scorching and hard, and Stevie wrapped his arms around Terry's shoulders, seeking more intimate contact.

Climax roared over his nerves, and Stevie drew his head back and shouted. His breaths came in starts and gasps, and he licked his lips, trying to clear his mind. His arms lay at his sides, boneless in his scattered state.

Terry stared down at him, his expression unreadable. "I...I should go. I have to call in. File my paperwork." He pushed up from the couch, looking more than a little rattled.

Stevie swallowed hard. He wanted to say something...to reassure Terry, to call him back. A primal, instinctive corner in his mind warned him not to.

He's über-alpha. Let him come to terms with this. Or not. His heart ached at the truth that Terry might choose to file this experiment under the heading of 'Never Happened'.

Terry scooped up his shirts and dragged them over his shoulders together. He pulled his leather jacket on over them, ran a hand over his sheath, looked back at Stevie, then averted his eyes. "Duty calls." Terry took a step toward the door, then stopped and turned halfway back. "I...uh... Do you mind if I come back again...sometime?"

Stevie nearly choked in surprise. "Sure. Anytime," he managed.

He nodded. In the next heartbeat, Terry was letting himself out of the apartment.

Stevie lay on the couch, his jeans at the top of his thighs, his shirt matted to his abdomen with jizz. Aftershocks wracked his body, and his head spun pleasantly.

God, that man is hot. He said he might come back. His heart leapt in excitement, and he smiled.

He probably won't. That quickly, his smile melted away.

Stevie levered himself off the couch and dragged his jeans up. "Time to get cleaned up, Cinderella."

* * * *

Terry mounted the stairs to one of the houses in town, one that was usually empty. He was still shaken by the strength of his reaction to Stevie, and until he was sure where it was headed, it was probably best to keep a wide berth between himself and his family.

He pressed the connection button on his headset and ordered the cell phone to call the manor. It rang twice before Tyler picked up.

"Armen Manor," his house lord grumbled.

"Terry, checking in."

"I take it we have a new protected?" he asked archly.

"Yeah. He's fine. The beast just got a tooth in him."

"You should have checked in earlier. I called our doctors to see if you'd taken him there."

Terry winced at the rebuke. "Sorry about that. He was a little shaken up. A few drinks in him, and he's feeling better."

"Good. Name?"

"Steve Cole. Twenty-three."

Tyler snorted at that. "No wonder he was shook up."

"But amazingly together, considering what he found out tonight." Terry respected that about him.

"Think he'll stick to the deal?" That was always a concern with a young man. Too many of them thought they were invulnerable.

If he even thinks *about taking the amulet off, he'll need a proctologist to remove it.* The fact that he wasn't taking 'no' for an answer shook him. He'd protect Stevie, whether the young man wanted to be protected or not.

"Terry?"

"What? Oh. Yeah. Steve will keep that amulet on." *I'll make sure of it.*

"You're sure of that?" Clearly, he wasn't.

"Absolutely."

"Good. Then give me the details."

Terry didn't even have to flip his notebook open. He'd memorized everything important he knew about Stevie already. "Five feet nine, runner's build, red-brown hair...a lot of red, blue-gray eyes." *One hell of a delectable body.*

Which I really need to stop thinking about, if I intend to get any work done. That sobered him and he went back to giving his report.

Chapter Forty-eight

Two days later

Terry took his time in the shower, washing away the smell and stress of the hunt. *The stress of the hunt but not my sexual stress.*

He considered beating off again, then dismissed the idea. There was little question what—or rather who—he would fantasize about. Not that there was a problem with that. *Well, aside from the fact that I want Stevie, not just the memory of Stevie.*

The problem was that there was also little question that the experience of beating off would be wholly unsatisfying. Terry had suffered more than his share of sex dreams in the last few days, sex dreams that made him want to experience more of a certain luscious redhead.

The night before, he'd gone to a bar with the thought that he was just in need because he hadn't had full-out sex with Stevie. In the end, he hadn't picked up anyone for the night. The women hadn't really enticed him, and the men hadn't held a candle to Stevie.

The idea that he might be printing on Stevie briefly occurred to him, but Terry rejected it soundly. To his knowledge, the only Warriors who'd printed on males had been *Blutjagdfrau*. It was more likely that he wanted something new, to experience something that had always held appeal for him but he'd always denied himself. *Just a new type of conquest.*

The idea of having Stevie beneath him, as he had on the couch, of pushing his cock deep into the smaller man's ass, had him stroking himself off to the fantasy.

He didn't doubt that Stevie's ass would be tight, and he clenched his hand down tight to stimulate it.

Memories of the kiss they'd shared before he left was all it took to send him over. *But still pulsing in want. Damn it all, I have to see him again.*

Maybe spending a night balls deep in Stevie would sate the need to know what it would feel like.

Who am I kidding. It's going to take a lot more than a night to explore all of Stevie and decide if this attraction is fleeting.

That in mind, Terry turned off the shower, then hurried through drying off and dressing. He had somewhere to be. He just hoped Stevie wasn't entertaining anyone else tonight, because the ache might well drive him toward madness.

* * * *

Stevie placed the Nook on the coffee table, abandoning the book he was reading to answer the knock at the door. Though he doubted Bradley had shown up here after the dressing down he gave his ex-boyfriend on the phone, Stevie checked the peek hole.

His heart stuttered at who he saw outside. *Terry.* Stevie rushed to open the door.

After a moment of stillness, Terry's voice rumbled between them. "Am I welcome?"

"Yeah. Sure." *Why wouldn't you be?* Stevie cleared the way to let Terry pass, then closed the door behind him.

Terry hesitated for a minute, then shifted from foot to foot.

Stevie eased back a step, his senses on high alert. Why had Terry come here? Did he want to experiment further? Did he want to convince himself the last time had been a fleeting moment and he didn't really swing that way? Was he frustrated or scared by his reaction and looking to strike out at an easy target?

Not knowing had his heart doing acrobatics. "Terry? Why did you come here?"

The Warrior shot a sideward look his direction. Then he was in motion, straight toward Stevie, every sculpted muscle strung tight. Stevie backed tight to the wall, cursing himself for not moving a direction that left him somewhere to run.

Terry pressed his hands to the wall on either side of Stevie's head and lowered his face. Stevie's gasp of surprise gave Terry all the room he needed to plunder Stevie's mouth. A moan fought its way up Stevie's throat, mingling with a similar sound from Terry.

At last, Terry pulled away, his breathing ragged. He trailed a single fingertip down Stevie's trembling lips. "Am I still welcome?"

To anything you want. Stevie managed a shaky nod and something verbal that sounded vaguely affirmative. "What..." He cleared his throat, but his mind was slower to oblige. "What do you want? Precisely?"

After a moment of stillness, Terry cupped Stevie's ass in his hand and drew him to his larger body. Their cocks brushed through two sets of jeans. Terry stroked a fingertip down the crease of Stevie's ass through the fabric.

Fuck, yes.

"I admit I'm not sure about repaying with the same, but—"

"S'okay," Stevie managed. It was. He'd always liked to be ridden hard by a stronger man, and Terry definitely fit the bill.

Terry's cock jerked, seemingly making an attempt at self-escape from the faded fabric. "Don't worry. I fully intend to repay it another way."

"What?" He wasn't offering to pay for sex, was he? Stevie would show him the door if that was his intent. He wasn't a man whore and didn't intend to start a new profession now.

Terry licked his lips, and Stevie's knees went weak in anticipation.

"I think we need a bed," Terry opined.

He pointed the way, and Terry lifted him and carried Stevie to the door, which already stood ajar. At the bed, Terry took his time removing Stevie's clothing, then settled him in the middle of the mattress. That left Stevie with a great view of Terry stripping himself nude and joining him.

Their mouths joined and parted, while Terry explored Stevie's body. There was something energizing about that, knowing he was the first man this highly sexual and very sexy man had touched this way.

Terry moved abruptly, leaving Stevie stunned, his lips sex-swollen. Before Stevie could right his senses, Terry had taken his cock into the heat of his mouth.

There was nothing gentle in what he was doing, not that Stevie wanted him to be gentle. Hot sex always had an edge of rough play, in Stevie's opinion.

Terry experimented, more suction and then less, faster and then slower, deeper... The change came abruptly, from experimental to full-on carnal knowledge. It took Stevie only a moment to piece together that Terry had been playing at his body, testing what he responded to most. Once he knew, he pursued it. Terry wasn't offering what Stevie wanted; he was demanding the most powerful climax he could force from his body.

It didn't take long for him to succeed. Stevie bowed up, gasping out incoherent noises while starbursts of color danced before his eyes.

A flick of Terry's tongue against the sensitive nerves along the bottom of his cock propelled him into aftershocks, and Stevie shouted, his hands closing into fists in the blanket, his toes curling. A full-out scream tore from his lungs.

At last, Terry released him, leaving Stevie shivering, his throat raw. The larger man wrapped himself around Stevie, Terry's cum-scented breath bathing his face.

Stevie struggled to form coherent sentences. "Oh... Oh, damn. That was..."

"Good?" Terry inquired, sounding more than a little amused.

"Fantastic."

Terry chucked darkly. "Glad to hear it. It was my first."

"I hope it *won't* be your last."

His expression took on a potent edge that made Stevie all the more aware of Terry's sexual nature. "I'd say that's a safe bet."

* * * *

Terry stared down at Stevie, his emotions rioting. He was proud that he'd managed to affect Stevie so markedly, hungry for more of him, and fascinated by the younger man. Everything about him drew Terry's gaze and made him want to touch and taste.

"Top drawer," Stevie offered.

"What?"

"Everything you need is in the top drawer of the bedside table."

"Oh."

His cheeks darkened a bit. "I mean...if you still want to—"

Terry captured his lips in a kiss. He drew away, his cock complaining any length of wait. "Damn right, I want to."

Stevie nodded and glanced at the drawer.

He took the hint and rolled over to pull it open. Terry surveyed his choices and pulled out the lube. The toys could wait for another time. He wanted himself inside Stevie, not a toy, no matter how much fun it would be to watch Stevie moaning in pleasure with a toy embedded in his ass.

"How do you want me?"

"Just like you are." He'd always taken women doggy style when he'd gone for anal, but the fantasies and dreams of Stevie on his back, facing Terry as he took his ass, were too enticing to abandon without a test run.

Stevie spread his ankles a bit, then pulled his knees back, making room for Terry between his legs. It was a dream come true. Literally.

He slid into place, and their cocks brushed. Terry sucked in his breath in shocked delight. Stevie wrapped a hand around both and started stroking. The soft underside of Stevie's cock brushing against his own propelled him toward release.

Stevie stopped abruptly.

"Don't you dare," Terry ground out.

"But I thought you wanted—"

"You have no idea how many times a night I can come. This won't stop me...unless you want me to stop."

"After that blow job? Are you nuts?"

Terry laughed in relief. It ended on a choked gasp, as Stevie started moving his hand again. Blissful bolts of pleasure had Terry arching his back, rocking his head back, closing his eyes. He wanted it to last longer, but there was no holding back. He came in a series of jerks, releasing days of pent-up need in a rush. He let his head drop forward, relaxed.

Not entirely relaxed. He admitted he was still hard, still in need of finding out how good it would be with Stevie.

Stevie released his cock, and Terry levered his head up and stared down at him. The way Stevie shifted, his eye movements, and the teeth dimpling his lip were impossible to miss.

"Why do you do that?" Terry asked.

He darkened and didn't offer an immediate reply.

"Stevie? What's got you so nervous?"

He cleared his throat, going a few shades darker. "Well, guys who are new to it..."

"Yes?"

"They don't always react...well to coming for another man. Sometimes, they react really badly. After you rushed out of here last time—"

"I shouldn't have done that." Terry's heart ached at the fact that Stevie was afraid of him, afraid that he might do this beautiful young man harm.

"No. It's okay. I mean... I understand why you did."

Terry shook his head. "No. It wasn't okay. There are rules for Warriors. We're big on rules."

"Rules?" His brow creased in seeming confusion.

"Well, one of them should put you at ease."

Stevie nodded and waved him on.

"A lover must always be treated with respect, and the lover must be given more pleasure than we take from him or her."

A long, slow release of air was Stevie's only immediate response. "So, you're saying it's against your rules to hurt me?"

"It's against the rules for me to hurt any innocent person, but especially not a lover. If you ever feel I've mistreated you, you call the manor number I gave you. You still have that, right?"

He nodded. "Yeah. In my wallet and in my address book."

Terry was glad to hear it. "If you ever believe I've harmed you, you call that number and ask for Lord Armen. You tell him, and he will take it out of my hide for you. He's my judge in matters like that."

Stevie tried to speak several times before he managed to spit out another question. "If he's a judge, he won't necessarily be punishing you. What if he thinks I'm overreacting?"

"He won't. If you believe you've been wronged, that's enough for him. It's my job to make sure you *never* feel I've wronged you."

Silence fell between them for a moment.

"Understand?"

"I think so."

"Good. Then you won't need to look so scared every time I come. Right?"

Stevie smiled, then laughed. "I guess not."

Terry cupped his cheek gently. "That's better. I prefer your smile any day."

"Know what I prefer?"

"I'd like to," Terry admitted. Gods, but that was the truth. He wanted to know how to give Stevie pleasure more than just about anything in life.

"You getting back to what I interrupted."

His cock bucked in excitement, and Stevie's started to harden again. At Stevie's groan, Terry opened the lube bottle and poured some into his hand.

Working his ass up took less effort than Terry was accustomed to with women, probably an indication that Stevie had taken at least a few lovers before.

None of my business, and it's not like I'm a virgin. Still, a twinge of jealously settled in Terry's chest.

He didn't have time to dwell on it. Stevie's reaction when Terry hit his prostate had his full attention. Part of him wanted to finish Stevie off with his fingers, but the need to be inside him won that argument.

Terry replaced his fingers with his cock, working his way slowly inside, a little further with each withdrawal and return.

"Yes," Stevie panted out. "Deeper. Almost—" He screamed at what Terry assumed was his cock rubbing against the prostate again.

Terry didn't hesitate. He thrust deeper and faster, losing himself in the sublime grip of Stevie's channel, the little wiggling moves the smaller man made, and the disjointed sounds that announced his rise to climax.

Stevie's cock jerked once, then again, and he came with another shout. His channel clenched down tight, every muscle contracting at once. That was the end for

Terry. He pressed deep and roared at the climax that drained him.

Coherent thought seemed to take an inordinately long time to return to his disordered mind. When it did, Terry feathered kisses along Stevie's face.

Stevie was just as slow to recover. He lay beneath Terry's bulk, glassy-eyed.

"Are you okay?" Terry asked. Had he hurt him in those fevered moments of climax? If he had, he would never forgive himself.

"It think that may be the understatement of the century. Of course, I'm not sure I'll be able to move for a while."

Terry slid free of his body and lay beside him on the mattress, pulling blankets over their bodies. "I vote for a rest, a snack, and then we'll see where it goes from there."

"Not sure what's in the fridge," Stevie half-yawned.

"How's pizza sound?"

"Mmmm hmmm."

His breathing went deep and even in the matter of a few heartbeats. Terry watched him sleep, his entire body relaxed as he hadn't felt it in years. Possibly since he faced the change.

Terry laid back and sighed, too energized to sleep but too relaxed to get up and do anything. The scene was peaceful, and peace was something in short supply in a Warrior's life.

Chapter Forty-nine

One week later

"Sure you won't stay and meet them?" Stevie asked.

"Wish I could." He did. Some days Terry cursed his duty. Any other man would be able to take a personal day once in a while, no matter the schedule he was expected to keep. Terry had to schedule things like that in advance and sometimes explain himself, to boot. "Why don't we set up to have dinner together next weekend?"

Stevie smiled and nodded. The fact that Terry could make him smile sent flutters through his stomach. He considered staying.

At least long enough to tap that ass again. Visions of Stevie riding his cock as he had that afternoon was enough to make Terry hard for it again.

Somehow I doubt Tyler would accept this as anything resembling an emergency. A Warrior who can't control his curse is no better than a beast. That in mind, Terry made his way out to the living room and settled on the couch.

His boots were halfway buckled when the lock on the hall door clicked. The door swung open, and a little girl with bright strawberry-blond hair bolted through, a full-grown version of the same in tow. The smaller stopped short, staring at him in open-mouthed wonder.

Terry smiled at that. Warriors were predisposed to finding little girls charming, and this one was cuter than most. With her hair pulled out into two fluffy ponytails and her blue eyes wide in wonder, Terry could easily find himself wrapped around her little finger.

"Well, hello. You must be Julie."

She nodded, seemingly at a loss for words.

Her mother looked up from the door lock and smiled. "And *you* simply must be Terry. Stevie's description didn't do you justice."

"Sharon!" Stevie stood in the bedroom doorway, his cheeks darkening.

She went to her twin and gave him a hug. "Well, he is gorgeous, I agree. You didn't lie. But you didn't tell me he was..." Sharon sized him up. "However tall you are of hunk."

"Six feet four," Terry offered.

Sharon fanned herself. "Wow." She smiled warmly. "So, is it popcorn for four?"

Terry's heart ached. "I'm afraid not. I didn't find out in enough time to switch with someone at work, but I suggested dinner on me next weekend, if you have the time?"

"On you? Sure. How else am I going to get to interrogate you?"

"Sharon!"

Terry raised an eyebrow at her. "With..." He snapped his mouth shut. "Sorry. Not appropriate in front of a little girl."

Julie piped up at that. "With what? Rubber hoses or whips and chains?"

He gaped at her, at a loss for words. How old was this child?

Stevie doubled in laughter. "Rubber hoses," he informed her.

"Oh. I think whips and chains would hurt worse, though." Julie climbed up on the couch next to Terry and plopped down beside him.

"Probably so," Terry agreed.

She kicked her feet. They dangled a full three inches over the carpet. "What do you do for a job?"

"Security. I protect people and objects." He wasn't lying...precisely.

"Do you use a gun?" she fired back.

Sharon raised an eyebrow in challenge, and she crossed her arms over her chest.

She disapproves. He bit back a wince at that. "No, I do not. Not all security men do."

"How about a radio?" Now that she was talking, Julie seemed full of questions.

"Actually, I use a cell phone with a secret earpiece like FBI agents wear."

"Really?" she squealed.

"Really, really." He nodded.

She started to ask another question, but Stevie picked her up. "Terry has to go, or he'll be late for work, Julie. And we have to go, or we'll be late for the movie."

Julie pouted. "But we'll see you again next weekend, Uncle Terry?"

He liked the sound of that, both the part about seeing them again, and the part about her considering Terry her uncle. "Yes you will. I want you to think about it hard, Julie. Tell Uncle Stevie where you want to go, and it's on me."

"Really?" The squeal was back in her voice.

Sharon winced. "You may regret letting Julie pick the place."

"Doubt it." Terry rushed through the last of his buckles, grabbed his coat, and rushed for the door. His only pit stop was to brush a kiss against Stevie's mouth on the way.

Sharon was already there, holding the door open for him to leave. She shot him a speculative look and dropped her voice to a whisper. "Nice touch, but fair warning..."

"Yes?"

"Hurt my brother, and you answer to me."

"Fair enough."

"Sharon," Stevie complained again.

"Hey. You watch my back, and I watch yours." She smiled sweetly. "Oh...and I *do* use whips and chains, when Stevie gets hurt."

"Someone hurts Stevie, and they'll see worse from me. I guarantee it."

The surprise evaporated into a laugh. "I like you, Terry, even if you do let my daughter choose the restaurant."

"When I treat you guys again, it's your choice," he promised. Terry checked his watch. "Gotta go."

She cleared the way and watched him trot toward the stairs.

Chapter Fifty

Three weeks later

"Are you sure you want to do this?" Stevie asked for the third time.

Terry laughed. "I said 'yes', didn't I?"

"Yes, but..." *Why am I still questioning this? Has Terry balked at anything we've done yet?*

"But?" he prompted.

"Well, you might be uncomfortable." Stevie squirmed a little on the seat beside him.

He smiled a wicked little smile. "If someone comes on to me, I promise to tell him I'm already with the best guy in the room."

His cheeks heated. "You *said* you were new to this."

"I said I'd never had sex with a guy before. Warriors are used to getting propositioned. Some people postulate that we have something of an animal magnetism that appeals to both women and men, if they're attracted to men in general."

"Oh. But you never...?" *Why hasn't he ever chosen to sleep with a man before? Why me? Why now? Am I just an experiment?*

Terry shrugged, seemingly unfazed by the question. "I've never known a gay Warrior. A few have experimented, but none I know chose to stay permanently with another man. And... Well, guys in my family tend to want to choose someone early, so I figured—"

"Why waste time," Stevie finished for him.

"Pretty much. Warriors tend to think of other Warriors when we make comparisons. We don't usually look to humans. If I had, I might have considered being with a guy sooner. Really short-sighted, when you think about it."

Stevie smiled, though he wasn't comforted by the answer. Terry had never considered a man before. What if he ultimately decided a woman was the way to go? That was the chance someone took when a potential partner was bisexual.

Yeah, right. It wouldn't matter if Terry found another guy he liked or a woman. Losing him would still be painful.

"Problem, Stevie?" Terry asked.

"No. Not really. Just thinking too much." Stevie was. There were no guarantees in relationships. He knew that. Instead of obsessing over whether or not it would work out, he should be trying to make it work.

"If *you're* not ready for this—"

Stevie smacked his arm, a smile curving his lips.

Terry laughed heartily. "Well, that's better."

"What is?"

"Your smile. You need to smile more." He pulled into the parking lot and found a space.

Though Terry had been joking when he'd asked if Stevie was ready for this, the truth was, Stevie wasn't sure he was. It wasn't just the remote possibility that Terry would go screaming into the night in search of the closest possible woman to bed. One of the reasons Stevie himself had avoided this bar for so long was the fact that Bradley frequented the establishment.

They'd only taken six steps past the door when Stevie spotted him. He cursed under his breath. When had Bradley started going out midweek?

Probably still in the 'impress him' phase with his new lay.

As if the thought drew him, Bradley unwrapped himself from the young man in question and made his way toward the door.

Well, too late to run. Besides that, Terry was already placing an order with Smitty at the bar.

Stevie pretended he hadn't noticed Bradley and eased into the crowd next to Terry. If he was very lucky, Bradley hadn't noticed him either and would leave without doing so.

I've never been lucky.

As if in conformation of that fact, Bradley slung an arm around Stevie's shoulder and dragged him backward into his broad chest. "Stevie, baby! I haven't seen you in forever."

"You always were fond of hyperbole," he replied drily. *Forever would be a reprieve.*

Bradley ignored him...and ignored Stevie's attempts to free himself from Bradley's hold. "Where you been, Stevie?"

"Somewhere I don't have to be mauled by you."

His hold tightened a notch in warning. "And what does that mean?" he inquired coolly.

Terry was abruptly crowded to Stevie's chest. "It means you should listen to the man and let him go." There was no mistaking the warning couched in the comment.

Bradley never was all that quick on the uptake. He looked up at Terry, not the least bit intimidated by the six-inch difference in their heights. "Says who?"

Terry pressed two drinks into Stevie's hands. "Hold these, please," he requested.

Stevie took them, battling between apprehension and interest in what Terry would do next. "Got them."

He wasn't sure what he expected, but it wasn't Terry gripping Bradley by the wrist and peeling his arm back as if it were a wet noodle.

"Ow! Hey! What the *fuck*, dude!"

Terry guided Bradley back to his young lover and released him there. Then he stepped between Stevie and Bradley. "What the *fuck*? I'll tell you what the fuck. Stevie doesn't want you touching him. I suggest you remember that."

"And what's that got to do with you?" Bradley inquired.

"A couple of things. You see, Stevie is here with me. Whatever claim you *think* you have on him, I guarantee he doesn't agree with you, and that is very much my business. Besides that, seems to me you're busy ignoring the person *you're* here with, and while that isn't my business, it's still not smart."

There was a tense moment of silence, and Stevie shivered in awareness of the rising testosterone in the air. There was little question that Terry would end anything Bradley decided to start.

Bradley snorted. "Never thought you went for the leather and chains scene, Stevie," he spat.

Terry tensed between them.

Stevie addressed him directly. "What I go for isn't any of your concern. You lost that place in my life when I found you in bed with...oh what...two, three, four ago for you?"

The heat coming off Terry's body seemed to ratchet up a dozen degrees at that pronouncement.

"Yeah. Whatever," Bradley brushed him off. "See you around, Stevie."

"Not if I have anything to say about it," Terry grumbled.

Stevie could see Bradley heading for the door around the formidable blockade of Terry's tensed arm. Terry eased at the distance, and he turned toward Stevie when the door closed behind Bradley and his latest lay.

"You okay?" he asked.

Stevie nodded, identified his drink, and swallowed a mouthful of it.

Terry took his own and downed it in two swallows.

He stared at it, wondering if drinking was a problem for Terry.

"I never drink more than two," Terry answered his unasked question.

"Okay." Stevie took another drink of his.

"You still up for this?"

"Not really," he admitted.

"Then let's go," Terry suggested.

Stevie settled his drink on the edge of an empty table, and headed for the door. Terry followed in his wake.

Outside, Bradley was trying to convince his young lover of something. From the sounds of it, it wasn't working out as well as he'd hoped it would, and his frustration level was rising with every word.

Terry wrapped an arm around Stevie's shoulder and shot at warning look at Bradley. Bradley scowled at the move, then turned back to the fast-becoming-an-argument he was involved in.

They were several blocks away before Terry addressed the situation. "You and Conan were...?"

"Bradley, and yes. I thought it might be going somewhere, but..." He shrugged. "He's an asshole. Glad I found out sooner rather than later. And glad I never went unprotected with him."

"So what's his problem? Besides being an asshole?"

"That covers it, actually."

Terry shot him a look of disbelief.

"Oh." Stevie's cheeks heated. "He seems to think he still has a right to be around me. I don't know why. I've done my best to dissuade him."

"Maybe I should do that."

Something in his tone said Bradley would regret it if it came to that. "Meaning?"

"Meaning I didn't hit him this time. He tries that again when I'm near you...or he hurts you, and all bets are off."

Stevie managed a smile. "People pay good money to see fights like that."

Terry laughed harshly. "Believe me, it wouldn't be much of a fight."

"Then let's hope he stays away."

A raised eyebrow was Terry's only reply.

"I don't want you to get in trouble for it. Bradley's not worth it."

* * * *

Terry raised his head at the sound of music from the kitchen. It was an older song, and it took him a moment to recognize it. ZZ Top's "Sharp Dressed Man."

Stevie started singing along, and Terry smiled. He pushed from the couch and headed for the kitchen.

The sight of his young lover shifting his hips to the sound of the music had him thinking hard about stripping Stevie right then and there. As if in answer, Stevie turned toward him and put his hands out toward Terry.

He didn't hesitate to sweep Stevie into his arms. *And not for a box-step or waltz either.* Like most Warriors, Terry had an inborn talent for grinding dance.

He just hadn't anticipated how much more appealing he'd find indulging in it with Stevie than he had with a woman. *I should have tried this years ago.* How many years had he noticed men? Truth be told, probably as long as he'd been noticing women.

A smile pulled up at the corners of Stevie's mouth. "You like this song?"

"I like you dancing. The song? It's okay. Not one of my favorites, but not bad. At least I can dance to it."

"What's your favorite?"

Terry considered that. "Depends on my mood. I like a lot of kick-ass songs, like "Hair of the Dog" by Nazareth or "Not Falling" by Mudvayne. But those are better for working out than for dancing. Sometimes I like the oldies, especially "Don't Fear the Reaper" by Blue Oyster Cult or...well, a lot of the Beatles' songs. *The White Album*...yeah, that's good music."

"What about for...?" Stevie's cheeks went dark, and his eyes glittered in mischief.

"Oh. Well, that's no contest. "Principles of Lust" by Enigma."

One eyebrow went up in surprise. "That's some serious sexy."

"I agree. I have it on my phone. Interested in testing it out?"

Stevie's smile announced it was going to be a long, hard night...in the best possible way.

Chapter Fifty-one

One week later

"Up for Mick's?" Patrick asked, cleaning the remains of the beast he'd taken from his sacred weapon.

Terry shook his head. "Nah."

His cousin sheathed his weapon and panned his gaze up and down Terry. "That's the fourth time I've offered and you've turned me down. What gives, cousin?"

"I've got someone... Well, it's not serious yet, but it might become serious." He was lying, he knew. Not only had he not had sex with anyone else since he met Stevie, he was finding less and less interest in the idea. It was getting serious, at least on his side; he wasn't sure how serious Stevie was yet.

Patrick chuckled. "Someone you saved?"

His cheeks darkened a notch. "Yeah."

"Then you're cooked. You know that."

"I know it." Armens were practically known for falling fast and hard for women they saved in the line of duty. *But this time, it's not a woman.* To Terry's knowledge, no Armen had fallen for another guy. Slept with guys? It had happened from time to time, but none of them had printed on a guy. *Until now.*

There's a first time for everything. There'd never been twins in the historical record until Katie and Corwyn. There'd never been a Warrior born outside of printing until Scott.

Patrick clapped a hand on his shoulder. "Good luck, cousin."

"Thanks. I might need it."

Patrick winced. "Hope not." He tipped his head and withdrew, heading for his car.

Terry did the same, his head spinning in facts and fantasies. He wanted to make Stevie his mate. If he ever questioned it, the surety that he would tear Bradley limb from limb in Stevie's defense cinched it for him. That was the kind of protection one was driven to give a mate.

He couldn't deny he wanted to make Stevie his mate, but was that possible?

If I'm printing—and I am—it's clearly possible from my side. But the problem wasn't simply whether or not Stevie would accept the idea of being bound to him for life. Every Warrior faced that.

No, Terry had to face the problem of choosing a mate others might feel was unacceptable. Stevie couldn't bring children to the house. Stevie wasn't someone of the opposite sex. What Terry was considering had never happened before.

And no one has the right to an opinion about who I sleep with or mate with. Terry reran that thought several times, his heart pounding in the realization that it was true. The Rules of Sanction didn't say the mate or lover had to be of the opposite sex. That meant the rules were clear. No one had a right to bitch about the choices Terry made regarding taking a mate.

I can take Stevie to mate, and no one can stop it.

If he accepts me. That was another issue, and it was one that would take time to resolve he was sure.

Terry uttered a series of curses. Printing and forced to wait. Damn but that sucked.

* * * *

Three days later

Terry pulled Stevie into the curve of his body, savoring how well they fit together. Sex between them wasn't enough. He wanted to know everything about Stevie. He wanted Stevie to be a permanent part of his life.

"Tell me about your family."

Stevie sighed. "What's to tell? You've met Sharon and Julie."

He had, and they'd had two dinners and a movie out together as a group since then. As predicted, Julie had Terry pegged as a sucker already.

But that was only his sister and niece. "Parents?" Terry prompted.

Stevie shook his head.

"Dead?" His heart ached at the idea of having so little family. Terry rubbed Stevie's shoulder, at a loss to offer comfort.

"Maybe. I don't know."

His hand went still in shock. "What?" What in the world was he talking about?

"My father left when Sharon and I were kids. Six or so. Went to work—or so he said—and never came home."

Terry bit back his *Blutjagd* at the idea of a father abandoning his children and wife that way. It was something no Warrior would ever do.

"Can't blame him too much. Living with my mother had to be maddening. It wasn't easy on us either, but we didn't have much of a choice in the matter."

"Unbalanced?" Scott's mother had been a piece of work, he knew. She'd been institutionalized before the Warriors found the young rogue existed.

Stevie snorted. "That's the understatement of the century. Religious. Way over the edge religious."

Terry winced. He'd met the type before.

"She kicked us out when we were seventeen."

"She what?" That stirred his fury again.

"We were quite the disappointment to her. In the same day, she found out Sharon was pregnant and I was gay. That was the end for her. She kicked us out that night. We had five minutes or so to pack a change of clothes and a few essentials. Then..." He made a moving whistle sound. "Gone."

Terry groaned. What lousy reasons to kick a child out.

Stevie kept going, filling in the details. "We hiked a few towns away, ended up in foster care for the next ten months. That at least allowed us both to finish high school, so I guess I shouldn't knock it."

"Wait. What happened when they went back on your mother for kicking you out? There are laws about that, aren't there?"

He shrugged. "Slap on the wrist, but she wasn't going to take us back. Besides, who would want her to?"

"I guess so." How bad a parent did it take for a kid to decide none is better?

"They put us in separate homes, but we made sure to keep in touch, and we went to the same high school. Once we were eighteen, we got a little place together. Sharon worked days. I worked nights. That way, we didn't have to pay someone to watch Julie.

"We depended on public assistance as little as we could. At first, we had WIC and food stamps and medical. Sharon was always the better student, so we got some loans to let her get her associate's degree.

She got a better job, medical for her and Julie. We dropped the WIC and food stamps. I got my associate's. Eventually, I want to get my bachelor's."

"Why do you live separately now? Did you have a fight?" It would surprise him to hear it was something like that. Sharon and Stevie seemed to get along so well.

"No. Sharon felt the need to prove she could support Julie on her own. I get it. I miss them, but I get it."

"Yeah. That makes sense, I guess. I'm glad you have her."

Stevie snuggled in deeper. "Me too. So what about your family? Sharing is a two-way thing, Sharon always says."

Terry smiled. "Huge, huge family. Warriors are like that. Parents, uncles, aunts, cousins. I have two brothers, both older. They're both married and have kids. Jarrett is the oldest, and William is next in line. Then me, of course."

Stevie was silent for a long minute. "What are they going to think of this?"

"This?"

Stevie pressed his ass against Terry's cock, raising more than a little interest.

"This. I mean, you said you need sex often but you'd never been with a guy before. Does your family know you're bisexual?"

"No, but they won't care. That's one of the nice things about being a Warrior."

Stevie was strangely silent.

Terry fished for something to say. "It's home. You know?"

"Must be nice."

"Having a big family?"

"Having someplace you consider home. Even this place..." He looked around at the sponge-painted walls. "I know it's probably temporary."

I could give you a home. A permanent home. But it was too soon for that. *Isn't it?*

Chapter Fifty-two

Two weeks later

Terry trudged into the manor house, his stomach grumbling. He'd rather be with Stevie right now, going to dinner together, but Stevie was working his second job tending bar, and there was no food service there. Food was a definite priority.

"Hey, Terry! Good to see you, Cousin."

He waved a hand Jaden's direction and kept walking.

Jaden trailed along behind him. "I hear you've been spending a lot of time with someone special. Rumor has it you're printing."

Terry smiled. Yes, he was printing, and as soon as he thought Stevie was ready, he was going to broach the subject with him.

"Damn. She's got you." His cousin laughed heartily.

Terry ignored him and went to the fridge. He opened it, then started searching out a meal, hoping the trainees had left more than bare bones behind.

"So, spill. What's this special one's name?"

"Stevie."

"Like Stevie Nicks?"

"Something like that."

"When do we get to meet her?" Jaden reached over his shoulder, grabbed an apple from the door bin, then hopped up on the countertop, barely missing the spigot for the coffee system.

"Don't let Sammi see you do that," Terry reminded him.

One thing the Lady Armen would *not* stand for was a breach of common manners. Sitting on tables and countertops was sure to get a Warrior a lecture he wouldn't soon forget.

"Yeah. Yeah. When do we get to meet her?" he managed around a mouthful of masticated apple.

No one gets to have an opinion on my love life or who I mate with. It's one of the few benefits of Warrior life. "I invited *him* for dinner this weekend."

Jaden stopped short, the apple halfway to his mouth for another bite. After a pregnant moment of silence, he laughed. "You got me, Cousin."

Terry closed the fridge and turned to him, quirking up a brow in challenge. "You think I'm joking?"

"Yeah. Good one, too. You sleeping with a guy named Stevie." Jaden rolled his eyes. "I almost believed you, for a second there."

"Tyler mated with a woman named Sammi."

"A woman. Sure. And you know as well as I do that Sammi is short for Samantha."

"Well Stevie happens to be a nickname for Steven."

Jaden's face lost color, and he gaped at Terry. "You're *not* kidding?"

"Nope. Not a bit."

Jaden slid off the countertop and moved to stand in front of Terry. "You're going to bring a *guy* home to meet the family?"

"Guys do it every day." *And the Rules of Sanction say who I sleep with or mate with is my choice.*

"Yeah, but you..." He seemed to wrestle with words, and the words were winning the battle, since none emerged.

Terry forced his arm muscles to loosen. "I what, Jaden?"

"Cousin, I *know* how many women you've fucked over the years. I've seen it. We've all seen it."

"You seem to have missed how many guys I've looked at before I decided on a woman for the night. It's called bisexual, *Cousin*."

Jaden sputtered.

"It never even occurred to you that I fucked all those women, because I was looking for something I wasn't finding. Did it?"

"What? A *dick*?"

Terry stopped short of pummeling him. He forced his *Blutjagd* back a few dozen notches and took a calming breath. "Maybe I was. The Rules of Sanction say it's none of your business either way. Is it?" There. The challenge was out.

"You *can't* bring him here, Terry. You know that. You have to know that."

His fury uncorked, and Terry shoved Jaden aside. His cousin rebounded off the counter, the apple flying toward the far reaches of the room. Terry stared at him for a second, then managed words. "Fuck you. We don't need your permission or acceptance. We don't need you."

He stormed down the hall and through the foyer. He didn't hesitate until he was at his car. It was Tyler's voice that reined him in.

"Terry? What's going on?"

He turned his head and glared at Jaden, standing a body length behind their house lord.

Tyler followed his line of sight. "Jaden?"

That unglued Terry's tongue. "Teach the damned pup the Rules of Sanction, or I will." With that, he pulled his car door open and slid inside.

Tyler appeared on the other side of the door. "Wait! What Rule of Sanction did he break?"

"Ask him. If I repeat it now, I'm taking it out of his hide." Terry took another calming breath. *Fuck it. It's not working.* "I don't feel equal to being his judge right now."

He reached for the ignition, key in hand.

"Where will you be?"

"Out. I'll probably turn off my phone for the night. But I've already done my hunting."

"Be sure to check in later." That was an order from his house lord.

"Later," Terry agreed.

Tyler closed the car door for him, then turned back, stalking toward Jaden. Terry didn't wait to see the fireworks. He turned the engine over, pulled out, and left the manor house far behind.

His mind teeming with plans, he checked the time. "Eight o'clock." Terry smiled. "Perfect." He had time to go shopping, clean up at one of the houses in town, and pick up Stevie from work.

His stomach grumbled. *First, some fast food.*

* * * *

Stevie smiled at the sight of Terry doing the walk of the dead into the kitchen. "Coffee?" he offered.

Terry grunted something that sounded roughly affirmative, then wrapped himself around Stevie's back. Stevie took a moment to bask in the comfort of being held close to Terry's body.

A knock at the door brought both of their heads around.

Terry tensed. "Expecting someone?"

"No."

"Then let me get it."

"Gladly." The last thing Stevie needed was Bradley or one of his goons trying to pay him a friendly visit. They'd play off it being a mistake if Terry answered the door.

Terry pushed off and headed for the hall, all muscle in a pair of jeans. Stevie tried to pay attention to the coffee, but he was too nervous. He turned at the sound of the door opening, moving from foot to foot as he waited for some sign of what was going on.

"What are you doing here?" Terry challenged.

Bradley. Stevie didn't question it.

A strange voice answered. "You didn't check in."

"I said later. I *said* I was going to turn my phone off for the night."

"Yes. You did. Well, it's later."

Another voice interjected. "May we come in?"

Terry hesitated a moment. "It's not my apartment. Not my place to invite you in."

Stevie edged out into the hall and looked at the three men at the doorway...Terry and two others, who were clearly both Warriors. "Come in," he offered.

All three pair of eyes focused on him. They weren't hostile, but Stevie wasn't comfortable under their scrutiny either. He felt underdressed in nothing but his knit sleep pants.

He backed off a step, then turned toward the kitchen. "Coffee, anyone?"

"That would be great," one of the Warriors commented. "Thank you."

The three didn't head for the living room. Instead, they crowded into his kitchen.

Stevie went to work on the coffee, delivering Terry's cup first, black and bitter. Terry needed the caffeine desperately when he woke, and he wasn't interested in watering it down in any fashion known to man. Stevie's lover was shit before his first two or three cups.

He started on the next. "How do you folks like it?" he asked.

"Extra milk...cream...whatever you have," the same one who'd asked for coffee requested.

"Pull the half and half from the fridge?"

He moved away to comply, and Stevie dumped the grounds from the last cup and pressed in more.

"Steamed, foam, or plain?" he asked.

"Whatever gets it in the body fastest. I'm not picky."

Before he returned, the cup was half-brewed; Stevie handed it over when it finished. Since the other hadn't asked for a cup, he didn't start brewing again.

"Nice apartment," the other commented. "It's very soothing."

"Thanks. I like it," Stevie replied. "So...why don't you tell me who you both are? I can tell you're Warriors, but other than that, I have no clue."

The one who'd asked for coffee appeared at his side and offered his hand. "Tyler Armen."

"He's my house lord," Terry imparted.

Stevie took his hand and shook it. "What did you mean when you said Terry didn't check in?"

"I told him to," Tyler offered with a shrug.

"I told you the phone would be off for the night," Terry repeated.

Stevie smiled. "If you know him, you know Terry is no good for anything before his first two cups, and that..." He pointed to the cup of coffee in Terry's hand. "is number one."

"Well, that's true enough," Tyler agreed.

The other man stepped forward. He was slower offering his hand, but he did. "Jacob."

Stevie took his hand and shook it as well. "Welcome to my home. Both of you." He panned his gaze over Jacob. "I know you're all related somehow, but you look a lot like Terry."

"He's my son. Terry has always looked most like me," Jacob imparted.

Stevie nodded, his heart pounding. "He's told me about his brothers."

Jacob pulled his hand back. "I hope that little scene last night hasn't convinced you not to come out to the house this weekend."

Stevie swallowed hard and looked toward Terry. He could only guess what kind of scene they meant, but it sounded like Terry had his first taste of good old-fashioned homophobia. *And from his family, no less.*

Terry finished the cup of coffee and moved to the machine to make a second. "Fuck Jaden." He offered the statement blandly, as if he really didn't care what was said.

Stevie knew him better than that. "What did he say?"

"Nothing he had a right to," Terry evaded the question.

"He's right about that," Tyler agreed. "Jaden has already faced my judgment. He faces yours when you feel able to be even-handed about it."

Terry grunted an answer that didn't make sense to Stevie. He suspected whatever it was wasn't English, and since Terry spoke several other languages, that was entirely possible.

"I'll make sure he's not around when you two come to the manor for dinner then." He focused on Stevie. "If you're still willing to come and let us prove we're more evolved than our more juvenile members make it seem."

Stevie considered that. "If it will cause a scene, I'd rather—"

"It won't," Jacob assured him.

Stevie stared at him, challenging that statement. Clearly, it wasn't as 'okay' as Jacob and Tyler made it sound.

Jacob darkened a notch. "I admit I had hoped all my children would mate and give me grandchildren to spoil, but not all Warriors choose to mate. I've never heard of a case of a Warrior mate who couldn't bear children before, but in sixteen hundred years? It has to have happened at some point, I suppose. Hell, for a while there, the Warriors weren't sure Sammi could produce viable Warriors, but she could."

"I don't have to carry the baby for Terry and I to *have* babies," Stevie pointed out.

Terry placed a hand on his shoulder. "We could adopt a baby girl, I suppose, but I'm not sure I would make it past whatever background checks the adoption agency ran, unless one of our protected was involved to help the process along. Private adoption maybe."

"Why only a baby girl?"

Tyler winced. "We've discussed this before. Our boys are fairly rough and tumble...and big for their age. They're taught to be gentle with little girls, but not so much with each other."

"You're afraid they'll accidentally hurt a boy who isn't a Warrior," Stevie guessed.

Jacob nodded. "The only other alternative is teaching the other boys to treat the human boy as they would a girl, and I don't think that would be healthy for his sense of self, being treated as less than the other young men."

"Wait! How could this even come up, if you've never had a woman who was sterile?" Stevie demanded. "This...Sammi person, before she found out she could have a child?"

Tyler scowled at him. "Sammi is my mate, and no. It actually came up, as you put it, because my mother was a widow when my father met her. The family knew she had two children from her first marriage, and they were discussing the difficulties of bringing human boys into the household. That was before my father informed them that she had two *girls*, and it wasn't an issue."

Stevie shook his head. "We don't have to adopt, anyway. We could have our own children."

Terry looked up from his second cup of coffee, his interest clearly piqued. "How?"

"Sharon told me, if I ever get into a serious relationship, she's willing to surrogate for my partner and myself. Obviously, we'd have to use my partner's sperm, since she's my sister, but the baby would have some of my DNA and—" Terry's look stopped him cold. "What is it?"

"I'm not... I'm not allowed to reproduce with anyone but a mate. Part of our laws."

"Wait a minute," Tyler interrupted him. "Don't write that one off quite yet. The spirit of the law is to avoid bastards we can't properly track, raise, and train. If Stevie's sister is willing and checks out... I could support that."

Jacob seemed to consider it. "She'd have to be protected, of course. Carrying a Warrior's child, we'd insist on it. But it's not the worst or wildest idea that's ever been advanced in Warrior society."

"It's not?" That seemed to surprise Terry.

Jacob cleared his throat. "There was a...misunderstanding with your mother. Preventatives failed, and your oldest brother wasn't precisely...planned. She hadn't told Corwyn she was carrying yet, and Geoff decided to play the gallant. He offered to raise your brother as his own son."

"Before you two printed?" Terry asked, clearly aghast.

"Well, of course. Why would he make that suggestion afterward?"

"And what about you?" he pressed.

"He honestly thought I'd walk away and accept that, if your mother was more comfortable with the situation. He took protecting her pretty seriously. Needless to say, that wasn't going to work for me. At all."

A string of what could only be curses in other languages burst from Terry.

"But we worked it out," Jacob hastened to add.

"Clearly, you did. Yes, that was a worse suggestion than a surrogate."

Stevie wondered what Jarrett would make of the story of his origins. From what Terry told him about his oldest brother, being conceived before marriage wasn't something he would embrace.

Still, they were using terms that confused him. He motioned for their attention. "What does...printed mean?"

Terry went an alarming shade of crimson. "Not precisely how I wanted to introduce you to the idea."

"Dare I ask?"

"When a Warrior meets someone he wants as a mate... Uh. You've heard of imprinting...in animals?"

Stevie nodded.

"Well, a Warrior becomes fixated on the prospective mate."

"And what about the mate?" Stevie wasn't sure he liked the sound of what Terry was implying. Did that mean he would eventually find a mate and move on, because he was forced by biology to do it? What was the point in being in a relationship with someone who had that built in need to reproduce?

Tyler broke in. "The prospective mate is always told and asked if she is willing to be tied to the Warrior for life. If she refuses, the Warrior has to walk away before he is driven mad by the need to be with her."

"So he can walk away and refuse to follow through." That was a relief.

"Scott tried that. Didn't work so well. Technically speaking, it doesn't look like the male can choose to break printing. The prospective mate has to refuse him. If that happens, he can go on to print again. Once he prints, it's forever. He never falls out of love, is never unfaithful... As long as his mate lives, he isn't even aroused by another."

Which means Terry will cease to be aroused by me, when he finds this woman. Unless she turns him away. His heart sank.

"Do you understand?" Tyler asked.

"I think so." He felt faint and sick. What they were telling him was that there was little chance for a future between them.

"I don't think so," Terry snapped in response.

Stevie stared at him, at a loss for words.

Terry stuffed his hand in his pocket and came out with a gold band. A central diamond was flanked by two smaller ones on each side. "I'm printing on you, Stevie. Unless you point me to the door, I'm with you for the duration."

He wanted to throw himself at Terry...hug him, cry, maybe even blubber out a 'yes', but he wasn't sure about the two men in the room with them. "I think we need to talk. There's...there's a lot I don't understand about Warriors. I need to ask my questions."

Tyler drained his cup and placed it gently in the sink. "I know my cue. Good luck, Terry. Let me know if you need anything."

By Terry's stiff nod, Stevie guessed there was a message in that.

Jacob wrapped an arm around Stevie and tugged him into a hug. "Know you *are* welcome, if you want to join the family."

With that, they both disappeared into the hall, let themselves out, and closed the door behind them.

The silence in their wake was deafening.

Stevie forced speech. "If you print on me... You won't ever want to leave me?"

* * * *

His expression was so hopeful, it was all Terry could do not to kiss him right then and there. *He has questions. He deserves answers.*

"Never." *I don't want to now.*

"Warriors are never unfaithful?"

"We're not capable of it, once we mate."

"What is involved in mating?"

Terry couldn't control his grin at that. "I think you know what mating involves. But to make us formally mates?"

Stevie nodded.

"I ask. You say yes...if you want to." He licked his lips at the thought of that word from Stevie. "We seal it with sex."

"That's all?" He seemed surprised by it.

"Magic words, remember? The right word, at the right time... That's all it takes with a Warrior."

Stevie didn't ask another question right away, and Terry's nerves buzzed in suspense. Just when he would have prompted him, Stevie found his voice.

"No wedding? Marriage? It does have its benefits, like...medical insurance and stuff."

"We can, if you want to. Some Warriors have legal weddings, if their mates want to. But that's not necessary. All medical for Warriors and mates...children...and Sharon, if she carries for us, are handled by our protected doctors."

"What about insurance and stuff? What if you get killed by a vampire?"

He smiled. "Warriors take care of our own. Mates automatically inherit everything the Warrior owned. In fact, mates are guaranteed a place in the family forever, even if the Warrior dies. We only file taxes on our investments, so tax code stuff doesn't bother us either.

"But if you want a wedding ceremony, just say so, Stevie. We'll do it however you want. If you want a full civil ceremony, we'll file all the paperwork. If you want a private celebration, we can bring in one of our protected priests or Tyler to officiate."

"Priests? You have protected *priests*?"

"Beasts. They just *love* fucking with the clergy."

Stevie's face twitched...then again. He burst out laughing.

It was good to hear him laugh, but Terry wasn't sure it meant Stevie was at ease with the idea of mating. "If you need time to decide, I'll give you as much as I can."

"Yes."

He nodded, biting back a sigh. "When you know for sure—"

"Yes, Terry."

He stared at Stevie, at a loss for words.

"I said 'yes'."

"You mean yes, you'll mate with me?" He couldn't.

"Of course, I mean that. Yes, I'll mate with you."

Terry scooped him up and kissed Stevie hard. After a moment, he pulled away. Both of them gasped for breath.

"But we are having a private ceremony. Sharon would kill me if I didn't invite her...if I said I eloped or something, and Julie wants to be a flower girl someday."

"Done. Priest or Tyler? Or do you have someone else in mind?"

"Tyler. I've never been much for priests and churches."

"Whatever you want," Terry reminded him.

There was another potent moment of silence. Terry waited to see if Stevie had any other requests.

"I believe there was another step involved," Stevie hinted.

Terry smiled. "Why, yes, there is." He carried his mate to the bedroom and pushed the door shut with his foot.

"Where are we going to live? This apartment isn't big enough for a baby. We'll have to move eventually."

"Up to you. The manor house has plenty of room. We could take over one of the townhouses or cabins. We could get a place of our own. Wherever we live..."

"Yes?"

"Keep saying that word."

Stevie blushed.

"Wherever we live, you can redecorate our rooms. If we live at our own place or one of the townhouses or cabins, you can redecorate the whole place."

"You'd like that?" He seemed surprised by it.

"Calming is something every Warrior needs...just a bit."

"But what if I want to excite you?"

"No problem." Terry's mouth closed on his mate's.

Chapter Fifty-three

Four days later

Terry slid the phone back into his pocket. "My mother said it's red meat tonight. As you would say, go with bold."

Stevie nodded and headed for the red wine. He picked up two bottles. "What do you think?"

"I told you, I'm useless at this. You pick it. I'll buy it." On some level, Terry felt like he was failing his mate. There were so many things important to Stevie that he didn't understand. *I'll learn.*

His cheeks darkened. "I'll buy it. I should buy the wine I bring my first time to the house."

"Then you buy one, and I'll buy the rest."

Stevie's brow creased in confusion.

"It won't be just my parents. We're going to the manor."

"Which means?"

"A lot of family, especially with a Warrior bringing home a new mate. Not all of them will have wine, but I'll make sure we have enough for all of them, just in case."

Stevie considered the two bottles. At last, he set one down and motioned with the other. "This one."

Terry put his hand out for it and examined the label. He glanced at the other Stevie had put back on the shelf. Then he nodded. "Go pay for this one. I'll take care of the rest."

Though it seemed to confuse him, Stevie nodded. "Okay."

He disappeared from view and Terry waved down a clerk. "A case of each of these. Can you deliver?"

She smiled, probably envisioning a good sale day. "Of course. Delivery before six?"

"That works."

Terry handed over one of the contact cards he left with protected and fished out his debit card. She disappeared to the front counter, spoke to the clerk taking care of Stevie...and his mate turned to stare at him.

"Are you nuts?" Though Stevie only mouthed the words, Terry didn't miss them.

He shrugged, the heat rising in his cheeks.

Stevie paid for the bottle he was buying and made his way back to Terry. Proving that large purchases resulted in fast service, the clerk had already returned the debit card and told Terry to come again soon.

His mate didn't comment until they were out on the street again. "Money really doesn't mean anything to you, does it?" he asked, more than a little rattled by the concept, it seemed.

"Not much. We don't waste money, but we don't hesitate to spend it either." Terry pulled out his wallet and handed it to Stevie.

"What does this mean?"

"Look inside."

Stevie flipped his wallet open and started flipping through the bills. His eyes widened. "More than five hundred dollars?"

"That little? I should hit the ATM and pick up more."

He stopped short. "Seriously?"

"The recommended carry cash for a Warrior is a thousand or more."

Stevie handed the wallet back, brooding. "So, I guess fifteen hundred or so for wine for the family isn't that big a deal?"

Terry tucked it into his pocket again. "No. But the good news is mates have the benefit of tapping that wellspring as well."

"Meaning?" He started moving toward the car again.

"Meaning you don't have to work any job you don't want to. You can start your own business if you want to. You can go back to school if you want to. It also means Sharon doesn't have to work while she carries for us." Terry smiled. "It also means you can have any coffee machine you want."

Stevie laughed. "That could get expensive."

"Try me."

"I should have picked a more expensive wine."

"It's not too late to change the order," Terry informed him. He started to turn back toward the store.

Stevie grabbed his arm, laughing and shaking his head. "No, Terry. I mean it. No."

"As my mate wishes."

* * * *

Stevie stared up at the manor, his heart pounding. "People live in this place?"

"About a ten full-time. The rest come and go. We also have a dozen and a half cabins and a dozen or so houses in eleven states."

"Wow. You weren't kidding. Were you?"

Terry's smile faltered a bit. "About?"

"Money really is no object."

"It is *an* object, but no, we don't really worry about it."

The parking area to one side of the house was packed with vehicles. Terry pulled along the closest line.

"It doesn't look like anything that close is open," Stevie noted.

"There will be." Before Stevie could protest, Terry spotted an open space and pulled into it. He shot Stevie a quirked brow and a smile.

"Okay. Explain."

Terry turned off the car. "The closest spots are for families with babies and toddlers...or for injured, infirm, or pregnant family members. The lord and lady get the next spaces. It's free game after that, unless it's a special occasion. Bringing a new mate to the manor *is* a special occasion. That gives us preferential treatment."

"So, don't expect to park this close every time we come here," he postulated.

"Pretty much. Until we have a baby to be considered, in which case, we get the prime realty."

Stevie laughed, then let himself out of the car. Terry did the same, and they made their way to the front door.

It opened before they reached it, and a young girl streaked out. She threw herself into Terry's arms from the top step. "Uncle Terry. Uncle Terry."

He hoisted her and tossed her into the air, catching the giggling girl as she plummeted into his grasp again. He repeated the move three times. Then he settled her to his hip with ease.

They started speaking, but they weren't speaking English. Stevie identified Spanish, French, and something that sounded Slavic.

His jaw dropped. "How old is she? Five? Six?"

Terry smiled and planted a kiss on her forehead. "She'll be five next month."

"And she speaks *how* many languages?"

"Two fluently, English and French; learning those started at birth. She's learning German and Spanish at the moment. I imagine Jarrett and her brothers will start her on Gaelic next year."

Words failed him. Four years old and already bilingual, well on her way to... He wasn't even sure what speaking four languages was called. Stevie had never known anyone who spoke more than three fluently.

Terry motioned to Stevie. "Meredith, this is your Uncle Stevie."

She waved to him shyly. "Hi, Uncle Stevie."

"Hi." He was momentarily at a loss for words. "Your niece?"

"Jarrett's daughter."

"Well, you're going to be a beautiful young Warrior someday," he complimented her.

Meredith shot a look of confusion at Terry.

He cleared his throat. "It doesn't work that way. Most of our girls aren't Warriors. It's rare, much rarer than girls are in general, in the Warrior world."

"How do you know which will be Warriors, then? Their size?"

The lines in Meredith's brow deepened. "No, silly. Only *Königs* are *Blutjagdfrau*."

Stevie shot a questioning look at Terry.

"More terminology," he explained. "One family produces all the *Blutjagdfrau.*"

"Oh. Well, I suppose I'll be learning more every time I have a discussion about the Warrior world." Every time he thought he had a handle on it, he learned there was more.

Terry nodded. "Most likely."

Stevie sized her up. "I have another niece. Her name is Julie, and she's five. I bet she'd love to play with you."

Meredith bounced on Terry's arm. "Really?" she squealed, sounding very much like Julie.

Terry chuckled. "Really." He smiled at Stevie. "Meredith is our only girl this generation...so far. I'm sure she'd love another girl to play with."

"Well then," Stevie decided, "I suppose I'll just have to invite Sharon and Julie out here to the manor one weekend. If you two like each other, maybe we can make it a regular visit."

She nodded emphatically.

They made their way inside. A group of boys of varying ages playing in the foyer stopped to stare.

Stevie shifted nervously. *And this is how it begins.*

Meredith pointed to Stevie. "*Se llama Tio* Stevie," she pronounced.

"*Excelente,* Meredith," Terry complimented her.

The boys lined up, largest to smallest. The first—a boy Stevie would guess was fifteen but, based on what Terry had told him about Warrior children, was probably only ten or so—offered his hand for a handshake. "Welcome to Armen Manor, Uncle Stevie."

Stevie took his hand, stunned beyond words for a moment.

Another moved forward. "Tyler says you make great coffee."

He took that offered hand as well. "Th-thanks."

The handshakes turned to hugs as the children got younger, and the comments and questions turned to more juvenile, things like asking him what his favorite color was or if he liked puppies. Stevie looked up at Terry, trying desperately to understand this scene.

Adults gathered in doorways, smiling. At last two women crossed the room to them. The first took Meredith from Terry. The second drew both Terry and Stevie into a hug.

"Hi, Mom," Terry breathed.

"Welcome home, Terry. Welcome home, Stevie."

Stevie tightened his hug slightly. *I think I am. For the first time, I think I am.* "Thank you."

Chapter Fifty-four

One week later

"Tell me again why Stevie isn't here," Sharon pressed.

Terry smiled. As usual, Stevie had been correct about his sister's inquisitive nature. "He and my mother are sharing recipes. At least, they were last time I checked on them."

Julie interrupted her mother's next question. "*How* many children did you say would be there?"

"Somewhere between eight and twelve, depending on how many of their parents made it into town for dinner. Plus the teens and babies, of course."

She made an expansive motion with her arms in the back seat. "I don't have that many in my whole classroom."

"You have fourteen other children in your class," Sharon corrected her.

"Well, they're never all there."

Terry laughed at her exaggeration. "They're not all your age. The youngest is two, and the oldest is nine. If memory serves, five of the twelve are between four and seven."

"But only one girl," she complained.

"Julie," her mother warned.

"I know. I know. It's not like ordering a hamburger with or without a pickle."

Terry swallowed another laugh at the comparison. He was starting to see where Julie got her unusual vocabulary from.

"That's right," Sharon agreed. "Unless you do a lot of doctors' visits and pay a *lot* of money, you can't control if you have a boy or a girl."

"Or one of each," Julie chimed in, clearly referring to her mother and Stevie.

"Or that."

Terry turned onto the access road, and Sharon focused on the manor house appearing over the rise. Her jaw dropped. After a moment, she shut it. "This is really where you grew up?"

He considered how to answer that. "Some of the time. The family owns several homes, and we lived wherever the head of the family assigned my father."

"Your family owns a company?"

"A venture...and investments."

"That's money."

"Yes. It is."

"And you actually work?" It was impossible to miss the note of disbelief.

"No free rides. All the guys work where we're assigned, unless our spouses want to stay in one place. The head of family always lets them stay in one locality, if the spouses don't want to travel."

Her eyes narrowed. "The *guys* all work. What about the women?"

"If they want to, they can. They aren't required to do it. Tyler's oldest sister, Michelle, chose to work for the venture. Michelle's twin, Melissa, didn't care for it, so she got her degree in an unrelated field and went an entirely different way with her life."

Terry pulled into a parking space and shut the car down. They'd barely stepped out of the doors when they were surrounded by a group of six of the children.

Meredith marched up to Julie and offered her hand. "*Bonsoir*, Julie." Though Meredith was four months younger, she towered over their new arrival.

Julie looked up at Terry in confusion.

"Julie doesn't speak French," he informed his niece.

"*Buenos*—"

"Or Spanish."

Meredith's forehead crinkled in confusion.

Terry squatted to her level. "If Julie wants to, maybe you and the boys can teach her another language. Right now, she only speaks English."

She didn't hesitate. "What language do you want to learn?"

"Meredith," he warned. "*Only* if—"

"German," Julie spoke over him. "My Mommy is German." She sucked at her lower lip, waiting for an answer from the children.

Meredith smiled widely. "I'm learning German now. I'll teach you some. Want to swing?"

Julie nodded, and the two girls darted through the parting throng of boys. In a heartbeat, the entire group was thundering away.

"Julie," Sharon called after her. Her heel sank into the grass, and she pitched forward.

Terry caught her and set Sharon back on her feet. He offered his arm to help her along, and she took it, her cheeks flaming...in embarrassment, most likely.

"She'll be fine. I promise. But I'll show you the play area, just to put your mind at ease."

They made their way to the children's training and play area. Sharon stopped short, panning her gaze from the obstacle course to rope course to the play area for younger children in awe.

"Don't worry," Terry soothed her. "The trainees keep the little ones off the teen equipment. No child is allowed on the rope course until they're ten, and anyone under the age of sixteen wears a helmet and a harness to avoid injury."

She nodded, then focused on the two girls ambling across the lawn together, deep in discussion.

Julie stopped and pouted. "The swings are full. Maybe we should—"

Meredith put up a hand, motioning for silence. She marched to the swings. "We wanted to swing," she announced imperiously.

All three boys hurried to offer their swings. Meredith took the center one and waved Julie to the swing to her right. Julie hesitated, then launched toward the swing, taking it from David's hand with a smile and a heartfelt "Thank you." David beamed at the praise. In moments, both girls were well under way, thanks to starter pushes from the boys who'd accommodated them.

Michael, a newly first nighted young Warrior, appeared at Sharon's side. "I've got the watch, if you two want to go in."

"Sure. Thanks," Sharon managed.

Terry shot his younger cousin a look ordering his diligent attention. "Have the children in before dark." He tapped his chest in the position an amulet would typically lie, then moved his gaze to Julie in a clear indication that their new arrivals didn't have their protection yet.

Michael straightened. "You have my word. I won't let the children out of my sight for a heartbeat."

"Carry on."

* * * *

Stevie looked up at his sister as she walked through the kitchen door with Terry in tow, her expression nothing short of stunned disbelief.

"It's quite a house. Isn't it?" he asked.

"Wow."

Stephanie laughed heartily. "Welcome to Armen Manor, Sharon."

"The name fits."

"It does. Armens have owned this land for nearly two hundred years, and this manor has stood for almost a century. It has been updated several times, of course: electrical, pipes, central air and heat, but much of the house is original."

Sharon spun a slow circle, looking at the expansive kitchen. She took a step toward the inner doorway and reached out to touch the intricate etching in the polished wood lintel.

"It's a blessing on all who live in or visit this home," Terry shared.

Stevie smiled at his sister's reaction. "Well, since you're in shock anyway, this shouldn't even make you twitch."

Her brow lowered a notch. "What shouldn't?"

Right on cue, Terry crossed the room and wrapped an arm around Stevie's waist. Stevie raised his left hand to display the ring.

Sharon gaped at it for a long moment. "You're getting *married?*"

"Shocked?" Terry asked.

Her disbelief melted into a wide smile, and a happy squeal filled the room around them. Sharon launched herself to Stevie and squeezed him tight. "When?"

"A month. I assume you and Julie will be part of the ceremony."

She bounced back a step, smiling widely. "Of course."

Terry nodded. "Stevie said the colors are black and silver. Dresses are on me."

"I must admit it. This *is* a surprise."

Stevie looked up at Terry, biting back a wince.

"What?" Sharon inquired, no doubt sensing Stevie's unease.

Terry offered his hand. "Stevie is part of the family now, and so are you and Julie, but being part of this family means I have to remove the blinders you've been living with."

"Blinders?"

He nodded toward his hand, and she took it. Terry led them to the library and offered the leather couch to Stevie and Sharon.

Stephanie took one of the chairs. Stevie didn't question that. They'd explained that one of the older women usually helped answer questions for a new woman coming to the house. Sometimes it was the Lady Armen; sometimes it was the mother of the Warrior bringing the woman in. In this case, it was the latter.

Terry seemed to consider where to start. "I told you I work security...protecting people."

Sharon nodded.

"I didn't lie about it, but it's not a job. It's a duty I was born to, and I'm not protecting people from what you might expect. We're called Warriors." He hesitated and met Stevie's gaze. "This part might go better if it comes from you."

"Gee, thanks," Stevie grumbled.

"Stevie?" she questioned him.

He took a calming breath. "Remember the injury on my neck a while back?"

"You *said* you cut yourself with the razor." There was an accusation couched in that statement.

"You've seen the peach fuzz I grow. Why would I need to shave that far down my neck?"

"Then what *did* happen to you?"

That was harder to admit. The words stuck in his throat.

"Damn it, Stevie!"

"The Warriors call them beasts. You'd... Um...you would call it a vampire."

Sharon gaped at him. She looked from person to person, then shook her head slowly.

"A vampire bit me, and Terry saved my life."

She pressed a hand to her mouth, tears misting her eyes.

"Really, Sharon. I'm not lying to you about this. It's not a prank. A vampire bit me."

Sharon lowered her hand into her lap. "Okay. Vampires. Let's say I believe you."

"It's all true," Stephanie imparted. "I know it's hard to believe, but it's true."

"So there are vampires in the world. What can I do beyond worrying about them?"

"Stevie," Terry prompted him.

He pulled the amulet from beneath his shirt, and Stephanie did the same. Sharon looked from one to the other, but she didn't voice a question about them.

Terry took over. "With your permission, I'll give you and Julie amulets and blessings. Once you have them, you never remove the amulets."

"What do they do?"

"Make it impossible for a beast to touch you or to feed on you. If one tries to do either, it calls a Warrior to protect you."

"And the catch is?" she pushed him.

Terry shrugged. "The Warriors have a duty to protect you both. You're welcome to live with us, since you're family. You can keep your own place if you want to.

"There are only three rules."

"I'm listening."

"First... Obey the Warriors in matters of your safety. If they tell you to stay somewhere, stay. If they tell you to leave an area, you do it."

Sharon nodded solemnly.

"Don't tell anyone about us. If you think someone needs us or is fishing for information about us, call us and let us know. We'll take care of it. Never tell anyone what you know."

"Okay. It may take Julie a while to learn it."

"We'll watch what we tell her until she's old enough to show discretion."

"And the last rule?"

"Never, *ever* remove the amulet."

She hesitated, forming her words carefully, Stevie suspected. "And if we remove them?"

Terry cleared his throat. "Once the beasts know about Stevie's relationship with me, they will do everything they can to use you against me. In specific, they will try to use both of you to make Stevie relinquish his amulet, which much as I love him, I have to admit would probably work. Then they would use Stevie against me to try and destroy my will to fight them. Without the amulets, it's much more difficult to prevent that."

Before Sharon could form an answer, Julie came rushing into the room, chanting "Mommy! Mommy! Mommy!" the whole way. She held up her wrist, bouncing in place. "Look. Meredith gave me a bracelet just like hers. Isn't it great, Mommy?"

Sharon stroked a finger along the line of miniature amulets, held together with a sturdy chain. She swallowed slowly. "That's...great, Julie. Why don't you show Uncle Terry. I think... I think he said there's a special..."

"It's a good luck charm," Terry offered.

Julie nodded. "Meredith said it's bad luck to take the bracelet off. *Really* bad luck." She ran to show Terry.

He reached down and drew Julie into his arms. He whispered the words, just as he had when he gave Stevie his amulet. Then he sealed the blessing with a kiss on the forehead. That completed, Terry set Julie on her feet again.

"I'm going to go find Meredith." She was gone before anyone could answer.

Terry nodded to Sharon. "I think I can find another bracelet, if you like. Or would you rather have an amulet?"

She hesitated long enough to make Stevie nervous. "I'd love a bracelet. Thank you."

Stevie let out a sigh of relief, and Terry smiled widely.

Chapter Fifty-five

Two months later

Stevie sat back on the bed in their bedroom at the manor house, rapt on the sight of Terry beating off to get the sample Sharon would be inseminated with. His mate came with a groan, his sweat-coated chest heaving in and out, as his semen splashed into the plastic receptacle in spurts.

Terry set it aside and fastened his jeans over his still-hard cock. That accomplished, he went to the door, opened it, and handed the sample off to one of their doctors. They started discussing something in low tones.

Stevie took a calming breath, trying to reason his way out of his arousal. It seemed wrong on some level to get a hard-on when you knew the results were going into your sister.

That didn't mean he went flaccid. Who could, looking at Terry's luscious back, the muscles flexing and bunching as he moved?

As if he overheard Stevie's internal argument, Terry spun back into the room and shut the door behind him. He made his way across the room, unbuttoning his jeans as he came.

Stevie swallowed hard, his head spinning lightly. He tried to make sense of Terry stripping off his jeans, but he couldn't. They weren't going in for the insemination. That was a little too much for Stevie's sensibilities. Instead, Stephanie—Terry's mother—was keeping Sharon company during the insemination.

"I...um... We have only—"

"I told them to give us half an hour," Terry interrupted him. He settled to the bed and started loosening Stevie's belt.

"I won't ask why," he gasped out. That much was obvious. Terry was intent on seriously hot sex.

"Maybe you should." Terry made it past his jeans and started stroking him up with one hand. He grabbed the lube off the bedside table with the other.

Stevie moaned. "Why?" He couldn't manage a whole sentence, but he was more than willing to play twenty question as best he could. He started pushing his jeans away to hurry Terry along.

Terry poured some lube into his hand and warmed it. "Conceiving a child is something every Warrior lives for. Just knowing he has permission to keeps him aroused, and knowing the mate is fertile will keep him hard for days on end."

"But I'm not the fertile one. I'm not the one who will be carrying the baby."

He started working the warmed lube into Stevie's ass, pushing one thick finger in to prepare him. "No, you're not, but you are my mate. How lucky for us that I'm going to be intent on you."

Stevie pushed back, helping him work him up for more. In moments, they'd moved on to two fingers.

"Lucky. Yes." *Oh damn, am I lucky.*

Terry grumbled out a series of curses in at least four languages. In the next moment, he was deep inside Stevie, moving hard and fast.

"Oh fuck," Stevie managed. He wasn't going to last. It took only a handful of thrusts for Terry to send him over.

His mate wasn't as quick. He'd pushed Stevie to two bouts of aftershocks before he came.

They lay together, breathing hard.

Stevie tried to make sense of what had just happened. "How long does this last?" God help him, a few days of this might well kill him with pleasure.

Terry trailed his lips from Stevie's ear to his mouth, kissing him before he answered. "Until Sharon is out of her fertile window. Maybe four more days. Definitely in earnest until after the next insemination."

Two days.

He pulled back, staring down at Stevie. "It doesn't bother you, does it?"

"Hell, no. But..."

"Yes."

"One thing."

"I'm listening."

"Next time, I'm giving you the hand job before the insemination."

Terry growled, and his cock bucked against Stevie's channel.

Chapter Fifty-six

Four and a half months later

"Need anything, Sharon?" Stephanie asked.

She groaned and put her feet up on the sofa. *I'll probably need Terry's help to get back up, but it's worth it.*

Stephanie laughed as she sank into a chair. "I remember those days."

"I shouldn't have demanded they do two inseminations."

Her smile went brittle. "It probably didn't matter. One sexual encounter resulted in Katie and Corwyn. Four or five inseminations or so resulted in Scott. Like Stevie told Terry, twins probably resulted from your side of the genetic code. Uh...no offense intended."

"None taken." Sharon couldn't argue that her own genetics probably resulted in the twins, not Terry's. "I guess you're right. At least the insemination was easier than what I'd prepared for."

"Ah, yes. The ability of Warriors to sense takes all the uncertainty about when to inseminate out of the mix."

The up side of conceiving for her brother and his mate was that there had been very little medical intervention to accomplish getting her pregnant. Rather than blood tests to confirm her fertility, Terry had been able to do that with a touch. There'd been no drugs or egg harvesting. Terry had simply provided the sperm the doctor had inseminated her with. Terry had assured Sharon that a single insemination would be enough, but she'd asked to be sure by doing a second two days later, and Terry had conceded to her request.

And I conceived twins. According to the ultrasounds, they were expecting a mixed set, just like Sharon and Stevie were. Terry had seemed shocked by it. Apparently a mixed set of twins like that had only happened once in recorded Warrior history. One way or the other, Stevie and Terry were going to have their hands full very soon.

While conceiving for Terry and Stevie had been much easier than she'd envisioned, carrying for them was another matter entirely. Warrior babies were big babies, in general. Carrying two of them compounded the size difference. At a little less than five months along, she was larger than she'd been at delivery with Julie.

Stephanie's next question broke her train of thought there. "What does Julie think about having a little brother *and* a little sister?"

"Cousins," Sharon corrected her. "We decided not to complicate it. It's easier for Julie to understand me carrying Stevie and Terry's babies than it would be for her to think of them as her brother and sister and wonder why I'm not raising them. She might wonder if I might want to get rid of her too or something."

"I guess so. The family is really excited about it, though."

Sharon laughed. "I think Stevie and Terry have bought more clothes than six babies could wear in the first year. Not to mention toys, car seats, a double stroller and—"

"Every possible baby health and bath product known to man," Stephanie added.

"Oh! The Burt's Bees products! Once Stevie said they were best, everything had to be Burt's Bees. I think Terry ordered a case of every product."

"I know. I know. Warriors are like that with their children. Especially little girls. You've seen how everyone spoils the girls, I'm sure."

"Yes, they do that."

The men and boys deferred to the little girls at almost every turn. The moment she found out Julie would be visiting, Meredith had all but demanded to have queen-sized bunk beds put in her room. It had been accomplished within twenty-four hours.

When Meredith learned Sharon and Julie were moving in, she'd insisted on having the smaller nursery next to hers adjoined and decorated as a suite for them to share. Now, she and Julie shared the very frilly rooms. When they got older, they might decide to have their own rooms, but for the moment, they were enjoying the novelty of having another girl their own age around.

Sharon raised her head at the sound of Terry's voice in the foyer. He was talking to someone, but whatever was going on, it wasn't a pleasant discussion. The voices escalated, and Terry and another Warrior moved into view.

"I've already apologized to your mate," the other Warrior offered calmly. "I'm trying to—"

"Not good enough," Terry cut him off. "You had no right to say what you did."

Sharon struggled to her feet.

"You'll want to stay out of this," Stephanie warned.

Sharon believed her, but something primal told her to get up and head to the doorway.

The other Warrior raised his hands for peace. "You're right. I'm trying to—"

"You still face my judgment."

Jaden. Stevie had told her about this Warrior.

Jaden's patience slipped. "What do you think I'm trying to do? I've stayed away from my home and family as long as could, to give *you* time to—"

Without warning, Terry punched him in the chest, driving Jaden a step back. The second punch—this one to Jaden's face—took the younger Warrior to his back.

Sharon gaped at Terry, shocked by the cold calculation in his attack.

"There's a reason for this," Stephanie whispered.

Jaden pushed to his feet again. He nodded to Terry. "Do you intend to do more damage, or are you done with me?"

Terry opened his mouth to say something. Based on his expression, Sharon guessed it wasn't going to be cordial.

"He's done," she ordered.

They both turned to look at her, and the fire bled out of Terry. "Yes, I'm done with him," he conceded.

Jaden tipped his head to Terry. "My apologies." Then to Sharon. He stalked toward the kitchen. Just before he disappeared from view, Jaden shot her a brittle smile.

Sharon's heart ached for him. She didn't doubt that Jaden meant what he'd said. He'd been cut off from everything he loved, waiting for Terry to be ready to take his pound of flesh. It was a double punishment. *A torture.*

Terry appeared at her side. "I'm sorry you had to see that. I shouldn't have—"

"No. You shouldn't have." Though Sharon was sure he wasn't about to say he shouldn't have hit Jaden, Terry was quick enough to catch her meaning.

His hand closed over her shoulder, kneading lightly. "You should lay down, Sharon. You're upset."

"And you're the one upsetting me." She turned toward the kitchen, shaking off his hand, and left him behind.

To his credit, Terry didn't follow her.

Sharon stopped in the doorway, beneath the blessing. Jaden sat at the table, a terry-cloth covered ice pack pressed to his cheek. He looked up at her, as lost as she'd ever seen a soul.

* * * *

My gods, she's beautiful. With her strawberry-blond hair and bright blue eyes, she was a ray of light in the darkness of a Warrior's existence.

There was no mistaking who she was. She looked too much like Stevie to be anyone but his twin. *Sharon.*

Which means the babies she's carrying are Terry's. Tread carefully, Jaden.

He dragged his gaze away from her. Looking at this particular woman wasn't good for his libido, and offending her wasn't a good way to keep his head. It would certainly net him a lot worse than a couple of punches.

Sharon sank into the chair beside him. She reached out and took the ice pack from his hand, then winced at the bruising beneath it.

"It's okay," Jaden soothed her. "It will heal in—"

"A few days. Yes, I've heard that. I'm sure it hurts now, though." She pressed the ice lightly to his cheek. "Here. Hold this."

Jaden complied, stunned that she was tending to him. And after what he'd said about her brother being an unsuitable mate. Which gods had favored him today?

She's a mother and a bearing woman. The hormones probably make her acutely aware of situations she can be nurturing in.

He sucked in his breath at the sensation of Sharon dragging his shirts up his chest.

"No. You can't," he breathed. He was already enchanted with her. Jaden wasn't certain his sanity could take the blow of so intimate a move, since it was certain she would hold a grudge against him for his earlier offenses.

She hesitated, her hand so close to his lower abdomen it warmed his skin. His cock came up at her proximity.

"You're hurt. I need to see—"

"I'll heal," he repeated. "You shouldn't do this."

Sharon stared at him, her brow furrowed in confusion. "There's some rule I don't know about that says I'm not allowed to help you? Is it because this was a judgment?"

Rule? If only it were that simple. *I need a reason she'll understand.* "No, but Terry—"

"Terry doesn't own me," she snapped back.

"Of course not, but—"

"Then sit still and let me check it."

Her earnest expression stilled his protest. "O-okay."

She yanked the shirts further up, and her fingertips stroked along the edges of the bruise, firing his nerves.

And my cock. Gods help me, maybe this isn't a blessing after all.

"Men," she grumbled. "I swear raising children is easier than dealing with the lot of you Warriors. Well, let's take care of this."

"You really don't hate me, do you?" The question slipped out without decorum.

Sharon's eyes widened. "Why would I hate you?"

"What I said. I was surprised when Terry announced he was bisexual. I was shocked by it, to be honest. I didn't mean it how it came out." Jaden braced himself for a smack. *If she does it, I deserve it. Might as well face all my judgments at once.*

It didn't come, and he relaxed his muscles slowly, wondering at it.

She smiled faintly. "I'll get you another ice pack." Sharon was halfway across the room before she spoke again. "I hear that Warriors are considered honorable again once they face their judge and pay their penalties for breaking the rules."

It wasn't quite accurate, but... "Yes. We have very real enemies out there. We don't hold many grudges between ourselves, especially within a house Too dangerous to have the Warrior you have at your back angry at you."

"Then you've proven your honor by apologizing and facing Terry." She pulled out another ice pack, slipped it into one of the terry cloth covers, and headed back. "Of course, if you disrespect Stevie again—"

"I won't, and Terry would kill me if I even considered it. Not that that's my reason, of course."

Sharon settled the ice on Jaden's bruised ribs gently. Then she met his gaze. "Terry would have to beat me to the punch. Literally. I protect my little brother."

Jaden realized he was staring at her. *Say something, dummy!* "If you feel the need to do that, do me a favor."

One brow went up. "And that is?"

"There's a baseball bat or three in the sports closet. Hit me with one of them. It will do a decent amount of damage to me, but it will protect you from harm. Hitting a Warrior is a lot like punching a tree."

The edges of her mouth twitched, and Sharon swallowed what was probably a laugh. "Thought that one through, have you?"

"Split-second tactical decision," he countered. "Warriors learn to do that early in life, even if it has to be beaten into them a bit."

She did laugh at that. Jaden smiled. Sharon's laugh was worth any self-depreciating remark he made to hear it.

A miniature version of Sharon stomped through the doorway, dropped a backpack on the floor, then headed for the fridge. Though Jaden had heard how much Julie resembled her mother, he hadn't believed it was possible until that moment.

"Bad day at school?" Sharon inquired.

Julie pulled out a bottle of apple juice and stubbornly tried to open it while the refrigerator door swung shut. "I don't see why I can't home school here like the other kids do," she grumbled.

"We said you would try this new school for six months."

"It's almost six months now."

Sharon left Jaden in charge of his own ice packs. She crossed the room and placed her hand out for the juice bottle. Julie handed it over with a sigh. Once the opened bottle changed hands, her mother answered.

"It's been four and a half months. Not six."

"I *hate* that school, and I learn a lot more here."

Sharon folded her arms in the space between her pregnant womb and her full breasts. "Like the name you called Michael?" she challenged.

Jaden winced, though he had no clue what offensive vocabulary she'd picked up from the other children. *Or the Warriors.* Since Michael was Jaden's youngest brother, he'd probably called the man worse than what Julie had. *It's still not appropriate for a little girl to be exposed to that language.* Or to use it, though most of their adult women grew into it eventually.

"I said I wouldn't say it again," Julie pleaded.

"I don't think you're giving the school a chance. Your teacher is really nice. You've said so yourself."

"The kids are mean." Julie pouted.

Jaden straightened, his temper simmering lightly at the idea of anyone being mean to this sprite of a child. He placed the ice packs on the table, preparing to take action. Though he hadn't been formally introduced to Julie, she was a child of his house. *A female child at that.* "Mean, how?"

Sharon shot him a look he was sure was intended to warn him off. As if seeking an ally, Julie approached him.

"She is my daughter," Sharon reminded him before Julie could speak up and answer his question.

"I know that, and I respect it, but now that I know there may be some threat to Julie, I'm honor bound to end it or to notify Terry that there's a problem, if I can't end it personally."

She winced and crept a look over her shoulder, as if assuring herself that Terry wasn't listening in. "They're five-year-olds. How much *threat* can there really be?"

Jaden raised an eyebrow at her. It was a silent reminder that Warriors took any threat to their women and children seriously.

Julie broke the tension by poking at the bruise on his chest. "Did another Warrior get you in training?"

"Something like that." He didn't want to admit his dishonor to her. On some level, not admitting it seemed dishonorable in itself.

"Next time, duck," she counseled.

Jaden laughed heartily at her advice. "I'll try to remember that. In the meantime, tell me how the kids are being mean."

Her face screwed up in a look of disgust. She plopped into the chair her mother had vacated. "It's mostly Billy and his friends. They pull my hair and say I don't have a soul."

"What?" What kind of idiocy was this?

"A really old *South Park* episode," Sharon offered. "Gingers don't have souls."

"Julie technically isn't a ginger," he pointed out. Though her skin was fair and would burn easily, he was sure, it wasn't pale and heavily freckled.

"Ah, but redheads are half-ginger. They are called *day-walkers*." She added an ominous undertone to the final word.

"They're saying she's half beast?" Keeping his temper in check for that one was difficult.

"I went through it too," Sharon admitted with a strained smile. "It seems to have been added to the book of common childhood taunts now. I suspect it won't die out anytime soon."

"What else?" Jaden asked, focusing on Julie again.

"Sometimes they push for no reason, and..."

"And?" he prompted her.

She put a hand in her pocket and produced a folded sheet of paper. Julie handed it to Jaden instead of to her mother. He unfolded it and started reading the report from the teacher.

"What is it?" Sharon asked.

Julie darkened in a blush.

"A behavior report," Jaden replied.

"What for? Julie has never had behavior problems."

"I kicked Billy," Julie offered.

"Why?" Sharon's exasperation bled through in the question.

"He tried to steal my bracelet, then threatened to punch me if I didn't hand it over. Meredith gave me his bracelet, and Uncle Terry said it's bad luck to take it off. *Ever.*"

Sharon gasped and covered her mouth with a shaking hand.

Jaden nodded solemnly. He wanted to tell Julie how well she'd done, but there was little doubt Sharon wouldn't appreciate that. "What don't you go find Meredith, Julie. I think your mother and I need to discuss this."

She hopped off the chair and started walking away. Julie stopped and looked back at him. "Are you another uncle?"

"No. I'm a cousin. My name is Jaden." He steeled himself for her condemnation. Who knew what she'd heard about him from the other Warriors?

Julie smiled. "Don't forget to duck, Jaden." Before he could respond, she was sprinting through the house, accompanied by a shout of reminders to slow down from a Warrior the foyer.

Sharon sank into the chair with a groan. "What now? We can't let someone take the amulet away."

Jaden put the ice pack back on his chest. "You have a couple of choices."

"I do?" That seemed to surprise her.

"She's your daughter. All I'll do is give you a few choices. Which one is palatable to you is what we'll follow through on."

Sharon nodded and waved him on.

"Choice number one... One of the Warriors will accompany Julie to school every day and stay with her while she's there."

"The school won't allow that."

"We'd have to ghost."

"And do what, precisely? These are children, after all, and as bad as they may be, they aren't beasts."

He hesitated. "Tell Julie when to run the other way. If the bullies go after her, arrange for them to trip over their own feet a bit."

"Classroom pranks?"

Jaden shrugged.

"No. Besides that, they'd probably say she was a jinx or something and add that to what they tease her about."

"Choice number two..."

"Has to be better than choice number one is. Seriously, I'd hate to put the Warriors out that way."

"It's a duty. They won't complain, and we're always looking for special duties to give trainees. Duty they can't hurt themselves performing as they might going up against a beast."

She waved him on. "Choice number two?"

"We move Julie to a private school."

"There are bullies everywhere."

"I agree. There are, but there are a few exclusive schools that allow security for high-profile children."

"I'm sure they cost a lot."

He waited for her to catch up.

"Oh, yes. Money isn't an issue. Where are these schools?"

Jaden sighed. "That's the down side. Nowhere near here."

"No. Even if Terry and Stevie and I all moved to wherever the school is, Julie and Meredith wouldn't get to see each other, and I can't ask either of the girls to leave the manor."

"Yeah. I figured you would think that. Choice number three..."

"Home school her with the other kids," she guessed.

"It's really not a bad choice. Learning goes on in class time and out of it as well. Our children excel at advancement tests. The girls who go to college average twenty-two fifty on the SAT."

Sharon seemed to consider it. "Sold. But...uh...can we *try* to teach the boys not to introduce Julie to any more curse words in German or any other language?"

"We'll do our best. Out of curiosity, what did she call Michael?"

"*Scheiße Kopf.*"

Jaden couldn't help it. He started laughing. To his relief, Sharon smiled.

Chapter Fifty-seven

Three weeks later

Sharon collapsed to Jaden's chest, laughing. His heart tripped in excitement, and he savored the moment.

She stepped away, through the door Julie had disappeared through moments before. Jaden followed her, missing the connection already.

"Julie has settled into being completely spoiled," Sharon stated.

Jaden closed the door behind them. "Not completely. Meredith has been spoiled since birth. Unlike Julie, Mere often forgets the little things: please and thank you, smiles. Julie doesn't *expect* to be spoiled. It makes a big difference."

Sharon turned to look at him, ticking her finger and her eyes narrowed. "You just may be right about that."

"May? I'm wounded."

She burst out laughing.

Jaden pressed a hand to his heart, feigning injury. "Seriously. Wounded here." He took a step closer to her, hoping she would collapse against his chest again. "I'm not hearing the proper tone of concern from you."

Sharon laid an ineffectual smack against his arm. "Warriors and their egos."

And their printing. If she showed the slightest interest in him as a man and not a playmate for her daughter, Jaden would be the happiest Warrior alive.

"Of course you're making the same mistake Terry made."

Panic made a home is his gut. "What mistake?" *How do I fix it? How am I failing her?*

"When there's an adult woman and a little girl, Warriors tend to spoil the little girl. Women like to be spoiled a little too."

"How?" If he felt invited to, Jaden would spoil Sharon to the limits she would allow. *Please tell me how to spoil you. I'll take that as an invitation to do it.*

"Going out to dinner, for example."

"I'm listening." *Intently.*

"Just like Terry, you automatically offered Julie her choice of where to go."

He had, but since he'd been taking Julie out, and her mother had been tagging along—on the surface, anyway—that had only made sense.

But if she was saying she wanted him to take her to a restaurant she liked... "I'd like to take you to a restaurant you enjoy. Or maybe introduce you to one I think you will, but it's not a family restaurant, so we'd have to have Terry and Stevie watch Julie." His heart pounded in anticipation of her answer.

"As if there's any lack of willing babysitters. Stephanie would love to watch Julie. Or a half dozen other Warriors and wives."

Not the answer I was hoping for. "Is that a yes?"

Sharon looked down at herself, seemingly self-conscious, though Jaden couldn't comprehend why she would be.

"You... You want to take a hugely-pregnant woman with swollen ankles out to an adult dinner?"

"I want to take *you* to dinner, Sharon. A..."

She peeked up at him, her expression pleading for something he couldn't name.

Lay it on the line, Jaden. "A candlelit dinner somewhere with a maître 'd and food descriptions I have to translate for you."

"I don't have clothes appropriate to—"

"I can fix that." *If she comes up with another excuse, she doesn't want to go out with me. If that happens... Damn it, I'll need a mad cabin. I know I will.*

"You really want to take me to dinner?"

"Yes."

"On...a date?"

"Yes."

She took a step toward him, bringing them nearly belly to belly.

"Sharon?"

She rose on tiptoe and brushed her lips against his. Jaden's thinking mind bowed out of the discussion. Their mouths parted and meshed. Jaden cupped her cheek in his hand, and Sharon snuggled closer to him.

Sanity returned with a start. Jaden slowed the kiss to a series of questing touches of lips to lips. At last, he raised his head. Jaden stared at her, his heart hammering.

Sharon took a tremulous breath. "Saturday? S-so I have time to buy a dress."

"Yes to dinner?"

She nodded. "As long as I find a dress. If not..."

His muscles tensed. Was this another excuse? *Probably not, if that kiss was an indication of her feelings.*

"If not, I suppose we'll have to go somewhere else for now and do the candlelit dinner later?"

"Yes!"

Sharon smiled at his enthusiastic response. "You thought I'd say 'no'?"

"I didn't know." Jaden stroked the pad of his thumb up the line of her jaw to Sharon's ear. "Not knowing was driving me mad. Just finding the words to ask you was driving me mad."

"Mad?"

"Pretty much," he admitted. Did she know what madness he meant? Jaden wasn't sure what, if anything, Sharon knew about printing.

She placed a kiss on his cheek. "I should go to bed now."

Jaden backed off a step, withdrawing his hand. "You should." Carrying Terry's twins had to be exhausting for her.

She turned away, a spring in her step that countered his analysis. "I need a good night's sleep so I'll be ready to shop tomorrow." Sharon wagged her fingers in farewell and headed up the stairs, leaving Jaden with what was no doubt a sappy smile pasted on his face.

* * * *

"So where do you want to go?" Stephanie asked.

Sharon sighed. She'd wanted to do this alone, but Terry had insisted she take someone with her.

"Sharon? Are you okay?"

"Fine. I want...um...I want to buy a dress."

Stephanie put the car in gear and started to pull out of the parking space. "Maternity store, here we come."

"No."

The car stopped, and Stephanie shot a questioning look her way.

She picked at the front of her blouse, then decided to spit it out before she lost her nerve. "I want to get an evening gown, not a sundress or a frock."

The moment of stillness ended with Stephanie pulling out and leaving the manor grounds. When they were halfway to town, when Stephanie broke the silence.

"What's the occasion?"

"A date."

"With one of the Warriors." She didn't question it.

"Yes. Dinner at some elegant, candlelit restaurant, yet to be named."

Stephanie let out a long, slow breath. "Okay."

"You're not going to have Tyler—?"

"Forbid it? Of course not!"

Sharon smiled, relieved at her answer.

"Look at it this way. He's taking you to dinner. An expensive, romantic dinner at that. Whoever he is, he wants something permanent with you."

"He said not knowing if I'd go out with him was driving him insane."

Stephanie laughed heartily. "Oh, he's far gone."

"Yeah. I know." Sharon had been hoping that was true. *Scared that it is too.*

"Is that a problem for you?"

"You're good at that."

"Knowing when you're upset?"

"Something like that."

Stephanie winced. "What *is* upsetting you about him being far gone?"

Sharon rubbed gently at her squirming children.

"Terry doesn't have the right to an opinion," Stephanie informed her.

"I'd take the baseball bat to him, if he tried to interfere. Terry doesn't own me," she snapped back.

"But?"

"I do not intend to be a pregnant bride...or mate or whatever."

Her brow crinkled in confusion. "I don't follow."

"If he's that close... What if he can't wait?" Tears pricked at her eyes.

Stephanie sighed. "Warriors will wait as long—"

"As they can," she complained.

"Do you *want* to be his mate?"

"Once I'm not a blimp bride? Sure."

Stephanie's look fluctuated between exasperation and shock. "He won't rush you. Especially not right now. If you're willing to...uhm..."

"Sleep with him?" Sharon's cheeks flushed at the memory of the night before. "Yes. It's safe to say I am."

"Whoa," Stephanie breathed. "I've got to know. Which Warrior is it?"

"Jaden."

She smiled.

That smile made Sharon distinctly nervous. "What?"

"We're going to find you the perfect dress. Screw that. We're going to find you two or three perfect dresses."

"We are?" Her enthusiasm made Sharon's head spin. "I mean— I won't be pregnant forever."

"Yes. We are. You've got a few months until labor day rolls around. If I know Jaden, he will want to spoil you rotten, now that he feels he's allowed to. I say we beat him to the finish line and get you several dresses."

She chuckled. "And *then* we'll make you an appointment with my spa."

"Why?"

"Can you reach around my grandchildren to shave your legs?"

Sharon looked down at the huge swell of her womb. "I see your point."

"Then the spa it is. A full day of pampering for both of us, including hair and makeup. Does that sound okay to you?"

"I've never gone to a spa before."

"Then this will be a treat."

* * * *

Jaden startled, as Sharon levered herself up from the chair, coming to his feet in response. Terry reached out to put his dessert plate on the coffee table.

Sharon huffed at him. "I *don't* need someone to escort me up and down the stairs. The balustrade exists for a reason, Terry."

The overprotective Warrior daddy started to protest.

Jaden cut him off mid-word. "I'm headed up anyway. I'll walk with her, if that's okay with you, Sharon. Finish your dessert, Terry."

His expression stated clearly that Terry was suspicious. Jaden pretended not to notice it.

Sharon smiled. "Sounds good. Thank you, Jaden."

He made a theatrical bow and hand motion for her, and Sharon started giggling. They fell into step together in the foyer.

Halfway up the stairs, Jaden started whispering inquiries. "I heard you came back with shopping bags and dress bags today. I take it you found a dress or two?"

"Three. And, yes, I already know which one I'm wearing on Saturday."

"Really?" He'd been afraid she wouldn't find one she felt comfortable in, and she found three?

"Really. And some shoes, a couple of wraps, purses, lingerie..."

That last word raised a lump in his throat. "Can I see?"

"On Saturday. Or whenever I wear an outfit on a date for the first time, anyway."

Jaden chuckled darkly. "You love torturing me, don't you?"

Sharon wound her arm through his and led the turn toward the Warriors' wing at the top of the stairs. "Not my intention at all."

This moment is about to end. "What *is* your intention?"

She opened the door to her room and tugged him along toward the doorway. His body tightened in anticipation, and he followed when she released his arm and stepped in ahead of him.

Terry's voice made Jaden's heart stutter.

"Jaden, do you have a minute?"

He forced his jaw to unclench. "Sure." Jaden leaned down and pressed a kiss to Sharon's lips. "Be right back."

"I'll be waiting." Her cheeks went an enticing rose color.

Jaden turned and left her behind, tapping down his *Blutjagd.* Whatever Terry's game was, Jaden was going to end it. *Quickly. Decisively. He better never try this again.*

"Calm down," Terry stated calmly, though his *Blutjagd* flickered as well. He led the way to the Warriors' office and preceded Jaden inside.

Jaden restrained the impulse to slam the door. He closed it slowly instead. "Talk, Terry, but make it good."

"Just a reminder. A *friendly* reminder."

"I'm listening."

"Sharon is very pregnant."

Jaden crossed his arms over his chest and planted his feet shoulder-width apart, in a fighting stance. "Strangely enough, I noticed that, and I know they are your babies as well. News travels fast in the Warrior world. But—news flash for you—the babies are yours, but Sharon isn't. You don't own her, Cousin."

"I didn't say I did. Just...be gentle with her."

"Gentle? You're insinuating I lack control?"

"No! I didn't say that."

"Well, then you're saying I am in the habit of ignoring the Rules of Sanction. Break one, I'll break another?"

"No, nothing like that. You've paid your dues. I just—"

"You're just breaking the *same* rule I did."

Terry darkened, averting his gaze.

Jaden's temper uncorked. "Even if all I intended was a lover, you would have no right to wave me off. Back off or spend the next few days explaining to your mate how you overstepped your bounds and took a debilitating nut shot for your impertinence."

Terry's jaw dropped. It took him a full minute to recover. "Even? So you're printing on her?"

"None of your business."

"No. It's not my business. Are you?"

Jaden tamped down his fury a notch. "Yes, I am. Have a problem with it?" He raised his hand to stop whatever Terry was about to say. "For the record, if you do have a problem with it, to quote you, fuck you if you do."

Terry smiled. "Nope. No problem at all."

His *Blutjagd* faded in surprise. "Really?"

"If you're printing, the idea of hurting Sharon would shred you. So... carry on, Cousin."

"Don't worry. I intend to." Jaden pulled the door open and headed back down the hall.

Terry's laughter chased him down, and Jaden considered going back to make his position clear.

No. There's a lady waiting for me. Never keep a lady waiting. He stopped at Sharon's door and knocked lightly.

"If it's Jaden, come in." There was an edge of challenge in her tone that said Terry wouldn't have been extended the same welcome.

He opened the door, stepped inside the room, and closed it behind him again. Jaden would have liked to claim he wasn't disappointed by the fact that she was still dressed, but he was. *Acutely so.*

"Is there a problem with Terry? Do I need to—?"

"No and no." Jaden made his way to the bed and settled on the edge of the mattress next to her. "Terry and I understand each other perfectly."

"You do?" Sharon moved closer to him, clearly hinting at picking up where they'd left off the night before.

Jaden cupped a hand around the back of her neck and drew Sharon's lips to his. "Yes. We do."

She wrapped her arms around him and kissed Jaden.

His head spun in pleasure. He eased out of the kiss. "He doesn't interfere in our relationship, and I don't hit him so hard in the balls he can't get it up for three days."

She winced.

"What do you think of that?"

Sharon's laughter echoed off the walls. "I think you should take off your boots and stay a while."

He hastened to comply. "Glad to."

* * * *

Jaden double-checked his clothes in the mirror. He had to look perfect for Sharon. He had to make the entire night perfect for her.

A glance at his watch later, he was in motion, out of the bathroom, then down the stairs.

Michael stopped short halfway across the foyer and gaped at him. He didn't find his voice until Jaden was at the foot of the stairs and straightening his suit jacket. "What gives with the monkey suit, big brother?"

Jaden smiled. "Never keep a lady waiting."

"You're printing?"

"Don't make it sound so inconceivable."

Michael jumped in with all the exuberance of a teenaged Warrior. "With who? Did you save her? Spill."

Right on cue, Sharon appeared at the head of the stairs, Stevie at her side to aid her down. Jaden ignored both of their brothers and focused on Sharon.

The dress she was wearing was a deep green that complemented her hair and eyes. The style made his heart skip in excitement. It was a sheath dress, cut for a pregnant woman. One shoulder was bare, and deep slits revealed her legs up to mid-thigh.

Michael gasped beside him. "I can see why you're printing."

Jaden shot his youngest brother a warning look and ordered him away in the language of the ancients. To his credit, Michael tipped his head in acknowledgment and loped away without a backward glance at Sharon.

The lady in question appeared in front of him, and Jaden gave her his undivided attention.

"Well, what do you think?" she asked, twirling on the silver silk flats she'd worn for Stevie's wedding. "The matching shoes would have taken weeks, but—"

Jaden took her hands and brought both to his mouth to kiss her knuckles. "I think you're the most beautiful woman I've ever seen."

Her smile lit his world.

Chapter Fifty-eight

Three months later

Stevie watched as Terry stroked a hand over Sharon's distended womb, cooing to the baby doing gymnastics inside her. "Soon," his husband breathed, a wistful note making it all the more poignant.

Warriors really are family men, through and through.

"Good," she replied. "No offense to you two, but I'd rather not do this for you again."

Stevie winced at that. "We won't ask. I promise." Sharon clearly hadn't anticipated how different carrying for Terry was when she offered to do it. Maybe she should have asked more questions of the women who'd carried Warrior babies before she agreed, but it was too late for that now. Of course, carrying twins probably made it all the worse.

Jaden strolled into the room, bringing a glass of milk and a plate of meat and cheese, bread and herb butter for Sharon. "Hmm... I suppose that means I shouldn't broach the subject for a while."

"Probably a good idea," she agreed.

Surprise of surprises, Jaden and Sharon had hit it off sometime in the second trimester, right about the time Jaden trusted that Terry wouldn't kill him on sight.

The entire household knew he wanted to seal printing with her, but Sharon had decreed she wasn't doing that until after she gave birth and recovered from it. Though the wait had to be nearly intolerable for Jaden, you'd never know it to look at him. Terry had postulated that knowing she was *willing* to seal with him was enough to cool Jaden's blood.

Not that the two weren't sleeping together. Sharon had been sharing Jaden's room for the last few months, and no one seemed to have a problem with that. Not to mention, Jaden had taken to being a dad to Julie like a duck to water.

The only tension had apparently come when Terry warned Jaden to be careful how he handled the woman carrying his children. With Terry protecting their babies and Jaden offended by the suggestion he would harm the woman he intended to make his mate, Stevie was amazed the two hadn't beaten each other senseless.

Two six-year-old girls bolted into the room, breaking Stevie's train of thought. They tracked in a formidable amount of mud, three larger boys—aged between two and six years old and muddied to their knees or above—hot on their heels. The girls bolted for the Warriors' backs, demanding protection.

Sharon started to lever herself off the couch to intervene, but Jaden put a hand on her shoulder and stepped toward the pursuing mass of children. All three boys stopped short and looked up at him, going wide-eyed at Jaden's warning look.

"Do I have to speak to you about this?" Jaden asked.

Alan, the youngest, piped up without delay. "She pushed." He pointed to the girls.

Julie stomped her foot, indicating that she was the aforementioned pusher, though it wasn't clear which of the boys was the pushee.

Knowing Julie, there is more than one pushee. There was too much mud on the boys to believe she'd done less than shove all three into the largest puddle she could find.

"They said we have to listen to them because we're girls. That's not fair. It's not right," she protested.

Jaden bit back what Stevie suspected was a laugh. He cleared his throat. "Are you Warriors yet? Are you cursed?"

The boys shifted nervously. One by one, they answered in the negative.

"Right. Which means...?" he prompted them.

Ben, the oldest, sighed. "They don't have to listen to us."

"Correct."

"Told you," Julie informed them.

Jaden did smile that time. "You boys get cleaned up. Then report back here. Ben, you have a carpet to clean."

He shot a horrified look at Jaden. "Why me?"

"My guess is the girls would have wiped their feet, if you had stopped this instead of joining the younger boys chasing them. You let all four of the others run in here without removing shoes or even wiping their feet on the mat."

His cheeks darkened. "Probably true."

"Good. Then the girls can clean up the mud in the kitchen, David can clean up the mud in the dining room, and you, Ben, get to clean the rug in here. Next time, remember to be a good example for the little ones."

"Yes, sir." He didn't sound pleased, but he didn't argue the order either.

David added his agreement and pulled off his boots before he took another step. Ben followed suit and nodded to Alan to do the same. The toddler plopped to his backside and started working his boots off. The move left a lot more mud for Ben to clean, but the older boy didn't complain about it.

"Was that necessary?" Sharon asked.

Jaden lifted Julie and settled her on the smaller sofa. Meredith scurried up after her. He started stripping off their matching mud-caked Mary Janes and lavender ruffled socks, seemingly considering his answer. The duo looked like a set of fraternal twins; they were dressed nearly identically, but Meredith was half a foot taller, with dark hair and eyes, while Julie looked like a short carbon copy of her mother.

The boys left the room, boots in hand.

At last, Jaden spoke. "They're thanking their lucky stars I gave them such an easy punishment. Presuming to order the girls around was bad enough. Chasing them down was way too much."

"He's right about that," Terry chimed in. "Tyler would have made that much more painful."

"Go on," Jaden ordered the girls.

They each planted a kiss on his cheek, then ran for the kitchen to perform their own chore.

Jaden watched them go. "I gave the girls that punishment for show, just to teach them not to push."

"But...they're doing it," Stevie pointed out.

Jaden and Terry shared a chuckle.

Terry answered his comment. "I guarantee the boys will be down there taking the task off their hands, as soon as they're changed. Ben will insist on it. He knows he shouldn't have allowed any of the little ones to break the rules. Even Alan will help the girls do their share, and then he'll probably help David do his."

"But Ben will do his own, as some matter of honor?" Stevie guessed.

"You've got it," Jaden replied. "One of us may be house lord someday, and—"

"Figure the odds that *you'll* be house lord," Terry teased.

Stevie snorted then shot an irritated look at Terry. "If *you* are, I am *not* being referred to as Lady Armen."

"Anyway," Jaden spoke over them. "The last thing they'll want to chance is a future house lord seeing them slacking off."

"Or seeing them breaking the Rules of Sanction?" Terry reminded him.

Jaden went crimson. "I've already paid my dues for that, and I have apologized more than once."

"And I won't mention it again."

Jaden pushed to his feet. "I should go oversee the punishment I gave."

A gasp from Sharon brought all their heads around. It took Stevie a moment to note the slow, deep breaths and the slight pallor of her skin. Sharon's hand was closed in a fist so hard her knuckles stood out a stark white.

"Sharon?" Jaden appeared at her side.

"I don't think you'll be overseeing that punishment." It came out slightly shaky.

Terry vaulted to his feet and reached for her. Jaden was there first. For a long moment, they stared at each other across Sharon's body.

"Play nice boys," she managed weakly.

Jaden scooped her up, shooting a warning look at Terry. "The babies are yours, but Sharon is mine. Don't forget it."

Terry laughed and dragged Stevie into a hug. "I couldn't have an interest in her if I wanted to. You know that. I have a mate."

His cousin relaxed a notch and offered a sheepish nod. "I know it."

Stevie smiled at that. *A mate. Terry will never consider another lover while I'm alive.*

"Boys," Sharon called for their attention. "The hospital is not getting closer this way."

"One of the vans," Jaden decided.

"I've got the keys," Terry shouted back, bolting for the key rack in the foyer.

By the time they reached the front door, it was clear half the household knew what was going on. Stevie marveled at it all the way to the van. This was home.

Terry leaned down to plant a quick kiss on Stevie's lips. "Time to start our family, Stevie. Ready?"

"More than ready." He'd been waiting for this his whole life.

Cory:

Damsel In Distress

Chapter Fifty-nine

Hannah tried to force herself to move, but the pain made her head spin. There was no chance she would make it to her feet, less chance she could find her way home in the near future. Even finding her way to a phone and help seemed beyond her wildest dreams.

She raised her head, focusing blearily on a doorway and light beyond. Light was good. The...things—whatever they were, because they certainly weren't human—didn't like the light. She knew that much. Hannah reached a hand out, dragging herself across the cold tile toward her only hope. Light.

Until the sun goes down again, and it starts all over. She shuddered at that, certain she'd be no closer to freedom when that moment came. Just the thought of claws and teeth—and their bodies touching hers—wrenched a sob from her.

Whatever they were—vampires or some other kind of monster—they reveled in blood and pain. They drank the blood from the cuts they inflicted, and they drank the blood torn from her battered tissues after sex. Part of her wished they'd drink enough to send her into shock and kill her, but they hadn't so far. They healed the wounds, just enough to make sure the blood wasn't wasted and that they didn't take too much at once. Anemic or not, she wasn't going to die of blood loss anytime soon.

The shaft of sunlight beckoned, and Hannah made her way toward it, each inch gained sending shards of agony through her thighs and abdomen. Even her bruised and scarred body didn't ache as much as the sorely-used center of her sexuality.

She needed to touch the light more than she needed water or food, needed this small victory more than she needed freedom. While her heart argued that last, her rational mind knew there was no chance of escape...save this small one.

It seemed to take forever to reach it. Her heart pounded with every muscle-clenching slide across the cold floor. Her head spun in the certainty that it was some trick, that it was a strong artificial light meant to give her false hope, that it would disappear the moment she reached it and the torture would start again. Alternately, she feared the sun was going down, that she'd reach the light just as it faded away naturally.

Hannah held her breath at the threshold of the larger room; her hand hovered at the edge of the light, shaking. She stared at the bright glow surrounding her fingers, blinking hard to make the tears clouding the beautiful vision fall. With one last gargantuan heave, Hannah pulled herself into the light, turning to catch the rays on her face, her entire body trembling.

They could kill her now. If she had this for just a few minutes, she could die without a qualm.

* * * *

Corey Armen slammed the door of his truck shut, cursing how far out of the way this attack was. It had been over long before he'd arrived.

It wasn't the loss of a kill that bothered him. It was the victim he was concerned for. If he or she wasn't in evidence, Corey would be stuck with tracking to offer protection. Worse, if he couldn't track the victim, there were too many unpleasant possibilities to consider, death nearly the least of them.

The smell was overpowering, and Corey recoiled from it. He calmed his nerves, then stepped into the abandoned mine refinery building. Abandoned by humans, that is. The place had been used by the beasts for years, it seemed, though the beasts must have bled victims without true feeding to hide it this long. The smell of death was thick and gut-wrenching, and Corey vowed to burn it when he left it. In the meantime, he had to search it, distasteful as that was.

As Corey half expected, based on the stench, the rooms were full of trophies of their kills. Bones and half-rotted skin peeled from helpless humans littered the first two rooms. The bile rose in Corey's throat, and he swallowed it down. Burning this place would be a blessing.

A sound intruded on his concentration. Was it a sob? The slide against the ceiling was too large to be a rat; something else was in the building with him. Something alive. Corey backtracked to the stairs, his sacred weapon in hand, though there was little possibility a beast was above ground at this hour. More likely, he'd found the victim still alive.

The second floor was office space, a more polished though weather-rotted area. The scent of fresh blood and sex was strong. This was where they took their victims. Downstairs was the slaughterhouse for the dead. He shuddered at the possibility that the victims hadn't been dead when they were slaughtered. He'd heard of flesh-eating beasts, but they were thankfully few and far between.

The first room was stacked with furniture from the others. The second was bare, save the bolts worked into the floor and ceiling, a metal plate full of rotting food, and an empty metal mug. The smell of sex was overpowering, and Corey didn't question that far too many had suffered degradation here. The trappings of forced sex lay about. There were whips, oral dams, and all manner of cutting tools, not that the beasts needed the last with the claws they were surely able to form.

At the third room, he stopped short, disbelief stealing his battle sense for an instant. The victim lay on the floor, her bruised face turned to the sunlight streaming through a high window. Her face was nearly without color; even the tear tracks on her cheeks hadn't reddened, as they usual would. He would have thought she was dead, if it wasn't for her shivering and the shallow movements of her chest with each breath.

Her torn blouse gaped open, revealing ragged tears on her chest and abdomen, healed by the beasts, probably for the sole purpose of extending her life for more torture. The blouse was the only clothing she wore, and Corey stared in dismay at the scars peeking from between her trembling thighs.

"Gods," he breathed. "Dear gods." He'd never seen depravity on this scale before. Corey hardly knew where to begin rebuilding a life after it. A simple rape and feeding, yes. But this?

Begin at the beginning. Get her out of here. Corey sheathed his weapon and knelt to her side, laying a hand on her shoulder gently.

A sob escaped her throat, and she tensed. The words to reassure her stuck in his throat. What could Corey possibly promise? That he'd make this right? He wasn't sure he could.

"I'm here to help. Trust me. I won't let them touch you again." That was something he could promise with confidence.

She blinked her eyes, searching his face. After a long moment, she nodded. He didn't waste time; Corey scooped her to his chest and made his way back to the truck. Then he wrapped her in a blanket and settled her inside. He took a deep breath and slid behind the wheel.

Begin at the beginning. But what now?

* * * *

Corey's fingers shook against the buttons on the phone, and it took him two tries to dial the manor. His gaze strayed to the woman asleep on the bed, an IV in her arm feeding her both glucose solution and a mild sedative.

"Manor," Tim answered.

"I need Tyler," he replied simply.

"Corey?"

"Tyler," he repeated. No one but his house lord would do, in this case.

"You've got it. Hang on."

The wait was maddening. By the time Tyler came on the line, Corey was certain his heart would burst from continued pounding.

"Corey?"

"I need men, and I need them fast."

"Tim! What is it?" his house lord inquired. "Start waking the men. Now." That was obviously delivered to Tim. The fact that Tyler didn't question his assessment heartened Corey.

"We have an enclave that needs to be expunged. Tonight. If we don't take them tonight, we may lose them entirely. If that happens..." He swallowed down a painful lump, flicking his gaze to Hannah again. "You don't want more victims like the one I'm caring for, Tyler. You don't want to lose more this way, either. We have to stop them here, before they set up shop again."

A sharply indrawn breath came back to him. "How bad is it?"

"Not to get too technical... And thank the gods her memories aren't clear, because I pray to Tes they never are. She's been bled and raped multiple times, over at least three nights so far. She's certain of three beasts, but there may be more. I almost burned the site, but this is all I can give her, the end to the ones who did this to her. But I can't do it alone. I need men, Tyler. I need them before nightfall."

"They've done this before?"

Corey ground his teeth at the truth. "I can't even calculate how many we've lost this way. They take trophies." His stomach lurched at the memory. "So many trophies."

"You have the men. Four hours. As many as I can roust and get to your location in that time. But Corey..."

"Yes?"

"Don't leave her alone. Not after dark."

Memories of Hannah's terror when he'd delivered her to Marcos for medical aid seared him. Corey had stayed with her through the entire ordeal, holding her hand and making promises for her safety. Part of him wanted to take the hearts of every beast who'd touched her. Another part wanted to stay by her side. It wasn't simply his duty to do it that drove him; he wanted to be there for her.

"Corey?"

"I'll lead them to the site during daylight hours," he decided. "They can take the enclave without me. Hannah needs me."

"Are you sure about this?" Tyler asked carefully.

He didn't need to be more specific. Warriors of Armen were known for falling for the damsels in distress, fast and hard. If there'd ever been a woman who needed help, it was Hannah.

"She needs me, Tyler. I have to be here for her, as long as she needs me...or as long as I can."

"Not too long," he cautioned.

"No. Of course not."

* * * *

Hannah shifted on the bed, stretching her hand out in search of Corey. He took it, as she knew he would. It was enough. Just the fact that he was there was all she needed to feel safe, though she didn't understand why he affected her that way.

It wasn't that Corey took her out of the torture chamber. Just the sound of his voice had convinced her that he wasn't like the ones who'd hurt her.

She opened her eyes, focusing on him with some effort. Corey sat in a chair at the bedside, stroking her hand, his expression soft and calming. He didn't waste words asking how she was. There was silence, but it was a pleasant silence...comfortable.

"They'll be here soon," he assured her.

Hannah furrowed her brow. "Who?" Her hand tightened in the unspoken fear that the people showing up were meant to replace Corey.

"I'm not leaving," he soothed her.

She nodded, her breathing easing. "Who?" she requested again.

"More like me. It's over. They've killed the ones who..." He met her gaze fully for a moment. "They've incinerated the site, Hannah. It won't happen again. You have my vow on that."

She choked back a sob, nodding. *Over.* She could hardly believe it.

Corey raised her hand to his lips. He didn't kiss her knuckles as she expected; instead, his breath and skin warmed her. He trailed a fingertip along the bracelet he'd given her as part of his protection. Whether it was a vow that he would protect her or a way to assure himself that she still wore it, she wasn't sure.

Time seemed to have no meaning. Corey didn't move, even when the door to the room opened and someone stepped inside.

Hannah took her time, turning to the new arrival slowly.

The man was dressed much as Corey was, older but not by much, she'd wager. He took a step toward her, and Hannah shied closer to Corey.

His eyes opened, panning to the new arrival. Corey guided her hand back to the bed but didn't release it. "Tyler," he rumbled.

Tyler dropped to one knee. "You have my vow, Hannah."

Her voice shook. "Vow?"

"All of Armen is at your service. If you have need, it will be provided. That something like this happened in our range..." He blanched. "It never should have happened in our range."

She nodded. "I don't understand what this means, but thank you."

Tyler tipped his head to Corey. "Cabin ten is at your disposal."

Corey sighed. "Good choice. Thank you."

Hannah's head spun. Following the conversation was tiring. "I don't understand."

Corey hesitated. "Do you believe you could walk down a crowded street?"

His voice was soothing, but the words sent a spike of fear through her. People touched you on crowded streets. They got close. The noise. The scents. She shook her head, working through the physical impossibility of staying at her apartment, returning to work, shopping... How was she supposed to live?

Tyler rose, taking a step back to give her space as she edged away. "We'll move your belongings for you. You have my word, Hannah. Everything you own will be moved for you before you arrive."

Her heart ached at that. The idea of being alone was worse. She started to protest.

Corey stroked his thumb over her hand. "You have my word, Hannah. I'll be there for you."

She met his gaze, sighing. "Okay." Why couldn't she come up with something better than that?

"I spoke to Marcos and Sherri," Tyler continued.

Corey nodded.

"When Hannah's ready..." He glanced to her then away.

"What?" she asked nervously.

Corey squeezed her hand lightly. "A psychiatrist, when you're up to it."

"I'm not crazy," she reminded him.

"No. But you may want to talk."

She considered that. "Not now."

"If you want to. When you want to."

Hannah closed her eyes, relaxing into the pillow.

"Take care of her," Tyler ordered quietly.

"I will," Corey replied. "I will."

Chapter Sixty

Three days later

Hannah sighed at the silence around her. The hospital had never been this quiet. There had always been the sounds of footsteps, Corey's breathing, water running, the beeps and whirring of machines... Moreover, there had been voices: overhead speakers, laughter, coughing, and the occasional tense conversations when the Warriors acting as her bodyguards had rebuffed journalists trying to sneak into her room.

But now? The only sound she could make out was the whisper of wind against the windows and walls.

She tried to remember where she was, but the last thing that she could bring to mind was riding shotgun in a luxury vehicle with Corey at the wheel. He'd pushed the wheelchair as far as the parking lot, as the hospital had required. Then he'd lifted her into the seat, wrapped a light blanket around her, and buckled her in. The drive had been so smooth and quiet, she'd dropped off to sleep.

That left her with the reality that Corey had carried her into the cabin and settled her to bed. As if in confirmation, the layer of blanket closest to her skin was the one she'd had in the car. The only change seemed to be that he'd stripped the tennis shoes they'd brought her from home off before leaving her to sleep.

Leaving. Her heart stuttered at the thought. Had Corey left her alone in the cabin? Or had he just gone into another room while she slept?

The certainty that it was the former had her struggling with the blankets, in a panic to be free to search for him. Or to run. Memories of the chains had her more frantic to accomplish the task.

The door opened, and Corey vaulted into the room. He grasped the top blanket—the one he'd tucked around her—and ripped it up. Hannah pushed the other away and threw herself into his arms, her breathing coming in gulps of cool air.

His hands smoothed her hair down. "Shhh. It's okay. I know. I shouldn't have tucked you in," he berated himself.

"You weren't here," she gushed out. Hannah cringed at how panicked that sounded.

"I won't leave you, but..."

His hesitancy gave her pause. "But?" she prompted him.

"If I stay in this room... I could get a cot brought out to us tomorrow, I suppose, but I had hoped the fact that my bedroom is on the opposite side of the bathroom from yours would be close enough. If it's not, it's—"

"It is." *I'm being ridiculous. Why should Corey sleep on a cot, when he could have a bed?*

He paused. "Is it, Hannah? If you aren't comfortable with me being that far, I can get the cot."

It wasn't comfortable. Hannah knew she'd rather have him in the room with her. "It is. I just... I didn't know where you were, and the blankets..." She took a calming breath. "I panicked. I'm sorry."

"Don't be. It's understandable."

That didn't mean she had to like it. *Now I'm being childish.*

But if being childish meant Corey would hold her a little longer, she could live with it.

"Do you want me to bring dinner in here for you?" he asked.

Though the offer touched her, it was another reminder of how sedentary she'd become. Hannah needed to feel strong. *Stronger.* She would never be strong like Corey was strong. Not against the beasts. "Can I come to the table?"

"You're allowed to do anything that doesn't compromise your safety. The question is, do you wish to go to the table? And do you need my help?"

Hannah shook her head. "No. I should be able to make it there." She'd been walking to the bathroom at the hospital for two days without more than Corey escorting her to make sure she was steady on her feet.

He nodded but made no move to set her aside.

Her heart tripped at that. At last, Hannah retrieved her wits and eased out of his arms. The sense of loss was immediate and potent, and she tried to reason her way out of it.

I have to be stronger than this. I have to find a way.

Corey hesitated a moment, tipped his head, and turned toward the doorway. "I'll get dinner on the table for you."

Chapter Sixty-one

Two weeks later

Hannah pulled at the V-neck sweater, trying to cover the scars on her chest, but no matter how she tried, they showed. Frustrated, she dragged the sweater off and pulled on a turtleneck.

Scooping up the offending shirts and sweaters, she stormed down the hall to the kitchen. Hannah shoved the clothing into the garbage can, sobs sticking in her throat.

Corey's hands settled on her shoulders, and she turned to him, seeking his broad chest. He rocked her, making soothing sounds.

"What is it, Hannah?" he whispered. "What can I do?"

"They show. I can't stand when they show."

His breathing hitched. "The scars?"

She nodded.

His arms circled her. "We could remove them," he offered. "Marcos could arrange for—"

"No. Not... Not yet. Not now." The idea of more pain, even pain that would ultimately remove the scarring, was too much. Not to mention that they'd have to touch her.

"Not now," he agreed.

Corey offered no further comment. He just held her. Hannah let him, needing the contact, needing Corey. He was the one calming constant in her life.

* * * *

Hannah stepped from the bathroom into the bedroom, going still in confusion. There were stacks of clothing, folded neatly on the bed. She looked at one item after another in awe, finally snagging out a hunter green sweater and jeans to wear. Dressed for the day, she went in search of Corey.

He was in the living room, kicked back in the chair, a book in his lap. His gaze panned from the book to her face, and he smiled. "Good. You like them."

Words failed her for an instant. "You did this?"

Corey nodded. "Anything for you, Hannah. I can't say that often enough. If you need... If you want anything, you just tell me."

A stirring in her stomach sent her back to her room. She closed the door between them and leaned against it. Corey made such a selfless offer, and her body had taken it in a completely unexpected and frightening way. She wanted. She needed, but she seriously doubted that Corey intended to fulfill that want, the one coiling in tissues still healing from brutal assaults.

More likely, he meant monetary fixes. His family had thrown a small fortune at that already, she was sure. They'd paid off all her bills—her car note, her college loans...even the fee to break her lease, when they moved all her belongings to the cabin. Though they hadn't presented her with the title to the cabin and the land it was on, they'd made it clear to her that it was hers. Everything was at her discretion, even who came and went.

Just thinking about 'coming' set off another twinge of reminder that—on some level—that's what she wanted from Corey.

* * * *

Three weeks later

I can do this. I can do this.

A man brushed past her, and Hannah recoiled to the storefront. Everywhere she looked, there were people pressing in. They were too close, encroaching on her personal space, touching her.

Her breathing went ragged. Hannah looked for a space to slip back into the flow of pedestrians, but they were moving too fast and traveling too close.

I can't stay here until the crowds clear out. By then, it would be dark, and there were worse things in the dark than other humans.

When she'd parted from Corey in town, she hadn't told him which way she would be going. How would he find her if she didn't return to the car?

I have to make this work. I have to get back to the car, at least.

Hannah tried again, stepping into the crush of people flowing past. A woman looking at her cell phone veered toward Hannah, and she fled the crowd again, pressing a hand to the brick wall, trying to force her breathing to even.

"Hannah?"

She turned to him blindly, burying her face in Corey's chest. His arms encircled her loosely, and he rocked her back and forth.

"How long did you watch?" she asked.

He didn't reply to that.

"I wasn't alone, was I?"

"Not for an instant," he confirmed.

Hannah smiled against his shirt. That was a comfort. "Have you ever really left me?"

"A few times, but never for long." He shifted. "Can you walk with me? Or...should I carry you?"

"Walk," she managed, feeling foolish for requesting either.

Corey turned her toward the car, wrapping an arm around her body. He didn't rush through the crowd, and the crowd didn't rush him. It parted, leaving them a bubble of room, a bubble that hadn't existed without Corey at her side.

This was what he was...her buffer from the world she couldn't come to grips with again. Hannah wondered how long it would be until she could handle the world alone, if she'd ever be able to do it for herself again.

Chapter Sixty-two

One week later

Hannah pushed the bathroom door open, intent on refilling her water cup. She stumbled in, then stopped short. Corey looked over his shoulder, his hand gripping the shower controls. For a moment, neither of them moved; Hannah wasn't certain she was breathing.

His chest drew her eyes. How many times had she sought solace against it and never seen it? She moved closer, reaching out to touch him. At the last moment, Hannah flicked a glance at Corey, seeking his approval.

A slight nod came in reply, and she touched him, tracing the etched muscles of his torso. Corey tensed, and she looked up into a fierce countenance. Some rational portion of her mind argued that that look should frighten her, but it didn't. Her body responded to it sexually, dampening, straining, her nipples aching.

Corey drew in his breath sharply, muttering a curse she almost didn't catch. Hannah glanced down, unsurprised to find that he'd come erect. Still, her heart stuttered at the sight.

"It's okay, Hannah," he assured her. "Nothing will happen that you don't want. You have my vow on that."

Nothing she didn't want. The truth made her mouth go dry. The problem was she did want him. The fact that she wanted him sent bolts of fear through her, but that didn't kill the arousal.

"You're confused," he guessed.

"Hell yes, I am."

He raised one large hand and stroked at her hair. "Nothing you don't want, but...you don't know what you want right now. Do you?"

Hannah shook her head. "I—I do, but just the idea of... of it... I don't know if I can."

He nodded. "You need a safe way to get used to the idea."

"I don't understand."

Corey nodded toward his bedroom. Hannah backed off a step, wrenching her hand away from his chest, her body in a riot.

"It's not what you think," he assured her.

"What then?"

"I'm going to go in there and..." He glanced to his erection, then back to her. "Take care of this."

Hannah swallowed hard at the thought of it. "And?"

"The choice is yours, Hannah. You can listen. You can watch. You can choose to do neither."

Her breathing hitched at the thought of it. "Why?"

"The things they did to you were unspeakable...unnatural. This is natural. If there is any chance you could take back your sexuality, I want to see that happen for you. I may be wrong, but I believe the only way you might is to see and hear a man naturally handling his arousal with no demands on you."

She didn't know how to respond to that.

Corey headed for the door to his room, leaving it slightly ajar. She stood there, frozen in indecision. Part of her urged running the other direction, despite her curiosity.

Then the noises started, low moans that stoked the heat in her womb. Hannah took a step toward the door then stopped, embarrassed at the idea of watching him stroke off.

His breathing went ragged and loud, and hers followed suit. His sounds grew louder, and she could hear the bed shifting beneath him. The end came in a guttural shout.

There was a moment of near-silence. Then Corey ambled back into the bathroom, semi-erect, his lower abdomen and pubic hairs coated in a slick of his fluids. He reached into the shower and started the water.

"I'll do the same every evening at about this time, Hannah," he promised. "What you choose to do, you do. If this is something you want to pursue, you have to take the first steps toward it. It's not something I can do for you."

"Like walking in crowds," she managed. "You can only make me feel safe while I find my feet."

His eyes said there was more, but his nod called her wrong. She went back to bed, her head spinning.

* * * *

One week later

Corey lay back on his bed, his muscles itching for action he might or might not be gifted with. The fact that he likely would not was immaterial. He'd made a promise, and as torturous as he found it, he would see it through.

Hannah's face as she watched him release himself the night before tantalized him. That was all it took to render him hard and aching. Corey stroked his fingertips along the sensitive underside, letting his gaze wander to the bedside clock. It was already after nine, but that didn't mean Hannah wouldn't choose to appear.

The first four times, she'd listened. She'd fled to her bedroom afterward two of those times, as if afraid to watch him stroll into the bathroom for a shower after hearing his intimacy. So far, she'd watched twice. The first time, she'd opened the door a bit and watched him through it. The second, she'd ventured just inside the door. Having her watch was ten times the aphrodisiac having her listen had proven. She'd only stayed away one night of the seven he'd been doing this, the night between listening and watching.

Another glance at the clock showed it was five after the hour. Corey sighed and circled his aching cock.

Watching or not, I vowed to provide the opportunity. The problem was, Corey wasn't entirely certain why he'd thought this was a good idea.

Control. It was a way to let Hannah feel in control of her sexuality, without force, without expectation, without touches that might shock her back into memories of the beasts.

But how he wished she'd choose to experiment further.

Time. Hannah needs time. While she might recover her ability to enjoy intimacy, it wouldn't be a quick turn.

Still, the visions of Hannah touching drove him on. Corey stroked himself, closing his eyes, daring to imagine...

The soft click of his bedroom door sent a shiver of anticipation down his spine. The knowledge that she was watching made him harder. Corey shifted, restless, wanting. A moan escaped his lips.

Her feet whispered across the rug, and Corey's heart skittered in excitement. She hadn't approached his bed before. It was another small step to healing, he was sure.

Hannah stopped at the bedside, her breathing ragged, her scent teasing Corey. He arched toward her, fighting back release to allow her a full show.

Heat from her body warmed Corey's thigh. Hannah was so close, she could touch him at any moment. As if in answer, her fingertips trailed up his thigh.

That ended his self-control. Corey arched up into her hand, shouting out his climax, his seed shooting over his hand and stomach. Hannah ran shaking fingers through the slick, and Corey shuddered hard, forcing his eyes open.

She didn't notice his attention. Hannah was rapt on the aftereffects of his self-release. Her eyes were wide, and her tongue traced her upper lip. Corey bit back a groan at that, his cock coming to aching readiness again. She sucked in her breath.

"I can go again, Hannah," he offered. He wanted to release himself a second time. He wanted her to take an active part in it.

Give her time. Don't rush her.

She sank to the bed, nodding.

Corey stroked himself. If she wanted to watch all night, he'd manage it. Her hands on him alone would keep him hard for her.

* * * *

Hannah's breathing hitched at the interplay of Corey's muscles beneath her hand. His hips pistoned back and forth, and his hand tightened and loosened, forcing himself toward another climax.

"What do you think of?" she asked.

Corey moaned, shaking his head.

"Please." She had to know.

His eyes slid open, pleading with her for something nameless. "You."

Her heart stuttered at that. "M-m-me?"

He slowed. "No pressure, Hannah. You have my word."

She nodded. Still, the idea stunned her. "What do you think about? What about me?"

Corey's hips sped again. "You touching me, kissing me... Gods!"

"And?" she prompted him.

A fresh spurt of his fluids trailed down his cock. "There are positions where you'd be in control, Hannah. If you wanted to experiment."

She gasped at the heat building in her. Just the thought of it had her thighs wet and her mouth dry. Hannah settled her fingertips on his length, letting it slide back and forth beneath them. Corey caressed his thumb over her fingers, encouraging her.

"What would I do, Corey? How would I..." It hardly seemed possible, but Hannah was looking forward to hearing it.

Corey's cock bucked against her fingers. "There are so many ways. You could climb on me, as I am now. You could take my fingers in the same way. You could let me—" He thrust his hips up, announcing his excitement.

She knew the technical aspects of how to have sex. That part wasn't what she really wanted to hear. It was the way his voice deepened when he talked about having sex with her, the way his cock jerked in excitement. "Tell me."

She considered climbing on him. What would Corey do, if she did? Would he expect to be inside her? Or would touching be enough for him? Would it be enough for her?

"If you straddled my face, I'd use my tongue to taste you."

Her fingers circled his cock reflexively, and he gasped. The idea of Corey's tongue was appealing, something she'd thought impossible after the beasts drinking her blood and their semen that way.

"Oh, yes. I'd do anything you wanted, Hannah."

"Anything," she mused.

Corey's breathing went choppy, and his cock slid back and forth between her fingers. What would it feel like inside her?

He climaxed again, shocking her back to reality, the reality of what a man's climax felt like inside her. *A beast's climax, at any rate.* Corey wasn't a beast; he wouldn't force himself on her. Still, she wasn't ready to experience that yet.

Hannah eased her hand from his cock, her fingers tingling from the contact. Corey didn't comment; he didn't press her for more...or even offer to touch himself again for her. He waited to see what she'd say or do next.

"Tomorrow night," Hannah breathed.

"Yes?"

"A kiss," she decided. The beasts didn't kiss. It was one thing she felt certain would hold no risk of memories for her.

"Anything you wish, Hannah. I will do anything you wish and no more."

She nodded, disconcerted by that concept. At a loss, she rose and fled to her bedroom.

Chapter Sixty-three

Hannah entered Corey's room, her heart pounding. She looked at the bed, but Corey wasn't in the bed. She wasn't certain if that was a relief or a disappointment.

"Hannah," he called softly.

Her mouth watered at the sight of him sitting in the easy chair, bare-chested. Corey put a hand out to her, and Hannah eased toward him, taking it. He kissed the back of her hand, his eyes locked on hers.

"Sit," he invited.

She hesitated.

"I could stand, if it makes you more comfortable," he offered.

"No." Sitting, he was less formidable. *But sitting means feeling his cock against me.* Even that held appeal.

Hannah lowered herself into Corey's lap, perching across one hard thigh. He didn't move on her immediately. He raked a hand through her hair, as he often did when she retreated to his chest.

"You're sure?" he asked.

She raised her face to him in answer. Corey's breath bathed her lips and invaded her mouth, making silent promises.

Then his lips brushed hers, lingering, enticing. Hannah's eyes slid shut, and she turned further into him. Corey nuzzled her lips.

"More," she breathed.

A soft sound of pleasure escaped his lips. "Open for me?"

Hannah hesitated, memories of the oral dam and beast cocks making her blood chill.

"Hannah? What is it?"

She opened her eyes to the sight of Corey, concern etched on his beautiful face. Sealing her mouth to his wasn't something she needed to consider for long.

Corey's tongue swept into her mouth, a slow, sweet exploration. There was no hard, thrusting cock, gagging her, unavoidable, hands bracing her head still for the assault. As if to prove that to herself, Hannah drew away from the kiss. Before Corey could question her, she returned to it, inviting his soft tongue inside, moving her head to a more favorable position.

His hands traveled the length of her spine, circling her waist. His words of the night before played again in her mind, and Hannah slid from his lap, breaking off the kiss.

Corey let her leave, averting his eyes. "If I've made you uncomfortable—"

She grasped his hand and tugged. Corey stood, his eyes questioning. Hannah led the way to the bed, settling to the edge.

"Are you sure?" he repeated.

She guided his fingertips to her mouth and kissed one after another. "I'm sure that I want to kiss you. I'm sure that I want to feel you touching me."

Corey placed one knee on the bed, slid his body around hers, and laid down on the other side of Hannah. He cupped her shoulders and turned Hannah toward him. He stopped there.

"Tell me how you want to be touched."

When she didn't answer, his gaze moved to her chest.

Hannah guided his hand through the slit in her robe, settling it on her inner thigh. He nodded his understanding, then relaxed to the bed. She followed him down, parting her lips to his.

At first, Corey kept it to kissing. His hand lay between her thighs, unmoving, warming her. Then it inched upward, stroking maddening circles on her inner thigh. The kiss kicked up a notch at that, taking on a hotter edge, a more urgent meeting of mouths.

The rough pads of his fingers circled over her clit, and she pulled back on a moan. Corey kept circling, seemingly waiting for something.

Hannah grasped at his arms. "Yes," she breathed. "Oh, yes." The edges of something momentous pulled at her, making her muscles weak. Coherent thought deserted her, and her body ignited in a way she'd never experienced before.

* * * *

Corey started to question if she wanted him to continue, when Hannah stiffened in his arms. Her scream echoed off the plaster walls, and she gasped and trembled in seeming shock.

His heart stuttered at the latter. "Hannah?"

She dropped to the bed beside him, her breathing harsh. Then she curled her body to his, laying her head on his chest.

"Was it okay?" he asked, worried that he'd pushed her too far, too fast.

Hannah straightened her robe. Her skin heated against his. She pushed to sitting, then to standing.

Corey sat up, staring at her in dismay.

At last, she looked back at him. "Tomorrow night?" she asked, her voice breathy.

He nodded. "As you wish, Hannah. Always."

She backed toward the bathroom door, then turned and walked away.

Corey watched her go, his body strangely silent. With the promise of sex so close at hand, he had expected to pay dearly when she called a halt. For some reason, that hadn't happened.

Realization that there was only one possible answer had his heart pounding in apprehension. If the Stone knew that he intended to aid Hannah through this trial, She might allow him a reprieve from his usual drives to facilitate it.

Was it presumptuous to believe such a thing? It took only a moment for Corey to come to a decision on that. "Fuck it if it is."

Chapter Sixty-four

Six weeks later

Corey went still at the buttons popping loose on his jeans. He licked his lower lip, starving for all of her. "Touch me," he pleaded.

Hannah's mouth covered his again, a hot, hard kiss. She pulled back, breathing hard. "Take them off."

A shiver of excitement worked down his spine. Hannah didn't ask him to remove his jeans often, and he hurried to comply.

Everything with Hannah was a learning experience, a work in progress toward making her comfortable with her own sexuality...and his. He'd already established that she was unlikely to be aroused by any position where she wasn't facing him, even during foreplay. Though Hannah knew he had no inherent desire to try anal with her, just the position brought too many bad memories for her.

As did the idea of fellating him. She still shied from French kissing when the wrong memory struck, and the idea of a cock in her mouth sent her into a near-panic.

Not that I need them. Corey was content to take whatever she was comfortable with. *And no more.*

Hannah loosened the front of the short silk wrap she wore, revealing her breasts. Corey didn't hesitate to cup them in his hands. When she offered, without thoughts of the scars making her shy, he never refused to take advantage of it.

In truth, Corey didn't find her scars off-putting. Strange as it seemed, he couldn't look at Hannah without finding all of her appealing. The scars were a sign of something despicable being done to her, but they were also a sign of this beautiful, strong woman surviving it long enough for him to save her.

Hannah gasped, and Corey searched her expression. Her head was thrown back, and her eyes were closed. There was no sign that she was in pain or troubled by memories, so he continued.

In moments, Hannah was moving against him, rubbing her wet slit against his cock. "You know what I want," she breathed.

He pushed up from the mattress and took the tip of one breast into his mouth. As her sounds became more avid, he went from licking to suckling.

"No."

The word stopped him cold. Literally. An icy shaft of fear settled in his gut. Had he done something that made her uneasy? Would she call a halt yet again?

His stillness gave her the opening she needed to push up on her knees, lever his cock up, and work her sheath partway down it. Corey gasped a series of ragged breaths in and out, shocked by the change. This was an unexpected treat, a delight.

But I have to be cautious. I can't spook her. Not now that she's finally chosen to experiment with this.

He met Hannah's gaze, questioning her silently. It was his only choice, since Corey wasn't sure he could form words.

For her answer, Hannah settled further onto his cock, gripping him tight in her heat. Corey moved slightly, pushing just a little deeper, his muscles tensing in anticipation of a negative reaction.

Instead, she moaned.

"More?" he managed.

Hannah nodded.

He raised his hips again, and her hands closed on his shoulders. Corey moved deeper, and her nails bit into his back. He hesitated, waiting for her reply.

Hannah pushed further onto him.

One experimental thrust led to another and a third. Before long, he was as deep as he could go. Her sounds went sharp in pleasure.

"Tell me what you want, Hannah," he pleaded. "Anything you want."

She didn't answer immediately; she just ground down on his cock, then wrapped her legs around his waist. Just when Corey would have continued in earnest, she found her voice.

"I want you on top."

He bit back a dozen curses, reining in his drives. The few times they'd kissed and touched that way had strained him to his limits and beyond.

"Corey?"

"Oh, yes." He turned Hannah beneath him and thrust deep, holding his position as she let out a cry that might have been pleasure or might have been pain. "Hannah?"

"Oh, yes," she repeated his words.

That dragged a smile from him, and Corey set a slow, easy pace. In moments, climax was beating at his nerves. He held off, trying to be sure she came first.

He managed it, but barely. Hannah's shout, the way she pulled at him, her inner muscles milking him over was too much for him. He climaxed with a groan, the rush of cum bleeding his stresses away more markedly than it ever had before.

Hannah was so quiet, it put his nerves on edge again.

"Are you all right?" he asked.

She smiled a crooked smile. "That was the...the best."

"The best, huh? Am I, really?" If she said 'yes,' it would be the highlight of his life thus far.

Hannah's smile disappeared and she darkened in a blush. She slid her gaze down and away.

Corey placed his fingers under her chin and tipped her face back up. "Hannah?"

She didn't respond.

It took him a minute to rerun their discussion and make some deductions based on her reactions. The results made his stomach clench.

"You were...? Before the beasts, you—?"

"Yes. So it's not like I have anyone to make comparisons with." She darkened a few more shades.

Corey wanted to kiss her, but that would be completely inappropriate given her upset. Instead, he eased her to his chest, stroking a hand down the back of her hair while he ordered his mind. His cock lessened and retreated, leaving her body slowly.

"It's your choice, Hannah."

She didn't move. "What is?"

"If you want, we'll continue with what we've been doing."

Hannah pulled her head back, looking up at him. "I want to, but..." She gasped at his body responding to that comment.

He cursed himself silently for it. For all intents and purposes, he'd just given a virgin her first pleasurable experience. Inappropriate as it might be, he wanted to give her more, as much as she would allow him to.

She visibly brought herself under control. "What are you offering?"

"To give you any and every experience you want to have. Just say the word. I'll give you all the basis for comparison you want." *With me.* He bit back that pronouncement. If Hannah needed more, he had to let her go.

But he wasn't going to like it. If the Stone was kind, she wouldn't ask that of him.

Hannah seemed to consider it carefully. "Would you...?"

"Anything," he reminded her.

"Just sleep with me tonight."

Corey nodded solemnly. "I'd enjoy that, Hannah. It's not just a duty. You're not just a duty to me. I want you to know that."

He turned off of her, and she sank to his chest, wrapping her arms around him. Within minutes, Hannah was a comfortable blanket over him.

Just give me the word, Hannah. I'll be anything you'll let me be...including your mate.

Chapter Sixty-five

Two months later

Corey raised his head at the sound of the car approaching. He'd known one of the others would be visiting sometime in the next few days. Two or three times a week, one of the Warriors came out to the cabin to train with Corey, in the belief that he would go insane if he wasn't training.

That was true before Hannah accepted him as a lover, but it wasn't true today. In some odd twist, his need to train had all but disappeared the first time his cock found a ready home in her body.

Not that he could admit that to Tyler. What possible explanation could he give for such an anomaly in a Warrior? And what if Tyler sent him away from Hannah? That was too horrific to contemplate in detail.

He rose from the porch swing and made his way down the front stairs, starting his warm-up before the car came to a halt. It was Tyler this time. He'd only seen his house lord in rotation once before, and that had been before Corey and Hannah had entered into a sexual relationship.

Tyler tipped his head. "How is she?" He kept his voice low, most likely in case Hannah was still asleep.

"She goes out to shop with me now, but she can only walk close beside me, so no one crowds her. Still, it's less nerve wracking for her than being here alone while I go."

"Good. That's good." He looked toward the cabin, but they both knew he wouldn't enter it. The cabin was Hannah's. Corey was only welcome inside because Hannah wanted him there. If she didn't, he would be banished from it as well. No one else was allowed to enter without her explicit permission, unless it was an emergency.

Tyler sighed. "Sorry it's been so long since we've gotten someone out here to spar with you."

Corey managed a strained smile. "I'm fine." He was. He'd be even more so if they finished training soon and Tyler left him alone with Hannah.

The woman in question opened the door and stepped out onto the porch, wearing a pair of jean Capris with an oversized button-down shirt, the top few buttons open to show an enticing—but scarred—vee of skin. "Corey, do you want—?"

She went still, gasped, and her eyes went wide and round. The color left her cheeks in a rush, and she pulled the top of the shirt closed, then launched back through the door and slammed it behind her.

Tyler winced. "Oh, damn. I didn't mean to upset her."

Corey sighed. "It's not you being here."

His house lord raised an eyebrow in disbelief.

"Well, the guys usually do call first, but it's not you being here. It's the scars. She usually wears something that covers them in public."

"But she doesn't mind you seeing them," he noted.

Corey managed not to grimace at the note of speculation. "She used to. Hannah has gotten used to me seeing them." A tight smile pulled up at his lips. "Besides, it's too hot to wear sweaters like she did the first few months. She'll be calmer once it's cold enough to start wearing them again."

"We could arrange for—"

"I've already offered. She's not ready for that yet...if she ever will be. The pain of surgery, coupled with doctors touching her... It's too much for Hannah."

Tyler grunted in reply, his muscles tensing, most likely in frustration that he couldn't do more for her. For centuries to come—if the current war lasted that long—this monumental failure would be a stain on the Armen name.

Tyler started his warm-up, and silence fell between them for a few long moments. At last, he found his voice. "We should arrange for another guard for a day or two."

Corey's heart stuttered. "Hannah won't be comfortable with that."

"Not in the cabin, of course. Maybe... Maybe he could pitch a tent."

"And where are you planning on sending *me*?" He tried to bite back the challenge in it, but that was a stretch.

Tyler offered a slight shrug. "Your parents miss you. I thought you might want to spend a day or two with them."

"I've never been away from Hannah that long. She likes knowing I'm two rooms away." But it stung to think of his mother missing him. "I'll speak to Hannah. I'm sure she wouldn't deny me a visit from my parents. She might even enjoy my mother's company. She's not a man, after all."

"You still need some time away, Corey."

"For what?"

"Just a few hours for yourself."

Corey stared at him, trying to follow Tyler's hinting.

Tyler sighed. "A night in town. Go to a bar, pick someone up..."

His stomach lurched at what Tyler was suggesting. Corey didn't need to consider it deeply to know no other woman would satisfy him now that he'd been with Hannah. *Hell, it probably wouldn't have once I met her.* "I don't need it."

His house lord straightened. "What about your drives? You'll be no good to her if you're thinking with the wrong head."

"I can't explain it, Tyler. Maybe the Stone knows Hannah needs me. We've always said She has a fondness for women and children. Whatever the case is, I don't get antsy when training is spotty. I don't seem to need to go find a lay for the evening. I'm always even-tempered when I'm with Hannah. If I didn't know better, I'd wonder if I'm still cursed."

Tyler was so still and silent, a bead of nervous sweat ran down Corey's back. After an announcement like that, who knew what a house lord would think or order. If a Warrior wasn't a Warrior, what was he?

"Well, I guess I don't have to worry about you printing on her and losing you to madness, then." After a moment, he shot Corey a look of pity. "Are you willing to give up your chance of printing, if that's what it takes to keep your vow to Hannah?"

"I will do whatever it takes to keep my vow to Hannah. Whatever, Tyler."

That seemed to rattle him, but he nodded his agreement. "Do you need to train today?"

"Not particularly," he admitted.

"We should, anyway. You need to be in top form, if you are Hannah's chosen protector."

"I agree." *I will never fail her. Never again.*

"When I go back to the manor..."

His hesitation sent a chill of warning down Corey's spine. "Yes?"

"I'll give your mother your love and tell her you'll call."

"Thanks, Tyler. That means a lot to me."

* * * *

Hannah looked up from the sandwich she was making, as Corey let himself into the cabin. In the distance, she heard the crunch of tires of gravel.

"Are you all right?" he asked.

She went still, trying to find the words to answer him honestly. In the end, a whispered 'no' was the best she could come up with.

Corey sighed. He crossed the room to her, then turned Hannah's face toward him. "What do you need?"

Answering that was more problematic than answering the last had been. The usual answer that she didn't know what she needed wasn't good enough.

"Hannah?"

"I need not to be broken," she complained.

Corey eased the butter knife from her hand and set it on the counter. Then he turned her toward him.

Hannah gasped at the sensation of his body warming hers. As if in answer, Corey's mouth parted hers in a heated kiss.

Potent need seared her, and Hannah pulled his button fly open. Corey didn't question her; he pulled her Capris open and pushed them and her panties away together. They pooled around her feet, and Hannah stepped out of them. His jeans retreated against her thighs, and she shivered in delight.

Corey lifted her to the edge of the counter and eased his cock inside her ready body. There were no words between them. One thrust led to another and another, faster and hotter with each repetition.

Hannah held to him, her heart hammering in excitement. She savored Corey's single-minded attention to making love to her. Climax washed over her, and Hannah screamed. Corey followed her over with a groan. In the aftermath, they traded lazy kisses.

He broke the silence first. "Does this feel broken to you?"

She smiled. "Not this. No." *Never.*

"But your ability to interact with other people," Corey guessed.

She nodded, her happiness eroding that quickly.

He sighed. "We could work on that."

"How?" If he had a new idea, something she hadn't considered before, she was all ears.

Corey trailed a fingertip down the length of her nose. "What would you think of spending some time with my mother?"

Hannah gaped at him for a moment. "Really? Your mother wants to spend time with me?" Why would she?

He didn't answer right away, and he seemed to consider that answer carefully.

Realization made her heart stutter. "Oh. I see. If you want to...to see your parents, you have to go." But her heart pounded in terror at the thought of him being gone long. Or of joining him, for that matter. Still, it wasn't right to make him miss out on seeing family.

He shot her a look of exasperation. "Are you saying you don't want to meet my mother?"

"Of course not. I just—"

One raised eyebrow brought her up short. Corey sighed. "My father doesn't have to come into the cabin at all, if you don't want him to. We'll grill some steaks. We'll—" He lifted her at the waist, his cock sliding free, and carried Hannah toward her bed. "—make some s'mores. If you're comfortable eating with my father, we can eat at the picnic table. If not, you and Mother can eat inside, and my father and I can eat outside."

He lowered her to the bed and paused, seemingly waiting for something.

Hannah considered what he'd said. "I'd like to meet your mother. Your father... We'll...see." It was the most she could promise with ease.

Corey smiled. He laid a kiss on her lips. "Next weekend?"

She tried to slow the drumming of her heart. "Okay. Next weekend." *One more baby step.*

Chapter Sixty-six

Five days later

Hannah watched the car pulling up the drive, her heart pounding in anxiety. Cory kneaded her shoulders, and she sighed in relief.

He didn't need to repeat what he had half a dozen times already. *Only what you're comfortable with. Nothing more. Let me know if something is too much.*

"You should go out to meet them," she opined.

"Yes. I should. I'll give you a few minutes, and then I'll bring my mother in."

"Don't give me too long. I may run for it." It was a joke, and they both knew it. Where would she run, even if she decided to? Why would she? If spending time with Renee was too much, Cory would just take his mother outside.

He chuckled and released her shoulders. In the next moment, he was outside and striding across the lawn toward the black SUV.

A woman slid from the passenger seat, coming to her full height of level with her son's chin. Renee had dark brown hair with heavy streaks of gray. She wore Bermuda shorts with a striped boat jersey and Docksiders. Corey wrapped his arms around her and kissed her cheek. She patted his cheek in return, and her laughter reached Hannah inside.

Wes, Corey's father, rounded the front of the SUV, wearing a nearly identical pair of jeans, boots, and black t-shirt as his son wore in summer. Corey offered his hand, but his father dragged him into a man-hug. Their voices rose, and Hannah smiled, remembering similar excited homecomings when her mother had still been alive.

They turned toward the cabin, and Hannah started to retreat. She talked herself out of it, then stepped forward again and offered a wave that felt shaky.

Wes tipped his head and continued walking. Renee waved back, her smile wide. Corey's father didn't presume to enter the cabin. Instead, Wes took a seat at the picnic table, while Corey escorted his mother to the door.

Hannah took a calming breath that fell far short of the calm she was seeking. She turned toward the door and pasted on a smile.

What do I do? Play hostess? She'd never had a serious enough boyfriend to have the potential in-laws over for dinner before. How did someone do that?

The door opened, and Hannah launched into a rapid-fire offer of refreshments before Renee was even through the doorway. Before she knew it, she was listing the possible choices.

Renee motioned for Hannah to calm down. "It's okay."

Hannah tried another calming breath. Her cheeks flamed in embarrassment.

"Corey, why don't you go keep your dad company. Hannah and I can sit and talk a while."

"Okay with you, Hannah?" His expression was starkly serious.

"Yes. That's a good idea."

Once he was through the door, Renee offered her hand. Hannah hesitated, then took it.

"That's better. Do you want to sit at the kitchen table, in the living room, or out on the porch swing?"

Hannah peeked toward the window. "I'm not ready to be that close to Wes. No offense."

"None taken. Why don't I make us a cup of tea and we can relax in the living room?"

"I... I don't really like tea, but you can have some. I'll just grab a glass of lemonade."

"Lemonade sounds wonderful. Much cooler than a hot cup of tea." Renee released her hand and went to the fridge.

Hannah pulled out two glasses, then reached up and pulled down a package of Fig Newtons. They retreated to the living room together and settled on opposite sides of the couch.

Renee looked around at the living room, seemingly deep in thought. Hannah did the same, trying to guess what her guest was thinking.

"I'm surprised you haven't redecorated. It's been a while since I've been here, but it doesn't look like you've changed a thing."

"Redecorate?"

"Of course. The cabin is yours, unless you'd rather have one of the city houses or one of the other cabins. You have that choice, you know."

Hannah poured a glass of the lemonade, working at that. "I didn't know I had a choice of other houses, but I like this cabin. I don't think I'd want to trade. I mean... Unless you'd like to be closer to Corey. I wouldn't want a house in town, but a cabin closer to town, maybe, just so you could see each other more often."

"Oh, we could see each other nearly every weekend, if you're comfortable with that."

She managed a smile that felt more natural. "That would be nice. I like not being in crowds, but it's nice to talk to another woman."

Renee reached out and covered Hannah's hand with her own. "I'd like to get to know you. If you want, I could bring out one or two of the other ladies as well. If you decide to redecorate, we could help with that."

Hannah surveyed the living room again. "I think I would like that. I know the cabin is mine. I don't know why I never considered putting some touches in it for me...aside from what came from my apartment, of course." She took a drink of the lemonade, considering what she would do with it. She'd been considering some sort of hobby. This would give her something to do. Especially since there were three bedrooms, the bathroom, the living room, and the kitchen to decorate.

"Do you have a working Internet connection up here?"

"Yes. I don't use it often, but I do."

"Use it. Start designing your dream house. Remember, price isn't a concern."

"That's so hard to get used to," she admitted.

Renee laughed heartily. "I know. You'll get used to it, though."

* * * *

Corey glanced toward the porch, where his mother and Hannah were chatting. Each had a plate of grilled steak and shrimp skewers on her lap. He smiled. He'd hoped Hannah would be more at ease with a single woman than a crowd of people. He was glad he'd called that one correctly.

He looked back at his father, just in time to catch Wes's raised eyebrow.

"What?" The challenge was out before Corey could rein his tongue.

"How did Tyler miss it?"

"Miss what?"

His father's look was hot in censure. "While I might believe you smell so highly of Hannah because you live in the cabin with her, you also reek of a man aroused. And a woman aroused."

"It's not what you think."

"I think you're taking release with a traumatized victim you're sworn to protect."

He winced. "Not...quite."

His father gaped at him. "Oh, shit. You're printing. Aren't you?"

"I'm controlled. The Stone is keeping me controlled...somehow. But yes, I have feelings for her." *I just hope the Stone will release me without too much pain, if Hannah someday rejects me.*

"Does she even know what printing is?"

"No. How do I start that sort of conversation with her? This isn't the usual way printing happens." His heart ached at that. How many times had he considered and rejected the idea of explaining it? Too many.

Wes took another bite of his steak, his expression far away. "You know, your mother told me she and the other ladies are going to help Hannah redecorate the cabin."

"Hannah mentioned it. She's very excited about it." Another thing to be thankful for. Isolation couldn't be good for her, in the long run."

"If the ladies mention it in passing, it will be less pointed than you explaining it."

Corey shook his head. "I don't want everyone knowing what's going on here. I don't even want to think about what Tyler would do if he knew."

"No. Nothing like that. Just your mother. If she starts the conversation, others will chime in. They don't have to know why they're doing it."

He considered that carefully, then nodded. "Good plan. Let's try it." The worst thing that could happen would be that Hannah showed no interest in printing. If that was the case, he was in no more dire a position than he currently was.

* * * *

Six weeks later

"How's this looking?"

Hannah looked over her shoulder, then gaped in surprise at the texturing on the wall Stephanie was painting. "Fantastic. How did you learn to do that?"

She smiled. "My son-in-law, Stevie. The man is a master at decorating. He taught me about accent walls and sponge texturing and all sorts of other wonderful tips that I've been dying to use."

No wonder she'd suggested them. "You'll have to thank him for me."

"If you want to, you can thank him yourself. He's right outside with the guys, directing the landscaping you wanted."

A shaft of fear settled in Hannah's gut at the idea of walking out into the mass of Armen Warriors.

"Or not," Stephanie hurried to add. "I'll thank him for you."

"Thanks."

Renee broke the tension by changing the subject. "So how are Stevie and Terry settling into their printing?"

"Great," Stephanie imparted. "And they're really excited about Sharon being their surrogate. I swear, Terry has already bookmarked a hundred sites with things he wants to buy. Printing changes a man so much, and becoming a father all the moreso."

Hannah tried to follow the conversation, but she didn't understand all the terminology. "What's printing?"

The room went unnaturally still for a moment.

Then Renee came to her side. "Warriors... When they find a person they love and want to spend their life with, their version of marriage is more like animal imprinting. They choose a mate for life...if the mate—he or she—is willing, of course."

Her heart leapt in excitement. "Really? That's interesting. How does it work?"

Stephanie turned from her work on the wall. "Like most people, they fall in love, but it's more intense. They become...sexually addicted to the person they are printing on and can't be aroused by another person. I think that's a good way to put it."

Sammi nodded. "Warriors are usually hounds when it comes to sex. If they don't get it often enough, they get antsy. Even hand jobs, masturbation and blowjobs don't do the job for long. It has to be full-out sex for any lasting relief. I know... I mean, Tyler told me Corey doesn't suffer that, since he's been your guard. Must be the Stone's doing."

Hannah tried to dissect that. Corey hadn't left her long enough to get laid the entire time he'd been guarding her. Did that mean he was printing on her? Or that being with her was stealing something from him he'd always enjoyed? How could she be sure without risking opening wounds with him?

Renee continued, seemingly oblivious to her upset. "But if the mate is willing, a Warrior cannot walk away from his printing. Don't get me wrong. They aren't unhappy about the idea. A printing Warrior with a willing potential mate is nearly the height of contentment for a Warrior."

She nodded. "I think I understand." *But how do you know if a Warrior is printing?* Could she even ask that question without revealing her hopes that Corey was?

The conversation moved on again. "You should consider coming to Christmas at the manor," Sammi intoned. "We could give you a room in a quiet part of the house, and if it gets too crowded for you, you could take a break there."

"I'll think about it." Hannah couldn't do more than that. Just the idea of being in a huge house with most of Corey's extended family made her nervous.

"Do that," Sammi counseled. "It's a nonthreatening crowd to face. It might help you over some of your fears."

That's true. I want to get stronger.

Renee's pained look caught her attention.

It's not fair to make Corey miss Christmas with his family. I can survive a few days, even if I have to hide out in the room a lot. "I think I will. I'll let Corey know."

That won her an ovation from the group of ladies helping her paint.

"You won't regret it," Stephanie promised.

I hope not. Hannah smiled and nodded, then went back to painting.

Chapter Sixty-seven

Two months later, Christmas Eve

Corey swallowed a mouthful of beer, watching Hannah retreat up the stairs. She'd lasted longer than he'd thought she would. In fact, she'd only taken two breaks all day. The first was midafternoon. She'd requested time alone in her room for the two hours before dinner. The second was now...after dinner. She hadn't made a request of him, which meant she might want his company...or not. He would have to tread lightly for the night.

Though she'd fared well in the crowd, she'd shied from any attempts by the men to engage with her. It had taken them less than an hour to decide, as a team, on a tactical response to it. Corey, the women, and male children under the age of ten were allowed in Hannah's vicinity. If a male or older boy had to pass through, he would do so behind her back, without speaking, which might startle her. It had worked much better than Corey had anticipated.

At the top of the stairs, Hannah looked back at him and smiled. Corey's heart tripped in excitement, and he offered a wave to let her know he would be up shortly to join her. She made her way toward their rooms.

He didn't hurry to finish the last few swallows of his beer. Hannah might want time to change clothing or take a shower. Of course, joining her in the shower would be quite arousing, he'd learned.

That in mind, he finished his beer, dropped the empty bottle into one of the recycling bins set up for the party, and headed for the stairs. He stopped to hug his mother, and his father offered a clap on the shoulder. Then he was off, loping up the stairs two at a time.

Corey slipped into her room without knocking, and Hannah looked up as if in surprise. He went still, questioning her silently. If she wanted him to go, he would.

She was in motion a heartbeat later, crossing the room, meeting him halfway in a heated embrace, her lips parting to his. Corey lifted her to the top of the bureau, his printing driving him. Gods but if he didn't find a way to ask her soon, he was going to be stark raving mad.

Over the next few minutes, they worked at each others' shirts, opening buttons, hands delving beneath. Hannah broke off from the kiss at his first stroke of his fingertips over her nipple, a sound halfway between a sob of pleasure and a sigh escaping her.

Corey cautioned himself to slow or risk spooking her. Though that hadn't happened in weeks, he wasn't willing to risk it. Her face tilted up to his, and the kiss resumed in earnest, letting him know that she was still in her comfort zone.

The sound behind him had barely registered in Corey's mind when a hand dragged back at his hair, and a blade settled to his throat.

"Release her," Tim ordered.

A squeak of fear escaped Hannah, and she started trembling in Corey's hands, wide-eyes locked on the blade at his throat. Corey opened his mouth to reassure her.

"I said release her," Tim barked.

Corey eased his hand out of her shirt. "Fasten it, Hannah," he managed in a soothing voice.

It would do no good to reason with Tim. Whatever he believed was going on, this was going to a judge. He only hoped this wouldn't traumatize Hannah into her shell again. Sex and blades were not an association Corey would have reinforced for her.

"Move."

Corey locked his hands on the bureau top, refusing. "No matter what state of undress you drag me out of here in, you have no right to demand Hannah reveal her body to you."

Tim hesitated, clearing his throat. "Agreed."

"Corey?" Hannah managed shakily, working the buttons.

He glanced down at her. "It will be all ri—"

Tim's hand tightened in Corey's hair and jerked his head back. "Don't look at her."

"Right." Gods, Tim had the wrong idea, he was certain.

Hannah finished righting her clothing and pushed at Corey's arm to indicate that he should move back. He did so, and she slid to the floor.

"Move," Tim repeated.

"Wait," Hannah requested. "What are you doing? Where are you taking Corey?"

"To be judged." Tim said it with conviction, as if there was no question what Corey had done wrong.

"Judged? Why?"

Corey sighed in relief. He couldn't argue with the one taking him into custody. She could.

Tim hesitated, seemingly as confused as she was. "That remains to be seen."

"Perhaps Hannah should come along to give evidence," Corey suggested.

"I suppose Tyler will insist on talking to her," he mused.

"And I give my word that you don't need the blade."

The sacred weapon moved from Corey's neck to the perfect position to take his kidney. "A show of trust. If you move against either of us—"

"I really don't understand this." Hannah's voice held an edge of panic.

Neither did Corey, but this was the wrong time to say it.

Tim guided Corey toward the door without answering her. Halfway to Tyler's office, Warriors started to notice their little procession. Tim requested Tyler then guided Corey to the empty office. By the time Tyler arrived, Warriors were being called from beds to attend to the proceedings.

Tyler marched in, looking wholly pissed off. He panned his gaze down Corey's body, probably noting the unbuttoned and rumpled shirt. He raised an eyebrow that spoke volumes. "What is the charge? I suggest someone make it good."

Tim pushed Corey toward Tyler, then swept his weapon into the sheath at his waist. "I'd wager on coercing a woman to willingness, though I admit I can't be sure."

"What?" Hannah asked. "Corey has *never*—"

Tyler put up a hand for silence, then offered his hand to Hannah. She stared at it warily, shied a step, then took it, letting Tyler guide her to a chair; she settled into it with a look around that announced her wish to run.

Tyler considered her for a moment. "You understand that we just want to protect you, Hannah?"

She flicked a look seeking help at Corey then nodded. "Corey does protect me," she offered.

His heart leapt at that. He liked the idea of protecting her far too much of late. He liked that she noticed and appreciated it, even that she depended on it. *I really need to seal printing, as soon as she seems willing.*

Tyler looked to Tim. "What makes you suspect Corey?"

His voice left no doubt that he still wasn't convinced. "He snuck into her room and—"

"I did *not* sneak," Corey protested. "I walked in."

"Without knocking," Tim fumed.

"I'm not in the habit of knocking to enter Hannah's rooms. Nor is she in the habit of knocking to enter mine." It couldn't hurt to make their relationship clear...he hoped.

Tyler waved to Tim to continue.

"And I heard..." He shifted beside Corey, seemingly discomfited. "I know it was a sob. I'm sure it was."

Hannah paled a notch. "I wasn't crying, I assure you."

"Corey?" Tyler asked.

"Hannah feels deeply," he offered diplomatically. "Acutely, though it's pleasurable. I have to slow down sometimes to make sure the sounds are... Well, to make sure she's not uncomfortable with what we're—"

Tim cursed fluently, and Hannah shot him a nervous look Corey wished he was free to soothe.

"I won't allow this again," Tim vowed.

The connection made in Corey's mind, he turned to Tim. "I am not Tom. I have never convinced Hannah to anything, and I never will." Gods, just the thought of it made him ill.

"She can't even look at a man," Tim argued.

"Other men? No, she can't. I wish to the gods she *could* meet your eyes."

Hannah gasped, and Corey turned to her, his mind working fast to make whatever connection she had.

"No," he soothed her. "I'm not saying I want you to look at other men *that* way. If you did... I'd let you follow your heart, wherever it led, but I'll be honest. The *last* thing I want is it leading you away from me."

"Can't you see the man's printing?" Wes demanded, no doubt afraid this might go against his only son.

Tyler motioned for silence, then moved toward Corey, demanding his full attention. "Are you printing, Corey?"

He sighed. "I am, but I won't rush her. I don't care how long it takes Hannah to be ready. Or if she never is, I'll have to deal with it as any Warrior does."

"I am."

Her whispered answer left his heart stuttering, and his cock rose fast and hard. Corey argued it back. She couldn't be saying what he thought she was.

"Hannah?" Tyler prompted her.

"Printing... As I understand it, Corey would be asking me to marry him?"

Tyler looked from Corey to Hannah, seemingly considering something. "It's more than that, Hannah. If Corey seals printing with you, he'll be tying himself to you, binding his heart and soul. There's no turning back for him. That's why he's giving you time to be comfortable and sure. If you change your mind later, he can't change his. If you refused him after he sealed printing, it would kill him."

"Tyler!" Corey bit back the rest of his protest and forced himself to calm before continuing, well aware that his *Blutjagd* was burning merrily. "Think what associations you're making for her, I beg of you."

His house lord cocked his head to one side, then nodded. "You have my apologies, but it is better for you that Hannah knows what she'd be entering into."

Hannah huffed. "I don't suppose any of you trust me to know my own mind?"

Tyler tipped his head to her. "I certainly do."

"That's why I was waiting for you to be sure," Corey grumbled. "If you're sure, that's good enough for me."

"Then, if Corey is serious, I want nothing more than to seal printing with him."

The wave of arousal that assaulted him nearly sent Corey to his knees. He forced slow, even breaths, trying to rein it in long enough to pay attention to the conversation.

Tyler chuckled darkly. "You are far gone," he noted.

Corey nodded. "Am I being judged?" he inquired. If not, he had more pressing matters to attend to.

"It seems Tim misunderstood."

"Good."

"Good?" Hannah asked.

Corey turned to her, offering a hand to help her to her feet. "Very good."

She launched into his arms, seeking out Corey's mouth.

He reveled in the moment then broke away, nuzzling her lips. "I'll show you good," he promised.

Chapter Sixty-eight

Mother's Son

Corey sipped at his beer, smiling at the sight of Hannah feeding their daughter. She was a wonderful mother. He'd always known she would be, even when she'd worried about her abilities while she carried their first child.

Quinton came out like most Warrior babies: squalling, hungry, and completely besotted of his mother. He was an easier baby than most, and when he was difficult, all it took was snuggling to Hannah to calm him again.

Their strong attachment remained, even when Callum was born four years later. After that, it had taken an agonizing decade for the Stone to decide to bless them with another child.

And She gave me a daughter. Was it sacrilege to wonder if the Stone had done so to reward Corey for his tireless protection of—and perhaps his love of—Hannah? If it was, he wasn't certain he cared.

Reward or not, Kyra was glorious.

Their daughter had been born only weeks before Christmas. Though Corey had expected Hannah to beg off their usual trip to the manor for the holidays, she'd embraced the trip whole-heartedly and had accepted the pampering the family had heaped on her with gusto.

Not that the men felt free to touch her, of course. That hadn't changed at all. Then again, even if Hannah had accepted it, Corey wasn't sure he would be able to control his anger at the sight of it. Warriors were a territorial lot, and Corey was no exception to that rule.

Movement out of the corner of his eye caught Corey's attention. From the flash of black, he knew it was one of the men or older boys. The women and children wore a wide array of bright colors for the holiday, so it wouldn't be one of them.

A spike of jealousy at the idea of another man staring at his mate while she was feeding their daughter had Corey shooting a glare at... *Quinton.*

Their older son stared at his mother, his expression a shifting, indistinct mix that confused Corey. Concern overwhelmed the irritation that simply.

Corey stood and made his way to his son. Quinton snapped a look at him and went cherry red in the face in response.

"Come on. Let's take a walk." Whatever the problem was, it was a safe bet it was something Quinton would be more comfortable talking about with Corey than with Hannah.

He nodded and headed for the door. A few heads turned to watch them go, including Callum's, but Corey and Quinton were quickly dismissed. The other Warriors probably believed Corey had to offer correction to his son, and it was no one's right to interfere with that.

They were outside, well past the children's play area and into the woods, before Corey broached the subject. "Does it bother you to see your mother breastfeeding Kyra?"

Quinton sighed heavily. "No. Most of the women choose to breastfeed. I don't really remember her breastfeeding me or Callum, but I know she did. I've seen plenty of women breastfeed. It's good for babies."

"Yes. It is good for them. Especially for Kyra, since she's a freed female and not a Warrior."

His son nodded in reply.

"Are you...confused by seeing it?"

Quinton shot him a look of irritation. "Confused? I already said no. I've seen plenty of women breastfeed before."

Corey fished for the words to clarify it. "You're a young Warrior in training."

"I noticed," he replied flippantly.

"I'm sure you did." The words stuck in his throat, and Corey prayed he was wrong. "Are your drives confused?"

Quinton stopped short, and his *Blutjagd* flared a bit. "No. By the gods, how could you even ask such a thing?"

Despite the fact that his son was angry with him, Corey's heart eased. "Because whatever you haven't manned up enough to say yet has me concerned. Concerned enough that I'm not sure you're safe to be around your mother and sister. I shouldn't have to worry about that, and I refuse to allow *any* threat to them."

The young Warrior took a step back, and his *Blutjagd* faded. "Then maybe you and the other Warriors should stop treating me like a child and tell me the truth."

That stung. It called to the forefront a perceived lack of honor in Corey and the other Warriors that his son harbored. No Warrior wanted to be thought of as dishonorable. Corey crossed his arms over his chest and glared down at his son. "And just what do you think I've lied to you about?"

"Let's call it lies of omission."

The sick certainty that he knew where this was going turned Corey's stomach. "Go on."

"You don't hunt. The only reason you're going to hunt in the near future is to first night me, because that's a father's duty." Quinton hurried on before his father could answer. "The other Warriors call mother 'Armen's glass angel', but none of them will explain the title. I've seen how she's treated. Not just how she's pampered; all the women are pampered, more or less. The men always keep themselves where she can see them, keep their distance, even wait for her permission to approach her. Even the König females don't get that sort of treatment."

His son paused for a moment, then launched in again. "And now...the scars. I don't remember her breastfeeding Callum or me, but it occurs to me now that mother has never shown her chest before. She wears high shirts, even during the summer. When she swims, she wears a short wetsuit that reaches her elbows and knees."

And she typically uses a light blanket to cover when she nurses Kyra. The only reason she hadn't been covered with one at this feeding was that Kyra had spit back a large portion of the first breast onto it, and Hannah had told Corey not to fuss with running all the way to their room for another.

"Well?" Quinton challenged him.

Corey's head spun in the silence following the verbal assault. His heart ached. He'd hoped never to have to explain this to his sons, but it seemed his reprieve was over. "Come on. Let's go sit in the meditation area."

His son paled a notch. "You think I'll need to sit down for this?"

"I think *I* do." Corey was abruptly weary. He felt decades older than he had inside the house.

"Okay." But his tone of voice said Quinton was rethinking his request to be told the truth.

"Be sure, Quinton. Once I tell you the tale, it cannot be unheard. From this day forth, you will be burdened with the same dishonor that paints all of Armen."

Words seemed to stick in his son's throat. At last, he bobbed his head. "I understand."

"You will soon," he grumbled.

They walked to the meditation area in silence, then took a seat on one of the stone benches. Corey looked around at the god marks engraved into short pillars around the circumference of the cleared space, focusing on Ani. *The protector of women and children. Would that Hannah would have had Your protection then.*

"It was a Beast, wasn't it? Did the beast take mother from you somehow?" Quinton sat, rigid, every muscle ratcheted down tight.

"Yes and no. It wasn't *a* Beast. It was three of the curs. They didn't take your mother from me. I took her from them."

Quinton looked as if he might puke. "Armen's dishonor is that they managed to feed from her?"

"Armen's dishonor is that they managed to hold her hostage for three days, during which they perpetrated all manner of atrocities."

His son staggered to his feet and lurched away.

He needs to know it all. "It never should have happened. The Beasts who took her had been operating for decades. They were wily. They were vicious. They took trophies of their kills. I can only assume one of them slipped up and let a tooth break skin."

Quinton wheeled around to gape at him. "The scars?"

"They used knives and other cutting tools to draw the blood. Then they healed her just enough to keep her from dying from blood loss. She has more scars. All over the portions of her body she hides from you. They didn't feed her anything sustaining, and they offered only enough water to keep her alive but weakened. Given another day...three at the most, she would surely have died in their hands. Just another trophy on their walls."

His son heaved his dinner onto the ground.

Corey gave Quinton time to decide if he wanted to question more. Perhaps telling him about his mother's past would convince him he didn't want to know the rest.

After several bouts with sickness, Quinton rubbed a shaking hand across his mouth. He made it back to the bench on trembling legs and sank to it. For a moment, he was silent.

Finally, he found his voice. "What about the Beasts?"

"They didn't live another day."

"You killed them?"

"No. I took your mother from them during the day. I called in the troops, and they expunged the guilty and incinerated the site. Your mother needed me. She couldn't be without me."

Quinton met his gaze, seemingly tortured by the truth. "And you fell for her. Didn't you?"

He nodded. "Very quickly. It took your mother much longer to decide she wanted more of our relationship than friendship and protection, but I never pushed for more."

"How did you stay sane?"

"The Stone helped with that. She keeps me sane, even if I'm not hunting. She kept me sane when your mother wasn't ready to seek out a man...and when she wasn't ready to commit to one. Thankfully, you were conceived after we sealed." He smiled at the truth that he wouldn't have cared if his son had been conceived before it, if that had been Hannah's wish. *Though that* might *have cost me my head.*

Quinton sat, lost in thought. When he spoke, his voice was subdued. "I'm surprised the Stone gave you any sons."

"What? Why?" More Warriors surrounding Hannah, even if they also hunted the night, were a good thing.

"What if a Beast kills me? What will that do to Mother?"

A protective surge welled up inside Corey, and his tone went gruff in response. "You and your brother had best dedicate yourselves to being the finest Warriors Armen has. If you die early, before your mother does, and cause her a moment of heartache and grief, I will curse you to wherever the Beasts are punished, until such time as Hannah reaches the Warrior's Rest and wants to see you again. I would never deny her that."

Quinton stared at him for a long moment, then nodded solemnly. "When we get home, we double my training." He didn't question it, which was presumptuous of him.

"We double it now. You work out with your cousins every morning and with me every afternoon."

"Done."

Corey bit back a smile. His son would make a fine Warrior someday soon. "We should go back. Your mother will be wondering where we've disappeared to."

"Absolutely."

On the way back the manor, Corey had to hurry to keep up with Quinton.

But he's calmer than I'd hoped he would be if it ever came to this. That's good.

Corey stopped him just inside the door. "You should clean up."

Quinton loped away, and Corey headed back to the library.

And my mate and daughter.

Hannah looked up and offered a smile for him. Her peek past him didn't escape his notice.

"Bathroom break," Corey explained in half truth.

She nodded, but her pallor worried him.

Corey came to her side, and ran a hand along her cheek. "Are you all right? Can I get you anything?"

"Just tired, but Kyra is wide awake."

His offer to take their daughter and let her sleep was cut off by Quinton's voice.

"I'll take her. Go get some rest before her next feeding."

Hannah's smile faded a notch. "I think she needs a changing. Maybe I should—"

"I'll take care of it. Won't be the first diaper I've changed."

Her look of amazement faded into one of pride. Hannah passed Kyra into her eldest brother's hands, and Corey helped her to her feet.

She paused for a moment and touched Quinton's cheek, looking up into their son's face. "Thank you. You have always been such a good boy." She sighed.

"And now you're becoming a man, right before my eyes."

Quinton leaned down and placed a kiss on her forehead. "No matter how old I get, I'll always be your son. Anything you need or want, just let me know."

Her eyes narrowed, but she forced a smile and nodded.

Corey could see the questions forming in her mind. He escorted her through the parting crowd and up the stairs, more than passingly aware of the tension in her back and shoulders.

Hannah held her tongue until they reached their room. Then she turned on him and speared him with a look that said he was in a lot of trouble.

Corey pushed his hands into his pockets, at a loss to explain himself.

"I know that promise, Corey."

As well she should. Every Warrior who'd met her in the last seventeen years, Armen or not, had uttered it to her. "He's an adult now, Hannah." *Or very nearly so. Another month, and he will be.* "He was asking questions. As a Warrior of Armen, Quinton needs to know about the dishonor of the Armen house...and to protect—"

"Quinton wasn't even *born* when I was attacked. How could he possibly be dishonored by it?"

Oh, shit. She's gone into protective mother mode. Corey sighed. "It's Warrior terminology. It—"

"So, it's like original sin? I've always hated that idea." Hannah ran a hand across her forehead, tears welling in her eyes.

She shouldn't be upset. She's still healing from having Kyra, and she's nursing. Not that a Warrior wanted to see his mate or mother upset at any time.

Women in general. They were hardwired to soothe and protect females.

"Corey!"

"No. Nothing like that," he hastened to answer her question. Quinton isn't personally dishonored. It's more of a cautionary tale. The Kaufmann house still clings to a mistake one Warrior made in the seventeenth century or so. Armen has more than a few cautionary tales out there."

Hannah's mouth moved, as if she was trying to string words together. Just when Corey would have hugged her, she spoke again. "Quinton didn't need to know that."

"He does. But not for the reasons you think."

She waited for his answer.

Corey reached out for Hannah and drew her toward the bed, trying to formulate words that would make sense to her. "Every Warrior, especially Warriors of Armen, has a special duty toward protecting you from harm."

"I don't want to *be* a duty to Quinton and Callum! They are my sons."

"Which means they love you more than anyone in the world, besides me. They want to protect you, just as I want to protect you. Let them."

Hannah didn't seem to have an answer for that. Corey lifted her and settled her on the bed, trying not to think of the first time he held her in his arms.

No. This is completely different. It will always be different, because I will never allow another Beast to touch her.

Before he could ask if Hannah was still angry, she wrapped a hand around his neck and urged him down to her mouth.

Corey didn't question her. If Hannah wanted him to kiss her, he was more than willing to follow through. His cock ached, a reminder that he hadn't been able to have sex with her for three weeks and probably wouldn't for that length of time or more.

The kiss went hotter and deeper, and Corey resigned himself to masturbating in the shower, if that's what it took. He went still at the feeling of Hannah working his belt open.

A groan escaped his mouth, and his head spun in possible ways to follow through. "Do you want to watch me come or do you want to trade favors?" *Anything. Just touch me.*

A sly little smile curved her lips up. "I want you inside me."

His heart hammered at the suggestion. "But it's so soon. Won't I hurt you?"

"You said 'anything I want', Corey." There was a hint of seduction in that.

"Anything," he vowed. Corey stood and stripped away his clothing, his cock going harder at the stark hunger in his mate's expression, as she did the same.

Hannah reached out and stroked the pre-cum from the head of his cock. His breathing went ragged, as she licked her fingertips. Though she'd started experimenting with fellating him more than a decade earlier, it wasn't something they engaged in often...and never without her offering it.

"Anything," he repeated, as he settled to the mattress with her.

There was no play at slow seduction. They'd been together for over seventeen years, and they knew each other well. Corey knew where to touch her, and he did. Hannah trailed her hands over his body, but she made no move to suck him, so he put it out of his mind and focused on what she *was* offering.

Touching turned again to kissing. Corey released her lips and inched inside her, prepared to stop if she was still too sore from childbirth to make love to him.

Hannah moaned, and he froze, looking for signs of distress...or of passion. The fingernails raking down his back gave him the answer he was seeking, and Corey started moving again.

He sank into her heat, reveling in every sound and movement. Cory trembled in pleasure. He gasped, forcing himself to hold back when he need to come so badly.

Not yet. Hannah first.

As if in response, she cried out in ecstasy. Her inner muscles massaged him, setting off his climax in response. His release shook Corey to his core, a slightly-less-potent echo of the night they sealed printing.

He smiled. That had been a Christmas Eve as well. The holiday season had always been kind to them.

Hannah snuggled closer to him with a yawn.

"Better?" he asked.

"Much. Just make me one promise?"

"Anything." How often would he have to say that?

"When Callum starts asking, warn me before you tell him what you have to." Hannah stared up at him, her eyes wide and pleading.

They are her sons. Hannah loves them beyond reason. "Yes. I will do that for you."

A sleepy smile was her only answer.

* * * *

Corey woke with a start. It took only a moment to orientate himself; his heart started pounding in response. Hours had passed. Hours! And Quinton had yet to return Kyra to them.

Kyra never goes this long between feedings. What is wrong?

The last thing Corey wanted to do was to wake Hannah before he knew what was going on. He slipped from the bed silently, then pulled on his jeans.

It didn't take him long to find his son. Quinton sat in a gliding rocker in the nursery next to their bedroom, Kyra asleep on his chest, one small fist clutched in her eldest brother's black t-shirt.

Corey forced his heart rate to ease. He ambled toward them, relieved that everything seemed to be okay.

Quinton didn't look up. "She's fine. I've given Kyra a bottle of Mother's expressed milk, so she can sleep longer. Mother needs to sleep longer."

"Yes, she does, but please don't give Kyra another. Your mother will be in pain if she doesn't empty her breasts often enough. It will also adversely affect her production of Kyra's milk."

A solemn nod was Quinton's only reply.

Corey started to turn away, then stopped. "Your mother asked that I not tell Callum without letting her know first. I will hold you to that promise as well."

He met Corey's gaze solidly. "I will be bound by it."

"You are your mother's son, Quinton. That comes with additional responsibilities."

Kyra wriggled against her brother, changing her position.

"I know it." Quinton reached up and started patting his baby sister's back.

Corey focused on the strip of black fabric wrapped around Quinton's hand. He circled his son, wincing at the sight of the blood on Kyra's forehead.

"What blood oath did you take?" Corey demanded. He kept his voice lowered, so as not to wake the baby.

"I took an oath to protect Kyra and Mother in your stead, should that become necessary, no matter what hardships I might face for it."

"I hope that never becomes necessary." Quinton deserved more. "You make your mother proud."

Quinton smiled up at him. "That's good to hear."

"Corey?"

He snapped around at the sound of Hannah's voice. "Do you need anything?"

"Is Kyra all right?"

"Just fine. Quinton is taking good care of her."

She wandered across the room and placed a kiss on Quinton's head. While she was distracted, Corey wiped the blood off the baby's forehead. Though the idea of Quinton's oath wouldn't bother Hannah, his bleeding would. She was soft-hearted that way. As if in agreement, their son hid his hand at his side.

"Time for bed," she announced, reaching for the baby.

"Let me," Corey offered.

"My sweet boys."

"Anything for you," they replied in unison.

The End

Excerpt from The First Book of Texts

By Gawen first Lord Schwertträger,
Stone Lord and master trainer
"The Rules of Sanction"
Part One (penned in 510 AD)

A Warrior must be mindful always of the humans around him. More than human, less than damned; the cursed have the potential to do great good. Inherent in that potential is the ability to do great harm.

A Warrior will have enemies, and to protect those humans bound by the Stone's sacred trust, the Warrior will kill in honorable battle those enemies.

A child is never truly an enemy. He may be disarmed and even rendered unable to continue the present battle, but though the child of today may grow to be the enemy tomorrow, today he is naught but a boy.

A woman may be slain in battle only as a last resort. If she raises her blade against a Warrior, he will first treat her as he would a child. Remember always that a woman battles most fiercely for child and home. Whenever possible, a Warrior should seek his true enemy elsewhere and leave her to protect what is hers from less honorable men—and less dangerous.

In battle, unforeseen events will occur. In battle, innocents will often die. The Warrior should never carry a battle to innocents that can be fought elsewhere. When there is no choice, the Warrior must be mindful of the innocents in his midst. An innocent life taken in honest error is lamentable. One taken in negligence is unforgivable.

More than human, less than damned. The Warrior must never forget that humans are powerless before him. This is not a reason for pride but rather a warning.

The Stone made a pact in its wisdom. One of the foundations of that pact is the Warrior's promise to do no harm. Those under a Warrior's protection and innocents all, the Warrior must protect to death.

Humans are fragile things in that they are frail and unable to heal as Warriors do as much as in that they fear and attack any perceived threat. Warriors possess the power to be perceived as a threat.

As the chain is only as strong as its weakest link, so the pact is only strong as the trust imparted by its weakest to its strongest. For the safety of Warrior and mate, no Warrior may threaten that trust and live.

Warriors are cursed. Stone-Chosen or passed from father to son, the curse manifests in the same fashion, generation after generation. Akin to the damnation of the beasts, never doubt the curse for what it is.

Blutjagd, the blood lust, comes first and foremost. Where the beasts are driven only by darkness, the darkness in a Warrior's soul will be very strong. The urge to kill the beasts is at its heart, for dark knows dark, as the Warriors and beasts each sense the other and seek each to destroy the opposing dark.

Blutjagd in its purest sense is naught but good, but that is not only how it will make itself known. The gift of *Blutjagd* is also the ability to protect what a Warrior holds dear to him and what he has a duty to protect, but there is a fierce streak in him that rivals his love and loyalty.

When a wrong is done by a human to him and his, a Warrior must not allow darkness to rule him. Capital offenses require the ultimate price. Of that there is no doubt, but the price must be exacted on the one who has wronged him alone. Revenge is not something a

Warrior indulges in. The ones who have not acted against him are innocents. The pain of their loss is more punishment than they deserve.

If the offense is injurious but not capital, retribution should be taken in kind. If no injury is sustained, no blood may be spilled in return, unless the guilty attacks in earnest.

A Warrior must ever be mindful of the nature of the crime against him. He cannot allow his pain to rule him. Capital crimes involve grave harm and disregard of innocence. Murder or rape or the attempt of either, an unprovoked attack on a Warrior's mate or child— In such a case, the interloper must pay the ultimate price, as the pact demands. The Warrior who exacts the ultimate price for a crime that is not capital or not in defense will face death himself from his true judge, having proven himself lacking in control and respect for the fragile sanctity of life.

Likewise, the Warrior must gauge his punishment of Warriors who wrong him by the rules of sanction. A Warrior has the right to face the Warrior he has most wronged as judge—or his house lord, as case the may be when the injury is to his own house or to a human not of a Warrior's household. One who acts as judge in another's stead faces sanction by both the true judge and the Warrior he judged out of place—or the Warrior's lord, if he is incapable of judging for himself.

The drive to print can lead to madness in *Endspiel.* Printing can make a Warrior the most stable of men, unless his mate or children are endangered, but the time of printing is the most dangerous and unstable time of all for a Warrior.

Warriors are not lawless soldiers. A Warrior must rule his curse, lest the curse rule him. The sanctions in taking women are understandably rigid because of the great danger printing poses.

The beasts take women brutally, without care and concern. Until a Warrior finds his mate—or after he loses his mate, he will require release with women aside from his mate. While he has a mate, she will provide the only true release he will find. She is a balm for his soul, calming his *Blutjagd* and appeasing his sexual appetite as no other woman can while she lives. He will have no need and no wish to perform with another, as long as he has her.

But, a Warrior who cannot control his curse is no better than a beast. A Warrior may not take an unwilling woman, even if she is the woman of an enemy or an enemy herself. Neither shall a Warrior use his whiles to sway an unwilling woman to some form of willingness to bed her. Such a move is dishonorable in that it exploits her innocence and does her injustice.

A lover must always be treated kindly and with respect. It is the Warrior's duty to repay the peace a lover grants him with pleasure. If she gifts him with her maiden's blood, he must ease it from her and repay her tenfold for her sacrifice.

A Warrior must never take a child to his bed. A woman shy of fifteen years, though she bleeds, is not a woman for the taking. Her body is not adequate to carry a Warrior's child until she matures, and her innocence is still largely intact.

If the woman of a Warrior's desire is the freed daughter of another Warrior, she may not be taken without her father's consent or that of her house lord, if her father is dead. The Warrior protecting his child is a dangerous man, and the interloper may be perceived as a threat to that family. For the safety of all, this rule must be adhered to.

The Warrior who takes simple pleasure without permission from her keeper owes a solid blow for every instance to the one who would give his permission.

Judgment of whether or not the Warrior is worthy of the woman will then be rendered by her judge.

If the Warrior takes his satisfaction in her in such a case, he must submit to that same man as judge. It is within his judge's rights to exact one of three punishments. If he deems the Warrior without either honor or control, he may take his life for it. He may take him to trial and forbid his interaction with the woman again. Or, he may take a single blow and give his consent—with any reasonable restrictions he deems fit the situation, from the question of when children are appropriate to loyalties in repayment for his trespass.

In any case—satisfaction taken or no—the judge has the right to strike the woman a single open-handed blow if he feels she is without honor in her actions.

A Warrior who cannot control his curse is no better than a beast. A Warrior who returns to a forbidden woman a second time faces the certainty of death.

A Warrior must always submit absolutely to his judge. If he raises a hand in his own defense to any Warrior—judge or no—or does not meet and live by his punishment gracefully—even unto a sentence of death, he will face death, as he has shown himself without control. If the Warrior lies to his judge to hide his misdeeds when asked for the truth, he will face any penalty up to and including death, as his judge wishes, for he has shown himself lacking in honor.

If the woman wronged is human not of a Warrior house, the house lord of the Warrior who wronged her will sit as his judge. If the accused is a house lord, the Stone Lord will stand as judge. If he is Stone Lord, a council of the lords will stand as judge. In the case of the house lord, he will no longer be deemed worthy of his position and shall forfeit his place as house lord to the next in line to hold the seal. The Stone will take care of its own succession as It always has.

Taking any woman—human or of a household—unwilling or attempting to do so, automatically warrants a sentence of death, as would attempting her murder or the murder of a child. The body of the Warrior would then be presented to the woman and her family and personal protection be granted them in repayment by the house lord.

If the Warrior is come upon in the act, the woman's safety is paramount. If he can be restrained and presented to his true judge, it should be done despite the fury driving the Warrior who comes upon the scene. If such a thing cannot be accomplished without the threat of further violence to his victim, the criminal should be executed as he is. She should then be tended to medically and returned to her family with proof of the attacker's state.

If a human family wishes to exact their own punishment on a Warrior, they will be permitted the right of inflicting their own beating, with the protection of the Warrior guard, before the judge passes his own sentence. Remember always that when a Warrior breaks the pact, the safety of all depends on restoring the peace with the humans injured.

Only in a challenge of trial is the Warrior to defend himself physically. Only to his true judge, at the appropriate time, is the Warrior to defend himself in words—if such is the case that there is any excuse or explanation for his actions—or to plead mercy for the woman involved. A Warrior should never plead mercy for himself, as his actions are his own, dishonorable or honorable, and honor demands he take responsibility for them.

The Warrior may demand his right of his true judge and no more of the Warrior who places him in custody. If he raises a hand to that Warrior, he will be restrained or killed as the situation unfolds. Should he survive the punishment of his true judge for his first crime, he still faces death at the hands of the Warrior holding custody for his lack of control. If the Warrior taken into custody attempts violence against an innocent— In such a case, no move will be made to restrain him. His life is forfeit.

The Stone Alphabet

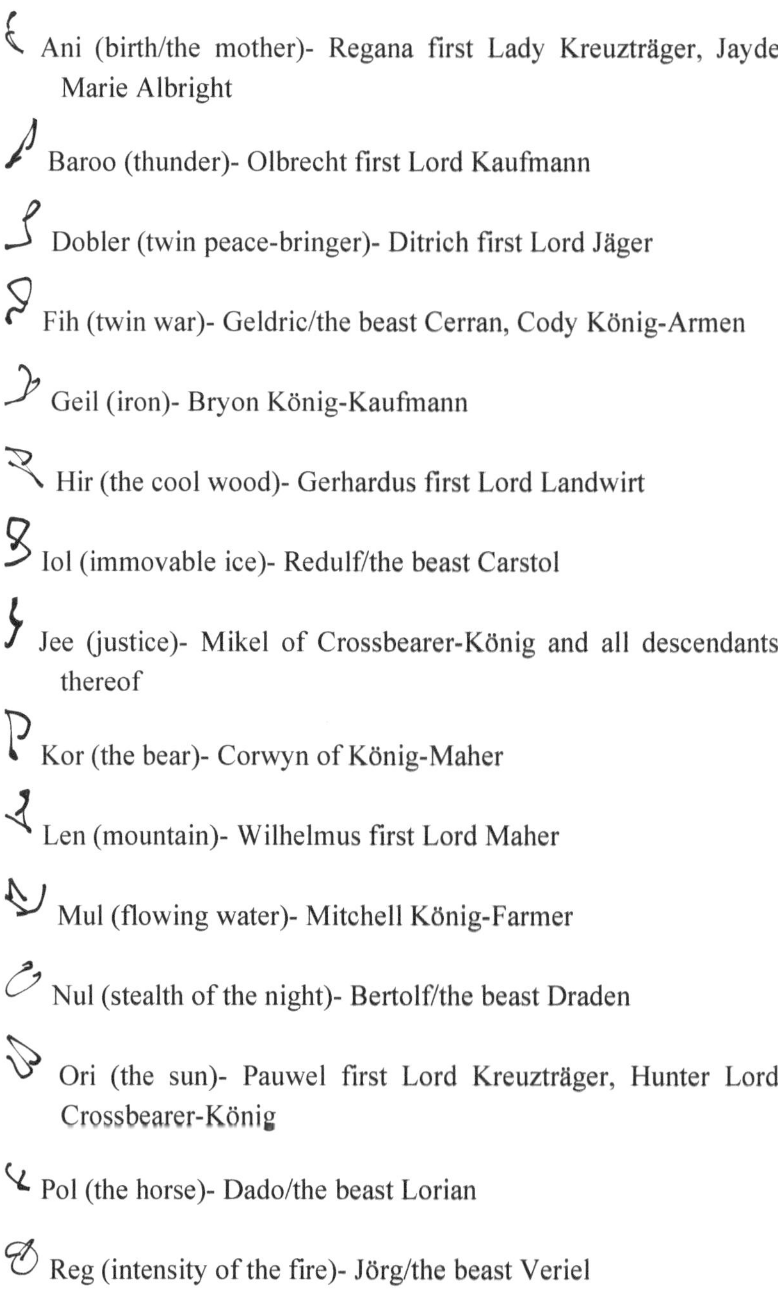

Ani (birth/the mother)- Regana first Lady Kreuzträger, Jayde Marie Albright

Baroo (thunder)- Olbrecht first Lord Kaufmann

Dobler (twin peace-bringer)- Ditrich first Lord Jäger

Fih (twin war)- Geldric/the beast Cerran, Cody König-Armen

Geil (iron)- Bryon König-Kaufmann

Hir (the cool wood)- Gerhardus first Lord Landwirt

Iol (immovable ice)- Redulf/the beast Carstol

Jee (justice)- Mikel of Crossbearer-König and all descendants thereof

Kor (the bear)- Corwyn of König-Maher

Len (mountain)- Wilhelmus first Lord Maher

Mul (flowing water)- Mitchell König-Farmer

Nul (stealth of the night)- Bertolf/the beast Draden

Ori (the sun)- Pauwel first Lord Kreuzträger, Hunter Lord Crossbearer-König

Pol (the horse)- Dado/the beast Lorian

Reg (intensity of the fire)- Jörg/the beast Veriel

Syth (the Stone lord)- Master Trainer Sibold, Gawen first Lord Schwertträger, Etienne Lord Kaufmann, Joseph Lord Armen, Carrick Lord Armen, Corwyn Lord Hunter, Lewis of Maher

Tes (stars and moon)- Kevin König-Smith

Vin (wind)- Cunczel first Lord Schmied

Wul (the wolf)- Tilbrand/the beast Resten

Zel (ending/death)- Erin of Crossbearer-König, Kaitlyn "Katie" of König-Maher, Skye of König-Armen, Victorious Ellen "Vick/Vicky" of König-Smith, Margaret Elizabeth "Maggie" König-Farmer, Colette "Lettie" Kong-Kaufmann

About the Author

Brenna Lyons wears many hats, sometimes all on the same day: former president of EPIC, author of more than 100 published works, owner of Fireborn Publishing, columnist, special needs teacher, wife, mother...and member in good standing of more than 60 writing advocacy groups.

In her first ten years published in novel-length, she's won 3 EPIC e-Book Awards (out of 15 finalists) and finaled for 3 PEARLS (including one Honorable Mention, second to NY Times Bestseller Angela Knight), 2 CAPAS, and a Dream Realm Award. She's also taken Spinetingler's Book of the Year for 2007.

Brenna writes in 26 established worlds plus stand-alones, poetry, articles and essays. She's a bestseller in indie/e fantasy and horror, straight genre and cross-genres thereof. Brenna has been termed "one of the most deviant erotic minds in the publishing world...not for the weak." (Rachelle for Fallen Angels Reviews) Milieu-heavy dark work is practically Brenna's calling card, with or without the erotic content.

She teaches classes in everything from POV studies to advanced editing, networking to marketing. Brenna enjoys hearing from people who read her work and can be reached by e-mail.

Website: http://www.brennalyons.com/

Facebook: http://www.facebook.com/brenna.lyons

Email: brennalyons4168@live.com

Also by this Author

Available from ***Fireborn Publishing***

KEIF'S DEN AND PACK
Keif's Pack
Mother of the Keif
Keif's Den (Coming Soon)

PROPHECY
Prophecy: Revelations
Prophecy: Rapture
The Prophet's Mate
Prophecy: Rampage - Meet Gavin
Prophecy: Rampage (Coming Soon)

THE FANTASY CLUB
The Consort

Beyond the Veil
Fairy Wishes (Coming Soon)
Mine for the Night
Once in a Blue Moon
Overtime Pay
Stay With Me
The Fire God's Woman
The Punishment of Phoebus Apollo
Werewolf U

Available from ***Phaze Books***

ANGEL-WING SAGA
Sons of Heaven: Beldon
Daughters of Man: Prize Match
Sons of Heaven: Unexpected Mates
Daughters of Man: Claiming a Princess

BRIDE BALL
Bride Ball
Poison, Lies, and No-Win Choices

COLOR OF LOVE
The Color of Love

FIRE AND ICE
Magmon's Hunger
Magmon's Lover

INSTINCT SERIES
Animal Instincts

KEGIN SERIES
Conquest
The Last of Fion's Daughters
Last Chance for Love
Rites of Mating
In Her Ladyship's Service
Matchmaker's Misery

KIELAN SERIES
The Lady's Lowborn Lover
Time Currents
Cubed

NIGHT WARRIORS
Night Warriors
Will of the Stone
Bearing Armen
Hunter's Moon
Maher Men
Choosing a Mate/Starting a War
Raised to Be His Own
Veriel's Tales I: Crossbearer Turned
Veriel's Tales II: Losing Regana
Blutjagdfrau Lost
The Warrior's Man
Damsel in Distress

STAR MAGES

The Master's Lover

XXAN WAR

Daahan Rising

Crossbred Son

Raashh Decisions

Enslaved

All I Want for Christmas is You

Fates Magic

All's Fair…

Black Sail

Mama's Tales

Dream Walk

Unexpected Daddy

Phaze in Verse

We Shall Live Again

May the Best Man Win

Nevermore

Marked

And It Was Good

Available from ***Mundania Press***

STAR MAGES

Written in the Stars

Fairy Dreams

Monsters of Myth Anthology

Available from ***Under the Moon***

RENEGADES SERIES

TYGERS

Renegade's Run

Max Sec

URBAN GRIMM
Catch Me, If You Can
Three Wishes
Temptation of Eve

With Great Power
Undead in Blue
Evil Overlords Union Issue #1 Anthology
Undead Embrace
"*Playing Games*" in *Forbidden Love: Bad Boys*
"*Marked*" in *Forbidden Love: Wicked Women*
"*The Master's Lover*" in *Forbidden Love: Sacred Bands*

Available from ***Logical Lust***

"*Mine for the Night*" in *The Cougar Book* Anthology

Available from ***Coming Together Charity Anthologies***

INSTINCT SERIES
"*Foundling*" in *Coming Together: Into the Light* Anthology

"*Claim Mate*" (available separately and as part of the *Coming Together: Against the Odds* Anthology)
"*The Fire God's Woman*" in *Coming Together: Under Fire* Anthology

Available ***self-published***

KEGIN SERIES
Earth-Born Lord
Graham: Training the Earth-Born Lord

NIGHT WARRIORS
Claiming a Lady

Stone Lord
Mother's Son

COLOR OF LOVE
A Safe Heart

Snapshots from a Poet's Life

Award-Winning Books

EPPIE/EPIC eBOOK AWARDS WINNERS
Coming Together: Against the Odds- 2010
Time Currents- 2010
Coming Together: Into the Light- 2011

EPPIE/EPIC eBOOK AWARDS FINALISTS
Fion's Daughter- 2004
Collected Poems: Book One- 2005 (now titled *Snapshots of a Poet's Life*)
Renegade's Run- 2005
Rites of Mating- 2006
All I Want for Christmas- 2006
Phaze in Verse- 2008
"The Fire God's Woman" in Coming Together: Under Fire- 2009
Three Wishes- 2010
Matchmaker's Misery- 2010
The Cougar Book- 2011
The Master's Lover- 2011
Bride Ball- 2011

DREAM REALM AWARDS FINALIST
Last Chance for Love- 2003

PEARL HONORABLE MENTION
Night Warriors- 2004

PEARL FINALISTS
Schente Night- 2003 (now included in *The Last of Fion's Daughters*)
König Cursebreakers- 2004 (now titled *Will of the Stone*)

JOYFULLY REVIEWED BEST BOOKS OF 2010
Written in the Stars- 2010

SPINETINGLER'S BOOK OF THE YEAR 2007
NOBODY: An Anthology of Dark Fiction- 2007 (Brenna's pieces of the anthology can be found in *Beyond the Veil*)

TRS's CAPA FINALISTS

Ultimate Warriors- 2004 (Brenna's portion is now available as *With Great Power*)

Written in the Stars

LOVE ROMANCE AND MORE CAFÉ BOOK OF THE YEAR RUNNER UP

Last Chance for Love- 2008

ROAD TO ROMANCE REVIEWERS' CHOICE AWARD

Prophecy: Revelations- 2004

LOVE ROMANCES REVIEWERS' CHOICE AWARD

Black Sail- 2003

ROMANCE JUNKIES BOOK CLUB STAFF PICK

TYGERS- 2003

FALLEN ANGELS ROMANCE RECOMMENDED READ

Devon's Price-2005 (now available in *Bearing Armen*)

JOYFULLY RECOMMENDED READ

Fairy Dreams- 2008

The Last of Fion's Daughters- 2009

TREBLE HEART FINALIST

Prophecy: Revelations- 2003

www.ingramcontent.com/pod-product-compliance
Lightning Source LLC
Chambersburg PA
CBHW030028030726
47500CB00001B/1
9781943528141